Dear Joel,

To my friend & my doctor who keeps me going from day to day! I love your stories, your words of encouragment! Keep your faith & stay on the journey! God has so much in store!

Be God's,

Judy

OUT OF MY LEAGUE

OUT OF MY LEAGUE

Love never makes a wrong choice

Judith Kay

To order additional copies of this book, contact:
Xlibris Corporation
1-888-795-4274
www.Xlibris.com
Orders@Xlibris.com
57060

CONTENTS

1 Mind Over Body...7
2 The Morning After...10
3 Reflections of the Inner Voice 15
4 Fragments 20
5 Everything is Changing..30
6 Stuck...38
7 Out With It..45
8 History Repeats Itself 54
9 The Threat of Exposure...64
10 The Score that No One Tallied.....................................72
11 Restlessness..80
12 Potential Opportunities 87
13 Issues of Adolescence..98
14 Heart to Heart..106
15 The Prick of the Thorn...113
16 The Catch of the Day 118
17 The Sanctuary...130
18 The Waiting Game...139
19 Meet Mike...145
20 The Confession...153
21 Just Say the Words..162
22 What Will it Take...172
23 Getting to Know You..176
24 A Line of Questioning..187
25 Prom Night..194
26 Blurring the Lines..203
27 A Bucket of Balls 210
28 The Recent Past..220
29 A Jealous Streak...232
30 Before the Judge..244
31 The Setup 254
32 More to Come 269

33 The Hand that Deals the Cards.................................282
34 Horsing Around..292
35 An Angel in Disguise..304
36 Bobby...314
37 The Analysis 324
38 Joseph Phillip..332
39 Around the Table...345
40 Status 356
41 Principle Matters 366
42 Making Amends 376
43 Baring her Soul...384
44 Tough Love...394
45 The Love Within...406
46 The Point of Decision..415
47 The Cry of the Heart...425
48 Old Habits...436
49 Charades 445
50 Letters of a Name 455
51 Making Contact..467
52 The Facts of the Matter..476
53 Wearing Hats...485
54 Breaking the Dam..494
55 New Beginnings...508
56 Freedom 518
57 Seeking Victory..527
58 You Belong to Me...537
59 Playing for Keeps 551
60 The Moment of Truth 560
61 Family 574
62 Dessert 586
63 The Defense..601
64 A Chance to Explain 614
65 Staking a Claim 626
66 Breaking News..638
67 The Secret Door 652
68 Peace 660

1

Mind Over Body

The room began to lighten with the first signs of daylight. Samira was awake in her own bed but nothing felt natural. *The man laying next to me isn't even my husband.* She lay perfectly still watching him sleep. *He shouldn't be here.* Just the same, his steady breathing was almost comforting. *Or maybe I shouldn't be here with him. Which is it?* Samira closed her eyes but caught herself the instant before she fell back to sleep. *Oh no! I'm not going there again. I need to get up while I still have control over my defenses.*

Samira stepped into a hot shower hoping to diffuse the uneasiness of the morning. *I was afraid I'd forget how to be with a man.* Samira smiled into the steam. *But he was so gentle and patient.* Her fears melted with his touch. Ever so gently he led her to a place she had purposefully forgotten.

In one way, Samira felt alive in ways she'd forgotten. In another way, intimacy was a thing of the past. *It conflicts with the code of ethics I've decided to live by until I get the girls raised and out on their own.*

Veiled in the mist of steam, Samira swallowed hard. A mix of emotions were threatening to spill over. *Dear God, what have I done?* One part longed for more of the same. The other scolded her personal desires. *Two weeks ago I knew who I was and what I stood for.* There was no immediate solace for her guilty conscience. *Today everything is muddled and confused.*

Samira pulled her hair over one shoulder. The rhythm of the water reinforced the shame that was mounting against her. *Now what I am supposed to do?* She felt guilty about the wine that diluted her defenses; guilty for enjoying the company of a man that wasn't her husband. *I enjoyed far more than his company!*

Samira stepped out of the shower and toweled dry. *How can he sleep so soundly while the voices in my head are screaming?* She slipped a short-sleeved sweater over her head and adjusted her hair. *The fact of the matter is, I chose to sleep with him!* She shook her head at her own lack of discernment.

Everything she had done since meeting him challenged her personal boundaries. From an over-extended lunch hour a week ago to intimacy last night. *I don't even know his last name, for Heaven's sake!* Samira stepped into a pair of khaki shorts.

She silently studied the man in the mirror. Signs of a morning beard darkened his chiseled cheekbones. *There's more silver in his hair than I noticed before.* Tan lines over his shoulders indicated he'd worn a tank top outside in the sun. *He's handsome even in his sleep.* Samira shook off a tingle of excitement that ran the length of her spine. *There are so many things I wish I knew about him.* She ran a brush through her hair. *Or maybe it's easier if I don't know.*

The wooden slats in the dining room window cast patterned sunlight across the kitchen floor. The aroma of freshly brewed coffee permeated the air. *Thank God for timers on coffee makers.* Samira poured a full cup into her favorite mug.

Everywhere Samira looked reminded her of the seductive, candlelit evening. Dirty dishes were stacked on the counter. Unfamiliar keys on the dining room table. A sports jacket hung over the back of a dining room chair. *Everything he did moved me in places I'd forgotten existed!* Goose bumps prickled her skin as she recalled the moment she crossed the line and surrendered to spontaneous foreplay.

How am I supposed to act the morning after? But the consequences suddenly seemed very threatening. *What do I say to the man who serenaded me all the way to my bed?*

Samira sipped the coffee. *Something tells me he won't be as intimidated by this morning's circumstances as I am.* That thought was almost maddening! *I've worked hard to develop the woman I've become.* She started to load the dishwasher more out of habit than anything else. *Who is he to waltz into my life and test my boundaries?* She rinsed the plates and put them in the racks. A single drop of wine was peacefully resting on the bottom of his glass. *It's been over six years since these glasses have been out of the cupboard.*

Samira poured the drop of wine into the ceramic sink and watched it stretch slowly toward the drain. *I could blame the wine for my flirtatious spirit last night.* Her memory skipped back to another candlelit dinner. *Wine wasn't to blame that night either, but at least that man was my husband.* She dipped her finger into the leftover wine in the other glass. *What made me suggest making dinner at home anyway? It's not like me to be so assertive.*

Samira scooped up her hair and locked her fingers together across the top of her head. *I need to get my thoughts in order before he wakes up!* She closed her eyes and stretched her chin toward the ceiling.

So much for my integrity! Samira's bare feet paced between the sink and the breakfast bar. *I have too much at stake to let the decisions of one night affect the rest of my life.*

Samira returned to her bedroom. He was still in the same position, content in his morning slumber. *What do I tell the girls when they ask me what I did on my date? And Norma. What do I tell her when she asks what I did all weekend while the girls were away?* She took note of the clock on the nightstand. *I'm sure Mrs. Barnes has already spotted his truck in my driveway and Lord knows she will talk. And my brother would have some words of wisdom for me under these circumstances!* But these thoughts weren't nearly as accusing as the one that nagged the hardest: *What would my parents say if they knew I slept with a man I hardly even know?*

Samira crossed the bedroom and gathered his clothes off the floor. *He said he had a late morning appointment.* Her eyes moved to the clock. *But it's only seven.* She carefully draped his pants over an easy chair. He was still sound asleep. *It's kind of sexy to have a man in my bed!* She decided to let him wake on his own. *Unless it starts to get too late. Whatever the case, I'll make sure I'm not the reason he's late.*

Back in the kitchen the coffee had cooled considerably. *What kind of appointment do you schedule on a Saturday morning?* Samira warmed her coffee before taking a seat at the breakfast bar. *I don't even know what he does for a living.*

Sex always comes with obligation.

Samira cringed at the voice in her head. *Tom said that to me the night he proposed.* She shuddered at her immediate circumstances. *What if I've created a new obligation for him?* The keys to his truck were within reach. Samira fingered them thoughtfully. *Or have I created an obligation for me?*

Several minutes passed. *Once he's awake, I'll offer him breakfast, and then he can simply be on his way.* She refilled her now empty coffee cup. *I'll be hospitable but firm.* Satisfied with her decision, Samira opened the book and picked up the story where she'd left off.

2

The Morning After

J.P. Ralston rolled into the empty space next to him and raised his arms over his head. It wasn't unusual to awake in someone else's bed. He checked the time on his watch. *No way!* He confirmed the lateness of the hour with the digital clock on the nightstand. *Shit! Chances of making the driving range before going to the office are slim to none now.*

J.P.'s eyes searched the room for his clothes. *In all my experience, I've never had a woman pick up my clothes for me.* He pulled the button-down shirt over his shoulders then removed the cellular phone from the belt on his pants.

Three messages scrolled across the display. *Mike, Denise, and the ex-wife.* He took time to view the digital message from Denise. "Affidavits arrived. See you at 10 AM." J.P. clipped the phone back on his belt and stepped into his pants. *Ten o'clock should be doable.*

He shook his head. *Gut feeling told me to leave while I still had the power to make that decision.* He slipped his foot into a shoe. *But it was all good.* He smiled at the recollection. *In fact, it was very good.*

J.P. leaned over to tie his shoes and came face to face with a photograph. The woman was smiling her gorgeous smile but her arms were wrapped around another man! *So who the hell is he?* The picture tied a knot in J.P.'s stomach. *The sooner I meet Mike, the sooner I don't need the answer to that question.* He couldn't help but look at the picture again. *How long ago that was taken?* His eyes cautiously scanned the room in search of evidence. *I don't see anything incriminating in plain site.*

Sunlight flooded the front rooms as J.P. stepped out of the bedroom. She was sitting at the breakfast bar with her back to the kitchen. J.P. took in her quiet presence as he buttoned his shirt. *I wonder why she let me sleep?*

Samira looked up from the book. "How long have you been standing there?"

"Long enough." *She's more beautiful in the morning than she is at night.* He smoothed the wrinkles in his dress shirt with his hands. "How long have you been up?"

"Long enough."

And she's quick too. J.P. had to smile at the rhetorical remark.

"Would you like some coffee?"

I really need to be on my way. Common courtesy told J.P. to stick around long enough to be polite. *But the gut feeling is usually right.*

"No thanks."

"Do you *ever* drink coffee?"

J.P. rolled the cuffs on his shirt and tucked the shirttail inside his khakis. "Rarely."

"Really." Her voice was full of curiosity. "You *rarely* drink coffee, yet you invited me to the Café Ole Shop . . . twice?"

You didn't seem the type to invite to a bar. "Stranger things have happened."

"Hmmm," she took a sip of coffee. "Not to me." She climbed off the stool and turned toward the kitchen. "What else can I get for you then? Orange juice? A glass of milk?"

J.P. watched her graceful moves. *In retrospect, it's a damn good thing she was already out of bed before I woke up.*

What I wouldn't do for a rerun of last night. "Orange juice." J.P. weighed his options. *Breakfast is cordial. I've already wreaked havoc with Mike this morning.*

"Cereal or toast?"

I never eat first thing in the morning! "Cereal." *Why am I still here anyway? Normally I'd already be out the door headed for the driving range.*

The tidiness and tranquility of the house somehow brought a sense of steadiness. *She's pretty settled here.* Subconsciously, he drummed his fingertips against the tiled countertop. *The last thing she needs is me spoiling her routine.*

"The cereal is on the turntable next to the sink." The sound of Samira's voice pulled his thoughts back to the present.

I should probably just go. "Samira . . ." Her name felt strange rolling off his tongue. *Did I pronounce that right?*

She turned with a look of anticipation.

I don't usually have trouble reading a woman's thoughts, but nothing is registering. "I don't have a lot of time . . ."

Something in her eyes stopped the thought.

"Don't let me keep you." She carried orange juice and glasses to the breakfast bar.

Shit, Ralston. You might actually want to see this one again. He took a deep breath. *I'll play this scene out and see where it goes.*

"You're not keeping me." *Cereal won't take long anyway.* He opened the cabinet expecting healthy bran cereals. *This is interesting.* "So what's your preference? Tony the Tiger, Toucan Sam or the Silly Rabbit?"

Samira's eyes widened.

She seems just as surprised as I am!

"Oh, anything is fine." Color was rising in her cheeks.

Let's see what we have here. J.P. scanned the colorful boxes. "Best hidden picture game in the cupboard." He slid the box over the counter then sat down on the stool next to her.

Samira's face was crimson with embarrassment.

J.P. grinned. "What's the matter? You don't like the silly rabbit?"

"No." She shook her head. "I just didn't realize that's all I had in the pantry."

Let's see where she goes with this one? "Are you saying you don't normally eat cereal in the morning?" J.P. poured cereal into both bowls. *I like the fact she's a little off center.*

"Rarely."

He poured the milk. "So do I understand correctly that you don't eat cereal even though you offered it to me?"

"Stranger things have happened."

She's damn quick. "Not to me." J.P. shared his easy smile. *Touche.* He turned the box around and placed it between their bowls. "Last one to find the hidden rabbit does the dishes."

The momentary light-heartedness relieved the awkwardness of the morning.

"It's been a million years since I read the back of a cereal box." J.P. pushed the empty bowl across the tiled countertop. "Silly rabbit anyway."

"I think you cheated."

Gutsy woman. J.P. leaned into the countertop and tipped the box on its side. He directed her eyes to the bottom edge with his finger. *Read the small print.*

"I knew it!"

Humored by the interaction, J.P. watched Samira set her empty bowl aside. The moment they made eye contact, she looked away.

Her eyes are intense. But I still can't read her thoughts.

No reason to fight the clock now. He leaned back into the armed barstool. *Mike's already half way through a bucket of balls.*

"What time is your appointment?"

Nope. Not going there. No personal discussions with a new woman. It's a cardinal rule.

"You did say you had to be somewhere didn't you?" Samira stepped off the barstool and walked around the breakfast bar headed for the dining room table.

Her hips moved with such grace that J.P. caught himself undressing her with his eyes. *Ignore her body and play by the rules.* "Yeah, I need to report in at the office around ten."

Samira returned to the breakfast bar and motioned for his empty bowl. A moment of silence passed between them.

"How long will you work today?"

J.P. picked up the empty juice glasses and followed her to the sink. "Until I get the job done." *Why are you answering these questions? Next thing you know she'll be expecting you to call when you're done.* He was very aware of potential expectation. *Don't set her up for failure, Ralston.* He watched her avoid his eyes again.

She set the bowls in the sink and turned around for the glasses. Their hands touched for just a moment. *How can something so quick affect me like this?*

"Shall I call you later?" *You know better than to go there, Ralston.* New tension rose between them.

Samira quickly wiped her hands on a towel. Her response didn't come right away. She pulled her hair back from her forehead and forced a smile. "If you like."

The sudden resistance in the woman's disposition was puzzling. *One moment she's joking around over a cereal box and the next she's holding her thoughts.* J.P. sighed. *Now what?* This was the part of new relationships he dreaded the most—knowing what to do and say *after* spending the night. *Especially when she's so damned tempting.* He watched her put the milk away in the refrigerator. *I should have skipped breakfast for the driving range.*

"Listen, Samira . . ."

This time when she turned, she held his eyes. "I don't want to make you late."

Fair enough. I have her permission to be on my way. J.P. lifted his sports jacket off the dining room chair. Samira followed only as far as the end of the table. The expression on her face was transparent to the mixed emotions of the morning.

She really is beautiful. And last night has to be one of the most incredible experiences of my life. An onslaught of thoughts rushed into his mind. "About last night . . ."

"It's okay . . ." Samira looked away as her voice trailed off in an open-ended thought.

I seriously doubt that. J.P. swallowed the wave of guilt that stuck in his throat. *I feel responsible for her confusion.* Instead of making an exit, J.P. walked back to where she was standing. *Be careful, but be honest.* Slowly, he ran his fingers through the ends of her dark hair against her shoulder. She stiffened slightly.

"Look, Samira . . ." *Say the words, Ralston. Tell her she was unbelievable.* "Thank you for last night." J.P. was instantly disappointed. *I want to tell her more!* He wanted to tell her how incredible the night had been for him. He wanted to tell her how beautiful she was. But nothing more came out.

J.P. caught her chin as it fell and gently lifted her face with his hand. *I think I need to kiss her. Or does she need to kiss me?*

Samira closed her eyes but turned away before his lips met her cheek.

Damn. Deflated and now equally confused, J.P. turned toward the front door.

"Phil."

The sound of his name stopped him. *Phil.* J.P. turned around in time to see his keys take flight. *What caused me to introduce myself as Phil?* He reached but missed the catch. The keys crashed loudly against the hard floor. *I haven't used my given name in years.* He scooped the keys up off the floor.

A perfect spring morning met him on the other side of the door. *I should have been on the driving range.* The sound of his name sounded in his ears again. *It sounds foreign, but it feels alright coming from her.* He stepped off the wooden planks of the porch with nothing more than an over-the-shoulder look to see if Samira was following. *Nope, not there.* He confirmed Mike's cell number vibrating on his cell phone cell before sliding into his pickup. *I'm going to skip the interrogation and call him back later.*

J.P. rolled down his window. Samira was watching him through the open door. *That's the face that made me use my name.* He couldn't remember a time when he was so taken by a woman's beauty. *Nor can I remember a time when I've been so tormented by a woman's unpredictable candor.* Suddenly, the anticipation of freedom lost its attraction.

J.P. drew a deep breath and closed his eyes for a quick moment. When he opened them she was gone. *Why is it so hard to leave this mornig?*

3

Reflections of the Inner Voice

Samira watched until Phil's truck was out of sight. *How many times did I stand here and watch Tom drive off to work?* Samira could feel Mrs. Barnes watching from across the street. *So much for privacy.* She calculated how long it would take for the elderly neighbor to circulate the news. *Just what I don't need.*

Something needs to speak louder than the silence resonating in this house! With a click of the remote control, Samira cued National Public Radio on the stereo. *J.S. Bach. That should help.* She stopped to straighten a stray magazine on coffee table, but her thoughts were still in the bedroom. Samira stepped into the hallway but hesitated at her bedroom door.

Samira Cartwright always made her bed. Every day. No exceptions. *Except today.* The throw pillows strewn about on the floor gave her an uneasy feeling. *Everything is out of order.* Her thoughts were reeling. So much had happened in a short two-week time. Routine habits were tainted with the anticipation that he might call; she couldn't stay focused on daily tasks. *And now even my house is in disarray because of him.*

Samira tucked her hair behind her ears. *I really don't know that much about him, yet he seems very familiar at the same time.* Samira reached for the top sheet. *Sometimes it's like I've known him forever.* She pulled the sheet tight across the mattress. *And then the next moment he's like a total stranger.* As she straightened the pillows, she ran her hand over the pillowcase where Phil had rested his head. *He certainly slept like he was comfortable here.* Samira stretched for the comforter at the foot of the bed. Her nightgown was hanging on a hook, untouched.

Without warning her conscience won out. Samira pushed the comforter all the way onto the floor and grabbed for the top of the sheets. A mix of emotion surged as she stripped the entire bed. *One moment everything seems so right. And the next so drastically wrong!*

Samira plopped down on the edge of the bare mattress and hugged Phil's pillow to her middle. She caught a whiff of his after shave. She had never invited a man back to her house. *Not even the man I married!* Samira breathed in his scent again. *What is it about him that makes me so assertive?*

Baffled by her boldness and frustrated by the confusion, Samira smoothed the pillow on her lap and carefully placed it at the head of the bed. *I'm not ready to wash his pillowcase yet.* She walked around the bed and organized the throw pillows in the corner of the room.

Samira gathered the bathroom towels and added them to the pile of bedding. As she turned around, she caught her own reflection in the mirror. *Who are you?* The woman she thought she knew so well looked back with a questioning expression.

"What?" Samira spoke out loud to herself. "I had a wonderful evening! There is no reason to be ashamed!" She ran a brush through her long dark hair, purposefully avoiding eye contact with herself. *I'm glad he stayed.* She stopped brushing her hair momentarily. *But I'm also glad he's gone.* Tom's picture caught her attention. Subconsciously she turned his wedding band on her right hand. Her own wedding rings were hanging over a hook with laced ribbon.

She recalled her wedding night with Tom in this same room. *I was so scared that night!* The brush caught on a tangle. Samira worked the knot until the brush moved freely again. *But I never told Tom.* She studied his face in the frame. *Did he know how scared I was?*

Samira's thoughts skipped forward in comparison. *I wasn't as scared last night.* Controlled passion permeated every touch. *Oh how I'd love to have his touch all over again.* A sudden uneasiness in the comparison caused Samira to turn Tom's photo so he wasn't looking directly at her. *Is it really his touch? Or am I still missing Tom?*

Until today Samira had never considered altering her lifestyle. *After Tom was gone I just never allowed myself to think about having another man in my life.* She had grown very comfortable raising her girls as a single parent. *Maybe too comfortable.*

But in light of last night, everything had changed. *Oh, Dear God, he made me feel alive again!* Samira ran her hand over his pillow. *I've been just a mom for so long now. He made me feel like a woman.*

But she also knew moving into a relationship with a man was not in the master plan. She felt selfish for wanting him to stay and guilty for enjoying him so much. *He didn't resist my seduction, but I seriously doubt this is something new for him.* A new surge of guilt swept over her.

"Just keep busy," she told herself. "Do whatever it takes to keep your mind busy!"

Disgusted with her mix of emotions, Samira carried the bedding to the laundry room and sorted it into whites and colors. *It feels good to be washing away the residue from last night.* She started the washer. *Maybe my guilt will wash away too.*

"I don't want my mind to be in as much disarray as this house!"

The light on the answering machine blinked four new messages but Samira walked on by. She stepped into the garage to recycle the wine bottle but something stopped her.

"Valpolicello Classico from Sartori." The Italian rolled off her tongue nicely. With a hesitancy she couldn't explain, Samira set the bottle on the floor next to the crate. Sunlight flooded the garage as the overhead door opened. Samira shaded her eyes as she headed toward the mailbox.

"Nice day to be out and about."

Ah, Mrs. Barnes. I knew she was watching. "Beautiful day." *Maybe she didn't notice.* "Your petunias are starting to bloom nicely."

"Petunias are the easy ones." Mrs. Barnes straightened her back with a great deal of effort and peered out from under the wide brim of her straw hat. "Have you had company today?"

I knew it, I knew it, I knew it! Samira mindlessly flipped through the mail. "Enjoy the sunshine, Mrs. Barnes." *Maybe she'll forget.*

"Thank you. You do the same."

Dear God, please make her forget! Samira shook her head and picked up the wine bottle on her way back through the kitchen door. *And while you're at it, maybe you can make me forget last night too!* She smacked the stack of mail onto the counter harder than necessary. *And what in the world am I doing saving this stupid wine bottle?* Nonetheless, it fit into a perfect spot next to the dish drainer under the sink. She thought again. *No, don't make me forget. I need to remember.*

The telephone rang, startling Samira. She caught the knuckle of her finger in the cupboard door. "Hello?" Samira squeezed her hand into a fist to help diffuse the throbbing.

"Hi Mama! What are you doing?"

"Oh Krissy! Hi! I'm just tidying up around here." Samira was jolted back into motherhood. *And trying to ignore Mrs. Barnes.* "What are you doing this morning?"

Kara's voice came on the line with her sister. "Hey, Mama! It's me too! We're helping Gramma in the kitchen. She's making salads for the big party tomorrow. I wish you were here!"

I really don't belong there. "Have you heard from Aunt Ellen yet?"

"Gramma doesn't think she's going to make it home in time." Krissy sounded disappointed. "Grampa says she has to work so she'll have to celebrate later."

Ellen always has to work.

"What did you do last night?" Kara asked excitedly.

"Yeah, how did it go on your—" Krissy was whispering loudly.

"Shhh," Samira quieted her daughters. *I can't lie to them, but I can't exactly tell them the truth either.* "We'll talk about it when you get home, okay?"

"Okay," Krissy answered. "Is he cute?"

"Krissy, please, not now!"

"Sorry, Mama," Krissy giggled. She changed subjects as quickly as she'd asked the question. "I can't believe Aunt Donna and Uncle Vern have been married for fifty years! That's like forever! You should see the cake Gramma ordered for them . . ."

" . . . Gramma says there will be a houseful tomorrow," Kara interrupted. "We are going to serve the punch . . ."

As the girls rattled on, Samira pictured Tom's family in her mind.

"I think we're going over to swim this afternoon . . ." Krissy brought Samira's thoughts back to the conversation. " . . . We have to get the salads done first so everything is ready to go. Gramma says she can't relax until everything is perfect for the party!"

"Gramma wants to talk to you," Kara interjected. "I miss you, Mama!"

Before Samira could say goodbye to her daughters, Norma Cartwright was on the line.

"Samira, dear, how are you? Did you have a nice evening at home last night? We're so pleased to have the girls with us here and I'm sure you could use the peace and quiet at your house for a few days too. Have you thought any more about joining us tomorrow afternoon?"

Samira took advantage when Norma took a breath. "I think I'll just stay here." She glanced around the living room. The keys and the sports coat were nowhere in sight. *At least the evidence is gone.* "There are several things I need to catch up on. But thank you for the invitation just the same."

"That's fine, dear. We just don't want you to feel left out. Well, honey, we need to wrap up this kitchen work so we can get over to the pool. Thanks for the call. We'll be fine here, don't you worry about us."

The girls called me, Norma. Samira shook her head at her mother-in-law's comments. Before she could reply, Norma said her goodbye and the line went dead.

She tilted her head and stared at the phone in her hand. *It's good for Krissy and Kara to remain active in their grandparents' lives, but I'll take the liberty to distance myself, thank you very much.*

NPR radio switched from J.S. Bach to a talk show. Samira clicked it off. The only sound in the house now was the gentle hum of the washing machine. She picked up her book from the breakfast bar and retreated to the rattan sofa in the sunroom. She curled up against the floral throw pillows and opened the story to the marked page.

Why can't I stop thinking about him? This time she didn't fight it. Samira closed her eyes and sank further into the cushions. *I can still feel the way he held me as we danced in the living room.* He was such a gentleman. She replayed the moment Phil broke from a kiss and suggested maybe he should leave while he could still claim an ounce of willpower. *No way!* She chuckled out loud. *There was no way I was going to let him leave by that time!* His gentle resistance gave way to her seduction.

Samira opened her eyes and stared at the living room floor where they'd danced. *I allowed my heart to speak louder than my head.* She drew her legs tighter to her chest and rested her chin on her knees. *In spite of all the promises I made to myself!* She sat reflecting on the tears that spilled over as this man she'd only just met brought her back to a place she had missed so desperately yet been so afraid to seek. *Intimacy. I'd all but forgotten.*

Stop it, stop it, stop it! The inner voice was screaming in her head. Samira sat up on the edge of the sofa and piled her hair on top of her head with both hands. His words sounded again,

"Thank you for last night . . ."

They were few but they were perfect. She hadn't realized until this moment how desperately she'd needed to hear them. *I hope he was sincere.* She pictured his face when he stopped to make eye contact. *He seemed sincere.* She shook her hair loose. *I didn't dare kiss him!* Now Samira was standing. *I had to separate my desires from my morals somehow!*

Samira's eyes searched the room. The perfect order was suddenly unbearable.

"Okay, girlfriend," she spoke out loud to herself. "You have got to get out of this house!"

4

Fragments

The telephone was ringing when J.P. Ralston stepped out of the shower. Shifting gears from Samira had been more difficult than he'd anticipated.

Another ring. *Yeah, yeah, hang on . . .*

Chase, J.P.'s black Labrador, moved out of the way as he reached for the telephone next to his bed. *This better be quick. I'm already late for the office.*

"This is J.P."

"J.P., buddy . . ."

Mike.

" . . . I stopped by on my way home last night but you weren't there. You owe me one now. I fed Chase for you." He continued to ramble. "Who was the broad? Haven't seen her around before . . ."

Ah, the dreaded interrogation. "About this morning . . .,"

"Sure hope she was worth it. It's not everyday I get stood up by my best friend." Mike forced an air of self-pity with a heavy sigh. "Well?"

I knew I didn't feel like facing his wrath. "I just didn't get up in time, that's all."

"Yeah, right. Gut feeling says you didn't have any trouble getting up." Mike laughed heartily. "Who's the chick anyway?"

I've already ignored gut feelings this morning. J.P. fastened his watch on his wrist as he talked. "When did you see her?"

"I was at the bar when you waltzed in at the club last night. Stirred up quite a fuss among the waitresses, I might add . . ."

Should have known he'd be at the bar. J.P. half listened. His mind was already on the affidavit waiting on his desk.

"Where'd you meet a broad like that?"

I don't like his inference. "The lady, if you don't mind."

Mike chuckled. "She looks a little out of your league."

"Thanks for your vote of confidence." J.P. sorted through a laundry basket for a pair of clean socks. "At the library."

Mike laughed loudly into the phone. "Yeah right. Where'd you really pick her up?" He was still laughing.

"No shit." He identified matching socks. "And I didn't pick her up; I invited her to dinner."

"You sure didn't stick around long for asking her to dinner! By the time I made my way across the room you'd split."

"How many drinks between the bar and my table?" J.P. squeezed the receiver between his ear and shoulder and stepped into a pair of clean pants. *I know Mike well enough to know he stopped to talk to someone along the way.* "Hey, Mike, I hate to cut you off, but I'm late for the office."

"What you hate is coughing up details! And to answer your question, two drinks." Another hearty laugh filled the phone. "Tell you what, I'd be more than willing to check in on your *lady* while you're at the office." There was a slight pause. "Hell, I won't even charge you for the service."

"You touch the lady and you die, good buddy," J.P. checked his watch again. "But you might check in with Denise this afternoon. We need your signature on an affidavit . . ."

"I'll check in with Denise in exchange for more particulars on the *lady!*" Mike interrupted playfully. "Where'd you end up for dinner?"

J.P.'s patience was growing thin. "Her place." *No more details on Samira just yet, Mikey.* "The paperwork arrived late yesterday . . ."

Mike's tone was firm when he cut in again, "No details, no favors, Counselor. And by the way, it's Saturday. Screw the affidavit! I'll be on the green by the time you get out of the office. Look me up later."

Must be nice to have a day of luxury on the golf course. And I know Denise is watching the clock.

J.P. ascended the outdoor staircase two by two. The red brick of the building radiated with heat from the morning sunshine.

"Mornin' boss!" Denise looked up from her computer screen. "Nice you could make it in *around* ten."

Denise's naturally blue eyes appeared more green with the help of colored contacts. Her auburn hair showed signs of new highlights.

"New do?"

She acknowledged the inquiry with a nonchalant gesture of her hand. "Nice try but you're still late."

J.P. reviewed the stack of mail.

"I don't have the affidavits yet . . ."

"No, they're on my desk. I haven't looked at them yet." *I've been a little distracted.* "And chances are good we won't see Mike until Monday anyway."

"He'll need to sign before we can move forward."

I know, I know.

Denise fastened some messages to a clipboard then guided her boss's eyes about halfway down the top sheet with an artificial fingernail. "Mr. Hughes has already called this morning needing specifics on his father's Estate. You'll want to call him back today as he's leaving for London on Sunday . . ."

"Tomorrow?"

"Yes, Boss." Denise frowned. "This is Saturday."

J.P. motioned for her to continue.

"You have a message from someone named Mary. She said something about an engagement or something on Friday night. She talked like you had already committed so you might want to check your calendar."

J.P. ran the name through his mind but couldn't put a face with it. "Do you know her?"

"Nope. This one didn't come through me."

"Did she leave any particulars?"

"No bust size or anything." Denise continued. "More importantly, the Mid-America Corporation left a message right before I came in that you should call Mr. Stephenson right away."

J.P. tapped the clipboard with his fingertips. "Call Mr. Hughes and tell him we'll have the documents ready for his review by one o'clock." J.P. moved into his own office. "This estate is taking more time than I'd hoped, Denise. How long will he be out of the country?"

"I'll ask for his timeline." Denise answered from the other room. "This is the very reason we stopped handling estates, Boss. Remember?"

I remember. "We won't make a habit of it." J.P. sat down in his high-backed leather chair and rolled up to the mahogany desk. With the click of a button he booted his computer and listened to the hard drive whir into action. "The only reason we're assisting with this estate . . ."

" . . . Is because Lloyd Hughes played such a huge part in setting up your private practice." Denise finished the thought. "I know that story."

Satisfied, J.P. continued in a professional mode. "Let's get Mr. Stephenson on the line and see what's on his mind this fine day."

"What should I do about Mary?"

I have no idea who this Mary chick might be. J.P. wrinkled his face in thought. "Let it slide. If it's important, she'll call back."

Soon after his divorce, J.P. learned it was wiser and more conducive to filter his personal calls through Denise. His home number was unlisted and most of his social calls went through Denise. *And it happens to work very well this way.*

"Mr. Stephenson's on line two."

Without hesitation, he picked up the phone to greet his newest client. "Mr. Stephenson, J.P. Ralston here. How can I be of service?"

"J.P., I appreciate you getting back to me on the weekend like this." The executive sounded quite serious. "It seems our on-line system was hacked over night. I don't have a full report from the technicians yet, but it appears the firewalls failed. Some accounts have been accessed and considerable assets seem to be misplaced . . ."

J.P.'s adrenaline started to pump. *This doesn't sound good.*

" . . . We may need legal counsel as the day progresses."

J.P. went over his morning agenda in his mind. "I can be there by noon, Mr. Stephenson. Is that soon enough?"

"Noon should be fine." There was a slight hesitation. "In fact, make it one o'clock. That will give the technicians another hour to reboot the system after we close for business." Mr. Stephenson addressed a third party then returned to the conversation on the telephone. "Meet me in the main board room, J.P."

"Let's get this Hughes file moving, Denise." He looked up to see his paralegal standing in the doorway ready for action.

"This is Saturday, remember? I want to be home by lunch."

"As long as this report is ready for Hughes, you're out of here at noon as promised. We're going to need permission from city hall to copy these plat maps." He handed Denise two cylindrical containers. "I have the plots and landmarks noted in the diagrams. Hughes will need copies of each page as well as documentation on the boundary lines."

Denise took the canisters. "I'll be at city hall as soon as the doors open Monday morning."

"I'd like to go over the precincts with the city attorney before we deliver to Hughes."

Denise was already on task. "What is the difference in the property tax if the city is right about the property lines?"

"A few hundred thousand dollars. Enough to make it a worthy discussion." The attorney skimmed a document as he spoke. "The key is to find the actual date Lloyd Hughes closed the purchase. If he closed before the city incorporated the township, the family is off the hook."

The boundary information Samira located on the library's computer was inconclusive. *But she gave me enough information to lead the city to believe we have the actual dates of incorporation, whether they're exact or not.* J.P. was still confident he could convince the city to lower the settlement.

Without another word, J.P. closed the door between the offices. He donned his rimless glasses and began to settle into the case at the table behind his desk. He'd spent several long weeks searching for specific information to secure a position against the city on behalf of the Hughes family. *The information from Samira gives us a running chance to win this case.* Another thought intruded. *I wonder if I have a fighting chance with her.* He pushed that thought aside.

A vibration against the attorney's waist indicated a new page on his cell phone. Slightly frustrated at an interruption, he waited a few minutes before checking the message. *Janet. That's the last person I need to talk to this morning.* J.P. cringed at the thought of a confrontation with his ex-wife.

It wasn't until after the Hughes report was compiled that J.P. turned his attention back to the call. Reluctantly he pressed the speed dial on his desk phone.

"It took you long enough to call back!" Janet sounded anxious.

Gotta love the attitude.

"I tried to call you at home. Where are you now?" Janet's tone already carried accusations.

"Believe it or not, Jan, it's a busy day at the office. Is there a specific reason for this call?" J.P. forced a business response. *It's the only way to survive her disposition.*

"I wouldn't bother you if it weren't important . . ."

Really? That comes as a surprise to me.

" . . . I'm in over my head with James and we need to talk. I've probably waited too long but kept thinking I could handle it but now I just don't know and Bruce is tired of . . ."

"Whoa, whoa, slow down." J.P. ran his hand through his hair. "One thing at a time."

"We just have to talk, Phil. This can't wait any longer."

Everything is always dramatic and urgent when it comes to Janet. J.P. gave her permission to speak her mind.

"Not on the phone, for crying out loud! This is serious!"

J.P. fingered the pile of research on his desk and ran the next forty-eight hours in his mind. The Hughes Estate had to be ready for deposition by mid-week and it was sounding like Mid-America could use up every other free moment. *No. I'm not leaving town this weekend.*

"Casework has dibs on my time, Jan. It's either now or sometime next week. Take your pick."

Several moments of silence followed the response.

"Can you even listen now, Phil? Or is your mind too full of legal issues to care?"

The attorney slowly turned the leather chair away from the stack of papers on his desk. *I'll give her a limited hearing.*

"I can listen." *Momentarily.*

There was a heavy sigh into the phone. "I don't know when you last talked to the boys," she finally began. "But James and I have been locking horns lately." There was a slight hesitation. "Actually, Bruce and James have been going at it for quite some time now; maybe since Christmas; maybe even since last summer . . ."

That would explain the distance I felt with James on the phone awhile back.

" . . . His choice of friends has been terrible, his grades have bottomed out and he insists on running his own life." Janet choked back a sob as she continued. "He left last night . . ."

Phil waited for an explanation but nothing came. "What do you mean, '*he left*'?"

"He walked out the door." Now Janet was crying. "Bruce said if he walked out he couldn't come home." Janet sobbed harder. "And . . . and . . . he didn't."

Phil closed his eyes and leaned forward and rested his elbows on his knees. "Look, Jan, James must have some issues to work through. I wouldn't get too worked up about it yet . . ."

"Too worked up?" Janet screamed into the phone. "You didn't hear those words, Phil! We told him to choose between his family and his friends and he didn't come home!"

J.P. ignored a tap on the door.

"Have you talked to his friends? Someone knows where he is."

"I've called everywhere. He's nowhere to be found . . ."

"Who have you talked to?"

"I'm going to call the cops."

"Don't call the cops, Janet." Phil rose from his chair and removed his reading glasses. "Call Jennie Johnson. Chances are good she'll know where he is . . ."

"Jennie Johnson!?" The shriek in Janet's voice caught Phil off guard. "That little tramp of a cheerleader?"

Herein lies the biggest part of the problem. Obviously they don't approve of his girlfriend. "Careful, Jan. She's tramping around with your son. She probably has a good idea where to find him if he's not with her."

"So help me," Janet warned. "If I find him with her . . ."

Case closed "For christ's sake, Janet. Do you want him home or not? That was what you insinuated a few minutes ago." J.P. waited for his question to settle. "If you want James home, then it will be in your best interest to not condemn him before you find him." *No wonder he walked out.*

J.P. motioned for Denise to come on into his office. "Make some calls and call me back when you know something more concrete. But don't call the cops." *The last thing James needs right now is for the authorities to get involved.* He pointed to Denise's answer on the clipboard.

"Good God, Phil, I have enough phone numbers for you to fill a book. Which number am I supposed to use?"

"Use the cell." *Eventually they all reach me.* "I'm tied up in a meeting with a client early this afternoon."

"That's just great. I can always count on you to be tied up . . ."

Time to end this phone call. "Call me when you know something."

The abrupt click of the line left a dial tone buzzing in the attorney's ear. *I hate the miles between me and the boys.* Worse yet he hated that James was in trouble at home. *But I wouldn't want to live any closer to Janet either!*

J.P. took a deep breath and exhaled very slowly. The Café Ole` coffee shop at the end of the alley was alive with the approaching rush of the Saturday brunch crowd. *Add this fiasco to my caseload and I'll be lucky to find another noon hour at the coffee shop.*

Time passed but J.P. Ralston was lost somewhere between fatherhood and broken relationships. He detested Janet's accusation of being preoccupied with work, but at the same time, he realized the truth in that statement all too well.

"Anything I can do?" Denise appeared at his side. "It's 12:30."

The only thing J.P. wanted her to do in that moment was reach a woman on the phone; one he thought might understand. *Samira.* He remembered the uncluttered order of her home. *My life is anything but in order.*

"Unfortunately not." *Hell, I don't even know where I stand with her after this morning. If I stand with her at all.* He looked up into the tinted eyes of his assistant. "I need to get over to Mid-America. I'll finish these files when I get back."

Denise nodded in understanding.

J.P. returned to his office a little over an hour later. *What's Denise still doing here?* He pushed open the glass door planning to address the violation of the Saturday noon deadline. He was surprised to find a young man standing with his back to the door. Denise was obviously in the middle of a lengthy discussion. *Who's she talking to?*

"Oh, J.P.," Denise seemed relieved to see her boss. "This is . . ."

"Uh, uh, . . . R-r-rick." The young man hung his head as he spoke. He stuck his arm straight out.

J.P. took the card from his fingertips and turned it over. *What's he doing with one of my business cards?*

A worn Hard Rock Café t-shirt hung loosely from the boy's shoulders and his baggy shorts showed signs of long-time wear. J.P waited for the young man to speak again but nothing happened.

"Would you like to sit down?"

"N-n-no thank-you." Rick glanced up then immediately looked back to the floor again. "Ah-h-I, I have J-James in my c-car."

What the hell? "Here?"

"Y-yes, sir." Rick's lanky arms remained pinned to his side. "In my c-car."

J.P. tried to gather his thoughts. "Denise, get Janet on the phone."

"N-n-no sir. J-James s-said to get him h-here."

J.P.s' eyes went from Denise to Rick then back to Denise. "Hold off a minute." He held out his hand to stop Denise from dialing. "Take me to him, Rick."

J.P. found his youngest son crumpled over in the back seat of an old sedan. The headliner hung low, barely missing the top of James's hair. The car reeked of alcohol and cigarette smoke. J.P. held his breath and pushed James upright into the seat. The boy opened his eyes a crack then closed them again.

"James." There was no response. *I need to get him out of here.* J.P. turned around and faced Rick, who was now standing next to a woman who was just as lanky and awkward. *But first I need any information he might have.*

He took a long hard look at the woman standing next to Rick. She held a burning cigarette between two fingers. Her thin hair was uncombed and her flimsy dress clung to her stark frame.

Rick avoided eye contact, staring into the space between him and the well-dressed attorney. "Th-this is my m-mom."

J.P. was anxious to get James out of the car but forced himself to remain calm.

"I'm James's father." *Where in God's name did James connect with these people?* "J.P. Ralston."

"I think he's going to be okay." The woman spoke gently in spite of her rough appearance. "But he had a hard night."

J.P. stared at his son, obviously hung over. *What happened to him?* He looked back into the tired face of the woman. "Tell me your name again?"

"Rita." She took a long draw on the cigarette.

"Rita." J.P. repeated the name as he organized his thoughts. "How did James end up with you?" He ran his hand through his hair.

"J-jennie called m-me to come get him," Rick began hesitantly. "Th-they went to the p-party at the p-ark . . ." His eyes were focused on his friend in the car.

It was all J.P. could do to wait on Rick's stuttered words. *Just talk to me, kid!*

" . . . H-he was m-messed up r-real bad. J-Jennie said h-he c-can't go home."

The woman flicked her cigarette butt onto the pavement and ground it out with the toe of an old shoe. She looked like she might have something more to say.

J.P. nodded silent permission for her to speak.

"James is a good boy, Mr. Ralston. Th-this is just a bad time for him." Rita's southern accent was more evident now. "Rick went and got him an' brought him down home. When I got home from work we got him here to you." Rita hesitated. "He told us to get him here."

J.P.'s mind was racing. "Rick, what were they doing at the party?"

Instantly the boy grew more uncomfortable. He wiped his hands on his ragged shirt and exchanged a frightened look with his mother. She encouraged him to speak.

"It was a r-regul'r party, sir." Rick stared at his feet. "B-but J-jennie says there was a f-fight . . . a bad'n." Rick's eyes moved to his friend again. "Th-that's all she said."

J.P. deliberated Rick's response. *Define regular party. Are we talking alcohol? Drugs? What's that term mean, anyhow?* "Was James in a fight, Rick?"

The young man gasped uneasily and froze in place. "If'n he was, ah-ah-I don' know 'bout it . . ." Rick stammered around. "Jennie says he drank too much too fast . . ."

"Mr. Ralston," the mother interjected. "We just picked the boy up. He slept for awhile then told us to bring him here." Her eyes softened as she looked over at James in the back seat of her car. "He had a bad night and needs a place to stay 'til he can go home again." She sighed. "Jennie says he can't go home now."

No, he can't go home to Janet, and it sounds like I need to talk to Jennie if I want any specific information. J.P. took a deep breath and began to process what little information he had.

"Rick, do you see that coffee shop at the end of the alley?"

The boy followed the J.P.'s finger and nodded.

J.P. opened his wallet. "I need you to go there and ask for a large black coffee to go." Intentionally he reached for the bony hand of the young man and placed the money tightly in his palm.

Without speaking Rick took off in an awkward stride toward the Café Ole. J.P. turned back toward the mother. "Rita, I need to go back upstairs and talk with my assistant. I'll bring my truck around to get James in a few minutes." He hesitated on another thought. "Is there anything I can get for you?"

Rita reached through the open window for a carton of cigarettes. She shook her head as she lit up. "I'll wait here."

J.P. pulled his truck around to the front of the office building. James was almost six and half feet tall. *He's not exactly easy to maneuver in this condition.*

Rick handed J.P. a large, steaming Styrofoam cup with a lid. J.P. placed the cup in a holder on the console. He was quite surprised to see Rick offer the change.

"Oh, no, keep it." J.P. closed the door on his son. Reaching once again for his wallet, he extracted two more bills and laid them in Rick's open hand. "Thanks for getting James down here. James is lucky to have you for a friend." *Damn lucky.* J.P. considered his son's condition. *He could have been left for dead along side of a road somewhere.*

Rita stepped forward and expressed a word of thanks. *It's no doubt been awhile since she's had a couple of extra fifties.*

"That's not necessary, Mr. Ralston . . ."

"It's the least I can do." *If I had more on me I'd give it to them.*

"He's a good boy. We just wanted him to be safe."

J.P. pulled a pen out of his shirt pocket and scribbled his cell number on the back of a new business card. On another card, he asked Rick to write his own phone number.

"Ah-h-I h-hope he's okay," Rick said meekly, glancing in James's direction.

J.P. followed the gaze and shared the same concern. *The worst of it may come after the hangover.*

Denise appeared with a stack of bound files and placed them behind the driver's seat. She made a face when the stench of James's condition hit her nose. She exchanged a worried glance with her employer.

I know. J.P. silently acknowledged her fear. "He'll be alright."

Saying that is one thing. J.P. took a long, hard look at his battered son slumped against the seat belt. *Believing it is another.*

5

Everything is Changing

Without a direct plan, Samira drove to the Maple Street Library and parked in her reserved space. *Next week would have a smoother start if I could get a little more paperwork off my desk.* Mrs. Haddock was redesigning the information board in the entryway when Samira arrived.

"Ms Samira!" The grandmotherly woman shook a finger at her supervisor.

"Whatever are you doing here? This is your day off!"

Samira quieted the assistant librarian with her finger. "I'm only here to pick up some paperwork." She slipped around the edge of the circulation desk and unlocked the door to her office. *I wouldn't mind working an hour if I had the office to myself.* "I'm not planning to stay."

Mrs. Haddock followed Samira. "Something tells me your girls are away this weekend . . ."

Samira pursed her lips as she flipped through the stack of mail on the corner of her desk. *Nothing that can't wait until Monday.*

" . . . If they were home you'd be busy with them somewhere instead of searching for something to keep you busy here."

Samira sighed. "You're right. Krissy and Kara are away this weekend." She smiled gently at the woman in the doorway. "I was just out and about and thought I'd pick up the finance reports for one more review before Tuesday's board meeting." *Anything to keep my mind busy.*

Mrs. Haddock rearranged her over-permed hair with her hands. "You really need to enjoy your time off, Ms Samira. I'm sure you have the reports in fine order already."

"Thank you, Helen." Samira slipped the reports into a manila envelope and with a swift twist, secured the string around the round plastic button. "Have you been busy today?"

Mrs. Haddock shook her head and nodded toward the window. "No ma'am. Too nice of a day for the library to be crowded. I have managed to catch up on the odd jobs however." She stepped aside as Samira closed the office door.

"The bulletin board out front looks great," Samira complimented. "It's nice to have a day to get caught up."

The wrinkles along Mrs. Haddock's mouth formed into a smile and her soft brown eyes twinkled slightly. "Thank you, Ms Samira. Have a nice afternoon and do something for yourself."

"You do the same." Samira waved with car keys in her hands. *I love working with Mrs. Haddock, but her insistence on being in my space is overwhelming sometimes.*

The car was hot from sitting those few minutes in the sun. Samira cracked the windows and turned on the air conditioner. *I really don't like taking work home.* She backed out of her parking space and turned in the direction opposite her house. *But I wouldn't have accomplished much with Helen hovering over me.*

Several blocks passed before Samira realized she didn't have a destination in mind. *I could take Helen's advice and do something for me.* She turned left onto the main thoroughfare and drove toward the new shopping mall. *I guess last night was for me as well.*

I can't remember the last time I've been to the mall alone! Samira stopped to admire the flower arrangements in the Hallmark window. *Krissy and Kara always drag me to their favorite stores. But not today.* Samira window shopped her way to the department store at the end of the concourse. *My only deadline is meeting Susan at the Civic Center at seven thirty.* She checked her watch. *Plenty of time.*

"May I help you?" a sales clerk asked from behind a rack of clearance items.

Samira's mind was a million miles from the merchandise. "Oh, no, I'm just looking today."

"Are you looking for yourself or for someone else?"

I'm really not shopping for anyone. "Myself, I guess."

"Well . . ." the short, stocky woman pushed a pair of big glasses up on her nose. " . . . You shouldn't be looking in the clearance area. The new summer line is over here." She motioned for Samira to follow. They stopped in front of brightly colored fabrics and summer accessories. "This is where you should be shopping."

It's certainly more cheerful over here! Samira smiled and began to scan the size 10 racks. *I really don't need anything new.* She pulled a skirt off the rack and held it out for a better view. *But then again, I haven't purchased anything new since . . .* Samira's eyes looked far into the distance at nothing in particular . . . *since I can't remember when!*

Before she realized it, Samira was in front of a three-way mirror in the dressing room. Assorted colors garnished an ankle-length skirt hanging gracefully from her waist. Samira piled her hair on top of her head so she could see the back view of the sleeveless sweater.

"It's definitely you."

Samira made eye contact with the same sales clerk. "I don't know . . ." She turned around. "I love the skirt." She ran her hands over the broomstick pleats and admired the splashes of color against the navy background. "But I'm not so sure about the top. I really prefer a jeweled neckline and this fuchsia isn't doing much for me."

The stocky sales clerk took a hold of the edge of the skirt. The design took on a new dimension when the pleats were erased. "You're right about the hot pink. Definitely not doing much for you. But I think the V-neckline is fine." She dropped the hem and allowed the skirt to fall naturally once again. "The new Vanderbilt twin sets are the answer. The colors are much softer."

Wearing the merchandise, Samira followed the woman back onto the sales floor. The clerk held up an open-weave crocheted tank.

"Yellow?"

The woman held it up to Samira's face. "Yellow or the neutral taupe." She held another color over the edge of the skirt.

"The open weave seems a bit risqué for me." Samira was already searching for another option.

"Just try it on," the clerk encouraged. "I think you'll be pleasantly surprised. It's not as revealing as it appears."

Samira reached for the taupe sweater and returned to the dressing room. Once again she admired the new outfit. *Much better color and she's right, the sweater is very elegant.* She turned in the mirror and put her hands against her stomach in an effort to flatten it. Samira turned around again. *Just for fun, I think I'll take it home.*

The clerk folded the sweater in tissue paper at the checkout counter and slipped it into a paper shopping bag with the skirt. "You do know about the Memorial Day Shopping Extravaganza coupons, don't you?"

"No, I don't believe I do." Samira signed a check for the purchase amount.

"You earn one coupon for every item purchased anywhere in the mall all day." The woman slid two coupons across the counter. "You can use them at the food court or movie theaters until five o'clock Monday afternoon of next weekend." She adjusted her large glasses. "If you don't get them used then you can keep them for the Labor Day weekend specials. Or if that doesn't work out, use them at the fall Bridal Fair." She smiled. "The trick is remembering where you put them if you save them that long."

"My daughters love the Bridal Show." Samira stashed the red coupons in the bill compartment of her wallet. "I bring them every year."

"There you go. Don't forget where you put them." The lady made direct eye contact. "How old are you daughters?"

"Thirteen and fourteen."

"I'd never have guessed." The clerk handed the bag over the counter. "Enjoy your new outfit ma'am."

I never shop for myself for no reason. Samira smiled. *With any luck, maybe I'll have a reason to wear a new outfit.*

Samira shifted the bag from one hand to another as she waited in line for frozen yogurt. *That is if Phil ever calls again.* Her thoughts returned to the circumstances of the morning. *I probably should have kissed him.* She ordered a small cone and a glass of water. *But I might not have stopped with one kiss, and where would that have landed me?* Samira found an empty bench and sat down. *Back in bed, that's where I'd have ended up!* She caught a drip on the back of the cone with her tongue. *Tom was right. Sex always comes with obligation.* She thought some more. *I don't know if I'm ready for that yet.*

Back at the house Samira remade her bed and started a second load of laundry. There were still a couple of hours before she had to meet Susan at the Civic Center. *It's the last chamber concert of the season.* She unpacked her new clothes and hung them on the closet door while she put things back in order. Tom's picture was still turned sideways on the dresser. She started to turn it back then thought again. *I don't want to face him every time I brush my hair!*

Samira sat down on the edge of her bed. *It feels good to sit down for a bit.* She stretched out on top of the quilted comforter and inhaled the trace of aftershave from the pillow case. As she closed her eyes, the passion in Phil's touch came alive. She allowed her mind to revisit the way he moved his hand into the small of her back asking for silent permission to continue. *How sweet that he took the time to wait for permission. But surely by then he knew I was going to follow through.*

Samira opened her eyes with a start. The digital clock read six-thirty. She checked her watch to be sure she wasn't dreaming. When the two matched, she moaned out loud. *There's no way I can be on time now!*

Samira quickly changed into dress slacks and a blazer. She fastened her hair at the back of her head with a clip and changed her earrings to something more suitable for the evening. Fresh lipstick and a quick brush of cheek color sent Samira out the door without eating.

Susan grabbed Samira by the arm as she traded her car keys for a valet ticket.

I knew she would be frantic!

"Where have you been? I was beginning to get worried." Susan was directing Samira toward the auditorium as she spoke. "I called your house and you weren't there so I called your mother and you weren't there either."

"You called my mother?"

"Not really . . ."

Thank goodness!

" . . . I just wondered if that's where you were." Susan was still guiding Samira by the arm.

They crossed the formal lobby before Samira brought Susan to a halt in mid-stride. "We can't go in during a number."

A tuxedo clad usher held his finger up for them to be quiet.

"I about freaked when you weren't here. You're never late, Samira. Are you feeling alright?"

"I'm fine, really, Susan." Samira tucked a stray hair behind an ear. *How much do I want to tell her?* "I went shopping this afternoon at the new mall then went home and took a nap. I just overslept, that's all." Samira shrugged her shoulders.

Susan's mouth fell open and her bright blue eyes lit up in disbelief. "You went shopping alone? Without the girls?"

The usher motioned again for them to talk more quietly.

Susan put her hands on her wide hips and lowered her voice. "No way! You never go shopping; especially alone!"

I know she'll be totally surprised with this piece of information. "I even bought a new outfit." She leaned away as Susan tried to put her hand against Samira's forehead.

"Something's wrong," Susan stated. "Is there something you're not telling me?"

If you only knew. But, Susan is not the one to talk to about Phil. Samira considered her options. *Then again, maybe I shouldn't bring him up to anyone until I know if I'm going to see him again.*

The sound of muffled applause from within the auditorium beckoned a safe reprieve from the pending conversation. When the usher opened the doors the women entered the aisle-lit concert hall.

Stage light illuminated the program just enough to make out the title of the second piece. *String Quintet G, Op.111: 1, 2 and 4.* Ordinarily Johannes Brahms would relax Samira. But her mind was busier than usual. She found herself squirming impatiently in the contoured chair. *I wonder what time he turned out the light?* Rarely did she need a nap in the daytime. *We must have stayed up later than I thought.* She turned her program to the dim light between numbers. *Vivace Ma Non Troppo Presto. Oh good, I'm ready to pick up the tempo!*

Samira breathed in the fresh evening air outside the civic center.

"Are you hungry?" Susan pulled a lightweight jacket over her shoulders.

Samira stepped aside so a man and woman could pass on the sidewalk. They were walking hand in hand. *I don't remember what it's like to belong to someone like that . . .*

"Samira?" Susan interrupted her thoughts. "Are you feeling alright? You seem quite distracted tonight."

"Oh, really, I'm fine," Samira lied. *I don't remember what it's like to be needed by a man.*

"You don't look very fine."

"Something just caught my eye, that's all."

Susan's blonde head spun around. "Someone you know?"

Samira brushed a strand of long hair from her face. "No one in particular." With a deep breath she changed the subject. "Don't you just love the crisp rush of the spring air?"

"I'm a little cool myself." Susan studied her friend's face carefully. "You parked with the valet, right?"

Samira flipped her parking ticket between her fingers.

"They're open until eleven. Let's grab something to eat then I'll drop you back here." Susan started for her car.

"Wait, Susan . . . I don't want to keep you from your family." *And I don't know if I'm up to a meal with Susan.*

"Nonsense." Susan linked her arm in Samira's and started for her car again.

Why do I let her control me like this? Samira skipped a step to pace Susan's sudden urgency.

Susan drove a few blocks and pulled into a neon-lit diner. The line at the door hinted at a long wait, but the hostess assured them it would only be a few minutes before a table would be available. Samira crossed her arms uncomfortably over her stomach. *I am hungry, but not in this noisy setting.* Her eyes followed a lime green and orange neon line around the top edge of the diner. *Dear God, make this meal pass quickly.*

I just want something light to hold me over.

Susan looked over the top of her menu. "That didn't take too long. You're not going to get a salad are you?"

I wish it didn't make so much difference to Susan what I eat and don't eat. When the waitress came to take their order she ordered a Chinese Chicken Salad with a glass of water.

"Always watching your diet," Susan mused. "Just once I'd love to see you sink your teeth into a big juicy steak."

"I'm not watching my diet. I just don't like to eat heavy before going to bed." Slightly annoyed, Samira shifted in her seat.

"At least you can go home and go to bed." Susan emptied her thoughts. "I'll have to check on Joey when I get home, put the house back together, and I'm sure Sam will want to get personal in bed." She tilted her head to one side. "Then maybe I'll be able to go to sleep." Susan slapped the menu down on the table and waved for a waitress.

Samira tried to remember what it was like to be a wife and a mother at the same time. It was hard to step back into those shoes. *But I don't ever remember not wanting private time with my husband.*

"How do you do it?" Susan looked Samira directly in the eyes. "You always seem to have everything under control."

Susan has no idea who I am anymore. "For one thing . . ." Samira had to raise her voice to be heard over the jukebox. " . . . I don't have a little one to care for anymore." *For another thing I've sacrificed a personal agenda.* She smiled quietly to herself. *With the exception of last night.*

The waitress delivered a huge plate of onion rings. Susan pushed the plate into the center of the table. "Dig in. I can't eat all these by myself."

Samira declined the offer politely.

"There you go, watching your diet again." Without warning, Susan changed subjects. "Did I tell you Sam signed me up for golf lessons this summer? He says that's the only place we're ever going to be able to hold an uninterrupted conversation so it's time I learned to swing a club." She continued to talk with a mouthful. "I think there's still room in the class if you'd like to join me."

Golf? That's one of the few personal details I do know about Phil. He plays golf. Samira turned a bite of salad on her fork. "Thanks, but I'll be busy enough with the girls' activities. They're going to baby sit for my brother's kids this summer."

"How many kids do they have now anyway?"

"Three," Samira smiled gently at the thought of her nieces and nephew. "Bonnie is just finishing first grade, Lizzie will go into Kindergarten next year and baby Mark just turned two."

"Holy-moly, no wonder they need your girls to baby sit." Susan tipped her head. "And what's up in your life? Anything tall dark or handsome?"

Samira almost choked on a bite of salad. "Why would you ask?" *Surely she doesn't know about last night!*

"Because . . ." Susan stopped talking to take a bite of shrimp. "If you're not seeing anyone, I have someone I think you should meet."

Oh good, she doesn't know . . .

"Would that be a yes or a no?"

That would be a definite NO! Samira avoided eye contact and rested her fork against the edge of the glass plate. "I don't know Susan." She composed her thoughts. "I'm really not in the market for a man right now." *Unless it's with Phil again.*

"Nor will you ever be." Susan's tone was accusing. "You need to step out of your comfort zone, Sister! It's time to experience life outside of your house for a change." Susan pushed her now empty plate aside and motioned for the waitress to pick it up. "Greg is really cute, he's a gentleman, and he's easy to get along with. I'll have him call you then you can make a decision."

"I really don't want him to call me, Susan." Her mind was reeling with memories of another time Susan set her up on a blind date. *I could live without that kind of humiliation again.* "I just prefer to handle my own affairs . . . or lack thereof." *Is that what I just started? An affair?*

"Honest, he's a really nice man, Samira. You might actually like him and fall in love or something. Then we could do family things together like we used to." Susan realized her words too late. "I'm sorry. That didn't come out exactly like I'd planned."

I know. Samira's eyes were fixed on the back of the booth behind Susan. *Everything always goes back to our family outings together.*

"Of course we could do some things together without a man too," Susan tried to smooth the tension that hung between them. "It's just hard for Sam to hang out without a guy in the picture, that's all."

It's just like Susan to point out the obvious. Samira shook her head as she took a bite of salad. *That was a long time ago. I wish she could let it be.*

The next thing Samira knew, Susan was fishing for her car keys. "Are you finished? The Royal's game is probably about over and I promised Sam I'd be back about then."

The salad on Samira's plate was only half eaten. She set her fork aside and wiped her fingers on a napkin. *This would be the answer to the prayer for a quick meal, I guess.* She nodded. *Even if I'm not finished, going home alone has to be better than sitting in this crowded diner with Susan.*

Samira silently longed for someone she could really visit with. *I used to have a lot in common with Susan Olinger.* She extracted a dollar bill from her wallet and slid it under the edge of her plate. *But I don't know if I can continue to participate in this friendship; if indeed it can still be considered a friendship at all.*

6

Stuck

J.P. half carried James into the house and took him directly to the bathroom. Without much resistance, he stripped James down to his underwear and maneuvered him into the shower. *God, I hate to do this.* J.P. turned the faucet. *But it's the only way to revive him.* Seconds later, cold water rained down on his son's weakened body.

James screamed obscenities at the top of his lungs. *At least he's saying something.* J.P. loosened his hold. When his legs gave out, J.P. allowed his son to slide down the wall into a sitting position. *What the hell?* J.P. stared at a single golden hoop hanging through his son's naval. *James, you and I have a long way to go.* J.P. closed the bathroom door and left James alone to sober up.

Chase's bark announced a visitor before J.P. could change out of his wet clothes.

Mike, no doubt. I wondered how long it would be before he'd look me up. He unbuttoned his dress shirt as he went back down the hall.

"Hey, man, most people shower with their clothes off." Mike helped himself to a glass of water. "Denise told me you'd be here." He downed the water in one gulp. "What the hell are you doing home? I figured the Mid-America leak would keep you occupied all afternoon."

J.P. slipped out of his wet shirt and draped it over the back of a kitchen chair. "It's James." He nodded toward the closed bathroom door. "I left him in a cold shower." He started down the hall toward his bedroom again. "How the hell do you know about Mid-America?"

"James?" Mike followed J.P. into the short hall and stopped in the bedroom doorway. "How'd he get down here?"

"When did you talk to Denise?"

"A few minutes ago."

"At the office?" *Why's she still at the office.*

"Yes, at the office! I figured you'd be involved with Stephenson somehow." He pointed an accusing finger at J.P. "By the way, I signed that affidavit. Now you owe me two."

"Two, where'd you get two?"

"I fed your orphaned dog last night. That was one. And signing an official document on a Saturday is definitely another. That's two."

Mike always keeps score. J.P. shook his head. *Denise should have been home before I got back from Mid-America.*

"So what's the scoop with James?" Mike crossed his arms and leaned on the doorframe.

"Long story . . ." J.P. changed into gym shorts and a sleeveless t-shirt while he explained how James was delivered to his office.

" . . . so, now he's in the shower sobering up."

He passed Mike in the doorway and headed back to the kitchen. Mike followed.

"Now I'm stuck here for the rest of the day." J.P. untwisted the tie on a loaf of bread. "Did you eat?" *I'm starving.*

"Yeah, I ate at the club." Mike straddled the back of a kitchen chair. "Who's tending to Mid-America if you're here this afternoon?"

J.P. opened the refrigerator to find the fixings for a sandwich. His mind was still on James. "His timing could have been a little better." J.P. opened a jar of mayonnaise. *He didn't answer my questions.* "So how do you know about Mid-America?"

Mike beat his hands against the tabletop in a rhythmic pattern. "One of our clients is missing some assets." He grinned. "I figured you were called in for legal counsel." Mike reached for a bag of potato chips.

"I thought you said you ate."

"I did." Mike fingered a chip. "I doubt James stopped to think about *your* timing when he walked out on his mother."

"Still pisses me off." J.P. stacked cheese slices and leafed lettuce on top of cold cuts. *The whole deal with Janet pissed me off.* "I've already met with Mr. Stephenson. There's not much he can do until Monday morning." He leaned on the counter and took a bite of his sandwich. "What are you doing off the course already?"

Mike helped himself to another chip. "I played golf with the mayor and this new guy named Sammy-O. Only nine holes this round. Just for the record, I'm playing them again on Wednesday."

Must be nice to have time to play golf whenever you want. "What kind of a name is 'Sammy-O?'"

"Don't know, but he's a damn good golfer. Still beat 'em by four strokes." Mike wiggled his thick blonde eyebrows and grinned. "Strictly business though."

"If this Mid-America case rolls, it's likely I'll need assistance. Think you guys might be able to spare an intern for a couple-three weeks?"

"Hey, hey," Mike interrupted the professional conversation. "I think a little congrats is in order here. I gave up a whole Saturday to challenge our fair mayor."

Half a Saturday. "Was the mayor keeping score?"

"Nope!"

I didn't think so . . .

"I need to stop by the office on my way home. I'll talk to Vince and see who's working where." Mike grinned. "On a second thought, I have a new little gal who's sharper than a pin. How much experience you looking for?"

"In what category?"

"How much work you lookin' to get done?" Mike rose from his chair to refill the empty water glass. "I don't have anybody on board like that model you picked up."

Bobbie Jo Sommers. J.P. finished chewing. "She picked me up, remember?"

Mike grinned fictitiously. "Oh, yeah. I forgot that detail. What was it she offered you again? S-N-S-A?"

J.P. returned the sly smile. *Good memory, Mikey.* "Sex—no strings attached." He laughed at the recollection. *And damn good sex too. But the SNSA was her rule.*

"How do you get so damned lucky?"

That time I happened to be in the right place at the right time. "Must be my looks."

"Certainly isn't intelligence."

J.P. displayed a choice finger but held the verbal assault. "What's wrong with the one shacking up at your place on the weekends?"

"Strings and plenty of them . . ."

He always ends up with these pushy broads who take advantage of his good nature.

" . . . I gotta get that one figured out." Mike filled his glass again. "Anyway, the modeling chick . . . what was her name?"

"Sommers. Bobbie Jo Sommers."

"Yeah. Bobbie Jo Sommers. I saw her picture on the cover of a magazine . . ."

J.P. pointed to a stack of mail. "Halfway down."

Mike started through the stack. "The girl at the office looks pretty experienced. Maybe a nine and a half. Great boo . . ."

"Spare me the stats." J.P. interrupted the physical description. *I don't need a distraction. I need a make-shift attorney.* "Who else you got?"

Mike pulled the cover model from the stack and whistled. "She does have a body, now, Counselor." He flipped through the lingerie catalog. "She should have made a killing with this release."

Every release.

"What exactly do you need assistance with?"

"The Hughes case will be ready for court next month and there's a couple smaller cases that need attention." He ate the last bite of the sandwich.

"Shit, J.P. You've never backed away from a nine and a half before. What's up with you?" Mike shot an accusing look in J.P's direction.

He's right. The thought of anyone new who wasn't Samira suddenly wasn't appealing. *But I don't know if I like Mike taking notice.* He turned away from the observation. *But Samira obviously comes with strings attached.*

"Okay, let me check it out." Mike let J.P. off the hook. "I'm thinking Derek Danielson. He's done with school, just waiting for the bar exam schedule to post." His eyes twinkled. "But this other gal . . ."

A loud crash in the bathroom interrupted the conversation. Both men stared at the closed door.

I forgot James was here.

Mike winced. "He must have hit it pretty hard, huh?"

"Plenty hard." J.P. closed his eyes and squeezed the bridge of his nose with his thumb and forefinger. *I just hope he made it to the toilet.*

Mike put a firm hand on his friend's shoulder. "Go easy on him, J.P. It's his first offense."

"It's his first *public* offense."

"Do you know that for a fact?"

"According to his mother . . ."

Mike looked J.P. square in the eye. "Then he's innocent until proven guilty."

I have my doubts.

"At least give him a towel or something." Mike was headed for the back door. "He's probably freezing to death. God, I hate it when you don't bring me a towel."

I remember the last time I sobered Mike up in a cold shower. That was a long, hard night. "Women have a way of bringing men to their knees over a toilet."

"Do you think James is involved with a girl?"

"Oh yeah." J.P. pictured the girl in his mind. "Jennie Johnson. She's a trip."

James was heaving again.

"Look, I'm going to take off and let you deal with James." Mike unlatched the screen. "Let me know if you need any help with Mid-America. I'll be around the rest of the weekend and my official day off is Monday, you know."

An official day off is the fringe benefit of owning a partnership with Vince Barringer. J.P. nodded and watched Mike disappear through the door.

Is there anything else that can go wrong today? J.P. unclipped the leash from Chase's collar when they reached the path that paralleled the creek. The phone call back to Janet had been anything but pleasant and James hadn't exactly been cooperative either. *But at least he's sleeping it off now.* Familiar scenery passed at a steady pace as Chase and J.P. ran in sync.

God, he's only fifteen years old. What caused him to end up like this? Sweat ran down J.P.'s sides. *Josh always seems to have his act together, but James follows a different path.*

J.P. had been out of his boys' lives for a long time. In fact, he couldn't remember the last time James and Josh had been inside his house. *It's just like Jan to wait until things are out of control to hand off to me.*

J.P. snapped his fingers. Chase followed him over the walk bridge to the concrete path on the other side of the creek. J.P. stopped running long enough to reattach the leash. "Too many weekend walkers over here for you to run free."

He wiped the sweat off his face with the front of his shirt. *A few more blocks and I'd be in Samira's neighborhood.* J.P. shook his head. *But no reason to bother her with James passed out in the guestroom.*

Invigorated, J.P. set the stack of research files on top of his desk. *I need to get this Hughes case done before Mid America picks up pace.* He removed his shirt and used it to mop up the sweat on his face and arms. He skimmed the contents of the research again. But nothing was sinking in.

So what do I do with James? Being a dad didn't come as naturally as he'd hoped. *Hell, I didn't have time to even plan to be a dad.* But then time passed. *I guess I never really grew into it over time either.* He thought some more. *Being a dad meant spending time with a woman who made me miserable.*

As J.P. sat down in front of the television, Samira's living room came into mind. *She seems to have her life in order.* He could picture her daughter's school photos on the wall. *Obviously she has solid relationships with her kids.* Another picture came into his mind. *Who the hell knows who the man in the bedroom photo is?* That thought was slightly unsettling.

It was late into the night before J.P. heard James moving.

"Need some help?"

James was sitting in a heap on the bathroom floor. The blanket from the bed was wrapped loosely around James's shoulders.

James was weak and hung over. "I throw up but nothing happens." Silent tears stained his face

"Your stomach is empty but your muscles don't know that yet," J.P. knelt and offered his son a tissue. The attorney in J.P. Ralston was slowly giving way to the father James needed. "It's going to take some time for this one to wear off, James." He studied his son's weary face. "How's your head?"

"Pounding." James blew his nose. "I don't even know which way is up."

J.P. flipped on the overhead light to get a better look at his son. *I don't know if his eyes are black from drinking or from fighting.* James cursed and put his head between his knees.

"Why don't you go back to bed? You'll feel better lying down."

J.P. offered a hand to help pull him up. James refused the assistance and staggered to his feet on his own weakened power.

Have it your way.

James stumbled to the kitchen and collapsed into a kitchen chair, still wrapped in the blanket. Carefully, he rested his head in his hands.

J.P. placed the Styrofoam cup from the Café Ole in the microwave and waited for it to heat. When it was good and hot, he placed it on the table directly in front of his son.

"I'm not going to drink that shit."

Watch the attitude, James. "Its better than the last shit you drank and the caffeine will help the headache."

James pushed the cup away, almost causing it to spill.

Stubborn, just like his mother! "You can either drink it or I'll pour it in. Your choice." J.P. waited.

James squinted his eyes in the light of the kitchen. For a long time he stared at the cup. Eventually he took a sip, swearing as it burned his mouth. He took a few more sips then pushed it away again. "It's not helping my head."

"Give it time, it will." *Trust me. I know.* The Café Ole logo on the side of the cup caused emptiness in J.P.'s stomach. There was supposed to be a woman on the other side of that logo. *You didn't even attempt to call her tonight.* He wondered what the consequences of that might be down the road. *Women like it when you check in again soon after.*

A few short hours of sleep was all J.P. could find. His mind was consumed with questions he needed to ask James or Josh. At the same time he was already starting to process the next step for Mid-America. He rolled over again, disgusted that sleep wouldn't come.

J.P. finally climbed out of bed resigned to the fact that he might as well begin the day. Chase was still fast asleep on the rug. James' breathing was heavy and steady. *Best he just sleeps it off.* He poured a glass of orange juice and stepped outside to retrieve the Sunday paper.

J.P. was at his desk when the room darkened slightly. James filled the entire door. *He's grown since I spent time with him.* The Ralston men studied one another for a moment. *He looks like a little kid stuck in a six foot four inch body.*

"Hungry?"

James leaned heavily on the doorframe. "Not exactly."

He needs nourishment. "You should eat something." J.P.'s voice was low but controlled. "There are English muffins in the cupboard, but if you don't want that then try some dry toast. You need something in your stomach."

James nodded once then leaned forward and put his head in his hands. Several moments of silence passed between them before J.P. spoke again.

"A hot shower wouldn't be a bad idea either . . ."

Now James looked his father directly in the eye and tightened his jaw. "A *hot* shower would be a hellluvalot better than the one you put me through."

So much for starting the day on a decent note. "You can choose the temperature of the water when you can stand on your own power." J.P. kept a close watch on his son. "Look, James, I don't know what happened up there the other night but before this day is out, we need to get to the bottom of it."

James looked away. The circles under his eyes gave insight to the pain in his temples.

"Why don't you get something in your stomach and shower up?" J.P. remembered his promise to his ex-wife. "And before you and I sit down to sort through this mess, you owe your mother a phone call." J.P. pointed to the phone on the wall. He let that bit of information sink in. "Your clothes are still in the washer so you'll have to find something around here that fits."

James stuck out his foot and examined the lack of length in the barrowed pair of sweat pants he was already wearing.

I know. He's got a good inch and a half of height on me already! J.P. rose from his chair. "Don't forget the phone call."

J.P. took note of the dread in his son's eyes as he stared at the telephone. *I don't blame him. I wouldn't want to call her either.*

J.P. knew another phone call that needed consideration. *Samira's probably up by now, but I don't know if a Sunday morning call is a wise decision or not.* The attorney traded one file folder for another. *Besides, I couldn't tell if she really wanted to hear from me again or not.* He opened the cover of the file but didn't recognize the contents. *There was no way to read her thoughts.* J.P. closed the folder and leaned back in his chair. *Mike might be right. She may be out of my league.*

7

Out With It

The organ prelude beckoned parishioners into the sanctuary. Samira reached the top step at her parents' church. *I'm not getting here any too early.* She spotted her parents already seated in their regular pew near the front. *Mama and Daddy will be surprised to see me this morning.* Samira politely sidestepped a few friendly greetings then slipped in beside her father.

The familiar words of the old hymn came easily. Samira blended her clear soprano voice perfectly with her father's tenor harmony. *I love singing with Daddy!* Samira bowed her head as the pastor offered the invocation. *Sometimes I miss the tradition and familiarity of this place.*

It felt good to be tucked in the nook of her father's arm. *I always feel complete here.* But as she recited the prayer of confession, Samira no longer felt so confident. *Maybe I shouldn't have come here after all.*

Samira studied the stained glass windows. *I used to love looking at these windows as a child.* She observed the patterns and the colors. *The angles in the glass remind me of my comforter.* Samira squirmed in the pew. *Dear God . . . This is NOT the place to be thinking of that!* She felt her father's hand rest a little heavier than necessary against her shoulder. *Daddy used to do that to keep me still when I was little.* Samira grew self-conscious. *Am I that restless?*

A wave of relief rushed over Samira's being as she stood for the final hymn. It was good to be standing. Raymond's voice sang out in clear tenor harmony once again, but this time it was all Samira could do to open her mouth.

There is no way Daddy would approve of Friday night. She sang a few words. *Phil is too intense for my father.* The song ended. *But I see some of Daddy's traits in Phil too.* She bowed her head for the benediction. *Like his work ethic.*

Without warning, hands and faces began to surround Samira. Warm welcomes and well wishes from old family friends flooded from every direction.

"It's so good to see you . . ."

"Welcome home, Samira . . ."

"Where is your family this morning . . . ?"

Samira pasted a smile on her face and patiently answered questions and exchanged handshakes in the aisle. *I know they mean well, but this is a little overwhelming.* She searched the room with her eyes, hoping to locate her parents. *Where's my father when I need him?*

"It's good to see you, Samira."

Of all the people I thought I might run into this morning, David was not one of them. Samira made an effort to appear composed. *I thought he quit coming to church soon after he and I . . .* Samira corrected herself. . . . *Well, soon after I stopped seeing him.*

"It's good to see you, David." She forced another smile.

Immediately following Tom's passing, David took it upon himself to try to fill the vacancy in Samira's life. *His intentions were good.* Samira shook her head at the sudden recollection. *And I know he was a good friend of Tom's, but . . .*

"Uh-hum." A woman cleared her throat.

David laid his hand on her shoulder. "Samira, this is my wife, Melanie."

Oh, good. David found a wife. Samira offered her hand and a word of congratulations on the expectant baby. *I wonder if she knows about me.* Samira listened impatiently as Melanie rattled on and on about their expectant child. *I really didn't mean to hurt him . . .*

"Samira, dear . . ."

Thank you, Mama! Get me out of here!

" . . . I see you've met Melanie."

"Just now." Samira allowed her mother to take her hand. "And their news is very exciting too."

"We think it's a boy," David announced proudly.

"It is very exciting, isn't it?" Ashleigh smiled genuinely. "You're father is waiting outside, dear." Ashleigh started to lead Samira down the aisle toward the double doors at the back of the sanctuary. "Do take care of Melanie, now David."

Thank goodness! Samira held on to her mother's hand just like she had as a child. *I just wasn't ready to see anyone else.* Samira sighed. *And David wasn't the one I needed.*

Ashleigh laughed heartily as she stepped into the narthex. "Everyone is always glad to see you. They don't mean to be overbearing."

Samira looked directly into her mother's dark eyes. *Mama grows more beautiful every day.* Her once dark hair was now streaked with gray and white. Samira had inherited her mother's chocolate brown eyes and tall frame.

"You look radiant this morning, Mama."

"Why, thank you, dear." Ashleigh's olive complexion glowed from within. "I had a feeling you might show up here with the girls away for the weekend." She smoothed a long strand of loose hair back from her face and skillfully tucked it into the bun at the nape of her neck.

I don't want to ask. But I do want to know. "When did David come back to church?"

"It's been awhile," Ashleigh thought out loud. "Ever since he got married. A couple of years anyway." She touched Samira on the shoulder. "I know it is still hard for you to see him."

"Really, it's alright." David aside, the sooner she was out of this church, the better. *It's just strange to be back sitting among old memories again.*

Samira shaded her eyes and spotted her father waiting patiently in the shade of an old oak tree. *He looks quite sprite in his sports jacket and dress slacks.* His hair had also grayed over the years but as far as Samira was concerned, he hadn't aged at all. Raymond's hazel eyes sparkled with delight as his hands connected with Samira's.

"It's good to have you here this morning, Princess. And you're coming for lunch I presume?"

"Of course!" *I have nothing else on my agenda.* "I expected Wes and Pam to be here with the kids."

Raymond looked deep into Samira's eyes.

Oh, Daddy, don't do that!

"Weston said something about Pam being away this weekend. I'm assuming he'll join us for lunch."

Ashleigh was already headed down the sidewalk.

Daddy knows me too well. Samira started to follow her mother, but hesitated in her father's gaze. *He's wondering why I couldn't sit still.*

Every room of Ashleigh's house was adorned with freshly cut flowers.

"The lilies are beautiful, Mama." *And they smell good too.*

"They're in full bloom now." Ashleigh fingered the bouquet as she passed by the dining room table. "Would you like some coffee? Almond spice made just this morning."

Samira knew the house well for she had grown up in this very place. Without hesitation she crossed the white painted kitchen and retrieved two cups from the cupboard. *Everything is always in its place.* The stenciled ivy vine along the bottom of the cabinet door matched the pattern in the tiled backsplash of the counter.

"Lunch smells wonderful!" Raymond shared a contented smile with his daughter. "Weston left a message that he and the children will be here for lunch."

As always.

Ashleigh nodded her head with approval. "I was almost sure he wouldn't attempt to feed the children Sunday dinner on his own."

"Where is Pam this weekend?" Raymond accepted a cup of coffee from his daughter. "Thank you, Princess."

"Pam went to Springfield with some girlfriends for the weekend." Ashleigh sipped her coffee. "Weston said she needed the time away."

I'm sure she did. Being at home with three little ones all day long definitely merits a weekend away. Samira enjoyed the aroma of the coffee as much as the flavor. *Although I'm not sure I personally ever took any time like that for myself when the girls were little.* Samira smiled at the recollection. *I always took Tom with me and left the girls here.*

"So, Princess," Raymond addressed his daughter gently. "Tell me, what's new in your life?"

"Well . . ." Without thinking, Samira started to mention the new man in her life. *No wait.* She took a quick sip of coffee. "I can't think of anything in particular." *I have never withheld anything from my parents before.*

The simple fact that she'd had an affair over the weekend caused sudden anxiety. *My parents would not approve.* Samira sighed into her coffee. "Nothing new, I guess. Just the same old routine." *I've never had anything to withhold from them before!*

"When do you expect the girls home?" Ashleigh turned her attention back to her daughter.

Samira recovered quickly. "This evening." She set her coffee cup on the counter and opened the cupboard to set the table. *They are probably on their way over to the clubhouse for the anniversary party as we speak.* "Norma and Dale will bring them back sometime after supper."

"I'm sure they're having a grand time with all of their cousins." Ashleigh glanced in her daughter's direction. "You'll have to get some plates from the dishwasher." Ashleigh checked the meat in the oven. "Did you go to the chamber concert with Susan last night?"

Samira nodded her head as she counted out seven forks and seven spoons. *But that may very well be the last time I go anywhere with Susan!*

"We called Friday night to see if you wanted to join us for dinner at The Elks. Did you get our message?"

Samira dropped a table knife against the white tiled floor with the mention of Friday night. *That would have been one of the messages I ignored on my answering machine.*

"Well, anyway," Ashleigh continued. "Since you didn't answer we went ahead. Wonderful meal. Ed and Phyllis met us there . . ."

"Who?" Samira turned around suddenly. *Who did she say?*

"Ed and Phyllis Jones," Raymond clarified over the top of the Sunday paper. "You know Ed . . ."

Samira didn't hear the rest of the sentence. *Oh! I thought she said she met Phil!* "Samira . . ."

"What."

Ashleigh laughed a jolly laugh. "I don't know what's gotten into you, dear, but I need the serving bowl from the china hutch. Would you mind getting it for me?"

The bang of a door followed by hurried little footsteps announced the grandchildren. *Thank God!*

"Granny, Granny!"

Samira watched her mother's eyes dance as she greeted her youngest granddaughters with a group hug. The little girls squealed with delight as their grandfather lifted them off the floor. *I remember when Daddy used to do that to me.* Samira finished setting the silverware around the table.

"Where's your father?"

"Coming in a minute," Bonnie, the oldest, answered. "He couldn't get Mark out of the car seat."

Wes always has trouble working gadgets.

Lizzie giggled and climbed into her grandfather's lap at the kitchen table.

Samira's brother appeared in the kitchen doorway carrying his youngest child. Mark's little blonde head was resting heavily against his daddy's shoulder. Without permission, Samira reached out her hands to the toddler.

Mark leaned into Samira's hands without thinking twice.

"How's my little Mark?" Ashleigh asked her grandson.

The boy turned his face away from the attention. *Let's go rock, little man. Did you just wake up?* She snuggled her nephew noting how much he had grown since she'd last held him. As he closed his eyes against her shoulder, Samira ran a finger through a lock of curls. Softly, she kissed the top of his head and nudged the chair into a rocking motion.

Tom wanted a little boy. She imagined herself as a new mother again. *We would have tried again if . . .* Little Mark sighed heavily indicating a deep sleep. *Well anyway . . .* Samira caressed Mark's soft hair as she continued to cradle him in her arm.

Casual conversation followed dinner as Samira helped her mother clear the dishes. She could see her nieces through the sliding door playing on the swing set with their grandfather. *Maybe I'll join them when we're done here.*

"Sorry about barging in on you, Sis," Weston apologized as he sorted through the Sunday paper. "I didn't realize you had plans to be here *without* the girls."

"Since when do you have to feel sorry about showing up here with the kids?" Samira closed the dishwasher and started the wash cycle.

Wes continued to shuffle the papers. "I know you don't get much time alone with the folks, that's all..."

Today is not the day to be alone with the folks anyway.

"...What happened to the business section?"

"Your father had it in the sunroom." Ashleigh answered as she entered the kitchen. "Look who I found sitting in the middle of the crib." She skillfully maneuvered about the kitchen carrying little Mark on her hip.

Wes disappeared into the sunroom and sank into the floral cushions of the couch. Samira watched him settle into the business news.

Weston always reads the business news first. Samira spent some time on the lawn admiring her mother's flowerbeds. Brilliant color accented every corner of the yard. *It's no wonder I love gardening so much.* She returned to the air-conditioned house through the sunroom.

Wes lowered the newspaper and addressed his sister. "I thought about calling you to help with the kids yesterday morning, but Mom said you had a day to yourself."

"You could have called. I was home." *Why do I make myself so available?*

"That's alright. Turned out Mom was home." Wes went back to his newspaper.

That's good. I had company anyway. Samira straightened some gardening magazines on the coffee table.

"So, what's new in your life?"

Why is everyone all of a sudden so interested in my life? She put her hands to her face when she felt her cheeks fill with color.

"Obviously you've got something to share." Wes's eyes twinkled at his sister.

Samira rolled her eyes. "It's just the sun." *Wes knows I'm lying.*

"What do you say we go for a walk?"

"Maybe I don't feel like walking." Samira headed for the kitchen.

"Isn't it a beautiful day?" Ashleigh exclaimed.

"It's a great day for a *walk*." Wes followed his sister with interest. His untied shoestrings tapped against the tile.

"Don't you have someplace to be?" Samira poured a glass of iced tea for herself. *If I tell anyone anything, it will be Wes. But he already knows I have something to tell.*

Wes shook his head and held an empty glass under the pitcher.

"Weston," Ashleigh called from the table. "Can you get Mark out of the high chair for me?"

Wes left his glass on the counter and went to assist his mother.

Maybe he'll forget about going for a walk. She watched little Mark toddle off toward the family room. *But if I'm going to talk to him, I don't want to talk here!* Samira stepped into her loafers and started out the front door.

"Hey, where are you going?"

"For a walk."

Wes scrambled to tie his shoes. He caught up to Samira halfway up the block.

"My ears are on little sister . . ."

Samira set the pace and avoided eye contact. "What if I don't have anything to tell you?" *But I know the words are going to tumble.*

Wes lengthened his stride in order to keep pace. "You always have something to tell me. I'm your confidant, remember?" He caught his breath and took a few more steps. "Might as well spill it."

Samira kept her eyes glued to the sidewalk. *I need to talk to him, but I don't want him to know all the details.*

"Okay, then I'll guess." He took a stab. "Somebody you met through Susan?"

How frustrating! "I don't need Susan to find a date!"

"Okay, so you found him on your own. What else you got?"

How does he know already that this is about a man? "Close. I think I might have a man in my life." Samira glanced to the left, then to the right before stepping off into an intersection.

"Short? Fat? Skinny?"

He's just right in all of those departments. "Handsome, tall, tender, funny . . ." *Taller than Tom.*

" . . . Whoa, whoa, whoa. Handsome and tall are good. Go back to the tender part."

Wrong adjective! " . . . We danced, we talked . . ."

"And . . . ?"

I have to tell him to clear my conscience. "And I let him stay."

They kept walking.

Why isn't he saying anything?

"It's not like I just let him stay, I mean," Samira searched her words, but nothing was coming to mind. "I've been out with him before . . ."

Unintentionally, Samira's pace slowed a little.

"I'm not passing judgment, Sis."

Why not. You usually do.

"So, how long have you known him? Is he married?"

Samira slapped her brother hard on the arm. *No! He's not married!* "Divorced. Has two teenage boys who live with their mother." *I can't believe he asked me that!*

"Where'd you meet him?"

"At the library."

"What's he do for a living?"

"He's an attorney. I think."

"You think? You should know. Successful?"

Now he's going to pass judgment. "I don't know!" Samira threw her hands up. "He drives a pickup, has designer labels in his suit coats."

"Smoker? Party animal?"

"Wes! You said you weren't passing judgment!" Samira paused briefly at the curb and waited for a car to pass before she started across the street. *I hardly know enough about him to answer these questions!*

"I'm not passing judgment on you, but he's another matter. So come on, out with it . . ."

It's not like I didn't expect Wes to ask questions. "Alright. But only one more question." Samira ran her hand through her hair, which had fallen out of the clip. "Non-smoker, plays golf, don't know anything about his personal life, and he drinks Italian wine."

"Last inquiry: history with women?"

Samira stopped mid-stride. Wes stopped a few steps in front of her.

Why would he ask me that? "Frankly, Wes, I didn't ask and he didn't offer." She pushed her hair back again.

"I just don't want you to get hurt . . ."

How can I possibly get hurt if I don't have any expectations for him? Samira turned a shoulder to her brother. *Sometimes I get so tired of being protected and babied.*

" . . . It's been a long time . . ."

"I know," Samira interjected. "But I . . ." She searched for an explanation. " . . . I really had a good time . . ." *I don't want to make eye contact with my brother.*

Samira pulled her head back as Wes removed her sunglasses.

"Just go slow, okay?" He paused momentarily. "Life's too short not to take a risk, but make it a calculated one, alright?"

Why do I feel like he can see right into my soul?

Samira recalled her brother's advice when she'd decided not to see David anymore. "You once told me to look for somebody with passion . . ."

Wes rolled his eyes, "Passion yes. Lust, no. You've got a lot to offer, Sis. I don't like the idea of some guy taking advantage of you . . ."

He's not just some guy! "I invited *him* to stay . . ." *At least I don't think so anyway.*

" . . . that doesn't mean he had to accept the invitation!" Wes frowned. "He could have kissed you goodnight and made his exit . . ."

It's not like he didn't try. "Maybe I didn't want him to leave." *Now there's a confession if I've ever had one.*

"You haven't known him that long. I'd just appreciate him more if he took his time getting you in bed, that's all."

He took his time once we were in bed. Samira caught that thought. *But that's not a detail I'll share with anyone. Not even my brother.*

Wes put his hands on his hips and looked into the distance behind Samira. "Truce, okay?"

That means we can't discuss this matter in the same way again. Samira nodded once. *Truce.*

Wes was looking hard into his sister's eyes.

I hate hearing what he has to say. But I do feel better having spilled my guts. She allowed Wes to press her head into his chest. His heart beat hard against her forehead.

"You're really out of shape if you can't pace me on a walk." Samira changed the subject.

"That was hardly a walk!" He nudged her around and they started back in the direction from which they had come. "I'd call that an almost-sprint!"

Comfortable silence walked with them for short distance.

"So you'll call if you need me?"

"Hopefully I won't have to call."

"But know I'll answer if you do."

Thank you, Wes.

8

History Repeats Itself

J.P. sat across from his son in the dining room at the athletic club. James fingered a French fry.

"You're not eating much." *He needs the nourishment after being so sick.*

James shrugged his shoulders. His face was solemn and the circles under his eyes were still dark and sunken. "I'm not that hungry."

J.P. wiped his mouth on a paper napkin and leaned back in the chair. *I'd still like a little more information before he goes back up home.*

"Look, James . . ." *Go easy, Counselor.* "I need to understand what happened the other night. I'm working with a blank slate here and can't be of much help to you if I don't know the facts."

The burger sat cold and untouched on the restaurant plate.

I've never known James not to eat. J.P. weighed his options. *Obviously open-ended questions aren't working.*

"Exactly how did Rick know to come pick you up?"

James was instantly on the defense. "I don't know."

That's the same answer I got last night. Trying to sound more patient than he felt, J.P. probed further, "You don't know, or your don't remember?"

James glared at his father and set his jaw. "I don't know *and* I don't remember."

"Listen, James." *This shouldn't be so hard!* "I'm not mad, I'm just in the dark. I need to know the circumstances so I can help mediate between you and your mother and Bruce . . ."

James interrupted with clenched teeth. "Just leave Bruce out if it! All right? I don't want anything to do with that bastard."

At least he's saying something. J.P. studied his son's face. *Obviously hit a nerve.* He motioned to the server across the room. *Let's see what else I can get.*

"All right." He signed the ticket for lunch. "We don't have to bring him into it." J.P. slid a five-dollar bill under his water glass.

Reluctantly, James followed his father toward the front desk. J.P. stopped in his tracks. *Wouldn't you know she'd be on duty today?* His eyes landed on the girl working behind the counter.

"My card please." *She knows my name even if I can't remember hers.*

The girl pretended not to notice him. J.P. waited. He knew James was watching with interest. *It would help if I could at least recall her name.* Once again J.P. addressed the young woman. "J.P. Ralston."

"Heard you been out of town." She tapped the edge of his membership card on the counter. Her short brown ponytail bobbed as she spoke, but her eyes were full of spite.

It would also help if she were wearing a staff name badge. J.P. chose his words carefully. "I've been working." *I'd have never picked her up if I'd known how resentful she was going to be.* J.P. reached for the card but she pulled it back and slowly slid it through the magnetic reader.

She squinted her eyes into an accusing look. "Is that your rehearsed excuse for broken promises?"

I don't make promises.

She placed the card flat on the counter between them but didn't remove her hand. *I wrote the policy about touching an employee while they're on duty.* He knew the security camera was focused on the registration desk. *I'm not going to take her bait.* Eventually she removed her hand so J.P. could have his card.

James broadened his step to catch up with his father. "What'd'ya do to piss her off?"

Now there's a sudden change from his sorry attitude. J.P.'s stride was resolute. *Just my luck James would witness that.* He weighed his options again, but this time the stakes were higher. *If I want answers from him, I'd best give him the answers he wants.*

"I slept with her." J.P. stopped in the middle of an empty parking space. "Once." *But I told her up front not to expect anything more.* J.P. pushed his hands into the pockets of his khaki shorts and looked into his son's gray eyes. *I never thought I'd be looking up at my own son.*

"She looked pretty wicked, Dad." James curled his mouth into a slight smile. "She didn't look that bad in bed did she?"

J.P. gave his son a look that told him not to tread much further. "To be perfectly honest, I don't remember." *I took her to dinner, got what I wanted, and was on my way.* He took a deep breath and looked beyond his son at nothing in particular. "It's not something I'm proud of and I don't plan to let it happen again." *At least not with her.*

James ran his tongue over his bottom lip. "She sure knew how to ruffle your feathers though, didn't she?"

J.P.'s patience was spent. *Enough discussion about my private life.* He took a step closer to his truck. "We have exactly two hours to get our butts to your mother's living room. Do you want to ride with me or shall I call her to pick you up?"

James opened the door of the truck and climbed inside. "I'll ride with you." He was still visibly humored.

Later that afternoon J.P. found himself sitting in a worn easy chair in Janet's living room. The discussion was not producing any results.

"We really can't finish this until Bruce gets home," Janet announced.

J.P. watched James close his eyes at the mention of Bruce's name. *I've got to get to the bottom of this.*

"I don't know what's keeping him," Janet admitted out loud. "He's usually home by now."

It's Sunday night. Where could he possibly be?

Janet was pacing the living room floor. *She has more gray in her hair than the last time I saw her.* He watched Janet's eyes fall on their son who was slumped into an old sofa.

"And you still have semester exams to take if you want to be promoted out of the freshman class." There was a sharp edge in Janet's voice.

James crossed his arms and shrugged his shoulders.

I'm beginning to think maybe he honestly has no memory of anything from Friday night.

Josh waved a rolled newspaper in his father's direction. Disgusted with the lack of progress with Janet and James, J.P. joined Josh in the kitchen.

"Page three, lower left corner." Josh pointed.

J.P.'s eyes came to rest on the sheriff's report. *Late Friday evening, area residents reported a scuffle at the picnic area in Madson Park. By the time authorities arrived on the scene the culprits had fled, but in their haste they left a broken picnic table and park bench. Anyone with information concerning the incident should contact the sheriff's department."*

"James?"

"Most likely," Josh replied half interested. "And his buddies."

"Your mother know?"

"Probably not." Josh shrugged. "I doubt she's read the paper today."

Josh reached for the phone when it rang, but his mother answered first from the other room.

She put her hand over the mouthpiece and spoke directly to J.P. "It's Bruce. He can't be home until late."

J.P. checked his watch. *It's already late, damn it.* "How late?"

"Ninish . . ."

Shit! I still have a couple hours of road time. "What's the hold up?"

Janet spoke back into the phone, but he could tell from the way she was hiding her face that she had no control. J.P. looked beyond Janet at his son on the couch. *James doesn't even want the bastard involved.* "Then we'll finish this up without him."

"You can't," Janet covered the mouthpiece again. "Bruce needs to be involved in these discussions."

Bullshit. J.P. knew he had to stay. *I told James I'd see him through this.* But at the same time, he could have easily walked away. He ran his hand through his hair.

Janet hung up the phone. "He's stuck with a client. That shouldn't be totally foreign to you, J.P."

He's in insurance agent. Reschedule the freakin' appointment.

"He says he'll be here as soon as he can break free." Janet sighed uneasily.

Prove to me he's even with a client. He watched Janet leave the room.

"I don't want to be here all night." J.P. spoke out loud without thinking. He looked at Josh. "Nothing personal. I can just think of some places I'd rather be."

"Missing a hot date, Dad?" Josh took a playful stab at his father.

"No."

But I can think of one I probably should have called. His thoughts rewound to the open-ended suggestion to call Samira when he was finished at the office Saturday. *It wouldn't have taken much to just pick up the phone.*

"I thought maybe you had somebody in waiting," Josh wiggled his eyebrows.

"Not this time, Joshy."

"Too bad." Josh hopped off the kitchen counter. "I have one meeting me in town in a few minutes if I can find a ride."

J.P. grinned at his son. *Now there's a subtle suggestion if I've ever heard one.*

He followed Josh into the living room and turned his attention back to James. *I'll try him one more time.* "Surely you can recall one of the issues between you and your mother before you left the house the other night?"

The teenager clung to his silence. *Come on, James. Just talk to me!* J.P. took a long breath.

"Grades." Josh answered for his brother. "That was one of the issues." He glanced at his brother for consent to continue. "They didn't think he should be going out to party because of his grades."

"I had all my homework done."

He's defensive, but at least we have a starting point. J.P. looked between his sons hoping for a breakthrough.

"They just don't want me going out period. Had nothing to do with my grades." James looked away. "Doesn't matter what I want to do, they keep me under lock and key anyway."

J.P. looked to Josh for confirmation. The older brother tipped his head to the side and shrugged one shoulder as if he couldn't dispute the accusation.

Janet returned to the room.

She looks like hell warmed over.

"After Bruce gets home we can decide how to handle the next few days," she announced.

The easiest thing to do is to tell the boys to pack and take them home with me until the dust settles. He thought about that possibility. *If it settles.* Something was telling him there was more domestic unrest than he cared to know. *Damned if I'm going to sit cooped up here while we wait.*

"You still need a ride to town, Josh?"

"Are you serious?" Josh was obviously surprised.

Janet's eyes shot a sharp look of warning across the room. "You can't take him to town."

"Why not?"

"Because Bruce isn't even here yet."

"Jan, it's not even seven o'clock."

"Josh has no business being in town tonight."

Josh rolled his head back in unbelief.

More bullshit. "We'll be back around nine." *But I hate to leave James here.*

"That will give James time to study," Josh suggested.

"The principal said he didn't have to take his tests until Tuesday."

"Good." J.P. looked at his son on the couch. "He'll have a head start." He tossed his keys to Josh. "We'll be back."

"J.P.!" Janet's voice was sharp. "Josh doesn't have any business going into town. It's Sunday night!"

What is she so afraid of? "Did you ask him if he had plans for tonight?"

Janet scoffed. "He can't have plans if he doesn't have a ride."

"Well, he has a ride. So now he can have some plans." *Case closed.*

"Don't you walk out that door on me!"

J.P. opened the door for his son. "We'll be back."

Once inside the truck, J.P. let out a deep breath. "What's up with the Sunday night bullshit?"

"She's always like that. If she doesn't want to drive us into town, then we can't go." Josh started his father's pickup and carefully pulled out of the driveway onto the gravel road.

These boys need some transportation of their own. I can't believe they're held hostage in their own house.

"She's always been that way," Josh explained. "She worries too much or something."

She's too damn controlling. J.P. decided to change the subject. "So who's the hot date?"

"You'll see," Josh smiled his father's smile. "She'll be there pretty soon."

They parked on the town square where a large group of teenagers were already gathered. The custom Dodge pickup drew a crowd. He watched closely, but didn't see Josh pay special attention to anyone in particular. *But he sure is having fun showing off my truck.* J.P. stepped away and allowed him the glory of the spotlight. *Looks like a harmless crowd.*

J.P. scanned the parking lot. Three other students were mingling on the far side of the parking lot. One face was familiar. *Rick.* J.P. studied him long and hard before deciding to be sociable. *He's not an active player here, but he doesn't appear to be an outcast either.*

"Hey Rick." He recognized the old sedan that had delivered his son to Joplin.

Rick looked up, made brief eye contact, and then looked away again. "H-hello Mr. Ralston."

"School's about out for the summer, huh?"

Rick nodded, then looked away again.

"What do you plan to do with all your free time, Rick?"

The young man stuffed his hands deep into his baggy shorts and dropped his head nervously. "I-ah-ah—I go work where m-my mom works."

I wish he weren't so self-conscious.

"I-is J-james home?" This time Rick looked directly at J.P. and actually held his eyes there for a few seconds.

"Briefly," the father reported. "I don't know how long he'll be around, but he's out home tonight." *My guess is he'll be better off staying with me for a little while.*

Rick raised his chin in a half nod. "Ah-I'd hoped h-he was okay."

A squeal of tires interrupted the lagging conversation. J.P. watched a rusted out Toyota pickup fish tail into another parking lot a few blocks away.

Rick watched too. When they could no longer see the truck, Rick spoke up. "Th-that's some of J-james's friends."

No shit?

"J-jennie's prob'ly over th-there."

This may be my opportunity to glean some information. "If Josh asks," J.P. peered into the distance. "Tell him I went for a walk. I'll be back."

Dusk was setting in as J.P. approached the small crowd of high school students. He hung in the shadows and evaluated their disposition before making his presence known. *Takes guts to make out in the bed of a pickup in public.* J.P. looked away from the couple heavily involved in personal activity.

You've got nothing to lose, Counselor. J.P. stepped out of the shadows. A few eyes glanced in his direction, but no one spoke. *I can be patient.* J.P. scanned the faces. *They look lost.* He waited some more. *I've seen this same look on James.* A petite, bleached-blonde girl wearing a skimpy mid-drift top was in the center of the gathering. She was wearing a hoop in her belly button that closely resembled that of his son's.

I'll take a stab. He watched her step forward, flaunting her heavy bust as she moved. *Jennie Johnson.*

One by one the teenagers began to pay attention. One of them lit a cigarette and offered it to J.P.

Gutsy, considering not one of them is of age in the first place. J.P. put up his hand in silent refusal. He leaned against a faded Pinto. "Anyone here know James Ralston?"

Time passed but no one answered. *I'll just wait this one out.*

"Who's asking?" a muscular young man with a tattoo on his bicep emerged from behind the Toyota with a young girl wrapped around his arm.

At least James isn't sporting a tattoo. Well, as far as I noticed. "His father."

Low murmurs passed among the crowd and a few students started to walk away.

The girl in the mid-drift top took a step forward. "You're his dad?"

Yep, Jennie Johnson.

"I didn't know he had a dad." The streaked ponytail that hung off the back of her head bounced with the front of her shirt "But I know him. Is he okay?"

With the raising of that question everyone seemed to freeze. Even the kids who were walking away stopped moving.

Let's string them along and see how much they're willing to give. J.P. looked directly at Jennie Johnson. "For the most part, but he's not out of the woods yet."

A sigh of relief rippled through the teenagers. *Let's see if anyone leaves now.*

Jennie asked another question. "Is he home?" She flicked ashes from a burning cigarette then put it between her lips and inhaled as she waited for an answer.

"Briefly." J.P. answered carefully. He slowly made eye contact with each person in the group. "In order for me to help James, I need some information about what happened at Madson Park. And I need it tonight."

Most of the eyes fell away from him and new murmurs rose from the crowd. *No one's going to fink on a friend in public.*

The tatooed boy spoke again. "Is he in trouble?"

J.P. shook his head. "I just need to understand what happened, that's all." He reached for his wallet and extracted a business card. "This is my cell number." He jotted the numbers across the back of the card. "I'll answer until midnight."

The attorney left the card on the back of the Pinto and walked away in the opposite direction from which he'd come. *We'll see if anyone has the nerve to call.* He circled the block on foot and arrived back at the bandstand where he'd left Josh.

Josh took his father by the arm and turned him slightly. J.P. thought maybe he was going to direct his attention to the crowd down the street. But instead, Josh nodded his head toward a group of girls sitting on the bandstand.

His hot date. "Which one?"

"The one in the middle."

Her long blonde hair was brushed to a glossy shimmer. *A lot different than the one your brother hooked up with . . .*

"That's the one I want to ask out."

J.P. frowned at his son. "What's the hold up?"

"I'm just waiting for the right time." Josh's eyes were fixed on the girl. J.P. bumped him in the ribs.

"Hey, Josh!"

Josh returned to his previous conversation as if he'd never left.

He's got a good head on his shoulders. Too bad he's so shy with the girls. Jennie Johnson's figure flashed in his mind. *Well, maybe.*

His thoughts were interrupted by a vibration against his hip. *That was faster than I expected.* J.P. checked the caller I.D. *It's a Harrisonburg number.*

"J.P. here."

"Is this James's dad?" A girl's voice was on the other end of the line. J.P. pressed the unit hard into his ear so he could hear better.

"It is."

"I was in the parking lot with Zach a minute ago but I'm home now." The voice stopped for a moment.

This may be my only eye witness.

"I know what happened the other night . . ."

Bingo.

"It's not James's fault that he got so drunk. There was a fight at home or something and Jennie went and got him." The girl was noticeably nervous. "One of the guys thought it would help him to have a drink but it didn't. He just got wilder and wilder and kept drinking more beer." The tension was becoming more evident. "We couldn't get him settled down so Marcus dropped a Valium in his beer."

She stopped talking.

Valium? "And then what happened?"

"And then James went ballistic. He started jumping around and breaking things up. I got really scared and Zach made me leave . . . everybody started running away." J.P. heard the girl choke and realized she was crying. "Zach said he passed out and wouldn't get up." She choked out in a sob. "Everybody thought he was dead."

Put her mind at ease. "He's not dead, but he was pretty sick." *Does she know anything else?* "Is there anything else you can tell me?"

The girl didn't respond right away.

She needs to know my intentions. "No one will know you've talked to me tonight. I'm just trying to help James."

" . . . well, there is something but I don't think I should tell . . . Jennie will kill me if she finds out."

"She won't find out. You have my word." J.P. listened closely.

The next sentence was only three words long but its impact was far longer than that. J.P. replayed it in his mind. The words fell exactly the same the second time.

"Jennie is pregnant."

Nooooooo! The voice inside of J.P.'s head was so loud he put his hand over the other ear. The phone went dead, but the statement was still sounding loud and clear.

The pierced belly button and full bust line seemed like a cheap trick in light of this information. *Now what?* He was stunned beyond belief. *This is exactly how I ended up with their mother!* His eyes dared to look down the street again. *If I've told them once, I've told them a thousand times to be careful.* J.P. put his hand on his forehead. *In fact, I've told them to be more than careful.*

The longer J.P. thought about it, the angrier he got. *Goddam! We've talked about this! I've even put the prevention in his hand!* Suddenly James's silent response from the weekend events wasn't enough. J.P. wanted answers and he wanted them right now. *I've been calm and I've been patient! But my patience is spent!* J.P. was tired of James's attitude. He was tired of Janet's controlling demands. But most of all he was tired of not having all the pieces to the puzzle.

It is time to end this charade. J.P. made sure Josh had a ride home and then set out to finish what he'd come up there to do in the first place. *And I'm going to start with the one who has the answers!*

9

The Threat of Exposure

When Norma Cartwright sets a time, she rarely misses the mark. Today was no exception. At exactly seven o'clock Samira could see Dale and Norma's Cadillac pulling into the driveway. *Here we go.*

"Samira, dear!" Norma exploded into the front room close on Kara's heels. Samira accepted the loose embrace from her former mother-in-law. Norma was still wearing her dress clothes. "It's so good to see you!"

You just saw me Friday. "Come on in."

"We had a grand time, just a grand time!" Norma clapped her hands together, her colored blonde hair shining. "The girls are turning into young women right before our very eyes." She tipped her head and admired the girls at length. "But we sooo missed you!"

It's just as well I stayed home. Samira greeted Dale with less exuberance. He looked more comfortable in shorts and a plaid shirt.

"Thanks, Grampa," Krissy reached up to hug her grandfather as he set her bag next to the door. Next she turned and hugged her mother.

I'm glad to have the girls back home. Samira savored the moment.

"Iced tea?"

"No thank you, nothing for me," Norma answered. "Krissy tells us your garden is starting to bloom. We'd love to take a peek . . ."

Dale raised his forefinger to interrupt his wife. "I might have a sip of tea, Samira," he indicated politely. *His eyes remind me so much of Tom.* She couldn't help but return his smile.

"Right this way," she motioned for Dale to follow her to the kitchen. "Krissy, go ahead and take Gramma out back. We'll be along shortly."

Samira took her time. "How have you been, Dale?"

"We've been mighty busy this week. But other than that life is treating us well." He took a long drink. "How about you, Samira?"

"Things are adjusting into the summer just fine."

"You're looking good," Dale complimented. His blue eyes twinkled. *Just like Tom's used to do.* "Thank you." She tucked her hair behind her ear. *Dale is always a gentleman.*

"Dale, dear," Norma called. "You must see this floral heaven!"

Samira watched Dale tip his head. "After you," he said with a quiet smile. *Norma always rules the roost.*

"It gets more beautiful out here every year," Norma complimented. She was sitting in the plastic lawn chair, her legs comfortably crossed. "You really should submit this work of art to a home and garden magazine, dear." She waved her hands over the area. "Really you should."

But if I was selected, I'd have photographers and reporters all over my sanctuary. Samira admired her work. *I prefer to keep it to myself, thank you.*

"You should have been at the party, Mama!" Krissy's eyes were bright with excitement. "There were so many people there!"

All the more reason to stay home. I wouldn't have known anyone outside the immediate family.

"We counted like over a hundred cards in the basket at the end of the day and all of the cake was, like, gone!" Krissy shook her head. "But it was a blast!"

"It was a grand success," Norma added. "Thank you so much for letting the girls join us! We just love showing them off."

As well you should. "Anytime."

"We took lots of photographs!" Norma announced.

"Gramma says she'll send them to us as soon as she gets them back."

"I'll send them in right away!"

"Oh good! I can't wait to show my friends!"

"Mama, Mrs. Barnes is here," Kara called from the back door.

Mrs. Barns? What in the world is she doing here? Samira exhaled slowly as she rose from the wooden garden bench. *Mrs. Barnes hasn't paid a personal visit in quite awhile now!* Reluctantly Samira left her guests in the garden to greet her neighbor in the kitchen.

Mrs. Barnes held out a plate. "I won't stay long because I know your have company . . ."

And chances are good she even knows who they are . . .

" . . . I brought you some fresh cookies. I thought you might be able to use them with the girls coming home and all."

Samira reached for the plate. *I should have known Mrs. Barnes would know the exact moment the girls arrived home.*

"It's not a problem to double the recipe, you know. Just as easy to make a double batch as a single." Mrs. Barnes glanced around the room as if searching for evidence. "I can't stay long," the woman repeated as she patted her bluish gray hair. "Mr. Barnes is waiting for me you know."

"Here," Samira removed a plate from the cupboard. "Let me transfer the cookies over so you can take your plate back home." *That way she won't have a ready excuse to make a second appearance.* Samira carefully stacked the cookies on her own plate. *The only time Mrs. Barnes pays a visit is when there's neighborhood gossip in the making.*

Mrs. Barnes didn't waste any time. "Did your brother get a new vehicle?"

Exactly what I thought. Samira handed over the empty plate. *The sooner I get her back across the street, the better off we'll all be.* Kara was suddenly involved in the conversation.

"What? Uncle Wes got a new car?" She snatched a warm cookie as she crossed the kitchen. "I didn't know that!"

"No, Uncle Wes didn't get a new car . . ."

"Who got a new car?" Krissy piped as she entered the kitchen from the other direction. She went directly to the pitcher on the counter and refilled her grandfather's tea glass.

Mrs. Barnes was politely waiting for an explanation.

"No one has a new car . . ." Samira corrected.

"I just thought the pickup must be your brother's. I haven't seen it around before . . ." the old lady baited the conversation with skill.

Oh, Mrs. Barnes, you do know something about timing, don't you? "A friend came by, that's all." *I hope Norma and Dale stay in the garden!*

"It's a good thing you're an early riser," Mrs. Barnes quipped. "He came by a might early for an ordinary visit."

Samira saw Krissy raise her eyebrows at her sister. They stifled a giggle. The mother sent a look of warning to her daughters.

Quick, divert her attention. "How's Mr. Barnes? Is he over his cold?"

Mrs. Barnes' eyes danced. "I was up with him several times in the night through the weekend, but he's doing much better now." The neighbor nodded once. "Thank you for asking . . ." With that the elderly lady turned toward the kitchen door.

She obviously made her point.

" . . . I won't keep you any longer. I know you're company is waiting. Somewhere . . ."

Samira watched Mrs. Barnes scan the room again.

"They're out back in the garden," Kara clarified without being asked.

No, we're not going to invite Mrs. Barnes to the garden. Samira opened the garage door for Mrs. Barnes to make her exit.

"Is she gone already?" Norma quipped.

Samira put her hand over her heart as it pounded in her chest.

Norma crossed the dining room and looked out over the white painted slats in the windows. "Why, she needn't run off like that on our account."

Yes, she did, trust me. Samira looked out to be sure Mrs. Barnes was safely across the street. "She just wanted to bring us some cookies." She placed the plate of warm snacks on the breakfast bar. Dale helped himself but Norma put her hand over her stomach.

"Oh, Samira dear, none for me," she lamented. "I ate more than my share at the reception!"

"Everybody did!" Kara agreed. "The food was soooo good! Gramma did a good job putting it all together." Her daughter changed the focus. "What did you have for lunch, Mama?"

Caught off guard, Samira had to remember. "Oh, I ate with Papa Ray and Granny." *And Wes and the kids.*

"I'm sure they appreciated your visit," Norma added.

She probably thinks I went over there simply to avoid Tom's family gathering. Samira caught that thought. *Well, I kind of did.* "When will Ellen be home next?"

Dale's eyes lit up with the mention of his youngest daughter.

"She'll be home for three weeks next month," the grandfather answered quickly. He winked at Krissy across the breakfast bar. "I'm sure she'll come get the girls to spend a few days."

From there the conversation flowed more smoothly, relieving the knots in Samira's stomach. *If they overheard anything about an early morning visitor, they certainly aren't letting on.*

Krissy was hot on the topic as soon as Dale and Norma were gone. "Was it your friend's truck that was here, Mama?"

I should have known Krissy wouldn't forget. "Yes, it was Phil's." *At least she waited for her grandparents to leave.* She started to cover the cookies with plastic wrap but Kara grabbed another one.

"He must be an early riser too, then?" Krissy followed her sister's lead and swiped another cookie from the plate. "So is he?" She started to follow her mother toward the hallway.

I don't really know, but he seemed quite content sleeping in. "Do you have homework?" Samira took a stack of clean towels out of the linen closet and headed for her bedroom.

"Mo-ther. We don't have homework the last week of school!" Kara's interjection showed signs of agitation.

"Was Daddy an early riser too?" Krissy asked, close on her mother's heels.

Where did that come from? Samira stopped in the doorway to her bedroom and faced her daughters. She closed her eyes and tried to stabilize the congestion in her mind.

"I think Mama needs a minute," Kara suggested out loud. She moved her hand and tapped Krissy on the shoulder.

"So, is he cute?" Krissy's eyes twinkled.

I guess they're not going to let me off the hook. Unwilling to jeopardize the memories still lingering in her bedroom, Samira decided to put the towels away in the main bathroom.

"WE-LL?" Krissy was impatiently perched on her knees with her freckled arms hanging over the couch.

I knew they would be curious. I didn't know they were going to be this demanding.

"She's blushing," Krissy whispered loudly across the room to her sister.

Samira touched her cheeks. They were hot with color.

"Yep, he's cute," Krissy assumed. "He must not drive a sports car."

"No," Samira answered quietly, her thoughts still somewhat distant. "He drives a pickup."

"A pickup?" Kara exclaimed. "What kind of a guy drives a pickup?"

A complex, sophisticated professional . . . Samira was surprised to hear such reluctance in Kara's voice. *Why does it matter what he drives anyway?*

"Well, he's actually very nice." *Why am I defending him?* "And he has a great smile." *But it's already Sunday night and I haven't heard a word from him . . .*

Kara rolled her eyes and flopped into the easy chair with her legs dangling over the edge. Her brown eyes met her mother's. "A pickup sounds like some kind of farmer or something."

"Or someone who hauls a lot of stuff," Krissy thought out loud. "How tall is he?"

Samira couldn't help but smile. "He's taller than me by a couple-three inches. I'd guess around six-two."

"Wow! That's taller than Daddy isn't it?"

I forget how curious they are about Tom when they've spent time with his family.

"Your daddy was almost six foot," she remembered for the girls. *But not quite because when I wore two-inch heels I was taller than him.*

"He doesn't wear cowboy boots does he?" Kara asked with skepticism.

"No cowboy boots." *Just designer clothes.* Samira chuckled. *Kara would appreciate that more than Krissy.*

Before any more questions were asked, the telephone rang. Both girls scrambled to answer but Kara got there first and quickly handed it over to her sister.

"Hurry, up," Kara warned. "I want to call Rene."

Krissy took the telephone and disappeared into her bedroom.

"Tell me when Krissy is off, okay, Mama? I'll be in my room."

I feel a little like the girls. When the phone rings, I hope it's for me! At the same time, she preferred not to take a call from Phil in front of the girls.

Long after Krissy and Kara were asleep, Samira still paced between the breakfast bar and the living room. Trying to keep busy, she moved the majority of her houseplants to the sunroom. When that job was complete she folded a load of laundry and unloaded the dishwasher. She tried to read the newspaper but couldn't bring her mind to rest on anything in particular.

The light on the answering machine had been flashing the entire weekend. *I might as well clear them out before starting a new week.*

" . . . beep . . . Samira, it's your mother. Ed and Phyllis Jones are meeting us for dinner. Daddy and I would like for you to come along if you don't have any plans. We'll leave around six. Just call if you'd like to go . . ." *Ed and Phyllis Jones.* Samira chuckled at her reaction to the name earlier in the day.

The machine continued, "Samira! Where in heaven's name are you? I'm calling your mother! . . . beep . . ." *Susan, Susan.* An unfamiliar male voice started the third message. *Oh, wow! Maybe he did call!* Samira leaned over the counter to listen more closely. " . . . Uuh . . . hello. My name is Greg. Greg Levitt, L-e-v-i-t-t-. Susan Olinger gave me your number thinking you might have an interest in going out with me . . . . so give me a call if you're free . . . I'll leave my number and you can . . ."

Oh for Heaven's sake! Samira didn't wait for the message to finish. She pressed the erase button and held it down until the machine protested with a loud buzz. *I can't believe Susan gave out my phone number AFTER I asked her not to!* She put her hands over her ears. *Go away, go away! I don't want a perfect stranger calling my house!*

Samira was angry at her friend's betrayal. *How many times do I have to say no?* She looked out the kitchen window as she turned down the lights. *Is it that important to her and Sam that I have a man in my life?* A light still shone in Mrs. Barnes front room. *I wish I understood her insistence that I find someone.* As she watched, the light across the street went out. *I knew Mrs. Barnes was paying attention Friday night.* There were times when a neighbor's attention was a blessing but today was not one of those times.

Emotionally exhausted, Samira retreated to her bedroom. *Just a week or so ago I was quite content reading my books and tending to my family.* Samira released the clip in her hair and let the ends fall haphazardly over her shoulders. *I didn't ask for him to interrupt my life.* The dresser drawer opened with ease. She selected a clean nightshirt from the folded pile. *Did I?* She couldn't remember praying for a relationship. *I used to pray that prayer, but somewhere along the line I knew it wasn't meant to be.*

Samira leaned into the pile of pillows on her bed and opened her book. The ring of the telephone startled her. *Maybe that's Phil!*

"Hey Sis . . . ,"

It's just Wes. He sounds tired.

"Did I wake you?"

"I wish," Samira admitted. "I'm tired, but I can't get still enough to sleep."

"It's probably the caffeine in all that coffee."

Samira leaned heavily into the pillows and propped her head up. "That would be too easy." She sighed heavily. "What bids your call?"

"Just wondering how your day panned out," Wes hinted. "Did he call?"

It's really nice that Weston cares. Still, she didn't want her brother to catch her disappointment. She strengthened her voice. "No, not today." *Or yesterday.*

"Were you expecting he might?"

Samira pulled her hair back from her face with her free hand. "We didn't part with any plans," she answered honestly. *Or if he had any, I squelched them by leaving the decision to call me up to him.*

"I was just wondering," Wes stated simply. "Are you okay with that?"

I can't lie. He knows anyway. "I don't know yet." Samira sank deeper into the pillows.

"I'm sorry, Sis." Wes was sincere. "I thought maybe he'd take time to check in."

He's setting me up in case Phil decides not to call again.

"I know," Samira sighed. "Maybe tomorrow." *Maybe.* Yet she was afraid to hope too hard.

"Well, hang in there, alright?"

"Alright." Samira promised. "I'll do my best."

"You are the best. And don't you forget that."

Samira smiled into the phone. "Thanks."

Once Samira hung up, the room became extremely silent. Hollowness crept into her heart. It was a feeling she hadn't felt in a long while and the memories that came with it were distant yet strangely familiar.

Now that I've discovered that innermost part of me again, I don't know if I can go back. Samira turned off her reading lamp. *I don't know if I want to go back.*

She burrowed down into her covers. His scent was still evident on her pillow.

10

The Score that No One Tallied

The screen door banged loudly behind J.P. as he stepped into Janet's living room without knocking. Bruce and Janet were sitting at the kitchen table. They stopped talking and stared at J.P.

Janet frowned. "You should knock . . ."

Don't give me any shit, Jan. "Where's James?"

"I sent him to his room . . . we need to talk first . . ."

J.P. headed for the staircase.

"You don't have a right to go up there," Janet yelled. "We need to talk to you first, J.P.!"

The time for talking is over! Two by two he ascended the stairs and stopped in front of the only closed door in the hallway. The door was locked from the inside.

"James, open the door." He wrapped the back of his hand against the hollow wood.

Nothing happened.

"J.P., leave James alone and come back down here!" Janet was frantic when she reached the top of the stairs. Bruce was close on her heels.

You don't have the answers I need. J.P. hit the door harder. "Open the door James, or I'll open it for you!" He could feel the force in his own voice, but this time he didn't even try to hold back.

"For heaven's sake, J.P . . . ." Janet touched J.P.'s arm.

He pulled away instantly. *Don't 'for heavens sake' me.* "Back off Jan, and let me get to the bottom of this."

"Bruce and I were just talking and we think . . ."

"I don't give a damn what either one of you think!" J.P. banged on the door again.

"James, open up!"

J.P. grabbed for the knob, but before he could apply any pressure, it turned in his hand.

James stood on the other side, defensive and erect. A pair of earphones blared music into his ears.

"Get your shoes on, we're going out."

James flopped back onto his bed and cranked the volume.

J.P. could feel his anger boiling. He physically removed the earphones and set his jaw. "I said we're going out!"

"J.P., don't . . ." Janet started to plead.

I have one issue to resolve and it does not concern you, Janet. J.P. held a long hard stare with his son.

James finally had to look away.

"Get your shoes on!" James didn't move. "Now!"

"You can't threaten anyone in this house!"

J.P. turned and looked at the face that had spoken. *Hamilton finally has enough gumption to open his mouth.* "I didn't threaten anyone." *Yet.* He looked back at James. "Move!"

James looked from his mother to his father, then back to his mother who was now crying. He finally reached for his shoes and slipped his size fourteen feet inside.

"Outside!" *I want him as far out of Hamilton's earshot as possible.*

J.P. prodded his son onto the front porch and stayed on his heels until they were standing in the driveway next to his truck.

My patience is spent.

James mirrored his father's angry glare.

"I have a few things to say to you James, and it's high time you listened and listened hard." J.P. was talking through clenched teeth and his eyes were narrowly focused on his son.

James looked away.

"Look at me when I'm talking to you, James!"

Defiantly James turned back to his father and locked glares again.

Don't you test me, young man.

"It doesn't sound like you have a welcome bed to sleep in at this house anymore." J.P. began his opening argurment. "Up until a few minutes ago you were welcome at my house but you have some unfinished business in this town and it's high time you leveled with me."

The look on James's face told J.P. that he now knew more details than James had ever planned to tell.

James squared his shoulders and set his jaw. "Since when have you been so goddamned interested in my life?"

J.P. held his ground and answered with force. "Since you arrived on my doorstep too hung over to stand on your own power, that's when."

Furious, James spit on the ground in front of his father's shoe. J.P. grabbed for his son's arm but a right hook caught him off guard under the edge of his ribs.

Holy shit! The father lunged forward and caught his breath. *He delivers a solid punch.* J.P. looked sideways in time to dodge the next swing. *You want to fight James Ralston?* J.P. blocked another swing. *You'll be sorry you ever doubled up your fist . . .*

Niceties were over and the tensions that had been building the past few days translated into pure rage. J.P. found himself delivering punches as fast as he was receiving them. He could hear Janet screaming in the background, but it took everything he had to defend against the built up anger in his fifteen-year-old son. *No words could ever settle what needs proven here, James.* J.P. took a hit high on the cheekbone.

Obscenities flew as flesh and bone connected in ugly blows. There was a vengeance between the Ralston men as blood mixed with tattered emotions. Neither cared who won or lost. This was a battle to earn respect and to settle a score neither had tallied over the years.

Get him down for the count! J.P. was tiring quickly and he knew he had to take James now or forfeit his dignity. With a final thud, J.P. knocked the legs out from under his son. Off balance and unable to catch himself, James crashed hard onto the gravel. J.P. pinned his son to the ground. He wrapped his leg around his James's to lock the hold. Finally, James surrendered.

"You listening now?" J.P. could feel blood running down the side of his cheek. *Jesus, Ralston, what have you done to your son?*

James looked at his father through teary eyes. His nose was bleeding and the look on his face showed stark confusion. J.P. still didn't let up on the pressure against his son's body. *Let's get it out in the open.*

"It's one thing to go around screwing up your own life, James," J.P. was winded but he was determined to close the argument. "But when you manage to screw up someone else's life, that's another story." He stopped talking to spit more blood out of his bleeding mouth. "No son of mine will engage in that kind of activity and walk away without taking responsibility." He looked hard into his son's eyes. "Do you hear what I'm saying?"

James tried to bite his bottom lip, but it was too swollen. He nodded in understanding and let his head fall back against the gravel.

J.P. let James go. He struggled up onto his knees, but James rolled into a fetal position and sobbed quietly. *What kind of a father are you?* J.P. closed his eyes to combat the guilt. There was a scuffle on the gravel. He opened his eyes to see Josh kneeling over his brother. When their eyes connected Josh looked confused and betrayed.

There may not be anything left to fight for. J.P. pressed his hands into his thigh to keep his balance. What had once been anger was now remorse. He watched as Josh and Janet helped James up off the ground.

Back inside the house J.P. cleaned his wounds in the bathroom while Janet tended to James in the kitchen. J.P. leaned into the mirror and examined the cut on his cheekbone. A cold compress took some of the sting away but nothing took away the hurt in his heart. *Never in a million years did I think I'd lose control of my temper like that with my own kids.*

Bruce stopped in the doorway. "You want me to wrap that fighting fist for you?"

I don't need any assistance from that bastard! J.P. refused the assistance. Upon closer examination he decided the cut could stand a few stitches. *I just hope the tooth that cut my hand is still intact.* He wrapped his fist with a damp rag.

Janet's eyes were swollen from crying. She had James' head tipped back against her chest, nursing his nose and lip, which were both still oozing blood.

J.P. looked at his son and then looked away. Shame came over him like a blanket. He sensed an unspoken respect between him and James that hadn't been there before. *But that's a hell of a way to find it.*

Josh was seated at the table. He held his head low and refused to make eye contact with his father. *It wasn't that long ago I relented to Janet's control over visitation with the boys.* He forced his eyes back into the face of both of his boys. *Now my chances of even having a decent conversation with them is in jeopardy.*

Spent from the fight and emotionally drained, there was still business that needed attention. J.P. knew he had to stay to see it through. Every muscle in his body ached and complained as he eased into a chair. Patiently he waited until James and Janet were able to converse.

Tensions were high in the discussion that followed. It was obvious James would not be allowed to stay with Janet and Bruce. *That leaves me.* J.P. thought about that for a moment. *I have no business becoming a parent at this stage in the game.* He studied his son's beaten face. *But I don't think either one of us have much choice in the matter now.*

Late into the night, it was finally agreed that James would stay with Janet long enough to take his semester tests. After that he was headed for Joplin.

Bruce started to get up from the table.

J.P. motioned for Bruce to stay put. "Wait a minute."

"It's late. I'm going to bed."

"There's still two items of unfinished business." J.P. spoke quietly. *We're all tired.* He waited for Bruce to sit back down. *But we need to get everything on the table.* Cautiously, he addressed his son one more time.

"Concerning Jennie Johnson . . ."

James looked away. Josh propped his head in his hands.

"Jennie Johnson is a slut!" Bruce accused.

Shut up, Hamilton.

Janet began to speak but J.P. put his hand out to stop her. " . . . any suggestions, James?" *He knows exactly what I'm talking about.*

Everyone waited as James prepared to respond. His lip was quite swollen by this time and his eyes were starting to darken.

The last hangover isn't even going to register compared to the headache he'll have in the morning.

James dropped his head and mumbled. "She says it's not mine."

"Doesn't think what's yours?" Bruce demanded without permission.

Go easy, Hamilton. We've been through enough already.

James squirmed in his chair. J.P. gave silent permission for him to answer the question.

"The baby." His voice was almost inaudible.

Bruce's chair went over backwards as he flew out of it. "You bastard! This is my house!" Bruce announced wildly. "And if you knocked up white trash like Jennie Johnson then your ass isn't . . ."

J.P. stood at the opposite end of the table in defense of his son. He stole a look at Janet and saw her hands come to her mouth in astonishment but she didn't move.

"Sit down, Bruce!"

"You're not in a courtroom, Ralston," Bruce retorted. "You have no right to order me around in my own house."

"Sit down!" *The only thing he thinks about is his own stubborn pride.*

Janet pulled Bruce's arm to his side. Tears were once again streaming down her face. Reluctantly Bruce reset his chair and eventually sat back down. He was visibly angered.

"How do you know, James?"

James shrugged his shoulders and hung his head. "I only slept with her once."

Again Bruce bolted from his chair. "How many times do you think it takes?"

Janet's face softened as she made eye contact with J.P.

"Only once." Janet whispered. Her eyes softed as they connect with J.P.'s. "Only once."

J.P. looked away quickly. He and Janet were all too familiar with the situation at hand. Josh sat at the table as living evidence to that fact. Blurred memories of his ancient past threatened to rock his focus. *That's one mistake I never wanted to pass on to my kids.*

It's out there now. J.P. reviewed the situation and decided to move things forward. *Whether it's his or not, we can work through the details later.* There was only one more item that needed addressed.

J.P. spoke calmly. "James, there's a plea in yesterday's paper from the sheriff's department asking for information regarding the incident in Madson Park." He waited for James to make eye contact. "Before you can take up residence with me, you need to pay a visit to the sheriff's office and tell them what you know."

Janet gasped. "How can you just stroll into town and know all this about my son?"

Our son, Janet.

J.P. watched Josh and James exchanged a knowing look. *That's what I thought. Both of them still know more about Madson Park than they're letting on.*

J.P.'s defenses wanted to attack Janet's lack of attention to their sons. *Just stay focused, Ralston, and wrap this up.* "When you give a report of the incident, you'll have to sign a statement of validity." He waited for both boys to show attentiveness before continuing. "I expect you to have a copy of that statement with you when you arrive at my house later this week." J.P. rose from his chair and tapped the tabletop with his fingertips. "We'll deal with Jennie Johnson on another agenda."

"I'll deal with Jennie Johnson right now." Bruce was standing again.

J.P. squared his shoulders. "No. You won't." He held Bruce's eyes long enough to let him know who was in charge. *Nor will you ever deal with anything else concerning my sons' lives.*

J.P. needed some fresh air. His entire body ached from the fight and his head was pounding from the emotional fatigue. He stepped outside onto the front porch.

Without permission, Bruce Hamilton followed. He stood with his back to J.P. and lit a cigarette. "He's a tough kid, Ralston." Bruce exhaled the smoke. "You handled him well."

J.P. didn't feel like dealing with Bruce. *Not now or ever again.* "I didn't *handle* anything."

"Let's just say you got your point across," Bruce snickered and puffed on the cigarette again. "The boy is messed up."

That boy you're talking about is my son! J.P. drew a deep breath in order to control his temper. *It wouldn't take much to take you out, Hamilton.*

"You should let me wrap your hand. It looks pretty rough."

I don't need your sympathy.

"The last few months around here have been quite a challenge. You have no idea how much crap James has brought into our lives." Bruce took another drag on his cigarette.

His sentiments are much the same for you.

"He's all but flunked out of school. He never comes home at night. And he's hanging out with a bunch of punks."

Give me one thing that would motivate him to come home to this confine. J.P. was still holding his tongue. *My patience is waning.*

Bruce turned around and leaned against the railing J.P. was facing. "I have no time for a kid like that in my life."

Nor do I have time for you, bastard. J.P. considered his options. *It's time for closing arguments.*

"You know, Bruce, I've tolerated the way things are with my sons because I figured it was better for them if I didn't interfere. I thought it was more important for them to have family stability than a regular visitation schedule with me. Recent discussions with my boys lead me to believe I was wrong. I should have stepped in when I knew they were dealing with your egotistical, self-righteous attitudes. I should have exercised the rights of shared custody and stayed involved in my boys' lives." Now J.P. faced Bruce Hamilton. "I don't know what's going on around here but something isn't adding up. I'm here to tell you that I'll get to the bottom of it."

Bruce started to speak but J.P. didn't allow a single word. "Understand that from this point forward *all* decisions concerning Josh and James will not concern you."

"If that's the case, then they don't have a right to live under my roof!" Bruce shouted in retaliation.

"So be it." J.P. wasn't going to back down. "I'll do whatever it takes to secure stability in my sons' lives, even if it means removing you from their jurisdiction."

Bruce flicked a cigarette butt off the edge of the porch. "You can't do that without a court order."

Consider it done. J.P. considered the ramifications. *Let's see how long he's willing to live without the child support payments.* "Stay away from my boys, Bruce." J.P. felt the depth of his concern rise from somewhere deep within. "They deserve better than you."

He'd finished his argument and was ready to take whatever steps were necessary to remove Bruce Hamilton from immediate custody. J.P. turned to walk away and came face to face with a beaten fifteen year old. *How long has he been standing there?*

James pursed his swollen lips. The look in his eyes was weary and dejected.

What are you doing, J.P.? As badly as he wanted to, he couldn't force his eyes away from James. *The marks on his face are from my fists!* James was crying out in silent desperation. *My God, James. I am so sorry.* Every ounce of energy that was left in J.P. screamed for him to put his arms around the boy.

James glanced sideways and broke the silent communication.

"We're going to get through this," J.P. assured his son quietly. *I wish Hamilton would go back inside and leave me alone with my son.*

James nodded as his eyes came to rest on his father's. J.P.'s heart broke with the anguish that was in James' expression.

He lifted his uninjured hand and placed it on James' shoulder. "We will. I promise."

"I thought you didn't make promises." James spoke the truth solemnly.

He heard what I told the girl at the desk. J.P. took in a long breath and held it there for a long moment. *She's not worth the cost.* "This is different." *You're different, James.*

James nodded once, but avoided eye contact with J.P.

J.P.'s eyes looked over James' shoulder. Josh was standing in the doorframe. His eyes were also mournful and sad. *I might as well have beaten him too.* James went back in the house. If there was communication between the boys in the doorway, J.P. wasn't aware.

Josh moved as his brother passed by. *He hurts as much as James does.* The door slammed again. Josh disappeared behind the screen door without speaking.

And maybe I do too. All the mistakes of his past piled up in his heart. *I thought I had it made with the boys living up here and me working to pay off the divorce, providing for them according to the law, and putting money away for when they'd finally be free to come and go according to their own agenda.* J.P. tucked his injured hand under his other arm to help deaden the pain. He hadn't realized how long he'd looked forward to the day when James and Josh could make their own decisions about his presence in their lives.

I'm right back where I started eighteen years ago facing the repercussions of the same bad decision. Time passed. *The road I've been on led me right back to the trap I fell into the first time around.* Standing there alone under the vastness of the universe, J.P. felt considerably insignificant. *Heaven's about the only thing that can save me now.* A single streak of light fell from the sky. J.P. watched it plummet and obliterate into the darkness. *And I'm not putting much hope in that anymore.*

11

Restlessness

He said he didn't have much time but wondered if I could meet for lunch.
Samira replayed their conversation as she walked the three short blocks from
the library to her house. *He just wants to talk.* The librarian walked around a
little red tricycle that was parked haphazardly in the middle of the sidewalk. *I
wish I knew what he wants to talk about.* She looked both ways before crossing
the street. *Of course I have time. I only wished I'd had a little more notice.*

Samira stopped at the mailbox. *It would also be nice to know where Mrs.
Barnes is about now.* She unlocked the kitchen door. *Bill, bill, advertisement,
and three fashion magazines. How do these publishers get my name and address,
anyway?*

Leftovers were easy to reheat. *A minute in the microwave and we have
a full-blown meal.* Samira set two plates on the breakfast bar. *I hope he's not
disappointed I wanted to meet here instead of the Café Ole.* She checked the
clock. It was a few minutes after twelve. *It would be so crowded and busy there
over the noon hour.*

There was a knock at Samira's front door. *He has yet to be late.* She wiped
her fingertips on a kitchen towel. *Breathe.* She opened the door to the man
she'd only seen in her dreams for the past several nights. He didn't speak and
she didn't move.

He looks just as inviting as he did the last time I saw him.

"May I come in, Pretty Lady?"

He said that Pretty Lady thing again. "Oh, yes!" She opened the door
further. "I'm sorry."

"I thought maybe you'd changed your mind."

"About what?"

"About lunch."

Out of habit, Samira relocked the door. *Oh, lunch! What is the matter with me?* "No," *Why am I so nervous?* "Come on in." Her hands were balmy with sweat. *He's clean-shaven but the fresh bruise on his cheekbone looks sore.*

"Are you afraid of intruders?" Phil tapped the lock on the door.

Just breathe, remember? She inhaled slowly through her nostrils and decided to speak the truth. "Maybe more afraid of an intrusion."

"Yeah . . ." Phil's eyes scanned the room uncomfortably. "Maybe I shouldn't be invading your lunch hour like this . . ."

"Oh, no!" Samira caught the misunderstanding instantly. "I mean, from my neighbor!" She pointed through the sheer curtains over the dining room window. "I have an elderly neighbor, well, Mrs. Barnes, who doesn't know the word 'knock'." Her eyes went back to the bruise on Phil's cheek. *I wonder what happened.*

Phil was nodding. "The one I waved to a minute ago."

I knew she'd be watching! "Yes. That would be Mrs. Barnes." Samira glanced out the window. ". . . well, I just don't want her paying me an unexpected visit." *Lunch. You should offer him lunch.* Samira tucked her hair behind her ears. "It is lunchtime though. You're probably starving."

"I don't have a lot of time, but wanted to see you for a few minutes."

A quick lunch is better than not seeing him at all. "How about ham and scalloped potatoes? Just takes a few seconds." Samira put the casserole dish in the microwave. "Would you like a salad?"

"You don't have to serve me."

I'm more nervous today than I was last weekend!

Phil smiled a genuine smile. "Here," he handed an empty plate to Samira. "You do whatever you do with the potatoes and I'll fill the glasses. Deal?"

Deal. "The glasses are in . . ."

" . . . the cupboard to the right of the sink." Phil finished her sentence. When Samira turned around Phil was already holding two glasses.

"Water for the lady?"

"Yes, please." *I can't believe he remembered.* Samira breathed in deeply, enjoying the scent of his aftershave. *He smells like my pillowcase.* When he turned toward her, she once again took notice of his cheek.

"Have you cleaned your cut?"

Phil glanced at her, then looked away. "I've showered. Does that count?"

"Not really." *It needs some attention.* She waited for him to finish filling the glasses. When he turned toward the breakfast bar, she studied it more closely. "It really should be cleaned. It will heal better."

Phil raised his eyebrows and shook his head again. "It doesn't hurt anymore."

"It looks like it does." The microwave beeped. Samira checked the casserole, but it wasn't hot enough yet. She pushed the reset button.

"Believe it or not . . ." Phil touched the cut with his fingers. "It looks better than it did."

Then it definitely still needs cleaned. "Wait here," Samira touched him briefly on the arm as she left the kitchen. *Here's everything I need. Hydrogen peroxide, cotton swabs, and a box of bandages.*

"Whoa, girl. What are you thinking?"

"I'm going to clean your wound." She set the items on the breakfast bar. "It won't hurt." She reached for his hand. "And it won't take but a minute." She gently pulled on his hand for him to sit down. Phil tensed and yanked it away.

I must have overstepped my bounds. Samira took a step back.

Reluctantly, he put his hand to his chest. It was wrapped in a soiled bandage.

The beep of the microwave interrupted the silence that hung between them.

"Okay, so this one hurts a little."

"I'm sorry." Samira apologized. *I have a feeling there's more to this story than I might want to know.*

"It's not your fault." Much to Samira's amazement, Phil took a step toward the barstool. "You're sure it won't hurt?"

"Not much." *If he's willing, they do need some attention.* "Are you sure?"

Phil sat down at the breakfast bar, even though his eyes still showed signs of distrust.

Samira poured a small amount of peroxide into a bowl and carefully dipped a cotton swab, studying the cut on Phil's cheek as she did so. Gently, she pressed the swab against his cheekbone and held it there for a few seconds. "Doin' okay?"

"Would it matter?"

He's very tense. Samira touched her fingertips against his other cheek in an effort to steady his nerves. The smoothness of his cheek sent shivers up her spine.

"Yes, it would." She removed the swab and examined the cut again. "It will heal faster if it's clean." She used the swab to clear away the dried blood around the edges. "To be honest, I'm more concerned about your hand." *I hate to think what's hidden under there.* "Did you consider seeing a doctor?"

"Didn't even cross my mind."

Why am I not surprised?

"Maybe you could just kiss it and make it better."

"I could, but that might not make it any better."

"I'd be willing to give it a shot."

Samira tried to ignore the chemistry that was building. She used her fingernails and gingerly removed the band aide. The wound underneath was still open. Phil flinched as she adjusted his hand against the counter. *If I didn't know better, I'd guess he was wounded in battle.*

"Where'd you learn first aide?"

"My mother is a retired registered nurse. In fact, she's a retired emergency room nurse." Samira looked into Phil's eyes. "If she were here she'd be dragging you in for stitches." She surveyed the cut on his hand again. "This one is deep."

The muscles in Phil's jaw line flexed as she Samira removed the last bit of bandage.

"I'm almost afraid to ask, but what did your father do?"

"Financial Management." Samira flattened Phil's hand against the counter.

"I'm glad he wasn't a surgeon!"

Samira was sincerely concerned about the lack of medical attention. "This one might hurt a little." She eased the swab into the cut.

Phil's jovial spirit faded quickly as the peroxide penetrated the wound.

Samira apologized when Phil caught his breath but she didn't remove the swab. *He asked a personal question. I guess I'll do the same.* "Who was the victim?"

Several seconds passed.

"What makes you think it was a *victim?*"

I wonder if he always answers a question with another question. "I'm assuming he fought back." She removed the cotton swab and started to soak another.

"Really," Phil started to pull his hand away. "You don't need to do it again."

"The second won't hurt as much because the nerve endings are primed." Gently, Samira took a hold of Phil's fingers and repositioned his hand. "Almost done." This time when the peroxide penetrated, Phil didn't respond. "How bad was the other guy?"

I don't know if he's holding out because of the pain, or because he doesn't want to talk about it.

Phil drew a deep breath and let it out slowly. "My hand hit his teeth about the same time his fist connected with my cheekbone."

Samira held pressure on the open sore. "Is he alright?" She looked up from the wound to his face. *The anguish in his eyes is far worse than the pain in his hand.*

Phil stared at his hand. When he answered, his voice was very quiet. "The *other guy* was my son."

Oh Phil . . .

Without further prompting, Phil filled in the details of his weekend, ending with the fight with James.

No wonder he hasn't called! Samira finished cleaning the cut as she listened. Using a butterfly bandage she pulled the flesh together as best she could. *It could still stand a few stitches.*

Phil summarized the situation. " . . . So he'll be arriving on my doorstep with a suitcase tonight." He stopped talking and looked at Samira. "I haven't been a full time father in more than ten years." His face was contemplative. "And to be perfectly honest, I haven't the slightest idea where to begin."

The worrisome look in Phil's eyes captured Samira's compassion. "You've already begun." There were many questions she wanted to ask but she knew the noon hour was quickly slipping away. "Just go slow. You'll both have some adjustments to make, but everything will come together. But right now, we need to get some food in your stomach."

Samira turned for the microwave, but Phil pulled her into a full embrace. This time when he started to kiss her, Samira didn't turn him away.

"Aren't you hungry?"

"Not anymore." He kissed her again. "At least not for lunch."

Without warning, Phil suddenly let go. He didn't push away; he just released his hold on her.

Oh my! Samira watched him raise a cell phone to his ear. *Did it ring?*

Phil checked his watch against the display on the cellular phone. "I need to check in at the office." He pressed a button. "It will just take a minute."

Samira pushed the reheat button on the microwave. She listened over the hum of the microwave.

"Yeah, Denise, it's me . . . what time?"

Who's Denise?

"I'm still at lunch . . . no, I can be there . . . call the city attorney and reschedule for morning . . . any word from Benson and Barringer?"

He reminds me of Wes when he's in a business mode. She carried the steaming food to the breakfast bar.

" . . . It could run late but I'll still check in before I leave for home . . . ,"
Samira continued to listen.

" . . . Anything else? . . . She did? . . . tell her I'll be there . . . no, just tell her to meet me at the office . . ."

He never says goodbye at the end of a phone call. "Busy day?"

"Busy week."

I'm beginning to think his entire life is scheduled to the hilt. "It's okay if you eat and run," Samira offered. "I need to get back to work too."

Phil sat down in the same barstool and picked up a fork with his uninjured hand.

That's funny, he ate with his right hand the other night. The playfulness of the previous moment was long gone. *His mind has definitely moved on to the afternoon agenda.*

"Thanks for the first aide, Samira," Phil offered between bites. He held out his injured hand and examined the new bandage. "I'll certainly look more presentable at this afternoon's meeting."

"You're cheek looks better too. You still might want to have a doctor look at your hand . . ."

Phil interrupted. "Nah, it will be alright." He nodded his head in approval. "Feels better already."

Something tells me he doesn't even have a family physician. She could feel his eyes on her as she finished taking a bite of potatoes.

"What?" she asked as she laid her fork alongside of her plate.

Phil was leaning back in the armed stool with his hands behind his head. He grinned. "I was just thinking," he began, "Last time I left with an agenda and now I show up with the same scenario." Phil rose from his chair. "I'm damn lucky you could even meet me on short notice like this."

I'm just glad we didn't go to the Café Ole.

"You don't have to be so kind." He refilled his water glass and took a drink before returning to the breakfast bar. "But I do appreciate the hospitality." He stopped right next to her. "I really wanted to call before today . . ."

"That's okay." *Under the circumstances.* "You were obviously a little distracted."

Without waiting for permission, Phil bent down and gently kissed her on the lips. *If this is his thanks, I like it.*

"There's a chair with my name on it in a conference room across town." Phil's voice was quiet.

Samira stood up and allowed Phil to kiss her again. But this time he didn't stop. His bandaged hand moved up her back on the inside of her shirt. *He doesn't have permission to do that!*

"Then you'd best be on your way." Samira doubted her defenses. This time Samira was close enough to feel the vibration between her stomach and Phil's hip. *So that's how he knows he has an incoming call.*

Reluctantly, he slid his hand out of her blouse. His eyes were suddenly distant.

"Duty calls?" Samira was somewhat relieved for the interruption. *I really don't want to make him late.*

"Unfortunately."

Samira noted a look of regret. "Don't let me keep you."

Phil put the phone to his ear. As he turned away, he ran his hand through his hair.

Samira waited. *If he's as passionate about his work as he is with me . . .*

There was an awkward silence when Phil turned back around.

"Thanks for lunch, Samira." There was a hint of hesitation. "And for the doctoring."

Samira's eyes re-examined the cut on his cheek. *It does look much better.* She stood completely still as Phil's arm gently pulled her in. Instinctively she closed her eyes and returned his tender kiss.

"I'll call you," he whispered.

I wonder how soon.

His lips brushed her forehead briefly. He stopped long enough to unlock the deadbolt.

Samira watched. He crossed the length of the porch and climbed into his pickup. His stride was confident. *He's already focused on work.*

He isn't anything like the man I thought I'd fall for. Even in her wildest dreams she had pictured a man with a typical nine to five workday. *Or maybe a school teacher who worked the same kind of hours as me.* She'd pictured someone older, more settled, and maybe even more adjusted. *I imagined a family man.*

But Phil is none of these things. He's restless, over committed to his work, and insecure about being a dad. He's as professional as he is rugged. Samira shook her head as she cleared away the lunch dishes. *He's so far from the man I had painted in my mind.* Samira started down the driveway headed back to work. *What is it about him that draws me?* She glanced across the street. *No visible sign of Mrs. Barnes.*

Samira crossed the second street. *So why do I only want more of him if he isn't what I'd hoped for?* His aftershave was still fresh in her memory.

I'm drawn to his restless nature. A smile crept across her face. *Yes, I am. There is something exceedingly romantic about a man who can't settle down.* She thought about his busy schedule. *Or maybe about a man who won't settle down.* Samira waited for a car to pass before crossing the intersection. *I wonder what drives him?*

Samira walked through the entryway of the library. Her eyes passed over the rows upon rows of organized books and periodicals. *Maybe it's time for something less predictable and orderly for a change.* A shiver crept up her spine as she considered the answers to these questions. *Maybe it was his intrusion I feared when I locked the door.*

12

Potential Opportunities

The board of directors were frustrated with the investigative reports. *They're not moving fast enough.* Evidence against the hackers was piling up and the documentation of the crime was complete. *But nothing is leading to an arrest.* It was becoming obvious that additional investigations would be necessary over and above that of local authorities.

J.P. was still deep in thought over Mid-America when he entered the office.

"You were a bit distracted over the lunch hour." Denise handed the communications clipboard to her boss without waiting for a response.

"I was behind closed doors." His eyes scanned the telephone messages. *Too many personal calls.*

"I'm sure you were." She pointed at his hand. "You must have decided to see a doctor."

Better than a doctor.

"The Hughes Corporation needed an RSVP for a dinner party before two o'clock."

"So how did I respond?"

"You accepted for you and a guest. You'll be sitting with Christopher and his wife at the head table the night after they return from England."

"When?"

"Three weeks from Friday in Springfield." Denise turned toward her computer and pulled J.P.'s calendar up on the screen.

"Business or otherwise?" Phil set the clipboard back on Denise's desk. "And who's on the guest list?"

"Formal and business, although it doesn't sound like you'll have a specific role. It's their daughter's engagement party. I'll inquire about the guests." Denise turned and faced her employer. "Should I secure an escort?"

"That won't be necessary." *I'll make that call myself this time.*

"I could call *Mary?*" Denise exaggerated the name. "She called again, by the way. She sounded like she might like to see you again."

"Screw Mary." *I still can't put a name with a face.*

"I'm assuming you already took care of that." Denise followed him into his office. "What do I do with the rest of these phone calls?"

The attorney sat down in his chair. "Call the vet back and schedule Chase for vaccinations." J.P. picked up a pen and jotted down his concerns about the incomplete investigation for Mid-America. *Why is she still standing there?*

"Any instructions for the rest of the phone messages?"

J.P. stopped writing and looked directly at Denise. *I don't have any desire to talk to any of them.* He considered the names on the list. *But I don't know why I can't tell Denise that.*

She was still waiting.

J.P. made another note concerning Mr. Stephenson's case. *You don't want to tell her because you know she's going to give you shit about it.*

"You can let them go."

Denise opened her green eyes wide and put her hands on her hips. "You don't even want me to call one for the Hughes party?"

"No."

"You don't happen to have a steady or something now, do you, Boss?"

I do not have a steady. J.P. chose not to respond. *She's right. Normally I'd be all over that list looking for a date.* "What's on for the rest of the week?"

Denise disappeared for a minute and returned with the clipboard. "Okay, at a glance . . . I've put off all the low priority items until the Mid-America business is underway. We have a court date for the Hughes hearing in two weeks." She looked up from her notepad. "I expect they'll settle before that though, don't you?"

"The city will do whatever it takes to avoid negative publicity with the Hughes family. I'm sure city hall is working on some kind of a compromise." Another thought entered his mind. "However, it might not hurt to have a representative at the city council meeting next week . . ."

"I'll clear my calendar." Denise jotted a reminder on the corner of the paper. "Derek Danielson from Benson & Barringer will be here to interview in an hour and Mike left a message about a special investigator?"

"Yeah . . . Our honorable police department isn't impressing me with Mid-America's computer glitch. Benson and Barringer have an inside track on a P.I. but I want to talk to Mike again before we hire." *The sooner the better.*

"I'll see if I can get him on the phone."

"Very well. Give me five minutes to recap the board meeting." He checked his watch. "How long before Janet gets here with James?"

"She said she'd be here around six. Derek Danielson will be here in about forty five minutes now."

"Before I talk to him, brief him on the Edmundson case study and quiz him on the details of a limited liability corporation."

"I can do that." Denise was taking notes. "And what about James? Is he coming to stay?"

"He could be here for the better part of the summer." *Just thinking that makes me nervous.* "Depends on how fast Mike gets to the paperwork." *I'm more comfortable unraveling the online heist at Mid-America than I am trying to figure out how to be a father to a wayward fifteen year old.*

Denise smiled. "Personally, I find it rather interesting that becoming a full time father has you turning down dates."

I may get more mileage out of James's arrival than I thought. J.P. glanced in Denise's direction. "That will be all, Denise."

The peace that came with the closed door was a welcome reprieve to the madness of the previous twenty-four hours. J.P. stretched his arms into the air then locked his hands behind his head. *You think I'd be anxious to get on with this case.*

He found the Maple Street Library number in his call history and pressed "send".

"Ms. Cartwright, please." A few moments later Samira's voice filled his ear. "Samira, it's J . . ." *No, she doesn't know me as J.P.* " . . . Phil. Do you have a minute?"

"I was just about ready to leave for home."

Which means she probably gets off about this time everyday. He logged that information into his memory bank. "Should I wait and call you there?"

Samira gave permission for him to continue.

"I just got back to the office and learned I have a business engagement in Springfield in about three weeks." J.P. moved the computer mouse to pull his calendar onto the screen. "I'd like to take you as my guest if you're free." *And I hope she is.* J.P. tapped his pen against the legal pad as he waited for a response.

"What's the date?"

Tell me you can make it. His eyes scanned the Fridays until he spotted the Hughes engagement. "Looks like the seventeenth."

The silence on the other end of the phone was not as encouraging as J.P. had hoped. "But if you already have plans, I understand . . ."

"No, no," Samira replied quickly. "It's nothing like that. Can I let you know?"

"Sure, no problem." *How soon?* "Should I give you a call later?"

"Give me a couple of days . . ."

J.P. waited. But no further explanation followed. *A couple of days before I call you again, or before you can give me an answer?*

The call ended without any clear direction. *I should have waited to call her at home.* He was used to immediate answers. *This woman, as beautiful as she is, has a way of playing me into her agenda.* Even this morning when he called to take her to lunch he had no intention of ending up at her house. *But that's exactly what happened.*

J.P. admired the clean bandage on his hand again. He could almost feel her body against his as he remembered the way she returned his kiss. *But, I couldn't have done that at a restaurant.*

Maybe I gave her too much personal info. He jotted a few notes on the pad concerning Mid-America, but his train of thought was elsewhere. *I don't know what made me open up like that.* His pen went over the letters of his notes again. *She's obviously easier to talk to than any woman I've been out with in the past.* J.P. shook his head. *Correction. She's the only woman I've ever discussed personal matters with.*

Derek Danielson turned out to be a promising prospect for legal assistance. J.P. rose from his chair and offered a handshake. Derek rose also, towering over the senior attorney with a lanky frame.

"Anyway I can be of service, Mr. Ralston."

"Be here in the morning and we'll put you to work." J.P. stepped back from the table. "And call me J.P." *Everyone else does.* He corrected his thought. *Well, almost everyone.*

"Very well, sir." His rimless glasses made his eyes look smaller than they really were.

He's eager to work. That's a good sign. "Denise will brief you on the case work at hand."

"Yes, sir."

We've got to lose the sirs.

The smile on Derek's face gave away his excitement. *I don't know if I've ever hired a male intern.* J.P. buzzed for his assistant. Denise appeared instantly.

"Denise, Mr. Danielson will be starting in the morning. Is there anything you need to go over with him before he leaves today?"

"Yes, I do. And your son is here, J.P."

He's early. J.P. followed Denise and Derek Danielson into the outer office. Janet was sitting cross-legged in a winged-back chair looking quite out of place. James had his back to the office, looking out the window over the main street down below.

J.P. motioned for them to join him in his own office. James turned around slowly. J.P. took a long, deep breath. *The bruises around his eye are from my fist.*

"How'd it go at school today?" He cleared the interview files from the table behind his desk.

James lowered himself into the corner chair. "Fine."

"Any specifics?"

James shrugged. "Took the semester tests and came home."

"James only had two tests today so he was out early." Janet was still standing in front of J.P.'s desk. "So we're here a little early."

"I noticed." J.P. ran his hand through his hair and sat down at the table. *It's hard to focus on family matters when this casework is screaming for my attention.*

"Have a seat, Jan."

"James has a paper to show you." Janet nodded toward her son. "He and Josh went down to the sheriff's office and told them what they knew about the Madson Park incident."

We could have reviewed that later, but since she brought it up, we might as well take a look. J.P. watched as James fished the paper out of the back pocket of his baggy shorts. It was crumpled and tattered.

He quickly skimmed the contents of the multi-carbon copied papers. *I'd prefer to discuss this with James in private.* "It appears everything is in order."

"Nothing is in order if you read the whole thing!" Obviously agitated, Janet rose from her chair and crossed her arms over her middle.

A buzzer sounded on his desk. "Excuse me, J.P. Can you take a call on two?"

Denise wouldn't interrupt if it wasn't important. He walked to his desk and picked up the receiver hoping to hear Samira's voice.

"I have a meeting set up with Sparky, J.P . . ."

Oh. It's Mike.

" . . . He's willing to listen but he doesn't want to meet downtown. I set it up at Mona's Cafe just south of the city."

J.P. turned his back to his ex-wife. "This isn't the best time." *James' affidavit needs my attention at the moment.*

"Best time for what?" Mike asked into his ear. "To hire the best computer spy in the world?"

"No, to discuss the possibilities." *Maybe Mike will read between the lines here. And what the hell kind of a name is Sparky anyway?*

"Well, excuse me for interrupting, but Sparky needs a confirmation within the next two minutes or he'll split."

"Split what?"

"Town, that's what." Mike laughed. "Do you want him or not?"

Sparky. The attorney considered the name again. *His credentials are outstanding.* "I don't know."

"Trust me, J.P. This is the P.I. you want. He's ex-KGB. His skills are second to none and he won't settle for anything less than goal. You tell him what you need and he'll deliver."

J.P. had no reason to not trust Mike, but at the same time *Sparky* seemed a bit far-fetched to be real. "Does he speak English?"

"Si`, si`," Mike replied seriously. "Along with probably five or six other languages."

All I need is English. "Where's Mona's?"

"Tenth and Collyer. Eight tomorrow morning. I already cleared that with Denise."

J.P. glanced at the schedule that was still up on his computer screen. *Sure enough, M. B. at Mona's is typed right into the agenda.* "Eight?" *Why so early?*

"Do you need a wake up call?"

"No, I'll be there."

Janet was impatiently pacing the length of his office.

I've got to get her out of here. J.P. turned his attention back to the paperwork from the sheriff's office, but this time he put on his glasses. He wasn't sure what he was looking for, but it seemed complete. Without looking up, J.P. turned to the second page. James Ralston's signature was scrawled on the bottom line followed by Janet's signature.

"Did you have to go with him today?"

"Yesterday," Janet corrected. "And no, I didn't take him down there. They called me to come over . . ."

J.P. looked from his ex-wife to his son.

" . . . Your ingenious suggestion for James to go talk to the cops now has charges filed against him!"

"Charges?" The attorney in J.P. looked at his son over the top of his glasses. "What kind of charges?"

"It's all there in those papers," Janet continued. "Now he's under arrest. Juvenile house arrest until he can see the judge a week from Thursday."

"What else can you tell me, James?" J.P. sat down at his desk and waited.

"I wouldn't fink on my friends so they are holding me accountable, whatever that means." James shrugged, keeping his eyes anywhere but on his father's.

J.P. removed his glasses and squeezed the bridge of his nose. *This isn't exactly the way I wanted to begin my custody stint.* Janet was rattling on and on. *God, I wish she'd shut up!* She finally stopped talking and looked at him as if maybe there should be a response of some kind.

"What do you want me to say?"

"You weren't even listening!"

How can I listen and think at the same time? You're relentless!

"Do you even care what the rules are?"

"Rules for custody or the arrest or what?" *What I need to do now is get this paperwork over to Mike.*

"You figure it out yourself," she said through clenched teeth. "I came all the way down here, waited for you to get out of yet another meeting, just so I could talk to you about this and you still don't care enough to hear what I have to say!"

J.P. couldn't deny the fact that he'd tuned her out, and he was pretty sure he couldn't convince her that he did care. *But given the set of circumstances, there's nothing I can do until he goes before the judge anyway.*

"Look, Jan, if he's under house arrest, then he's under house arrest. We can't change that before he goes to court . . ."

"Do you know exactly what that means?" She didn't wait for an answer. "That means he must be in the presence of a parent or guardian twenty-four-seven unless he has a job. If he has a job he has to sign in and out with a designated supervisor even when he goes to the bathroom!" Janet's voice was getting higher as she spoke. "He cannot be out of sight from an adult for one minute for the next ten days!"

Okay. J.P. thought about that information. *That's a little overwhelming.* In light of the current casework, the attorney could see some issues arising. *Then we'll find him a job so I know where he is all day long.* The father leaned back into his leather chair and took a deep breath. *And Denise is going to hate the fact that she's legal guardian #2.*

"Then we'll deal with it." *It's time to end this conversation.* "At least James went down to the precinct and reported what he knew . . ." *or at least part of what he knows.* "You're off the hook, Jan. You can go home. I'll pick Josh up at the usual meeting place on Saturday morning."

Janet blinked the tears out of her eyes obviously surprised at the dismissal. J.P. appreciated the moment of silence as she gathered her thoughts.

"His things are in my car."

J.P. reached his right hand into his front pocket, careful not to rub too hard against the fresh bandage. He handed his truck keys to James. Without a word James followed his mom out of the office.

"Denise. Can you get Ernie McElroy on the phone for me?"

"At the club?"

"Yeah. He's the maintenance man." *Surely he has something James can do around there.*

"Will do."

"Then I need to talk to Mike again as soon as you can locate him." *He's probably already at the gym.* J.P. checked his watch. *Looks like I won't get a workout in today.*

"Line two, boss. Ernie."

"Ernie, I need a favor. My son is moving in with me for a while and he needs a job. Have anything out there he can give you a hand with?"

The elderly voice of the maintenance man was thoughtful. "Well, I can surely find something for him to do. How old is he, J.P.?"

"Fifteen. And he's big—six four and about one-ninety." J.P. thought again. "And he's an athlete." He waited while Ernie thought again.

"How soon's he gonna be here?"

"He's here now. The sooner he's employed the better."

"I could use him in the morning to pick up golf balls off the driving range. After that he can help the mowers out on the green. Can you have him out here by five thirty?"

J.P. glanced at the clock reluctant to give up another minute of the quickly passing afternoon. "I can run him over right now. How long do you need to keep him?"

The elderly voice chuckled. "Five thirty in the mornin', J.P."

"In the morning?" *Shit. I thought eight o'clock was early.* "Do you know how long it's been since I've seen five thirty at that end of the day?"

"That's the beginnin' of the day," Ernie chuckled again. "Not the end. Have him over here and I'll see to it he gets a good workout."

J.P. wrapped up the details of the arrangement and thanked Ernie for his help. By the time he was finished with the phone call James was back upstairs in the office.

James was staring at his father's hand as he tossed the truck keys across the room. "You go see a doctor or what?"

J.P. admired the bandage. "A friend doctored me up over the lunch hour." *I don't think I've ever referred to a woman as a friend.*

"It looks damn serious now. You end up with stitches?"

J.P. shook his head. He could see evidence of the split in James's lip and the darkness of his eyes gave indication that he was also still recovering. "How are you?"

James shrugged his shoulders. "Alright, I guess. A little sore."

Denise buzzed the desk.

Probably Mike.

"Mr. Hughes, J.P. Line one."

J.P. picked up the call without hesitation.

"J.P., this is Jefferey Hughes."

Interesting. I usually work with Christopher Hughes. "How can I be of service?"

"I'm needing some information on a real estate tycoon in Joplin. He goes by the name of Sean Bridges. Do you know him?"

"I know the name but nothing specific." J.P. turned to a clean sheet of paper. "But we can do some snooping around. Something specific you're looking for?"

"He's contacted us regarding an industrial tract for sale northwest of the city . . ."

The city of Joplin has shown interest in that same tract. Across the bottom edge of a legal pad he wrote: *Sean Bridges.*

" . . . We need to understand Bridges' motives before we move forward."

J.P. nodded his head into the phone. "I'll see what I can do, Mr. Hughes. Are you working on a timeline?"

"As always, J.P.," Mr. Hughes tone was dead serious. "Do what you can."

"We'll do." *But I'm hesitant to take on another assignment.* J.P. ran his hand through his hair. *But it is the Hughes Corporation, just the same.*

"We appreciate your effort."

J.P. shook his head as he hung up the phone. *Derek Danielson isn't coming on board any too soon.*

"Denise, what do you know about a Sean Bridges?"

"He owns and operates Bridges Property Management. Why?" She appeared in the door between the offices.

"Jefferey Hughes wants the run down on him as soon as humanly possible. Anything you can get on him."

"I can put Danielson on it first thing in the morning."

"I'd rather have it today." *I'm going to owe her for this one.* "And if you can find anything on the industrial tract for sale on the edge of town we could use that too."

"The one out by the airport?"

"That's the one."

"The city is considering it for airport expansion. It will no doubt be on the agenda for next week's council meeting."

I know. "Get the low down, anything you can find will be useful." J.P. spun around in his chair and reached for the newspaper folded on the cadenza. He pulled out the real estate section and handed it to his son along with a yellow highlighter. "Mark every listing you can find with Bridges Property Management or Sean Bridges as the agent."

James spread the paper out across the conference table behind his father's desk and went to work. The additional assignment at the end of the day rewound J.P.'s mind back to the weekend before.

"Hey, Denise, what were you doing here late Saturday afternoon?"

"Oh, I finished the report for the Lloyd Hughes Estate so we could get it off in time Monday."

Shit. I forgot all about finishing that report. "Did we get it over there in time?"

"Of course."

I owe her big time. "I'll make it up to you . . ."

"A simple thank you would suffice, but I'm always up for a cash bonus." Denise flashed a quick smile and disappeared through the doorway. "I hate to add excitement to your day but while you were on the phone with Mr. Hughes, another call came in . . ."

Don't make me play games, Denise! "And that would be from?"

"I don't know much about her," Denise started. "But she called earlier and wondered why you didn't call back. She's in the area this weekend . . ."

Obviously not Samira. "Out with it." J.P. opened the Mid-America file.

Denise came back and stood between the offices. "Bobbie Jo Sommers." She instantly disappeared around the corner.

The attorney stared at the empty doorway. *Just who I don't need making an appearance.* Leaving the folder open, he followed Denise.

"What'd you tell her?"

"That you were behind closed doors."

"Very funny." *I didn't figure I'd see Bobbie Jo anytime soon.*

"Seriously," Denise added. "I told her you'd call when you got a free moment." She handed him a memo with Bobbie's phone number.

Doesn't look like I'll be any too free this weekend. He remembered the house arrest. *Or any time soon.*

"Who's Bobbie Jo Sommers?" James asked as he poured over the real estate listings.

Surprised by his son's inquiry, J.P. tried to shrug it off. "A girl I . . ." *I what? I didn't exactly date her. I just spent a week in her bed!* " . . . I was with awhile back." The details of the affair were still fresh in the attorney's memory. *Let's change the subject.* "What are you finding on Bridges?"

"Nothing yet." He didn't look up from the paper. "So you might have a hot date this weekend then?"

"Doubtful." *But she does have a figure that will stop you in your tracks.* He pictured Bobbie's lingerie shot in his mind. *But the last time she was in town I lived alone.* Another pretty face came into focus. *And the last time she was in town, I didn't know Samira Cartwright.*

J.P. tried to concentrate on the case in front of him. *What is it with this Cartwright woman? She didn't even accept my invite to the Hughes engagement.* The one-sided conversation continued. *Face it, Ralston, she's already got her hooks in you.*

J.P. didn't know if he liked being hooked or not. *It messes with my mind.*

13

Issues of Adolescence

The Cartwright girls danced anxiously waiting for their mother to finish a phone conversation. *For heaven's sake, what is so important that they can't wait another minute?*

"Guess what! Guess what happened after school today?" They giggled simultaneously.

"What? What?" *I don't know what's triggering their excitement, but I do know it's about time for us to meet my parents for dinner.*

Kara nudged Krissy in the arm.

"Well . . . ?" *Spit it out, girls!*

"Kara has a boyfriend!"

A boyfriend? "Really?" *Oh my. I don't know if I'm ready for this.* Samira's excitement instantly turned to queasiness.

Kara's skin turned a dark crimson. "Well, maybe not a boyfriend yet, but he asked me out."

Asked her out.

Krissy hugged her sister. "This is soooo exciting. I can't wait to tell Tiffany!"

Samira removed Krissy's freckled arms from around Kara's neck. "What's his name?"

"His name is Ryan and he's so cute! He's Rona's brother and he's in high school and everything!" Before Kara could take a breath, Krissy spilled. "He wants Kara to go to the movies with him Saturday."

Ryan. "Saturday?" *Knowing his name doesn't help me feel better about this.*

"You should see him, Mama! He's . . ."

Samira held out her palm. "Thank you for the report, Krissy, but I would rather discuss the details with your sister." *Alone.*

The telephone rang into the excitement. Krissy pounced on the receiver and quickly disappeared behind a closed door. *Okay. We have about twenty minutes to figure this out.* Samira studied Kara's face. *She's waiting for my permission.*

"This is very big news, Kara." Samira sat down in the desk chair. "Ryan." *Wow. Is Kara old enough to date?* "Is he really in high school?"

"Going into the tenth grade." Kara's eyes were dancing. "But Mama, I am going into the ninth grade, remember?"

It doesn't seem possible. Samira studied her daughter's excited face. "Do I know Regan?"

"Ryan."

"I mean the sister."

"Rona."

"Rona. Do I know her?"

"Rona Parkison. They live on Walnut Street not too far from the old depot." Kara's face lit up. "The movie starts at 2:00 Saturday. It's PG-13 and his parents can pick me up and . . ."

"Oh, Kara . . ." Samira interrupted. She stood up and ran her hand through Kara's hair. *She is so beautiful.* She hugged Kara more in an effort to buy time to gather her thoughts than anything else. *And growing up so fast! How do I know this Ryan won't take advantage of her?*

"Can I think about this through dinner?"

"You're not going to talk to Uncle Wes about it first, are you?"

"Why do you ask that?"

Kara dropped her voice. "I don't know . . . it just seems like you always have to talk to him about these kinds of things first. I don't want him involved in my private life like that this time."

I can appreciate that. "Then I won't talk to Uncle Wes. But let me think it through, okay?

The restaurant was busy when Samira and the girls arrived. *We all have our assigned places to sit, as always.* Her parents sat one at each end of the table. *They're kind of like bookends to our lives.* But the chair opposite Samira was empty. *It's not like Wes to miss a family gathering.*

"I'm going to order for Wes." Pam was getting Mark situated. "He said he'd be along in a few minutes."

As soon as the waitress had taken everyone's order, Papa Ray was right on task. "Let's see the end of the year grade cards." He was beaming at his granddaughters.

Both grandparents examined the girls' report cards with animated enthusiasm. Samira felt her father put his hand over hers. *That's daddy's way of telling me how proud he is of my girls.*

Samira's mind slipped back to conversation with Phil earlier in the week. *I don't know what I'd do if one of my girls was having issues in school.* She unfolded her napkin and put it on her lap when the waitress delivered her salad. *I am so thankful for the way my girls take the initiative to be successful.*

Ah, here comes Wes. Samira glanced at Pam, who was busy feeding Mark croutons from her salad. *She'll feel better when Wes gets in his seat.* It felt really strange having one empty chair. *I remember the first time we came here after Tom was gone.* She forced that memory from her mind. *I'm glad Wes's chair won't stay empty.*

They were halfway through the main course before Samira was addressed in conversation.

"You've been awfully quiet this evening, Sis." Wes was looking across the table into his sister's eyes.

Samira shrugged. "I didn't mean to be."

"Something on your mind?"

Plenty. Samira shook her head and forced a smile. She could feel Kara watching her. "I'm just enjoying the chatter, that's all." Now she could feel her father's eyes on her as well. *Why do I always feel so transparent with Daddy and Wes?* She wiped her mouth on a napkin.

Wes nodded but Samira knew he didn't buy her explanation. *Nor did Daddy.* She added a pad of butter to the baked potato. *And Kara is scared to death I'm going to talk to Wes about her social agenda.* The butter melted quickly. *That's kind of how I feel. Melted from the inside out.*

The stars were faintly visible in the sky beyond the city lights. *It's a beautiful night.* Samira walked along the sidewalk in front of the restaurant. It was warm enough she didn't even need a jacket. She watched her brother help fasten the children into their car seats.

If I don't discuss Kara's social issues with Wes, where do I turn for advice? For a brief moment Samira wished Tom could be there to celebrate the end of another school year with his daughters. *Sometimes I wish he were here to help me through these parenting decisions too.* A new thought entered her mind. *I wonder what he would say to Kara wanting to date a sophomore in high school?*

"The girls' grade cards are very impressive indeed," Raymond spoke quietly.

"They had a good year. I just can't believe this will be their last year together at the middle school."

Samira liked the way her father put his arm around her shoulder. "They wouldn't be nearly so well adjusted without your constant nurturing, Princess." A genuine smile crossed his face. "You're doing a fine job with them."

"Thank you, Daddy." *Does he know I'm struggling with a parenting issue tonight?* Samira followed his eyes to where her daughters were standing. *He must know, or he wouldn't have said that.*

"Sometimes it's really hard, Daddy." *I think I have to make up my mind on my own dinner invitation before I can deal with Kara's.*

"I know it is." Raymond pecked his daughter on the cheek with his soft lips. *That's exactly how Phil kissed my forehead when he left the other day!* Samira smiled and glanced at her father's face. *No wonder it feels so natural when Phil does that . . . it's just like Daddy!*

"Sorry I was late to dinner." Wes apologized as he stepped up onto the sidewalk.

Wes is talking to Daddy, not to me.

"Everything alright at the bank, Weston?" Raymond dropped his hand from Samira's shoulder and tucked it into his front pocket.

They rarely discuss business outside the office.

"A little hectic, but under control." Wes answered casually but Samira knew he was thinking otherwise. "Just happened to have an early meeting that ran late."

"Unusual for a Friday afternoon, isn't it?"

Wes nodded. "First time in a long time."

Krissy and Kara joined their mother.

Wes grinned broadly at his nieces. "I didn't know if I'd see you two here tonight. Won't be long and we'll be adding chairs for boyfriends at this end of the school year dinner."

The comment was made in complete innocence, but the look on Kara's face wrongly accused her mother of discussing private issues with her uncle.

"It's not our social schedule you have to worry about, it's Mama's! She's been . . ."

Krissy! Please don't bring me into this! She stopped her daughter with her eyes.

Wes ruffled Krissy's hair. "Your mother deserves a little personal time, don't you think?" He winked at his sister.

Samira could feel her father's eyes studying her face as it reddened against the night sky. *It's not time to talk to my parents about Phil.* But she did know if she chose to accept an evening invitation to Springfield she would need a place for the girls to stay the night.

"I was thinking I might take Pam out tomorrow night."

Samira wondered if Wes changed the topic of conversation for her benefit. "It's been awhile since we've had a moment alone."

Pam did seem unusually quiet at dinner. "Do you need help with the children?"

"Maybe," Wes admitted. "If you're free."

Krissy turned abruptly and faced her mother with a pouting lip.

"Your father and I could take the children for awhile," Ashleigh volunteered as she joined her family. "We'll be through with the hospital auxiliary function around five."

Something tells me Wes would rather not accept that offer.

"That's okay, Mama," Samira assured. "We don't mind, do we girls?" *Maybe Wes and Pam would reciprocate the favor if I do decide to go to Springfield.*

Kara rudely pulled her mother's arm toward the car. "It's getting late and we still have some . . ." Kara whispered the next word, " . . . *discussing* to do."

Samira fastened her seatbelt as Krissy let loose. "How come we're always the babysitters when Uncle Wes decides he needs a night out?"

"They just went out for dinner together tonight," Kara added.

Believe me, it's not the same. Samira sighed and turned her car into the night traffic.

"But we start babysitting Monday. Maybe we didn't feel like sitting with them tomorrow too." Krissy sighed obnoxiously. "You didn't even ask us." Krissy's annoyance was relentless and her irritation showed. "How come Uncle Wes always plans on us to stay with the kids? Granny offered too . . ."

Enough! "I offered, Krissy. Wes is more comfortable with us coming to the house than he is taking all three kids to Granny's for the night."

Kara clarified the statement: "Why is Aunt Pam more comfortable with us than Granny? You've always trusted Papa Ray and Granny to be our overnight babysitters, right Mama?"

Except when I go with Phil to Springfield. She reviewed that thought. *Does that mean I'm leaning toward accepting?*

Tensions ran high back at the house. It was late and Samira was emotionally drained from analyzing her own pending date. *And now I have to factor in a date for my daughter too!* Samira pulled the clip out of her hair. *How am I supposed to handle this?*

"You talked to Uncle Wes, didn't you," Kara pulled a brush through the length of her hair.

Samira gathered the stray towels and pulled the hamper drawer out far enough to deposit the dirty laundry.

"No, Kara, I haven't spoken to anyone about Ryan."

"Then why did he say he thought we might not come to dinner because we'd have a date?" Kara squeezed toothpaste on to her toothbrush and mindlessly laid the tube on the counter.

Samira moved the toothpaste and the hairbrush into a drawer. "Wes just knows you're growing up. One of these days Papa Ray will call to schedule the end of the year dinner party and you'll have to tell him you can't make it because you have other plans." *I just hope that day doesn't come any too soon.*

Kara spit into the sink. "Well, he sure talked like he knew something." She wiped her mouth on a towel and left it on the counter.

Instantly, the mother hung the towel back on the holder. Kara rolled her eyes. "Will you stop cleaning up?"

"I just want it tidy in the morning."

"Well, I'm not done in here yet!" Kara's voice was sharp. "So, have you made any decision, yet?"

"I'd like to talk to Ryan's parents first."

"Did you read the movie review? I left it on the dining room table."

"Yes. I read it. The movie is not the problem; it's the company I am concerned about. I just don't know them." *And you're only fourteen.*

Kara left the bathroom in a huff. Samira followed. *It's usually Krissy who speaks her mind. Not Kara.*

"Just let me call them in the morning, okay?"

"You're making a bigger deal about this than you need to!"

I don't mean to. I just have to be sure. "I'll call first thing." *And I'm the mother so that gives me the prerogative to make deals out of issues.* She watched Kara organize the piles of school paraphernalia on her bed. "I'm sorry I can't give you an immediate answer, Kara. This is all new to us. We have to work through it together."

Kara carried a stack of notebooks to her desk, her long hair shimmering in the light. "I know. But all of my friends can go to the movies with boys. But I have to keep waiting for an answer."

"All of your friends are not you."

"You can't protect me forever, Mama."

Samira sat down on the edge of her daughter's bed. *Well that pretty much says it all.*

Kara immediately retracted her remark. "I'm sorry, Mama. I didn't mean to hurt your feelings."

Samira bit her bottom lip. *Am I really overly-protective of them?* Samira's thoughts went back to Phil's analysis on his son's family life. *I guess I'd rather have Kara mad at me for caring too much than wondering if I cared at all.*

"We'll discuss this again in the morning when I'm not so tired, okay?" Samira's voice faltered a little as she spoke to her daughter.

Kara nodded meekly as her mother left the room.

It had been a long, full day. Samira dimmed the lights in the front room and picked up her book from the coffee table. The house was still and peaceful, just the way she liked it at this hour. The steady light on the answering machine haunted her as she climbed into bed. *Phil has a way of not being very predictable.* On one hand his spontaneity was quite erotic; on the other it drove her crazy.

I don't have an answer for him yet anyway. Why did it have to fall on the seventeenth? Any day but my anniversary.

Samira processed the Saturday agenda. *Kara's only going into the ninth grade.* She fingered the novel on her lap. *Daddy made me wait until I was 17 before I could date and even then I wasn't allowed to date without a group of friends.*

Samira's eyes fell on her husband's face in the photograph on the tabletop. *What I wouldn't do to have you here tonight.* She turned his wedding band on her right hand. *Tom would know how to handle these situations.* Samira moved her hand across the empty pillow.

Slowly, as if in a dream, another man's face appeared in her mind.

She tried to dismiss the vision. *What if Phil needed an answer right then?*

Nothing felt right. *Am I more upset because Phil didn't call or because my daughter is invited out on a date?* A single tear slipped out the corner of her eye and rolled down her cheek. *I can't even give a response to my own invitation! How am I supposed to give an answer to Kara?*

Without warning, Samira could suddenly hear Norma's voice loud and clear as it rang out in the hospital chapel the day Tom died. "*Samira, promise us you won't take Tom away from them . . .*"

I haven't taken their father away from them. Samira looked around the room. His pictures still graced the shelves. *His memory is alive and well. They will always know their father.* Samira rolled her neck from side to side. *But maybe that's part of the problem. I will always know their father too. But he can't fill me up anymore.* She blinked away another tear. *What happens when the girls grow up and get lives of their own? Dear God, am I wrong for wanting him to call me again?*

Her memory rewound to lunch with Phil. She felt Phil's hand slip up the inside of her blouse. *Phil's a grown man and he made that move without permission.* That thought made Samira shudder. *What will Kara do if that happens to her?*

Maybe I'm out of sorts with the girls because I'm out of sorts with myself. After Kara's outburst this afternoon, there was no doubting her resentment against

Wes having any input on her life. *At one point in time I would have used Susan as a motherly sounding board, but even that relationship is slipping.*

That thought alone spurred an entirely new set of questions:

How can I possibly allow myself to think about a relationship with a man when I can't even keep the relationships with my girlfriends intact? But at the same time, how can I possibly be complete as a mother and as a woman if I don't have a life to call my own? Surely there's a way to strike a balance without forfeiting one relationship for another. Isn't there?

These questions nagged on into the darkness of the night.

14

Heart to Heart

"Sit for a minute, Phillip." Aunt Maggie's wrinkled hand patted the leather cushion on the sofa. "It's been a long time since we've talked."

It has been a long time. J.P. stopped in the kitchen doorway. *But it sure feels good to be at the ranch.*

"These fellas need their sleep if they want to be at the lake by dawn, Maggie Jean." Uncle Roy was turning out the lights as he spoke.

Maggie waved him off with her hand. J.P. watched his sons disappear around the staircase landing. "Night, Dad."

Aunt Maggie smiled sweetly. "I see so much of your father in Joshua."

"Hate to admit it, but I see a lot of me in that boy too." J.P. relaxed into the sofa. "Kind of frightening."

"Don't be so hard on yourself." Maggie's eyes were still on the empty staircase. "Josh has your very best qualities. And you both have Joe's smile."

A yellowed photograph of his parents hung on the wall next to Maggie and Roy's wedding picture. For a brief moment J.P. recognized the man in the frame.

"Do you ever think about looking him up?"

"Nope." *No reason to.* "Not anymore. He had his chance and didn't show."

"That was a long time ago, Phillip. Time may have changed him over the years."

I don't want to waste my weekend talking about the Captain.

"How tall is James, now? Do you think six-four?"

"About." *I'm right at 6'2".* "I never thought I'd be looking up at my boys, Aunt Maggie."

"I've looked up to everybody all my life. But the Ralston genes do run strong."

There were several moments of comfortable silence. J.P. could feel himself settling into Joseph Phillip.

"James says he's spending the summer with you."

"He doesn't have much choice." J.P. rested his head on the back of the sofa. "James and Janet . . ." *No, that's not right.* ". . . James and Bruce aren't seeing eye to eye on much these days."

"It will be good for you to spend the time with James. He needs you."

I hope. "It's going to take some getting used to."

"Of course it will, Phillip." Maggie rocked back and forth in the platform rocker as she visited. "Lord knows how badly your boys have needed your touch over the years."

If the Lord knows, he hasn't gone out of his way to inform me.

"You don't give yourself enough credit as a father, Phillip."

Here comes the pep talk. He waited but she didn't say any more for awhile.

"I've heard from your father, Phillip. He would like to see you. Bobby went . . ."

". . . Out to see him over Christmas." J.P. completed the sentence. "I know, he told me."

"He has some things of your mother's he'd like to give you," Maggie continued. "I know it's hard, but he's an old man now." Maggie paused. "He took the Navy business very seriously, Phillip. Too serious if you ask me. But just the same, he would like to mend some fences."

I know she means well, but I have no feelings of sentiment for my father. No matter how old and decrepit he might be.

"Bedtime, Maggie Jean." Uncle Roy appeared on the landing.

"Well, anyway, I don't want to spoil your time at home, but I'll put the letter on the desk. It will be there if you want to read it." Maggie reached out and patted her nephew on the knee. "You look tired, son. I imagine those boys will have you out of the sack before day break."

"Your bag's at the top of the stairs, Phillip." Uncle Roy turned around to head back upstairs. "You comin' Maggie?"

"In a minute," she replied softly. "Anything I can do for you before I turn in?"

Aunt Maggie used to always ask me that at bedtime. J.P. shook his head.

The short little woman wriggled out of her rocker. She walked behind the sofa and squeezed J.P.'s shoulders as she passed. "Good night, dear. The guest suite is ready if you like."

"Thanks, Aunt Maggie, but I think I'll bunk in the back room." He looked into her gray blue eyes. "It's nice and quiet down there."

"It's quiet everywhere here, Phillip. But I made your old bed too, just in case."

J.P. watched the platform rocker as it swayed back and forth and then slowed to a stop. The grandfather clock chimed ten times. *She's right. It is quiet here. No traffic. No sirens.* The only audible sound on the main floor was the steady sway of the pendulum on the clock.

Time passed. J.P. contemplated the letter on Maggie's desk. *I have no desire to make contact with the man who took my mother away.*

Slowly, J.P. pulled himself off the sofa and turned off the only remaining light. He made his way up the wrap-around staircase. As promised, his bag was waiting at the top. James was stretched out over the entire length and width of the double bed in the first room down the hall. *I have no idea what I'm going to do with that boy for the rest of the summer.* A glint of light shone on the rhinestone earring in his son's ear. *I wonder what made him do that?*

The only light shining at the end of the hall was under the crack of the bathroom door. J.P. passed Josh's empty room. He turned the switch on the bottom of the wall lamp. *Nothing has changed.* The bed was still against the far wall and the walnut dresser was still in its place next to the window. He set his bag down and reached behind his head to remove his t-shirt. *Sleep is going to come easily.*

There was a slight tap on the open door. *Hey Josh.* "Too early to be turning in?"

"Way early." Josh flopped into the worn swivel rocker.

"James didn't have any trouble calling it a night." J.P. sat down on the end of the double bed. The stitched pattern of the old quilt top felt familiar under his hands.

"James never has trouble sleeping."

"Probably growing."

"Maybe." Josh shrugged casually. The Ralston men studied one another in comfortable silence.

"It's good to have you guys here, Josh."

"It's been awhile, huh?"

"Too long." *Since Thanksgiving last year.* "Too many miles . . ."

" . . . and too many schedules."

J.P. looked away. *I know. Caseload.*

"We were beginning to think you might not make it this afternoon."

I should have watched the clock closer. "I didn't realize we were running that late until your mother pointed it out."

Josh rolled his eyes. "You missed the bulk of her pointing." He eyed his father carefully. "I tried to call you when shit hit the fan with James last weekend. I figured you were at the driving range with Mike or something."

J.P.'s mind went back to breakfast with Samira that morning. "I missed that driving range appointment with Mike too."

"Heck, if you stood Mike up, I don't feel nearly as slighted."

"I didn't say I stood him up."

"But you didn't say you didn't either." Josh grinned. "So, you were working right?"

Not exactly. "I went in around ten."

"I tried calling the house . . ."

Is he inquiring for himself or for his mother?

"Late night, then?" Josh leaned forward and rested his elbows on his knees. "That's what I thought. All nighter?"

Some dates I might brag about, but Samira is more of a treasure than a trophy.

"Speak now or forever hold your peace." Josh's eyes were twinkling. "Should have known it was girl that held you up."

Why should I have to answer to a seventeen year old anyway?

Josh was suddenly serious. "So you know a lot about girls, right Dad?"

"Not nearly as much as I wish I knew." *I still can't read Samira's thoughts.*

"You never seem to have any trouble finding one."

That's true. "But that doesn't mean I know much about them. Finding a girl is one thing; keeping her is another." *Not that I've wanted one around for very long at a time anyway.*

"Good point." Josh laughed a little.

"What's so funny?"

"You're track record with women. You don't stay with one woman too long at a time, do you?"

Let's not go there. "So do you have something specific in mind for this line of questioning?"

Josh's blue eyes became solemn. "I'd love to have specifics to talk about, Dad." The young man sighed heavily and sank into the old chair. "Most of the guys I hang out with have steady girlfriends and plenty of specifics to go with. I'm lucky to have a date on Friday nights."

What about that pretty blonde you pointed out to me in the parking lot? "If the girls are turning you down, Josh . . ."

"That's not it." Josh was visibly flustered. "That's not it at all. I don't even know what to say when I have the chance to ask somebody out."

J.P. thought back to his own tongue-tied episode with Samira the day he went back to the library looking for her. "You might come by that more honestly than you think, son."

"You always know what to say, Dad. Same with James. He could have several dates every weekend if he wanted." Josh's voice faded away and he closed his blue eyes.

"You're wrong, Joshy." J.P. decided to confess his blunder. "I tripped over my tongue so bad that I invited a woman out for coffee."

Josh opened his eyes and looked doubtingly at his father. "You don't even drink coffee."

"Case in point. This lady was so gorgeous, I forgot everything I'd planned to say and ended up inviting her for coffee."

"You're a lawyer, Dad. You always know what to say."

J.P. popped his son on the arm with the back of his hand. "I have notes in the courtroom, Josh. Seriously, I felt like a fool."

"So what'd ya do to get over it?"

"I ordered a Coke."

"No, about the knowing what to say stuff."

"Nothing. I'm still not over it." *I have never been so nervous asking a woman out. Ever.*

"No, I mean how'd you finally learn to ask a girl out? You do it all the time now!"

Oh. Josh thinks this is past history. He shook his head and ran his hand through his hair. "This just happened a couple of weeks ago, Josh." *Shit, I've known her less than three weeks and already she's messing with my mind.*

"What?" Josh chided. "Mr. Sly fumbled a date recently?"

I don't know if I appreciate his sudden interest or not. "You're not going to tell this story to your mom are you?"

"Nah, I never tell mom your good stories."

Wonder what he does tell her then. "Okay, here's the deal. I think the reason I stumbled around and forgot what I was going to say is because this lady was so incredibly pretty . . ."

"You mean like sexy?".

Sexy? "Well, no . . ." *Yeah. Sexy is a good word.* "Well . . . okay." J.P. couldn't hide his boyish grin. "She's just a really classy lady . . ."

Josh motioned with his hands for his dad to continue.

Why am I explaining this to Josh? "Anyway, I was kind of short with her at the library one afternoon while she was helping me research a case." *No. I was really impatient with her.* "I was working against the clock and didn't give her much credit for the information she discovered. But then after I left

I couldn't stop thinking about her. A few days later I decided to go back and apologize for the way I'd acted."

"No doubt. Did she remember you when you went back?"

That's an interesting question. J.P. opened his mouth to say something but nothing came out. *I have no idea if she did or not!*

Josh leaned in further. "Well?"

"It's really weird," J.P. admitted. "When I went back to the library, I didn't see her anywhere and I didn't know her name. So, I'm standing there trying to describe her to this old woman behind the counter when all of a sudden she just appeared right there in front of me." J.P. could see her just as plain in his mind now as if she was standing in his room right then.

"And . . . ?"

"And nothing." J.P. laughed at his own lack of poise. "I couldn't think of a thing to say." *And I don't think I ever apologized either.* "I think she finally introduced herself or something and I asked her out for coffee."

Josh was laughing. "That blows me away! You always have something to say."

"You're mother is the one who always has something to say." *I don't know if I like his response or not!* "I use notes, remember?"

"Even with girls?"

"Not with every girl, Joshy; just the really pretty ones." J.P. walked over to the dresser and started to unpack his bag.

"I hear that!" Josh flopped onto his father's bed. Suddenly he became serious again. "There's this girl in our school. Her name's Amy and she's new this year. She's the one I showed you in the parking lot." Josh paused momentarily. "I wanted to ask her to prom but never got the words to come out of my mouth."

"Maybe you should have asked her out for coffee." *It saved my ass.*

"Maybe." Josh was thinking. "But you always have a date, Dad, so you must know how to ask a girl out."

"Getting a date is one thing, Josh. Getting knocked off your feet by a woman is an entirely different story." *Is that what Samira did to me?* That thought took J.P. by surprise. *I think she did.* "This woman is different somehow. I can't explain it and I can't deny it." His voice was softer when he spoke again. "Somehow you just know she's the one you have to ask out so you do whatever it takes to get the job done."

"So, are you saying this is *the* one?"

J.P. looked his son directly in the eyes. "Hell, I don't know. But I figure if I can't stop thinking about a woman before I even know her name, I have nothing to lose by asking her out." *Funny to hear those words come out of my mouth.* J.P. shook his head.

"So . . ."

"So what?"

"Did she go out for coffee?"

"She did." J.P. grinned at the memory. "And we went out to dinner a few nights later."

"Now I *know* why you didn't answer the phone Saturday morning!" Josh slapped his hand against the mattress in victory. "I knew I could get it out of you!"

He baited me! J.P. put his hands on his hips and studied his son. *And I fell for it.*

"So I guess I just have to open my mouth, even if I do make an ass out of myself like you did, huh?" Josh climbed off the bed and stood directly in front of his father.

I did not make an ass out of myself . . . did I?

"You crack me up." Josh turned for the door. "Morning's going to come too soon. 'Night, Dad."

That's it? A little father-son dialogue then 'night dad? He stepped into the hall and watched Josh disappear behind a door. *Good night, Josh.*

J.P. finished undressing and climbed into the freshly made bed. *Even the sheets smell like cedar.* The conversation with Josh replayed in his mind. *And I know I didn't make an ass out of myself.* The grandfather clock struck eleven times in the distance. *Or if I did, it didn't seem to phase her.* J.P. rolled over into the empty space in the bed. *What I wouldn't do to fill this space with Samira tonight.*

15

The Prick of the Thorn

Just because I can't talk to my brother about Kara's love life doesn't mean I can't talk to him about my own. She picked up a business magazine and flipped through the pages without reading anything. *For pete's sake, I can't believe I've let this decision take over every waking thought!* Samira put the magazine back down on the small table. *And I can't imagine what's keeping Wes on a Sunday afternoon!* Samira's hands were sweating as she paced the floor of her brother's office. *I liked Daddy's office better.* Samira glanced at the walnut accent table next to the bookcase. *The furniture is too heavy for this sunny room.* She stopped in front of the full-length windows overlooking downtown.

"Samira." Wes appeared in the doorway. "Sorry to keep you waiting."

She turned to face him. *He's trying to look enthusiastic, but the fact is, he's exhausted.* Samira was surprised to see him still in his church clothes. "I didn't mean to interrupt . . ."

"Interrupt? I'm here on a Sunday afternoon of a holiday weekend . . ."

He's busy. "This really isn't important, Wes. You can just call me later if you like." *But I hope he lets me stay.*

Wes was shaking his head. "Nonsense. Here, take a load off." He motioned for Samira to sit down. "So what's on your mind, Sis?" Weston took a seat in the winged-back chair.

Here goes. "You told me to call if I needed you, right?"

"I'm answering."

Samira couldn't sit down. *Just get it out there.* She leaned on the edge of her brother's massive desk. "It's about the seventeenth." *I wish he already knew what I was going to say so he could finish my sentences.* "I've been invited out for an evening in Springfield."

"Okay." Wes was frowning. "And you're here to what? Ask my permission?"

"I don't know, exactly." Her fingers tapped against the desk. "It's a big step for me, I guess."

"Help me out here, Sis. I'm assuming it's with the same guy."

Samira nodded.

"What exactly did he invite you to?"

"He called it a business engagement." *I don't know much more than that.* "It includes dinner."

Wes opened his palms to the ceiling. "Maybe I'm missing the gist of this, but a business dinner shouldn't be threatening." He shrugged his shoulders. "I think you should go, Sis. Obviously he thinks highly of you if he's inviting you to join him on business."

I hadn't thought of it that way.

"Seriously," Wes added. "I'd be extremely cautious of taking someone along to meet with my clients. He probably is to."

"Do you think he's meeting with clients?"

"Samira." Wes stood up and put his hands on his hips. "You said he was a lawyer, right? So, I'd guess is that a business meeting might possibly include a client." Wes raised his eyebrows.

"I guess so." *I want him to talk me out of it.* "But it's clear over in Springfield! We're talking about an entire evening here. It's not like I can leave work, get ready to go, and then be home by midnight . . ."

"Look," Wes squared his sister's shoulders and looked her in the eye. "You're not exactly up against Cinderella's curfew here." He narrowed his dark eyes. "I don't know what's eating at you, but you're going to have to get over it before you make a decision."

Someone tapped on the open door. Samira watched her brother cross the room and exchange information with a short dark man.

"Hey, Sis, I need to initialize the mainframe computer so they can reboot. It won't take very long."

That's okay. I'll wait. Samira studied her right hand. *My finger feels naked without Tom's ring. I didn't think I'd ever take it off.* Her mind tripped back to the day in the hospital when the nurse removed it from her husband's finger before surgery. *He told me to keep it safe.* She touched the faint line it had made around her finger. *I didn't know it would be the last time he'd ever have it on.*

Samira sank into the chair her brother had been sitting in. *So what is it that's really holding me back?* She thought for a moment. *Wes is right. I should be honored he included me on a business engagement.* She held her hand out at arm's length. *And it's not that I don't want to be with him again.*

Suddenly the chair was too confining. Pam's picture was smiling back on her from the corner of Weston's desk. *June seventeenth has always been reserved for my husband.* Samira fingered the frame around the photo. *I don't know if I can give myself to any other man on that night.*

The sidewalk below her brother's second story office window was amazingly lifeless. *If I accept the invitation, then I accept the potential that comes with being alone with Phil.* She breathed in deeply. *And if I don't accept, then I remain locked in my past without any potential at all.*

"So?"

Samira jumped at the sound of her brother's voice.

"What'd you come up with?" Wes proceeded to sit down in his oversized executive's chair.

Samira wrapped her arms around her middle and shrugged her shoulders. *I feel silly needing his approval.* Wes studied her face until she looked away.

"Samira," he said gently, "If you're looking for my blessing, you have it. Pam and I will even keep the girls for the night so you don't have to worry about watching the clock. Besides, we owe you one for watching our kids last night anyway." Wes tipped his head to the side. "But if you're looking for my consent, I can't give that to you."

Samira closed her eyes. *Of course not. No one can give me permission except the voices inside my head!* Very slowly Samira realized her brother was standing right next to her. Without asking, he cradled his arms around her from behind and pulled her up against his chest.

"It's still the seventeenth of June, Wes."

"I know."

"That was our anniversary."

"I know."

"Any day but that one and . . ."

" . . . You know, Sis, just because you're going to dinner with a man who isn't Tom doesn't make you any less of a mother or wife . . ."

How can I be sure?

" . . . And if the evening turns into breakfast again, you'll know it's time to let the past be the past. Your time with someone else will not erase your memories with Tom. I promise."

"But what will the girls think?"

"How will they know?"

"How will they know what?"

"Whatever it is you're trying to hide from them." Wes squeezed his sister harder.

"They'll know what the date is on the calendar."

"So?"

"So it's not with their dad."

"It can't ever be with their dad again, Samira. Accept that fact and move on. It's time to live for your future instead of hiding in the past."

Samira pressed the back of her head into her brother.

"Look at me." Wes turned Samira around to face him. "You need to get over whatever obstacle you've created. You're a beautiful woman with a whole life ahead of you." Wes ignored the intercom buzzer on his desk. "Maybe going out with someone new on your original wedding date has some sort of symbolic significance. Maybe it doesn't. But you can't keep your heart in the past and ever expect to share your future with anybody new."

Samira didn't like the insinuation. *But he's speaking the truth.*

"Pam and I will keep the girls that weekend. The whole weekend if you like. We'll be glad to have them around and you'll be glad to not have them around. Okay?"

"But you're the one who said to 'go slow', Wes . . ."

Wes didn't break eye contact. "You are."

This time when his intercom buzzed, Wes responded leaving his sister to her own thoughts.

If is becoming a bigger word than I imagined possible. Samira cleared the dinner dishes still contemplating what she would tell Phil *if* he called for an answer. *I was gone most of the afternoon and he still didn't call.* Deep down she wondered why he'd never offered his phone number to her. *Maybe it's a control thing.*

When the dishes were done, she stepped into the sanctuary of her back yard. The aroma of fresh flowers was invigorating. She breathed in through her nose and allowed her senses to be filled. The Magnolia was in full bloom. Samira followed the brick walkway to the bed of roses in the center of her garden. A tiny pink bud begged for her attention. *It's so beautiful.* Gingerly Samira fingered the flower.

It must take a lot of courage to open such fragile petals to the world. I'd be scared to death.

She sat down along the raised edge of the rose bed. *Maybe that's what's really holding me back.* She touched the pink bud again. *What happens if I open up and things don't work out? Then what?*

"What happens if you open up and the wind blows your petals all over the yard?" Samira spoke out loud to the flower. "But if you ever want to share your blossom, you have to let go and open up."

Samira stayed in the garden for several minutes of contemplative solitude. *Life wasn't always so complicated.* Tom had swept her off her feet and asked her to marry him before she'd really even had a chance to tell her parents she was in love. *Not that they didn't know that from the way I talked about him and spent time with him.* Saying yes to Tom's marriage proposal was a given—something she knew she was supposed to do. *Why is it so difficult to say yes to a simple dinner invitation fifteen years later?*

. . . Because Tom is gone and you have the responsibility of his offspring for accountability.

But Tom is gone. Forever. She fingered the tiny rosebud again. *I can't change who he was in my life. But maybe it's time to make those changes in me and move forward.*

As Samira released the rose bud her finger caught on a thorn. Instantly dark red blood oozed from the wound and stained the pink petals. She applied immediate pressure to the wound. *That's exactly what I fear might happen.* A slight throb caused her to press the wound harder. *I'm afraid the old wounds will open and I'll be hurt all over again.* She felt badly for staining the rosebud with her blood. *But this time if I get hurt, Krissy and Kara will suffer too.*

Samira dared to look at her finger. The bleeding had stopped but there was a mark where the thorn had penetrated her skin. *What if the bleeding in my heart doesn't stop that easily?*

"Mama!"

Samira looked back toward the house. Krissy was standing on the back step waving her arms.

"Mrs. Barnes wants to know if you can take her to the store."

Of course I can take Mrs. Barnes to the store. I have nothing better to do. Samira sighed. "Tell her I'll be over in a few minutes."

She stood up and inhaled deeply. The fragrance of the roses was thick. *I'll never know what new love is like if I don't put myself out there.* The now stained rosebud looked so vulnerable at the end of the long stem. "I think I know how you feel." Samira spoke to the bud. "I just hope I don't get stained like you."

16

The Catch of the Day

An obnoxious clanging brought an abrupt end to J.P.'s slumber. He rolled over in Aunt Maggie's bed and moaned.

"Rise and shine! Didn't you hear the breakfast bell?"

Is that what that noise was?

James threw his body weight into his father's bed. "You're missin' Aunt Maggie's grub."

"Do you know what time it is?"

"Time to fish."

The hands on his wristwatch indicated four thirty. *No fish is worth losing this much sleep over.* Reluctantly J.P. forced his legs over the side of the bed. *This is supposed to be vacation.* The faint aroma of bacon hinted at a big breakfast. *Breakfast before dawn doesn't feel like rest or relaxation.*

Maggie's voice called up the stairs.

"No time for a shower this morning, Phillip! Roy's afraid the sun's going to beat you to the lake."

I only fish at this ungodly hour to appease Uncle Roy and the boys. J.P. ran his hand over a second-day beard. *And I'd feel a hell of a lot better with a quick shower.* Instead, he heeded Aunt Maggie's advice and rinsed his face with cold water.

After breakfast the boys and Chase piled into the bed of Uncle Roy's faded blue pickup.

"Open your eyes, son!" Uncle Roy bellowed as they bumped over the gravel road. "You're going to miss the sunrise."

J.P. put on his dark sunglasses and closed his eyes. "There will be others."

"Not on this day."

He's way too chipper for me at this hour.

"Now sit up and take notice!" With a flip of his calloused hand Roy tapped J.P.'s arm then pointed toward the sky. "There's a hawk up there scouting out morning grub."

J.P. leaned forward in the seat and removed his sunglasses pretending to watch the hawk. Then he closed his eyes behind the glasses again.

The sky was just starting to turn pink as Uncle Roy pulled to a stop under a grove of cottonwood trees.

"A boy can't come of age unless he's experienced the dawn at the lake . . ."

I oughta be of age by now. J.P. had to smile at his uncle's consistency. *Never once have we skipped a fishing trip during a summer visit.* He helped the boys unload the gear.

"Sit back and watch carefully, men. I'm going to show you how to catch the best fish of the day on the first cast." Uncle Roy was preparing his line.

Josh shook his head as he made his first cast. "If you catch the biggest fish of the day first thing, I'll clean it for you." He grinned boyishly at his great uncle. "Deal?"

Roy nodded once and adjusted his fishing hat. Skillfully he dangled his rod over the edge of the dock and made some mysterious maneuvers with his elbows and hands.

"What's he doing?" James asked with caution.

He always makes those moves. "He's getting ready to reel in the catch of the day," J.P. whispered.

"Oh. Riiight."

J.P. searched the tackle box for the perfect bait. *It's all Greek to me.* He fingered a brightly colored orange and yellow bug.

"What's the matter, Dad?" James poked his finger into the miniature box. "Can't bait a hook?"

It's hardly a fish I care to bait, J.P. thought to himself. *Wrong species.* He allowed James to bait his hook, then cast his line with rusty skill. J.P. sat down on the dock and leaned into a sturdy support post. The sunlight sparkled on the water like glitter.

Now this is one view I wouldn't mind sharing with Samira. Never once had he considered bringing a woman to the ranch. *Where did that thought come from?* He'd always figured that would interfere with the little time he had with Josh and James. *Besides this is my escape from reality.* The thought lingered. *Wonder how the boys would like sharing their territory with two junior high girls?* J.P. contemplated that possibility. *Probably not.*

Then again, their next regular trip would be in July. He might throw out the possibility just to see what she said. *Shit, J.P. You don't even know if she's going to Springfield with you yet. Maybe you should offer one invitation at a time.*

A sudden scurry of activity drew J.P. back to the dock.

"Here she comes, boys!" Uncle Roy had a snag on his line. Whatever was on the end of the line wasn't going to give up easily. Roy worked the rod and reel with expertise. "Well, don't just stand there, give me a hand!"

Chase barked at the excitement as James and Josh both grabbed for the rod. Between the three of them they hauled in a feisty bass.

Roy stood tall holding the line a few inches above the fish. "Now there's a beaut' of a fish, fellas!" He cut the line and smiled broadly. "Let me see you match this!"

"Whatdaya think she weighs, Uncle Roy?" James was admiring the catch.

Roy suspended the fish in midair. The scales glistened in the morning sunlight as the fish flipped in resistance. "Four, maybe five pounds," he estimated. "Joshy, you might want to sharpen your knife."

Josh moaned and picked up his own rod again.

Somehow J.P. couldn't see Samira getting much enjoyment out of a slimy bass, but he smiled at the possibility of sharing the story.

In the solitude of the morning, J.P.'s thoughts bounced back to the letter on Aunt Maggie's desk. *Eventually I'll read the letter out of respect for Aunt Maggie.* He didn't have that much respect for the Captain. Too many burned bridges between him and his father. *Joseph Phillip.* Most people earn the right to be called by their name. *To date the Captain hasn't earned any honors for being a family man. Why's he trying to start now?*

James disappeared for a period of time leaving Josh in charge of his rod. J.P. watched his youngest son walk along the edge of the woods and disappear. *I suppose if he's still under house arrest I should follow him.* At the same time, he was quite comfortable with his legs tanning in the morning sunshine. *I'll cut him some slack.* By the time James returned, Josh had landed a catfish.

"Whose rod was it on?"

Josh shrugged his shoulders. "Doesn't matter. I reeled it in either way."

James grabbed for his rod but Josh pulled it out of arm's reach. James slipped on the wet dock and stumbled toward the edge of the lake. He came up swearing and swinging at his brother.

"There'll be none of that on my fishing trip," Uncle Roy warned. He kicked a small item toward James. "Seems you might have lost something there, boy."

James exchanged a quick look with his brother and snatched it up. He pulled his baseball cap low to avoid eye contact with his father.

J.P. ran his hand through his hair and rested his weight against a wooden post. He didn't see what the item was, but he did see the exchange of silent communication between the brothers. *I wonder what other secrets he's hiding underneath that cap?*

By the time the sun was high in the sky, Uncle Roy was taking inventory. "A catfish, a walleye, two blue gills, and a beaut' of a bass." Roy removed his fishing hat and wiped the sweat on his brow with the back of his hand. "Should be enough for grub tonight."

"What time is it, Uncle Roy?" James asked.

"Time to head back to the ranch. Church starts in an hour and Maggie Jean won't want me to go smellin' like a fish."

James narrowed his eyes. "Are we goin'?"

Roy shrugged. "That's up to you."

Given my druthers I'd rather stretch out in the hammock between the Ash trees than go sit on a hard pew.

"The fish are probably done biting til' nightfall anyway, aren't they Uncle Roy?" Josh was reeling in his line.

Roy looked out across the water. "Chances are good they've gone deep." He reached into the cooler with his bare hands and pulled out the first catch of the day. "We have just enough time to clean these before heading out."

Josh moaned out loud.

"And you thought the old man would forget, didn't ya?" James chided from the edge of the dock.

J.P. quieted the younger brother with a motion of his hand. "What do you say we start packing up the gear?"

Obediently James pulled his line in and started to gather the tackle boxes and equipment. "Are we keeping the rubber boot?"

Roy was already bent over Josh, guiding his knife with his experienced hand. He answered without looking up. "We keep every catch."

I have a catch I want to keep too. It seemed a little too soon to be making that assumption. *Why is this woman so fresh in your mind this morning, Ralston?*

James tossed the boot on top of the pile and headed for the truck.

I wonder how much I'd have to pay James to remove his earring before introducing him to Samira?

That's it, J.P. told himself. *You have way too much time on your hands out here in the wide open space.* He folded Roy's lawn chair and leaned it against the post. J.P. looked out across the lake. *If there ever was a place to behold, this is it.* The water gave a rippling reflection of the sky.

J.P. looked back at the cleaning lesson. Josh drew in a breath and held it as Uncle Roy led him through the steps. Roy would make a cut in a smaller fish, and then Josh would copy in the bass. *Who's coming of age this time? Josh or Uncle Roy?*

James returned to the dock and peered over his brother's shoulder.

"Hey, Joshy. You missed a spot over there."

Without speaking, Josh threw his body weight into his brother. James went sailing off the edge of the dock into the cold lake. Caught up in the excitement, Chase bounded into the water as well.

J.P. leaned back on his heels and watched as James surfaced. He was spitting water and spouting obscenities at his brother. *I think Josh made his point.* J.P. didn't dare laugh.

Josh ignored the lack of affection and finished cleaning the bass. James swam back to the dock and hoisted his soaked body out of the water.

"Seems to me you might want to save your advice 'til you're a little closer to shore," Uncle Roy looked up over his photo gray lens.

James swore again and glared in his father's direction. J.P. watched with interest as he removed his shirt. He fingered the contents of his pocket then disgustedly wrung it out over the water. *Eventually I'll have to investigate that stash.* James leaned against the post and removed his high top shoes. When he straightened up, sunlight reflected from the hoop through his belly button. *I will never understand what possessed him to do that!*

James looked away defiantly as he passed his father on the dock.

"Scumbag," James retorted.

"Fool." Josh evened the score.

Back at the house, J.P. fingered the plain white envelope on Aunt Maggie's desk. Shaky handwriting addressed *Margaret Jean Tennison.* The return address was a pre-printed label from the Captain's residence in Lexington, Virginia.

"Ready, Dad?" Josh clamored down the wooden stairs. "James is already outside."

I'm ready for a nap! J.P. tapped the bottom edge of the letter firmly against the desktop. "Yeah, I'm coming."

The door closed with a solid thud leaving J.P. alone in the room. *Twenty five years. That's how many years separate us.* He remembered sitting alone at the rail station in St. Louis an entire day waiting for the Captain to step off a train. That moment never came. *Nor did an apology that explained the absence.* That was the day Joseph Phillip Ralston II dropped his first name.

But today is not the day to dig up old wounds. He left the letter on the desk and joined his sons on the front porch. They drew straws to determine who carried the backpack first then headed into the state park that led them back toward the lake. At first the conversation was limited, but as the men hiked, the silence dissipated.

"Remember when we used to camp out here when we were little?" Josh asked. "We carved our names in a tree trunk somewhere around here."

James pointed to a downed tree. "I remember Uncle Bob helping me climb over that trunk." He stepped over the tree with ease and rolled it enough to clear the walkway.

"You'd probably have to help Uncle Bob over it now," Josh commented with a laugh. The boys scouted about until they found their names in the side of a Maple tree.

"That tree has grown since we were here last," J.P. observed out loud. He reached out and ran his fingers over the rugged letters.

"What's Uncle Bob doing these days, anyway?" James started back toward the path.

"He's still in Boston working telecommunications." J.P. stepped over a small limb. "He'd like for us all to come out this summer if we can find a mutual date."

"Like with a girl?" James asked.

"No," J.P. chuckled. "Like on the calendar."

"Be more fun with a date."

Chase bounded by his master in pursuit of a chipmunk. The boys took off after the dog. Moments after they dipped out of sight, Josh called back.

"Dad! Look down there!" He pointed over the edge of a hill. "I thought the lake was a lot further out than this!"

J.P. laughed as he caught up to his son. "It is when you're legs are short!" James was already at the water's edge throwing a stick into the ripples for Chase to retrieve. "This is the best camping site on the property." J.P. remembered days gone by. "Kindle, shade, water, fish . . ." He momentarily lost track of time.

"I remember when Uncle Bobby pushed mom off the end of that dock!" Josh chuckled.

J.P.'s eyes landed on the end of a worn wooden ramp. "Bobby didn't push your mother into the lake. She stepped back too far and lost her footing."

"Tell that to Mom," James retorted. "She's still pissed!"

"That's the same trip we caught too many fish and the game warden made us throw some back," Josh recalled.

"Same trip you got a fish hook stuck in your thumb and we had to quit fishing to take you to the hospital," James reminded. "You about ruined the whole weekend!"

Josh examined his thumb as if looking for remnants of the scar.

J.P. silently remembered a time he had to carry James on his shoulders because his legs were too tired to walk that far. *Where does the time go?* Crouching down, he picked up a small stone. As he turned it in his hand, his mind wandered back to times at the lake with Janet. The early memories were full of adventure and new experiences. The last trips to the lake were tainted with hollow conversations and hurtful accusations. *I brought the family up here hoping to mend that relationship.* J.P. shook his head. *Nothing I did by that time was going to satisfy Janet.*

He straightened his body and squeezed the rock in his hand. It was warm from the afternoon sun. *How can something so hard have any warmth at all?* Somehow he knew that his heart had hardened with the ruling of the divorce decree. *Joint custody is a farce.* Instead of challenging the paperwork and fighting the system, J.P. forfeited his scheduled rights to see his sons. *At the time I thought it would be easier on the boys to sign off and keep the peace.*

With a full arm extension, J.P. threw the rock far into the water.

That was ten years ago. Seeing his almost grown boys stretched out in the sun on the wooden planks conjured feelings of regret. *I should have gone to bat for them.* He felt out of touch in ways he couldn't describe. *Hell, they don't even know who I am. All they know about me is what Jan and Bruce have insinuated over the years.*

Tired of fleeting thoughts, J.P. called his boys back to shore and headed them off in another direction. Forty-five minutes later they arrived at the top of a bluff overlooking the lake.

"Out of breath, old man?" James teased.

"Hardly." It felt good to be out on the terrain. J.P. removed the backpack from around his shoulders and passed it off to his youngest. James opened the zippered pouch and took a long drink from the water bottle. Without waiting for permission, Josh stretched out on the leaf-laden lawn under the trees.

"So talk to me. What do you guys do when you're home?" J.P. joined them on the ground.

James handed out peanut butter sandwiches and homemade cookies from Aunt Maggie's lunch stash. Both boys remained silent for a moment.

Finally, Josh spoke. "Well, we aren't really home all that much, Dad. Between school and games and other stuff, we aren't home much."

"There isn't much time between school and games so we usually just hang out with friends after school." James added between bites. "If we don't have a game, we have practice and that usually runs late . . ."

"Your practice runs late," Josh corrected. He looked at his father. "James always hangs out longer on the court."

"So, exactly what does 'hanging out' consist of these days?" *I'm curious.* "I'm out of the loop."

James winked at his father. "We wouldn't have to hang out so much if we had a car of our own . . . ."

J.P. took a bite of an apple and ignored his son's comment. *I hear you. If Janet and Bruce would allow me, they'd already have their own transportation.* J.P. nudged his son for an answer.

Realizing he wasn't off the hook, James filled in some blanks. "Okay, so sometimes we play cards, do video games . . ."

" . . . Homework," Josh added. He rolled his eyes at his brother. "One of us did our homework."

James shrugged.

"Someday you'll wish you'd have done your homework," Josh remarked under his breath.

James put up his fists in an imaginary fight. "Ooooo, go ahead. Take a stab, Joshy!"

J.P. kicked his youngest son gently in the foot. "So don't you ever just go home and hang out?"

"No!" The boys replied in unison. Then they laughed at their father's bewildered look.

"Look, Dad, its no big deal. It's just the way it is." James answered casually.

J.P. tossed an apple core into the shaded woods. *J.P. knew the answer to the next question but decided to ask it anyway.* "Do you two hang out with the same friends?"

Simultaneously James answered the same, but Josh answered different. *That's interesting.* J.P. raised his eyebrows.

"Well, some of them are the same," James offered. "Not all of them."

Josh climbed up off the ground. He bumped his brother harder than necessary. "Not many are the same. We usually go our separate ways after school then meet up with Mom for a ride home." By this time Josh was headed back to the trail.

There's more dissention in the ranks than I thought. J.P. didn't like where it might be leading. "You two need to stick together. Whatever the circumstances. Alright?"

James stood up and stretched his arms toward the sky. "Just like you and Uncle Bobby used to do, right?"

J.P. laughed a little. "I looked out for Bobby because he had a way of not looking out for himself." *In more ways than one.*

Josh ignored the humor but James related. "So that's what big brothers are for, huh?" James held his hands out for his brother to return a high five.

Josh turned away leaving his brother's hands hanging in mid air.

"Lighten up, Joshy."

J.P. placed his forefinger and thumb between his lips and let out a shrill whistle.

"Christ, Dad!" James retorted. "Whatya do that for?"

Chase bounded out of the woods and beat his master's leg with a wagging tail.

"Just calling my dog." *And ending the sibling assault.* J.P. reached down and patted Chase with his hand, but his eyes were on Josh who had already started down the other side of the bluff.

The boys challenged J.P. to a game of basketball late in the day. Uncle Roy carried the old metal lawn chairs off the porch and positioned them at the edge of a concrete apron in front of the barn while the boys rolled the portable hoop into position.

J.P. played a few rounds then dismissed himself. *I don't want to wait any longer.* All afternoon he'd fingered his phone in his pocket. He found the number in his contacts and pushed the button. No one answered.

"Did you leave a message?"

J.P. spun around on his heels, unaware that Josh had followed him. He shook his head as he pushed END on the cellular telephone.

"No message."

Josh wiggled his eyebrows. "How's she gonna know ya called if you didn't leave a message?"

"How do you know I'm calling a her?"

"Just a hunch," Josh teased. "A little late to be makin' a call, don't you think?"

I don't know if I like where this might be heading. "Your definition of late and hers might not be the same."

"Told you it was a her!" Josh pointed his finger at his father. "Never know. Leaving the right message might make all the difference."

"A difference between what?"

"How will you know if you don't leave a message?" Josh crossed his arms over his chest and leaned against the truck.

"Alright, alright. I'll call back and leave a message if you'll leave me alone." *I could live without the badgering.*

Josh nodded eagerly in anticipation.

J.P. fumbled with his phone. "Maybe you could go over and wait on the porch or something."

Josh smiled brightly. "I'd rather wait here." He pointed at the phone. "You know, Dad, you don't have to redial on a cell phone if you're calling the same number twice in a row."

I know that. J.P. deliberately turned away from Josh and pushed SEND. *I was hoping to buy a little time.*

One ring.

I prefer not having an audience and I hate answering machines.

Two rings.

The sun was getting low in the sky. J.P. looked back toward the barn and caught a glimpse of James dribbling a lay up across the ready-made court. He pointed for Josh to join his brother.

Three rings.

"Maybe later," Josh antagonized. "I'd rather wait for you."

Four rings.

What if she doesn't want to talk to me? After all, even Mike thought she looked a little out of my league.

"Hello?"

The voice on the other end caught J.P. by surprise and he failed to respond.

"Hello?"

J.P. cleared his throat. "Hey, Samira, it's me, J . . . Phil." J.P. swallowed hard and tried to ignore Josh, who was now doubled over in laughter. "I didn't think you were going to answer."

"Oh, Phil!" There was amusement in her voice when she spoke again. "You called me but didn't expect me to answer?"

How does she do this to me? J.P. was flustered. *And it doesn't help that Josh is laughing hysterically.* "Well . . . not exactly . . . I mean, I called a few minutes ago but you didn't answer . . ." J.P. looked up at the sky and took a deep breath. " . . . So I didn't think you'd answer this time either." *She gets me totally worked up and she's only on the other end of a phone!*

Samira laughed. "Well, I didn't make it to the phone a minute ago, but you didn't leave a message either."

"No, I guess I didn't," J.P. confessed. "Are you busy?" *Because I could call back later.*

"I was outside watering the roses." There was a pause on the line. "Are you home?"

"No, no, I'm up at my aunt's ranch." J.P. dug his shoe into the gravel. "I just thought I'd check in."

"I didn't realize you were leaving town."

J.P. ran his hand through his hair. "No, I guess I didn't tell you." *Should I have told her?* He tried to ignore Josh who was now mimicking his every move. *Maybe I should explain.* "I bring my boys up here every year at this time. We come up here and fish and hang out for the long weekend."

"You go, Dad!" Josh yelled from the tailgate of the pickup.

I wish he'd go away. "You won't believe what I'm doing now."

"Are you underestimating me?"

J.P. was taken aback by Samira's candor. "No, not at all." *I would never underestimate her.* "But any self-respect I might have had is lost to my son."

Josh laughed loudly and pointed at his father.

" . . . Anyway, we did a little fishing earlier and spent some time out on the trail."

"Catch anything?"

The only thing I want to catch is you, Pretty Lady. "There's nothing out here I'd like to catch."

Samira played along. "I thought maybe you'd tell me a big fish story. Like Moby Dick."

Moby Dick. I haven't heard that title since undergrad literature class.

"Hemmingway?"

"Melville, Herman."

"World Lit?"

"Mostly likely American."

Damn.

Josh was getting a little too much enjoyment out of his father's conversation. *I need to know what she's thinking about Springfield, but I'm not going to bring it up with Josh standing here.* "I'll have to brush up on my authors."

"Maybe you should."

"Listen, it's good to . . ." *To hear her voice.* " . . . be in touch." *Why don't my words come out?* "I'll be back sometime Monday."

"I'll be around."

Is that an invitation or just information? "I'll give you a call."

"I'd like that."

There's a little confirmation, anyway. There was a long pause. *So how do I end this now?* Josh was making faces and imitating his father with exaggerated movements.

Samira finally spoke. "So I'll talk to you then?"

I'd like to do more than talk. "Yeah, I guess so."

With that Samira said her goodbye and left J.P. hanging in front of his son. J.P. tossed his phone into the grass and immediately lunged in Josh's direction.

Josh was bent over in laugher. "That's the best entertainment I've had in a looooong while!" he gasped.

J.P. wrestled Josh to the ground playfully. *I had no idea he had this much strength!* He had to put up quite a fight to avoid being pinned. With more than a few quick turns, J.P. finally twisted Josh's arm into the small of his back.

"I give, I give!" Josh surrendered but he was still laughing.

J.P. released the hold and rolled over onto his back, exhausted from the romp but invigorated by the success of his phone call.

"You really like her, don't you Dad?"

J.P. closed his eyes and put his hand over his forehead. *Yeah. I think I do.* A sharp jab in the ribs made J.P. catch his breath.

"Well? Do you or not?"

J.P. propped himself up on his elbows. "Do I what?"

"Like her."

Humored by Josh's insistence, the father smiled his easy smile.

"You must really like her if you can't even talk about her." Josh offered a hand to help his dad up off the ground.

J.P. accepted the assistance. *Just say it.*

"Chicken."

I am not a chicken. "Okay. I admit it. I like her." J.P. trotted to catch up to his son.

"A lot," Josh added. He lengthened his stride.

J.P. caught up to Josh with ease. "Maybe."

Josh laughed out loud and ran onto the court. "Chicken."

"I thought the basketball game was called HORSE," Uncle Roy bellowed from his lawn chair.

"It is." Josh accepted a pass from his brother. "It's Dad." The boy turned and shot the ball through the hoop. "He's the chicken."

Roy laughed. "Your father's only a chicken when it comes to women."

What? J.P. stopped in the middle of the court and threw his arms out to his sides. *Where does he get the gall to say that?*

"Dad!"

A pass bounded off J.P.'s shoulder. He retrieved the miss and took the ball to the basket. *Score!* One quick pass and James made a shot over his brother's attempted block.

"Well?" Josh dribbled the ball back out to center court.

"Okay." J.P. stole the ball from his son and took it in for an easy lay up.

Josh rebounded. "Just say it, Chicken."

"Say what?"

"A lot."

He's relentless! J.P. blocked Josh's shot. *But I am not chicken.*

"A lot." He leaned over to catch his breath. "Satisfied?"

Josh laughed. "Yeah. For now."

Well I'm not. J.P. stepped aside and allowed his boys to jockey for the shot. *I'd like to know what she's thinking about Springfield.*

17

The Sanctuary

Samira surveyed the flowerbed with a gardener's scrutiny. *If I keep at it, I should be able to finish weeding these two small beds before dusk.* She pointed to the wheeled work cart.

"Krissy, would you hand me my gloves and trowel, please?"

Krissy obeyed silently.

I love how every season brings new life to this garden. In the aftermath of Tom's death Samira created a sanctuary where she could experience a continuous life cycle. Everything from the small pool and fountain to the brick walkway worked toward that goal.

"So, tell me more about the last day of seventh grade." *It's hard to believe my youngest daughter is already going into 8th grade!*

Krissy settled into a green patch of grass. "Let's see, where did we leave off?"

She thought for a minute. "Tiffany and Jayma were really nervous that the boys would sit by them at lunchtime so we ate our picnic lunch early and hurried outside." Krissy stopped. "Do you know Gramma gets really nervous too?"

Where did that thought come from? Samira glanced at her daughter.

"She kept clicking her fingernails on the hymnal during church. Grampa says she gets that way when something big is in her mind . . ."

The narrow spade in Samira's hand turned the dirt around the dahlias. *Norma is always slightly on edge,* Samira thought to herself. *Interesting Krissy noticed.*

" . . . Once Uncle Steve and the cousins arrived Gramma seemed to relax. Did I tell you that Aunt Donna wore a bright red dress and made Uncle Vern wear a tie with his suit? They all looked so proper and everything." Krissy pulled her knees up to her chest. "Why do people make such a big deal out of being married for fifty years anyway?"

"Because fifty years is a very long time to have a relationship with one person." Samira tapped the trowel on the edge of the flowerbed. "Anymore, five and ten year anniversaries are something to celebrate."

"Do you think you and Daddy would have made it to fifty if he hadn't been sick?"

Wow! I didn't expect to go into that tonight. "Yes, I do. We knew when we said our marriage vows that it was a forever thing."

"Well, at least until the death and parting thing anyway."

That would be the finality of it all, wouldn't it? Many months had passed without a direct conversation about Tom. *I wonder if Krissy is thinking about June 17ᵗʰ as much as I am.* The anniversary remembrance was marked on every calendar in the house.

"Your Daddy liked to celebrate, Krissy." Samira leaned further into the flowerbed to reach the far side. "We celebrated every year in style, he made sure of it." *He always made me feel so special on our anniversary.*

Krissy rested her chin on her knees seemingly lost in thought for a moment. "That's pretty cool." She grinned. "I must get my party attitude from him, huh?"

Samira chuckled. "That and many other traits." *Like your quick wit and talkative nature.* She finished her work and sat down on the edge of the raised bed. *And her little freckled face and crystal blue eyes. Those are her father's too.* "You most certainly have his zest for life."

Krissy giggled and started to get up. "Does that mean I can go to the mall with Tiffany tomorrow night then?"

Samira shook her head. "The trip to the mall has nothing to do with this conversation . . ."

Kara's voice called from the house.

"Over here," Samira waved a garden glove but didn't bother to stand.

"Mama, there's someone at the door for you," Kara called.

"Who is it?" Krissy skipped toward the house with enthusiasm.

Samira checked her watch. *Almost eight. I'm not expecting anyone.* She kicked off her garden shoes outside the kitchen door and stepped inside with bare feet. Krissy was standing at the breakfast bar staring at the door.

Samira looked from her daughter to the guest.

Oh my!

"I tried to call but the line's been busy . . ."

Kara ducked her head at the mention of the busy signal.

Phil shared an easy smile. " . . . So I decided to stop over on my way across town."

Krissy cleared her throat obnoxiously.

Wow. With a quick exhale of breath, Samira tried to gather her thoughts. *Whew! Okay, regroup.* She had hoped Phil would check in when he got home. *But it didn't occur to me he might just drop in.* She smoothed her old t-shirt with her hands. *I must look like a wreck, just coming in from the garden and all.*

"So . . . ?" Krissy prompted.

"Yes," Samira's eyes were locked with Phil's. *Of course I should introduce the girls.*

Phil ran his hand through his hair and shook his head once. "Maybe I should have waited for the line to clear."

"No, it's okay." *I doubt Kara would have been off the phone before bedtime anyway.* She swallowed again and tucked a lock of loose hair back into her ponytail. *Just focus.* "Let me introduce you. Krissy, Kara, this is Phil." Samira still hadn't taken her eyes off the man. "Phil, this is Kara."

Kara had been studying Phil's face, but now she looked away shyly.

"And this is Krissy," Samira continued. *And I'm still Samira . . . I think.* Krissy tried to stifle a giggle when Phil acknowledged her by name.

Samira left her gardening gloves on the breakfast bar and started across the room. *Just act casual and in control.* "Phil has been fishing with his boys this weekend."

"Well, that would definitely explain the whiskers," Krissy blurted.

Phil rubbed his chin as if just remembering he hadn't shaved in several days.

Krista! Samira watched Kara send a daggered look across the room at her sister. *I never know what she's going to say.* Krissy's eyes were full of orneriness.

Phil flashed an easy smile in Krissy's direction. *I love that smile.* She felt the color rise in her cheeks.

Kara's dark brown eyes reflected more maturity than her sister. "We're very pleased to meet you, Phil." She looked at her mother. "We'll be in my room if you need us."

"We will?" Krissy's expression indicated total surprise. She waved to the visitor as her older sister took her arm and drug her toward the hallway. "Bye Phil!"

Thank God for Kara's insight! Samira hid her face in her hands. "I am so sorry."

"No need to be," Phil leaned back on his heels and stuck his hands in the pockets. "I should have called first."

"That's okay, really," Samira started to explain. "I just hadn't prepared them to meet you, that's all." She melted under his gaze. *No, I hadn't prepared me to share you.* Silence lingered between them.

"I was thinking I should have called more for your sake." Phil's voice was gentle when he spoke.

Obviously he noticed. "Maybe so . . ." Samira sighed heavily. *Where's my manners? I should offer him coffee. Oh no . . .* ". . . something cold to drink?"

"I'm alright," Phil assured. He glanced over his shoulder. "But I might take some water out to Chase. I left him in the truck . . . ."

"In the truck?" Samira's reaction was genuine. "Invite him in!"

"Oh, no," Phil started to explain. "You don't want him in here. He's been at the lake all weekend. He needs a serious bath . . ."

What a terrible thing to say! Samira stepped over to the window and adjusted the wooden shutters so she could see the driveway. "Nonsense. It's silly to leave someone in the truck! Bring him in for a drink."

"Oh, wait . . ."

Samira frowned when Phil laughed.

"Chase is my dog."

Chase is his dog? Dumbfounded, Samira stared at the rugged man in her entryway. *I didn't know he had a dog!* Suddenly the realization became very humorous and she burst out laughing. *He's more inviting by the minute.* Samira covered her mouth with her hand and tried to compose herself. *Now that's funny!* "Maybe you could just let him into the back yard then," she suggested through stifled laughter.

Phil obliged and met Samira in the garage with his canine friend. *And he's a big dog too.* Chase bolted into the backyard. Samira closed the walk in door and crossed the yard to the pool. *I'll give him some fresh water.* She bent down and turned a faucet near the ground. A spray of water burst into the air at the far side.

"I don't have a bucket or a bowl out here . . ." Samira could feel Phil watching her with growing interest.

"This will work just fine."

She watched as his eyes took in the garden.

"This is a sight for sore eyes."

Samira assumed he was talking about the landscape. She touched a leaf on a flowering tree as she spoke. "This is my hideaway. I love it out here. I planted this garden when . . ." *Wait. I've never talked to another man about my husband.* "Well, anyway . . ." she tried to refocus. "There is something in bloom in every season." *He probably doesn't care much about flowering trees and rose bushes.*

When she looked up she realized Phil's eyes were fixed directly on her. Samira crossed her arms over her middle trying to ignore the chemistry that was building. Chase found the pool and noisily helped himself to a long drink.

Change the subject. "So how was your weekend?"

Phil moved slightly closer to Samira as he answered. "It was good to get away but it's good to be back just the same."

Samira cleared her throat. "I meant with your boys." She glanced over her shoulder wondering where her daughters were.

Phil thought for a moment. "A weekend is hardly enough time, but it was good to hang with them for awhile." He grinned and ran his fingers over his scruffy beard. "I guess I took my sabbatical seriously."

In spite of the beard, Samira couldn't help but notice how well the cut on Phil's cheekbone was healing. "I don't mind." *The rustic look is rather sexy.*

"The beard or the dropping in?"

"Your cheek looks better." *Of course it will probably show up more when he's clean-shaven.*

Phil reached up with his right hand and touched the wound. "Not bad, huh?" He held his hand out for Samira to examine. "Even this one is healing up pretty good."

Samira noticed the dark scab. *There will be scar when that one heals.* "Does it still hurt?" When Phil didn't answer, she looked up.

Without waiting for permission, he took a step closer and drew Samira into his body. *No wait!* Passion took over in a heartbeat and there was no way Samira was going to ignore it now. She succumbed to his kiss and enjoyed the prickly whiskers against her cheek. *This is definitely okay.* Samira wrapped her arms around Phil's waist and kissed him again.

Screams from the garden entrance brought a sudden halt to the intimate moment. In an instant Samira's personal desires were shattered by motherhood defenses.

"There's a big black dog in the yard!" Krissy raced past her mother and Phil. "Did you see it?" She continued to search around the flowerbeds. "How did it get in here anyway?"

Phil separated himself from Samira. With a snap of his fingers Chase appeared obediently at his side. Samira listened through a filtered ear as Phil introduced his dog to Krissy.

"You didn't tell me he had a dog!"

There are many things I didn't tell you. Samira looked out across the garden. *And there are many things I still don't know.* Samira put her hands in her hair. *I just need a moment to compose myself!* Somehow she managed to suggest that her daughter wait back inside the house.

"I'd rather stay out here and play with Chase." Krissy rubbed the dog's head. "Obviously no one told him about the 'no dog' rule."

Phil smiled guiltily.

Samira rolled her eyes at her daughter's accusation. "No *stray* dogs allowed." *Why doesn't she just go back inside?* "Chase hardly appears to be a stray." *Although I don't think I've ever had a dog in my back yard before.* Samira tried to remember.

Samira watched Phil's eyes scan the garden. "He's definitely not a stray, but he could probably find something to dig up." He bent down and looked Krissy in the eyes. "Krissy, thanks for telling me about the dog rule . . ."

Oh, no! Don't let Krissy spoil everything. Samira started to interrupt but Phil stopped her with the motion of his hand.

" . . . Maybe you should take him back through the garage and put him in my truck."

"Okay." Krissy bounced off the ground. "Do you think he'll go with me?"

Phil snapped his fingers twice and Chase stood at attention. The master gave a command with his hand and the canine obeyed.

That's absolutely amazing how the dog responds to Phil's hand commands. "I'll meet you inside, Krissy," Samira called as her daughter disappeared. *He handled that exceptionally well.* "Thank you . . ." *for talking to Krissy like that.*

Several feet now separated them.

"Thank you."

"I meant for giving Krissy something to do," Samira avoided Phil's eyes. *It's too dangerous to look at him again.* Her stomach was churning with uneasiness. *He makes me do things I shouldn't do. It's almost like I don't have any control.* Suddenly her life was looking very complicated. *I can't let him do that to me when the girls are around!*

"I know what you meant."

And I know what you meant too. Samira looked high into the branches of the magnolia tree. *And it was good for me too. You're welcome.*

Phil took a step toward her, but Samira took a step to keep her distance. *What if passion is all there is to this?* Her heart pounded hard in her chest. She wondered how much of the kiss Krissy had witnessed. *Worse yet, I wonder what she'll tell her sister? Or her friends?*

Phil sighed heavily. "Look, Samira . . ."

I've disappointed him again. " . . . I know," she interrupted. "It's just seems so soon." *Too soon for what, Samira?* She struggled to balance her emotions between womanhood and motherhood. *Given your history, anytime is going to be too soon.* She glanced at the house. "I should probably get back inside." *It's too soon to juggle Phil with the girls at home. That's all.* She didn't convince herself.

Phil nodded but the look on his face gave insight to his own confusion.

"I'm sorry," Samira whispered. "This isn't the way I had things pictured . . ." *Not even close!*

"It's alright." Phil's voice was very low when he spoke.

No, it's not. Samira was doubtful. Nothing seemed right anymore. "I think I have some things to figure out." *I could easily let him in if I were single and looking for a companion.* Every ounce of her being wanted to continue what they had started. *But I'm not single. I have to make sure the man I bring in to my life is good for my girls too.* "I am so sorry . . ." *Or do I just have to make sure I'm ready?*

Samira could feel his eyes on the back of her shoulder as he spoke. "Take your time, Samira." There was a slight pause. "I can wait."

I don't know how long it will take to figure me out! Several awkward moments separated their thoughts. *And I still owe him an answer on the Springfield thing.* Samira took a deep breath. *If it's even still open for invitation.*

Phil spoke again. "Why don't you give me a call when you're ready."

Samira looked out across her garden. "With school just getting out things could be quite hectic . . ." *I can't believe I'm making excuses! I waited all week for him to call and now I don't even know how to talk to him!!*

"Like I said," Phil interrupted. "Take your time." He ran his hand through his hair. "I'll be around."

I don't want him to be around. Samira stared at the brick walk under her bare feet. *I want him to be right here!* She wanted so desperately to be cradled in his arms yet held firm to her defenses. *I should just ask him about Springfield and get it off my mind.* When he stepped closer, she felt her heart skip a beat. Looking up, she met his dark blue eyes again. *This is just too risky.*

Ever so gently Phil placed his hand under her ponytail and kissed her on the forehead.

Samira closed her eyes. *Just like my father.* She watched Phil turn and head for the gate. *I really don't want him to leave like this.* She couldn't bring herself to speak and he didn't say a word until he reached the exit.

"Be in touch, Samira."

Be in touch? Samira bit her bottom lip. *That's it? He walks away and leaves the ball completely in my court.* Guilt engulfed Samira as the gate closed between them. *How can I possibly be a good mother while I'm dying to share my innermost being with a man that isn't their father?*

Everything about this man felt right yet the exact things felt terribly wrong. *What right does he have to waltz into my life and conjure up all those feelings I buried so long ago?* Samira fought against her conscious. *How can he bring me so much pleasure and cause me so much distress at the same time?* Samira stretched her chin to the heavens. *He can make decisions too! What if he decides he can't wait long enough for me to be ready?*

O dear God, what am I supposed to do? Samira whispered. She bent down and turned off the water spicket. Instantly the fountain stopped flowing.

"He's really cute!" Krissy commented as her mother tucked her into bed. "You didn't tell us he had a dog!"

"I didn't know he had a dog until tonight, Krissy."

"Does he always have a beard?"

"Not that I know of . . ."

"Nice truck. Does he have a car too?"

"I don't know . . ."

"How old are his kids?"

Samira's patience with the questions was growing thin. "I just don't know yet, Krissy." The mother tried not to sound edgy. *But I don't know any of these things!*

"It's kind of hard to learn everything about one another after just one date," Kara added from the doorway to her sister's room.

Two coffee shop dates, dinner, and an overnight, Samira silently corrected. *But how would Kara know how much you can learn about someone from a date?*

"Right, Mama?"

Samira pulled the top cover over her youngest daughter and quickly pecked her on the cheek. "We're just starting to get to know one another." *But if I don't hurry up and reply, he may move on.*

"I can still smell his aftershave." He smells alright for coming home from camping."

Oh good grief! The scent is on me! Samira ignored the comment and turned off the light as she left Krissy's room.

"I hope he comes back," Krissy chimed as the room went dark.

I hope he calls first!

Kara turned off her light and slipped under the covers of her own bed. "He looked like a mountain man."

What kind of comment is that? Samira sat down on the edge of the bed, watching Kara's face in the dimly lit room. "He'd been camping for several days. The last time I saw him he was clean shaven and very professional looking."

Kara's eyes widened. "I can't picture him that way."

Samira smiled. *I don't mind the rustic look.* "Well, maybe you'll have a chance to meet him under different circumstances." *Kara always has trouble visualizing.* She smoothed Kara's long dark hair back from her face.

The fourteen-year old turned onto her side. *She's done talking for the night.* Relieved to be off the hook, Samira left the room.

So what made Tom's name almost fall out of my mouth when I was talking to Phil anyway? It didn't seem like the natural thing to do, yet at the same time it was right there. *The entire garden was created in Tom's memory. But I've never talked to anyone about that.* Being able to give life to something new every season was therapy in and of itself. *Why I felt compelled to say something about it tonight is a mystery.*

Samira slipped into her nightshirt. In front of the bathroom mirror she washed her face with cool water and toweled dry. The texture of the towel reminded her of Phil's beard against her cheek. *I feel awful that I pulled away from him like that. And then I couldn't even explain.* Krissy's questions echoed in her mind. *I'd like to know the answers to those questions too.*

With a book in hand, Samira climbed into bed. The words on the page read easily under her eyes, but they weren't sticking. Reluctantly she closed the novel and turned out the light. But even in the dark of the room there was no peace of mind.

Oh, God, have I sacrificed too much already? The prayer fell silently into the night. *Is it all right for me to seek solace with a man that isn't Tom?* Samira hugged her pillow and closed her eyes tight. *I don't know if I have the strength to be with someone again. And I really don't know if I have the endurance to survive if I turn out to be his passing phase . . .*

There was no sanctuary in the hollow of the night.

18

The Waiting Game

Mr. Stephenson stood facing the window overlooking downtown. His back was to the board of directors. The meeting had been in session most of the morning. *It is high time to make a decision so I can be on with my day!*

J.P. removed his glasses and spoke into the silence of the room. "Either we take a chance on the new information from Sparky, or we sit the week out waiting on local authorities." He waited but there was no immediate response. "The deciding factor is how quickly you want to move the investigation forward."

"How are the local investigators going to take it when they know we've undermined their efforts?" Mr. Stephenson looked worried when he turned around.

J.P. pushed his chair away from the table. *He is one of the most conservative clients I've ever served.* "Two things, Mr. Stephenson. First, we are not undermining an investigation. We are enhancing the timeline. Second, hiring a private investigator is going to communicate that you're serious about finding the suspects." *It doesn't make sense not to move forward with Sparky.* "The longer we wait, the less chance there is of an arrest. Bottom line."

A buzzer on the intercom interrupted the meeting. Mr. Stephenson nodded for a board member to answer. "For you Mr. Ralston . . ."

For me? J.P. rose from his seat and identified himself to the caller.

"It's Denise, Boss." Her voice was energetic. "Sparky checked in. He thinks he's found the missing link. He needs access to the mainline server at closing."

Perfect timing! J.P. covered the mouthpiece and addressed Mr. Stephenson. "Sparky's found the link he was looking for. He needs access to the server at closing. Is that a possibility?"

Mr. Stephenson narrowed his eyes in thought. *Come on, just make a decision. We need to make this work.* Slowly Mr. Stephenson's head nodded once.

"Send him over, Denise."

"Sparky's weird about that, you know," she reminded. "Stay on the line. Let me ask him for a specific time . . ."

Why is she calling on their phone anyway?

"He needs access before they close out today's business."

"On site?"

"Nope. Told you. He's weird about that. He prefers to work from a remote site but in order to do that, he'll need new access codes."

Whatever that means. J.P. shook his head. He'd never worked with an investigator as intense and secretive as Sparky. *I wonder if I'm going to have to pay him in unmarked bills.*

"Mr. Stephenson," J.P. addressed his client who was once again looking out the window. "We'll need new access codes so Sparky can access the server before the close of business today."

A single nod gave silent approval.

"Tell Sparky it's a go."

"Will do," Denise confirmed. "And by the way, your cell phone isn't on."

It's not? J.P. felt his phone through his jacket pocket.

"You might want to fix that as you leave the meeting."

If I ever get out of the meeting. J.P. hung up the telephone feeling a new sense of energy. *If Sparky pans out as successful as Mike promised, I'll owe the biggest favor of my life.*

Mr. Stephenson picked up the telephone and notified his technicians to allow access for the investigator.

I have never known a businessman to be so slow to make decisions! J.P. spoke to each board member as they parted ways.

"You're making the right decision, Mr. Stephenson."

Mr. Stephenson nodded but avoided eye contact. "I hope so."

What is it going to take to earn his trust?

"I don't like not knowing and I like waiting even less."

I understand the waiting part. J.P. activated his cell phone before repacking the contents of his briefcase. "We should have a good report in the morning."

With any luck. "I'll be in touch."

Mr. Stephenson's face was still contemplative. "I appreciate your attentiveness, J.P."

What is it about him that feels so familiar? "Not a problem." J.P. exchanged a handshake before Mr. Stephenson left the room. *I can't believe how long that meeting lasted.* J.P. exited the building through a back doorway. *Shouldn't have been that difficult.* He unlocked his truck with the remote. *Either we hire the private investigator or we don't.*

The downtown library was busy with the noon hour activity as J.P. passed by. *I wonder if Samira ever has business downtown?* The same thought made him mad. *In light of her inability to make a decision, it's just as well you keep your mind on your work.* He turned the corner at the Café Ole and followed the alley to his private parking space. The café was busy too. *I'd passed that place a million times without giving it a thought until I invited Samira there.* Again he caught his thoughts. *Give it up, man. She may not even call you back.*

"Hey, Boss."

Denise was at her desk when J.P. entered. Derek was busy in front of a computer in a makeshift work space in the corner.

J.P. addressed Denise. "Nice work with Sparky. Did he leave any indication of what he was thinking?"

Denise shook her head as she handed over the message board. "Nope. He's very secretive, you know. Kind of like he lurks in the shadows of some crime movie or something." She wiggled her shoulders from side to side. "I'd love to meet him and get his autograph when this is all said and done."

J.P. skimmed the messages. "He's not very social. Doubt if he's much into signing his name for a fan." He returned the clipboard to Denise's desk and addressed the first message on the list. "What's the scoop with Christopher Hughes?"

Denise followed J.P. into his office. "His secretary emailed that you should be receiving documents from England concerning the affair in Springfield."

"What kind of documents?" J.P. removed his sports coat and hung it over the back of a chair.

"She didn't say."

"Find out." *I knew I'd be on official business once I returned the RSVP.* "I'd prefer to work that evening in the know—without surprises."

"In that case," Denise continued. "She also indicated that the guest suite was reserved in your name at the convention center complex. Sounds like it could be a late night."

J.P. tried to ignore the pit in his stomach. *I can't even get Samira to make a decision on dinner, let alone an overnight.*

"Are you sure you don't need me to secure a date for the evening?"

You mean night, so you'd might as well say it. "No." He tried to withdraw the sharp remark. *I'll give her a few more days to reply.* "That won't be necessary."

"Not even a backup?"

J.P. balanced his weight on his fingertips as he leaned slightly into his desk. *Read my lips, Denise.* "I said 'no.'"

"There's no word from a Sean Bridges," Denise changed the subject without further harassment. "We did have a call back from a Jessica Hutchison who says she's a senior associate for the Bridges Property Management Group. Should I call her back?"

The attorney sorted a short stack of piles into order of priority for the afternoon. "If she's the only connection then we'll have to run with it." He opened a file marked *Hughes Estate.* "Any word from the city attorney on possible settlement?"

"Nothing yet. Should I call him?"

"Let's wait him out."

"How long?"

"Give him until Thursday. They should be able to make a decision by then." *Which is more than I can say about Samira. I don't think she has a timeline.*

"You're out of town for a juvenile court hearing on Thursday. Don't forget." Denise tapped her pen on the clipboard. "When did James get back?"

"Yesterday." *Left him at home long enough to run up here to pick up a file and to make a personal stop.*

"Is he working at the club today?"

J.P. glanced at his watch. "For a few more hours." *Short hours at that.* "Did Mike call about the hearing?"

"Yes, Mike called." Denise tapped the edge of the clipboard. "I was getting to that. He says he'll brief you on the way up there. You're scheduled at eleven but Mike says they run late so plan to be bored."

I can think of a million places I'd rather be than sitting in the lobby at juvenile court. "Anything else?"

"Not at the moment, which is probably just as well since you're a little on edge." She started to leave the office. "Derek and I can handle the Thursday agenda if you're worried about that. And he's doing a fine job, so far, in case you're interested." Denise turned in the doorway and faced her boss. "If there's something else eating at you then it might be in your best interest to either resolve the issue or let me in on it so I can fix it for you."

J.P. sat at his desk staring at the closed door between the offices. He hadn't even spoken to Derek Danielson who was diligently handling the case overload. *And now I only have three short hours before James is done at the club.* He fingered the files on his desk. *What the hell am I supposed to do with him while I continue my work day?* Irritated with the new responsibility, J.P. opened the army green folder as if a new bit of information might jump off the page concerning the boundary issues between the city and Lloyd Hughes estate.

And what is Christopher expecting of me in Springfield? That thought was irritating as well. *I like handling their business affairs.* The Hughes Corporation was his biggest and most profitable client. *But they've managed to blur the lines with this estate.*

J.P. turned his attention back to the file in hand. *All I need is one historical, dated document that proves the city was unincorporated in 1912 and we could close this file for good.* That document had yet to be discovered.

"Mr. Hughes, Christopher," Denise's voice sounded on the intercom. "Line two." *Damn it, I didn't want to talk to him!* J.P. closed his eyes for a minute. *A simple explanation from Hughes' personal secretary would have sufficed.*

"Mr. Hughes, J.P. Ralston here. How can I be of service?" *There I times I'd prefer not to make myself so available.*

"J.P., it's good to hear your voice. I understand you're wondering about the nature of your presence in Springfield. Are you concerned about the accommodations?"

"The invitation and the accommodations are quite satisfactory, Mr. Hughes. However, I can only meet your expectations when I am informed of my duties." He drummed his fingers against his desk in anticipation of the client's response.

Mr. Hughes chuckled. "This is the very reason I have you on board, J.P. You're the best in the business . . ."

Skip the niceties, Christopher. Let's get down to business.

" . . . It seems our family attorney, I'm sure you remember Sebastian . . ."

"Very well, sir." *Sebastian and I have our differences . . .*

" . . . Sebastian will be tied up here in Great Britain; unable to make the Springfield engagement. I'd appreciate you looking over my daughter's prenuptials so we can make it official at the ceremony."

I despise family law. J.P. closed his eyes and pressed his fingertips into his forehead. *But this is Christopher Hughes.*

"It would be a great favor to the family, J.P.," Mr. Hughes continued to thicken his plea. "No one would appreciate it more than Mrs. Hughes and myself."

"Who prepared the agreement?" *Tell me it wasn't Sabastian.*

"Sebastian and the legal representation of the betrothed . . ."

Figures.

" . . . I would appreciate your taking the time to go over it, you know, make sure everything is in order."

Maybe he doesn't trust Sebastian either. "I'm assuming you'll need it notarized as well?"

"If it's not too much trouble, J.P."

It was suddenly obvious that Mr. Hughes wanted the agreement signed and notarized without Sebastian's presence. *I wonder how many of my own documents have been proofed and edited by Sebastian over the years?*

"Very well, Mr. Hughes. I'll review the agreement so it can be notarized that night." He took a deep breath knowing full well how tedious and time consuming it could become.

"Fine, fine, J.P.," Mr. Hughes sounded into the telephone. "As you know, we've reserved the private suite for you and a guest at the civic center so plan to stay the night. I'll be sure it is well stocked . . ."

"That won't be necessary, Mr. Hughes." *I don't even know if she's going to accept the invite to dinner yet.*

"Just the same, we'll plan on you staying." It was obvious the businessman was turning his thoughts to other matters. "The documents should reach you by the weekend. We'll be in touch."

Damn it. J.P. had known Stephanie Hughes since she was born and she had yet to be denied anything she wanted. *Including the Duke of Ellington.*

He's twice her age, J.P. guessed. With that thought came another. *I wonder how old Samira is anyway?*

The attorney slammed a folder hard against his desk. Every time he turned around Samira was creeping into his thoughts. *I should have told Denise to secure a date for the seventeenth.* He left his desk and stepped into his private bathroom. Trying desperately to clear his thinking, he turned the ceramic handle on the faucet and cupped his hands to catch the cold water. He rinsed his entire face.

I have never left the ball in a woman's court. J.P hid his face in a dry towel for several moments. *What was I thinking? She can't even relax enough to kiss me, let alone pick up the phone to call.* J.P. left the towel hanging over the edge of the sink. *No woman has ever been so appealing and downright maddening at the same time!*

J.P. grabbed his sports coat and headed for the front door of his office.

"Boss?"

"I'll be at the gym."

"It's only two o'clock . . .".

I know that. James wouldn't be off work until four and Mike never arrived before five. *This workout is for me.*

" . . . Leave your phone on so I can I call you if I hear from Sparky." Denise paused. "Or should I not call you?"

J.P. held the door open with one hand. "Only if you deem it necessary." *There is no reason to be short with Denise.* When he turned to look at her it was obvious he'd hurt her feelings.

I should probably apologize. But J.P. Ralston wasn't in the business of making apologies. Instead he turned away and stepped out into the hot afternoon sunshine. *The sooner I'm at the gym the better off we'll all be.*

19

Meet Mike

"Are you going to lunch, Miss Samira?" Mrs. Haddock located the head librarian in the research center.

Samira had been at the computer all morning. "Oh, is it lunchtime already?"

"Any luck yet?"

"No. Nothing." *How frustrating.*

"Anything I could help you with?"

Samira shook her head. "I'm looking for a phone number . . ."

"Who is it for honey?" Mrs. Haddock adjusted her bifocals to read the computer screen."

"I don't really know." *I can't believe I slept with a man who isn't showing up in a phone listing!* "Why don't you go ahead and take lunch, Helen. I'll go when you get back."

"Alright. It seems to me it would help to have a name if you're looking for a number to go with it." Mrs. Haddock patted Samira on the shoulder. "Good luck. I'll be back at one."

Samira was relieved to be alone with the computer again. *He said to call when I was ready.* Her eyes skimmed the professional listing again. *Well, I don't know if I'm ready or not, but I'd at least like to be able to call him.*

"Attorneys. Lawyers. Legal Advice. Nothing!" Samira's finger tapped the mouse. *This isn't that big of a town! He shouldn't be so hard to find.* She opened the Chamber of Commerce site. *No Phil. No Phillip. No anything.* She closed the site. *It would have been helpful for him to leave a number!*

There was a tap on the door. "Samira? Are you busy?"

Busy. But not successfully so. Samira turned in the steno chair. "Oh, Kelly! Hi. Come on in." The green eyes of Kelly Davis were a sharp contrast to her dark red hair. "What brings you to Maple Street Library? School is out for the summer."

Kelly smiled and sat down in a chair across from Samira. "I know. You'd think a school teacher would hide from books all summer long!"

"What can I help you with?"

"Well . . ." Kelly hesitated, but her eyes were still bouncing with energy. "I'm here on a personal matter with a professional motive."

Samira raised her eyebrows.

Kelly reached around her head and unbound her naturally curly hair. "I need some informational books on American Government; maybe something on US History."

"Government?" Samira rose from her chair. *But you're Krissy's English teacher.* "Do you have a new teaching assignment?"

"Oh, no. Nothing like that." Kelly re-wrapped her hair with an elastic binder. "You know Brian Wilson, right?"

"Mr. Wilson. The science teacher." *Young. Single. I know him.*

"Yes." Kelly followed Samira into the main library. "He's invited me on a continuing ed trip this summer. For two weeks! All the way to Washington D.C. and back."

This must be the personal part. "Do continuing ed credits in Social Studies count for English teachers?"

"Only if I fill out the paperwork correctly!" Kelly giggled. "That would be the professional part of my visit today."

So Kelly is taking a two week vacation with Brian Wilson. Interesting.

Kelly ran her hand over a bookshelf as they walked through the historical section. "We'll go through Philadelphia on the way out, so any history on the sites there would be helpful too."

Samira slowed to a stop and began skimming the spines. "You know, the high school library has a vast collection of historical books on Washington D.C . . ."

" . . . Oh, I know!" Kelly interrupted. "But I'd prefer Mrs. Billings not get wind of my trip with Brian . . ."

Understood. I can appreciate that!

" . . . not that we shouldn't be going together, but . . ." Kelly pretended to skim the titles with Samira.

"You don't have to explain to me, Kelly." Samira pulled a big colorful book off the shelf. "Start with this one. It's a pictorial directory of the nation's capital." She pulled another. "And this one has more documentation."

Kelly took both books with interest. "So, what about you, Samira? Do your summer plans include a man?"

Taken aback, Samira turned and stared at Kelly Davis. *Where did that question come from?*

Kelly waited. "Well?"

I don't know Kelly all that well. But I don't see any harm in talking to her either. "I don't know yet." Samira took a deep breath. "I've had a couple of encounters with a man here lately but I have no idea where it's going. If anywhere." *Encounters? What kind of a word is that?*

Kelly tipped her head playfully and then leaned toward Samira as if she had a secret to share.

"I have to be honest. Krissy told me you had a hot date a week or so back . . ."

A hot date? Samira shook her head. *Why am I not surprised by that?*

" . . . but don't be mad at her," Kelly cautioned. "She was so excited for you, Samira." Kelly shook a few loose curls back away from her face. "So how did it go?"

A genuine smile appeared on Samira's face without hesitation. "It went well, I think." *But I can't even be myself with him when the girls are home.* "But you know, Kelly, it's really hard to have a man with my life the way it is." *Do I really want to share this with a woman I only kind of know?*

"Maybe you're trying too hard, Samira."

What is she talking about?

Kelly reached across and touched Samira's hand. "What's the worse case scenario?"

Kelly just told me she's driving half way across the country and spending two weeks with Brian Wilson. Samira crossed her arms over her stomach.

"Think about it. What's the worse thing that could happen? You'd end up liking him and then it wouldn't work out?"

What's the worse thing? That I already do like him. That he's too intense for my father. That he'll have nothing in common with Wes. That he's not enough of a family man for my girls . . . "I really don't know. There's just so much to juggle and think about and plan around . . ."

"And you're the only one who knows. Right?"

Knows what?

"I mean, you probably haven't been able to talk to him about any of the complications or anything so it's all just stuck in your mind." Kelly was looking Samira right in the eyes.

Amazing how she can read my thoughts. Samira looked away. *Susan used to be able to do that.* "I guess I'm just afraid to get my hopes up." *Maybe afraid to get the girls' hopes up, too.* That last thought hit the nail on the head. *Plain and simple, I don't feel like getting hurt. And worse yet, I'm not ready to get the girls' hopes up only to have them crash with me if things don't work out . . .*

Kelly began to walk as if she realized the conversation had gone deeper than Samira was ready to share. "Let me see, how can I say this and not come across sounding too simplistic?"

Samira followed, listening; hoping Kelly could relieve her mind.

"Let me say it this way . . ." Kelly turned back and looked at Samira again. "The only way he can break your heart is if you put it out there for him to take."

Samira translated the comment back through her mind slowly: *The only way he can break my heart is if I put it out there for him to take.* She stood stock still for several moments. *Do I want to take that risk?*

"You're the only one who knows, so you're the only one who can make that decision," Kelly added through the opposite side of a bookshelf.

So let me ask her this. "How is it with Brian Wilson?"

"It's not." Kelly picked up another book. "I mean, we have a great time together and I enjoy his company but he's just not the forever type." She laughed a little, "I have a hard time picturing myself settling in for life with anybody, but especially with Brian." She continued to talk as her hand pushed her bushy curls back again. "Personally, I think Brian found this continuing ed trip so he could show me how adventurous he is." Kelly smiled casually. "But he's really not that way at all." She shrugged her shoulders. "But I have yet to get a better offer so I'm going to go explore the world, spend some more time with him, and see where it all goes from there."

She's so nonchalant about the whole affair. "Isn't it uncomfortable spending time with him if you know he might not be the one you want to end up with?"

Kelly laughed. "Only if I let it be." She set the books down on a study table and once again refastened her hair. "I figure I can either stay inside my room for the rest of my life or put my heart out there to test the water. Who knows? It might lead somewhere if I give it a chance. Or it might not." She cocked her head with a brilliant smile. "My guess is you'll be glad you gave him a chance."

I'll have to revisit this conversation later. By myself.

Kelly Davis left with an armload of books about the same time Mrs. Haddock came back to work. *The only way he can break your heart is if you put it out there for him to take.* A sudden urgency took over Samira's need to reach Phil. *What if Kelly Davis is right?* She informed her assistant that she might not be back right on time. *If I can't find him in a phone listing, maybe I can find him at the club where he attempted to take me for dinner.*

Samira's heart pounded hard in her chest as she opened the full-length glass doors of the athletic club. *I am totally OUT of my comfort zone!*

"Excuse me."

The girl behind the desk stopped folding towels and made eye contact.

Samira smiled. "I'm wondering if you might be able to assist me. I'm looking for someone who is a member here . . ."

"We have a lot of members' ma'am." Her dishwater blonde ponytail flipped over the top of her head when she bent over to pick up a fallen towel. "Does this person have a name?"

Samira cleared her throat. "Well, yes he does, but I'm not sure I have it right." Her palms were sweating profusely. *I can't believe I don't even know his whole name!* "His first name is Phil and I think he's an attorney . . ."

The desk attendant grinned mischievously and focused her blue eyes directly on Samira. "Phil?" The girl laughed. "That's interesting."

What's interesting? Samira decided not to ask. "Do you know him?"

"Oh, I know him." She moved a stack of folded towels to the shelf behind her.

Samira took a deep breath. "Well, I've been trying to get in touch with him . . ."

The girl grinned. "You and every other woman around here." She popped her gum. "Try Ralston." The girl snapped a towel. "I hear he's out of town but with him you never know if that's a fact or not."

Samira wiped her hands on her thighs. *Well, he told me he'd be around.* The voices inside her head were screaming for her to leave. *I've come this far, I'm not going to give up quite that easily.*

"Ralston, thank you." Still watching the girl, Samira continued with hesitation. "Would it be alright if I left a message for him here?"

"You can leave a message . . . ," the attendant turned her back as she sorted through a pile of unfolded towels. " . . . but no guarantee he'll ever get it."

The attendant glanced sideways at Samira. "Plenty of women ask for him but we're not his answering service . . ."

I don't know what I was expecting, but this wasn't it!

" . . . but here's a piece of paper if you dare to give it a shot." The girl sneered. "Last I knew his weekends were booked through November . . ."

Through November? What is she talking about? Samira didn't dare inquire about the nature of the bookings. *Maybe this wasn't a good idea.*

" . . . If you're not already on his weekend agenda the chances of getting in now are slim to none." The girl snapped another towel and forced a laugh. "And I'd say your chances of getting in with him are probably even slimmer than most."

Now Samira was sure she had made the wrong decision. The pit in her stomach was quickly rising to her throat. *I hope to God she's talking about the wrong man.*

Samira pushed the paper back toward the girl without speaking and turned to leave. *I made a terrible mistake in coming here.* Samira felt exposed from the inside out. *I should have known better than to go out on a limb like this.*

Samira's eyes were already focused on the parking lot on the other side of the glass doors.

"Excuse me, ma'am?"

Samira stayed focused on the exit.

"Miss?" A man caught up to her and touched her arm.

Oh Dear God, what is going on? She pulled her arm away from his touch. *Was he talking to me?*

"I didn't mean to startle you . . ."

He is talking to me. Samira looked up into dancing blue eyes.

" . . . I really am sorry to be so rude," the man offered gently. "But I couldn't help overhearing your conversation with the attendant. I apologize for her inappropriate behavior." he continued to explain. "I'll see to it that her manager is aware of this most uncomfortable situation."

Maybe he works here. Samira glanced at the bartender across the room. *But I'd think he'd be wearing a uniform or a nametag or something.*

"Would you mind?" The man motioned her toward the empty lounge. "I'd like to visit if you have a moment."

Samira hesitated, but something about the energy in his eyes made her oblige. She stepped into the lounge and allowed him to lead her to the bar. He pulled up a barstool and sat down so he was just under Samira's eye level.

"My name's Mike, Mike Benson." He offered his hand.

Mike Benson. I don't know a Mike Benson. Samira examined his long, curly blonde hair and bushy mustache. *He better not be trying to pick me up.*

"Do I understand that you're looking for someone in particular?"

He eavesdropped on my conversation. Samira crossed her arms *I should have just stayed at the library.*

The man folded his hands on his lap. His eyes were still fixed directly on hers. Samira shifted her weight against his gaze.

"I really am sorry."

He should be. Samira took a step toward the door.

"No. Wait, please. I know about everyone who comes through here," the man offered in a gentle tone. "I thought I might be able to deliver a message."

Mike Benson. Samira was still skeptical. *How do I know I can trust him?*

"Look," Mike tried to explain. "I have a feeling you're looking for a good friend of mine." When Samira didn't respond he offered the name. "Did I hear you mention Phil Ralston?"

At least he knows the name. With Phil's name out in the open, Samira breathed a sigh of relief. *And he doesn't seem to be derogatory about it either.* She returned his inquisitive glance. *I should probably say something.* She took a deep breath.

"Yes." she finally admitted. "I was supposed to call him but haven't been able to find a phone number." Samira looked around the room finally. *Oh. This is the same bar where Phil and I waited for a table that didn't materialize.*

"Somehow, that doesn't surprise me." "The man laughed and shook his head making his blonde curls bounce. "I've known J . . ."

Who?

"—Phil Ralston longer than I can remember." Mike wiggled his eyebrows. "Let's see, I went to undergraduate school with him, roomed with him in law school, and try to keep him out of serious trouble these days . . ."

So he is a lawyer. Samira studied the man in front of her. *Maybe Mike is too. Although he isn't as clean cut as Phil.*

A broad smiled peaked out from under the full mustache. "Anyway, I have a feeling he'd like to hear from you."

I'm so relieved to hear him say that! Samira smiled back, thankful that she might actually get a step closer to locating Phil.

Mike almost laughed at loud. "My buddy has a way of forgetting himself in the presence of a pretty lady."

Pretty lady? Samira put her hand to her face when she blushed. *Does he know Phil called me that?* "Well, I would like to talk to him. If I could get a number or something."

"That's no problem." Mike moved his hands for the first time since sitting down. Samira could feel the depth of his thoughts as he studied her face. "I'd be glad to give him a message."

Samira glanced over her shoulder. "The girl said he was out of town . . ."

Mike followed her eyes to the front desk. "That girl is highly misinformed." He left the barstool and walked across the room. Samira watched Mike exchange a few words with the bartender and return with a pad of paper and a pencil.

"Here you go." Mike handed her the paper and pencil. "Any message you want will be personally delivered at the earliest possible convenience."

That's really nice of him. Samira wrote her name on the paper. *Even if his approach was rather abrupt.* Underneath her name she wrote one word: *Ready.* "Just ask him to call me." *He has my number.*

Much to Samira's dismay, Mike opened the paper and read the note. "Pronounce your name for me."

"Samira."

"Very pretty." Mike refolded the paper. "I'll see that he gets this." He stashed it in the hip pocket of his dress shorts. "Anything else I can do for you, Samira?"

Samira could feel her cheeks burn with color as his eyes penetrated hers.

"Buy you a drink? Give you a ride home?" Mike's eyes twinkled. "Anything? I'm at your service."

How does he look at me like that? It's like he's seeing through me. "Just deliver the message, Mr. Benson." She could feel her voice shake a little as she spoke.

Mike crossed his heart with his hand and then patted his hind pocket. "You have my word, Miss Samira."

I hope so. With a word of thanks, Samira turned to leave. She could feel Mike Benson's eyes on her all the way to the front door. *I hope he delivers the message soon.* She didn't breathe a sigh of relief until she reached the safe haven of her car and even then she was short of breath. *Not only does Phil take my breath away, but his friend has a way of doing the same thing!*

As she drove back across town, Samira replayed the meeting with Mike Benson. *He's an interesting character. I wonder if he's a lawyer too. Must be if he roomed with him in law school.* She also wondered how much of the conversation with the attendant he'd actually overheard.

"You and every other woman," the girl had said. It was hard to know how to interpret that remark. *"And your chances of getting in with him are probably slimmer than most".* Mike had said the girl was misinformed, but the comment still hurt.

Samira's mind went back to that magical Friday night. *He was so patient and so gentle. I can't imagine him any other way.* She desperately wanted to dismiss any unprecedented concerns. *The girl had to be thinking of someone else.* Samira pulled into her parking space at the library. *Or is it possible she's one of Phil's weekend agendas?*

A new train of thought entered Samira's mind as she ascended the steps to the front entrance. *Maybe there's a reason I can't locate a phone number.*

20

The Confession

"Hey, Mike, my man." The kitchen door slammed behind J.P. Mike was in the living room watching major league baseball. Empty pizza boxes graced the coffee table where Mike's stocking feet rested.

"Hey man." Mike lifted his tall frame off the leather sofa. "How'd it go?"

"Very well, thank you."

They exchanged a high five as J.P. passed through the corner of the living room.

"So I take it Sparky impressed the weebie-jeebies out of the Mid-America board?"

"You have such a way with words, Mikey." J.P. set his briefcase on the table in his office. "Sparky was right on the mark. Where's James?"

Mike pointed toward the bedroom. "We watched the first four innings waiting on the pizza. He ate. We talked. Then he crashed."

J.P. scanned his computer screen for messages from Denise. "Did he eat much?"

"You doubt a growing boy's appetite? He put away enough pizza to feed an entire baseball team."

Nothing from Denise. That's a good sign. "What'd he talk about?" J.P. loosened his tie and unfastened the top button on his dress shirt.

"Do I look like a fink?" Mike ignored the question. "So what's the scoop with Mid-America?"

Let's get the chaff out of the air. "What's the connection between Mid-America and your client?"

Mike wrapped his first two fingers around.

That's what I figured. "In that case, my discoveries are confidential." J.P. raised his eyebrows. "All I can say is there should be enough evidence for an arrest." *Eventually.* He removed his suit coat and draped it over the back of his desk chair.

Mike seemed satisfied.

"No raw confessions out of James, huh?"

"Nada. We talked baseball, basketball and a little football. I walked him through tomorrow's hearing in detail. I think he'll do fine before the judge." Mike turned his head toward the television and followed scores as they scrolled across the bottom of the screen. "Damn, the Cubs are two runs up on the Cards." He returned to the previous conversation. "He sure has the hots for Jennie Johnson. Talked about her a lot. Gut feeling says he's holding out the truth on her account."

J.P. pulled his tie completely off and hung it over the suit jacket. "Could be. Did he happen to mention she's knocked up?"

"Shit." Mike's face turned serious. "James?"

"He doesn't think so. Says she talked to him about that possibility *before* they got it on." J.P. unbuttoned a cuff on his shirt and began to roll it over his wrist. "How's that going to play into his testimony?"

Mike chewed on his mustache for a minute. "I'll definitely need to address that with him *before* he goes in." He paused for a moment. "The last thing we need is a surprise on the witness stand."

"No shit." *We've had enough surprises.* He rolled his other cuff out of habit.

"Hey," Mike's eyes twinkled with orneriness. "Speaking of having the hots for a girl, what'ya do to piss off the little gal who works the front desk?"

"What *little* gal at what desk?"

"The dishwater blonde who works check-in at the club . . ."

J.P. pictured the girl in his mind. *She just doesn't go away, does she?*

" . . . She had some choice words to describe your weekend behavior." Mike distorted his face. "In fact, she seemed to think you were out of town this week . . ."

J.P. squinted his eyes as he pictured the girl in his mind again. Ever so slowly, a nametag came into focus. "Oh my god," he announced as his palm met his forehead. "That's the mystery Mary!" He shook his head. "She's been calling but I couldn't put a face with that name for the life of me!"

"Go on . . ."

I've already had to tell this story once.

"Counselor?"

"Oh, I was supposed to have a date or something with her last weekend. Denise handled it." *I still have no recollection of promising her anything after our first meeting.*

"So, you've been out with her then?"

"Once." J.P. tried to act casual. "I took her to a business dinner when I needed to impress potential clients . . ."

"Were they impressed?"

"I didn't get the job if that's what you're after . . ."

Mike pumped up his chest and blocked the doorway so J.P. couldn't pass through. "That's not what I'm after."

Maybe I can distract him. "Wouldn't you rather hear more about the Mid-America link?"

"Not anymore. This Mary story is very intriguing. Let's finish this saga first."

There is no escaping Mike's interrogation.

Mike laughed and allowed J.P. to exit.

"Look, there's not that much to tell," J.P. headed for the kitchen. "I had her once. No big deal. I couldn't even remember her name for christ's sake." J.P. tipped a wineglass in Mike's direction.

"None for me, thanks." Mike grinned. "I have a few plans of my own later tonight." Mike straddled a kitchen chair and rested his chin on his fist. "Nothing like *Bobbie Sommers* though."

There is no one like Bobbie Sommer, my friend. "You have a hot date on a Wednesday night?"

"Since when were week nights ruled out?" Mike shook his head full of hair. "Besides, it's one of the few nights Rachel isn't at my place."

At least I don't bring them home with me. "Mikey, that is one item of business you need to take care of." J.P. removed a cork from an already opened bottle of wine.

"It's on my list of things to do."

He's doesn't want to face Rachel's wrath. J.P. could feel Mike eyes on his back. "What exactly is it you want out of me, Counselor?"

"Let's see." Mike tapped his hand against the table. "How about the name of my interception at the club this afternoon and meal expenses for pizza with James?"

What interception is he talking about? J.P. reached for his wallet and tossed a twenty on the table. "It's all I've got on me. Float me the rest until morning."

Mike folded the bill and stashed it in the pocket of his T-shirt. He smiled broadly. "Okay, are you ready?" His blue eyes glistened with anticipation of a new story. "This is one you're going to want to hear . . ."

Ah, Mikey, you're always good for a story. J.P. eased himself into the chair across the table and enjoyed the smoothness of the wine as it went down. "Anytime, Mikey, I'm listening." He offered a silent toast with his glass.

"Okay, get this. You know I was at the club today, right?"

" . . . Playing golf with the mayor again . . ."

" . . . rematch you know,"

"Okay . . ."

"And Sammy-O . . ."

"Whoever . . ."

"Remember the new guy I played with a couple of weekends ago?"

J.P. took another drink. *Unnecessary details, good buddy.*

"Anyway, I'm on my way out the front door and this *lady* walks up to the desk and asks if she can leave a message for you . . ."

What do you mean, lady?

"Mary was working. What a bitch! She bad mouthed you. I couldn't take it." Mike stopped the story and pointed an accusing finger. "You really need to learn how to let them down easy. You're killing your reputation, man."

Better than allowing one I don't even like to live in my house. J.P. flipped a choice finger back at Mike. *I'll handle my affairs my own way, thank you.*

Mike ignored the gesture. " . . . So anyway, this lady is trying to leave a message and Mary is carrying on. She spouted off something about you being out of town and being booked until November or something . . ."

Let's cut to the chase. "So, I'm assuming you intercepted the message?"

"Right. So now you owe me another one!" Mike rose from his chair and approached the counter. "I think I might have that glass of that wine after all."

You're funny, Mike. J.P. patiently watched while his friend poured a glass of Merlot.

"And the message is . . . ?"

Mike leaned on the counter directly behind his friend's chair. "Please call."

Give me a break! J.P. looked over his shoulder. "That's it? You set me up for a *please call?*"

"Yep!" Mike's eyes danced wildly. "I got her name too." Mike reached for his hip pocket. "If you can't remember her name I'd be hap . . ."

J.P. bolted from the chair and grabbed Mike by the shirt. "Samira!"

Mike held the wine glass high to keep from spilling. "Good god, J.P.! You don't have to fight me for it!"

J.P. smoothed Mike's shirt. *I should probably explain.* "I've been waiting for her to call all week."

"Relax, man!" Mike took a folded piece of paper out of his pocket. "It's only Wednesday. And it would help if you'd leave a number." Mike sat back down in the chair at the table.

I didn't leave a number? J.P. opened the note and ran this thumb over the ink. *Ready.* Samira's handwriting was fluid and graceful across the paper. *Ready for what?*

"Same one from two weekends ago, right?"

"Yeah," J.P. leaned against the counter. "Same one."

"Well . . . ?"

I'm not talking to him about Samira. "Well what?" He couldn't hide the smile on his face or the color in his cheeks.

Mike's tone softened. "She's quite a catch, J.P. Be advised to take care sporting her around the club."

Maybe so, J.P. thought to himself. *She is not my usual date.*

"Look, good buddy, I'd love to stick around and hear the rest of the story but I need to take a shower before I meet up with my date." He reached into his shirt pocket and removed the twenty-dollar bill. Deliberately, he stuck it in the empty wine glass. "Thanks for the drink and congrats on the progress with Mid-America."

"It's almost ten."

"She promised to wait."

I hope Samira is still waiting too. "What time are we leaving in the morning?"

"Eight and I'll be on time," Mike promised. "Oh, by the way, James said Ernie is picking him up at 4:45 to work for a couple of hours before we leave. He wants to come home and clean up before we head north so you'll need to retrieve him about seven . . ."

"Hey, Mike . . ."

The rambunctious attorney turned around at the back door and rested his forearm against the top of the refrigerator.

"Thanks for hanging out with James tonight."

"And for making that awesome interception . . ."

"And for the interception."

"And for hooking you up with Sparky . . ."

Yeah, and for that too. "And for Sparky."

Mike waved off the appreciation. "You owe me at least four favors, good buddy. And believe me, you'll pay."

J.P. grinned at Mike's insistence on keeping score.

"I'll see you at eight." Mike stepped outside. "And next time you want a pretty woman to call you back, leave your number."

I really didn't leave a number? J.P. ran his hand through his hair. *I'm surprised she went out to the club looking for me.* The last drop of wine in the bottom of Mike's wineglass was working its way into the corner of the folded bill. *That took guts.* J.P. pulled the money out of the glass with two fingers. *Same wine I served Samira at her house.* The note was laying on the counter. J.P. ran his fingers over Samira's name. *Payback on this one's going to be hell.*

J.P. didn't want to wait any longer to talk to Samira. He returned to his office and picked up the phone. *I already know her number, which is frightening considering Denise usually makes these calls for me.* He stopped dialing when he felt a presence and remembered he wasn't alone. J.P. turned in his desk chair and looked into the gray-green eyes of his son. *I guess she'll have to wait.*

James lowered himself into a chair. "How was the meeting?"

"It went well. Good progress on the case tonight." *Nice he asked.* "How'd it go with Mike?"

James leaned his head back against the wall behind him. "Okay, I guess. He says the meeting with the judge could be intense."

"Are you worried about that?"

"Maybe."

I'll prompt him, see where he goes with it. "The best way to handle this whole deal is to come clean, James. It's possible the authorities already know the details from Madson Park, so holding out isn't going to gain you any points with the judge." The father folded his hands and allowed James time to think about that. *Just ask the question.* "Do you know what happened, James?"

For the first time in over a week, James nodded with affirmation.

I knew he did.

James looked away. Then came the long awaited confession. "It's Zach's baby . . . the one Jennie is pregnant with."

Zach? "Isn't he Gina's boyfriend?" *The one who called my cell phone?*

"Yeah."

"So how does that work?" *I'm not sure I want an answer to that question.*

"It's complicated."

"Try me."

James took in a deep breath. "Jennie slept with Zach to get some goods."

Well, she got the goods! "Then Zach needs to be responsible for the baby."

"If Jennie tells him about the baby then, well . . ."

Spit it out, James. No use holding out now.

" . . . well, then we don't party. Zach will pull out of town and Jennie will be left high and dry." James shrugged his shoulders.

She's already left high and dry. "What are *party goods*, James?"

For a brief second James made eye contact with his father. *I've seen that look before. It's the same way he looked at Josh that night in Janet's kitchen and again on the dock the morning we were fishing.*

James shrugged his shoulders again.

It's a look asking for trust. "Here's the deal, James." J.P. leaned forward and put his elbows on his knees. "Keeping secrets right now is not going to help Mike plead your case. We need the truth in order to give you fair representation." James was looking at the floor. *That's not enough, is it.*

James lowered his voice. "But anything I say can or will be used against me, right?"

J.P. nodded slowly. "Basically." *But there's more.* "But it can also work in your favor." The father knew what else needed to be spoken. *Just say it, Ralston.* J.P. inhaled very deeply. "But that only holds true in the court of law, James. Whatever you tell me . . ." *If I say this out loud, then I have to follow it through.* ". . . I won't hold it over your head."

"You won't be mad at me?"

That's not what I said. "I said I won't hold it against you—once it's out there you and I will deal with it together. I won't throw it back in your face." *Like Bruce does.*

A few more moments of silence separated the men.

"Zach gets us whatever we want," James confessed. "Booze, smokes . . ."

"Anything else?"

"Maybe . . ."

"Like what?"

"Like whatever we ask him to get . . ."

"Specifically . . ."

James rose from his chair. "Smack."

Heroine? J.P. followed his son into the kitchen. "Are you in possession?" *Of course he is. He had it at the lake.*

"Maybe . . ." James stopped in the hall that separated the kitchen from the guest room.

J.P. spoke very calmly. "How often, James?"

"Only when I'm with the guys and not even every time." James sighed. "It gives me a headache."

It may give you more than that! J.P. ran his hand through his hair. *I don't know what I expected, but this isn't the confession I'd hoped for.* He knew what had to happen. "Whatever you've got, James, it has to go to the judge tomorrow."

"But I'll get busted."

"We'll both get busted if you don't turn it in."

"But, Dad . . . you don't understand . . ."

"No, James, this time I call the shots." *And then I have to let it go if I'm going to maintain any kind of trust with this kid in the future.*

Slowly James turned toward his bedroom. J.P. followed and watched James dig his hand deep into the over-sized duffel bag. It came out holding a miniature bag of white powder. James studied the packet in his hand a moment before slapping it into his father's waiting palm.

"Is this all of it?"

James nodded silently.

"You're not holding any back?"

"That's it."

"This will change the outcome of your hearing tomorrow, son." J.P.'s heart ached as he thought about the potential ruling. "You'll be looking at a summer of probation." *Could be facing juvenile time.* "Maybe longer." *Probably longer.*

"What about Jennie?"

He's got to let her go! "It's not your responsibility unless you got her pregnant."

"And what if I did?"

Don't be the hero, James. "If you did, then we deal with it." J.P. fingered the illegal substance in his hands. "But if you know for sure it's not yours, then you need to let it go."

James sat down on the edge of the bed and placed his elbows on his knees. "It's Zach's. She told me before we did it. She'd already done one of those tests and everything."

"Then she's going to have to figure it out."

"But I'm her friend."

"Friends get friends help."

"But what if she doesn't want anyone to know?"

"Somebody has to know, James."

"Why?"

He really doesn't get this, does he? J.P. knelt down so he was eye level with his son. "Because there's a baby involved James . . . a human being. You just can't let that fact go untold."

"She says she'll take care of it."

"Maybe she will, maybe she won't." J.P. hesitated before finishing his thought. "But your responsibility as a friend is to see she gets the proper kind of assistance either way. Letting people think it's your baby isn't going to let her off the hook. Either way she's pregnant." *She needs more help than you can give her, James.* "As a friend, it's not your job to protect her. She needs your support to do the right thing."

James tucked his head between his knees.

I wish I could fix everything and make it all go away.

When James looked up, his eyes were damp. "If I do that she's not going to see me again."

"Probably not." *Which would be my preference given the state of affairs.*

There was a very long period of silence as the Ralston men each processed their own thoughts. *Maybe he just needs to think this through on his own.* Just as J.P. reached the hall James spoke again.

"Then I need to call her, Dad. I need to tell her what I'm going to do."

That takes guts. J.P. started to offer the phone in his office and thought better of it. He handed his son the cell phone. The he closed the bedroom door to give James privacy.

I might as well call Mike with the new information. He left a message on the voice mail. *I thought his confession would relieve my mind somehow. But this is a lot.*

J.P turned off the lights in the living room and sank into the leather sofa. The television flickered in the darkness of the house, but there was no motivation to turn on the sound. He stared at the screen. Sports Center scores scrolled across the bottom but they weren't coming into focus.

James appeared and took a seat in the chair adjacent to his father.

"Did Mike tell you I'm going in to work for awhile in the morning?"

J.P. nodded.

"I figured I could pick up a few bucks before we leave town. I'll just do the golf balls then call you for a ride."

That's fine. J.P's brain and emotions had grown numb. "Did you talk to Jennie?"

"Yeah."

There were no other words between them. *Really there's nothing left to say.* Tomorrow was going to be a very long day. *I have no idea how to be a father after all this time.*

James left the room.

"I'm sorry, Dad."

I am too, James. The scores on the television screen were repetitious. *Sorry for leaving you to fight your own battles.* J.P. clicked off the television and turned to face his son. But the space in the doorway was empty, just like the space in his heart.

21

Just Say the Words

I was only gone for a few minutes! Samira listened to the short message again. Phil's smooth baritone voice sent excited shivers up her spine.

"Is the machine broken or something?" Kara leaned over the counter next to her mother.

"Oh, no, nothing's broken." Samira was embarrassed to be caught. "I just couldn't hear the last message very well."

Kara started to reach. "Turn up the volume."

Oh, no! Don't push play! Samira grabbed Kara's arm abruptly. "I've got it now." In the same motion she picked up the notepad where she'd written Phil's phone number.

"Are you sure there's not something else on the machine you need to hear?" Kara looked sideways at her mother.

"No, nothing else." Samira could feel sweat beads forming on her forehead. *I feel like a teenager!*

Kara laughed. "Whatever, Mama."

I wish she wouldn't use that word!

"Uncle Wes isn't going in early tomorrow so we don't need to be at their house until you leave for work." Samira watched her daughter tie her hair in a knot at the back of her head as she talked. "After lunch we're going to meet Paula and Renee at the pool. Aunt Pam said she could drop us off."

Samira was listening, but it was hard to keep her mind away from Phil's message. *I just want to listen one more time.* "I'll pick you up at the pool after work then."

Samira watched as Kara disappeared into the hallway. *Thank God she didn't push play!* Samira stared at the little machine. *He said he'd be home this evening.* She glanced at the clock and decided to wait awhile longer before returning the call. To pass the time she flipped through a magazine. Next she watered the plants in the kitchen windowsill. When that was finished she checked the clock again. *I used up a whole four minutes, for pete's sake!*

I feel like a schoolgirl just with a new crush! She decided to water the flowers in the front yard. *It's been two days since I gave the note to that guy named Mike.* Samira adjusted the garden hose. *But I haven't talked to Phil since I pushed away from him in the garden.* Mindlessly, she pulled a small weed out of the flower bed. *I want to tell him I've decided to go to Springfield.*

Back inside the house a half an hour had passed. *It's officially evening now.* But when Samira picked up the receiver, Kara was talking to a friend. It was much later before she retreated to her bedroom and actually dialed the numbers. *It's ringing.* Samira wiped her sweaty palms on her bedspread.

"Joe's pizza."

I know I dialed correctly. She double checked the numbers.

"Will this be dine in or carry out?"

Samira was still studying the series of numbers written on the notepad.

"Well? Are you going to order or not?"

Don't tell me it's the wrong number! Disappointment was settling in quickly.

"I'm sorry. I think I have . . ."

"This is J.P." A different voice came on the line.

J.P. isn't the man I was hoping for either!

" . . . I think I've dialed . . . ."

"No, wait!"

Is this the same voice on my answering machine? You should ask for Phil.

"Who's this?"

I'm not giving him my name until I know who it is! "I'm calling for Phil Ralston."

There was a delayed pause. "This is Phil."

It is? Samira pressed the phone harder into her ear. *He seems very distracted.*

"This is Samira."

There was a different tone in the voice when he spoke again. "Hey, lady," he replied with recognition, but he still sounded preoccupied. "Hang on a minute, okay?"

This is almost as crazy as the Mike Benson thing! She took a deep breath. *Talking to this man on the phone should not be so nerve wracking.* She leaned into the pillows on her bed. *But nothing with Phil ever seems normal.*

"Samira."

Now I recognize his voice!

"Sorry about that. James answered while I was outside with the dog. He has no business picking up like that."

Oh, that was James! Samira almost laughed at the prank. "He just caught me off guard that's all."

"I imagine he did." There was a slight pause on the line. "Hey, I got your message."

Now that was a whole other experience! Samira thought to herself. "I was hoping your friend would get it to you." *Actually, I was hoping he was really your friend.*

"Mike's a good messenger."

He certainly has a style of his own. "He seemed trustworthy enough." *At least once I got to talking with him.* "Calling is difficult without a telephone number."

"My fault."

Samira wished she could see Phil's face.

"You're note says you're *ready.*"

Whatever that means! Samira subconsciously twisted her hair with her fingers. *Maybe he'll offer an explanation for not being listed in a telephone directory.* Samira took a deep breath. "About next weekend . . ." she forced her voice sound stronger than she felt. "Ready or not, I've been thinking and I'd like to try to go with you." *I mean, I definitely want to go . . .*

Phil didn't reply immediately.

Samira waited. *Phil?*

He didn't reply at all.

Samira removed the phone from her ear and made sure it was still powered on. *He's still not responding!* A sudden panic came of her being. *What if he found another date?*

" . . . that is if the invitation is still open . . ." *Please still be open.*

Still nothing. A few seconds later a dial tone buzzed in her ear.

Stunned, Samira stared at the receiver in her hand. The pit that was already in her stomach felt like erupting. A wave of emotion seemed to rise from the tips of her toes and form a lump in her throat.

Samira put her head in her hand and leaned her shoulder into the arrangement of pillows. *What kind of a response was that? . . . Did he find someone else? . . . Why wouldn't he at least respond?* Samira didn't know if she was angry or hurt, or both. What she did know was that he was very confusing and very frustrating. *He drives me crazy!*

Samira climbed off the bed. She grabbed a damp washcloth and began to wipe down the counter in her bathroom. When the phone rang, she chose not to answer. *Surely one of the girls will pick up.* Samira ran the cloth under the faucet and rinsed it out.

"Mama!"

Samira chose not to respond.

"Where are you?" Krissy's voice was getting closer. She appeared in the bedroom. "Oh, there you are!" She smiled a mouthful of braces and wiggled her eyebrows. "The phone is for you but I can't find the other phone."

Samira pointed to her bed. Krissy spotted it and cheerfully, clicked it on and handed it over.

"I'll give you some privacy!" Krissy slowly closed the bedroom door.

Privacy! Like that's really what I need here. Samira inhaled deeply, trying desperately to control the emotions that were on the brink of spilling over.

"Hello."

"Samira, it's Phil. The battery went dead on the phone."

Oh, really? Samira didn't know if she believed him or not.

"I had it on the charger before you called, but obviously it wasn't a full battery yet."

"I thought maybe you hung up on me." *I can't believe I just said that to him!*

"Not a chance."

Samira's anger began to fade into relief, which faded into more confusion. She sat down on the edge of her bed and waited through an awkward pause.

"Samira, what are you doing right now?"

Just talking to you. "Not much." *Unfortunately.*

"Listen, this phone thing isn't working out very well." Phil was obviously thinking out loud. "And James and I could use a little space. Can I just come over for a few minutes?"

Right now? The mother's defenses started to kick in. "The girls are home."

"I know. I just talked to one of them . . ."

Oh, yeah. I guess he did. Do I want him to be here with Kara and Krissy home again? Samira took note of the late evening sky out her bedroom window.

" . . . I don't have to stay long."

He sounds disappointed. Samira resigned to her self-imposed fears. "Okay, for a few minutes." *He's right about the phone part not working out very well!* Deep down she was excited to see him in person. *But I don't want to spoil the moment again.*

"Give me twenty minutes to get across town."

Twenty minutes didn't sound like a long time, but now that she was waiting, it seemed to take forever. *I'll just meet him out doors.* Her heart raced and the sweat in her palms went from hot to cold the minute she realized he was approaching the front door.

Samira opened the door before Phil had a chance to ring the bell. He grinned a boyish grin and tipped his head in greeting. She couldn't help but return a smile.

This is silly. I'm a grown woman and he's a grown man! It shouldn't be so uncomfortable inviting him into my own house! Instead, she stepped out onto the porch. *If I don't turn on the porch light, maybe Mrs. Barnes won't notice us out here.*

Samira turned her back to the invisible neighbor and leaned against the wooden railing. *It doesn't matter what he wears. He still takes my breath away.*

"So you really didn't hang up on me?" Even as the words fell, Samira was surprised to hear them come out of her mouth. *The cut on his cheek is almost completely healed.*

"No ma'am, I did not hang up on you." Phil's eyes were intense. "But your conversation with James wasn't fair." He made a worried face. "There's a lot of things I didn't calculate into fatherhood."

I don't think he knows how to be a father yet. "How did the meeting go today?"

"How do you know about that?"

She stifled a smile as she realized he'd answered a question with a question. *That's Phil's trick.* "You said you had an out of town meeting concerning your son during the day but you'd be back this evening."

Phil's face was still blank.

"On my answering machine."

"Oh yeah." The look on his face showed a hint of humor but the tone of his demeanor took on a serious front. "The meeting . . ."

Samira waited. *Maybe I shouldn't have asked. He seems uncomfortable.*

" . . . the meeting was a court appearance." Phil's eyes looked out across the yard. "It wasn't all bad news, I guess."

A court appearance? This is more serious than I thought. "Is everything alright?"

"Well, let's see," Phil counted on his fingers. "How do I put this?" He looked up at the porch ceiling for a minute. "James has been with me ten complete days now and my schedule is completely challenged, my homelife is nonexistent, and I'm beginning to feel like a full time chauffeur. And all this before he took a job at the club that starts at five in the morning." Phil looked past Samira into the distance behind her. "And that's all in addition to the fact that he is now under my custody for the remainder of the summer, facing several hours of community service, and answering my phone without permission." His dark blue eyes settled on Samira's. "Let's just say it's a test I'm not sure I can pass."

I'm sure it is. Samira held his eyes. "And how is James adjusting?"

"I don't know." A slight grin appeared on his lips. "I guess I hadn't thought much about how James is taking it all." He shrugged his shoulders and stuffed his hands into the pockets. "He seems to be getting on alright far as I can tell."

Obviously he is out of practice. "You'll both adjust over time." *But if he works at it, I think he'll make a fine father.* Samira smiled gently.

"Hope so." Phil cocked his head to the side and studied Samira's face. "But I didn't come here to talk about James." The hue of his eyes darkened. "I came here to talk about you."

Samira felt immediately awkward again. She scooted onto the porch railing and balanced her body weight with her toes wrapped around the spindles. *I'd rather talk to him about his life than mine.* "So what might there possibly be to talk to me about?"

"No," Phil corrected. "Not talk to you about—I want to talk *about* you." He took a step to the side and sat down in the wooden rocker. He leaned forward and placed his elbows on his knees. "I'd like to take you to Springfield with me."

The directive caught Samira slightly off guard but she was determined not to let it show. "And why do you want to take me?" *I'd really like to know the answer to that question.*

"Because, Pretty Lady . . . ,"

Pretty Lady? I love the way he calls me that . . .

" . . . Because you are the lady I desire."

That was it.

Is he going to say something else? She was more stunned with this statement than she was when the dial tone sounded in here ear.

"The question seems to be whether or not you want to go along." Phil slowly leaned back into the chair.

Oh! His phone must have died before he heard me. Samira's heart was pounding hard against her sternum and her breath was shallow and weak. *And evidently he hasn't found another date.*

She stared at Phil without answering.

"Well?"

"I do." *I really do.*

Phil's questioning look faded into an easy smile. "I'm really glad to know that." He rose from the chair and took two steps toward Samira. He stopped immediately in front of her. There was just enough space between them that she could have moved away had she chosen to. When she didn't, Phil stretched out his arms against the porch supports on either side of her.

His presence, his body language, his easy smile—everything draws me in. Afraid to move, Samira stayed frozen in place. The firmness of his biceps flexed against his body weight as he leaned in closer.

And this is the man I desire.

About the time Samira was seriously thinking about kissing him, the porch light unexpectedly flooded the entire area!

What in the world? Samira covered her face with her hands.

Krissy exploded onto the front porch. She seemed just as surprised to see Phil and Samira as they were to see her.

"Oh, my!" Krissy exclaimed. "I didn't know your were out here, Mama!" The girl put her hands to her face.

Phil stepped back and silently acknowledged Krissy's presence.

"Krissy!" *Krissy how could you do this?*

"Did I just talk to you on the phone?" Krissy was looking at Phil.

Oh, Krissy! Don't empty your mind now!

Phil concurred.

"Then why are you here now?"

Now Samira was humiliated!

"Because I wanted to talk to your mother in person instead of talking to her on the phone." His tone was gentle and his eyes were soft as he looked at Krissy.

Wow. Samira liked the way he looked at her daughter. *Obviously he's not afraid to hold his own with her*

"Did you bring your dog this time?" Krissy's eyes went immediately to the truck.

Phil knelt down and balanced himself on the balls of his feet. "No, I didn't. Maybe next time." He raised his eyebrows in humored acceptance of the interruption. Samira had to look away.

"Oh." Krissy looked back to her mother. "Um, well, anyway, I couldn't find you in the garden so I came out here." She was seldom at a loss for words and Samira found it interesting that Krissy was searching for them now. "Tiffany called and wants to know if I can go over Saturday afternoon."

Samira shook her head. "Can we discuss this in a few minutes, Krissy?" Shifting into motherhood with Phil sitting right there was very awkward. *Or am I uncomfortable shifting out of womanhood with Krissy right here?* Whatever the case, Samira refused to succumb to a repeat scenario like the disaster in the garden. She forced herself to remain on the railing and did her best to appear unaffected by Krissy's abrupt interruption.

"Yeah, sure," Krissy answered. She turned to go back in the house and then turned back around toward her mother. "Should I tell Kara you're out here?"

Samira chuckled at Krissy's confusion. "If you want to." *I wish she'd turn off the light!*

Samira realized she was holding her breath. She attempted to let it out slowly but her heart was beating so fast she almost couldn't contain the nervous excitement.

Phil was chuckling. "She's a ball of fire, isn't she?"

"That's one way to describe Krissy." *You could also call her overly assertive.*

Phil's eyes were once again focusing on Samira's. He stood up and faced Samira again.

Obviously he hasn't forgotten where we were.

"About Springfield," Phil continued. " . . . If you're comfortable staying the night, there are accommodations available at the Civic Center Complex. If you'd rather drive back late that night, then I don't have a problem with that either." Phil lowered his voice a little more. "However you're most comfortable."

I'm most comfortable wherever he is and my girls aren't. A chill ascended the length of Samira's spine as Phil's hand ran over her left shoulder and down her arm.

" . . . so I'll let you think on that and you can let me know."

I have to appreciate the advanced permission to think it through. "At least I have your number this time."

Phil displayed an easy smile but his eyes were watching her hand. "And I should be the one to answer the next time you call . . ." his voice trailed off as he lifted her right hand off the rail.

Samira allowed him to link his fingers between hers. Unable to speak, she just nodded, wondering if he'd notice she was no longer wearing the wedding band. She could feel his thighs between her knees as he leaned in closer. In spite of her personal promise to not ruin another intimate moment, Samira was horrified at the thought of Mrs. Barnes watching from across the street. *I wish the lighst were off.*

Very gently Phil's lips touched her forehead. Samira wanted so desperately to answer the initiation but she couldn't. She rested her head heavily into Phil's cheek.

"Very well, then . . ."

He knows I'm not going to kiss him out here. I hope he's okay with that.

"You can let me know." He squeezed her fingers in his, touched her on the temple with his lips once again, and then turned and walked away.

Samira couldn't make her legs move. She sat frozen in place on the porch rail.

No longer had Phil backed out of the driveway than Krissy and Kara were on the porch. *I knew they were watching!*

"Did you see the way he looked at you?" Krissy asked.

"Mama! He is so good looking," Kara added.

"Why didn't you tell us he was coming?"

"Is he coming back?"

"You should have kissed him!"

"Enough!" Samira left the security of the porch rail in spite of her weak knees. "Back in the house before Mrs. Barnes hears you two."

"Like she didn't see everything anyway," Krissy sneered.

Great! Samira shooed her daughters behind the front door and turned off the outside light.

"What was he doing here?" Kara asked all too seriously.

That tone deserves an honest answer. Samira bit her bottom lip as she walked to the kitchen. Safe behind the breakfast bar, she turned and faced her daughters.

"He wanted to ask me out."

"I hope you said yes after the way he did that . . . ," Kara's voice trail off.

"Did what?"

"Well . . . came over here and *everything* . . ."

Krissy butted in, "Like what is *everything*, Kara?"

"Girls," Samira interjected. "It's really not that big of a deal, is it? He just wanted to invite me to a business dinner, that's all." *But it's really more than that!*

Krissy giggled and grabbed her mother's arm. "And you said yes, right?"

Samira simply nodded. Krissy threw her arms around her mother. "Oh, this is really exciting. What are you going to wear?"

What am I going to wear? Samira sat down on a barstool. "I haven't any idea." *What do you wear to a business engagement?*

She observed her daughters with caution. Krissy's exuberance was quite unnerving. But as she looked into Kara's eyes, she saw a shadow of doubt. *Or maybe it's a feeling of betrayal somehow.*

Krissy flitted off into the bedroom. Samira questioned Kara with her eyes.

"Really, I'm glad you're going."

"Are you sure?"

"It's okay." Kara's dark eyes were contemplative. "I think he really likes you."

"You do?" *How do you know?*

"Well, the way he looks at you and all," Kara tried unsuccessfully to explain. "And he just seems really gentle, like, well, not like the mountain man guy who was here the first time . . ."

Yep, they were watching. Samira smiled softly.

"Do you want to go out with him again?"

"Yes, I do."

Kara nodded once. "Then I think you should go."

Samira hadn't realized how badly she needed her daughter's support. "Thank you, Kara." *Maybe she just needs to feel involved.* "Maybe you can help me decide what to wear,"

Kara nodded in affirmation then quietly slipped away into her bedroom.

Because you are the lady I desire. Phil's words replayed again and again in Samira's mind. There wasn't the slightest hesitation in his voice when he answered her inquiry. *I like the sounds of that.*

A manly shower-fresh scent was still apparent in the air when Samira stepped back onto the front porch. Either that or the scent was on her again somehow. *He shared just enough personal information to make me feel trustworthy. He spoke to me directly so I know he's sincere. And he touched me just enough to show me he cares.* And he was the gentleman she'd experienced that first night together. *Just as I hoped he would be.*

He's complex. Samira leaned into the support post and allowed the weight of her body to slide down into a sitting position on the top step. *He's intense and demanding, but in a gentle sort of way.* For a moment it didn't matter if Mrs. Barnes was watching or not. *And he called me Pretty Lady. Daddy would like that about him.*

A gentle breeze blew her hair away from her face. *Now I really know how the little rose bud in my garden feels.* She rested her head against the post. *Absolutely scared to death!*

22

What will it Take

J.P. was oblivious to the twenty minutes back across town. Three things had him totally stumped. *First, she led me right into another personal discussion before I realized what was happening. Then she dared to ask me why I want to take her to Springfield.* J.P. scratched his head. *No woman has ever asked me why I invited her on a date!*

What's up with that? J.P. looked both ways at an unmarked intersection. *And then to answer her like that! Any word but "desire". For god's sake you're a lawyer, Ralston. Use your vocabulary training!*

He turned off the ignition in his driveway. *I have worked damn hard to call my life my own. Until a few weeks back I had a perfect world where I could come and go and think and do as I pleased.* The entire house was ablaze with lights. *Now I have a son who needs a father.* The next thought all but paralyzed his independence. *And I think I have a woman who might need me too.*

J.P. closed his eyes and pressed his neck into the headrest. *It has nothing to do with that. What if I'm the one who needs her?* He opened the door. *Now that is a frightening thought.*

J.P. Ralston never needed anything or anyone to make his life complete. He reminded himself of that as he greeted Chase. He subconsciously reached down and patted the dog's head.

"Chase. I have never let anybody have this much control over me." He snapped his fingers for Chase to follow him to the back door. *But the way she was sitting there tonight . . . There isn't much I wouldn't do for her.*

James was sitting on the kitchen counter with the telephone wedged between his ear and his shoulder. He was munching out of a bag of pretzels.

172

I hate it that she has this much control over me.

"It's for you." James spoke through a mouthful.

J.P. took the phone, irritated to have his private thoughts interrupted. He covered the mouthpiece. "Who is it and why are all the lights on?"

"Mom. And I was tied to the wall. Couldn't reach the switches." James crossed the kitchen and turned off the hall light before disappearing into the living room.

J.P. waited a few seconds before putting the receiver to his ears. *It's almost impossible to shift gears to Janet.* He cleared his throat.

"Jan, what's up?" *I spent all day at the courthouse with her. Who knows what she wants now.*

"It's a little late to be running errands, isn't it J.P.?" Janet was picking the fight. "I've been on the phone with James for quite awhile now."

I am not going there tonight, Janet. "Then you should be all caught up." J.P. helped himself to a pretzel. "What can I do for you?"

Janet was speaking but the voice J.P. heard in his ear was Samira's. *"I do." Holy Toledo. She said those words without even a slight hesitation.* He shuddered at the recollection.

"Holy shit!" J.P. spoke out loud.

"What's the matter now?"

J.P. stood stock still in his kitchen trying to clarify what had happened. *"I do" is not a phrase I'd ever planned to hear again.* Samira was clear and fresh in his memory. *But at the same time, the way she was sitting there was totally erotic.* J.P ran his hand through his hair. *Given my vulnerability, I might have replied with a commitment I am nowhere near ready to make!*

"J.P.?"

Who the hell is on the other end of this phone call? "Jan."

"Have you heard anything I've just told you?"

This is definitely not Samira. J.P. decided Janet wasn't worth the effort. He had more important things to contend with. *Namely a pretty lady across town who is threatening my independence.*

"Look, Jan, it's getting late and it's been a long day for all of us." *I've got to get her off this phone.* "Let me call you back in the morning."

"I'll be at work in the morning."

"So will I. I'll call you from there."

"What do I do about Jennie Johnson until then?"

J.P. tried to remember what his ex-wife had just told him. *Nothing. I didn't hear a thing she said.* "Is it an emergency?"

"Good god, J.P.," Janet sneered. "I don't know how you can possibly function with clients when you can't even communicate for one minute on the telephone . . ."

Doesn't sound like there's anything pressing. "I'll call you in the morning." *Spare me the verbal assault.* "Sleep well, Jan." Without waiting for a formal close to the conversation, he reached over and hung up the phone.

"*I do.*" The quiet confidence in Samira's voice was still the same.

Damn it. She's definitely out of my league. He opened the refrigerator. *I need something to slow down these thoughts.*

James pulled a t-shirt off over his head as he entered the kitchen. He stopped in the doorway and made an exaggerated effort to turn off the living room light behind him. "I'm turning in. Four thirty comes mighty early."

Hope I'm asleep by then.

"Thanks for bringing my bike down, Dad. That's going to make it easier to get around during the day."

For both of us. J.P. acknowledged the appreciation in a single nod. He twisted the cap off a cold Corona.

James grinned.

"What?"

"I don't know what she did to you in that short amount of time but whatever it was, she did it up good."

Who? Your mother? J.P. lifted the bottle of beer to his lips.

James continued to observe his father.

"What the hell is that supposed to mean?" J.P. sat the bottle against the counter top a little harder than necessary.

"Nothing," he stated with the same sly smile. "But your eyes are all glazed over and you act like you . . ."

"Like what?"

"Like maybe there's more to come . . ."

"More of what?"

"More of whatever it was you didn't get tonight."

He's definitely not talking about his mother! J.P. watched his son vanish around the corner. J.P. rubbed his eyes with his fingertips. *If that had been Mike I'd have had a few choice words for him.*

"Good night, Dad," James called from the bedroom. "I'll see you when you get to the gym for your workout."

A door closed the space between the father and son.

Any other night he would review a case or catch Sports Center on ESPN. Tonight his mind was too busy to attempt either. He lowered himself into the oversized armchair in the living room and propped his feet up on the coffee table. Sitting there in the dark he allowed Samira's dark eyes to penetrate his again.

There's definitely more to come. But she's the one who's calling the shots.

He took another drawl on the bottle.

One kiss wouldn't have done it tonight. There's no way I could have stopped with that.

Chase lumbered into the room and rubbed against his master's leg.

Maybe that's why she wouldn't look at me.

J.P. was at the bottom of the bottle before another cognitive thought emerged.

Obviously she's going to want more than I've had to give in the past. He thought about that for awhile. *How much of me am I willing to give her?*

The empty bottle looked out of place on the coffee table.

Or maybe it's me. Maybe I'm the one wanting more than I've had in the past.

Chase sighed heavily indicating a deep canine slumber.

What is it about her that keeps me from walking away? J.P. asked himself the question as he rose from the chair. *God knows the smartest thing to do is turn and run like the wind.*

The brew was doing its job. *I might be able to relax enough to get some sleep eventually.* He left the bottle on the coffee table and turned off the lights in the kitchen. The house was quiet.

On his way into the hall, he cracked the door on the guest bedroom. *I guess this is his bedroom now.* J.P. watched his son sleep for a few minutes. *He has to be tired after the long day in court.* An unopened duffel bag sat at the foot of the bed. *Just because the marriage ended didn't give me any right to believe that fatherhood ended with it.* J.P. closed his eyes for a moment. *He's a good kid. I just hope we can figure this mess out together.*

J.P. removed his clothes and brushed his teeth. *Everything is in order for tomorrow.* He checked the alarm clock before turning off the light next to his bed.

He should have been able to surrender to the day. But as he lie in his bed consumed by the darkness of the night, the seductive, contented face of the woman on the porch haunted his memory.

I want to be able to give her what she needs, but what if I don't have what it's going to take?

23

Getting to Know You

Samira took a mental inventory. *Casual clothes for Saturday daytime, a change in case the day fades into evening, and a cotton nightgown.* Samira held the gown at arms length. *No. Not a cotton nightgown. Too conservative.*

The top drawer on the dresser was still open. *How about a long nightshirt?* Satisfied, she added it to the wardrobe collection on her bed. *I don't want to over pack, but I also want to have everything I might need.* She would wear her dress shoes and pack sandals. *The only thing I know for sure is that the evening party is formal.*

Samira removed the plastic from the only formal dress she owned. She held it against her by the hanger and surveyed the tea length in the full mirror. *This is definitely better than wearing one of Pam's.* She turned to the side. *It's more me.*

At least it still fits. The last time she wore it was to an officer's ball when Krissy was three or four. *That was a long time ago now.*

Commotion in the other room drew Samira out of the bedroom.

"We're home, Mama!" Krissy skipped across the living room to greet her mother. Bonnie and Lizzie were close on her heels.

Lizzie grinned and batted her big blue eyes at her aunt. "We're going to help you get a date!"

"Mark is asleep," Kara informed. "Aunt Pam is going to bring him in to my bed." She moved her little cousins out of the way so Pam could make her way through with the sleeping toddler.

"How long before Phil gets here?" Krissy asked.

Samira's eyes went directly to the clock on the kitchen wall. "He said four o'clock or shortly thereafter." *And he has yet to be late.*

"Great!" Krissy exclaimed. "We have exactly an hour to turn you into Cinderella!"

Samira sighed as she made eye contact with her sister in law. *Does she have any idea how nervous I am?*

"Why don't you let your mother and I get organized, then we'll come get you to help with the finishing touches." She motioned for Samira to follow her to the bedroom while Kara and Krissy busied themselves with the little girls.

"Thank you!"

"No problem. I could take them all over to the pool so you have more time to get ready by yourself." Pam pushed the bedroom door closed.

Samira shook her head and started to pack her clothes into an overnight bag. "No, I think it's important the girls are here when he comes." She tucked her still-damp hair behind an ear. "And I'm glad you're here too. I'm a little nervous." *Correction. I'm terrified.*

Pam laughed as she eased into the chair. "I can understand that! So tell me, what did you decide to wear?"

Samira pointed to the black dress on the closet door. "I tried them all on, but Kara settled on this one and I think she's right. It's simple, it's plain . . ."

" . . . and it's you," Pam interjected. "But I bet Krissy went for the sequined gown."

"Funny you should know that!" Samira had to laugh. "That girl is the queen of fashion."

"They're both excited that you're going away. That's all they've talked about this week."

Samira sat down on the edge of the bed. "It feels really strange, Pam. Sometimes everything feels out of sorts with this guy, and then in the next minute everything feels really right." *I have a whole boatload of emotions with him.* "It's really hard to explain."

"Maybe there's more to him than meets the eye," Pam suggested. She rose from the chair and lifted the dress off the hanger. "Finish packing and let's get you into this dress. I can't wait to see it on!"

Ever so patiently, Samira stood stock still in front of the bathroom mirror while Krissy and Kara rolled her long dark hair into a French roll and fastened it securely with a transparent comb. *It's pretty.* A few strands at a time Kara formed the loose ends around her face into long vertical curls with the curling iron. *But I don't know.*

"Perfect." Krissy looked at her mother in the mirror.

Almost too perfect.

"Now, add these and you're set." Very carefully Krissy fastened a strand of pearls around the jeweled neckline of the dress. Samira stood up, inserting a pair of dropped pearl earrings as she moved.

"Where are your shoes?" Krissy sounded almost panicked. "It's almost time for him to get here! Don't you feel like you're going to a prom?"

Samira noticed the clock next to her bed. *Krissy's right. Almost four o'clock.* "I don't know. I never went to the prom."

Krissy shook her head. "A mother who didn't go to the prom? Every girl should get to go to the prom."

"Maybe this is Mama's prom." Kara was studying her mother in the mirror.

Krissy left the room in search of her mother's dress shoes.

"So, what do you think?" *Be honest, Kara! I'm counting on you . . .*

Kara walked completely around her mother, taking care to notice every detail. She stopped and straightened the bow at the waistline in the back.

"Honestly?"

"Of course." *Please.*

"The hair needs something." Kara made a worried face. "You need to do something because it doesn't look like you."

Thank you! Loosening only the top edge of the comb, Samira reached underneath the twist and released the ends. The loose hair cascaded over the top of the rolled bun. *Much better!*

"Now that looks more like you," Kara admitted. "What do you think, Krissy?"

"That's it!" Krissy put Samira's shoes on the floor. "Now, step into your shoes and let's go show Aunt Pam."

The girls hurried out to find their aunt, but Samira stayed in the bathroom. The woman in the mirror looked vaguely familiar, like maybe someone she had once known. She sucked in her stomach against the fitted bodice. *It's snug.* Samira smiled. *Control top panty hose aren't hurting anything either!* She leaned into the mirror and touched up her lipstick with a finger.

When the doorbell rang, her heart skipped at least two beats. *I don't know if I'm ready!* This time when Samira put her hand over her stomach it was to stop the fluttering of butterflies. *I can't believe I'm going away for an overnight and my girls know it!*

"Mama! Come on!" Kara whispered at the bedroom door.

Samira crossed the bedroom trying to look more confident than she felt. Every nerve in her body was on edge but she didn't want that to show. She stopped and made eye contact with Pam before stepping into the living room. Little Mark was perched on his mother's hip. Pam smiled brightly and nodded her approval

Breathe, Samira. Breathe! The dress shoes sounded against the hard wood floor as she crossed the room to greet her date. *There he is! Tuxedo shirt. Formal pants. I love the narrow buttoned suspenders.* Samira smiled. *And he always rolls the cuffs on his sleeves.* A bowtie hung loosely around Phil's neck. *I should have known he wouldn't be completely dressed.*

When their eyes met, neither spoke.

"Auntie, you're so pretty!" Six-year old Bonnie was standing between Phil and Samira. Her hands glided over the satin fabric of the skirt.

Samira touched the girl's blonde curls. "Phil," she motioned toward Pam with her hand. "I'd like you to meet my sister-in-law, and little Mark." Then she pointed her finger playfully at her niece who was peering over the back of the sofa. "And this is Lizzie."

"And me. What about me?"

"Yes," Samira smiled at the hem of her dress. "This is Bonnie."

Phil acknowledged the woman at the breakfast bar but Samira knew he was mostly watching her. She excused herself to get her things. Kara followed her all the way to the bedroom.

"I put your hairbrush and lipstick in the bag. Do you have everything else?"

"I hope so." Samira looked into her daughter's eyes. "I feel really strange." Samira realized her honesty but it was too late.

"You're just nervous like it's your first date." Kara sounded mature beyond her years. "Once you get out of here you'll feel fine." Kara zipped the overnight bag. "You look so pretty, Mama."

"Really?" Samira glanced at the full-length mirror.

"Really." Kara patted her mom's shoulder. "Wait right here and don't move." She returned a few seconds later with a bottle of body glitter.

"Oh, Kara, I don't know . . ." *But I don't want to disappoint her either!*

"Just a little across your shoulders." Gently Kara rubbed the gel into her mother's skin. "It's the perfect touch. You'll dazzle him for sure now."

Kara carried her mother's bag and set it down at the front door.

"I think I'm set."

"Mama, the phone is for you," Krissy announced. "Should I take a message?"

Samira looked to Phil. *Who in the world?* He indicated that she had time. She walked back to the desk and took the phone from her daughter.

"It's Susan . . ."

Oh no. Not Susan! "Hello?" *I should have had Krissy take a message.*

"Hey, girl," Susan was full of energy on the other end. "Sam and I have this great evening planned for tomorrow night but we need a fourth. A man he's golfing with has invited us to dinner. Sam says he needs a classy date so naturally I thought of you . . ."

" . . . Oh, that's very kind of you, but I have plans." *It feels good to tell Susan I'm busy!* "I'll have to pass this time."

Susan went into recruitment mode immediately. Samira shook her head and rolled her eyes at Pam.

" . . . I'm sorry, Susan," Samira finally interjected. "I really need to go. I have someone at the door . . ." A few more brief exchanges were made before Samira was finally able to hang up the phone.

Krissy was engaged in conversation with Phil when Samira turned around. *Lord only knows what Krissy is telling him.* "I'm sorry."

Phil shrugged his shoulders as if the interruption didn't bother him.

"You're going to have a great time," Krissy announced. The girl turned back to Phil. "So, you'll probably have her home . . ." her voice trailed off in a question.

Phil's eyes sparkled at Krissy's candor. "Whenever she's ready to come home."

I'm so glad he's patient with Krissy.

"Ready?" Phil reached for her bag and opened the door. *He needs to get out of here.* She turned and told her daughters and Pam goodbye. *And so do I!*

"Have a great time, Mama!" Kara handed her mother a small black purse and a folded shawl.

Samira couldn't hide her excitement. She flashed a full smile at her daughters and stepped out the door in front of her date. She walked around the front of Phil's pickup and waited as he opened the door for her to get in. As he reached around to place her bag in the extended cab their eyes met.

Samira swallowed hard. Her back was against the open door and she could feel his presence move somewhere deep within her being. *Am I really going to have him all to myself until I'm ready to come home?*

Phil stood there with his hand on the top corner of the window. "You are a sight to behold, Pretty lady." His eyes looked her up and down. "If we didn't have an audience standing in that front room window and another one sitting on that porch swing across the street, I'd kiss you right now."

Samira smiled and rolled her eyes. *Now I know he's noticed Mrs. Barnes.* When he took a hold of her hand to help her into the truck, her heart skipped another beat. As soon as he closed her door she let all of her air out so she could breathe more steadily.

"Honestly, Samira," Phil said as they started down the street. "You take my breath away." He glanced in her direction when they stopped at a red light. "I don't know if I can focus on business with you along."

Samira looked out the window to hide her blush. Before she could speak, Phil was lifting a cellular phone to his ear. *Did he make a call or did someone call him?*

"J.P. here."

There's that name again. Samira listened. *Obviously someone called him.* She saw him check his watch.

"We'll hit traffic this time of day so I'm just going to head out . . . no, I haven't, I'll stop on the way out of town . . . you're going to have to transfer the file when it comes in then . . ."

I wonder who's on the other end? The tone in his voice had changed dramatically and everything was business now.

" . . . I'll call you as soon as we're settled . . . I know, I don't appreciate this last minute review either . . . can you make changes from this end if need be? . . . alright, I'll go through it as quickly as I can . . . Use the business center . . . Alright, keep me informed . . . I'll call from Springfield."

Phil didn't say goodbye, he just clicked off the phone. "The client I am representing tonight has a way of not providing pertinent information until the very last minute." Phil turned off a main thoroughfare and started into an older neighborhood lined with quaint brick houses. "I need to stop at home and pick up my bag and let the dog out one more time before we leave town."

He's taking me to his house? Samira nodded, not sure how or if she was supposed to respond. *He's obviously tuned into the business at hand.* He turned into an alley, which led to a driveway. He stopped under a carport.

"Let me get the dog out of the way before you come in."

Chase. Samira waited while Phil disappeared into the house. *So this is where he lives.* He returned a few seconds later and led the black Lab around the corner of the house and through a gate. Samira's eyes examined the quaint, brick house with interest. *I expected something bigger.*

Phil opened her door. "Okay, the coast is clear." Samira took his hand as she stepped out of the truck and then followed as Phil led her to the side door.

"I just need to grab a couple of things. Make yourself at home."

Like that is really going to happen. She looked around the dated kitchen. *No dishwasher.* The light pine cupboards with their round stainless steel handles were obviously original to the sixties era of the house. A sports coat hung over the back of a kitchen chair with the plastic cover from the cleaners piled on the table. *It's very quaint.*

She dared to cross the room and peek into the living area which opened into what appeared to be another room. *I wonder what books are on his shelves?* Samira admired the brick fireplace. *A tv and a stereo. Nothing too extravagant.* A matching leather couch and chair were the only pieces of furniture with the exception of a coffee table laden with newspapers and magazines. *Definitely more simplistic than I imagined.*

"Let me check the email one more time then I'll be ready to head out." Phil returned to the kitchen with an overnight bag. "Come on in." He motioned for her to follow him into the other room. "It's nothing fancy but it's a roof over my head."

Samira stepped through the arched doorway into the living room. Windowpane linoleum changed to a low piled carpet. French doors separated the living area from the office. One magazine on the coffee table was a sports journal, but the one next to it was a glamour magazine. *Why would a bachelor have a woman's fashion magazine on his living room table?* Then Samira remembered James. *Maybe that's something teenage boys are into.* She recognized the title. *A bit risqué for my taste.*

As she stood there still not speaking, Phil's hand touched her arm. A shiver went down her spine and she turned to face him. His face was serious.

"This is for you." In his hand was a long stemmed pink rosebud. Samira could smell it even before he handed it to her.

She accepted the gift and put it to her nose. *It's just like the timid little rosebud in my garden!* However, the rose she held in her hand had already begun to open.

"It's beautiful."

"And so are you." Phil was looking into her eyes. "We don't have an audience now . . ."

No, I guess we don't. Without waiting for further permission, Phil kissed her gently on the lips. Samira didn't know how long the kiss lasted, but the next sensation she was aware of was his hand against her bare back right above the satin bow. She allowed him to hold her closer than necessary. The room seemed to spin around her. *He makes me feel so alive!*

When she looked up into his face, she noticed a smudge of lipstick. His skin was smooth and silky under her fingertips when she wiped it away. *I like it when he shaves late in the day.*

Phil chuckled and pulled her in tight against him, hugging her with both arms. As he started to kiss her again, a telephone rang. He hesitated to let her go, but by the third ring he'd stepped around the corner into the kitchen and answered a phone on the wall.

Samira took a deep breath. *It's probably just as well. I don't know if we could have stopped on our own!* She smoothed her skirt as she listened to yet another one-sided conversation.

"Josh, what's up? . . . You guys make it up there alright? . . . Are you worried about Bruce? . . . Where's your mother? . . . No, I don't want to talk to her." Several seconds of silence passed as Phil continued to listen. Samira could see his shoulder blades tense through the back of his dress shirt. "Oh, for christ's sake, put James on the phone." Phil ran his hand through his hair. "Then put your mother on."

Feeling like she was intruding, Samira stepped further into the living room and picked up the *Vanity Fair*. A scantly dressed model graced the cover. *Her smile is bigger than the lingerie she's wearing.* Irritation was evident in Phil's voice when she listened in again.

"You get one phone call this weekend, Jan, and this is it." . . . Samira waited. "It's comforting to know he's been there less than an hour and you're already at odds with him . . . No, you listen. James is up there for two and a half days. You can either pick up where you left off, or you can take the high road and attempt to build some bridges . . . Jan, I'm not finished yet. Just remember, whatever you choose is what you live with for the rest of the weekend because I'm not coming up there to settle any discrepancies."

Several more seconds of silence passed. Samira mindlessly thumbed through the magazine and set it back on the table. *I wish I knew how to help him. He doesn't need any family problems going into a business meeting.*

" . . . listen, I have got to hit the road. I'm already pushing the clock. You're the mother, Jan. If you force the issue right off the bat you face a living hell until James leaves again . . . That's all I have to say about the whole damn thing . . ."

Samira cringed. *This is a side of him I have yet to know.* She sat down on the arm of the big chair and waited until she knew Phil was off the phone. When he didn't come for her right away, she dared to go find him.

Phil was facing the window with his back to the kitchen. His hands were shoved deep into his front pockets.

He must be so torn right now. "I'm sorry." *He seems to be trying hard to make things work with James, but it doesn't sound like it's going so well on the other end.*

Samira waited. Slowly Phil turned and faced her. *His thoughts are so far away.* She waited until she was sure he knew she was there and then crossed the kitchen to where he was standing. *I know he's hurting, but I also know he has a schedule to keep.* "Is there anything I can do?"

The hue of his eyes had darkened considerably. Phil shook his head slowly and looked away. *He is so tense.* Samira slowly moved her hands from his wrists all the way to his shoulders. "You're just going to have to trust everything is going to be alright until you get back." She didn't know enough about James' home situation to offer anything more than that. Samira touched Phil's face with her fingertips. The close shave exaggerated the tension in his jaw.

This time when their eyes met Samira read into the soul of a father. Very slowly Phil embraced her, drawing her whole body into his. *It's different from the way he held me in the living room.* This time Samira could feel passion beyond what words could describe. She put her arms around him and held him until he was ready to let go.

It took a few minutes to break the ice again once they were back inside the truck. Samira watched the scenery change from Joplin's city limits to the open highway.

"That Krissy of yours is quite a talker."

"Krissy has a way of not knowing when it's best to talk and when it's best to be still."

"She's entertaining." Phil was nodding his head. "She tells me you went to school in Springfield."

I wonder what other pertinent information Krissy shared without my permission? "Oh, she did?"

"Undergraduate?"

"And library science."

"SMSU?"

"I started at Drury. Finished at SMSU but I didn't go straight through." She stopped not knowing exactly how much of her history she wanted to share. *I'd have finished a year earlier had I not met Tom.*

"So you know Springfield pretty well then?"

That was a long time ago. "The city has changed a lot since then." *I've changed a lot since then. Everything has changed since then.* She didn't realize how lost she was in her own thoughts until Phil spoke again.

"What's on your mind, Pretty Lady?"

That was the second time he had called her *Pretty Lady*. Several things ran through her mind, but the biggest question was the one she decided to voice.

Here's my opportunity. "I'm curious," Samira grinned at Phil. "Who is J.P.?"

Phil threw his head back with an easy smile. "Fair question." He signaled to pass another car. "Joseph Phillip." Phil looked from the road back to Samira. "My father was Joe. I'm just Phil. My clients know me as J.P."

"Who should I know you as this evening?"

Phil looked over at her with that same easy smile. "You have my permission to know me as anyone you like."

I'm not sure which one of you to know. Another thought crossed Samira's mind and she decided to voice it before she lost her confidence. "You're not exactly easy to find in a phone listing."

Phil raised his eyebrows but didn't look at Samira. "Is that so?"

Samira nodded. "I didn't find any of your names in the directories."

"That's because I'm not in them."

He's purposefully avoiding eye contact now.

"Keeps my life simpler." Now he looked at her. "Unless there's a pretty lady trying to reach me."

Well, at least he admits to having an unlisted number.

Without any further explanation he changed subjects. "So where are your girls staying the weekend?"

The weekend, or the night? We agreed on a night. "They're staying at my brother's house until I get home."

"The brother that is married to the sister-in-law at your house this afternoon?"

Samira picked up the playfulness that first drew her to this man. "That's the one."

She felt his eyes on her face and dared to glance in his direction. The rolled shirt cuffs and loose bow tie brought a comfortable charm to the formal apparel. There was something sexy about a man in a tuxedo—*or at least part of a tuxedo.*

Samira could feel Phil's impatience in the traffic as they approached the city limits. She fingered the five-leaf pattern on the rose.

"Traffic is one reason I don't live in the city."

There was a long pause in conversation as they changed lanes.

Just then an over-anxious driver honked and forced a shiny red sports car between Phil's truck and another car. *Something in the way he set his jaw makes me think Phil kept his thoughts to himself.*

"I hope you aren't disappointed in this evening's affairs, Samira." Phil was shifting into more of a business mode as they approached downtown. "Until I get my hands on my client's documents and get a feel for what I'm up against, I don't really have a clue how much personal time I'm going to have." Phil ran his hand through his hair.

He does that when he's thinking.

"My goal will be to finish with the business as efficiently as possible so . . ."

"You don't have to explain," Samira interrupted. "I know this is a work night for you." She turned the rose between her fingers.

Phil stretched his arm over the back of the seat and touched the back of her neck with his fingertips.

"Well, let me put it this way . . ."

Samira tipped her head slightly to defer a shiver as it crept up her spine. Just the touch of his hand was enough to trigger anticipation.

" . . . I have yet to attend a business meeting that's lasted all night." Phil didn't take his eyes off the road.

There's an expectant invitation if I've ever heard one. Samira studied Phil's profile. *I wonder if I'll ever know Phil without J.P.?* She thought about that for a moment. I think he's more accustomed to being J.P. without having to be Phil.

24

A Line of Questioning

J.P. reread the email from Denise. *There's barely enough time to double check the amendments in the prenuptial agreement before reporting in to Mr. Hughes.* For just a quick moment his eyes wandered from the laptop to the woman patiently waiting in the velvet wingchair. *She seems content.* He forced his eyes back to the computer screen. *Wish I could say the same for me.*

Concentrate, Ralston. J.P.couldn't help it. He glanced in her direction again. The wispy dark curls framed her face perfectly. *I wonder what's in that book that holds her attention so long at a time.*

An abrupt knock against the motel door snapped the attorney back to attention.

"Your printout, Mr. Ralston." A motel employee handed J.P. a document when he opened the door.

"Thank you, Barbara." He tipped the woman with a folded bill then closed the door promptly. When he turned around the woman who had been lost in a book was now studying him carefully. *What?* He returned to his seat at the high counter where a barstool acted as an office chair.

No matter how hard I try, I still can't read her thoughts. J.P. pulled the lengthy document from the file folder. *I'm just going to ask and see where it goes.*

"What's on your mind, Pretty Lady?"

The attorney laid the unneeded sheets aside and dared to look at his date, who was still watching his every move. When their eyes met she looked back toward her book.

The telephone on the wall sounded a double ring. *Mr. Hughes, no doubt.* He could feel Samira's eyes on him once again. *Once I pick up that phone I'm on the Hughes time clock until who knows when.* His eyes met Samira's. *She could be thinking anything.* He picked up the phone.

"Mr. Hughes, J.P. here."

"Very well," Christopher's strong voice sounded into the receiver. "I trust your drive over was uneventful."

With the exception of the event sitting in that chair. J.P. had to turn away from Samira so he could think straight. "It was, thank you." *Get the formalities out of the way.* "And you have outdone yourself with the accommodations, Mr. Hughes." J.P.'s eyes passed over the ornate décor in the main room. He stopped on Samira's quiet presence again.

"Good, good. Do you have a copy of the amended agreement?"

"I'm just to the final review now. It looks good." *I'd still like to take one more look though.*

"You know Mrs. Hughes and I appreciate you doing this for Stephanie on such short notice, J.P. We'll see to it you are well compensated . . ."

The price I pay working on site for Hughes family business is calculated in time. Most generally he could spare the time, but with this particular lady in his room, J.P. was wishing he had less business commitments and more time for personal discovery.

"Hors d'oeuvres and cocktails are being served before dinner . . ."

In other words, he expects me to be there.

"I'll finalize the review and be right down, Mr. Hughes."

The call ended without a formal conclusion. *Unfortunately it's time to make a public appearance.* When he turned to tell Samira it was almost time to go, she was no longer seated in the chair.

He ran his hand through his hair. *I really don't have the time for this final review.* J.P. typed an instant message back to his assistant.

"*Is it good to go?*"

A few moments passed. J.P. could hear water running in the other room.

"*Looks good to me,*" Denise typed back. "*I didn't find any new errors and the changes we made are correctly documented.*"

"*Then I'm rolling with it.*"

"*I'll be at home. Call me if something comes up. ~D*"

The attorney closed the dialogue window and rose from his chair. He started to unroll his cuffs. *I don't know what fragrance she's wearing but it's enticing.* She was now standing only a short distance from the counter.

"You didn't answer my question, Pretty Lady." J.P. grinned as he pulled his tuxedo jacket over his shoulders.

Samira didn't blink and her expression was more serious than J.P. preferred. *The last woman I brought to a Hughes engagement ended up spending the evening at the bar. I picked her up after dinner.* He fastened his cuffs. *But I don't want this one out of my sight.*

She's still thinking something. J.P. raised his eyebrows and waited for the response she seemed to be weighing in her mind.

Samira put her elbows on the back of the high-backed stool. "How did you know the attendant's name at the door?"

J.P. smiled. *That wasn't even close to what I thought might be on her mind.*

" . . . Do you know her?"

"No, I don't." He straightened his jacket and clicked the mouse to disconnect the server.

"Do you know the concierge?"

"No."

"Then how did you call them both by name?"

I think I'll keep her guessing. "Maybe that's for me to know and you to wonder about." J.P. taunted with a twinkle in his eye.

Samira crossed her arms over the black satin evening gown. "And how did you know who was going to be on the other end of that phone call?"

That one I can answer. J.P. placed the revised agreement back in the file folder and laid it carefully in his briefcase.

"Because, Pretty Lady, I knew Mr. Hughes would call as soon as he was aware of my arrival."

Samira's eyes indicated a hint of understanding.

"Anything else?"

Her look was still serious. "You still haven't answered my first two questions, Mr. Ralston."

She'd be good in litigation. "Mr. Ralston?" *Sounds mighty formal if you ask me.* He closed the lid on his briefcase and secured the latches.

"They all seem to know your name."

"So they do." J.P. thought for a moment. "But you don't have to use that name."

"You said I could know you by any name I wanted."

"So I did." *Damn, she's quick.*

"So the hotel employees call you by name, yet you don't know them?"

Maybe I should share my secret so as to not piss her off. The attorney grinned through his response, "Only by their name badges."

Samira's mouth curled into a slight smile.

"Satisfied?"

"Not yet."

Me neither, Pretty Lady. That part is yet to come. "Well, the Hughes party is beginning and I believe it's time that we make an appearance." He opened the room door and waited for Samira. She took her time crossing the threshold. *The end of the Hughes business won't come any too early tonight.*

Samira hesitated slightly at the doors of the glass elevators. J.P. wondered if she didn't like the motion.

"No, it's not the motion . . ."

I don't dare take a hold of her yet. Samira's slight figure was held tight by the satin dress. *But I would like to read her mind.*

" . . . I'm curious about this elevator." Samira turned slightly and looked down at extravagant lobby. J.P. followed her eyes. "Why are there only four floor options when there are at least twelve or fourteen floors in the complex?"

I've had other woman in this same elevator and not one of them has ever paid attention to that detail.

The carriage stopped but the doors didn't open. J.P. realized Samira was holding the door closed with the button on the control panel. *Oh, that's very funny.* J.P. reached for the hand holding the button.

Samira stopped him with her free hand. "Not until you answer my question."

So that's how she's going to play the game. "Which question do you want me to answer first?"

Samira raised a single eyebrow. "As long as you answer with something other than another question, you may have your pick."

There wasn't a doubt in J.P.'s mind that he would be held captive until he answered. He wanted to kiss her. *But I know better.* "The Hughes family has exclusive rights to seven suites in this complex . . . ."

He started to reach for her hand again.

Samira stopped him again. "But that doesn't tell me why I can only choose one of four floors."

I wasn't finished yet but I thought the people waiting outside the elevator might be getting impatient. J.P. held her eyes. *Or is she holding mine?*

Samira smiled as she continued to wait.

She knows she has me in a corner now. "Okay . . ." J.P. had to laugh. "All seven suites are located on the seventh floor." He watched Samira glance at the open balconies to the seventh level. "This elevator has access to the ground floor where we are now, the conference rooms on the second floor, and to the executive's club on the top level."

Very gently J.P. removed her hand from the elevator button and guided her steps with his hand on her waist. The people who were waiting to use the elevator were impatiently looking Samira and J.P. up and down.

"You sure know how to draw a crowd."

"I wouldn't have to stall if you would answer more directly." Samira's voice was playful.

J.P. laughed out loud. *She does keep me guessing.*

"I'm serious." Samira had a playful glint in her eye.

"Good evening, Mr. Ralston." A young man working a counter next to the elevator greeted the attorney.

J.P. nodded in acknowledgement.

Samira's eyes came back to his. "You're not wearing a nametag."

"Anything else you would like to ask before we go down to the ballroom?" J.P. folded his hands over the handle on his briefcase and waited patiently for a response. *I'd rather get the line of questioning out of the way before we meet the Hughes family.*

Samira didn't back down. "So how do they all know your name?"

J.P. leaned in close to Samira's ear and lowered his voice. "Because, Pretty Lady, when I'm under the employ of the Hughes brothers everybody knows who I am." He straightened his back and looked into Samira's now smiling eyes.

This is entertaining, to say the least. "Anything else?"

"No, Mr. Ralston," the chocolate brown eyes were dancing with a new energy now. "I think I'm just beginning to understand."

The space that separated the couple was less than an arm's distance, but to J.P. Ralston it could have been a mile. *Beginning to understand what?*

Tuxedo-clad men escorting high-society women graced the corridor. J.P. slowed his step when Samira's eyes came to a stop on a painting in the hallway.

"What do you see?" *I've been down this hallway before and never even noticed the artwork.*

"It's by Phillipe De Champaigne." Samira was carefully studying the canvas. "I've never known his oils to be in the public domain like this."

J.P. also studied the painting. "Nor have I." *But she sure uses a nice accent when she says that name.* He suddenly wished he knew exactly who De Champaigne was so he could converse knowledgably.

Without further reference to the artist, Samira turned her attention to other paintings. J.P. walked beside her as they made their way slowly to the next display. *What is going on in that beautiful mind of hers?*

"Mr. Ralston, Sir . . ."

J.P. turned to face the voice. Several couples in ceremonial formals were making their way to the ballroom but none seemed to be looking for anyone in particular.

A hotel employee suddenly appeared at his side. Slightly out of breath the young man in uniform extended a linen envelope toward the attorney's hand.

"J.P. Ralston?"

I have no idea what this is. The attorney nodded a silent identification. "This is for you."

J.P. took the envelope expecting the messenger to disappear. Instead the employee stood at attention as if he were waiting for an immediate reply.

J.P. turned the envelope in his hand. His name was scrawled across the front in a woman's handwriting. *Definitely not correspondence from the Hughes family.* Curious, he started to open a folded note, but a loose object fell into his hand. J.P. turned it over and read silently. *Admit One. Private Viewing. Runway Seating. Table Ten. Saturday June 18th, 8 PM.* The handwritten message simply read: *I'm free after the show. 516.*

Bobbie Jo Sommers. J.P.'s heart skipped a beat under his tuxedo shirt. *June 18th is tomorrow.* Instinct told him to turn around and scan the lobby, but experience told him to put the note back inside the envelope and show no immediate reaction.

"Is something the matter?" Samira's soft voice was sincere as she touched his arm.

The last thing I need this weekend is a skeleton jumping out of my closet. J.P. folded the note around the ticket and stashed the entire envelope in his interior jacket pocket. Guests were beginning to form a line at the entrance to the ballroom. *I know she's probably watching me.* The hotel employee was still there. *Waiting for a response he's not going to get.*

J.P. looked the employee directly in the eye. "There is no reply at this time." The young man nodded before disappearing into the crowd.

J.P.'s heart was in his throat. He knew he was being watched and most likely being watched very carefully.

Samira's eyes showed signs of concern. J.P. remembered her question.

"No everything is fine . . ." *Not.* He glanced down the hall that led away from the ballroom in the opposite direction. " . . . But I do need to make a quick call before meeting my client." J.P. reached for his phone and flipped it open. He pressed an auto dial button and waited for the phone to ring. *Pick up the phone, Denise.* Needing to distance himself from his date, J.P. put a finger in his other ear. Samira took the hint and stepped away. J.P. widened the distance with a few more steps in the other direction. *Now I have two women watching me!*

"Hey boss, what's up?"

"More than I'd bargained for . . ." *God, I hope she knows something.*

Denise interrupted. "The agreement is in complete order. All you should have to do is make sure the proper people sign on the proper lines . . ."

"I know," J.P. stopped the review. "I know that." *Of all times for Bobbie Jo to show up.* "I need to know if I had any messages from Bobbie Sommers today."

"Bobbie Sommers? No. Why?"

J.P. turned in a half circle and dared to scan the lobby area. "Because she's in this building." When he turned back he caught sight of Samira several yards down the corridor studying another painting. Her quiet presence summoned guilty conscience deeper than anything he had felt in recent history. "Can you reach her to tell her I'm working this weekend? All weekend!"

"All I can do is leave a voice mail. She never picks up. Should I do that?"

The pit in J.P.'s stomach was getting bigger by the moment. *A good stiff drink wouldn't hurt anything at the moment.* "Do something." He glanced back toward Samira. "The last thing I need is her on my tail this weekend." *Shit. What am I saying? She's already on my tail.*

"Obviously your mystery date accepted."

Not now, Denise.

"I'll do what I can but after that you're on your own. Anything else?"

That's all I can ask. Samira was making her way toward him now. As she walked her body seemed to glide along the carpet.

J.P. ran his hand over his breast pocket to be sure the incriminating envelope was tucked deep within. "It's better than nothing." He disconnected the call without saying goodbye.

The evening ahead was suddenly looking far more complicated than he'd anticipated. *Just conducting business with this Pretty Lady by my side is enough.* But now the S-N-S-A escort was lurking around a corner.

Samira smiled slightly sending chills all the way up J.P.'s spine. *Just get her in the ballroom.* He ran his hand through his hair and took a long, deep breath. When he offered his arm, Samira accepted. They fell into step behind the others waiting in line for the engagement party. *Why would Bobbie Jo Sommers be in Springfield?*

"There are two by Phillipe De Champaigne," Samira noted out loud.

Two what? J.P. turned his head and glanced at the sophisticated woman who had her hand loosely around his sleeve. *Oh, paintings.* "Really?" *I had no idea.*

Samira's dark eyes caught his. "Really."

She knows I have no idea what she's talking about.

"Oh, J.P.!" Mrs. Christopher Hughes was suddenly wrapping her ring-clad hands around his neck. "It's bloody good of you to be here!" she hugged the attorney without permission.

J.P. breathed a welcome sigh of relief as he prepared to introduce his date to Elizabeth Hughes.

25

Prom Night

Samira could feel Phil's hand against the small of her back. *It makes me feel like I belong with him when he touches me like this.* He addressed the woman inside the door by name. *Mrs. Hughes is definitely a woman of high society. Sequined gown, diamond earrings and choker.* Samira felt plain and simple in comparison.

"J.P., Christopher was so pleased you could squeeze us in," Mrs. Hughes gushed through a British accent. She continued to talk as she again hugged Phil loosely around the neck. "You will be at Stephanie's wedding won't you?"

A wedding?

J.P. accepted the ceremonial embrace. "You're looking more beautiful all the time, Mrs. Hughes."

He avoids her questions too. J.P.'s hand was once again against Samira's back.

"I'd like to introduce Samira Cartwright."

Mrs. Hughes opened her eyes wide. "My, my, J.P." Her deep red lips parted into a broad smile as she reached for Samira's hand. "Ms Cartwright, we are very pleased to have you joining us this evening." The woman waved at someone behind Samira and then turned her attention back. "Do help yourself to the bar and mingle, do mingle. Lots of people to meet." With more seriousness she looked at the attorney. "Christopher will be most delighted to see you."

Samira felt Phil's hand touch her own. *I'll gladly take his hand.* She smiled and nodded to Mrs. Hughes. "I'm honored to meet you."

Samira was relieved when J.P. excused himself. "Exactly what does the 'my, my' refer to?"

Phil rolled his eyes. "What does anything she says mean?" He seemed uninterested in Mrs. Hughes' disposition. "Elizabeth Hughes is . . . well, let's just call it eccentric. You'll see by the end of the night."

She does have a way with words. Phil was zig-zagging around linen wrapped tables. *He must have spotted Mr. Hughes.* A server carrying an empty tray stopped in front of them.

"May I bring you something to drink, Mr. Ralston?"

Even the waitress knows his name! When her eyes connected with his she realized she was supposed to order a cocktail.

I don't know protocol.

"Two club sodas on the rocks." J.P. answered for both of them.

Thank you. Samira smiled at the server. *I wonder if Phil ever drinks while he's working.*

As they approached a large gathering of people, Phil moved his hand to gently guide her by the waist. *I like the way he takes care of me.*

"Christopher Hughes is standing on the far side of that circle." Phil was speaking quietly as he moved her toward a group of tuxedoed executives. "He's talking to his brother, Jefferey. The man on his right is the company's Chief Financial Officer."

Samira's eyes studied the businessmen with care. *Evidently the other three men are not pertinent.* When the elder Hughes spotted J.P. he nodded and immediately excused himself from the men.

"J.P." Mr. Hughes called with an outstretched hand. "J.P., I appreciate your efforts to be here." Right away his sparkling brown eyes stopped on Samira. "And it appears you've outdone yourself tonight, Counselor."

With gentle pressure against the small of her back, Phil moved Samira a step closer to the executive. "Mr. Hughes, Samira Cartwright."

Samira extended her right hand expecting to shake but the balding man raised it to his lips instead. "Welcome, welcome." He released her hand. "Have you met Elizabeth?"

Well, that is most flattering. "Yes, a few moments ago."

"Very fine," the man assured. "We'll be dining together a little later." He motioned with his hand. "J.P., if I might have a few words . . ."

Samira felt a sudden urge to dismiss herself from the pending conversation. She moved with Phil to the edge of the room. His hand was still against her back when she leaned to speak into his ear.

"I'm going to step aside." *I don't think I belong in this conversation.*

Phil started to shake his head. "I'll be back." Samira excused herself politely. *Something tells me Phil doesn't want me wandering too far off.*

The private ballroom was even more elegant than the lobby of the hotel. Samira marveled at the artwork and décor. *Krissy was right about this being my prom.* Samira's eyes took in the extravagant attire of the guests. *And this is much more entertaining than spending my anniversary night alone with a book.* Diamonds and rubies accented women's hands and earlobes and glitzy dresses shimmered in the indirect lighting.

"Your drink, ma'am." The waitress appeared out of nowhere.

"Oh, thank you." *I can't believe she found me amongst all these people.* The girl handed her a stemmed glass. *And without Phil.* Her eyes went immediately back across the room where her date raised his glass in her direction. *Obviously he's still keeping an eye on me.*

The soda was refreshing. Samira wound her way to the self-serve buffet and picked up a china plate. *It's been a very long time since lunch.* She selected a few slices of cheese.

Across the table, another woman was filling a plate full of appetizers. Her hair was piled high on top of her head and her gloved hands displayed large diamond rings on the outside of the gloves. *Now that is an interesting way to wear your jewelry.* When the woman looked up, Samira expected an older face than the one that met her.

"Are you here for the bride or the groom?" The woman spoke with a foreign accent.

Oh! Am I supposed to have a role here? "The bride, I guess." *But honestly? Neither.*

"Beautiful girl," the lady said as she continued to fill a plate. "She's marrying a duke, you know. I hear they will settle in Wales."

Maybe it's best not to say anything than to try to carry on a conversation about something I know nothing about.

"It's a bloody shame the last one didn't work out, it is. Stephanie could have lived a life of pure luxury had she married the ambassador. Oh, what was his name?" The woman looked to the ceiling as if something up there might trigger the memory. "Shit. I can't remember his name."

Oh my! I didn't expect that!

The woman continued to heap food on the little plate. "I can't remember, but you know who he was, the old ambassador from France. He wanted her for show. Stephanie should have done it. He would have given her whatever she wanted." Without further conversation, the woman noticed someone more familiar on the other side of the serving table and immediately engaged in a new conversation.

Samira realized she was still staring at the gloved woman and quickly turned away. She wasn't sure what was more astonishing—the woman's sudden use of profanity in the middle of an otherwise straight conversation, or her initiation of family gossip at the serving table. *Definitely more entertaining than I'd imagined.* She added a few crackers to her plate and stepped away from the table. Orchestra members were tuning their instruments near the dance floor. She was still thinking about the young woman when she felt a familiar hand against her bareback.

"Hey, Pretty Lady. You didn't have to leave." Phil helped himself to a piece of cheese on the edge of her plate. "You should have stayed. I don't think you should be mingling around by yourself."

"Well, Mr. Ralston, I'm perfectly comfortable alone in a crowd." She offered him another piece of cheese. *I've spent half of my life alone in a crowd.* Phil took a hold of her wrist and guided the cheese to his mouth. Samira laughed as he took a bite from her fingertips.

"Next time I'll let you know if you need to step aside. Otherwise, stick with me."

I appreciate his concern, but I'm more comfortable mulling around in a crowd alone than I am engaging in a conversation that doesn't pertain to me.

Samira noticed Mrs. Hughes rearranging the name cards at the head table. She removed two cards from the table altogether and handed them to a hotel employee, using her hands to make her instructions clear. *Obviously the woman knows what she wants and isn't afraid to make it happen.*

"Do you know everyone at this table?" Samira asked as they gathered to be seated for dinner.

She watched as Phil's eyes scanned each face standing in the vicinity.

"Not one," he answered with a matter of fact. Then he grinned at Samira. "With the exception of you and the Hughes."

Mrs. Hughes was reaching toward them as she made her way around the table toward Samira and Phil. "J.P.," she addressed as she walked. "Do sit over here. I've seated you next to Christopher." The woman ran her hand over the back of a draped chair. With a brilliant smile she turned to Samira. "And you, my dear," She touched Samira's shoulders lightly. "You will sit next to me."

Oh please don't separate me from Phil! Phil immediately took her hand. She forced a smile for the hostess.

"Right here, Ms Cartwright . . ."

Mrs. Hughes touched the chair next to the one she had indicated for Phil. *Oh good.* Samira realized what had happened. *Interesting. Mr. And Mrs. Hughes have us sandwiched between them.*

Elizabeth started to step away then whispered into Samira's ear, " . . . it is a pity he hasn't put a ring on your finger." She smiled and stepped away as if she hadn't said a word.

Eccentric may be an understatement.

Phil pulled out the chair for Samira to take her assigned seat as a server appeared and placed a lettered name card next to her plate. Ms Cartwright it read. *Impressive. Mrs. Hughes must have taken care of that detail a few moments ago.* She caught sight of the hostess a few tables over hugging yet another guest.

Tête-à-tête flowed easily among the dinner guests at the head table. It turned out most of those sitting with the Hughes were members of the perspective groom's family. *That must be the bride and groom over there.* It seemed odd they were sitting alone without their families. She glanced around the room full of strangers. *There is much I don't understand about this event.*

At her own table, Samira listened to chatter about the wedding plans, the stock market, and the unpredictable weather in Wales. Mrs. Hughes' comment concerning a ring on her finger was still fresh in her mind as she allowed her own thoughts to crowd out the table conversation.

"How are you doing?" Phil asked when there was a break in business discussion

"Very well, thank you." When her eyes met his, she realized how serious he was. "Honest." she added. *I'm just here as an observer, and a very patient one at that.* She gently touched his leg under the table for assurance.

Samira watched as Phil passed his fork from his right hand to his left. *So is he right handed or left handed?* Samira vowed to pay closer attention.

A trumpet fanfare announced the honored couple as the final dinner dishes were cleared by the wait staff. The entire room full of guests rose from their chairs. Phil helped Samira with her chair. *I wonder what happens next?*

Christopher Hughes motioned for Phil to follow him.

Wait. Where are they going?

"I'll be back."

Obviously all business now. Samira followed Phil with her eyes. He stepped onto a platform with Mr. Hughes. *I wonder what he has to do up there?* Samira felt deserted.

"It was so good of J.P. to come tonight, Ms Cartwright."

I wonder if Mrs. Hughes senses that I'm a little uneasy.

"Our family attorney stayed behind in England so J.P. will notarize the agreement."

She's explaining on my behalf. Samira turned her attention back to the stage. *I appreciate that.*

Mr. Christopher Hughes spoke into the microphone. "It is with a great deal of pride that I introduce to you my daughter, Stephanie Elizabeth Hughes, and her betrothed, Sir William Bradford Coddingham, the fourth."

The fourth? Thunderous applause filled the large ballroom and for the first time Samira got a good view of the bride to be. *Very petite and much younger than I'd imagined.* Dressed less extravagantly than her mother, Samira guessed Stephanie to be more reflective of her father's character. The groom was slightly older than the bride. *I wonder if this marriage is arranged? Or are they actually in love.* From what she could tell there was no outward sign of affection between them. *But then again, how do you show affection in front of such a crowd?*

"Please do be seated," Mr. Hughes suggested to the assembly. As he continued to offer words of praise to his daughter, Mrs. Hughes turned back to Samira.

"I was thinking about tomorrow evening," the woman whispered loudly over her husband's speech. As if just having a revelation, the woman scanned the room and quickly flagged a server.

I'd think she might want to hear what her husband was saying!

Mrs. Hughes whispered something in the waiter's ear then settled back into her chair. "Just sit tight a moment."

As if I had anywhere to go. The father of the groom was now speaking. His wife, who was sitting next to Mrs. Hughes, appeared to be attentive to the speech. Samira watched as the two fathers shook hands and then took turns signing an agreement that was placed before them on the podium. J.P. Ralston and another man signed the agreement. *The bride and groom look like statues on a cake.* Samira felt a tinge of sadness for the couple. *It's like they don't have any say for themselves in this matter.*

Without warning, the trumpet fanfare cut loose again. Samira jumped. She put her hand to her chest to steady her nerves. Four trumpeters were obviously playing according to cue. Behind them, seated on the far side of the dance floor, a chamber orchestra was preparing to play. *Everything is formally orchestrated.*

"About tomorrow . . ." Mrs. Hughes patted her hand against the table.

What about tomorrow? Samira turned her attention back to Mrs. Hughes. *I like her accent.*

" . . . The Springfield Symphony is performing Copeland's Fanfare in its entirety in the auditorium." Mrs. Hughes picked up the conversation just like there had not been a break in thought. "I was thinking, if you were still in town, J.P. should escort you." Mrs. Hughes' eyes lit up with enthusiasm. "Now I know J.P. might prefer to find other entertainment, but it wouldn't hurt him, wouldn't hurt him a bloody bit, to sit in on the orchestra." With that she placed two tickets to the symphony in front of Samira. "Give these to him and see what he says."

Tomorrow night? I don't think we'll still be in town.

"Do you know the Fanfare?"

"The Fanfare for the Common Man?" *I assume.*

"I knew it," the woman exclaimed as she started to rise. "You are a gem, Ms Cartwright. Do talk to J.P. about the concert." She put the tickets directly in Samira's hand. "Now keep these close. If you don't use them, it's no loss. But we'll all be sitting together in the box. The ushers will know from the tickets."

"J.P.," Mrs. Hughes announced Phil's return to the table. "You need to step it up for this pretty lady." She patted the attorney on the arm then turned and addressed another guest.

Before Samira could speak, Christopher Hughes was at their side. "Thank you, kindly, J.P. I trust you'll take care of the agreement until morning."

"It will be in the hotel safe, Mr. Hughes."

"Very well, then we'll see you first thing tomorrow. I'll be interested to learn more about Bridges' property. He's sending a representative with a diagram. Jefferey will be most interested as well."

It sounds as if Phil might have an appointment yet tomorrow. I wonder if he knew that.

Mr. Hughes took Samira's hand. "And you have been most gracious to share the counselor with us this evening, Ms Cartwright."

And maybe again in the morning? She smiled and acknowledged the host as he kissed her hand again.

"Now, don't stay up too late," Mr. Hughes advised with a twinkle in his eye. "First thing tomorrow in my conference room."

He has his own conference room?

"Yes sir, Mr. Hughes."

Phil doesn't seem any too pleased to have another commitment. Samira studied his face while he wasn't looking at her.

The orchestra had started to play while Mr. Hughes was talking. Samira mentally tuned into the Mozart minuet. She assumed from the conversation with Mrs. Hughes that her date would not be interested in the orchestra. *But it would be fun to step onto the dance floor.*

This time when a waitress stopped to take a drink order, Phil ordered a JD and Coke.

He must be off duty. He looked to Samira for a request.

"I'm fine." *Although a cup of coffee would be nice.*

"Wine? Champagne?"

Samira shook her head with a quiet smile. *My last experience with a glass of wine left me fuzzy in the head!*

"Bring the lady a cup of coffee." Phil gave the instruction with authority.

Samira touched her hand to her heart. *How did he know to do that?* The Mozart melody was still playing in the background. *That was very sweet of him.* She took a step closer as Phil slipped his hand around her waistline.

"Would you be so kind to honor me with a dance?"

I thought he might not ask. Samira allowed him to guide her through the tables and clusters of people to the edge of the dance floor. Every pore of her being came alive as Phil took her right hand in his left. As she looked up into his face she was suddenly aware how much taller Phil was than Tom. *It used to make Tom uncomfortable when I wore these shoes.* She relaxed into her date's embrace. *I stood exactly even with Tom in these heels.*

Every time Samira glanced away, Phil's eyes remained on hers. *This just might be my prom.*

The first number ended, but Phil didn't move toward the edge of the dance floor. Instead he stood still, holding her slightly closer than necessary. His eyes were only focused on her.

He's so intense.

"Where'd you learn to dance?"

Samira could feel his body against hers. "My father." *Who doesn't even know I'm here.* The fleeting thought caught her off guard. "And you?"

"You're a good lead."

I know better than that. Phil's steps came naturally with a gentle authority. *He does know how to flatter me.*

Samira stood in front of the mirror over the bathroom sink. She loosened the comb the girls had placed so carefully in her hair. Shaking her head slightly, the hold released, dropping her dark hair over her shoulders.

Phil stepped into the reflection behind her and placed a glass of wine on the counter. *He is not my husband, but he is the one I want to be with tonight.* Ever so gently Phil ran his hand across the front of the fitted satin dress. Passionate signals radiated all the way through Samira's being. *I hope he doesn't notice how hard my heart is beating!* She continued to remove her jewelry in spite of his seductive attention.

He took a sip from his own wine glass. The bowtie was long gone and his pleated shirt was unbuttoned to the waist with the sleeves rolled twice. *Just like they were earlier in the day.* As she reached for the second earring, Phil's lips followed her hands. He kissed her gently behind the ear. *I love the way he draws me in.*

"I'm assuming you're officially off duty now."

"I was off duty the moment Hughes indicated a morning meeting." He kissed her on the neck again.

Samira tipped her head, enjoying his playfulness in spite of her nervous anticipation. "What time in the morning?"

"Nine."

"At least you were right about the meeting not going all night." *Maybe one sip of the wine won't hurt anything.*

"That leaves all night for our own business." Phil reached around and set his glass where hers had been. Without asking for permission he slowly unzipped the dress.

No, the wine isn't going to hurt a thing! Samira took another sip. "But Mr. Hughes said not to stay up too late."

Phil's blue eyes met hers in the mirror. "What I choose to do on my own time is none of Hughes' business." Although he made eye contact, the look was suddenly firm.

Now there's a lesson to be learned. Samira logged the moment into her mind. *Once he's off duty, there's no reason to bring up business until he does again.* She set her wine glass down on the counter. *But I'm almost positive I can lure him back.* Samira turned toward her date and initiated a kiss that lingered longer than she expected.

There is nothing I want more than to ease his tension and make him forget his worries. For the first time Samira realized she wanted to give him more than an evening affair. *I want to give him something so lasting nothing can compare.*

"Tell you what . . ." Samira spoke softly into his ear. "If you'll be so kind as to find a light for those candles . . ." she pointed through the doorway into the sitting room. " . . . I'll run a hot bath in that big tub." She watched as Phil's eyes looked over her shoulder into the luxurious bathroom.

Hughes' business is finished for the night.

26

Blurring the Lines

Sunlight was illuminating every corner of the hotel bedroom when J.P. opened his eyes. *Who opened the curtains?* It took a moment to recall his locale, but didn't take any time at all to remember the woman with whom he had spent the night.

J.P. rolled over under the covers and found Samira sitting next to him against a pile of pillows. A book was open against her bare thighs. *She's totally oblivious to everything except whatever is holding her attention in that book.* J.P. was slightly humored by the way she could totally escape reality without going anywhere.

When her eyes wandered from the book to his face he grinned.

"How long have you been awake?"

J.P. touched her arm with the back of his finger. "How long have you been in that book?"

Samira rested her head against the ornate headboard. "Do you always answer a question with a question?"

What kind of a question is that? He wiggled his eyebrows and lifted the cover of the book from her lap. "What's so intriguing that it pulls you in so deep?"

"You did it again."

Did what?

"*I Know this much is True.* It's for the literary club review. From Oprah's list." Samira ran her hand over the hardback. "Do you know it?"

You know how much is true? "Are you an Oprah fan?"

"There you go again, answering a question with a question." Samira closed her finger on a page. Her dark brown eyes were deep in thought.

She's not going to let me off the hook until I answer. "No, I can't say I'm familiar with that one." He put his arm under his head. "Read it to me."

The woman smiled slightly. "I doubt if you'd like it."

How does she know if I'd like it or not? He chuckled. "Too deep for me?"

"It's very complex."

Does that mean I'm too shallow to follow the storyline?

Samira dropped a bookmark in the page and unfolded her legs. "Are you hungry?"

Not for breakfast. "What time is it?" When she didn't answer he looked up. Samira's head was cocked at an accusing angle. *Ah. I answered her question with a question.* "No, not yet." *She's paying attention.*

"A little after eight." Samira set her book aside. "There are pastries on the counter when you're ready to eat."

J.P. sat up on the edge of the bed. *There weren't any pastries in the room last night.* "Where'd they come from?"

"Downstairs . . ." Samira crossed the room. She was wearing a long nightshirt and her hair looked damp from a shower.

Now there's one inviting woman.

" . . . From the continental breakfast bar."

"You went down there by yourself?"

Samira stopped in the doorway and turned around. "Of course by myself."

Her coy smile gave J.P. the chills. *She's bold.* "Wearing that?"

"That's for me to know and you to wonder about." She turned and stepped out of sight.

J.P. laughed. *Touché. She doesn't miss a beat.*

Following a quick shower, J.P. found Samira sitting on a bar stool with a steaming cup of coffee. Once again she was immersed in her book. *I don't think I've ever opened all the curtains in a hotel room.*

"How late were you going to let me sleep?"

Samira looked up from the book and tipped her head. "I was going to finish the chapter and then wake you."

So exactly how long would that have been? He watched her mark the page again and stand up. *I could skip the meeting and lay back down next to her for a while.* J.P. stopped her from going into the kitchen. He wanted to tell her how incredible she had been the night before. *She has a way of taking my words away.* Instead of speaking, he ran his fingers through her damp hair and kissed her. Samira responded without hesitation. *Everything about her is inspiring.* Instinctively one of his hands dropped over her hip as the other moved up her side.

Without warning, Samira removed his hand from her shirt. J.P. held her close in spite of her sudden resistance. *Whoa, Pretty Lady, we've been here on the morning after and this time I'm not going to let you walk away.*

"I don't want to make you late." She was gently resisting his embrace.

Mr. Hughes would have to understand. He tried to kiss her again but, this time she wasn't as receptive. "Wouldn't be the first time."

That was all it took. Samira put her palms against his bare chest and pushed away.

What in the . . . ? "That's not what I meant, Samira. I meant I've been late before, not that you made me late . . ."

"Mr. Hughes said nine o'clock. He's expecting you." She tucked her hair behind an ear.

Screw Christopher Hughes. There was no indication of a morning agenda when I agreed to a Friday night business engagement. J.P. ran his hand through his hair. *Now she's on edge.*

J.P. returned to the bedroom to finish dressing. *I'm known for calling my own shots. In fact, Miss Samira Cartwright, I like showing up at the last possible minute to avoid idle conversation.* But that wasn't the way the statement had sounded. *She's holding me to a schedule I never agreed to.*

J.P. picked up a roll on his way out the door. *Since she went to the trouble of bringing breakfast.* "I'll be in the Hughes conference room on the second floor." The tension from the moment before was still evident. *Hope it dissipates before I get back.* "With any luck this won't last more than an hour." Samira was now curled into the corner of the oversized sofa. *She's the most tempting woman I've ever known.* J.P. studied her carefully. *And the most unpredictable too.*

"I'll be here when you get back."

I'm counting on that. He started to leave and realized she might want the room key. *Hell she's already used it once this morning.* "I'll have to call you to come back up." *There's a first, Ralston. Calling my own room to get back in.* J.P. gathered his files and briefcase off the makeshift desk at the kitchen bar.

"I don't have any plans to leave the room." Samira's voice was quiet. "All the entertainment I need is right here." She lifted the book slightly.

That's amazing in and of itself. J.P. appreciated her offer. *But I think I'll leave it anyway.* He tapped the key card on the countertop. "I'll just ring the room when the meeting is over."

Samira nodded.

Why am I so hesitant to leave her here? J.P. took one last look at her before he closed the door. *Although I don't get the feeling she's going to miss me much.*

He pulled the door closed with weighted regret. Everything about last night had been so perfect, more fulfilling than he could have imagined. *She's gorgeous and simple and intelligent.* He pushed the elevator call button. *No, take back the simple part.* J.P. rubbed his eyes with his thumb and middle finger in thought. *Complex. She's definitely complex.* He stepped into the glass carriage and leaned against the golden handrail. *And she scares the shit out of me.*

Christopher Hughes met J.P. as the elevator door opened. The attorney took a deep breath and forced his mind to shift gears.

"Good morning, chap." Mr. Hughes clasped his hand with a business handshake. "Sean Bridges sent his assistant. She's inside with Jefferey. Help yourself to some coffee and I'll be right in."

I'd prefer to meet with Bridges in person. J.P. continued to listen, but his mind went immediately back to the woman in his room. *She drives me crazy.*

He opened the conference door and found Jefferey Hughes leaning over a table-sized diagram. The woman standing on the far side of the table was quite young. It took only a moment for J.P. to realize the hem of her skirt was just below table height. *I wonder what kind of impression Bridges is trying to make on the Hughes Corporation?*

The woman crossed the room with an outstretched hand. *I seriously doubt if she's wearing much under that double breasted jacket.*

"Jessica Hutchison." Her green eyes accentuated her dark complexion. Her short dark hair was stylish and thick. *Not bad for a real estate assistant.*

"J.P. Ralston." He returned the handshake and set his briefcase on the table. The woman followed him to where Jefferey was standing.

"This is the property the Hughes Corporation is considering."

I can see that. J.P. put on his reading glasses and scanned the enlarged plat map. He walked all the way around the table trying to get a feel for the lay of the land. *If this is the same property I'm thinking it is, the view is skewed.*

"Ms Hutchison, where is the airport in relation to this property?"

Christopher Hughes joined them at the table with a steaming cup of coffee.

Miss Hutchison walked around the table and then leaned over the top of the map. *I was right. Not much on under that jacket.* Her bright red fingernails clicked against the tabletop as she pointed to the top right hand corner.

"The airport is here." She tapped her nails against the map again. "The proposed commercial development site is just west of there."

J.P. chose to ignore the busty cleavage hanging over the map. *I beg to differ.* He walked around the map again and then turned. *She's either misinformed or she's trying to mislead my clients.* "North is here." *I know that for sure.* He put his finger on the top right hand corner. "That puts the airport over here." He rested his other finger on the exact opposite corner and looked to Miss Hutchison. *Let's see where she goes with this.*

When she finally spoke she was slightly flustered. "If you look at it this way . . . ." She tried to turn the map back the way she had it on the table, but J.P. held it down.

"It's better if we view it true to direction." Without further delay he gave an overview of the entire area on his clients' behalf. *The city is looking at this same piece of property for airport expansion.* The more he looked, the more discrepancies he noticed. *I'm not convinced this map gives accurate dimensions either.* Denise had briefed him otherwise. *And I trust Denise over this Miss Hutchison.*

"Mr. Hughes," J.P. addressed Christopher but was well aware that Jefferey was also attentive. "I'd advise we take a look at this property from another diagram before moving forward." *Let's look at the map provided by city hall.*

Christopher crossed his arms and stroked his chin in thought. "Jefferey?"

"I agree. I'd like to fly over and take a look from the air."

"Very well," Christopher stated. "We appreciate your time this morning, Miss Hutchison, but we won't be needing your assistance any longer." Christopher shook her hand. "Tell Mr. Bridges we will be in touch."

On another occasion, I might be inclined to follow up with an assistant like this. J.P. watched her turn away slightly irritated. *But this morning I have other interests.* Without asking permission, he began to roll the diagram.

"I'll be glad to do that for you . . ." There was a bite in her tone.

J.P. released the document into Ms Hutchison's hands. *A little touchy this morning.* He set the canister on the tabletop to hurry her along. *Seems to be going around.*

Once Miss Hutchison was on her way, Christopher and Jefferey Hughes were ready to work on their father's estate. *I wish I had something concrete to offer them.* J.P. still needed that one document to seal the case. *I'll just put it out there so they can chew on their options.*

"We don't have enough evidence on either side to take your father's estate before a jury." J.P. sat down in a chair across from the Hughes brothers. "If you're serious about commercial development in Joplin it will be wise to offer fair settlement against the back taxes and call it done."

"Our intension is to move commercial development into the city within the next year. You know that J.P. How much are we talking in settlement?" Christopher was looking him directly in the eye.

J.P. set his jaw. "They're still too high, but if the city is willing to drop the base to around two hundred and fifty thousand, I'll advise you counter them with half that in cash."

"That's still a hundred twenty five, J.P.," Jefferey stated. "We're talking about a city property line that was not even established until eight years after my father purchased it."

"I understand, but at the same time, there's no sufficient evidence to prove where the actual boundary was when Lloyd signed the deed. If you refuse to pay anything and we end up in court, the risk is high. Chances are good the jury will rule in favor of the city." J.P. waited for that information to settle in. "That ruling could potentially hamper any future development in Joplin."

"I say we do it," Christopher announced. "I'd like to have a commercial complex going up over there within six months. The longer this estate drags out, the longer it slows expansion."

J.P. observed the brothers exchange a look that indicated there would be more discussion behind closed doors. *Jefferey's not convinced.*

"Talk it over." J.P. stood up. "Then get back to me. I can meet with the city attorney as early as Monday morning." J.P. shifted the point of discussion. "And I'll be back to you with more information concerning Sean Bridges." He looked directly at Jeffery Hughes to let him know that topic was not forgotten. "We're still investigating pertinent out of state transactions that may or may not impact any form of agreement with his company. As soon as we have the details, I'll let you know."

"And what about the plat map?" Jefferey asked leaning back in the chair. "You obviously weren't comfortable with the diagram Miss Hutchison brought along."

He pegged that. "You're right, I'm not impressed. The dimensions were exaggerated and the directions seemed off." He thought about the way she had the map turned on the table. "Something doesn't measure up."

"Sometimes they enlarge the details for easier reading," Christopher pointed out.

"Sometimes. But that's not it." *I have a feeling Ms Hutchison is hiding something.* "Tell you what, I'll get a copy of the abstract from the courthouse Monday and we'll take a look. It will surprise me if Miss Hutchison was even showing you the same piece of land."

"Interesting." Christopher punctuated the thought.

Jefferey Hughes was finished with business for the day. He thanked J.P. for his time and politely excused himself from the table. Christopher also rose from his chair.

"J.P., it's been mighty good of you to give so much of your weekend on our behalf." He made eye contact. "If you don't have anything else planned for tonight and tomorrow, feel free to stay on. We'll pick up the tab."

As always. J.P. offered a word of thanks.

"Seriously, J.P.," Christopher stopped at the door and turned around with an obvious twinkle in his eye. "May make a suggestion? The lady by your side last night . . . maybe you should latch onto this one."

Define latching on. J.P. closed his briefcase but refused to look Mr. Hughes in the eye.

"I'd advise you do whatever it takes to keep her happy. She'll do you good."

You pay me to give you advice. "Who's the counselor here?" J.P. reached for the house phone next to the door.

"Need a lift?" Christopher grinned.

"Only picked up one keycard."

Mr. Hughes opened the door and motioned for J.P. to follow. They stopped at the private elevator. "Mr. Ralston is my guest," Christopher told the man behind the small desk.

"Very well, Mr. Hughes."

A moment later the carriage arrived.

"I imagine she'll answer a knock at the door." Christopher started to walk away. "Think about what I said, J.P."

I'm thinking already. He stepped into the elevator. *Thinking about what Mike said about her being out of my league. Thinking about what Elizabeth Hughes said about stepping it up for her. Now Mr. Hughes says to latch on to her. Thinking about the way I could have taken advantage of her this morning.*

Trouble is, hanging on to a woman is not one of my strongest traits. He was still thinking when the elevator stopped at the seventh floor. J.P. stepped off the elevator. His mind was full of unanswered questions. *I don't like the way she gets into my psyche.* No woman had ever affected him like this. *Normally I can keep business and pleasure separated.* He could see her in his mind's eye. *But she has a way of blurring the lines.*

He tapped on the door to his suite. *Or am I the one blurring it all together?*

Momentarily the door opened. J.P. took in Samira from head to toe. *She's doing it again.* She had changed into a long flowing skirt and an open weave sweater. J.P. noticed the contour of her collarbones. *She's just standing there and I can't think of a thing to say.* His eyes traced the veins in her hands. *Even her feet look sexy in those criss-crossed sandals.*

She's definitely the one blurring the lines.

27

A Bucket of Balls

"Would you like to come in?" Samira cocked her head and grinned playfully.

Phil finally crossed the threshold, but he was still contemplative. *He's watching me, yet I can't hold his eyes.*

"Did you finish your book?"

That's not the question he has on his mind. Samira closed the door and watched him set his briefcase on the bar stool. *Maybe he's still thinking about the meeting.* "No, but I found a good stopping point."

Phil opened the laptop computer and pushed a button.

"How was your meeting?"

"So what do you usually do on Saturday mornings?"

I should have known he'd do that question thing again. "You first."

"Okay." Now Phil made eye contact. "I'd say fair . . ."

When he left for the meeting he was mostly Phil. Now there's more of J.P. Ralston.

" . . . The first part was not to my satisfaction, but the remainder covered some solid territory." Phil was watching something on the computer screen. "Your turn."

For what? Samira almost forgot. *Oh! Saturday morning.* She grinned at the mundane answer that was about to fall from her lips. "Laundry."

"Every Saturday?"

Samira nodded once. "Every Saturday, first thing. Then I'm done for the weekend." *Very boring isn't it?* She waited for him to type something into the computer. *I have nothing to lose by posing the question.* "And what is your usual Saturday morning routine?"

This time Phil answered without hesitation. "I usually hit a bucket of balls at the driving range with a friend." Phil seemed very intent of completing whatever he was doing on his computer.

At least he didn't answer with another question. Samira slid onto the barstool next to his briefcase. *I wonder if his friend is Mike Benson?* Samira got an idea. "Is there a driving range here?"

"Do you golf?"

There, he did it again. She crossed her arms.

The knowing grin on Phil's face gave insight to the realization. "I'm sure there is."

I do like that easy smile. The hair on Samira's arms tingled when his blue eyes connected with hers. *I'd like to spend more time with Phil before our time is up.* "I'm curious as to what is entailed in *hitting a bucket of balls.*"

Phil laughed out loud. It was the same easy laugh she remembered from their first night together.

Maybe he's starting to relax. "Are you officially off duty now?"

Phil ran his hand through his hair and looked away. "I am as soon as I check in with the office."

Samira stepped off the barstool. "I'll finish packing while you wrap things up." *Obviously it's hard for him to shift gears.*

Most of her things were already in the overnight bag. *I'll give him some time to clear his mind.* She pulled a clear plastic bag over her evening gown and laid it across the bed. Then she went into the bathroom to get her hairbrush. *How does he keep track of his things when they're all over the place?* Instinctively, Samira organized Phil's toiletries on the counter.

The pink rose was the last thing to go in her bag. She put it to her nose. *Even without water it continued to open.* She ran her fingertips over the silky petals. *It doesn't seem so afraid to face the future now.*

When Samira turned around Phil was sitting in a chair across the bedroom. Samira jumped. "I didn't know you were in here!" *How long has he been watching me?*

Phil folded his hands and leaned forward as if he was going to say something important. Samira waited. *He has that unsure kind of look in his eye again.* She sat down on the bed next to her dress.

"You really want to go to a driving range?"

That's not what he's thinking. "Sure. You can show me your normal Saturday morning routine." *It has to be more exciting than laundry.*

His eyes were walking her up and down. She had to break the silence. "What are you really thinking?" *Maybe I don't want to know.*

Phil walked over to where Samira was sitting. He moved the dress to the side and sat down right next to her.

Now what's he going to do?

"What am I thinking?"

Is he mocking my question?

He put his hands on the edge of the bed and leaned forward. "I'm thinking . . . I have this absolutely stunning woman in my room who wants to go to the driving range?"

That's it? Samira took a quick breath. *That doesn't feel like what he's thinking.* "Or we could get a bite to eat if you like." *I don't think he's thinking about golf or food.*

"Are you hungry?"

Samira admired his tanned profile. "A little." *Actually, I'm famished!* She had eaten long before Phil was even awake. "Are you?"

Now he turned his face and looked at her. *That's the same look he had in his eyes before he got ready for his meeting with Mr. Hughes.*

"Yeah, I'm hungry." Phil was watching her closely now.

I meant hungry for food.

Very slowly he put his arm against her lower back. His other hand gently reached up under her ear.

If I return his kiss, I might not get lunch. At the same time, she could feel herself melting into the same passion she'd initiated the night before. *Then again, lunch can wait.* Samira closed her eyes and allowed Phil to take the lead.

Samira could see the entire lobby below. *I'm standing here in this glass room yet no one down there knows how I just spent the last hour.*

The elevator began to descend. *He's still watching me.* The doors opened onto the main level. Samira hesitated to follow Phil, but he politely waited for her to exit first. *Always a gentleman . . .* Their hands brushed in passing. Her mind went back to their intimacy. . . . *In every possible way.*

"I need to touch base with Antonio at the concierge desk," Phil informed. He was sorting through a small stack of notes and hotel cards in his hand.

Antonio must be wearing a nametag. "Are you sure they'll bring the luggage?"

Phil smiled his easy smile. "It will be in the truck before we are, trust me." He ran his tongue over his bottom lip. "Mr. Hughes would have it no other way."

I'm beginning to like this Mr. Hughes.

Phil put his hand behind Samira's back to guide her. "I'll wait over by the paintings." *I think I need a moment to gather myself.*

"Anything you wish, Pretty Lady." Phil selected a single envelope from his collection. "I'll just be a minute."

That's all I'll need. Samira turned and walked toward the gallery. *I can't believe I survived June seventeenth! And I have just made love to a man who is not my husband.* As she neared the fountain she could hear a piano in the distance. *Schumann, I think.* She followed the music. *And strangely enough, I don't feel any guilt.* Samira stopped to admire one of Champaigne's paintings again. She felt like her feet weren't even touching the floor. *He handles me so . . .* She stared at the painting hoping to find the word she needed to complete that thought. *He's so passionate and strong . . . and patient.* Her own reflection revealed a glow Samira didn't recognize in her own face. She laughed out loud at the realization. *He completes every part of me somehow.*

Samira turned around. *I want to see him from over here.* Her eyes went immediately to the concierge's desk. *Where did he go?* The music stopped for a minute. When it started again, Samira didn't recognize the piece. *I should probably go back.*

A marquee at the entrance to the auditorium announced the Springfield Symphony. *Oh!* Samira remembered the tickets from Mrs. Hughes. *I need to get these to Phil so he can return them.* Samira opened her purse to the bill compartment. *I put them right next to the food court tickets from the mall.*

Once again, Samira's eyes scanned the area. *I don't think he said he was going anywhere else, did he?* She could feel the smile that was still radiating on her face. *I wonder how far away the French Café is? I'm starving!* Phil was nowhere near the concierge's desk.

Oh, there he is. Samira started in his direction. *Don't forget to give him the tickets.* Suddenly, she realized Phil wasn't alone. *And the woman he's talking to is certainly not one I'd want to compete with.* Samira slowed her steps. *And he certainly seems engaged.*

Maybe he doesn't want me in that conversation! Samira noted the woman's youth and contemporary attire. *She looks vaguely familiar.* Samira couldn't help but stare. *Where have I seen her before?*

The glow in Samira's face faded. *I don't know who she is, but Phil certainly seems to know her.* She watched him nod his head in conversation. When the woman reached out and touched Phil's face, Samira looked away.

She squeezed the symphony tickets in her hand and turned around. *Maybe he should just come find me when he's finished doing whatever it is he's doing.* There was a sitting area in the far corner of the room. *If I had my book, I could just wait over there.*

Samira felt lost. She wandered reading various marquees. *This is a busy place. Every ballroom has a booking for tonight.* She read some more. *There's even a Runway show for Victoria's Secret. That's amazing.* Samira had to concentrate to keep her eyes away from Phil and that girl. *I wonder what kinds of people buy tickets to a lingerie runway show?*

Time seemed to stand still. Phil was still talking to the girl. *They're really not any of my business.* Samira forced her eyes in the opposite direction. *Well, she is not any of my business, but I would like to think Phil might be.*

Eventually she felt a familiar hand against her back. *Finally.* Samira took a deep breath. *Do I bring her up, or let it go?*

"Samira." Phil spoke her name quietly. "That took longer than I expected."

I noticed. Samira glanced over his shoulder wondering if his companion was still there.

"I bumped into someone I haven't seen in a while . . ."

He admits to knowing her.

" . . . I stopped to get caught up on her news."

He's not trying to hide her.

"I didn't mean to take so long."

Probably not.

"But now I know the luggage beat us to the truck."

He's definitely more anxious than he was earlier. Again Samira looked over his shoulder, but there was no sign of the girl. She hesitated when he started to slip his hand into hers.

"An old friend then?" *She's hardly old enough to be an "old" friend.*

Phil's blue eyes came to rest on hers but he didn't answer right away.

I shouldn't have asked. Samira looked away. *I have no right to be jealous.* She watched Phil look around the room. *I wonder if he's looking for her too?*

"That was unfair, Samira." Phil ran his tongue over his bottom lip. "I should have . . ."

No, I'm out of line.

" . . . introduced you."

Introduced me? Samira started to shake her head. *No. I just made love with you. I have no desire to meet a woman as pretty as her before my feet even touch the floor.*

Phil was looking very unsure of himself.

"I'm sorry," Samira apologized. "It's none of my business." *I'm over reacting.* She started to take the hand that he'd offered. *I still have Mrs. Hughes' tickets!* "Oh, here." Samira opened her hand. "I have some tickets for tonight's . . ."

"Tickets for what?" Phil's tone was suddenly defensive.

This is all very confusing.

Phil took the tickets out of her open hand.

"Mrs. Hughes gave them to me last night . . ." *Maybe I shouldn't have brought them up.* "They're for the Springfield Symphony. I thought if we weren't using them we might leave them so Mrs. Hughes could give them to someone else." Samira wiped her now sweaty palms on her skirt. *If things weren't awkward over that girl, they sure are now.*

Samira watched Phil tap the tickets against his other hand. Momentarily his eyes ascended the open balconies of the hotel above them. *I wonder what tickets he expected?*

Phil puckered his lips thoughtfully. "Mrs. Hughes," he stated simply. "She's always . . . well, giving something away,"

That is nowhere near what he's really thinking.

"We could use the tickets tonight if you like." Phil suddenly seemed relieved.

Still in town at eight o'clock? Samira tried not to appear too anxious. *That would put me home too late to pick up the girls.*

Phil held the tickets out for her to take again. "It's up to you, Pretty Lady. If you want to go, then by all means we'll make it happen." His voice was sincere and his blue eyes were once again focused only on her.

He called me Pretty Lady again! Samira was relieved now. "I'd love to go. But maybe another time. I'm thinking I should be home for the girls by then . . ."

Phil hesitated as if contemplating his next thought. "Very well. I'll leave these with Antonio for Mrs. Hughes."

This time I'm going with him to see the Concierge. Phil explained the situation to Antonio and then turned to face Samira.

"About that friend . . . It is your business."

No. He really doesn't have to go there. "You don't have to explain . . ." *Oh wow. They brought his truck around AND put the luggage inside?* She watched Phil tip the parking attendant.

"Maybe not." Phil offered his hand as Samira stepped onto the running board. "But just to set the record straight . . ."

Please don't disappoint me now. Samira held her breath. *Not today.*

"You're still the lady I desire."

Thank you! When he closed the door she breathed a sigh of relief. *That's really all I need to know.*

Samira found herself standing next to a set of golf clubs in the warm sunshine. *I feel so much better with food in my stomach!*

"This, Pretty Lady, is a bucket of balls." Phil held up a wire bucket bulging with golf balls.

"So it is." *I've never seen so many golf balls in one place before.* "What exactly do you do with them?"

Phil set the bucket on the ground and finished putting his wallet away. "Well, I'm going to position them on a tee and then practice my swing."

I wonder if this is what Susan does at her lessons. Men and women were coming and going along the sidewalk. *Everyone is dressed the same and they're all wearing funny shoes.*

"Do you take your golf clubs everywhere you go?"

"Are you . . ."

He's going to ask me a question.

" . . . Almost . . ."

Nope. He caught himself. Samira smiled.

"So you really don't golf then?"

Samira shook her head and smiled. "Nope, no golf. My brother plays though. In fact, he built a house in the middle of the new golf community north of town."

"He lives in Country Club Estates then?"

I really don't like admitting my brother lives in a gated community. She nodded. *That's all he needs to know about my brother.*

There was a bench behind the green strip were golfers were practicing. "I'll watch from here."

She watched Phil select a club from his bag. He placed a white ball carefully on the ground. Samira observed casually. "Okay, Tiger, show me what you've got." Phil gave her a sideways look. *I already know what he's got!*

Several strokes later Phil turned directly toward her. "You want to give this a shot?"

Oh. No. Not me. "I don't think so. I'd rather watch you." *In fact, I rather like watching him.*

Phil walked over to the bench and took her by the hand. "Come on, I'll help you."

Susan would love this! Reluctantly, Samira perched the dimpled ball on the tee according to Phil's instruction. The next thing she knew Phil was moving her feet with his own. *What's he doing?* Her sandaled feet looked out of place compared to the other golfers.

"About shoulder width apart."

He's really going to try to coach me through this! Samira moved her feet a little.

"Alright, close enough." He handed her a club. "Now, take the iron with your left hand . . ."

"This is an iron?" *It doesn't look like the iron I use on my clothes!*

"Yes."

Now he knows how little I know about golf! The club felt clumsy in Samira's hands. *It's heavier than I expected.*

"Are you right handed or left?" Phil was looking at Samira's hands.

I've been wondering that about Phil since I met him! "Are you right handed or left handed?"

Phil shook his head. "I golf left-handed."

That doesn't really answer my question. "Do you do everything left-handed?"

"No, Pretty Lady, I don't."

"Do you eat left-handed or right?"

"Right, why?"

"Just wondering." Samira thought again. "Which hand do you write with?"

"My left," Phil ran his right hand through his hair. "Which way do you hold a club?"

"I don't." *I'm not a golfer, remember?*

Samira noticed the man next to them. He appeared to be listening in on their conversation. When he saw Samira looking at him, he looked away.

Is he laughing at me?

Phil squared Samira's shoulders and tipped his head to look her in the eye.

Wes does that to me when he wants me to listen.

"Are you right handed or left?"

"Right-handed." *I am listening. I was just curious.* "For everything."

"Okay then," Phil attempted to hide his easy smile. "Then you need to stand on the other side of the ball."

"Why?" Samira was confused. "You stand over here."

"But I swing left handed. You're going to swing right-handed." Again he started to position her feet.

This is not my turf! I came here to watch Phil in his comfort zone!

Phil returned to his golf bag and began to sort through his clubs.

I wonder if Susan has this much trouble. "How do you know if it's left or right if you're standing sideways to the ball?"

"Trust me."

The man next to them was also sorting through his clubs. *Obviously neither one of them know what they're looking for.*

"Here," the man said handing Phil one of his own clubs. "Try this. It's my wife's. It might fit her a little better."

Phil accepted the club with a word of thanks.

Does Phil know him? He's not wearing a nametag.

Phil returned to Samira and once again adjusted her stance.

"I want you to hold your hands like this." Phil demonstrated.

"But this isn't even your club . . ." *This may be more trouble than it's worth.*

"No, but it fits you better and now you can swing the right way . . ."

He's obviously not going to give up!

"Okay, watch."

"Do you know him?"

Phil shook his head. "Not yet."

"Are you going to know him?" *Does he get to know everyone he meets? Maybe it's a form of networking for work.*

Phil was still serious.

Humor him and pay attention.

She studied the way Phil's fingers were clutching the club. When he handed it to her, she imitated him perfectly.

"Nice." Phil reached for her hands. "Choke up on it a little."

I have no idea what he means.

"Grip lower on the handle."

Oh. She moved her hands slightly and gained a nod of approval. The next thing Samira knew, Phil was standing behind her with his arms wrapped around hers. He placed his hands over her grip.

I like this part.

"We're just going to get a feel for the swing." Phil started to rock the club back and forth to the side of the ball.

This is strange. "I thought we were supposed to *hit* the ball." *Why is he laughing?* When she started to turn her head, Phil wouldn't let her move.

Obviously, Phil's in charge. Samira turned her attention back to the ball.

"First we need to get a feel for the swing." Phil continued to hold her in position. "Can you feel the weight of the club?"

"I can feel something." *But it's not the club.* She felt funny standing in this long row of regular golfers. *I'm the only lady wearing a long skirt and sandals.* And as far as she could tell, she was also the only one receiving personal coaching.

"Now we're going to feel the ball with the club . . . Feel that?"

"Maybe." *What exactly am I supposed to be feeling for?*

Suddenly, Phil forced the club back and took a swing. Much to Samira's surprise, the ball went flying towards a flag.

Samira looked on in amazement. "How do you know which ball is yours?"

Phil let go of her hands and stepped out of her stance. "Just keep your eyes on the ball."

Sounds easy enough. Samira scanned the grassy field stretched out before her. "How'd we do?"

Phil gazed out over the field with his hands on his hips. "I've done better."

Phil was chuckling but the gentleman next to them was doubled over laughing.

"I think I'm a better spectator."

"You are . . ." Phil started to say something and stopped. His eyes were dancing with renewed energy. "What do you say we bag these balls and find something else to do?"

I don't care what he does with the balls, but I do want him to finish his sentence. "I'm what?"

Phil lifted the club out of Samira's hands and returned it to its owner with a word of thanks.

"No problem." The man placed another ball on the tee. "Best entertainment I've had in a long time."

Oh, that's nice. Samira put her hands on her hips. *I didn't come here to be his entertainment!*

"Play these out on me." Phil set the bucket of balls down beside the man.

I'm not going until he finishes his sentence. Phil returned to the platform and nudged Samira.

"After you finish your sentence."

"Let's walk."

I'll walk, but he's not off the hook!

"Well?" They were headed for the parking lot.

Phil lifted his golf clubs over his shoulder. "You are . . ."

What? Finish your sentence!

" . . . Absolutely amazing."

I seriously doubt that's what he was going to say.

"What made you want to come here, anyway?"

Samira's face broke into a brilliant smile. "I thought maybe I'd find Phil here."

"Did you?"

Parts of him. "There was less of J.P. Ralston here than at other places . . ."

Phil was thinking. He put his clubs in the bed of his truck and snapped the tarp.

The only place I didn't experience J.P. was in his bed. He was all Phil there. Samira allowed him to open her door. *At least I think that's who he was then.* She climbed into the seat.

"Come here."

Where? I'm already here.

He wiggled his finger for her to move closer.

Why?

Phil pushed a loose hair out of Samira's face and tucked it behind her ear.

Oh. Samira succumbed to his kiss. *There is very little of J.P. Ralston in this.*

28

The Recent Past

J.P. sat in his own office as Mike reviewed the latest charges pressed against his son.

"These charges are damn serious, J.P.," Mike flipped the document in his hand and skimmed the second page. "Assault and battery with premeditated intent? If Hamilton takes James to court, they could try him as an adult . . ."

I'm well aware of the allegations. In fact, he'd watched as James was cuffed and booked at the county jail. J.P. didn't move. His eyes were still fixed on the coffee shop at the end of the alley.

"I'm surprised they released James into your custody."

"I didn't give them much choice in the matter."

"Somehow that doesn't surprise me." Mike's voice trailed off as he continued to read. He turned another page. "What'd you find on Bruce, Denise? Anything useful?"

Denise presented a short stack of memos. "He's been picked up for public intoxication and driving under the influence more than once in the last six months. Other than that I didn't find much." She handed the paperwork over to Mike but her eyes were glued to her employer. "When did you know there was trouble in Harrisonburg?"

J.P. shrugged his shoulders and took a deep breath. "Josh called on my way home from Springfield and told me Bruce and James were at odds. I hadn't planned to go get him until Sunday night but Josh wanted me to come on up." J.P. ran his hand through his hair. "When I arrived a few hours later there was a sheriff's car and an ambulance in the driveway."

Mike spoke up. "Did Josh give any indication of a motive for the blow up?"

"Maybe you should ask Josh."

"I will. Don't worry. I have a few questions for Janet too."

Denise waited patiently. "Is there anything else I can do?"

"Well, let me go to work on it." Mike suggested calmly. "I'll see how far I get with Hamilton's attorney and Janet. I'll catch up with you later if I need anything more. As it stands, James won't appear in court until Thursday. That gives us a couple of days to build a case." Mike lifted his sturdy frame from the surface of the conference table where he'd been sitting. "You going to be alright?"

J.P. nodded with false confidence. "I'm fine. James will be at the club with Ernie McElroy until one of us picks him up."

Mike puckered his bushy mustache. "Alrighty then." Mike nodded his head. "Don't let the boy out of your jurisdiction and avoid any contact with your ex-wife until you hear from me. I'll find you later and let you know what's up."

It's a helluvalot easier to be an attorney than it is a father.

The last thing J.P. needed on a busy Monday morning was more trouble concerning James. *I should have known it was too soon for James to go back up there.*

Denise tapped her pen against the edge of the communication clipboard as she re-entered the office. "You have exactly one hour before meeting with the city attorney. Are you up for it?"

J.P. nodded again. *Anything to keep busy at this point in time.*

Denise continued. "There's no indication they've dropped the settlement as of yet." She checked the item on the list. "You meet with Mr. Stephenson at one o'clock. No board members, just Stephenson, one on one."

"Do you have an update on the case?" J.P. was sitting at his desk fingering through a stack of file folders.

"Third file down," Denise informed without looking. "Sounds like you'll be out of the office all day on Thursday. Mike says there's no way around it."

I hate the fact James has to face the judge again. "So be it." J.P. surrendered. "What's the rest of today look like?"

"Before you came in a Jessica Hutchison called from Bridges Property Management. She's requested a private consultation concerning the property for the Hughes Corporation."

"That's the Bridges rep I met Saturday morning in Springfield. I'm not impressed so far." *Not impressed with her business anyway.* "Give her an early lunch, nothing more. No plat maps. I'd like to see the authentic documents without her edits." He pulled the Mid-America file out of the stack. "Any chance you can get a copy of the tract in question from the courthouse today?"

"I can call ahead for you to pick it up after you meet with the city."

"That works." *Just take care of business.* "Anything else pressing?"

"One more," Denise hesitated.

She looks concerned. "Spit it out."

"Bobbie Sommers called this morning. She's in town and wants to see you tonight."

Shit, Ralston. You should have told her you were unavailable when you had the chance. Slowly he shook his head. "Can't do it." *Not after the weekend I just spent with Samira.* J.P. thought again. *But I don't necessarily want Denise knowing that either.* "I need to give James my full attention tonight."

"She didn't leave a number," Denise informed. "The message said she'd stop in this afternoon."

That's just great.

"You know, boss," Denise's tone softened. "If you have a steady or something I can head some of these calls off before they . . ."

I don't know if I have a "steady". "That won't be necessary." *At least for the time being.* He touched the computer keyboard and cued the monitor.

Denise slid forward in her chair. "Forty five minutes before meeting Miles. He'll be in the third floor conference room at the courthouse. Sparky is already in Baltimore. He's supposed to call in before noon today."

"Noon our time or Baltimore time?"

"I didn't ask. Does it matter?"

J.P. watched as she walked away. "No, I was just curious."

Denise tapped her acrylic fingernails on the brass door handle. "Let me know when I should start forwarding Miss Sommers' calls to Mike."

J.P. closed his eyes for a brief moment. *God, she knows me well.* When he looked back at the door Denise was gone. *SNSA. Bobbie Jo Sommers.* The attorney opened Sparky's update and skimmed the overview for Mr. Stephenson. *Something tells me that's not the case with Samira.* He tried to concentrate on the file again. *I don't know what I want with her.* His mind went over the abrupt end to his weekend. *It just stopped.*

I kissed her goodbye twice. Once inside her house when he carried her bags in and then again in the doorway as he was leaving. *How hard would it have been to ask when I could see her again?* He turned the page absent-mindedly. *Because, J.P. Ralston, your mind was on the chaos in Harrisonburg.* He turned another page. *But you still should have given her some indication of your intentions.*

J.P. closed the file on his desk confident he could plead his case with Mr. Stephenson in spite of the distractions playing with his mind. *How else are you supposed to end a date?*

Maybe that's it. J.P. ran his hand through his hair and removed his glasses. *Maybe I don't know what my intentions are. Maybe there's more to come and I'm just too damned stubborn to want it.* Most dates he could kiss goodnight and walk away. *But Samira is not like that.* He pictured her in the evening gown. *I walk away but somehow she walks with me.* Her smile had left a vivid imprint on his memory. *She's not going away any too easily.*

J.P. closed his door before dialing the Maple Street Library. He asked for Samira. *I should at least explain why I needed to leave so quickly Saturday night.*

"I'm sorry, sir, she is on the other line. Would you like her voice mail?"

J.P. declined the offer. *I don't know what I was going to say in person, let alone on a voice message.*

An hour later J.P. was across a conference table from three city council representatives. Miles Johnson, the city's attorney, was acting as the mediator.

"You're missing the point, J.P.," Miles reiterated for a third time. "You know fair and square that Lloyd Hughes owed tax money for all those years he owned that property. We're not willing to negotiate anything less than the taxes due."

J.P. sat back in his chair. *I've argued this point numerous times. They should be ready to settle.* He looked his colleague in the eye. "I don't disagree. Lloyd owed property tax, Miles." He pointed to the deed on the table between them. "And the Hughes brothers do not have an issue paying what was due in 1959. But they are not going to pay for damages beyond the lost tax. Period." J.P. ran his finger down the left hand column of the page. "Do the math. If Lloyd were sitting here in this room right now he'd write you a check for a hundred twenty five thousand and close the deal. That's what was due at the time that property sold." *Never mind that the attorneys in charge of the sale happened to misprint the back tax in 1962 and forget about the fact that the paperwork for the new owner was misplaced for two years following the close of the sale.* "Lloyd was a sound businessman. He always paid his debts."

"Well now he owes closer to half a million," a councilman interjected. "If you seriously think we're going to let the Hughes Corporation walk away for less than a quarter of that, think again . . ."

Miles put out his hand to stop the council member from saying anymore but it was too late.

I'm finished here for today. "The only way you can come up with five hundred grand is if you charge out under commercial tax. When Lloyd purchased that tract it was still residential and it remained residential until 1968 at which time the name on the deed was not Lloyd Hughes." *I am sick and tired of reminding them of that fact!* "You are still missing the point." *I'm going to lay it on the line. There's nothing to lose at this point in time.* "The issue at hand is not about back taxes. The crux of this matter concerns the future of Joplin." J.P. looked Miles in the eye. "If you stick them for the whole amount against the estate now, the opportunity to gain economic development from the Hughes Corporation in the future is nonexistent."

A councilman spoke up. "We've seen healthy economic development for years without support from the Hughes Corporation. Why should we be concerned about their money now?"

I could name twenty or thirty commercial developments in Joplin funded by the Hughes Corporation. "You might verify that information before taking it before a jury, councilman." J.P. looked back to Miles. "Call me when you're ready to do business."

Done. I've said my piece. They can take it before the jury for all I care. J.P. lifted the deed off the table and placed it in his briefcase. "Good day, gentlemen."

All we need is one printed document—one stinking document would close this deal in a heartbeat. His mind was reeling. *We've been over it a million times, but I'm not willing to compromise my client's integrity.*

J.P. opened his phone. *Three calls. Denise. Mike. Janet.* He scrolled through a list of numbers and pressed the one he needed most.

"Samira Cartwright, please."

"She's in a meeting. May I take a message?"

No. J.P. disconnected the call. *I don't know why I'm thinking about her right now anyway.* J.P. stepped outside into the hot sunshine. *Business before pleasure. You know the rule.*

"Counselor!"

J.P. stopped and turned around.

"Where's your head, man? I've been trying to catch you since the second floor." Mike grinned through his bushy mustache.

"What brings you to the courthouse?"

"Hughes."

"They settle?"

"Not yet."

"Think they'll hold out for a jury?"

"I hope not."

"You don't sound any too confident, J.P." Mike wiggled his eyebrows over the top of designer sunglasses. "Where's the scrap in the dogfight?"

"I prefer fair settlement over scraps, Mike."

Mike's curly hair bobbed when he nodded. "You take this business way too serious, man." He patted his friend on the shoulder. "I talked to Hamilton's attorney. So far no dope but gut feeling tells me there's more to the story. I'll stay on it."

Mike opened a new pack of chewing gum. "Meet me at the club at six o'clock. Maybe I'll have something by then."

J.P. silently refused the gum. "Alright." *I'm ready for a hard workout.*

"So, tell me, Counselor," Mike paused. "You never filled me in on your romantic weekend with the classy chick."

"Lady . . ."

Mike wrapped his tongue around the gum. "*Lady.*" He grinned. "Okay. So how was she?"

"Good." *Incredible.*

Mike chewed on his gum. "That's it? Just good?"

He's not getting any details. "Yeah. It was a good weekend." He tried to shrug it off. "We had a good time." *I couldn't put her into words if I tried.* J.P.'s mind tripped back to the moment he looked down from the podium and saw her visiting with Mrs. Hughes. *She's sophisticated and smart and . . .*

Mike laughed out loud. "I kept your dog for a 'good' weekend?" Mike laughed again. "Next time call Denise. If I'm going to dog sit I want more than a 'good' report."

J.P. checked the ID on a new incoming call. He *knows I'm holding out.*

Mike started to walk away. "I'll take the silence as an indication that things went better than 'good'. In the meantime, I'm late for an appointment, good buddy. Six o'clock, alright? We have a lot of ground to cover with James before Thursday."

J.P. opened his cell phone to Denise. *Why is it so hard to talk to Mike about Samira?*

Mr. Stephenson looked tired and concerned as J.P. took a seat in his office. This was their first private meeting since the discovery of the hacker's damage. *He acts like we've already been defeated.* He watched Mr. Stephenson pour a cup of coffee.

"Mr. Stephenson, the news is good. The suspects are in custody. We should be able to summon a grand jury fairly quickly."

"Coffee?"

Is he listening to me? J.P. declined.

Slowly, Mr. Stephenson crossed the room and sat down in a big leather chair adjacent to J.P. *Something about him seems more familiar to me than usual.*

"There are many things I have yet to understand, J.P." Mr. Stephenson was reserved. "I have read the latest update, but I don't understand why we can't just charge the suspects with a crime and take them through the normal court proceedings."

"It's a complicated case." *Go slow enough he can follow and quick enough he won't change his mind.* "The whole nature of the case is complex. For instance, if these suspects would have physically robbed the bank at gunpoint and escaped with the 1.8 million there would be physical evidence to trace. As it is, the suspects broke into the bank in cyberspace. There are no fingerprints, no videotapes, no witnesses that we are aware of, and no bundles of money to uncover."

"I understand all that." Mr. Stephenson set his cup on the walnut table. "But why Baltimore? Wouldn't it be easier to bring the suspects here for court appearances?"

"That's complicated too." *How do I explain this?* "Exactly where did the crime take place? The only part of the robbery that happened here in Joplin is the part we can see on the computer screen. Funds were moved from one international account to another over wire. No one came inside this building and actually touched a machine to make that happen." *At least not as far as we know.* "Furthermore, the suspects are believed to have worked it from their home in Maryland." *I'll let him chew on that for a second.* "As inconvenient as it seems, the crime was actually committed in another state, therefore, the judicial system has to try them in Maryland."

Mr. Stephenson took a deep breath and folded his hands. "What exactly does that mean for me and my employees?"

In other words, how much expense is involved traveling back and forth. "It will be necessary for Mid-America to have a presence on the East Coast, no doubt about that. But we'll try to schedule the appearances before the court as conveniently as possible."

Mr. Stephenson lifted his tall lean frame out of the chair and walked across the room. He folded his arms and turned back to face J.P. "Explain to me again, the involvement of the other law firm . . ."

"With the board's approval, Benson and Barringer will come on board to assist with litigation." J.P. followed his client to the window and looked down upon the main street. "Vince Barringer and Mike Benson are the best in the business, Mr. Stephenson. You can't hire any two attorneys better equipped for federal prosecution. Each one of us will handle one phase of the trial, which will give Mid-America the upper hand. Vince will work the case from Baltimore. Mike will work the case from here with the assistance of Denise Burke. And I'll be wherever they need me to be."

Mr. Stephenson nodded once but he was obviously still deep in thought. "And Ms Burke, what exactly is her role?"

"Denise Burke is my personal assistant. She is communication central." *Among about a million other tasks that she performs to the "nth" degree.*

A long silence separated J.P. from his client. *What is it about him today? It's something about the way he's just standing there looking out the window. Or the way he's holding his cup?*

"Very well, then. We'll talk to the board in the morning. I'm sure they will support moving forward with the grand jury."

"We can't move forward without the grand jury, Mr. Stephenson. This jury will decide if there is enough evidence to indict the suspects. Without the indictment there can not be a verdict of guilt."

"I understand, J.P., I read the report." This time when Mr. Stephenson's eyes met J.P. he seemed more at ease. "I do appreciate your efforts in the case. I realize these requests are above and beyond your normal responsibilities to Mid-America."

Whatever it takes, Mr. Stephenson. "I'm glad I can be of service." *For the most part.*

By the time he was finished with Mid-America business it was late in the afternoon. J.P. returned to the parking lot with his mind already skimming the evening agenda with James and Mike. *No free time to speak of in the immediate future.* He pushed the redial button on his phone.

Damn it. Busy. *Again.*

Derek Danielson was standing at Denise's desk when J.P. returned to the office. Denise glanced at the clock and then back at her boss.

"James just called to be picked up. Should I send Derek or are you available?"

J.P. nodded a greeting to the intern as he passed through to his own office. "You tell me." *It seems strange it takes three adults to keep track of one teenager.*

"You stay."

J.P. heard Denise give the order but had no idea to whom it pertained. *Me or Derek?* He sifted through a small stack of folders while he waited for more direct instructions.

"Hey boss, did you pick up the plat map at the courthouse?"

Damn it. I knew I was forgetting something. J.P. slapped a folder onto his desk.

"I'll take that as a no." Denise appeared in the doorway. "I sent Derek to pick up James. You and I have some business to wrap up before you leave for the day."

I have business of my own I'd like to wrap up. J.P. sat down in his chair as Denise made her way toward his desk with the message clipboard.

"First things first . . ." Denise made eye contact. "This Bobbie chick is starting to get on my nerves. Either I get rid of her for you or you do it yourself. She's stopped in twice and called at least three times this afternoon. She acts like you're going to be just as excited to see her as she is to see you. And from the look on your face, my guess is otherwise." Denise took a seat and crossed her legs.

I don't know what to do with Bobbie Jo Sommers . . .

"Obviously we're not going to make much progress on that topic." Denise checked her list. "Next item. Jessica Hutchison. Lunch tomorrow or Wednesday? You need to tell me what time and where. I'll call her back. She's promised '*information you will be pleased to see*'."

I'll believe that when I see it. J.P. ran his hand through his hair but did not verbally respond.

"I know you're upset about James, boss, and you have a right to be. This whole custody thing is all new. But at the same time you still have work to do. You know, like an agenda to keep?"

I don't like the tone in her voice. J.P. started to retaliate but was met with firm resistance.

" . . . I'm hanging on to more than a few loose ends and they're starting to fray at the ends. Either you give me some direction or you end up working with the threads as they unravel when I go home."

I hear what she's saying, but can only juggle so much. Let's fix one of the issues.

"Tell Hutchison Wednesday, eleven o'clock at the pub across the street from Mid-America."

"O'Flannigans?"

"That's the one."

Give her my schedule and let her fill in the blanks.

"I'll be with Stephenson and the board of director's starting at nine. We need to get a hold of Benson and Barringer and set an appointment for them to meet with Mid-America as soon as they can spare an hour."

Denise made a note on the corner of the notepad. "Very well. Now we're getting somewhere. Are they officially on the case now?"

"As soon as we get the board's approval."

Denise made another note. "J.P., Derek is doing a fine job on the Andrews' photography case but I think he could use a little mentoring. I've been giving him all the attention I can spare, but he needs a little encouragement from the expert."

I don't need another assignment right now. "I can do that."

"Today?"

"If you think it's that urgent."

Denise stood up from her chair. "Maybe tomorrow when you come in you can leave the bullshit at home." She continued to attack as she left the room. "We all feel the caseload, Boss, but you act as though maybe you'd rather be somewhere else."

Maybe I would. J.P. walked around his desk and closed his office door slightly harder than necessary. *The city didn't budge on their charges against Lloyd Hughes; Something about Mr. Stephenson wasn't right today; the plat map I need is still at the courthouse; my son is now facing assault charges; and as if all that isn't enough, the goddamned line is still busy.*

J.P. stepped into his private bathroom to relieve himself. *There is no reason for me to take it out on Denise. And I know I need to be spending more time with Derek.* But another entire day had passed and he still hadn't made contact with Samira.

That's it, isn't it Ralston? He looked into the mirror above the sink. *You're pissed because you can't get her on the phone.* J.P. Ralston wasn't used to waiting for a woman to respond. *I'm not used to a woman permeating my every thought!*

If you had any sense at all you'd back out now—before you're in too deep. J.P. studied the face in the reflection. *Unless I'm already in that deep.*

That thought gave him the chills. J.P. turned the doorknob and stepped back into his office. Denise was waiting by the door between the offices. *I don't like the look in her eyes.*

"Someone to see you, boss."

Shit!

J.P.'s eyes started at the high-heeled sandals that laced up the long, shapely, stockingless legs to the edge of the short, brown leather skirt . . .

Sure enough.

. . . A casual belt hung loosely around her waist and a tight cotton tank clung to the curves of her breasts. Long brown curls rested silently over her shoulders and the neutral lip color faded into a sultry smile.

"Hello, Bobbie."

"You're a hard man to track down, J.P. Ralston." Bobbie swung her hip in his direction and crossed her arms under her heavy bosom.

"I'll hold your calls, *Mr. Ralston.*" Denise closed the door silently.

One time I broke my own rule and brought a woman to my office. J.P. looked over the cover model again. *And I'm still paying for that mistake.*

"What can I do for you, Bobbie?"

Bobbie Jo took a step toward J.P.

Wrong question.

"You can do anything you want for me. We didn't seem to have any trouble finding things to do the last time we were together . . ."

I really don't need this today. J.P. sat down in his chair. Bobbie leaned her heavy chest over his desk and touched his hand with a long fingernail.

Exactly what do I do with her now? Temptation was readily available. *But there's a woman across town . . .*

"What do you say, J.P.?"

. . . who's not answering her phone.

Bobbie Jo ran her finger under J.P.'s chin.

It wouldn't take much to relieve some tension . . . no strings attached.

J.P. allowed Bobbie to taunt him with her eyes.

I've changed since then.

J.P. pushed that thought away. Very slowly he linked his fingers in hers. *There was a time when she was a game for me.* He watched her move a little closer. *She was something I desired but didn't want to keep.*

Bobbie Jo walked around and slid her hip onto J.P.'s desk. *She's the same woman.* He remembered. *Same green eyes and full lips.* He dared to run his hand across her thigh. *I know the shape of her breasts and the scent she's wearing.*

Bobbie Jo put her hands in J.P.'s hair. *I know what lingerie she's wearing.* There wasn't anything about her J.P. Ralston didn't remember. *And everything is for the taking right here and now if choose.*

The slit in the already short skirt revealed what little she was wearing underneath. But slowly, J.P. began to realize something else. *She's not the one I desire.* He half expected his instincts to kick in, but nothing was happening.

"J.P., if I didn't know any better," Bobbie cocked her head dramatically, "I might think you were putting me off."

Am I?

Seemingly unaffected by J.P.'s lack of participation, Bobbie proceeded to stretch out over his desk. She propped her head in her hand and let her long curls fall to one side.

"Remember the last time we used this desk?"

I remember. Bobbie Sommers' face was only a few inches from J.P. *But she's only right about one thing—that was the last time.* "You should be on your way, Bobbie."

The girl didn't move. "Maybe this is *my* way. And if it is, I don't have anywhere else to be going today, J.P. Today is my day off. I drove all the way over just to be with you."

I can't believe what I'm about to do. J.P. stood up and walked away from the desk. "Today is not my day off." *And even if it was, you couldn't have me today.*

Very slowly Bobbie moved into an upright position but she was still on a mission. "I was surprised to see you in Springfield . . ."

No more surprised than I was to get that runway ticket.

"I thought you'd join me in my room."

"I wasn't in town for that long . . ." *Why can't I tell her the truth?*

She began to walk toward him. "But I'm here now. And I won't take long."

Everything about her is sexy and fresh . . . and yet nothing about her is . . .

Bobbie wrapped her body around his uninvited. *Walk away, Ralston. Before it's too late.* Her lips made contact with his as the intercom on his desk buzzed. Bobbie hesitated just long enough for J.P. to unwrap her leg.

"You have a call on line four."

We don't have a line four. J.P. picked up the intercom line. "Had enough?"

Denise. "That would be fine." He stared at the closed door between the offices. *She's enjoying this way too much.* Bobbie's hand ran up the back of his shirt and into his hair. J.P. stepped away from her touch.

"Derek has just arrived with your son."

Good timing. "Very well. Send him in."

"Which one?"

I don't care. "Mr. Danielson."

Bobbie was still standing next to J.P. when Derek made an unprepared entrance.

"Have a seat, Mr. Danielson."

Derek looked from J.P. to Bobbie and then back to J.P. Obviously unsure of what else to do, he took a seat at the conference table.

"That will be all." *Goodbye Bobbie Jo.*

Denise appeared in the doorway and motioned for Bobbie Jo to make an exit. "Will there be anything else for Miss Sommers?"

"Nothing else." *I can't believe I'm doing this.*

This time as she walked by, her hips didn't swing like they had. *Funny. Her scent isn't even appealing at the moment.* Denise followed Bobbie out.

J.P. pulled up to the conference table where Derek was waiting for further instructions. *What the hell just happened here?* "Show me where you're at with . . ." *What case is he working again?*

" . . . the Andrews case." Denise returned to his office. "I closed the last case for you, Boss."

I bet she did. J.P. opened the file. *Someday I'll ask her for the verdict.*

29

A Jealous Streak

Samira ran her ink pen over the letters she'd already written.

Noon. O'Flannigan's Pub. Across from MidAmerica Blg.

"Sure, I can be there." *But I was supposed to have lunch with Krissy, Kara and Susan's girls.*

"You know where Mid-America is, right?"

Everyone knows where the Mid-America building is. "Of course."

"The pub is right across the street from their parking lot." Phil informed. "Just tell the hostess you're there to meet me . . ."

No doubt he'll know hostess' name.

" . . . Once you get there I'll wrap up my appointment and we can grab a bite to eat somewhere else."

It seems strange we have to leave a restaurant to get a bite to eat. "Wouldn't it just be easier to stay there for lunch?"

"I'd rather not."

Okay. Her ink pen made another pass over the notation.

"Still there?"

Samira smiled into the phone. "Still here." *Just the sound of his voice makes me tingle.*

"Alright, I'm on my way into a meeting. I'll see you in a couple of hours, okay?"

He is certainly all J.P today.

"I'll be there." *But my next call isn't going to be so pleasant.* She hung up the receiver and ran her hand over the cover of a magazine on her desk. *It's the same periodical that was on Phil's coffee table.* The scantly dressed model on the front was smiling back at her. Samira turned to the cover story and read the lead.

Supermodel, Bobbie Jo Sommers, is the newest member of the Victoria Secret Family . . .

Samira took a deep breath. *That's definitely the same woman Phil was talking to in Springfield.* There was no mistaking that face. *Or that body, for all that matters.* The article highlighted the Bobbie Sommers' success story then moved into more hype about the live runway shows the company was sponsoring around the country. *I don't understand the motive behind putting lingerie on live models in public.*

Samira remembered the way the model had touched Phil's face. *My assumption is they're more than just acquaintances.* Samira turned back to the cover photograph. *It's definitely a body that has never had babies.* Samira sighed. *But not one I care to compete with either.*

Samira opened her desk drawer and pulled out the local phone directory. *Now that I know his name, I wonder if I can find him in the directory.* She opened the yellow pages to the A's. *Attorneys.* She ran her fingernail over the listings. *There's a Benson and Barringer. I would guess that to be Mike Benson's practice.* Samira's eyes continued to search the page. *There he is.* She tapped the page. *Ralston, J.P., Business Law.*

Samira flipped to the white pages. *Let's see what we can find here.* Several passes over the R's revealed an absence for J.P. or anything of that nature. *Nope.* She closed the heavy book. *So the number I have for him on the back of his business card must be private.*

"Ms Cartwright," Helen Haddock poked her head around the door. "Should I take the dated periodicals downstairs for you?"

"That's okay, Helen, I'll get them in a few minutes."

She fingered the numbers on the telephone but didn't dial right away. *What do I tell the girls and Susan?* Samira thought for a moment. *They're going to be disappointed I'm canceling lunch with them.* She dialed her brother's home number.

"Hello, this is Kara."

Here goes nothing. "Kara, this is your mom."

"I know," Kara acknowledged. "The library number is on the caller ID box. What's up? Aunt Pam's in the shower. Should I have her call you back?"

"Actually," Samira hesitated slightly. "I called to talk to you or Krissy." She paused again. "Something has come up at lunch. I'm not going to be able to meet with Susan and the girls at the park."

"So that means you won't be meeting us either then."

"That's right, Kara. I'm sorry. We'll have to reschedule."

"Like that's going to be easy. Susan only has this week off from work, you know. That's why she set up the picnic for today."

"I know, Kara, I . . ." *How do I tell her I'm going to meet Phil instead?* "Maybe Susan can meet tomorrow. I'll call her at home and see what she thinks."

"She's going to be really mad . . ."

She's probably right about that.

" . . . You know how she thinks you're always avoiding her these days? This is just going to make it worse."

The words on the notepad were starting to blur as Samira's pen ran over and over them. "Maybe it won't be as bad as you think." *We can hope.*

"Whatever!"

Whatever. I hate that word. Samira promised to call Kara back after talking to Susan.

It really shouldn't be so hard to talk to a girlfriend. Samira carried the periodicals to the basement. *If Susan were a real friend, she would understand without any explanation.* She sorted the magazines into alphabetical order and stacked them on the worktable for her staff to file later. *This is her week off, not mine.* Samira re-thought that statement. *Heck, if Susan knew I was dumping the picnic for a man she'd be ecstatic.* Samira piled her hair on top of her head with her hands then shook it down to her shoulders again. *But I don't know if I have it in me to involve Susan in my personal life.*

Time was passing. *Now I don't have any choice but to call Susan.* Her hands were sweating when she lifted the receiver to dial.

Four rings later the answering machine picked up. *Oh good. I'll just leave a quick message.*

The last hour of the morning passed very quickly. "I'll be back sometime early this afternoon, Helen."

"Take your time, Ms Cartwright. Enjoy the picnic with your girls."

There's a guilt trip if I've ever known one. Just as she climbed into her car, Susan pulled in and parked next to her. *What is she doing here?*

"Wait," Susan hurried around the front of her car. She leaned over, her short bobbed hair bouncing with every move. "Why don't you just ride with me and then I'll drop you off on my way back home?"

Now what do I tell her? "Did you get my message?"

Susan stood up straight and let her hand rest against Samira's open car door. "What message?"

"I called about an hour ago, maybe a little more." *Well, more like forty-five minutes ago.* "Something has come up, Susan. I need to be downtown in a few minutes."

Susan waved her hand in dismissal. "Well, that's alright. I'm a little early anyway. I was just in the neighborhood. Go on downtown and then meet us when you're done."

Samira realized the misunderstanding. "Not to the library, something else." She took a deep breath. "I don't know when I can break free."

"You mean I hired a sitter for Joey so we could have a mother daughter picnic and now you don't know if you're going to make it or not?" Susan was instantly frustrated. "My girls are already over there!"

"I'm sorry, Susan. I tried to reach you as soon as I knew." *But I really need to be going. Downtown parking over lunch is going to be a nightmare.*

"Did you call your girls?"

I can't believe I didn't call them back!

Susan put her hands on her thick waist. It was obvious she was mad. "Alright. I'll go get Krissy and Kara just like we'd planned." Susan adjusted her wristwatch. "No clue when you'll be done?"

Nothing seems right now. She was so torn. *But I've waited three days to hear from Phil. I didn't want to let him down either.*

"I'm picking up Joey at one thirty so if you're done by then, stop by, alright?"

The pit in Samira's stomach grew heavy as she drove downtown. She circled the Mid-America parking lot without any luck. *Phil said noon, and he sounded like he meant noon straight up.* Reluctantly, she circled around behind the three-story building and parked in a reserved parking space. *I don't usually do this.* She stuck her reserved parking pass on the rearview mirror. *But without it, I'm never going to find a place to park.*

O'Flannigan's Pub was dark compared to the bright sunshine. It took a moment for Samira's eyes to adjust even after removing her sunglasses.

"Just one for lunch?"

Angelina. She's wearing a name tag. "Oh, no." Phil's instructions replayed in Samira's mind. "I'm here to meet Phil . . ." *No wait.* " . . . J.P. Ralston."

The hostess nodded knowingly. "Right this way."

Samira's khaki skirt and plain tee didn't compare to the business clad men and women gathered in the bar. *It feels like everyone is watching me.*

Very few guests were in the dining area when the hostess held out her arm toward a table in the far corner. Samira could see Phil's profile against the window. He was sitting across from a woman. *But not the model from the magazine. Thankfully.*

It only took a moment for Phil to notice her. Samira could feel the intensity of his thoughts from across the room. *There is something powerful about his presence.* Phil rose from his chair and motioned for her to come closer.

" . . . If you'll excuse me," he said to the woman who still had her back to Samira. "Tell your employer I'll be more interested when he starts conducting business in person."

"But Mr. Bridges is rarely in town . . ."

She doesn't seem as interested in ending this discussion as Phil does.

"I understand." Phil was addressing the woman directly. "When he gets back into the area, call my assistant and I'll make myself available."

Without any reserve, Phil took her hand. "Shall we?"

Sure. Samira nodded as her fingers interlocked with his. *It feels good to touch him again.* She kept her eyes on Phil although she was dying to get a better look at the woman he was deserting.

Phil tossed a folded five-dollar bill onto the table and began to walk away.

He's obviously immersed in business. Samira skipped a step to keep up with Phil. More people had gathered for lunch and a line had formed at the hostess' desk. Phil stopped briefly and exchanged a few remarks with the girl behind the counter. *I bet he tips her.* Phil handed the young woman a folded bill. *Sure enough.*

Phil led Samira from the central air of the pub into the hot sunshine. *His thoughts are somewhere between that meeting and his next one. I can tell.* They walked about halfway down the block before speaking.

"It's good to see you."

Samira thought back to the scene at the restaurant. "I feel kind of bad leaving that woman there alone like that." *But I feel worse for standing up Kara and Krissy.*

Phil's eyes were still focused on the sidewalk ahead. He shook his head slightly. "Don't. She had an hour to make her case and failed to provide anything substantial."

But she seemed a little distraught.

"But you," Phil slowed his steps and turned to look at Samira. "You made your case simply by walking across that room."

"Was I late?" *I didn't mean to be late.*

Phil laughed out loud. "No. You were right on time. Thanks for the rescue."

Oh. He set me up to be his excuse to leave.

"You were extremely sexy walking toward me in the dining room."

"I should have changed out of these clothes." *And would have with more advanced notice.*

J.P. moved his hand to her waist and pulled her toward him as they continued to walk. *Just like he did in Springfield.*

"You don't have to change a thing."

People were gathered at the corner waiting for the walk light to signal. *I wonder if I know anyone here?* It hadn't been that long ago that she'd longed for a man's hand to hold. *But today, in broad daylight, walking along this familiar sidewalk, I don't know if I should . . .* Samira stopped her thoughts. *Springfield is one thing. In Joplin, it's another.*

Phil turned toward her. *Please don't kiss me here. Not in public.* Samira forced a smile when Phil caught her eyes.

"What are you thinking, Pretty Lady?"

I'm thinking I should be at a mother—daughter picnic. Samira bit her bottom lip, thankful for her dark glasses. "I'm thinking you promised me lunch." *I should tell him about the picnic.*

"Then by all means, let's find a place to eat."

When the light changed, Phil slipped his hand back into hers.

"I believe there's a deli on the next block with a gourmet coffee shop."

Sounds good to me.

"Great sandwiches, but I can't speak for the coffee. You'll have to be the judge of that."

Coffee is good. Samira nodded. *A deli won't take long. I might still have time to swing by the park on the way back to the library without having to make up too much time at the end of the day.*

Samira stood in the crowded lunch line. *I really do feel plain and simple compared to all these business women in heels.*

"Anything you like." Phil nodded toward the menu.

First things first. Samira ordered a Cappuccino. Next she ordered half a club sandwich with mayo but no pickles. She sat down in a wire chair to hold the table while Phil waited on the order. *I wonder what Susan and the girls are talking about?*

"Samira Stephenson?" an unfamiliar voice called an unfamiliar name. *No one has called me that for a long time.*

Oh, wow! "Ricardo!" Samira rose from her chair and greeted him with both hands. "It's Samira Cartwright now." She stepped into a quick hug with her former classmate.

"So, it is. So it is." A huge smile crossed his dark complexion. "It's been a long time. Missed you at the last reunion. Are you still living in the area?"

"Yeah, it has been a long time. The reunion fell during a difficult time . . ." Samira's mind went back to the spring Tom had been so sick. "I didn't make it." *Ricardo. It's so good to see his smile again.* "And yes, I'm still living here in Joplin. Same house and everything." *Well, almost everything. Everything but my husband.*

"You're looking great, Samira!" Ricardo took the liberty of walking all the way around her in spite of the busy patio. "Life must be treating you well."

Samira turned her head to follow her old friend's path. "I'm good, Ricardo." *I really am.* "What about you?"

Ricardo's eyes lit up as he caught sight of something behind her. "Still in Joplin. Still a pharmacist at the hospital. Still scouting out new prospects and the one approaching your table is quite nice." Ricardo grinned and nodded toward Phil.

Samira suddenly realized she was caught standing between two men. *Wouldn't Susan love this?*

Phil stuck out his hand. "I don't believe we've met." His tone was all business.

"Oh, I'm sorry." Samira recovered her hospitality. "Ricardo Martinez is a former classmate of mine. And Ricardo, this is . . ." *Which name do I introduce his by?*

" . . . J.P. Ralston." Phil turned back toward Samira. "There's a table inside if you want to move in where it's cooler."

Samira returned Ricardo's ornery grin. "Do you want to go inside?" *After all, he's the one wearing the business suit.*

Samira watched Phil remove his suit jacket and hang it over the back of his chair. He proceeded to roll his shirt cuffs. *He always rolls his cuffs twice.*

"No, I'm fine." Phil's dark blue eyes penetrated hers as he spoke. "Will you be joining us, Ricardo?"

Ricardo was standing with his arms crossed. *You really never know what he's going to say next.*

"No, no, but thank you for the invitation. Maybe another time." Ricardo winked at Samira and leaned over and whispered in her ear. "When you're finished with him, send him my way. He looks like a dream."

Samira's mouth dropped open. *I can't believe he said that!*

Ricardo flashed his million-dollar smile in Phil's direction and raised a hand. "Nice to meet you J.P. Ralston." Ricardo hesitated.

Samira watched him study Phil's physique. *Oh, please! Don't say anything more!*

"Do take good care of Miss Samira. She's a doll. A real doll." Ricardo's eyes passed over Samira again. "It was good to bump into you, my friend. Look me up at the pharmacy sometime. Let's catch up."

I'm sure that would be entertaining. Samira pulled up to the table and watched Ricardo set out across the busy city street.

Phil unwrapped his sandwich. "So Ricardo was a classmate then?"

"Yes."

"And obviously you knew him well?"

"Yes." Samira took a sip of the cappuccino. *He sounds a little concerned.* "We were good friends."

Phil nodded. He looked like he might ask another question but instead sunk his teeth into his sandwich.

"I haven't seen him for a long time . . ." Samira added more for her own thought than for Phil's information.

"He didn't act like much time had passed."

I could have asked a few more questions in Springfield but chose to take the high road, Mr. Ralston. "What makes you say that?"

Phil avoided any kind of eye contact.

If I didn't know better I'd think he was a little jealous.

"He didn't hold much back when he saw you."

For the first time, Samira realized Phil had been watching her while she waited at the table. *Let's see if Phil can figure it out.* "Because he hugged me?"

"That and the way he looked at you. And I don't know that he needed to whisper in your ear."

Samira was smiling and she knew that was irritating Phil too. *He's jealous.* She put her fingers over her mouth to finish chewing before she spoke. *He really didn't like someone else paying attention to me, did he?* "That's just Ricardo." She remembered Ricardo from years ago. "He's always been that way."

Phil nodded again but this time he was looking directly at her. "So, did you like the way he was looking at you?"

Did you like the way that model touched you in the lobby? "No, Mr. Ralston, you have it all wrong." Samira waited on purpose. *Let's see how he likes this.* "I liked the way he was looking at you."

"What's that supposed to mean?"

Samira tipped her head and raised an eyebrow. "He was far more interested in you than he was in me." Phil's eyes were full of doubt. *He's going to freak.* "Seriously. Would you like to know what he whispered in my ear?"

Phil leaned back in his chair. "I don't know if I do or not."

Okay, then. Samira picked up her sandwich again.

"So what did he say?"

I knew he'd have to know. "Are you sure you want to know?"

"I asked, didn't I?"

So he did. She put her sandwich back on the wrapper. "When he whispered in my ear he told me to send you his way when I'm done."

Phil put his elbows on the table. The look in his eyes told Samira he didn't want to believe what he was hearing. "You're full of sh . . . ."

Uh, uh, you can't go there with me. Samira put her hand out. "I know Ricardo," she reminded. "And I know he liked what he saw."

"You know what?"

"What?"

He's speechless.

"You make me crazy."

"Is that a good crazy, or a bad crazy?" *I should probably know before I tease him again.*

"I don't know yet." Phil held his sandwich with one hand but he didn't take a bite. "I can usually figure out what a woman is thinking, but you never cease to amaze me."

"That's funny," Samira replied immediately. "Because I've always felt like my emotions were completely transparent." *I don't think I've ever voiced that to anyone outside of my own family!*

"You're wrong, Pretty Lady." J.P. shared his easy smile. "Emotions, maybe. But you hold your thoughts and I'm not exactly sure what to do about that." He took another bite of his lunch.

I don't hold my thoughts. Samira realized her internal defenses all too well. *Okay, so maybe I do. Sometimes.* She looked up the street in the direction of the Mid-America building. *I think he just finished what I started.* She decided to change the subject. "So where do you usually have lunch in the middle of a busy week?"

"What makes you think this is a busy week?"

There he goes, answering a question with another question. "You just sounded busy when you called. And you looked busy when I arrived at O'Flannegan's." *I might as well just state those facts.*

"You're right. It's been busy and looks like it's going to continue to be that way for a while. That's why I thought maybe we could catch a quick lunch today."

At least he said quick. Samira remembered the picnic. *Maybe I still can pop in on the girls for a few minutes.*

"You're week must be a bit hectic as well."

"What makes you say that?" *Few people ever refer to my life as being busy.*

"Well, let's see," he took a drink of water. "It seems Monday you were either in meetings or on the phone when I tried to reach you during the day. Then your line was busy all evening. Yesterday they said something about you being downtown most of the day . . ."

So he did try to call. "For training." *I should explain.* "I was teaching a new software program to some of the other librarians." *At least he tried to find me.* "So, I guess I was busier than sometimes." When she looked up Phil, was looking right at her. "What?"

"It's really good to see you, Samira."

He said my name this time. In spite of the warm day, goose pimples formed on Samira's arm.

Phil's voice was gentle. "I didn't know if you could break free in the middle of the day but I know my next two days are jam packed. I was hoping you could spare a few minutes . . ."

He spoke with such honesty Samira almost forgave herself for deserting her daughters. "I didn't feel like . . ."

Samira waited but Phil didn't complete his sentence. *No, please don't leave me hanging again!* She took the last bite of her sandwich and waited some more, but he didn't say anything. She caught Phil stealing a glimpse at his watch.

"Where are you parked?"

He's is NOT going to walk me to my car. "At the end of the block."

Phil crumpled his wrapping with his hands and offered to take her trash as well. Samira obliged. Instinctively, she picked up his sports coat and handed it to him upon his return.

"Thanks."

I hate it when he leaves his thoughts hanging like this!

"I'm assuming the end of the block this way?" Phil pointed toward the Mid-America building.

Samira nodded. Without speaking they started to walk in that direction at a slower pace than they had arrived at this location. Phil didn't offer his arm or try to take her hand this time. He was obviously deep in thought. *I don't know if I should try to extract those thoughts or just leave him alone.*

They were almost back to the stoplight when Phil finally broke their silence. When he opened his mouth his hand touched the side of hers but they didn't lock fingers as they had earlier.

"I've been thinking . . ." He was contemplative. "Saturday night didn't go quite like…"

Like what?

" . . . I don't know, like maybe it should have . . ."

I thought about inviting him to stay a little while, but he seemed anxious to go. "So which parts should have gone differently?"

Phil ran his tongue over his bottom lip. "Like maybe the part where I kissed you but didn't ask when I could see you again." J.P.'s eyes were focused in the distance. "Because, I've decided I don't like not knowing when our paths might cross again."

Neither to do I.

The walk signal flashed but Phil didn't follow the rest of the pedestrians across the street.

"Then I guess it's a good thing you called this morning."

I didn't know if . . . well, anyway, I was just glad you were in the office to take a call. Next time maybe we could plan a little further in advance."

"I'm glad you called."

Another group of people were gathering at the corner to wait for the light to change again.

"I'm glad to hear that because at first I wasn't sure you wanted to come." Phil looked away as he spoke those words as if maybe he didn't want a direct response.

He deserves to know. "You're right. But it didn't have anything to do with you, Phil." Samira took the liberty to touch his elbow where it was bent holding his jacket. "I'm supposed to be at a picnic with my girls right now. They're still waiting on me." *And if I were to be completely honest here, I'd tell him I noticed his Springfield friend on the cover of a magazine. But I'm not quite ready to be that honest.*

This time when the light changed, his hand guided her to follow the crowd. "Well, I was preoccupied when I left on Saturday too. I'd heard from the boys and things weren't going well up at their mother's."

I knew something wasn't right. "You should have said something," she replied sincerely. "We could have been home earlier . . ."

"That was the call I took on the way home, so being earlier wouldn't have helped any. I just had a hard time shifting gears." Samira caught his eyes for a moment. "I'd rather have given you my full attention."

Like the one in the magazine? Samira caught her thoughts. *That's really not fair. I need to let him off the hook.*

"Truce then?" She offered her right hand.

Phil questioned her with his eyes.

"You were distracted Saturday and I was distracted today. We cancelled one another out." She offered her hand again. "Truce."

Phil grinned as he slowly offered his right hand to seal the deal. "Truce." They shook but Phil didn't let go. "But before you get too far away this time I was thinking maybe we could go out for dinner one night this weekend."

The light changed and this time they crossed to the side of the street in the shade.

"Maybe," Samira answered with caution. "After standing Krissy and Kara up for lunch today I need a little time to redeem myself. Can I check with the girls and see which night they're going to the movies?"

"Do you think they'll forgive me for stealing you away this noon?"

"Maybe." *Then again, who knows? They're teenage girls.*

"James has another court appearance day after tomorrow. Barring any major changes in parental requirements I should be able to break free either night."

I wonder if these are new charges. "I'm sorry, Phil. I hope things will go his way in court."

"There's no way to know how the judge is going to rule. This is one time James is just going to have to live with the consequences." Phil seemed to stop in mid-thought. "But there's nothing I can do about it now."

He really doesn't know if he should be discussing his family with me.
They slowed to a stop in front of O'Flannegan's Pub.
"Well, we're back where we started from."
Samira thought for a moment. "I think we made a little more progress than that."
Phil shared his easy smile but he didn't speak.
"Should I call to let you know about the weekend?"
He nodded slowly. "You might have to leave a message if I don't pick up."
"I know. Busy week." *I'm okay with that.* She could feel his eyes trying to see through her dark lenses. Out of courtesy she removed her sunglasses.
"If we didn't have an audience . . ."
" . . . You'd kiss me right here on the sidewalk?"
Phil nodded with a grin.
Samira leaned closer and let his lips touch her temple. *I love the way he does that!* The tenderness of his lips sent ripples of pleasure all the way to the tips of her toes.
"You'll call me then?"
"I have your number this time."
An awkward silence held their thoughts. J.P. finally checked his watch.
"Yeah, me too. I should be getting back." *Or stopping to check on the girls and Susan.* She started to step away but couldn't help the next thought from falling. "I'm sorry I teased you about Ricardo."
Phil shook his head and grinned at the recollection. He put his hands out in warning. "Just make sure he keeps his distance, alright?"
"From you or from me?"
"From both!"
Nice we ended on a lighter note. Samira unlocked her car. *Obviously he has a jealous streak.* She slid behind the wheel. *He didn't want me out of his sight in Springfield either.* She started her car and backed out of the reserved parking area. *Just the same, I don't mind him staking a claim on me as long as he'll let me do the same on him.* Samira checked for on coming traffic and then pulled into the four-lane street. *And eventually I'm going to need to know the whole story behind the woman on the magazine cover.*
But that was a conversation for another day.

30

Before the Judge

"My car would've gotten us here faster." Mike climbed the steps to the courthouse two by two. "Saved on gas too."

"As it is we're right on time." J.P. followed his friend. *Less time to sit around waiting our turn.*

"Is there a crime in being early?"

I never thought I'd be approaching this courthouse on behalf of my son. Twice.

James caught up. "I don't think your Corvette would have held us all."

"All the more reason to leave your dad at home." Mike grinned mischievously,

It's probably a good thing he didn't offer. J.P. started to open the oversized door to the ancient entry hall, but Mike's hand brought it to a sudden halt.

What? J.P. looked into Mike's reflective lens.

"Whatever happens in here, I'm the attorney. You're the dad. Are we clear?"

He knows my temper, my motives and my tongue. J.P. could feel James watching him.

Other people were trying to pass through the door. *James has the best counsel.* He exchanged a resolute look with his son. *Today he needs a father.*

Mike let go of the door and they crossed the threshold into family court.

"We meet with social services first." Mike was already scanning the crowd. "Why don't you guys go stand in that line while I check things out inside."

I hate standing in lines. J.P. knew Mike was still trying to find a way to have the charges against James either dropped or reduced. J.P. led his son toward the door marked Department of Human Services.

"How are you doing?" J.P. wanted to sound like a father. *But I feel more like an attorney.*

"I'm alright. I guess." James leaned heavily into a marble wall. "I could live without this shirt though." He made a pass over his chest with his hands.

He's only talking about the shirt because he doesn't want to talk about what's really on his mind.

"You should try wearing one everyday." J.P. smoothed his own shirt.

"You couldn't pay me to wear your shirts everyday."

"I get paid to wear them."

James laughed. "Yeah, I guess you do."

"Do you know why Mike wanted you to dress up?"

"To improve my image." James raised his eyebrows in a facetious air of authority.

Not quite. "He wants you to make a good first impression on the judge."

"Same judge isn't it?"

"Yes, but it helps to lose the tough-guy image."

"I feel stupid."

J.P. bumped his son playfully with his elbow. "You look good."

Mike reappeared in the hallway. There was a purpose in his step that made J.P. meet him halfway. Mike took James by the sleeve and directed him toward a conference room door. The first one was occupied but the second one was empty.

Mike's eyes were alive with energy. *He knows something.* J.P. could sense sudden surge of adrenalin.

"James." Mike was direct. "Tell me exactly what you're going to tell the judge about the actual fight with Bruce."

James questioned his counsel. "Just like you told me to?"

"I told you to tell the truth." Mike reminded. "Tell me, right now, word for word what happened during the fight."

James took a breath. "He . . ."

"Who's he?"

"Bruce."

"Use his name in court. Continue."

They've been over this.

"Bruce shoved mom into the kitchen table and then he yelled at me to stay out of the argument."

"Were you involved in the argument before that?"

"I'd told him to leave Mom alone."

Mike was holding eye contact. "Was there any dialogue between the two of you before you told him to leave your mother alone?"

"No."

"Okay, go on."

What's Mike looking for?

"He . . ." James stopped and corrected himself. "Bruce, pushed Mom into the table and told me to stay out of the argument then he started toward Mom again. When he raised his arm to hit her, I laid him out."

"Define 'laid him out'."

I can personally testify to what he means by laying somebody out. J.P. checked the scar on his hand for proof.

James shrugged seemingly unaffected by Mike's insistence on using the right words. "Knocked him down."

"Better. And that was it, right?"

James nodded. "Yeah."

"Did he take a swing at you?"

"He didn't have a chance."

"Had he hit your mom before you walked in?"

"I don't know," James answered honestly. "Josh and I got home in the middle of the fight."

"Don't call it a fight in court. Call it an argument."

I still don't know what Mike's thinking.

"Where did you hit him."

"Bruce?"

Way to correct your counsel, James.

"Yes. Where did you hit Bruce?"

"Under the edge of his ribs with my right fist."

Yeah, that's the punch I know.

"One punch?"

James nodded. "One punch. He went down like a . . ."

"No explicits in court, James. Just the facts."

"One punch."

I need to know what's up. "What's with the clarification?"

Mike slid a hip onto the polished conference table. "Bruce is in there all bandaged up like an accident victim. His hand is wrapped and he's wearing this brace thing around his rib cage." Mike made a motion with his hand.

"On the outside of his clothes?"

Mike nodded. "His eye is all bruised up too."

"That's odd."

"Exactly." Mike agreed. "My guess is he's going to try to make it sound like he and James had a knock down drag out fight when in truth James took one swing in defense of his mother's safety." Mike stroked his mustache.

"Is Janet in there?"

"Not yet." Mike stood up and lifted his cell phone from his suit pocket.

Ah. He's going to summons Janet to testify now. J.P. checked his watch. *There's still time to make that happen.*

James suddenly looked concerned.

"Just tell them the truth, James. That's all you can do." *And hope your mother has the guts to do the same.*

James nodded as he lowered himself into a wooden conference chair.

An hour and a half later J.P. found himself sitting alone in a chair along the back wall of the courtroom. *At least this hearing is closed to the public.* But sitting there in the back row he didn't feel helpful whatsoever. *I certainly don't feel like an attorney and I barely feel like a father.* He glanced at his son. *He looks confident enough.* J.P. took a deep breath. *James shouldn't even be here.*

J.P.'s eyes went to his ex-wife. Janet was sitting a row behind Bruce with her head bowed. *She looks scared out of her mind.* J.P. recognized the little old lady Janet used for legal counsel. *She's the same witch who demoralized my character before a judge even though it wasn't me that stepped outside the boundaries of marriage.*

The proceedings began. Bruce was called to the stand to state his case. It was all J.P. could do to sit in his chair without making a verbal objection. *The ONLY thing that's keeping me quiet is the promise I made to Mike before we came in here.* The more questions Bruce answered, the more dramatic he got. *Half this stuff is irrelevant to the charges.* J.P. shifted in his seat and folded his arms hard against his chest. *Counsel is leading the witness, for god's sake!*

Mike began his cross-examination. "How many times did James make physical contact to your ribs?"

Bruce held his head high. "I can't remember. Once I was down everything got all blurry and . . ."

"How many times did James hit you, Mr. Hamilton?"

Hold him to it, Mike.

"One time that I remember."

"How many bones did he actually break?"

There was a long silence in the courtroom.

Bastard. J.P. leaned forward and sat on his hands to keep from crossing the bar. *I could take him out right here and now . . .*

"Mr. Hamilton, you are required to answer the question." The judge spoke with authority.

"There are no broken bones but . . ."

"Thank you." Mike interrupted Bruce's explanation.

"How long would you say the conflict between you and James lasted?"

Again there was a moment of silence.

"Let's see if we can narrow it down, Mr. Hamilton. Would you say five minutes or less than five minutes?"

He'll fall flat on his face with this one.

"Less than five minutes."

Thank you.

"And Mr. Hamilton, who placed the call to the authorities to summons the law enforcement and an ambulance to your residence?"

Who the hell cares who called for help? J.P. watched Bruce lower his head. When he answered, his voice was too low to be heard.

"Please speak into the microphone, Mr. Hamilton." The judge folded her arms.

"I made the call." Bruce raised his head. "But . . ."

"There are no further questions."

Now I know why he's the attorney and I'm the father.

James took the stand calmly and with confidence. *Mike has either prepared him extremely well, or James is extraordinary under pressure.*

The prosecuting attorney crossed his wrists behind his back.

"Can you describe for the court your mother's state of mind during the argument?"

"Objection, Your Honor." Mike rose from his seat. "Counsel is asking my client to speculate."

The judge raised her hand. "I'll allow it."

You can do it, James. J.P. fixed his eyes on his son. *Just tell them the truth.*

The judge allowed time for James to think his answer through.

"She seemed to be upset, but I don't think she was hurt . . ."

Mike took the floor to restate the most important issues but by this time J.P.'s mind was no longer in the courtroom. He'd slipped years into the past. *What was I? Six or seven at the time?* He'd taken a running leap at his own father in an effort to stop a verbal assault on his mother. In his memory he could still taste his father's blood as he sunk his half-grown permanent teeth into the Captain's shoulder. *I paid for that attack with solitary confinement in Uncle Roy's barn.*

"Objection, Your Honor . . ." Bruce's lawyer drew J.P.'s mind back into the courtroom. "Counsel is leading the witness."

The judge puckered her lips in thought. "I'll allow it. I believe the questioning is valid."

Mike restated his original question with caution. "Is this the first incident of physical attack from your husband, Mrs. Hamilton?"

When did they call her to the stand? J.P. ran his hand through his hair and watched Janet bow her head.

"You are required to answer the question, Mrs. Hamilton," the judge urged.

J.P. shifted in his chair. *I forfeited my visitation rights with Josh and James thinking it would give them more stability at home.* He still felt responsible for Janet's decision to separate. *I figured if I stayed out of their lives as much as possible that would give them one less thing to contend with.* Now, as he waited with the rest of the courtroom on Janet's answer, J.P. sunk deeper into his own self-doubt.

"Yes." Janet finally answered the question. "This is the first time my husband has attacked me in any physical way." Her eyes were moist when she looked up.

She's lying. J.P. studied Janet's face.

Cross-examination did not reveal any new information. Seemingly satisfied, Mike informed the judge that there were no more questions.

When the judge dismissed Janet from her seat, her eyes connected with J.P.'s for a brief moment.

It doesn't matter if she told the truth or not. Josh and James have options. J.P.'s eyes moved to Bruce Hamilton. *She's stuck with him anyway you look at it.* He tried to feel sorry for her but he couldn't. *Hamilton undermined my marriage and won the bride.* That was a fact forced upon J.P. long ago.

Following Janet's testimony, the judge clapped her mallet hard on the podium. "The court will be in recess for twenty minutes. I will see counsel in my chambers."

Mike turned in his chair and gave a nod of approval. *Obviously Janet's testimony got the judge's attention, just like Mike had hoped.*

As soon as Mike and the prosecuting attorney disappeared behind closed doors, J.P. moved to the chair directly behind his son.

James lowered his head. "Mike says this is a good sign."

"It is," J.P. assured. "The judge sees major discrepancies in the accounts. She needs to ask some more questions before making a ruling."

James nodded. Momentarily the boy's eyes scanned the room. *He's studying Hamilton.*

"I didn't give him that black eye," James whispered. "He looks like me the day after my fight with you."

J.P. recalled Bruce's exact words. *"He came at me like a Wild animal!"*

Very slowly J.P. realized that the fight scene Bruce had described was the one between him and James. "Holy shit!" J.P. spoke the words out loud.

James was staring at his father. "Are you thinking what I'm thinking?"

"I think so."

That pisses me off! "What's the motive behind that?" J.P. dared to look in Bruce's direction. *That's exactly what he did. He described my fight with James.*

"Mom looks really scared."

She knows the truth.

"All rise." The bailiff's voice announced the judge's return. As the people rose from their chairs, J.P. moved back to his seat at the back of the room.

"The charges again James Allen Ralston have been dismissed for inconclusive evidence." The judge wrapped her mallet against the podium.

That was that. The next case was announced without any further discussion.

J.P. fell into step behind James and Mike. Janet was also making her way up the aisle. Politely, but without speaking, J.P. waited for her to pass before making his own exit.

Mike turned seemingly unaware of Janet's presence. "James and I have some business to attend to with DHS, then we have a quick meeting with Janet and her attorney."

Why the hell do we have to meet with them? Mike led James away. J.P. realized he was standing alone with his ex-wife. *This could be interesting.*

"James didn't give him the black eye." Janet spoke without prompting. She was looking into the empty hallway.

What did she just say?

"I did." Janet sighed. "Last night."

Janet, this is not the time nor the place to make that kind of a confession. The attorney in J.P. told him not to speak a word.

"Bruce has it in for Jennie Johnson's dad. I think he's trying to take it out on James or something." Janet's confession came but not without cost. Her eyes were damp and her hands were shaking.

J.P. looked around. *Let's not let the real testimony be overheard in public.* There was an empty conference room not too far from where they were standing. Without speaking, J.P. led Janet into the room.

"Is this what you do for all your clients?" Janet asked with sudden sarcasm.

She just spilled her guts to me now she's going to attack? "I don't recall you ever being my client."

"I was on a lower priority list than your clients." She sat down in a chair.

I promised Mike . . .

"You never made time for me."

J.P. leaned on the back of a chair. *Nope, I'm not going to let that one go.* "That was partly by your choice, Jan."

"Maybe . . ." Janet found a tissue in her purse and blew her nose. "You're the only one who still calls me Jan."

"I met you as Jan, I believe." *Where did that come from?* "Would you prefer I call you Janet?"

"That's all right." The look in her eyes told J.P. her thoughts were far away. "I still wonder what we could have done to remedy our differences for the boys' sake?"

My legal counsel would not approve of this conversation. J.P. glanced through the open door. *Maybe coming in here wasn't such a good idea.* J.P. ran his hand through his hair. "Look, we've been over that a million times. We can't go back and recreate what didn't happen so let's just leave it where it is."

"I know," Janet wiped her nose again. "But sometimes I wish I would have given you a little more time to come around. I was so sure you didn't want to be with me that I think I hurried things along just so I could get on with my life."

Quit playing the martyr, Jan. J.P. wasn't moved by her tears nor taken by her honesty. *I need to get out of this conversation.* He started toward the door hoping for an escape.

"Phil . . ."

Phil?

J.P. stopped at the sound of his name. For a brief moment he heard another woman's tone in the voice. When he turned around that face faded back into Janet's.

" . . . would you have been more willing to reconcile had you not known of my involvement with Bruce?"

That question caught J.P. completely off guard. "You're involvement with Bruce was your choice. How I responded had nothing to do with your decision to end whatever was left of our relationship."

"But Bruce looked at me differently than you did, Phil. He talked to me. And he didn't always have to rush off to some meeting . . ."

J.P. widened his stance. "I'd have treated someone else's wife differently too, Jan!" The attorney could feel his blood pressure rising but decided against leaving the room. "And how the hell do you think his wife felt when she found out about you? Did you ever stop to put yourself in her shoes?"

Janet rose from her chair but it didn't change her height much. "Their marriage was over long before I ever entered the picture . . ." she looked J.P. in the eye. " . . . Maybe ours was too."

"Our marriage was over the day I came home and found you in my bed with another man." *That's a day I'll never forget.* "You made your choice."

"But you didn't even fight for me." Janet's eyes were wide with accusation. "You could have at least acted like you wanted me back. Maybe I just wanted to win your attention back! Did you ever think of that?"

Promise or no promise, she's going to hear me out this time around. "You won my attention, Jan!" J.P. started into his closing argument. "Your decision to sleep with one of my clients in my bed was enough indication. There was nothing more I needed to understand about your feelings for whatever was left of our marriage."

J.P. walked completely around the table and faced his ex-wife. *I've spoken these words a million times in my mind.* He balanced his weight on the tabletop with his fingertips.

"Until that day I would have gone to bat for our marraige; I'd have bent over backwards to give our boys a fighting chance at a family. But I was not going to stoop low enough to take my wife back after she willingly climbed onto another woman's husband. The choice you made is the one we've all learned to live with, Janet Hamilton. And now you get to live with that bastard for the rest . . ."

"Counselor!"

Mike.

"May I have a word with you?"

J.P. took one last look at his ex-wife. The tears that had formed in her eyes were now spilling onto her cheeks. *I waited ten years to speak those words. Now that they're out, I'm content to let them lie.*

Mike was walking very quickly toward the front doors of the courthouse. "I don't know what in hell's name was going on in there, and to be honest I don't care if I ever know," Mike continued to walk. "But I need you to pull yourself together and get a grip before you sign the paper with the judge that says you are now legal custodian of your son." Mike's pace didn't slow as he pushed the heavy door open into the sunshine.

J.P. stepped outside, glad to be out of the building—glad to be out of Janet's presence. His mind was reeling with memories that hadn't surfaced for years.

"Damn it, J.P., I leave you alone with the woman for five minutes and you're engaged in a domestic discussion from eons ago . . ."

"How much did you hear?"

"Enough to know you were out of line."

"She opened the can of worms . . ."

"I don't give a shit who opened what!" Mike took a step down from J.P. "You're the dad today. Did you forget? James needs a father and you're on the verge of denying him any hope of stability."

"I didn't forget."

"Then act like it!" Mike reached up and straightened J.P.'s shoulders. "Whatever was going on in that room is ancient history. Let it go."

J.P. tried to pull free of Mike's hands. *She had no right to bring that bastard into my bed . . .*

"You hear me?" Mike's voice was calm but firm. "Let it go. Walk it off. Run it off. Do whatever you gotta do to get it out of your system because in twenty minutes you're going to stand before the judge and sign for custodial rights. They need you to be in a stable presence of mind."

"What do you mean *they?*"

"I'm putting both Josh and James on the custodial papers. Josh can decide where he wants to live, but you're going to have legal rights for both of them until DHS is done with the case." Mike released his hold on J.P.'s shoulders. "Twenty minutes and she's a timely judge." Mike lifted his wrist so J.P. could check the time.

J.P. took a deep breath.

"Be in her chambers in twenty minutes and leave the baggage behind." Mike started to go back inside the building but turned with one last instruction. "And you don't have permission to talk to *anyone* between now and then. You hear?" Mike disappeared behind the heavy door.

J.P. wished for his running shoes and a pair of shorts. *I didn't involve myself with the intent of becoming a fulltime father.* He started down the stairs toward the parking lot. *But James doesn't have anywhere else to go either.*

Shit. He stopped walking in the shade of a maple tree. *Just like she controlled the circumstances in the divorce, she's controlling them again.* J.P. put his hands on his hips. *Things didn't work out so well for her with Bruce, so once again she's tampering with my life.*

J.P. noticed Janet's Jeep Cherokee drive into the parking lot. *Josh must be off work.* In a moment's time Josh was out of the car headed for the courthouse. *He's a good kid.* Josh ascended the steps two at a time. *He deserves better than he's getting.* Josh disappeared into the building. *They both deserve better.* J.P. sighed heavily. *But how am I supposed to work them into my schedule after all this time?*

It was almost time to meet the judge. *As much as I'd like to spend more time with the boys, signing for custody now feels like wicked revenge.* J.P. began back up the concrete staircase. *It's like Jan finally has me right where she wants me.* He opened the heavy doors. *And there's not a thing I can do about it.*

31

The Setup

Even though it's Saturday, I'm glad I went in to work. Samira stepped into the kitchen from the garage and came face to face with her daughters. *It feels good to get a head start on next week already.*

"We got the towels folded and put away." Krissy's eyes were hopeful.

"And I unloaded the dishwasher," Kara added. "And dusted the living room for good measure."

Wow! They really worked for this privilege.

"And . . ." Krissy emphasized the word. "We got the downstairs all ready for a sleepover complete with air mattresses and everything."

Step aside, ladies. Samira waved her hands. The girls backed up into the kitchen as their mother moved forward. "I'm impressed."

"Please, please can't we go to the movies and then have Paula and Renee spend the night, Mama?" Krissy's hands were folded like a prayer.

"You promised if we got our chores done while you were at the library . . ."

I know what I promised. "Have I ever not followed through on a promise?" *And it is nice to have a head start on the housework too.* "Thank you for going the extra mile too. Go ahead and call the girls."

Neither girl budged. *So why are they not racing for the telephone?* Samira raised an eyebrow.

"We called them already." Krissy wrinkled her face. Her freckles all bunched together around her nose. "And Susan said you were going to help her pick out fabric for her curtains."

"She said she'll be here in an hour or so to pick us up." Kara added carefully.

"Oh, she did, did she?" Samira sighed. *I knew there would be repercussions for missing the picnic, but I didn't know it would entail spending an entire Saturday afternoon with Susan!* Now there was no backing out.

Samira sank into the sofa and pulled a throw pillow onto her lap. "Great. I don't feel like being Susan's decorator today." *Or any other day, really.*

"At least she's taking you out to dinner while we're at the movies," Kara pointed out.

Maybe that's a good thing. Samira sighed. *And then again, maybe not.* Meals with Susan were stressful for a variety of reasons. *All I want to do right now is unwind for a few minutes.* When the phone rang Samira chose to let the girls answer.

"It's for you, Mama," Krissy announced with a smile. "And I don't think you're going to want to miss it."

Probably Susan. "Hello?"

"She's quite a chatter box."

Phil! Samira put her hand to her forehead and pushed her hair back from her face. "Yes, she is. I'm sorry about that."

"No need to be." Phil paused. "Sounds like your evening is a little tied up though."

"Oh, so you know my social agenda do you?" The question slipped out of Samira's mouth before she realized her tone. "What did Krissy tell you?"

"That you have a hot date."

"No way!" Samira immediately stood up. *Surely that's not what Krissy said!*

"Not really." Phil was laughing "I just wanted to get your reaction."

Well he got one. "That's not fair," Samira sat back down.

"Probably not." There was a slight pause. "I didn't get you called back yesterday. I forgot I had to make an appearance at a study session for my intern. That appearance lasted until almost midnight."

He doesn't sound any too thrilled about that. "How'd he do?"

"Do with what?"

"The studying."

"Oh . . ."

He always seems to be surprised when I ask a personal question.

"They did fine. There's four of them working together. Derek should pass without any trouble." The business tone that had slipped into Phil's voice shifted again. "So you're all booked up tonight, huh?"

Samira drew her knees into her chest and allowed the cushions on the sofa to close in around her. "I'm afraid I am." *But not by choice.* "I get the lucky job of helping a friend pick out fabric for new curtains. And if I understand correctly, I think we're meeting her husband somewhere for supper while our girls are all at the movies."

There was a delay in Phil's response. "Well, next time we'll have to plan a little further in advance. Unless you're free later on . . ."

Samira shook her head slowly into the phone. "The girls are having a double slumber party." On a second thought she added, "But you're welcome to stop over."

"At a slumber party?" Phil sounded surprised. "I don't know if that's a good idea or not."

"Well," Samira twisted her hair in her fingers. "You can think about it. They'll be downstairs eating snacks and watching movies."

It seemed like Phil wanted to talk about something more, but as had happened before, the telephone just didn't seem to be close enough. *I feel badly I had to turn him down for this evening. He sounds lonely. Or maybe he's just tired.*

She was just ready to put the phone back on the charger when Susan rang the back doorbell and let herself into the kitchen. *So much for my down time.*

"Ready to go, girlfriend?" Susan looked anxious. "Joey is with my mother, Sam is on the golf course and the girls are in the van. Where do you want their sleeping bags?"

Samira pointed to the laundry room. "Right there is fine. They're sleeping downstairs so they can have their privacy!" *And maybe so I can have mine.*

Krissy and Kara appeared in the living room. *My goodness. Make up. Hair done. Different clothes. Must be a serious shopping spree.* The girls looked so much older all done up. *Won't be long and there will be boys picking up Krissy and Kara for the movies.* That thought sent a shudder up Samira's spine. *I'm not ready for that!*

Samira followed behind Susan at the fabric store. *It's a beautiful day.* She ran her hand ran over a patterned bolt. *I could be in my garden.*

"What do you think?" Susan tossed a sofa pillow onto a swatch of fabric. "Is it close enough?"

No. That's not it. "Not if you want the greens to match."

Susan was impatiently turning the fabrics over and over. *A few more mismatches and she'll make the decision whether the fabrics match or not.*

An electronic version of the William Tell Overture sounded. Susan flopped her oversized purse onto a fabric table and began to dig for the ringing cell phone. *The best-suited fabric for the project is over here.* Samira pulled a perfect match from the rack and unrolled a yard to get the effect.

This is definitely the one I would choose. Samira carried the bolt back to where Susan was standing. *But convincing Susan will be another issue.* The sofa pillow matched all the colors perfectly. *I knew it.*

"Oh, do you think?" Susan sounded doubtful. "I'd pictured a solid."

"Everything else in your living room is a solid. A pattern will add texture and depth to the room."

Susan wrinkled her nose. "Your living room could be on the cover of 'Country Living.' Mine will be lucky to have matching greens." The woman turned the bolt this way and that. "But I trust your opinion. You're the decorator. But Sam's going to hate it."

Samira could have lived without the rhetoric reply. *If Sam's going to hate it, then why buy it?*

"Speaking of Sam," Susan continued without realizing the insult. "He's off the course now so we can meet him as soon as we're ready."

Samira checked her watch. The movie was just starting. *This is going to drag on way too long. I can feel it coming.*

"We'll go eat and then come back for the girls," Susan rambled on as she carried the decorative fabric to the service counter. "Twelve yards, please," she told the clerk. "Did I tell you Sam's new golf partner was eating with us?"

What? "Tonight?" *I should have known a Saturday evening outing with Susan would include a set up.*

"In a few minutes . . ." Susan paid the clerk. " . . . It's no big deal or anything so don't get all worked up about it. I haven't met him yet either."

But I don't want to meet him. Anxiety set in on the way to the restaurant. Susan chattered on and on about her golf lessons but Samira's efforts to act interested were in vain. *I hate it when she does this to me!*

Susan barged into the dining area. Samira followed with sweaty palms and a nervous stomach.

"Relax, girlfriend!" Susan patted Samira's arm. "I'm sure you'll like him. Sam talks about him all the time."

I wonder what they've told him about me? A few moments passed before Sam appeared. He waved across the room as the hostess escorted them toward the table.

"He looks like a dream!" Susan chirped.

I don't even want to look. Samira put her hand on her stomach. *These setups are always a disaster.* Samira arranged a cloth napkin on her lap. *I don't even have my own transportation so I'm stuck here now.*

"Hey Samira." Sam gave Samira a squeeze around the shoulders.

Samira forced a smile and returned the friendly gesture. *It's always good to see Sam.*

"Susan, this is my golf partner . . ."

Samira's eyes widened as she recognized the face. *What are the chances?*

" . . . and this is our friend, Samira Cartwright." Sam continued the introductions. "Ladies, meet Mike Benson."

Susan gushed an overly friendly greeting and invited Mike to sit down. Contrary to Susan's suggestive motions, Mike chose to sit across from Samira. Susan mimed for Sam to switch places. *Either Sam is ignoring Susan, or he really doesn't care where he sits.*

Samira dared to glance over the top of her menu. Mike wiggled his bushy eyebrows and returned a boyish grin from under his full moustache. *Obviously he remembers me.* Samira looked back to the menu, but nothing was coming into focus. *If I had any appetite before now, it's vanished.*

"That's breakfast," Sam whispered. "Dinner is over here." Without permission Sam turned the menu pages then went back to his own menu.

I really need to focus. Samira inhaled very slowly. She could feel Mike's eyes on her again. *I hope he doesn't let Sam and Susan know we've met before.*

Are you ready to order?" A waiter knelt down beside the table and made eye contact with Samira. She opened her mouth to speak.

" . . . Just bring me the Club Sandwich with fries. Ranch dressing on the side, please." Susan closed her menu and handed it across Samira to the waiter. The waiter jotted a note on his pad then looked back to Samira.

I have no idea what I want. "Go ahead," she told Sam quietly.

Sam and Mike both placed their orders while Samira scanned the choices again.

"How about an Italian salad and a gilled chicken sandwich?"

"She's always watching her diet," Susan announced as if Samira couldn't hear. "But just look at her figure. You wouldn't think she'd need to be worried at all, would you?"

She's always making remarks about my eating habits. Samira handed the menu to the waiter. Her shoulders were now stiff with tension. *What I really need is a glass of water.*

Mike stopped the waiter and requested him to bring more water. *That was very insightful of him.* Samira thanked Mike with her eyes and he nodded slightly in return.

Dinner conversation was mostly about golf. Samira listened. *I don't know enough about golf to offer anything anyway.* Samira took another drink of water. *However, I do know more now than I did a few weeks back!*

"You haven't eaten much," Susan pointed out as she pushed her clean plate to the center of the table.

My appetite faded when you mentioned a guest at dinner. Samira glanced across the table. *And it dissipated completely when the guest turned out to be Mike Benson.*

Sam tried to smooth over Susan's frankness but it just magnified the issue. *I wish they wouldn't talk about me while I'm sitting right here.* Mike winked over the marital discussion going on between them.

Samira was relieved when Susan's telephone finally rang. Just like before, she flopped the heavy bag onto the corner of the table and began to dig.

"Sorry, Samira.," Sam apologized as Susan stepped away. "She just doesn't think before she speaks."

"Actually she speaks what she thinks," Samira corrected gently. "It's okay." *That's just Susan. Unfortunately.*

Sam patted Samira's hand. "You're too forgiving."

Sometimes.

"Sam are you finished?" Susan returned to the table and leaned over the back of her chair. "Mom has to leave and needs us to pick Joey up before we get the girls from the movie."

Sam frowned and waved his hand over his plate. "I wouldn't mind finishing." There was new tension in his voice.

Now even Sam is uncomfortable in front of his friend.

"Where's your car?"

"At the club." Sam took a bite.

"I can drop you off there on my way to Mom's."

And my car is home in my garage.

"I guess I can be ready," Sam sounded disgusted. He rolled his eyes at Mike as he pushed his chair back from the table. "What about you, Samira, are you . . ."

"Oh my god," Susan remembered out loud. "I forgot you were with me too. I told Mom I'd be there in a few minutes."

"I can take her home, not to worry." Mike jumped into the conversation.

The lump that had been in Samira's stomach immediately lodged in her throat. *Oh, No. That's not okay.*

"Are you okay with that?" Susan asked abruptly.

No!

"I'm okay with it," Mike answered. "You guys go do what you have to do and I'll take care of the lady."

Sam grinned at his friend. "Are you sure?"

If I didn't know better I'd think Susan had this planned.

Mike stood when Sam stood. "It's not a problem, really." He winked at Samira. "I don't mind at all."

Sam walked backwards, eyeing his friend. They exchanged a thumbs up sign.

"Sam will bring the girls by after the movies, all right Samira?" Susan called out as she walked away.

"As if you've had a say in any of this . . ." Mike added as he returned to his dinner. "She's quite a character."

Samira blinked in unbelief. "I'm sorry . . ." *What just happened here?* "I can call my brother for a ride. He lives close . . ."

"Nonsense," Mike interrupted. "Relax and enjoy your meal. I'll run you home."

Samira surveyed the situation. *I don't know what it is about Mike Benson, but I trust him.* She thanked him and went back to her now cold sandwich.

Mike flagged the waiter. "Would you care for anything to drink?"

You know, I would. "Iced tea would be very nice."

Mike ordered a cold draft along with the tea. "So, how have you been, Samira?"

I'm not very good at small talk. "I've been good." *I wonder if he knows I've been to Springfield with Phil.* "Summertime is always an adjustment at my house but we're settling in."

"Are you a schoolteacher?"

"No, I work at the Maple Street Library, but my girls are out of school for the summer. Their freedom seems to affect my schedule." *I haven't given out that much information to a man in a long time.* Samira glanced at Mike and found his blue eyes twinkling with energy.

"How old are your girls?"

"Thirteen and fourteen."

"I can understand why your life gets a bit hectic in the summer then." Mike smiled easily. When his beer arrived he took care to enjoy the first sip.

"How do you know Sam and Susan?"

Samira wiped her fingers on a napkin. "Let's see, I've known them since, well, I guess since Kara, my oldest, was in preschool. Our girls are the same ages. They were good family friends while . . ." Samira pictured park picnics with Tom and the girls. "I've known them a long time." She immediately forced the memories back into the archives.

Mike nodded as he took another drink from his draft. He sat the beer on the table and leaned into the table.

"So what brings you to dinner with them tonight?"

Samira was somewhat overwhelmed with all the questions. *At least he's easy to talk to.* "That's a good question." *I've wondered that myself.* "I think I'm here as a result of a guilty conscience."

"Really," Mike seemed intrigued. "Do tell."

Samira had to smile at his demeanor. *This is kind of like a personal counseling session.* "Okay, I stood Susan up at a mother-daughter picnic earlier in the week so tonight I'm paying my dues."

Mike opened his arms to the space around the table. "I don't see any mothers with daughters here."

True statement. She was beginning to enjoy his company. "Okay, then let's just say I was strong-armed into dinner with her and Sam. You just happened to come along as a surprise."

"Ditto." The curls on the top of Mike's head bobbed when he nodded his head. "I think we were set up."

Samira set her sandwich to the side. *I think I'll just finish my salad.* "You may be exactly right about that."

Mike cocked his head in thought. "I don't know much about Sam and Susan, but I have this friend. I'm thinking you might know him. He has many aliases. One such alias is Phil Ralston . . ."

"Another being J.P. Ralston?"

"One in the same," Mike continued. "I know a lot about him. If he knew I was sitting here with his date, he'd kick my ass."

I'm glad he brought Phil into this. "And what do you think we should do about that?"

Mike leaned into the table again. "I'm thinking when we leave here I take you straight to your house and we forget we ever saw one another. I happen to like my ass as it is."

Samira laughed. *Surely he's exaggerating.*

"No, seriously, Samira." Mike's face became very earnest. "He'll beat the shit out of me if he thinks I stole his date tonight. Trust me on this one."

"Maybe I could talk to him for you." Samira took a bite of salad. *It's the least I could do.*

"Here . . ." He handed his cell phone to Samira.

I was joking!

"When he answers act like you don't know me."

What in heaven's name am I going to say if he answers?

"Mike, what's up?"

Oh, he thinks I'm Mike! "This is Samira."

There was a long pause.

"Samira Cartwright." *I don't think this was such a good idea.*

Mike leaned back in his chair attentive to the conversation. "Tell him we're having a drink together."

I think not!

"That's not the number on the I.D."

Caller ID? Samira took a deep breath. *He knows I'm with Mike.*

"I guess not." She looked at Mike. "Here, I'll let you talk to him."

Mike shook his hand and moved out of reach. "You said you'd talk to him for me, remember? Get me off his hit list and I'll take you home."

This is getting complicated. Samira gave Mike a look of warning as she put the phone back to her ear.

"Where the hell are you?" Phil's voice sounded more forceful.

I don't want to make him mad! "T-Bone's Family Restaurant."

"I thought I was talking to Mike. Why T-Bone's?"

"It's a long story," Samira began. "I'm here with Mike because my girlfriend had to leave. He's going to take me home."

"Told you he'd be pissed." Mike shook his head.

I don't like being in the middle of this friendship.

"I thought you were busy tonight."

It's not what he's thinking. "I was, with Susan," Samira reminded back. "I just didn't know she was going to leave me here."

"Are you headed home now?"

He sounds so serious. "I think so." She looked at Mike. "Are we going home now?"

"Sure. If that's in the best interest of my well-being." Mike crossed his arms.

I wonder where Phil is. She decided to ask. "Where are you?"

"At the office." Phil hesitated a moment. "I need to finish what I'm working on then I'll meet you at your house."

"You don't have to do that." *I'd hoped he'd come by tonight, but not because he didn't trust me!* "I'll be fine."

"He's going to meet us at your place, isn't he?"

How does Mike know that?

"I knew he wouldn't trust me."

"Here, maybe you should talk to Mike . . ." Samira stood up and handed Mike the phone. "I'll be right back." *I'm not going to give him the chance to back away again.*

A few minutes later Samira stepped out of the ladies' room to find Mike paying for her meal.

"Please, let me get it." She opened her purse.

Mike returned his wallet to his back pocket. "Too late," he stated. "Besides, I'll bill it to J.P. anyway." With that Mike wiggled his eyebrows and motioned toward the exit. "My guess is we have about five minutes to get to where ever it is you live before I'm accused of kidnapping or something far worse."

Samira was humored by Mike's inference to Phil's jealousy. When he opened the door on a shiny red sports car for her, she stopped in her tracks. *This is a far cry from Phil's practical pickup truck!*

Mike's hand guided her into the leather seat. "Stay low and remember, you don't know me."

Samira laughed. *He's actually quite fun.*

The drive across town was speedy and a bit too careless for Samira's taste. *But at least I can say I've lived to tell the story.* She pointed to her driveway.

"Here you are, Samira Cartwright, delivered to your house as promised." Mike pulled the emergency brake between the bucket seats. "I'd walk you to your door but am afraid that would not be in my best interest."

Samira thanked Mike for the ride. " . . . And for dinner." She fumbled for the door handle.

"Here, sit tight." In a flash Mike was at her side opening the door for her.

Just as Mike took her hand to help her out of the low seat, another car pulled into the driveway. Kelly Davis smiled her brilliant smile and greeted Samira.

"I brought the girls over from the movies. I hope that's all right!" Kelly popped out of her car and flipped her seat forward. Three teenage girls bounded out of the backseat and Krissy climbed out of the front.

"We made her scoop the loop with the top down!" Krissy informed as she eyed the man standing next to Samira.

"What happened to Sam?" *I thought he was going to bring the girls home.*

"We didn't see him anywhere and the crowd was thinning out," Kelly answered with a matter of fact. "I didn't want them standing around in an empty parking lot."

I agree. "When did you get home?"

"Monday." Kelly pushed the driver's seat back into position.

"How was the trip?"

"Fine."

"My car can do that too." Mike jumped into the already confusing conversation.

Oh, I forgot about Mike.

"Do what?" Kelly asked.

"That convertible thing."

I should introduce him to Kelly.

"Really?" Kelly put her hands on her hips and turned into the breeze to blow the curls off her face. "Prove it."

"Do we know him?" Krissy asked her mother.

No. No one knows Mike.

"Yeah, we know him. That's Mike. Dad's golf partner." Paula answered.

Paula and Renee know Mike?

"Thanks for the ride Miss Davis." Paula turned directly to Samira. "Can I use your phone? I think I should call Dad and tell him to never mind about picking us up."

"Sure." *I guess.*

Mike was busy unfastening clips along the edge of the windshield. With the push of a button, the white vinyl top lifted into the air and began to fold automatically into the space behind the seats.

That's amazing.

"Not bad, Mike." Kelly emphasized his name as she reacted to the challenge. "But I bet your car can't do this." She climbed in behind the steering wheel and cranked up the sound system.

It's Aida! My favorite opera.

Mike crossed his arms and leaned back on his heels. "*Miss Davis . . .* "

Apparently they don't need an introduction now.

" . . . I can name that tune in 3 miles."

"Do you mind?" Kelly was looking at Samira.

"Mind what?"

Kelly removed the band holding her hair and immediately wrapped it back into a bun. "He said he could name the tune in three miles. I'm inclined to take him up on it."

"Oh. No. He's not with me."

"But she was with me." Mike jumped into his car. "Let me park in the street. I'll be right back."

Kelly turned the volume down on the sound system. "If he guesses *Giuseppe Verdi,* then he's worth hanging onto. But he's going to have to be able to spell the first name correctly." Kelly climbed into the driver's seat. "I'll let you know how he does." Kelly flashed her bright smile.

Samira suddenly realized what Kelly was thinking. "He's really not with me." She watched Mike get out of his car. "He just gave me a ride home."

"And it was my pleasure." Mike opened the passenger door. "I must say, I've played golf. Played just today in fact. But I can't say that I've ever ridden in one."

"Buckle your seat belt," Kelly instructed. "Three miles to name the tune and the composer and I'll bring you back."

Mike waved a hand into the open air above the windshield. "Tell our mutual friend I'm sorry I couldn't stick around."

Kelly put her little black car into reverse. "We'll be back".

Take your time. Samira started for the house. *That was quite a set up.* She picked up the afternoon newspaper off the porch. *Both of them.*

Samira had been home quite some time before headlights pulled into her driveway. *That was a long three miles.* She leaned into the kitchen window. *Nope, I know that truck now.*

Phil stopped just inside the front door. "Who's little black car?"

Samira craned her neck around the doorframe. *What do you know?* The top was up on Kelly's car and it was now parked in front of her house. Mike's was nowhere to be seen. *I wonder when they made that exchange?* She closed the door. *I bet Mrs. Barnes is having a hay day with all of this activity.*

"It belongs to my girlfriend." Samira closed the door. *I think I'll leave that story in Mike's court.* "Have you eaten?"

"No, I haven't." Phil was looking around the room.

"The girls are downstairs with their friends."

"It took me longer to finish up than I thought," Phil explained. "I trust Mike delivered you in a timely fashion."

Samira smiled. "Very much so," she assured. "Straight home, no detours or anything." *However, he was a little liberal on the neighborhood stop signs.*

"Mike's a good guy." Phil's eyes were watching her every move.

I wonder what he's really thinking. Samira offered a plate of leftover tacos.

"Mike seemed to think you might not appreciate his assistance tonight, Mr. Ralston." She removed the hot plate from the microwave. "He was worried you might try to rearrange his features somehow."

Phil swiveled in the barstool as Samira walked toward him. As she slid the plate onto the countertop he intercepted her at the waist. The next thing Samira knew she was standing right against him.

"Mike knows not to mess with my territory." Phil's eyes were softer than they'd been a moment earlier.

His territory? Samira crossed her wrists behind his neck. *Then I'm guessing Mike also knows I went to Springfield.* The potholders in her hands hung loosely against his shoulder blades. "I wouldn't want to create a rift between friends." *I think I'm going to kiss him.*

Samira closed her eyes and allowed his lips to touch hers not only once, but more than once. By the time she was aware of footsteps on the stairs, the tacos were no longer steaming on the counter. Samira reluctantly backed away. *Just look normal.* She hung the potholders on the hook next to the stove. *Even though normal is never easy when Phil is around.*

Four girls appeared in the kitchen.

"Are you cooking tacos, Mama?" Krissy sniffed the air. "They smell great. Are there any more?"

Phil's back was to the girls.

"No more tacos, but plenty of chips and salsa." She poured some chips into a wooden bowl and handed Kara an already opened jar of salsa. *Back downstairs, please.*

"Can we have melted cheese?" Kara asked.

I guess.

"Here," Krissy took the chips and salsa from her sister. "You melt the cheese. We'll take this downstairs."

It's like the girls haven't even noticed I have company!

"Do we know him?" Renee` asked. Her eyes were looking at Phil's back.

"It's not Mike." Paula announced.

It's definitely not Mike.

"No, that's Phil." Krissy punctuated. "Hi Phil. These are our friends."

That's enough information. Samira put the jar of cheese in the microwave.

Phil turned around at the informal introduction and politely greeted the young women.

"Okay then." Paula turned toward Kara. "Bring the cheese when it's ready."

Like mother like daughter, Samira thought to herself. *Paula is going to have all of Susan's lack of tact.*

By the time the girls went back downstairs, Phil was checking his phone.

I don't want him to have to leave. Samira noticed the clock on the wall. It was after ten o'clock.

"James," Phil informed. "I left him on a basketball court with my intern. They were supposed to page me when they were done."

"Do you need to pick him up?" *I hope not.*

Phil put the phone back on his hip with a natural ease. "No, Derek is dropping him off at the house. The page is my way of knowing they're on the way."

"Is James still under adult supervision?"

"To some degree." He was finished with the plate of food but he wasn't moving away from the bar.

"How did things go for him on Thursday?" Samira slid onto the stool next to Phil. *He looks so tired.*

Phil sighed. When he spoke his voice was distant. "Things went all right. Mike managed to get the immediate charges against James dropped, but an investigation is still pending . . ."

Oh, yes, Mike is also a lawyer. Samira surmised. *That would account for way he questioned me at the dinner table.*

"... All things considered, we're better off now than we were before the hearing."

"And that's good, right?"

"The only thing better would be if I didn't have to get back home to be a father right now." Phil's eyes reflected a gentle honesty.

Samira smiled softly and touched Phil's arm. Motherhood was not exactly her first choice at the moment either.

"I don't think you ever get to stop being a parent." *His eyes look heavy.* "We'll just have to make our own time."

"With the kids or without?"

I was thinking without. "Why do you ask?"

Phil pulled Samira's barstool closer to his and rested his arm behind her. "I have to go out of town on business the first part of this week, but when I get back I was thinking I'd take my boys up to my aunt and uncle's ranch." Samira could feel Phil's fingertips in her hair. "I was thinking maybe you might bring Krissy and Kara up with us."

Go out of town with my girls? With Phil and his boys? Samira ran her calendar in her mind. "That's the fourth of July weekend."

"I know." Phil's eyes were serious. "I take the boys up there every year."

And I spend every year celebrating Kara's birthday and watching fireworks with my family.

"Since you missed their little picnic thing on my account I thought maybe we could make it up to them."

Samira considered her options. *This is definitely a matter for family discussion.*

"Where exactly is this ranch?"

"North of Macon. It borders Mark Twain State Park."

I've never been that far north. Samira tilted her head in thought. "And what kinds of things do you do while you're there?" *Because I'm really not an out—doorsy kind of person.*

Phil smiled quietly. "We eat really well because my aunt is a great cook. We sleep really well because it's really quiet there. We hike and fish and ride horses sometimes. Sometimes we take a dip in the lake." Phil raised his shoulders. "Basically whatever you want to do." He winked. "You can read your book for long periods of time without any interruption if that's what you choose to do."

Samira smiled. *I like the way he thinks of me.* "I'll talk to the girls." *Hard to tell what their reaction will be.*

"You can let me know." Phil seemed to be shifting gears. "I fly out tomorrow afternoon and get back late Wednesday. I won't leave for the ranch until after work on Friday."

Samira avoided eye contact but she nodded her head. *What I'd really hoped was to see him maybe tomorrow afternoon when he isn't so tired and it wasn't so late.*

Phil's finger lifted her face to his and she returned his kiss again. This time he didn't hang on. When she walked him to the door she could feel the weight of his unspoken thoughts lingering between them.

"Be in touch, all right? My cell phone rings even when I'm out of town."

At least I have permission to call. "Hurry back."

"Only three days."

Three long days.

He kissed her on the forehead then turned and walked out the door.

He has no idea how much comfort that little kiss brings me.

Samira waited until he drove away before she closed the door. Kelly's car was still parked out front. *It must be nice to have such freedom.*

Suddenly the restraints of parenting seemed overwhelming. Samira leaned heavily on the door with her face in her hands. The emptiness deep inside echoed the reality of her singleness. *My desires taunt me even more when he's here and I can't have him.*

"More chips, Mama!"

Until I met Phil, I was simply a mom, and that was enough. Samira slowly lifted her weight off the door. *But now I've crossed the line. Motherhood almost feels like a burden sometimes.*

Samira refilled the wooden bowl with tortilla chips.

"Did Phil leave already?" Krissy asked innocently.

"Yeah, he went home to . . ." *He went home to be a dad.*

Krissy tipped her head in anticipation.

" . . . It was getting late."

"Too bad he couldn't have stayed longer." Krissy turned toward the basement steps again. "Thanks for the chips!"

'Too bad' is an understatement. Samira gathered Phil's dinner dishes. *I have a feeling he needs me too.* Girlish laughter echoed up the stairwell. *How will we ever be able to fulfill our needs for one another and still carry out the responsibilities of parenthood?* She rinsed the dirty dishes. *The way I see it, things could get complicated very quickly.*

32

More to Come

Josh grinned. "Relax, Dad. She's still back there."

"I know." J.P. had to look anyway. *Just to make sure she's still following in her car.*

"I'll let you know if she drops out of my mirror." Josh was driving his father's pick up. "We're not that far out now anyway."

That's true. J.P. was glad Josh was driving. *This has been a hellacious week.* "So you and James got along alright with Derek then?"

"He's cool." Josh answered with a shrug. "I can see why you needed me around to chauffeur James during the daytime." Josh raised his eyebrows. "You got him scheduled tight enough?"

"That's so I can keep track of him." He looked at James, sound asleep in the seat behind him.

"Do you really want to know where he is at five in the morning?"

"Yep." *The earlier he gets up, the earlier he goes to bed at night.* "But Derek did alright?"

"I like having Derek stay over better than hanging out at Denise's place while you're out of town."

Denise would agree. If he looked just right, J.P. could see Samira's car in the right hand mirror. *Samira sounded excited to be coming up here when I talked to her on the phone.* He watched her car in the distance. *But her disposition in person wasn't as promising.*

"You can sleep if you want to, Dad." Josh was looking at his father.

Do I look that tired? "That's alright . . ." *But it would feel good to close my eyes for a little while.*

"I'm going to get you to the ranch either way. You might as well take advantage."

J.P. studied his son. *He's confident. He's dependable.* The father adjusted his seat to tilt a little further back. *And he's got a really good point.* J.P. closed his eyes.

The engine shifted into a lower gear. *Are we there yet?* J.P. forced himself awake. James was stirring too.

"Slow down on the gravel. The dust will make it harder for Samira to follow." J.P. gave the instruction as he moved his seat back into the upright position.

Josh obeyed and let off the accelerator. "What kind of a name is Samira, anyway?"

The kind of name for a really pretty lady. "I don't know."

"Never heard it before."

Me neither. J.P. twisted in his seat to stretch his back muscles. He was relieved to finally be arriving at the ranch. *I just hope bringing Samira here with her daughters is a good idea.* J.P. watched the dust behind his truck drift off into the field. *Something in the way she looked at me today tells me she is having second thoughts.*

Josh pulled into the driveway and parked at the end of the sidewalk. J.P. watched Samira pull her car in behind. *And here comes Aunt Maggie. She's always happy to see us, even if we bring an entourage of strangers into her house.*

"Oh Phillip," Aunt Maggie gushed. "It's so good to see you!" She threw her arms into the air so J.P. could give her a hug. "Uncle Roy went into town for supplies."

Supplies. J.P. shook his head slightly. *You'd think they lived in the outback or something.* He watched Samira climb out of her car. *Uncle Roy probably went to town to get a gallon of milk.* Krissy and Kara joined their mother in the driveway. *I still can't believe I brought a woman, and her daughters, to the ranch.* J.P. ran his hand through his hair.

James bumped his father's arm as he walked past. "She looks a little uptight."

I hate to admit it, but he's right.

"Maybe she's just nervous," Josh added with a firm pat to his father's broad shoulders.

We can only hope.

J.P. took a deep breath and opened his arm to Samira as she stepped up next to him. *If the tension in her shoulders is any indication, I'd say she's more than a little on edge. Let's get the introductions out of the way.* "Samira, this is my aunt, Maggie."

" . . . And these must be your beautiful girls," Aunt Maggie exclaimed. "Welcome to the ranch."

J.P. took the liberty to properly introduce Krissy and Kara to Aunt Maggie. *I guess they only spent a couple of minutes with the boys.* J.P. decided to reintroduce James and Josh as well.

"This looks like a blast!" Krissy's eyes were wide with wonder. "Do we get to sleep in that big cabin?"

At least one of them has a sense of adventure.

"Absolutely," Aunt Maggie answered with a hearty laugh. "Come on inside and the boys can show you around."

J.P. intercepted a look of dismissal on James's face. He raised an eyebrow of warning. *You will do as Aunt Maggie suggests.* James waved his arm for Krissy and Kara to follow him into the house. *Thank you.* J.P. watched Krissy skip up the sidewalk to catch up. *Where's Kara?*

J.P. turned around and found her face to face with her mother. Kara's arms were crossed and she wasn't showing any signs of Krissy's enthusiasm whatsoever.

This could be trouble. He observed the two women exchange a nonverbal point of contention. *This is no doubt half of Samira's problem.*

"I bet you're famished," Aunt Maggie clapped her hands. "I made cherry pie this afternoon." She turned toward the house. "Come on in, we'll get the bags later."

Samira had already opened her trunk. *I guess she's going to get her bags now. The least I can do is help carry them inside.* There were only two bags for the three women.

"You pack lighter than any woman I've ever traveled with . . ."

"And how many women might that be?"

Where did that come from?

Samira lifted the first bag from the trunk.

"Here, let me help you . . ."

"That's alright," Samira stopped J.P. from helping. "We'll get them."

Alright. J.P. pulled his hand back. *This is certainly a new side of her.* He watched Kara take one of the bags and start for the house. *Let's just hope she loses the attitude.*

Kara dropped her bag at the end of the sidewalk and impatiently crossed her arms.

I could offer to fix Kara's attitude for her . . . He glanced in Samira's direction. *Or I could stay out of it and give her some space.* J.P. decided on the latter. He walked back to his truck and began to unsnap the tarp. *What the hell?* He watched Josh pick up Kara's bag. *She's following him into the house.* Now Samira was waiting on him.

J.P. lifted his own duffel out of the truck. It felt strange to carry his own bag but not hers. *But she had her chance and turned it down. I'll be damned if I'm going to offer again.* He opened the front door. Before crossing the threshold, he took one last purposeful breath of fresh air. *Just in case the walls start to close in.*

"Go on up, honey," Aunt Maggie was talking to Samira. She waved her hand toward the staircase. "Your room is the first door on the right. Just make yourself right at home." Aunt Maggie smiled warmly at Phil. "I'll have your pie ready when you come back down."

As soon as Samira was around the bend in the staircase Aunt Maggie spoke. "It's okay, Phillip. She just needs to get settled. Why don't you come on in and have some pie."

Obviously Aunt Maggie is aware of the tension too. He stared at the staircase. *Cherry pie doesn't even sound good at the moment.*

"I think I'll go shut the barn up." *Anything to get out of this house for awhile.*

"Oh nonsense. Roy will be back in a jiffy. You just come on in and relax a bit."

Relax? J.P. shook his head and opened the door. *I don't know if that's an option.*

"Dad?" Josh's voice stopped J.P. in his tracks. "Aren't you coming in for pie? It's still warm and Aunt Maggie has homemade ice cream to go with."

"I'll be back." *Eventually.* "You guys go ahead." *Don't wait on me.* He watched Kara follow Josh into the kitchen. *Whatever Josh did to win her over seems to have eased her attitude.* He could still feel the sting of Samira's tone. *There's still an attitude to contend with at the top of the stairs.*

J.P. stepped out onto the porch. *It's a little damp, but not too cool yet.* He placed his foot on the porch railing and stretched one leg and then the other. *The sooner I work off my own stress, the sooner the weekend can begin.*

Chase fell into step as J.P. picked up his pace. *A good, hard run won't hurt a thing.* By the time he reached the lake, J.P. was in full stride. The sun was just starting to dip over the horizon. It cast an orange glow onto the water.

J.P. slowed to a stop. He leaned over and put his hands on his knees. Chase bounded on by and rushed directly into the cool water. The canine returned a few moments later soaking wet. J.P. took off back toward the house. *Before Chase has a chance to shake himself dry!*

At least she has her own car in the case she decides she can't stick around. J.P. approached the barn. Sweat was pouring off his body but he felt better having spent his own energy. *What made me invite her here anyway?* He pulled his shirt off over his head and used it as a sweat rag as he began to slow his step. *Had I anticipated the attitude, I'd have skipped the notion.*

Once inside the barn J.P. leaned into the wall and stretched the tendons in his leg. *Maybe she'll decide she can't stay.* J.P. changed his stance and stretched out the other leg. *And what's with the cheap shot about how many women I've traveled with anyway?*

Chase trotted into the barn and greeted the horses before heading back out into the twilight. *I might as well finish up for Uncle Roy while I'm out here.* J.P. started toward the horse stalls to close the windows. *Don't know if I'm ready to face her yet or not anyway.* Instead of opening the gate, J.P. simply lifted himself over the metal rungs. *She pisses me off.* He stopped to greet Claire and allowed the old mare to nuzzle her soft nose into his hand. *Women. There's a breed I have yet to master.*

J.P. thought he heard Chase. *I don't want him to startle the horses.* He turned to slow the dog's approach, but instead came face to face with the brown eyes of the woman he'd deserted at the house.

Samira.

She stopped walking.

She is beautiful. He turned away long enough to close the wooden shutter over the open window. *But I don't have the slightest idea what makes her tick.* When he turned around Samira hadn't moved. *And she sure knows how to piss me off.* She was still watching him. *What am I supposed to do with her now?*

J.P. slowly lifted himself back over the gate. Several yards separated him from Samira. *The last attempt to communicate with her didn't exactly go well.*

"What's on your mind, Pretty Lady?" *As if that's something I really want to know right now.*

Samira's head fell forward and she put her hands behind her back. He watched as she gathered her thoughts. When she looked up her face was serious.

She probably told her girls to meet her in the car . . .

"I came to . . ."

Just get it over with, then we can both get on with our weekend. J.P. draped his arm over the gate and stared at the wall on the far side of the barn.

" . . . well, I came to apologize. I'm sorry. I was out of line."

That's not what I was expecting. J.P. listened to Samira's apology replay in his mind. *Tell her she doesn't have to be sorry.* J.P. opened his mouth to speak, but she was moving toward him and he couldn't force any words to officially form.

"This has been a really stressful week," Samira was explaining as she walked. "And then Kara, well . . ."

You don't have to explain anything to me . . .

"Kara and I are experiencing some differences in opinions, and . . . well, . . ." Samira stopped walking just a few feet from the stall. " . . . I'm just sorry, that's all."

Chase suddenly lost attentiveness in the discussion and quickly darted back outside.

Say something! Anything, Ralston! J.P. finally found his tongue. "You don't have to be."

"Yes, I do." Samira threw her head back and shook her hair off her shoulders.

Don't do that, Samira. The summer breeze coming in through Toby's window was cool against J.P.'s bare, damp chest. *Hard to stay pissed at her if she's sorry.* J.P. crossed his arms to divert a shiver.

Samira's eyes were still low when she spoke again. "Maybe we could start all over. You know, pretend like we're just arriving or something," Samira suggested. Her serious face was fading into a girlish grin.

At least she's not packed to leave. J.P. decided he could play along. "Like go back to the driveway again?"

"Well, maybe not quite that literally, but at least start our time together all over." Samira's hair was gently blowing in the breeze.

I could easily keep her alone in the barn with me for the rest of the night. "Welcome to the barn, Ms Cartwright." J.P. put his foot on the bottom rung of Toby's gate. With little effort he swung his leg to the other side. *The further I stay away from her, the better chance she has of making it back to the house with her clothes on.* "I'd like for you to meet Toby." J.P. patted the horse's shoulder as he walked across the pen. "And next door is his mate, Claire." J.P. pulled the window closed.

Samira stepped up to the stall. When J.P. walked back to the fence, Toby followed. He stuck his big horse nose over the top of the gate. Obviously startled, Samira took a step backwards.

J.P. folded his arms on the top of the gate and watched Samira through the top two rungs. *She's definitely out of my league.* Her brown eyes sparkled in the dim lights of the barn. *Gorgeous. Complex. And plain irritating sometimes.*

"Very pleased to meet you," Samira told the big brown stud. "And the same for you, Claire." Her eyes turned to the old mare.

Chase bounded in with a quick bark and gave Toby a start. The big horse tapped his hooves quickly in place. Samira jumped as well.

"Whoa, boy." J.P. steadied Toby with his hand.

The barn suddenly filled with an obnoxious, husky singing voice. "Oh give me a home where the buffalo roam . . . and the deer and the ante . . ." Uncle Roy stopped mid lyric. He stared at Samira.

Uncle Roy, you are a trip! J.P. climbed out of the stall and offered his uncle an open hand. "Uncle Roy, this is my friend Samira." *At least I think she is.*

Uncle Roy let out a hearty laugh. "Well, she gave me a start, she did." The old man wrapped his big hand around his nephew's. "What happened to your shirt, boy?"

"I took it off after my run." *Probably does look a little misleading.* He glanced at the nail where he'd left it hanging and noticed it was no longer there. Next thing he knew Roy was handing it over to him.

"Best to keep your clothes on," Roy winked. "Mighty pleased to meet you ma'am," the wise old uncle nodded a greeting to Samira. "You've got a couple of good looking girls in my kitchen."

J.P. shook out his shirt but it was saturated in sweat. *I have no intention of putting this thing back on.*

"Let me get the grain sack ready for morning then I'll close her the rest of the way up." Uncle Roy looked at J.P. "I hear Aunt Maggie's cherry pie calling your name so you won't want to tarry."

Now the pie sounds good. J.P. reached for Samira's hand and led her into the barnyard. Josh and James almost had their tent assembled in the yard.

"Did Uncle Roy find you?" The voice came from inside the tent.

"Yeah, he did." *I can't tell their voices apart anymore.* He pulled back the flap to see which of his sons had spoken. James was standing right inside. He grinned. Josh appeared from around the outside corner.

"Hey, Dad," Josh looked frustrated. "Can you hold this stake so I can pound it into the ground?" J.P. followed Josh into the darkest side of the yard. "I can't hold it and keep it taunt."

J.P. tossed his shirt in the grass and knelt down to get a good grip. He gave a big tug. The first time nothing happened, but Josh indicated for him to pull it tighter. Just as the hammer connected with the stake, the opposite corner pulled loose collapsing the entire structure.

Samira laughed out loud.

It is good to hear her laugh. Maybe we can salvage this rendezvous after all.

But the boys weren't laughing and they weren't appreciating Samira's humor either. James climbed out of the canvas ready to accuse his brother.

"He did it!" Josh pointed to his father.

J.P. threw his hands out in surrender. "All right," he told the boys as he stood up again. "Here you go . . ." He handed Josh one corner and James another. "Samira, are you honed up on your camping skills?"

Samira wasn't laughing now.

This will be good for her. J.P. walked around and handed her a third corner. "Hold this," he instructed. He picked up the small sledgehammer and claimed the fourth corner. "Okay, pull." Two of the tent corners pulled tight, but the third was hanging loosely in the breeze.

"Hey, Samira, you're supposed to hold on when we pull," Josh teased.

Samira was once again pulling her corner and the look of determination on her face told J.P. she was going to give it a good shot.

Alright, let's try it again. He gave them the indication to pull it again. This time he was able to get his stake in the ground without anyone letting go.

The next two corners staked quickly. *This old tent might actually be useable again.* J.P. moved around to the last corner and told Samira to pull it tight. As she did, J.P. hooked a stake through the loop and proceeded to pound it into the ground. *One more strike ought to hold it.*

It was almost secure when Samira let out a scream and let go of the string!

What the hell? They're both going down. J.P. looked in time to see Josh dive over the stake and break Samira's fall.

"Hey, get off of me!" James was yelling from somewhere in the heap of canvas.

Now Samira was laughing hysterically.

At least she's laughing. J.P. located the sledgehammer in the pile of rubble. *But I have no idea what triggered that.*

"What happened?" James asked as he beat the tent off his body.

A dripping wet Chase was sitting in the darkness with his head low in embarrassment.

"Looks like the mutt did a little fishing." Josh pointed. A partial fish was laying on the ground next to Chase's foot. "He didn't mean to scare you. He was just showing off his catch."

Samira pushed her hair out of her face and took a step away from the wet dog. When she backed up she bumped into J.P. That made her jump again.

Whoa, just relax, Pretty Lady.

Samira caught her breath and laughed again.

This trip might be more than either one of us bargained for. Just touching her made his entire body tingle.

"All right!" James spoke with force. "That's it. The tent goes up come hell or high water." Without hesitation he took the hammer from his father and handed it to Samira. "You knocked it down so you get to put it back up."

No. You're not putting Samira in the middle of this. J.P. reached for the hammer but Samira held it off to the side where he couldn't reach.

"No . . ." J.P. wasn't going to let her pound the stakes into the ground. *Especially in the dark.*

"Do you doubt my ability?"

Is she challenging my authority? J.P. put his hands on his hips.

Josh slapped his dad on the arm. "Sounds like a challenge to me, Dad."

I would never doubt her ability. Her judgment maybe. But never her ability. J.P. was beginning to enjoy the game. *Okay, Pretty Lady. If you have something prove, who am I to stand in your way?*

James took charge and pulled the first string back out into the grass. "Here you go, Samira. I'll put the stake through the loop, you pound the stake into the ground."

Samira followed the instructions and the first corner went up without a hitch.

J.P. watched, surprised. *He trusts her more than I do.*

Samira did the same with Josh's string and by the time she was around to the far side James was holding the third stake. J.P. listened as the hammer connected with the metal stakes three, then four times.

Not bad. I must say she has . . .

"Oh, no . . ."

What now?

"…Look out!" one of the boys sounded distressed, but J.P. didn't know which one. "Oh, man! Are you all right?"

J.P. wasn't going to wait and longer. He let go of his corner and hurried around to where the boys were hovered over Samira. *What is going on?* J.P. still couldn't see what was wrong. *Back off!* He pushed Josh out of the way and dropped one knee to the ground. Samira was sitting on the ground and she appeared to be laughing, but it was too dark to tell for sure. He started to reach for her hand but the next thing he knew, the tent was coming down over the top of both him and Samira.

And this time it isn't Samira's fault! J.P. caught his balance in a full straddle over her. He held out his arms to keep the canvas from separating him from Samira.

Samira covered her head with her hands. "I think we've been set up!"

Is that what's going on here? J.P. realized the situation too late. He took advantage of the private moment and stole a kiss from the lady on the ground before James and Josh pretended to rescue them.

J.P. couldn't see Samira's face very well, but he could feel her. *And she feels mighty inviting.* He took her hand in his and gently pulled her into a sitting position. James and Josh were working to uncover them from the topside, all the while exchanging staged bickering.

J.P. was half straddling Samira when the canvas lifted. He looked up into the thick lens of Uncle Roy's glasses. *Where the hell did he come from?* It seemed like a long time before Roy broke the mutual stare.

Suddenly Roy handed a damp t-shirt back to J.P. "I thought I told you to keep you clothes on, boy."

J.P. took the shirt. *Where does he get off telling me when to get dressed anyway?* With that Roy straightened his back and clapped his hands together.

"James, get me that hammer and let's get this thing staked to the ground. The sun is going to be up before you ever get your heads on a pillow."

James handed the sledgehammer to his great uncle. "At least he's going to let us have a pillow."

What I wouldn't give to stay concealed under that tarp. J.P. helped Samira all the way to her feet.

"Shouldn't we help them?" She was still stifling a laugh.

I think Uncle Roy has it under control.

J.P. showered before accepting Aunt Maggie's invitation for cherry pie. The house was quiet when he descended the stairs. He carried his plate into the living room. *Where'd the kids go?* No one was in sight. *Aunt Maggie could win contests with this recipe!* He watched Samira across the room while he savored the bite. The tension from earlier in the evening had dissipated. *She seems more at ease now.*

When the pie was gone, J.P. set the empty plate on the coffee table. Without permission, he walked up behind Samira and wrapped his arms around her middle. She was facing a wall full of family photos. She laid her head back against his shoulder.

"Are the girls asleep?"

"They're in bed but I doubt they're sleeping yet. It takes Kara a long time to settle down."

"Is she doing any better?"

J.P. kissed her hair. *I like the way she feels up against me like this.*

"I never know about her," Samira admitted. "One minute she's fine, the next she's in a tiff about something or the other." She leaned forward so J.P. loosened his hold. "Maggie turned in for the night. I don't know where your uncle went."

J.P. nodded toward the staircase. "Their light is out. Uncle Roy will be up with the sun so I'm sure he's down for the count."

"Who's this?" Samira's manicured fingernail pointed to an old photo on the wall.

I don't know if I want to address these old pictures or not. "That's my mother, and that's Maggie."

"And this must be your father," Samira guessed. "Strong resemblance in the cheek bones and smile." Samira tilted her head away from J.P. "Josh must have a lot of Ralston genes too."

It's a curse. J.P. tried to dismiss the derogatory thoughts. *He'll be hell bent on ambition and miss the same things in life I have.* He started to back away.

Samira caught J.P.'s hand. "No, come back. I want to meet the others." *Why?* "No you don't."

"Yes, I do," Samira tugged on his arm. "I love family pictures."

J.P. shook his head. *There's no reason to spend time on them. They're hardly family.*

"Please?" Samira pouted her lip.

J.P. considered his options. *How can I turn her down now?*

"Let me guess . . ." Samira studied the prints. "This is definitely Josh so I'm assuming this is a little James following along behind."

J.P. nodded.

"Who's with them?"

"That's my brother's oldest daughter, Alicia."

"Where do they live?"

"New England."

"Younger or older brother?"

"Younger." *I should have called him when I was out there this week.*

J.P. watched Samira study another set of photos. *She could ask me anything right now and I'd answer.*

"She's beautiful." Samira lifted his parents wedding picture off the table. "What's her name?"

Yes, she was. "Leona."

"Leona."

I like the way she said mom's name.

Samira's eyes admired the photo some more. "Was he in the service?"

J.P. nodded the answer as he moved toward the old leather sofa. "Career Navy man."

Samira set the photo back down where she'd found it and picked up another. "Who's this with you?" She carried the framed photo to where J.P. was sitting.

J.P. knew who it was without looking. "That's my brother."

"Who's car?"

"Mine." *This is ancient information.* He shifted in the sofa. "That was a '69 Impala. Great car." *I loved that car.*

"Who's the girl?"

She would have to ask. J.P. looked at the photo again even though he didn't need to. *I didn't love her.* "Well . . ." *Let's not reopen the discussion about how many women I've traveled with.* "I don't have any sisters . . ."

"I assumed as much," Samira sat down on the edge of the sofa. "What happened to the car?"

J.P. took the frame out of Samira's hands and set it down on the coffee table. *Pick a different picture.* "I sold it to make a dent in expenses during law school."

"How long did you have it?"

"Longer than I had the girl." *Let's see what she makes of that.*

Samira's elbow caught him under the ribs.

Hey. J.P. grabbed for her hand, but she was too quick. "True statement."

J.P. watched Samira fold her hands. "It's really nice here, Phil. I'm glad you invited us."

I like the way she says my name too. "I'm glad you decided to come." *And glad you didn't decide to leave.*

A comfortable silence separated their thoughts for a moment.

"To be honest . . . ,"

You don't have to tell me if you don't want to . . .

"It was really hard with the girls and all." Samira's eyes were distant. "And my brother too."

Why would her brother care if she went away for the weekend?

"Kara's birthday is coming up so she wanted to stay home and be with her friends . . ."

That would explain the sour attitude upon arrival.

"And my brother . . ."

Yeah, let's hear about this brother of yours . . .

"Well . . ." Samira hesitated. " . . . I don't know. This is all just very new for us, that's all." She was looking across the room at nothing in particular.

Me too. He'd never once brought a woman to the ranch. *Bringing someone here is new for me too. With the exception of Janet.* But she was his wife before she ever set foot in the cabin.

But Samira is still holding her thoughts on her brother. J.P. wondered what made her so concerned about her brother's opinions. *Let's see where she goes with this.* "I'm feeling a little guilty here, Samira. Last week I interfered with a mother-daughter picnic and now this week you tell me I made your brother mad too?"

"Maybe."

Shit. She didn't have to be so honest.

"But he's the forgiving type."

A faraway look in Samira's eyes caught J.P.'s attention. *I don't know what triggered it, but I've seen that look before.* Very carefully he moved closer to her. *She had that same look the morning I was leaving her house.*

"What's really on your mind, Pretty Lady?"

Samira tucked her hair behind her ears with both hands. "I think I'm getting really sleepy."

Doubtful. J.P. hated the way she held her thoughts. *She may be tired, but that wasn't what was in her eyes.* He ran a finger under the edge of her tank top and continued over her bare shoulder. She didn't move away so he linked his fingers through hers. Samira allowed him to pull her into a standing position.

"May I tuck you in for the night, Ms Cartwright?"

She answered with her chocolate brown eyes.

Of course this time her thoughts are loud and clear. Damn.

"But you may kiss me goodnight."

There's an invitation I'm not going to refuse. Very gently he brought her into him. *She completes me in ways I've never known.* When she laid her head against his shoulder, J.P. gathered her in completely. *I could hold her like this all night.* Slowly he rocked her back and forth until he felt her lips on his cheek.

"Good night, Mr. Ralston. Sleep tight."

J.P. watched Samira disappear around the bend in the staircase. *She takes my breath away.* He sank down into the sofa.

Chase sighed heavily in his sleep. J.P. sighed too but it wasn't a sigh of sleepiness. It was a sigh of contentment that he hadn't known before. It was a sigh of satisfaction he hadn't anticipated. *Without a doubt there is more to come.* The pendulum in the grandfather clock swayed with a steady beat. *I can't remember the last time I felt this much at peace.*

Good night, Samira Cartwright.

33

The Hand that Deals the Cards

Morning brought a peaceful awakening. Samira lay silently in her bed and soaked up the sunshine that was warming her bed. The hand sewn quilt showed fading from sunlight of days gone by. *Being here is like stepping back in time.* Samira slid out of the covers and opened her door a crack. *It appears no one else is awake yet.* She decided to take advantage of her own bathroom, but even after showering, her watch still only read six thirty.

This is my favorite way to start the day. Samira opened her book. *With the exception of a cup of coffee.* She sank into the worn swivel rocker and propped her feet upon on the low footstool. She was well into the second chapter before a tap at the door drew her out of the story.

"Come in." Samira looked up at the rugged man who had once stood in her living room. *Unshaven and still a bit sleepy . . . he's more than just a bit inviting.*

"Mornin', Pretty Lay," Phil's voice was low and quiet. "Did you sleep well?"

Samira had to smile. *I dreamt of you all night long.* She closed the book on her thumb. "I did, thank you." Samira rested her head against the back of the easy chair. "You're up early." *Phil's eyes are bluer than they are sometimes.* She wondered what made them change hues like they did.

Phil came on into the room and sat down on the corner of the already made bed. Samira pulled her knees in tighter. *It's hard to keep that promise to myself with him sitting here in my bedroom.* Samira replayed the reasoning in her mind. *I can't afford to compromise my judgment with the girls here.*

"I couldn't sleep anymore." Phil shaded his eyes in mock seriousness. "The sun was in my eyes." He grinned slightly. "No one's up yet." His eyes moved to the window overlooking the ranch. "Except Uncle Roy. He's probably out choring . . ."

Samira had to steady her breathing on purpose.

" . . . If you're not too far into that book I was thinking maybe we could walk down to the waterfront."

"I could probably find a bookmark."

No one was more excited to be on an early morning outing than Chase.

He's so full of energy! Samira watched the dog zig-zag across the path, back and forth.

Wildflowers dotted the tall grassland. They had only walked a short distance before Samira caught sight of the water. The iridescence shimmer on the horizon took her breath away.

"It's really something, isn't it?"

I've never seen anything like it! The sun-glittered water stretched as far as Samira could see. "It's beautiful."

Without asking, Phil linked his fingers in hers.

How can one tiny touch stimulate every ounce of my being? Samira didn't pull her hand away. *But I am not going to let myself go there this weekend. Too risky.*

It was still a distance before they reached the water's edge. *I can smell the flowers mixed in with the wet grass.*

No words were spoken. Nor did they need to be. It was as if everything that could be said was simply understood. *I wish I could bottle this moment and keep it in my heart forever!*

The shore was rustic, without a formal beach. Phil led Samira right to the point where the lake met the land. Without missing a step he leaned down and picked up a thick stick. *What's he going to do with that?*

Chase came bounding out of the wooded area. Phil let go of Samira's hand and stepped into the water.

Obviously he doesn't care if his shoes get wet!

With purposeful effort, Phil raised the stick behind his head and then threw it far into the water. Without the slightest hesitation, Chase ran down the end of a wooden dock and took a flying leap into the water. Samira laughed. *This is obviously a game Chase and his master have played before.*

Samira removed her sandals and stepped into the water next to Phil. *The sun is warm, but the water is cool!* She shook off a slight shiver.

Samira watched Phil hunt another stick. Just as Chase reached the shore, he tossed the second stick into the water, but not quite as far as the first.

He's never been so . . . There was a quiet spirit in him that peaked her interest. *So what?* The way he moved and worked with Chase was tranquil and tender. *Very much like the way he moves with me in intimate moments.* Phil was waiting for Chase to return. *He's perfectly at ease . . . nothing to prove and nothing to lose when he's out here.*

The third time Phil threw a stick into the water it didn't go far from shore at all. Chase swam right to it and obediently brought it back. However, this time the dog didn't stay in the deeper water. He dropped the stick at his master's feet. Phil leaned down to pick it up about the same time Chase decided to shake dry. Phil cried out in disgust as he raised his arm against the canine shower.

Now that's funny! Samira laughed right out loud. She couldn't help it. The stillness of the morning was suddenly awakened. Chase barked happily before taking off down the dock again.

"You find this funny?" Phil dried his face with his shirt.

"Very." She turned around to see Chase take another fearless leap off the dock. *And I must say, I've never seen a dog have so much fun!*

Without warning, Phil's strong arms had her in a full embrace and it felt as natural as the water lapping against her ankles. *I don't even know if my feet are even still on the ground!* She felt suspended in mid air by something more magical than anything she'd ever known. *I want to stay like this forever!* Samira wrapped her arms tight around Phil's neck. *He's a reason for living . . .*

As Phil completed a full turn, she felt her toes touch the shallow water again. She closed her eyes and allowed his kisses to take her back to the dreams she'd left in her bed at the break of dawn.

Chase rudely interrupted the tender moment by brushing his saturated fur against Samira's bare legs. *Oh, he's cold and wet!* Samira danced her feet in the water so Chase would back away.

Phil laughed as he released his hold. *What a healthy, contented laugh that is.* It drew Samira in even deeper. *Don't let me go yet.* She laughed right out loud, thrilled to be a part of his morning.

"One more time, boy." Phil took a stick out of Chase's mouth and threw it deep into the meadow.

Now that was a good idea. Samira knelt in a grassy spot to put her sandals back on. *There is so much passion and electricity right now.* She looked over at Phil on the shore. He was still watching Chase.

He is passionate and tender and handsome and . . . and intense. Samira needed to walk away in order to stop the voices in her head. *Very intense.* They were loud and they were suggesting things she wasn't going to allow. *And I like all those parts.* Samira glanced over her shoulder. *He should scare me but he doesn't. He should be too much to handle but he isn't. He should be everything I'd never need but he's not.*

She ducked under a low branch on a tree. *When I prayed for a new someone in my life I prayed for someone more traditional, more fatherly. I didn't pray for intense and passionate and . . .*

She stopped and turned around. Phil was jogging to catch up. . . . *He is everything I'll ever need.* She returned his smile. *Oh my. Where did that thought come from?* Chase took off headed back toward the house.

"There you are, Chase!" Krissy opened her arms to the dog as he dashed toward her. "Oooooo! Ick!" She wrinkled her nose. "Where have you been?"

"We took Chase down to the lake." Phil answered softly.

"He must like to swim or something."

"And chase sticks." Samira was watching the dog roll on his back in the grass.

Phil was also watching the dog. "That's how he got his name."

"It's a verb."

Phil frowned slightly. "What's a verb?"

"His name." *Did I state that thought out loud?* "Most names are a noun."

"Well," Krissy put her hands on her hips. "Now it is a noun because it's his name."

Phil waved his hand to stop the conversation.

"Is Kara up yet?" *I have no idea what we're going to find to keep her satisfied all day long.*

Krissy shrugged her shoulders. "I don't know. I'll go check." She quickly disappeared inside the house.

"She's a free spirit." There was amusement in Phil's eyes as he said that. *That's one way to describe her.* "Definitely."

"And Kara?"

Now Samira shook her head. "Much more like her mother. Calculated and deliberate . . ." *Set in her ways . . .*

Phil leaned into the porch support. "They're lucky they have you for their mom."

As if they had any choice in that matter. Samira sighed as her thoughts tripped back to the day before. "That would not have been Kara's opinion yesterday." Phil looked interested so she continued. "Somewhere along the line she decided she was going to stay home. In fact she made arrangements to stay with my parents without my permission." *And that was the first my parents actually knew I was going away for a couple of days.*

"Obviously you convinced her otherwise."

"Let's not say convinced." Samira recalled the harsh words exchanged during the late day argument. "Mandated, maybe."

Phil ran his hand through his hair in thought.

I wonder if he knows he does that thing with his hair?

"Well, I guess I can see her point. How many perks can there be on a holiday weekend in a totally strange place with totally strange people?"

And a man that Kara still isn't too sure about. "So what do you do when your boys don't want to do things with you?" *Any advice would be helpful at this point in time.*

Phil studied the grass in the yard as if he were watching it grow. When he finally answered the tone in his voice was distant. "I guess I don't know." Phil's eyes connected with Samira for just an instant. "I really haven't had them any too much in recent years. Our times together are determined by a schedule that fits someone else's agenda . . ."

He sounds so sad. Until then it hadn't occurred to her that this strong, able man could be manipulated in any way. *He must have a lot of hurt buried down deep inside.*

" . . . I know their mother struggles with them not following her rules and plans though. It's tough, you know? They have their friends and their plans and we have ours. We want them to be independent yet conform at the same time." Phil shrugged his shoulders. His eyes were looking at the tent where his boys were still sleeping. "I haven't been a father for a long time so this custody thing with James is a challenge . . ."

The look on his face indicated the same worry and concern she felt.

" . . . . I guess I just blunder through and hope I can remember the basics of parenting."

Samira shook her head in disagreement. "It's more than that." *I'm not sure where this is going, but I think he's missed the point.* "I don't believe you ever actually stopped being a father. Just because James and Josh didn't live with you doesn't mean you weren't their father . . ."

"But I didn't have a say in their decisions and activities . . ."

" . . . But you were still their father. You still had their love in your heart and they had yours in them. No one can take that away." Samira touched Phil's arm. "They know you differently than anyone else simply because they're a part of you. And because of that, you're already becoming that father you think you've forgotten how to be." *I hope he followed that.*

Phil wasn't saying anything. He was deep in thought.

I hope I didn't say something wrong.

"Good mornin' young'uns!"

Samira jumped at the sudden interruption. Phil's uncle appeared from around the corner of the porch. Krissy was close on his heels. *How funny! He's calling me and Phil the 'young'uns!'*

"We're going to gather eggs," Krissy announced. "Kara is up but she didn't want to go to the henhouse."

I don't blame her! Uncle Roy was swinging a wire basket. *He reminds me of a character in a Norman Rockwell painting.*

"Do you want to come?"

"Oh, no thank you!" Samira immediately refused the invitation.

"I wasn't talking to you, Mama!" Krissy pointed at Phil. "I mean him. Are you coming or what?"

Phil shared an easy smile with Samira. "I guess I'm going to the henhouse."

"You don't have to."

"Oh yes I do." Phil started across the grass. "Who am I to pass up a perfectly good invitation from a Cartwright woman?"

At least he qualified the Cartwright part. Samira instantly scolded herself. *He's been such a gentleman! Why do you doubt his character?* She opened the front door of the cabin. *Because I still need to know more about the woman on the cover of that magazine.*

The magazine was in her car. *I wish I could just let it go, but I can't!* The only thing left to do was talk about it, and there was only one person with whom she could do that and he was on his way to the henhouse with her daughter. *And then again maybe I'm just making way too much out of it . . .*

Phil's aunt called from the kitchen and offered a cup of coffee. *Now that's an invitation I can't refuse.*

Much to Samira's dismay, Kara's discontentment permeated the afternoon.

"Here's the deal," Kara pointed out. "You said we'd come up for a night or two. There's nothing more for us to do here, so we might as well go home."

"James says there are fireworks here tonight," Krissy piped up from the porch swing. Her legs were criss-crossed and a magazine dangled over her knees.

"Big deal." Kara rolled her eyes.

Samira's patience was being tried and she didn't like the trapped feeling closing in around her. *I'd even hoped, against all odds, that maybe, just maybe, Krissy, and especially Kara, would find something in Phil that captured their interest.* If the truth were known, Samira had even prayed that they might come to understand more why she needed this man in her life. *But that prayer has yet to be answered.* The cabin door closed behind her.

Kara took one last stab. "Well there's nothing to do here."

"What do you mean, 'nothing to do'?"

Phil's challenge surprised Samira. *Now what?* Kara wasn't used to being confronted by anyone, let alone a man.

Kara frowned and crossed her arms in defense. "At least I can't *think* of anything to do." Her dark eyes were studying Phil with caution.

Phil looked out across the lawn into the distance. "The boys and I are going to hike the Woodcutter's Trail down to the waterfront. Maybe you'd like to come along."

Please go with them, Kara. It would be so good for you.

"Can I come?" Krissy hopped up and left the magazine upside-down in the swing.

"Sure." Phil glanced in Krissy's direction. "But you'll need to change into long pants. The grass along the trail is long and scratchy."

Krissy was off in a flash.

Come on, Kara. Go! Take him up on the offer.

"How far is it?" Kara finally asked into the silence.

Phil tilted his head in contemplation. "Maybe an hour and a half total. Forty-five minutes each way."

Just do it, Kara!

"We can cut it short if you get tired," Phil offered casually.

That will do it!

Kara was instantly defensive. "I doubt I'll have any trouble keeping pace!"

"Only one way to find out."

Now there's the response of an experienced father if I've ever heard one. Samira thought again. *Either that or the response of an experienced attorney.*

Kara narrowed her eyes. "Whatever!" She disappeared behind the door.

Oh, how I hate that word!

Phil questioned Samira with his eyes.

"I hate that word."

"Whatever?"

"That's the one."

"It's all in the way you allow it to be heard."

Samira shook her head. "It's all in the way it's meant to be taken."

Phil draped his arm over her shoulder. "*Whatever.*"

She jabbed him in the ribs with her elbow but had to smile at his jibe. *He thinks this is funny!* She sighed with relief. *But I do like the way he baited Kara.*

Time passed but neither the boys nor the girls came outside.

"Wonder what they found to do in there?" Phil checked his watch.

All was quiet inside the house except for hushed conversation coming from Uncle Roy's game room. The door was open. Samira could see Josh sitting on the floor next to Krissy. *At least Krissy changed her clothes.* She tuned into the conversation best as she could.

" . . . There's some cards missing . . ." One of the boys sounded concerned.

"What's missing?"

I can't tell their voices apart!

A few moments passed without an answer. "The ace and the king of spades."

"I say they're cheating."

"We are not cheating!" Kriss's voice was serious.

This doesn't sound good! Samira started for the game room but Phil motioned for her to stay still. *He doesn't seem nearly as concerned as I feel!*

"Show your cards," one of the boys demanded.

"All of them." The other voice followed.

A few more moments passed.

"Stand up."

"There. Happy now?" Krissy mouthed back. "I'm standing."

I wonder what this is all about?

"Not yet."

Samira watched Josh climb up off the floor. "Turn around."

"Told you we're not cheating," Krissy taunted. "See? No cards."

"Now you, stand up."

Kara, I assume.

"I say she's wearing them . . ."

Suddenly Phil bolted from his parental eavesdropping.

What triggered that sudden reaction?

"That's enough!" Phil called the game with a single command. "Put her down!"

Put who down?

"They're cheating!" one of the boys complained.

"I don't care who's playing fair and who's not. Put her down." Phil's voice was forceful.

Samira stepped into the doorway just in time to see James and Josh set Kara back down on the floor. *What in heaven's name is going on in here?* As Kara put her feet out to catch her balance, two playing cards fell to the floor.

"I knew it!" James darted for the cards. "She *was* wearing them!"

"Kara Elizabeth!" Krissy snapped. "I can't believe you'd do that!"

"That means we win the bet," Josh surmised. "You two owe us big time!"

Kara's arms were crossed and her face was red.

Why would Kara cheat? Samira didn't know what to make of her daughter's behavior. *And what are they betting on anyway?*

"And paybacks are hell," James added.

"Watch the language," Phil instructed.

Thank you.

"I sent you in here to get ready for Woodcutter's trail awhile ago. What happened to that plan?"

Krissy jumped into the chaotic conversation. "They said we had to play hearts to see who was going to carry the gear. The losing team had to carry the heaviest packs."

Leave it to Krissy to air the grievance. Samira crossed her arms. *Let's see how the father handles this?* She watched James try to make an exit into the garage.

"Hold it!" Phil's voice reverberated in the room.

Obviously he's not going to let it go!

"Kara, if you're going, you need long pants." Phil pointed toward the stairs. "Krissy, if you're going you need to round up Chase and meet me in the driveway."

Samira stepped aside as the girls passed her in the doorway.

"James and Josh, you know damned good and well there isn't any 'gear' to carry down the trail."

"Uh, Dad, there's a lady present. You might want to, uh, you know, the language . . ."

Phil put his hands on his hips and took a step toward his boys. They both took a step closer to the garage exit. "Anyone who makes a run for that door meets me on the other side."

Josh threw his hands into the air. "Honest, Dad, we just invited the girls into a friendly game of cards. Low stakes, no kidding."

Phil pointed a finger at Josh. "You, get the water bottles, and you . . ." he pointed at James. "I want to see you in private."

Josh ducked his head in respectful defeat and passed by Samira without speaking. Much to her dismay, she watched Phil lead James out through the garage door.

I hope he doesn't blame James any more than the others. Samira felt an uneasiness rise in her stomach. A few minutes later Phil returned alone.

I wonder what happened to James? Samira was still standing in the same spot unsure of what she should do or say.

Kara descended the stairs wearing jeans and a fresh t-shirt.

"I'll be out in a minute." Phil turned around and hollered toward the kitchen. "Josh!"

"Yeah, yeah! I'm on my way." Josh rounded the corner with an armload of filled water bottles." He avoided eye contact with Samira as he passed through.

Phil leaned on the banister and crossed his arms. "I didn't mind the friendly interrogation until the boys assumed she was 'wearing' the cards."

He's trying to explain but I still don't understand. "What is that supposed to mean?"

Phil looked at her in disbelief. "That means they thought Kara was hiding the card in her clothes somewhere."

"And that means . . . ."

"That means the boys were dead-bent set on finding the cards no matter where she'd stashed them."

Oh, for pete's sake. Suddenly Samira understood the assumption. "Only a man would even think of that!"

"Only a woman would think to hide them there."

Phil started for the door.

Hey! "What's that supposed to mean?"

"Take it any way you like, Samira, but I wasn't going to have my boys conducting a body search on your daughters!" Phil opened the door.

"They would do that?"

Phil kept walking. "Only if they thought it would prove their point."

Samira thought for a moment. *They did have a point to prove, I guess.* The door closed between her and Phil. *I wonder where Kara hid them anyway.* The door opened again.

"Did you want to come with us?"

Samira laughed at Phil's sudden afterthought. "I'd prefer to stay here with my book."

Phil nodded. "That's what I assumed."

I'm glad he made that assumption. Samira stepped over to the window and watched as they headed out. *They're not exactly children anymore. But not mature enough to be young adults either.* Samira saw Phil take a playful punch at one of the boys followed by a gentle attack from her youngest daughter.

God help him. It's probably just as well I stay here. Maybe this is the outing Kara needs. Samira climbed the staircase to her room and located her book. *And maybe this is the peace of mind I need too.* She curled into the armchair where she'd started her day.

The story was the same, but her frame of mind had changed. *I don't know how long I can resist his presence.* Even though it startled her to watch Phil take charge of the children, she still found herself drawn to him. *What is it about him that makes me want him so badly?*

Or is it more of a need than a want?

That thought struck Samira. *At least while I want him, I am still in control of my actions. However, if I need him . . .* Samira shifted in the chair and closed her book. *Oh dear God, if I need him then I'm afraid it's out of my hands.*

34

Horsing Around

J.P. could hear Aunt Maggie chattering as he crossed the living room.

" . . . I worry about him. He works too hard and takes life so seriously . . . He's very much like his father in that way . . . but he has his mother's love of nature and her understanding of people . . ."

Aunt Maggie, do you have to air all your concerns for me to Samira?

"Oh, Phillip!" Aunt Maggie was quite surprised. "I didn't hear you come in. How was the trail today?"

Nice cover, but it's too late. J.P.'s eyes cast an accusing look on his little old aunt.

"We were just having a dandy visit." Aunt Maggie avoided his eyes.

"I'm sure you were." *I really don't appreciate her analysis of my character.* Samira's face was quiet when their eyes connected.

"Here," Maggie walked around the oversized kitchen table. "Denise called an hour or so ago. She needs you to call her back as soon as you can."

J.P. took the paper from Aunt Maggie and read the phone number. *She's at the office? On July 4th? What's up with that?* Work hadn't crossed his mind since arriving at the ranch and the though of it now was invasive. *I'd better get her called.*

"And Bobby called to find out when you are going back out east."

How did my brother know I was out east in the first place? J.P. cast another accusing look at his aunt.

"We were outside. The message said to call in later." Aunt Maggie offered to refresh Samira's cup of coffee.

Dear Aunt Maggie. Without any further discussion, J.P. went to get his phone out of the truck.

Kara and Krissy were balanced in the hammock between the trees when J.P. crossed the front porch. He had to smile. *They remind me of their mother with their noses in a book.* Across the barnyard James and Josh were involved in a one-on-one basketball match.

J.P. unplugged the charger and pushed the auto dial. *No answer at the office. I'll try her at home.* This time Denise picked up.

"Hey boss. Happy fourth of July. Sparky called."

"Good news?"

"He has key witnesses lined up for interviews in Baltimore."

J.P. watched James dribble a lay up the length of the driveway.

"So, what do you want me to do, Boss?"

How can I be a father when I have business dragging me back to Baltimore? "I can get you out late tomorrow." Denise was obviously focused. "Where do you want to fly out of?"

Samira appeared on Aunt Maggie's porch. *And how am I supposed to maintain any kind of connection with that pretty lady when I can't even stay home for a week?*

"Boss?"

"Home. I need to get James settled again before I leave." *And figure out what to do with him while I'm gone.*

"Derek is available to help. I already talked to him."

Damn, she's good. J.P. was watching Samira walk toward him. *And she's even better.*

"Hello?" Denise called J.P.'s attention back to the phone.

"Yeah, go ahead . . ." *What was she telling me?*

"The only flight out is through St. Louis at eight PM. Puts you in late but Sparky can pick you up and get you to the motel . . ."

I really don't want to talk about work today.

" . . . That will give you all morning to prep. However, that also means a private hopper out of Joplin."

Do what you have to do, Denise. I need off of this phone.

"J.P.?"

"That's fine." The attorney ran his hand through his hair. "Anything else?"

"No. I guess not."

"Okay then. I'll most likely talk to you from Baltimore next . . ."

Really? "Most likely." J.P. greeted Samira with his eyes. "I'll talk to you at some point tomorrow." He half-listened to Denise's final instructions. "That will be fine." J.P. tossed his phone back inside the truck.

"Did you get your calls returned?" Samira was close enough to touch.

"Only the urgent one. The other one can wait."

"Is everything alright?"

Yes. He could lie but somehow that didn't feel right. *No. Everything is not all right.* J.P. sighed. "Not exactly . . ." *She's not going to like this.* " . . . Sounds like I have to leave town again tomorrow night."

"But that means the case is progressing, right?"

She's sharper than I give her credit for. "That would be correct."

Samira turned slightly and glanced back over her shoulder. "Then that's good news right?"

"Right." *Let's not talk about my work today.* "The travel just makes for short weeks at home." *Leaving town hasn't been an issue in the past.*

He noticed Samira's eyes watching her daughters in the hammock. "Your girls seem more content now." *Especially Kara.*

"I think they're enjoying themselves finally." J.P. watched her face him again. "Thank you for taking Kara on the hike. She had a great time once she decided there was something to do after all."

"Maybe she just needed to quit thinking about the options she left at home."

"Maybe." Samira pushed her hair out of her face. "We'll get up early tomorrow and head back in time to spend time with my brother's family tomorrow afternoon."

And maybe her mother needs to stop thinking about her options at home too. J.P. closed the door of his truck. *But at least she's staying the night again.*

"So where did you go on the hike?"

J.P. pointed beyond the barn. "Do you want to see?"

"How far is it?" Samira sounded hesitant.

Like mother, like daughter. "We can ride faster than we can walk." *Toby would be up for an evening stroll.* "But you'll need to change into jeans."

Samira agreed to change and promised to meet J.P. in the barn.

This may be the only time I have alone with her before she leaves. J.P. had the stud saddled before Samira appeared in the doorway. Samira's steps slowed as she realized what he was suggesting.

J.P. smiled to himself. *You'll be fine. Trust me.*

Uncle Roy appeared from the back of the barn. "Toby, it looks like you're in for a treat." He ran his calloused hands over the saddle and checked the bridle with skill. "You'd best lower the stirrups, Phillip," Uncle Roy suggested without looking up. "I was the last one in the saddle."

J.P. followed the advice without questioning.

"Shall we saddle up Claire?" Uncle Roy adjusted his thick glasses and looked toward Samira.

No thanks. I'd rather have her with me.

"I don't know about this . . ." Samira shook her head. "I thought you meant riding like in the truck . . ."

"Are you headed down the trail?" Uncle Roy asked.

J.P. nodded as he ducked under Toby's neck to adjust the other stirrup. *Roy will set her straight.*

"The truck won't go down the trail, ma'am." Uncle Roy patted Toby's shoulder. "But this ole' boy will take you there in no time." He motioned for Samira to come closer.

I wonder if she's ridden before.

Samira removed her sunglasses. "Are you sure?"

"Absolutely." Roy answered.

I'm not going to give her enough time to change her mind. J.P. put his left foot in the stirrup and swung his right leg over the saddle with ease. He grinned at Samira's doubtful look.

"But he's so big!"

Uncle Roy was maneuvering her toward the animal. "He's no bigger than he was when he was standing here next to you," Roy commented with honest misunderstanding. "And he'll be the same size when you get back off too."

"I didn't mean Phil..."

Good ol' Uncle Roy.

"Climb up the fence one time and then put your left foot in here . . ."

J.P. moved his foot so Uncle Roy could position the stirrup for Samira to use.

" . . . then swing up your other leg over the back of the saddle . . ."

J.P. reached out his hand. With a great deal of uncertainty Samira locked her left hand in his. *Once she puts her foot in the stirrup, I'll just pull her around. It won't be any trouble at all.*

Toby stood stock still as Samira's weight landed behind the saddle.

Good boy. J.P. was impressed that she'd actually mounted without putting up a bigger fight. *She's too stubborn to not rise to a challenge.*

"How are you doing?"

"Fine, I guess . . ."

Toby started down the path.

" . . . Where do I hold on?"

J.P. chuckled. She was grasping his t-shirt with all of her might. He put his hand over hers more for comfort than instruction. "Wherever you want."

"What do I do with my feet?"

"Whatever you do," J.P. instructed. "Don't kick the horse."

"Why?"

"He'll take off on a full run." He could feel Samira's grip tighten with that remark. *Easy girl.*

Toby's steady gate took the couple all the way to the cove where J.P. had hiked with the kids. The longer they rode, the less frightened Samira seemed to be. *At least she's not clutching her fists anymore.* However, he could feel Toby's resistance to the slow pace.

"Patience, boy, patience." As they reached a shady spot near the water, J.P. pulled back the reins. *I know how he feels. Patience isn't one of my best qualities either.*

"Whoa, boy." The horse stopped immediately. *We could turn around and go right back.* J.P. considered the other option. *Or we could dismount here and spend a little time without company.* With a few encouraging words he finally convinced Samira to dismount with his assistance. J.P. put his own foot back in the stirrup and dismounted as well.

Samira pushed her jeans over her knees. "It feels funny to walk now."

J.P. led Toby to the edge of the water and allowed the horse to drink. *Tell me about it.* He looped the reins over a low branch and allowed Toby the freedom to graze on the tall grass.

J.P. turned around to find Samira sitting against the trunk of a large tree. *This woman is beautiful in any setting.* Her face was serious when she made eye contact.

"How often do you come here?"

His initial hope for a moment of intimacy was diffused by her cautious demeanor. *Maybe Aunt Maggie's shared a little too much.* J.P. crouched down so he could see her eyes.

I have nothing to hide here. "I used to bring the boys up every holiday but we're down to about three times a year if we're lucky. I doubt I'll have them back up here before Christmas now."

Samira looked surprised. "You should come more often. Your aunt really enjoys your company . . ."

Aunt Maggie has been sharing information that is better left alone.

" . . . Do you ever come without the boys?"

J.P. shook his head more at Aunt Maggie's liberty than at Samira's question. "Rarely. It's hard enough to get away when Josh and James are available."

Samira was studying his face.

Now what's she thinking? J.P. looked over at Toby who was contentedly pulling at the long grass with his teeth.

Let's see how she responds to this. "Where's your escape, Samira? Where do you like to take your girls?"

"I don't take them many places." Her eyes were distant. "We spend holidays with my family and they're all right there in town."

"No vacations or getaways?" *Is she that much of a homebody?*

"I'm pretty content just to stay home." With that, Samira stood up and walked over to where Toby was eating grass. "What about you? Any other hideaways?"

J.P. followed. *So much for taking advantage of some private time.* He tried not to let his disappointment show, but as she stood there in the sunlight it was all he could do to not take a hold of her. *I have no idea where this conversation is headed.*

"If I do get out of town there is usually a business connection of some sort."

Samira had her back to him when she asked the next question. "Do you travel alone?"

Something is obviously on her mind. J.P. wasn't sure how he should respond. *Might be time to head back to the ranch.* He decided to guard the answer until he had a better feel for her motive.

"Once in awhile I have the opportunity to take someone along," he answered carefully. *Take Springfield, for example.* "Most generally I travel solo."

Samira turned and faced him.

There's that same distant look she had last night.

"It's really strange for me to be here with you this weekend." Samira ran her hands through her hair and lifted it off her shoulders. "I mean, and don't get me wrong, Phil, but to be here with you and have the girls along and all, it's really very much out of character for me."

Maybe she's feeling guilty for not being home with her family.

"I don't think I told you . . ." Samira dropped her hair. "But the decision to go to Springfield was a really big step for me. To actually leave town to spend a night with a man in a hotel . . . well, that was a really difficult decision for me to make."

That explains why it took her so long to respond. "I'm glad you decided to go." J.P. pulled a fox tail out of it's shaft.

Samira smiled briefly. "Oh, I am too." Then her eyes dropped. "I had some personal issues to overcome that night, but I'm glad I . . ."

You what? J.P. was chewing on the end of the foxtail.

Samira turned completely away from him.

Why is she bringing this up now? J.P. wished he could see her face because he wasn't sure how to respond. *Maybe she just needs to know how much that night meant to me.* He walked up behind her and ran the fuzzy end of the weed over her the back of her neck.

"What you gave me that night is still with me, Samira." He wanted desperately to turn her around but resisted the temptation.

"I gave you everything I had . . ."

"I know . . ."

Samira interrupted his thought by stepping out of reach.

Now what?

"Do you really?" She took a few short steps and then turned around. "Do you know how much I gave?"

I thought I did, but maybe not. J.P. weighed his options. *I have no idea what she's talking about.* Toby's reins were coming loose from the branch but there was no way J.P. was going to walk over and fix it right then. *I'm going to plead the 5th.*

She turned toward the lake and let the breeze blow her hair off her face. "It's just that I haven't done that for very many others."

Holy shit, Ralston. Whatever it is she's given you, you'd best know how to reciprocate. He knelt and picked up a flat rock. *Because the way she's standing there in the breeze is a silhouette of pure desire.* J.P. flung the rock across the water. *There isn't much I wouldn't give to find a soft grassy spot where we could get comfortable together.* He watched the rock skip three times before disappearing into the lake.

"Three. That's how many times I've given myself away."

Away for what?

Samira's eyes were fixed on the place where the rock had sunk. "Obviously with my husband. One time as a result of bad judgment. And then you." She paused. "That's it. Three."

She's talking about more than sex. J.P. tried to get his thoughts straight. *She's talking about something far deeper than that.* He rubbed his face in his hands. *I've given those parts away too many times to count.* When he lifted his eyes out of his hands, Samira was standing directly in front of him.

No. That's not true. I've never given anyone as much as I've already given her.

Samira's dark eyes were focused directly on his. "Maybe you should take me back to the house, cowboy . . ." Her voice was tender. " . . . because I'm dangling way too close to the point of no return."

And that's a bad thing? "Do I go against your better judgment?" *I don't think I really want her to answer that question.*

Samira looked past J.P. toward the water. "Let's just say you test my boundaries."

She's only had sex with three men in her life? Ever? J.P. was running that reality through his mind. *That's impossible. A woman this beautiful? There has to be more than three . . . Doesn't there? And I've never spent the night in the same house with a gorgeous, available woman without making sexual contact.* J.P. corrected himself. *That is until last night.*

"My hope is . . ."

What is that hope, Pretty Lady?
"That the third time is a charm."
I'm the third.
Samira continued. "My fear is otherwise."
What the hell is that supposed to mean? J.P.'s thoughts were reeling as she started to kiss him. *This is the moment I've been anticipating for two days.* J.P. wrapped his arms around Samira's waist. *But now I'm playing on her terms.* He felt the curves of her body in his hands. *Hell, I don't even know how to define her terms . . .*

Suddenly Samira's words were playing again. *"My fear is otherwise . . ."*
Fear of what? J.P. allowed her to kiss him again but this time he wasn't as anxious to respond. The passion he'd waited on so patiently was suddenly more ominous than enticing. *I'd love to give her everything she needs, but gut feeling tells me I don't have whatever it is she's expecting.*

Samira's fingertips ran over his day-old beard and she pressed her face into his shoulder. *God, Samira. If I had it, I'd give it to you in a heartbeat.* J.P. held her tight fearing if he let go she might not be there at all.

Toby's nose brushed the back of J.P.'s shoulder. He let go of Samira when she jumped at the nearness of the horse.

There is no way I'm going to take anything else from her without clarifying what she's hoping for. "I think Toby's thinking about supper."

Samira's eyes were cloudy and J.P. could feel her spirit pulling away. *I can't afford to take advantage of her any longer.*

Samira was trying to appear unscathed by the confession, but J.P. knew better. "Maybe we should go back."

"And I suppose we have to *ride* him back?" Samira was studying the stirrup again.

I wish I knew exactly what she wants from me. J.P. decided he needed more time to think. *But I don't want her to know I'm thinking.*

"Yes, Pretty Lady." J.P. avoided her eyes. "We're going to ride him back, but this time you're going to drive."

Samira backed away quickly. "I don't know the first thing about riding a horse!" She looked at Toby. "And he's so big . . . ."

J.P. took her by the hand. "Up you go." He knelt and started to pick up Samira's left foot.

"But what about you?"

"I'm getting on behind you." *So I can think without being observed.*
Samira shook her head.

"Do you trust me?"

With that, Samira took a deep breath and nodded her head.
Trust is a start.

Samira put her left foot in the stirrup and allowed J.P. to push her on into the saddle. Even when Toby stepped sideways, Samira stayed in the saddle.

At least she's determined once she makes up her mind. J.P. mounted behind the saddle and placed the reins in Samira's hands. The diversion of the riding lesson relieved the tension that had built between them. *Given a choice I would make her third time all she needs it to be.* J.P. tapped his ankles into Toby's sides. *But what happens if I don't have all she's hoping for? What then?*

J.P. guided Samira's hands and legs with his own as Toby ambled up the trail toward the ranch. *Given my history and temperament, I don't know if I can play by her terms.* Suddenly his desires for Samira were shadowed by a threat to his independence. *I don't know if I'm ready to give that much.*

The rhythmic click of the grandfather's clock was the only sound in the house when Samira appeared at the bottom of the stairs. Freshly showered and wearing only her nightshirt J.P. caught himself once again fighting against instinctive tendencies. *Why does she tempt me like this then keep me at bay?*

Samira crossed the room and sank down in the corner of the cushy leather sofa. "Big day," she stated simply. "The fireworks were really pretty over the lake."

J.P. was sitting on the floor leaning against the matching chair.

"Did the girls like them?"

Samira curled her feet up underneath. "I think so. They were thinking of their little cousins watching fireworks without them."

She's the only woman I know who purposefully doesn't show me what she's wearing underneath. J.P. nodded for lack of a better response.

"Are you tired?"

The question came out of context. J.P. wasn't sure if he looked tired or if Samira was thinking he should be after the day's activities. He rested his elbow on his knee.

"A little."

Samira's eyes were soft as she studied his face. *She didn't allow me to tuck her in last night so I'm not holding out hope for tonight either.*

"You look sleepy."

"Maybe more relaxed than sleepy." *And extremely spent in the mental capacity.*

"Tell me about your parents, Phil." Samira's eyes had moved to Joe and Leona's wedding photo on the wall. "What happened to them?"

Do we have to go there? J.P. followed her eyes as he took a deep breath. There wasn't that much to tell really, yet at the same time he rarely allowed himself the memories. He subconsciously ran his hand through his hair.

"There's not much to know . . ." *Or at least not much I want to tell.* He flipped the magazine upside down for no reason at all. "My mother raised my brother and me on her own for the most part. Joe was in the Navy my whole life so I didn't know much of him." *Nor do I care to know him now.*

"Where did they meet?"

"Virginia Beach, Virginia." J.P. knew the story like he knew his own life. But sharing it was another thing. He decided to cut the dramatic details. "My mom was out there visiting her oldest sister, Naomi. She ended up staying out there until they were married the next year."

Samira curled deeper into the sofa and rested her head against the back. "Love at first sight?"

J.P. shook his head. "Doubtful." He couldn't imagine his father knowing anything about love. *I wonder how much Aunt Maggie has already told her?*

Samira's eyes were on the photo again. "What happened to them?"

J.P. studied his bare feet against the pattern of the area rug. "My mother died in a plane crash the summer I turned twelve." J.P. took a breath. *God, I hate those memories.* "And the Captain . . ." J.P. glanced at the man's face in the photograph. " . . . My father is in Virginia. Retired Navy now."

There was a long, silent span of time between that statement and Samira's next comment. When she spoke her voice was almost inaudible.

"Do you see him?"

J.P. shook his head. *There's no reason to see my mother's husband.* She was gone and as far as Joseph Phillip Ralston II was concerned, the Captain was gone too.

"I'm so sorry, Phil." Samira's eyes reflected a deep compassion.

Suddenly his thoughts were too intimate for sharing. *Move on.* "No need to be. That was a long time ago." He leaned back on the chair again and crossed his ankles on the rug. *But since she opened the door, I think I'll follow suit.* He studied her wishing he could touch her.

"So what's your story, Samira?" *Tell me about your husband.* "What did *he* do for a living?"

"Tom?"

Yeah, Tom. J.P. nodded.

"He was a city police officer."

"How did you meet him?"

Samira smiled slightly. "I was set up. I met him during his last year at the academy through a mutual friend . . ."

J.P. watched her eyes dance with the memory for a quick moment.

" . . . My friend Susan invited him to dinner. That's the same friend, incidentally, who also invited me and your friend Mike to dinner last week." Samira raised a single eyebrow to punctuate the confession.

J.P. raised his eyebrows in response. "She must be some friend." *Still pisses me off they had dinner without me.*

"She tries."

"What happened to Tom?" *Why is it so hard for me to say his name?*

Samira's eyes dropped. Suddenly J.P. wished he hadn't asked anything at all.

"You don't have to answer . . ."

" . . . That's okay." Samira shook her head slowly. Her hair fell down around her face. "Tom died of cancer. Kara was eight and Krissy was six." She tucked her hair behind both ears.

I had no idea. Without permission he eased onto the couch next to Samira. She didn't resist when he slipped his arm behind her shoulders. "That must have been really hard." *Harder than anything I've been through.* He pushed her hair back from her face with his fingers.

Samira didn't respond right away. Her thoughts were obviously somewhere in the distant past.

I didn't mean to make her cry.

"I'm sorry." She wiped her cheeks with her fingertips. "I haven't talked to anyone about that for a long time."

I understand that all too well. He continued to stroke her hair, grasping for words that might make everything all right again. *There are no words.* He pulled her in against his body and kissed the top of her head.

"He tried to hang on." Samira's voice was distant. "But in the end the cancer won." J.P. felt her lungs expand against him. "That was six years ago now."

"That's a long time ago . . ."

Samira's head moved back and forth slightly against his shoulder. "In some ways. In other ways it seems like yesterday."

Time passed but no other words were spoken. The grandfather clock chimed at eleven o'clock but neither Samira nor J.P. moved. They were kindred in spirit. Neither spared from life's injustice and heartache. They had both been left behind, yet forced into the future.

The outside door clicked loudly causing J.P. to sit up unexpectedly. Samira also sat up—both just awakened from a light sleep. J.P. watched as James disappeared into the bathroom behind the staircase. *How long was I asleep?*

Samira leaned forward on the sofa. She was obviously trying to get her bearings as well. J.P. reached out and pushed the hair back from her face. Her eyes turned toward the staircase.

"I'll walk you up." He offered his hand. His shirt was still warm where she had fallen asleep against him. *The last thing I want to do is leave her alone in a cold bed.* Samira took his hand. *But just the same, I'll respect her wishes.*

J.P. climbed into his own bed drained from the day's activities and fatigued by the memories that plagued his weary mind. He rolled over on his side and checked his alarm. *She's an early riser if I ever met one.*

In the moment before drifting off to sleep, the crack in the bedroom door widened. Thinking he might already be dreaming, J.P. rubbed his eyes. *She's still here.* He laid perfectly still, for fear if he moved the apparition would disappear.

Silhouetted by the moonlight trickling in the window, he continued to watch as she undressed and slipped silently into his bed.

This is my chance to make sure her third time is a charm.

J.P. awoke the next morning unaware of when Samira had gone back to her own room. He pulled on his jeans from the day before and stepped into the hall. *Her door is ajar.*

Samira lay sound asleep under one of Aunt Maggie's quilts. The sunlight was just starting to warm her room. J.P. stood silently in the doorway and observed her slumber.

She'd given him everything once again and he was better for it. *I'm more complete somehow.* There was something about the way she needed him; something about the way she gave of herself. *It's so much more than I've ever received from anyone else.* Her dark hair fanned across the cotton pillowcase.

Not once have I known a woman like I've known Samira Cartwright.

35

An Angel in Disguise

Samira pulled the laced curtains back from the window so she could get a better view. Phil was jogging toward the house, Chase leading the way. *I love the way Phil interacts with his dog.* There was a gentleness about him that was not always apparent in other relationships. Samira watched as he stopped to stretch. *I wonder if he runs every day.*

I should probably pack my things before going downstairs. The weekend had been more fulfilling than she'd anticipated. *But there are still so many things I wanted to talk to him about. Like the woman on the magazine.* She glanced at the picture on the cover before setting it aside. *But it sounds like Phil is flying out for business somewhere out east.*

Samira glanced out the window again. Phil was headed up the sidewalk, shirtless and sweaty from the early morning run. *He really does take his sabbaticals seriously. He hasn't bothered to shave since we arrived.* She grabbed the magazine. *I'll pack later so I can catch him before he gets in the house.*

"Well, good morning, Pretty Lady." Phil skipped the bottom step and joined her on the wooden porch.

Even in his sweat-drenched body he's still the most inviting man I've ever known. "You're up nice and early this morning."

Phil grinned. "I thought I'd get my run in before it got too hot."

"It's already plenty warm."

"So it is." Phil put his hands on his hips and bent his neck in thought. *He's looking at me like he wants to say something.*

"So? What's on your mind?"

"I'm thinking . . . ,"

How funny that he can't put his thoughts into words sometimes. Samira walked past Phil and took a seat in the porch swing. *I'll just wait while he thinks.* Her feet dangled as she pushed it into motion.

Phil's eyes followed her all the way to the swing, but he didn't make an effort to follow her. When he finally did speak he was shaking his head.

"I was thinking I either had the most incredible dream of my life last night or . . ." he stopped talking again. His eyes were fixed on hers.

I want to hear him say it out loud. "Or . . . ?"

"Or . . ." Phil took a step in her direction. "Or an angel visited me in my bed." He crouched down and leaned his back against a porch support.

An Angel? Oh my! I've never been likened to an angel before. She had to break his gaze. "You must have been dreaming . . ."

"Somehow I think I may have evidence to prove otherwise . . ."

Evidence? Samira felt her cheeks fill with color. *There was so much I wanted to give him.* She ran the night backwards in her mind. *I didn't feel right leaving him alone in his bed.* His dark blue eyes were watching her very closely. *I couldn't have lived with myself had someone found us in there together.*

The model's picture on the magazine came into Samira's focus. *Maybe she isn't a discussion for today.* Fearing Phil might realize what she was holidng, she quickly laid it aside, face down.

"You're welcome to stay as long as you like . . ."

If I were here alone, or single without my daughters, I'd be very tempted. Samira shook her head slowly. *But staying on with Krissy and Kara isn't as appealing.* "I really can't stay. Once the girls are packed and ready we'll need to start toward home . . ."

Phil's eyes fell at that statement. "That's alright," he said as he stood. "It's been really nice having you up here with me." His eyes scanned the outskirts of the yard. "I don't share this part of my life with too many people . . ."

I'm honored to have shared it with him. Samira stepped out of the swing and joined Phil at the railing.

"I'm really glad I came too." *I wonder if the magical moment out of at the lake will ever replay?* "And thanks for spending so much time doing things with the girls. They had a good time in spite of their initial misgivings." Samira leaned against the railing so she could see Phil's face.

He stretched out a well-sculpted arm and balanced his weight on a high support beam. "I didn't mind. It was good to get to know them a little more."

"Your boys will probably be ready for them to go home."

Phil chuckled. "They'll probably miss Krissy's stories. She's a live wire out there on the trail."

"She's a live wire anywhere." As an afterthought she added. "I hope Kara behaved." *Lord knows her teenage attitude has been showing lately.*

Phil nodded slightly. "She has to work harder than her sister to have fun, but she does alright." His eyes met Samira's again. "Give her a good challenge and she'll rise to the occasion."

He's already figured Kara out.

Chase bounded onto the porch with something green hanging between his teeth. *I hope it's not another dead fish!* Samira pulled her legs up abruptly. *Go away!*

Phil tried to divert the dog's aggression with his knee, but Chase was too excited to share his treasure. Samira pulled her legs up even further. *Please! Make him stop!* Before she realized what was happening, she lost her balance and started to fall backwards.

In an instant Phil had Samira's hand and was pulling her back toward him. He was still jockeying the dog with his foot, but hung on long enough that Samira could catch her own balance again.

Thank goodness!

"Here, boy," Phil knelt. He steadied the dog with one hand and examined the object with another. "You are going to get your butt kicked if Aunt Maggie finds out about this."

I don't want to know. Samira closed her eyes and turned her face away, afraid to look.

Uncle Roy appeared from behind the corner of the house. "Keep that thief out of Aunt Maggie's garden."

Where'd he come from?

Samira watched Roy disappear behind the house again.

"A green tomato." Phil examined the object. "Or rather, what's left of it." He rubbed Chase between the ears. "That'll give you a belly ache, buddy." Phil tossed the juicy remnants of the tomato into the bushes along the front edge of the porch.

Samira took note of the bushes. *At least I'd have fallen there instead of onto the hard ground!* She pushed her hair behind her ears. When she looked up Phil was standing over her. *My knight in shining armor.* A slight shiver ran up Samira's spine.

"What are you thinking, Pretty Lady?"

"I think you just saved my life."

"I'm thinking maybe you just saved mine."

His beard is softer this morning than it was last night. She ran one hand up under his ear and let the other one navigate against the bare, sticky skin on his lower back. *This is the part of him I want to take home with me.*

"Phillip!" Aunt Maggie's voice called out a sharp interruption.

The kiss left Samira catching her breath. *Wow.* She pulled her hair back with one hand and held it in a ponytail.

"There's a phone call for you Phillip, dear," Aunt Maggie announced, seemingly oblivious to the intimate moment taking place on her porch.

Phone calls always alter Phil's demeanor.

"On your phone? Who is it?"

I hope it's not that Bobbie person again. Samira glanced at the magazine still laying on the swing.

"Well . . ." Maggie looked apologetic. "It's Janet. I told her I'd see if you were back from your run yet."

Samira could see a sudden tension form across Phil's shoulder blades. *Case in point.* Samira remembered. *The same ex-wife that called his house as we were trying to leave for Springfield.*

Phil walked through the open door with purpose. It closed loudly behind him leaving Maggie and Samira on the porch.

So much for a private moment. The half-eaten tomato was stuck in the bushes. *That is disgusting!* "There's a book entitled, 'Fried Green Tomatoes'," Samira recalled out loud. *What in the world triggered that thought?*

"My mother used to fry up green tomatoes." Aunt Maggie responded as if she'd always been a part of that conversation. "I never much enjoyed them myself." Maggie wiped her wrinkled hands on her apron. "I should have told her Phillip wasn't back yet." Maggie's eyes were fixed on the solid door. "He's had such a nice weekend."

I hope it's nothing serious.

"I wonder what could be on her mind at this hour on a Sunday morning?" Maggie worried out loud. "Janet has a way of turning things sour for no reason, no reason at all." The old woman shook her head as she headed for the door. "I just hope Phillip doesn't let her change his mood. He's been so relaxed . . ." Maggie didn't stop talking as she opened the door into the house. "It's so good to see him so relaxed . . ." the woman continued to chatter as the door closed behind her.

I should go check on the girls. She could see Phil in the kitchen, the phone to his ear. His back was to her but Samira could sense the tension just the same. *Janet does have a way of pushing his buttons.*

Samira checked on the girls then stopped in the guestroom to finish packing her own things. *It's harder to leave here than I thought it was going to be.* Her hair was almost dry now. She ran a brush through the length and then wrapped a quick bun with her free hand. She carried her bag down the stairs and set it by the front door. She looked around expecting to find Phil. Instead she found Krissy.

"I think you'd better go after Phil, Mama. He's really mad and James is really going to get it . . ."

What in the world? Samira's questioning eyes moved to Maggie's worried look.

"It's true, Samira. Whatever Janet had to say turned up the heat . . ." Maggie was wiping her forehead with the back of her hand. "I'm afraid the weekend won't end as good as it began . . ."

Samira didn't wait for Maggie to finish. *There's no reason for the weekend to end with tension that arrived in that phone call.* She opened the door and scanned the front yard. *He's headed for the tent!* There was determination in Phil's stride. *I'm going to have to hurry!* She recalled Phil's regret when he told her about his fight with James. *Surely there's a better way to handle whatever it is.*

Chase was sitting at attention on the top step of the porch. *This is serious if Chase isn't following Phil!* Phil was almost at the tent. *I'm never going to catch him at this rate.*

Samira called out his name, but if he heard, it didn't slow his steps.

"Phil!" She called louder this time.

Phil stopped walking but didn't turn around.

Samira stopped a few feet from where Phil was standing. He had his hands on his hips and he was breathing heavily.

For whatever it's worth . . . "Phil?"

He turned around ever so slowly. His jaw was set and his eyes were angry. *This is neither J.P. or Phil.*

"Samira, don't . . ."

Don't what? Samira felt her confidence grow. *What does he think I'm here to do?*

" . . . You don't know . . ."

I know he's too mad to confront his son! "Maybe there's another way to handle this . . ."

"Handle what?" Phil snapped. "It's already started."

"But maybe you should . . .

" . . . should what? Do you think you know these boys better than I do?"

I would never question his relationship with the boys. "Not at all, I just thought . . ."

"Thought what?" The irritation in his voice was showing more with every statement.

"If you'll let me finish . . ."

"Finish? I'm going to finish what she started!" Now he was beginning to raise his voice.

Exactly my point. What she started has little to do with what you're about to do. Samira didn't appreciate his tone. *Phil's anger has nothing to do with the boys in that tent. That's obvious.* She put her hands on her hips and locked her eyes with his. "Maybe that's the point!"

This time when Phil tried to interrupt, Samira wouldn't allow it. "No, hear me out." *He needs to cool down.* She was careful not to match his tone. "Whatever Janet said to you on the phone just now may have more to do with her control over you than it does with the boys." *I can't believe I just said that to him!*

"What the hell is that supposed to mean?" Phil set his jaw and lowered his head to make a stronger point. "You don't have a goddamned idea what she told me on the phone . . ."

Well, there's no turning back now. "You're right about that, Mr. Ralston." *And there is no reason to swear at me.* "But I do know that she knows how to push your buttons and she's found just the one to gain your attention this morning." *I can't believe I'm standing up to him like this!* "And she also knows how to put an end to a perfectly good morning." Samira stopped talking. *I may as well finish my thoughts now.* "And there is no reason for you to raise your voice at me and even less reason for you to swear at me . . ."

Phil was still staring her down but Samira refused to let him intimidate her.

" . . . and my suggestion, in the case you might be listening at all, is that you let that phone call go and enjoy that last few hours you have with your sons before you have to leave town on business again." *There. I spoke my piece.* Samira put her hand over her stomach in an attempt to relieve the pit that was forming.

Phil shook his head hard and glanced toward the tent. "I just don't let things go." His eyes were steel gray. "If there's an issue that needs addressed then by god we're going to address it . . ."

Addressing it with God would be a better alternative than what you're about to do now. "Then address it on your time frame, not hers . . ."

"What the hell is that supposed to mean?"

"You don't need to swear at me." Samira's patience was running thin. *Is this the same man I made love to in the dark of the night?*

Phil looked away.

"All I'm saying . . ." *How do I speak the truth without setting him off more?* " . . . is that you need to get your thoughts in order before addressing the issues. Maybe she called on purpose to prompt a fight or something . . ."

Phil threw his arms out. "Who are you? Some kind of authority on my ex-wife?"

I could live without his petty insinuations. She'd hit a nerve. *But if I back down now, the boys, or at least one of them, is in line for the next punch.*

"No, but something Maggie told me makes me . . ."

"Maybe Aunt Maggie needs to keep her thoughts to herself . . ."

"She wasn't speaking directly to me," Samira interrupted. "And she only says what she does because she loves you . . ."

Phil closed his eyes and let his head fall forward. He put his hands behind his neck. Samira waited but he didn't speak.

Now what do I do? Her heart was pounding hard in her chest and James and Josh were now watching from the unzipped screen of the tent. *I guess I'll make one last suggestion. He can take it or leave it.*

"Listen, Phil," Samira lowered her voice so the boys couldn't hear. "I just don't want you to have any regrets about the weekend."

Nothing else came to mind. *I guess that's all that needs to be said.* Samira turned toward the house. Maggie quickly ushered Krissy off the porch. *Obviously they witnessed the whole thing.* Chase was still perched at attention on the top step. *Even his dog avoids his temper.*

"You did it, Mama!" Krissy announced as Samira set foot inside the cabin. "You saved James from being in big trouble."

Samira pursed her lips. *We'll see.* "Why don't you run along and see how Kara is doing." She needed a minute to gather her own thoughts. When Krissy was out of sight Samira stepped back to the window where she'd watched Phil jog across the yard less than an hour before. *He went from being thoughtful, passionate and incredibly irresistible to insanely angry in no time at all! I don't know . . .*

"You were very brave. Not many people dare to stop Phillip when he's in a rage like that." Maggie's voice was still shaking.

Samira turned to face Aunt Maggie.

"I've always sent Roy but I didn't know where he was . . ." Maggie caught a tear on her cheek with her fingertip.

The front door opened and Josh stepped through. He greeted his great aunt with a natural smile. "What's for breakfast, Aunt Maggie? I'm about starved to death!"

Samira looked back out the window. James was on his way to the house but Phil was nowhere in sight. *Chase is gone too.*

After breakfast James and Josh convinced Samira to allow the girls one last jaunt to the waterfront before heading home. She helped Maggie clear the last of the dishes as the kids took off across the yard. Maggie was chattering on about something or the other when Phil's broad shoulders darkened the kitchen doorway.

Samira stopped wiping the table and studied his eyes. *They're not angry anymore.* She wanted so badly to touch him, but his stance still showed signs of tension. *And he's showered and shaved.*

Aunt Maggie changed subjects without taking a breath. "Oh, Phillip, I fixed you a plate . . ."

He waved his hand. "I'm not hungry right now, Aunt Maggie . . ."

"You really should eat something, Phillip . . ." Maggie wiped her hands on her apron and glanced in Samira's direction. "I'll just take these scraps out to Chase . . ." The old aunt gathered the leftover sausages and made her way toward the front door.

Samira leaned against the sink. *I think I'll let him do the speaking this time.*

Phil walked across the kitchen and balanced his weight against one of Aunt Maggie's kitchen chairs. "You didn't have to do that."

Oh yes I did. Samira knew better. *Who knows what might have happened had I not stepped in . . .*

"I didn't mean for Janet's phone call to involve you."

Phil's voice was apologetic but he still hadn't said the two words Samira thought he might. "Better to involve me than the boys."

Phil shook his slowly. "Not so."

Just say you're sorry and we'll be all right.

"You're right about one thing," Phil added. "Janet does know how to push my buttons and this morning was no exception."

At least he's admitting that much. Samira dried her hands on a dishtowel and crossed the room to where Phil was leaning. "You just need to remember you have control over the buttons." She brushed the dishtowel over his arm hoping to relieve the tension hanging between them.

Phil looked beyond her but didn't speak.

"I just didn't want you to say or do something to jeopardize the good times the boys had with you throughout the weekend," Samira explained carefully. "They deserve a break from everyday pressures just like everyone else." *And I didn't want you to put a damper on what we shared this weekend either.*

Phil ran his hand through his hair.

He can't say it. Watching him try to cope with the awkwardness of the moment, Samira knew he wasn't going to be able to form the words of apology. *He is sorry. But he can't say it.*

"Are the girls packed?"

"They left their bag by the door."

"What time are you leaving?"

"As soon as the kids get back from the lake." Phil nodded his head in understanding.

So what do I say to him after this? Samira felt completely numb from the entire experience. *I might as well load the car and get ready to go.* Phil followed her to the living room and picked up her bag. They walked to the car without speaking.

Samira could hear the kids' voices in the distance. *My time with Phil is growing short.*

"You deserve better," Phil announced out of the blue. He had his hands in his front pockets and was looking off into the distance to a place Samira couldn't see.

Maybe, maybe not. She recalled the way he touched her the night before. *Most parts of you are perfect.*

"I didn't mean to swear at you."

Samira knew Phil was working toward an apology but it was not forthright in coming.

"I . . . I wasn't mad at you, Samira."

"I know that."

"But that doesn't make it all right."

"I know that too."

"And you're right again. The issues Jan called about aren't as urgent as they seemed."

"I didn't think they were."

"I wish we could just start the morning over again."

Like the way we started our arrival again? "We could start around midnight maybe . . ."

Phil's eyes suddenly returned to hers. The reminder of the night before caught him off guard. "That would be . . . well . . . , yeah, . . . I'd like that." His voice trailed off but the voices on the trail were getting closer.

"I'm sorry, Phil." She spoke his words and she knew it. Yet she couldn't stop them from coming.

"No, don't be." Phil's fingers lifted her hand. "There's nothing for you to be sorry about . . ."

His eyes were searching hers but she was afraid he wouldn't find the answer he needed. There was more to his unspoken apology; more than Samira could possibly begin to understand.

She allowed his lips to touch hers. Ever so gently he gathered her into a full embrace and held her just like he had at his house the night they were leaving for Springfield. *I can love him, but I can't give him what he needs most.* What he needed was beyond her capability. *He needs to find himself somewhere in the midst of this confusion.*

Phil let her go just as the kids appeared at the end of the trail.

The next few minutes were a blur of goodbyes and an exchange of hospitable thanks between Samira's family and Maggie and Roy. Even Chase got in on the departing excitement delivering yet another green tomato just as Samira climbed into the driver's seat.

Phil threw it far into the barnyard beyond the driveway. As the dog took off, Phil knelt down at Samira's open door.

"I'll call you from out East."

Samira nodded. *I'd rather see him in person, but a phone call is a good start.*

"I don't know when I'll get a break but . . ."

"I'll be there when you're free." *There's no need for him to feel pressure from me too.*

Phil nodded. His eyes were full of unspoken thoughts but it was obvious their time was up. He squeezed her hand as he stood up.

Samira started the engine just as Chase returned with the tomato again. This time it was dripping between his teeth. She laughed. *I don't mind leaving the ornery hound behind!*

Samira dared to look in her rearview mirror before turning onto the gravel road in front of the ranch. Phil was still watching the car, his fingers tucked inside his front pockets. *Yes, he's everything I prayed for.* Dust from the road blocked her view of the driveway. *Yet he's so much more.*

She turned left onto the blacktop just as Phil had instructed.

What if it's the more I can't handle?

36

Bobby

Uncle Roy's face appeared hidden behind his thick glasses. "If you ask me, that there looks like a woman you need to latch onto."

J.P. was trying to see Roy's face but couldn't make it out. "Uncle Roy, I don't know any more about latching onto a woman than I know about taming a lion."

"Seems to me the woman's not the one who needs tamin'."

Uncle Roy's words stung. "She looks a little out of your league, J.P."

"You might be the one who needs tamin' . . ."

" . . . a little out of your league . . ."

"Mr. Ralston."

"The woman might not be the one who needs tamin' . . ."

The voices were getting louder and louder.

"Better be careful dragging her around . . ."

"Mr. Ralston."

"You might need some taming . . ."

"Mr. Ralston . . ."

J.P. opened his eyes but he didn't recognize the woman looking back at him. Her hand was on his arm. Uncle Roy's husky voice was still playing tricks in J.P.'s mind.

"We've begun our descent to the runway, Mr. Ralston. Please put your seat all the way into the forward position."

Very slowly the roar of jet engines drowned out the voices from his dream. *That's the flight attendant.* J.P. leaned forward and rested his face in his hands. *If you're planning on hanging on to her, you need to get your shit together.* He pictured her face in his mind. *Samira.*

314

There were only two other people flying first class. He watched the stewardess prepare for landing. She looked over her shoulder and smiled in J.P.'s direction. *Nice looking girl, but the smile I'd like to see isn't hers.*

J.P. took the magazine out of the pocket in front of him. He was sure it was the same magazine Krissy and Kara had on the hammock. *And I know it's the same one Samira left lying on the porch swing.* Bobbie Jo Sommers smiled back at him.

The plane touched the runway once.

Why would Samira have this magazine?

There was a bump as the wheels touched the tarmac again.

And what does she know, if anything, about Bobbie Jo? He turned it over. *It's a newsstand copy. Not a subscriber.*

This time when the plane touched down it stayed. A few short minutes later the jetliner decelerated to a complete stop. *I suppose it's possible Samira saw me with Bobbie in Springfield.* He left the magazine in the empty seat next to him.

Sparky was waiting along the wall outside the boarding area as promised. J.P. tucked his return ticket inside his jacket and stretched out his hand to greet the former KGB officer.

Sparky made very brief eye contact and shook the attorney's hand only once. "Der is a car waiting."

I can't believe I put my trust in a man of so few words. J.P. adjusted his shoulder bag and fell into step behind the bald little man. The air outside was smoggy and thick. *Gotta love Baltimore.* They walked to a waiting limousine. Instantly two chauffeurs stepped onto the curb and opened the doors on either side of the car.

What the hell? J.P. watched Sparky walk to the far side. He barely had to bend over to climb inside. The uniformed chauffeur offered to take J.P.'s bag. He parted with his garment bag. *I think I'll keep my briefcase and computer handy.*

The doors closed and locked immediately. J.P. found himself facing Sparky. He turned in his seat and took note of the security glass between them and the drivers. Sparky poured a shot of vodka and offered one to his employer. *No thank you on the Vodka.*

"This is really nice . . ." J.P. continued to examine the car. "Am I paying for this?"

Sparky suppressed a smile. "No, sur." He offered a toast in mid air. "I have a good friend in area." Sparky's imperfect English accented his words. "Ah, but Hyatt Regency is very nice. Dat you do pay for. Tank you."

Must be a hellova friend. "Denise tells me you have a full day planned ahead."

Sparky's black bushy eyebrows raised considerably. "Ah, Denise is good vorker."

"She's the best. What time do we start in the morning?"

Sparky pointed a finger at his wristwatch. "Tomorrow is now today."

J.P. sighed. *I've just added an hour to what was already a long day.*

"Ve start at eight o'clock sharp. I vill brief you on the vay in."

That's good because I'm too tired to digest anything now. J.P. could see the reflection of the Hyatt's signage in the back window.

"Your key, sur."

J.P. accepted a business card-size envelope.

"I checked you in on the account." Sparky folded his hands politely. "Denise say she take care of everyting."

Wonder what else she's managing while I'm out here?

"I vill meet you in lobby at six thirty." The limousine slowed to a stop under the Hyatt's canopy.

"Six thirty?"

Sparky stepped out of the car. "Much briefing to do sur."

J.P. waited for the chauffeur to bring his garment bag.

"Four-tvelve." Sparky tapped his finger on J.P.'s room card. "Five-feefty." He tapped his own. "Good night, sur."

Five fifty. I need to remember that. J.P. found himself standing alone outside the Hyatt Regency. He could hear airplanes taking off and landing somewhere not so far off. Traffic dotted the horizon with multicolored lights. There was nothing familiar about this place; not even the scattered thoughts in his own mind seemed familiar.

Four-tvelve. He entered the hotel and pressed the call button on the elevator. *I don't care what number the room is as long as I have a pillow for my head.*

The morning began right on time. Sparky was more than prepared for J.P.'s arrival. The briefing was detailed and exact. By the time they were interviewing potential witnesses, J.P. felt completely confident in the case. It was nearing lunchtime when J.P. checked his watch for the first time.

"You do good work, Sparky." He packed his briefcase. "I appreciate the time you've put in out here." *Very timely and complete.*

Sparky's face remained serious as he nodded acceptance. "Dis afternoon you vill meet the judge handling the case. You also vill meet the defense team."

"How long before the actual hearing?"

"Long lunch in Balteemoor." Sparky studied his watch. "Courthouse will close 'til two o'clock. Den da hearing start." The little man finished scribbling a note on a yellow legal pad. "I vill brief you over lunch."

Sparky had lunch scoped out at a quaint café not far from the courthouse. It didn't take but a few minutes for Sparky to launch into the new briefings.

Mike was right on the money with Sparky. He doesn't miss a beat.

"My vork here in Balteemoor is almost fineeshed." Sparky wiped his dark mustache with a cloth napkin. "Ve must get the suspects to agree to the plea bargain if ve are to know der employer."

Sparky's right. Without that, chances of identifying their employer is slim to none.

"Der is something more I need to discuss vith you," the investigator leaned in as if he had a secret to share.

J.P. leaned in too. *I hope it's not a major hidden expense—like a limo.*

"Mmmm, I don't know vhat to tink." Sparky scratched his chin. "But I tink der is another link to dis case."

"What kind of a link?"

The investigator knitted his brow as he thought. "I don't know yet. Der are many vires back and forth to Joplin still."

"Are you still monitoring the communication traffic?"

"Absolutely!" Sparky seemed surprised to be questioned over that. "Alvays keep alert! Zometing is feeshy. Don't know vhat it is yet."

J.P. crossed his arms and watched the little man think. "Do you need to go back to Joplin to trace the link?"

"No. I don't think so. Caleefornia maybe. I maybe need to go to Caleefornia."

"California?" *How do I know he's not using this as a way for me to pay his way to the west coast?* "What's the connection there?"

"Mmm, lots of traffic to Caleefornia. Nothing from here to der anymore. All from here to Joplin to Caleefornia."

"And you think you could go out there and link somebody to this case?"

"Very posseeble."

Sparky is dead serious. J.P. studied the little man. *If this is a solid lead, we're going to have to slow the whole thing down to accommodate new evidence.* "How soon do you need to go out there?"

"Soon. Maybe tomorrow."

J.P.'s telephone rang. *Probably Denise wanting the latest update.* "This is J.P.".

"Hey, hey! Big Bro! What brings you to the eastern sphere?"

J.P. hadn't heard Bobby's voice in a long while. He excused himself from the table and carried the phone outside the café. "How the hell do you know I'm on the East Coast?"

"Aunt Maggie doesn't keep family secrets."

"Tell me about that!" *I'm sure she shared a few with Samira.* "When did you talk to her?"

"This morning first thing. She says you're in Baltimore."

J.P. looked up at the street sign and gave an exact location.

"Get this. I'm in Newark on business. I can be down there by 8:00 tonight and we can find some seafood and catch up."

I can make that work. It isn't everyday I spend an evening with my brother. "8:00 it is then. I'm at the airport Hyatt. Meet me there."

"Will do. Hey gotta run."

J.P. closed his phone. *It'll be good to see Bobby.* Sparky was waiting for him at the entrance to the café. "Let me pick up the tab."

"Ah, dis one is on me," Sparky spoke with appreciation. "You been very good to me on dis case."

J.P. stood at least a foot taller than his investigator. He had to chuckle as they walked side-by-side back toward the courthouse. "California, huh?"

"Yes, sur." They walked a few more lengths of the sidewalk before he spoke again. "And I think, if I am not meestaken, de links vill lead right back to Joplin again."

Very interesting.

A pounding on the hotel door ended J.P.'s shower sooner than he'd hoped. He wrapped his lower body in a towel. Bobby's smiling faced was looking back at him through the peephole.

"You said eight."

"So I'm early. Is it a crime to be early?" Bobby stepped into the room with his usual vigor. Slightly shorter and less fit than J.P., he still smiled the easy Ralston smile. "Get your ass in some clothes and let's hit the streets, find some entertainment, eat some seafood, drink some ale . . ."

I'm barely unwound from my case, damn it! Samira's smile was stuck in his memory. *And I also have a phone call I'd like to make before we leave.* "How'd you get my room number?"

"It was tricky, let me tell you. Had to read the desk book upsidedown." Bobby stood on his tiptoes and indicated how he'd had to stretch his neck to see over the counter.

Doubtful. The light was flashing on the hotel phone indicating a message. *He watched the desk clerk dial my room.* He shook his head and returned to the bathroom.

"How long did you wait downstairs?"

"Ten minutes before I decided to take matters into my own hands. Don't you ever check for messages?"

"I was in the shower for god's sake."

"Whoever's sake it was, you could have at least ordered me a drink while I waited," Bobby walked across the room and opened the curtain.

Samira opens curtains too.

"Aunt Maggie tells me you took a little family to the ranch." Bobby's voice was playful. "Don't mind if I go through your wallet to find her picture do you?"

No picture, but getting one's not a bad idea. J.P. watched in the mirror as his brother examined the contents of his billfold.

"No photo? But hey, you've got all the protection you could need for a night." Bobby flashed a set of condoms between his fingers. "That's my brother the attorney. Always prepared."

And that's my brother, Robert. J.P. shook his head. *Always full of shit!"*

The Ralston brothers called for a taxi to take them to the reef. A live band entertained on the beach while cocktail waitresses worked the crowd. When they'd had their fill of happy hour ale, they made their way inside the restaurant.

"Steak and lobster!" Bobby rubbed his oversized stomach with his hand. J.P. ordered the seafood platter and requested a bottle of house wine.

"So, how are Megan and the kids?" J.P. watched his brother fill the stemmed glasses.

"Fine, doing fine." Bobby shared the Ralston smile again. "Megan's accounts are still growing which keeps her on the cutting edge of the investments. Besides that she's awesome as always." Bobby grinned. "I'm not on the road quite as much as I used to be so I'm catching more ballgames and school concerts. Makes me feel like a real dad for a change." His eyes grew more serious. "What about you? How often do you see the boys?"

J.P. tipped his head back slightly. *Ale on an empty stomach might not have been a good idea.* He lowered his head to stabilize his vision.

"Well, James is currently living with me so I'm finding out all over again what it's like to be a dad." J.P. turned the stemmed glass in his hands but didn't lift it off the table. "I just spent four days with Josh and it sounds like he'll come down and stay a week once I get home."

"So, what's up with James? Did he finally grow wise to his mother's ways?"

Janet and Bobby never did exactly bond. "Something like that." Bobby was too wild for Janet's taste and Janet too stale for his. "He and Bruce aren't seeing eye to eye anymore . . ."

"Like they ever did."

"Maybe not," J.P. concurred again. "DHS decided it best for James to not live at home this summer."

"What's that do to your lifestyle?"

"Puts a new twist on everything from what time I wake up in the morning to when I can take a shower without running out of hot water." J.P. rested his head on the back of the booth. "But James seems to be adjusting all right. He has a job at the golf club. That keeps him occupied most of the day."

The waitress delivered a loaf of warm bread and clam chowder.

With the soup dish pushed aside Bobby asked another question. "So what can you tell me about this 'little family' that accompanied you to the ranch?"

The chowder and bread were taking the edge off the alcohol. J.P. tried to hide the grin that was forming on his face.

"Uh-huh . . ." Bobby pointed a finger at his brother. "Aunt Maggie's hoping this is the one to settle you down."

Suddenly Uncle Roy's words replayed in J.P.'s mind. *You're the one who might need tamed . . .*

"So, give me the lo-down bro. What's she like? How long you known her?"

J.P. hadn't talked to anyone about Samira. Not even Mike. *Can't hurt to let Bobby in on Samira.* "I guess I've know her a couple of months now."

"Just a couple of months, huh? She must be movin' pretty fast."

"Not really," J.P. admitted. "She's actually taking things rather cautiously."

"Smart woman." Bobby grinned with a hint of brotherly torment. "If she knows anything about you at all she's very wise to move slowly . . . a snail's pace even . . ."

How is it my past always seems to get in the way of my future? Bobby was still talking, but J.P. was no longer listening.

" . . . So, she must be stunning if you're still showing interest after eight weeks."

Stunning is close. The confrontation in Aunt Maggie's front yard replayed in his mind. *Amazing is more accurate.*

" . . . And she must have kids if you took a *family* to the ranch . . ."

That's a question I can answer. "Two girls. Thirteen and fourteen, I think."

"Right between Alicia and Angie." Bobby pulled out his wallet and pointed to pictures of his daughters. "Alicia will be thirteen in the fall and Angie just turned fifteen."

"So that means Justin is driving?"

"He's a senior this year, Phil! Same as Josh, remember?"

Wow. Josh is going to be a senior in high school? Suddenly J.P. was aware how quickly time was passing.

The waitress replaced the empty soup bowls with fresh salads. J.P. picked up his fork. *A little more food in my stomach won't hurt a thing.*

"So, if you were to propose tomorrow you think she'd accept?"

Bobby was never one to beat around the bush. J.P. took a bite. *Doubtful on the accepting part after yesterday's scene in the yard.*

"For being newly in love you don't seem to have much to say . . ."

"Who the hell said anything about love?" *I'm a far cry from being in love, little brother.*

"Aunt Maggie said she looks at you like she loves you."

J.P. put his fork down and rested his elbows on the table. "Do you believe *everything* Aunt Maggie tells you?"

Bobby made the sign of the Boy Scout with his hand. "Everything. Scout's Honor."

The wine was suddenly looking inviting again. J.P. took a sip. Then he took another. The whole time Samira's silhouette in the bedroom was playing in his mind. *Give him enough to keep him satisfied.* "Let's just say eight weeks is hardly enough time to expect too much more than an occasional night out on the town." *Does she really look at me like that?*

"Bullshit," Bobby challenged. "You think I'm going to buy that?" He took another bite of the salad. "It's written all over your face, Big Brother. She's got you wrapped around her little finger and I bet you haven't even had the guts to tell her that yet . . ."

Maybe she does, but I have no intention of telling her anytime soon.

" . . . But don't wait too long, Phillip, 'cause gems like that don't stick around too long." Bobby raised his wineglass in a toast. "Here's to sticking it out."

J.P. raised his wine and felt the tingle as the glasses touched. *He's spoken his piece. I doubt he brings her up again.*

The seafood platter was more than J.P. could eat. He pushed his plate away and sat up straighter in the booth.

"I almost hate to bring this up . . ." Bobby was still working on his lobster tail. "But I'm here and you're here so I'm just going to say it." Bobby laid the lobster pliers on the edge of his plate and lifted a piece of meat out of the shell with his fork.

Now what's he got on his mind?

"You know, you're only a couple of hours from the Captain out here. Maybe you could take an afternoon and drive down to see him."

Where the hell did that come from?

"Seriously, Phil. He'd like to see you and you're not that far out of the way." Bobby worked another bite of lobster.

"Since when have you become so chummy with the Captain?"

"I don't know," Bobby spoke carefully. "He and I are getting along these days. I went down at Christmas you know. I've taken Megan and the kids down there a couple of times now. He always asked about you."

"What do you tell him?"

"What's there to tell? You work hard. You play hard. Then when you get a break you usually spend it with the boys."

J.P. sighed heavily. *I successfully avoided this conversation with Aunt Maggie only to run head on into it with my brother.*

"You know, I don't officially have to be back in Boston until day after tomorrow. I could stay on and go down even tomorrow if . . ."

"No," J.P. interrupted the suggestion while he still could. "I have a flight out in the morning and I really need to be getting back." *If I get in early enough I could catch Samira before she gets off work, maybe meet her at the Café Ole . . .*

Bobby stopped chewing. He was looking directly at his brother. "You know, he's aged a lot and he's mellowed over time. You might actually have a decent conversation with him if you'd just pick up the phone even . . ."

"I don't have anything to say to the Captain."

Bobby wiped his fingers on a napkin. "Maybe that's not the point anymore, Phillip. Maybe the Captain has some things he needs to say to you."

This is exactly the reason I choose to keep my distance from my family. New tension hung over the table.

"Hey, it's your life. You're going to live it as you choose and honestly, that's okay with me . . ."

At least he's still honest with me.

" . . . But if you get a sudden urge to maybe pop in on the Captain sometime, just know he won't turn you away at the door." Bobby offered another refill on the wine but J.P. refused. *One more glass of wine is not going to help me in the morning.*

Bobby picked up a more positive conversation just as easily as he dropped the last one. When the taxi driver let them out under the Hyatt's canopy, J.P. offered his extra bed for the night.

Back in the room, J.P. listened as Bobby checked in at home. *She's got to know he's been drinking the way his words are slurring together.* J.P. tried to block out his brother's conversation. He flipped through Sparky's notes. *I don't need to hear what he's talking to Megan about anyway.* But still, he couldn't help but hear. *Every time I turn around Samira's smile is taunting my conscience.* Bobby lowered his voice as he told his wife he loved her. *But I don't know if I'm ready to say those words to her yet!*

I don't even know what those words mean anymore. *Her sleeping image under Aunt Maggie's quilt was comforting somehow though.*

Morning came too early. J.P. left Bobby sleeping off the wine and ale. *Happy trails, Little Brother. We'll have to do this again soon.* His own head was still pounding from the affects of the wine but duty called and he knew Sparky was waiting.

Denise had successfully changed Sparky's flights so he was off to the west coast. J.P. looked around the airport for an empty chair. *Two hours to kill before boarding.* He needed to sit down and get his thoughts together.

Too much wine and not enough sleep.

There were no available chairs in the boarding area so J.P. went back out on the main concourse. He leaned on a wall next to a large lighted map. The longer he stood there the more he was drawn to the coastline glowing on the wall atlas. He followed the main highway out of Baltimore with his finger.

Richmond Virginia. Less than two hundred miles. But that puts me back in late tomorrow instead of this afternoon. Immediately he dismissed the idea and returned to his stance along the wall. " . . . *maybe the Captain has some things he needs to say to you . . .* " *Now both Bobby and Aunt Maggie have said those words.*

I wonder if they can get me out later tonight? J.P. fingered the return ticket in his hands. *Can't hurt to find out, I guess.* J.P. inquired at the ticket counter.

"Well, sir, coach is full but first class has a few openings. You could probably get out standby." She ran her long fake fingernail over the screen. "The last flight out leaves at eleven fifty-three . . ."

J.P. signed on the line to release his seat on the morning flight. *I hope to God I'm doing the right thing, here.* He retraced his steps to the main level and signed on another line and rented a car. *I'll just pop in, pop out, return the car, and fly home.*

37

The Analysis

The honeysuckle filled the garden with sweet aroma. *One more bed to water after this.* Samira adjusted the spray nozzle on the end of the garden hose and gently showered the herb garden. She'd stayed in the house after dinner hoping Phil might call. Now that it was almost dark, Samira wished she'd started earlier. *Now the mosquitoes are starting to bother.*

Tidbits of conversation with Phil played in her mind. *He was just a little younger than Krissy is now when he lost him mom.* She couldn't imagine growing up without her own mother. *Such a tender age.* But at one time she couldn't imagine her life without Tom either. *I guess that's something we have to accept if it comes to pass.*

The fountain was making shallow ripples in the garden pond. Samira knelt down and ran her fingertips through the cool water. *It reminds me of the lake.* As she listened to the running water she allowed her mind to whisk her back to Phil's kiss. *I've never been kissed like that before. Not once.* She could still feel his whiskers brush up against her cheek.

"Guess who, guess who?" Krissy was on the run from the house carrying the portable phone.

Samira had only one guess.

"You're not going to believe this . . . ," Krissy announced with her hand over the mouthpiece.

Just hand me the phone, Krissy!

"Not yet," Krissy taunted. "First I need to know if we're busy Thursday and Friday."

"I don't know yet," Samira reached for the phone again. "Just let me have it."

"She doesn't know yet," Krissy said into the phone. "I don't think there's anything going on. I'll go ask Kara while you talk to Mama . . ."

Ask Kara what? "Hello?"

"Samira! Hi! How are you? I'm surprised I actually caught you at home . . ."

The woman's voice was not even close to the voice she'd hoped for. *I'm always at home.*

" . . . It's Ellen. I had a chance to come home for a few days so I hopped the first plane north and here I am."

"Ellen." Samira tried not to sound too disappointed. "Ellen, how are you? When did you get in?"

"I'm great. Doing great . . ."

She repeats everything just like her mother. Ellen was Tom's youngest sister. *Every time she comes home there's an array of festivities.*

"I came in this morning. Mom and I did some shopping and then I caught up with some friends for lunch . . ."

And she's still a social butterfly, also like her mother.

" . . . I was hoping to pick up Kara and Krissy for a few days at the end of the week."

Samira sat down on the edge of a raised flowerbed and subconsciously began plucking miniature weeds from between the hydrangeas. "I can't think of anything going on. The girls have been babysitting . . ."

"Oh I know, for your brother . . . ," Ellen interrupted. "Yes, Krissy told me. Do you think they could spare the girls for a couple of days?"

"I'll call Pam and see if she had anything planned."

"Oh would you do that? That would be so good. I have to leave on Monday but I really want to spend some time with the girls . . ."

It will be good for the girls to see her.

" . . . I'm thinking Thursday and Friday for sure. Saturday if they're still putting up with me."

Samira promised to get back to Ellen with an answer. *But right now, I'd like to keep my phone line open.*

"Do call me right back, do that, will you honey?" Ellen's voice sounded more and more like her mother's. "I'll be sitting on the phone."

I'll call her back after I finish out here. Samira snipped a collection of fresh flowers. *A couple of carnations, a coneflower, three cheerful zinnias, and a handful of daisies, and baby's breath for accent. Perfect.*

Krissy was on her way out as Samira was on her way in the kitchen door. They almost collided.

"Oh, Mama! So what did you tell her?"

"I told her I'd call her back after we talked it over."

"So what is there to talk about?" Krissy threw her freckled arms into the air. "Aunt Ellen is home! We are in slumber party heaven!" She pointed toward the hallway. "Kara is like in there packing her things."

There was still plenty of dirty laundry from their trip to the ranch. *I sincerely doubt they have enough clean clothes to pack!* "Ellen's thinking maybe Thursday and Friday. There's plenty of time to get your things together."

Kara joined into the conversation. "But we should call Aunt Pam first, right?"

"Exactly. Give her a call and make sure she doesn't have anything major planned." *And try not to talk too long, please.*

"Here, Mama," Krissy reached for the flowers. "I can get these in water for you."

Samira handed off the flowers then stepped into the laundry room to wash her hands. When she got back to the kitchen Krissy was busily arranging the fresh cut flowers. *She's using my wine bottle for a vase!*

"Krissy! Where did you get that bottle?" *Why did I ask that?*

Krissy stopped, bewildered. "Under the sink." She pointed to the still open cupboard door. "I saw it down there once and thought it would make a pretty vase."

Samira started to reach for the bottle. *That wine bottle is mine and Phil's from our first night . . .* As she reached for the bottle she caught a glimpse of Krissy's saddened, confused face.

What is the matter with me? She wanted desperately to hide the wine bottle back in safekeeping, yet at the same time she didn't want to destroy Krissy's array. *How do I fix this now?* "Do you think they will all fit?"

Krissy shrugged her shoulders. "Maybe. You didn't let me finish."

"I'm sorry." *I over reacted.* But at the same time that was a treasured memory. "I'd just never thought of using it for flowers." Silently, Samira watched Krissy go back to work. A few moments later Krissy held up a small batch of leftover flowers.

"I think we should put these in another vase." Krissy scrunched her face. "Do I need to *ask* before I pick one out of the china cupboard?"

Samira closed her eyes as she shook her head. "No, go ahead." *A couple are just a tad too tall.* When Krissy turned her back to cross the room, Samira took the liberty of rearranging a couple flowers to give it a better balance.

"I knew you would do that."

"Do what?"

"That. Move the flowers." Krissy returned to the counter with a crystal bud vase. "You always do."

"I can't help it." Samira shrugged her shoulders. "It's in my nature."

"Just like Granny."

Funny, I just compared Ellen to her mother! "Yes, I do get that from Granny, don't I?"

Krissy giggled. "You get a lot of you from Granny!" She turned the bud vase all the way around for her mother to admire. "What do you think?"

"Perfect," Samira announced. *Personally, I'd cut that carnation a shade shorter, but I'm going to let it go.*

"Really?" Krissy carried the smaller bouquet to the dining room table. "Thanks, Mama!" She admired her work. "I'm going to check the flowers later and make sure you don't move any!" She flashed a quick smile in her mother's direction.

Leave it, leave it, leave it, the mother told herself. *It's only a carnation in a vase.*

The entire evening passed without a phone call from Phil. Disgusted with her own impatience, Samira tried to relax. She was curled into the downstairs couch trying to watch a movie with the girls. They were totally engrossed but it was all Samira could do to sit there.

I'm sure he's tired after flying in late and then working all day. Samira glued her eyes to the television screen. *But he did say he would try to call.* The bright screen against the darkened room made Samira's eyes water. *He just didn't say exactly when he would call.* She rubbed her eyes with her fingertips. *But he is out there on business. I really shouldn't even expect to hear from him until he's home and caught up . . .*

"Are you crying, Mama?" Krissy leaned back against the sofa.

"No," Samira shook her head. "I'm not."

"Me neither," Krissy noted. Then she lowered her voice. "But I think Kara is. She always cries at this part."

Oh, so they've seen this before. Samira couldn't believe she was having so much trouble settling into the film. She took a sip from her coffee cup. *Cold. Any excuse to go upstairs.*

Kara climbed up onto her mother's bed and pulled her knees into her chest. "Look at this, Mama," the young woman ran her finger over a welted spot around her right ankle.

Samira adjusted her reading light to take a better look. "Does it hurt?"

"No, it just itches like crazy."

"Have you been putting something on it?"

Kara nodded. "The cream stuff that Aunt Maggie sent home with me."

Aunt Maggie? Samira ran her hand over Kara's ankle. "It looks like a couple of bug bites have swollen together. If it's not better in a day or so we might want Granny to take a look."

Kara nodded. "I'll put some more cream on before I go to bed." Pulling all of her hair to the side she began to weave the long strands into a braid. "The next time we go to the ranch I want to sleep in the tent."

Now there's a complete turnaround. "The next time? You didn't want to go at all this time!"

"I know," Kara smiled shyly. "But it wasn't as bad as I thought."

Well, let's hear the whole story. Samira laid her book face down on the comforter. "What was your favorite part?"

"Hmmmm . . . ," Kara finished braiding her hair and wrapped the end with a band from around her wrist. "Maybe the hike after the boys found the missing card."

"Hey, what was that all about anyway?"

Kara giggled. "James told us the loser had to carry the heaviest backpack and do chores with Uncle Roy . . ."

Uncle Roy? She's talking like she's related to these people!

" . . . I didn't know if he was serious or not. James is tricky that way. But I didn't want us to be caught out there in the barn scooping horse . . . well, you know . . ."

"I know."

"But we were losing really bad!"

Samira reached for her own hairbrush and began working it through her hair. "So you thought you could win by cheating?"

Kara flipped her heavy braid behind her shoulder. "Just for a minute." She giggled again. "But it didn't really work out that way and the boys really soaked us down at the lake!"

Amazing how that all worked out.

"But the hike down to the lake was fun too. It was really pretty up there, Mama. I wished you could have seen the view. You could see the whooooole lake from there!"

I did see that view, but not with you.

Kara's eyes came back to her mother. "Phil's pretty nice." She thought for a minute. "And he's pretty funny too."

He's much more than that. "Funny like how?" *Tell me what you think, Kara.*

"Funny like you never know what he's going to say. And he's always teasing Josh and James." Kara's eyes lit up. "Oh, and he plays into Krissy's stories really good. You know how Krissy starts chattering on, right?"

Of course.

"Well, yeah, like Krissy would start into this long, drawn out story and Phil would constantly interrupt her. He would say things like, 'Then what?' and 'Tell me that part again . . . ' Krissy would get really flustered because she's just used to talking until we tell her to hush. But Phil kept her on her toes. A few times she couldn't even remember what she was going to say and she'd have to, like stop talking!" Kara was smiling. "He wasn't mean or anything. He was just really funny with her."

Samira could picture Krissy's antics. *I'm so glad Krissy didn't scare him off with her babbling!*

Kara crossed her legs and pulled her ankles in with her hands. "So do you really like Phil, Mama?"

Oh wow. Am I ready to answer that question yet? She stared at her daughter who was watching her very closely.

"I mean, like, are you like going steady or anything?"

Does sleeping with him constitute going steady? Samira put her hand to her forehead and rested her elbow on her knee. "I don't know. I guess I hadn't really thought much about that yet . . ."

"Well, he must like you if he asked all of us to go to the ranch and everything . . ."

"True."

Kara drew an invisible design with her finger on the comforter. "And when he looks at you he seems like he . . ." Kara paused in thought. " . . . like maybe he really likes being with you or something." Now Kara's dark eyes met her mothers. "Do you like being with him?"

I can answer that question. "Yes, Kara, I like being with him." *I like it more than I want to admit.*

Kara was deep in thought. Several long seconds passed.

"He looks really different when he doesn't shave . . ."

That's for sure! Samira liked the rustic, laid back Phil.

"I think he's funnier when he's just hanging out and not all dressed up for work and stuff."

Me too. "What makes you think that?"

Kara raised her eyebrows and shrugged her shoulders. "He's more serious when he's like dressed up. Like when we were getting ready to leave he'd shaved and then he was all business-like again."

That's an interesting observation. And not so far off the mark. "By the time we were leaving Phil was already thinking about going back to work. He had to fly out to the east coast later that night . . ."

"Yeah, I know." Kara slid to the edge of the bed. "Josh told us. That's why he and James were staying a few more days at the ranch." Kara stood up and stretched with a big yawn. "Does he have to go out of town a lot?"

Now there's a good question! "I don't know." *But it's something I might want to find out.*

"Well, anyways," Kara started walking toward the door. "It was fun to go up there. Maybe he'll invite us again sometime."

Maybe. If I ever get to talk to him again!

"By the way," Kara stopped in the doorway and turned back toward her mother. "You know that magazine you bought for us?"

It was for me.

"I can't find it. I thought I had it with my things but when I started getting stuff ready to go with Aunt Ellen I couldn't find it."

That's because I took it so I could talk to Phil about the model on the cover. Samira suddenly remembered. *On the swing!* Her heart rate increased. *I left it laying on the swing!*

"What is it, Mama?"

Samira threw her legs over the side of the bed. "Are you sure you didn't get home with it?" *I can't believe I asked her that. I know exactly where I left it!*

"Pretty sure." Kara yawned. "I'll look again tomorrow. Good night, Mama. I'll see you in the morning."

Samira watched until Kara was completely out of sight before burying her face in her hands. *I had it with me all weekend just so I could talk to him about it only to leave it out there for the whole world to see!* She made her way to the bathroom. *Now what? Do I ever ask him about it or did he even find it before he left? What am I supposed to do now?*

Samira brushed her teeth. *I bought it for the sole purpose of discussion. But that didn't come as easily as I'd hoped.* She wiped her mouth on the corner of a towel. *And then again, maybe I've just read something into it. Maybe that Bobbie has no relevance in his life whatsoever.*

Samira left her bedroom and walked the nighttime routine through the house. *But then again, why would she call and leave a message for Phil to be in touch the next time he went out east?* She turned off all the lights in the front part of the house with the exception of the one under the kitchen counter. *A little light adds comfort.* She peeked out the window. *It looks like Mrs. Barnes is already in bed for the night.* She double-checked the deadbolt locks on both doors.

The house was perfectly quiet. *So Kara thinks he's funny.* She lifted her feet off the floor and tucked them under her covers. *He is. But he's more than that.* She reached over the nightstand and touched the brass base of the lamp. The light gently faded away. *And I happen to like the non-shaven Phil too.* Samira closed her eyes wishing he could be there with her. *I like them both. Phil and J.P.* She was beginning to understand the difference between the two. *Maybe Aunt Maggie found the magazine and tossed it out.*

Samira sat straight up in bed and immediately touched the base of the lamp again. The room was illuminated at once.

Aunt Maggie?

Samira put her hand to her forehead. *Where did that come from? She is NOT my aunt.* Samira grabbed her book and left the bedroom. She curled into the throw pillows in the corner of the sofa. *He can permeate all of my thoughts yet he can't be here with me. In fact, he can't even seem to find the time to call me from wherever he is!*

Another series of thoughts came to mind. *What if he's out on the east coast with that magazine woman?* It didn't seem so far fetched after hearing Maggie tell Phil to call her when he got out there again.

Surely not. Samira's logical side kicked in. *How could he possibly spend a weekend like that with me only to turn around and spend time with someone else?*

The model's figure formed in Samira's mind. *That's the drawing point, isn't it? There's no way I can compete with that!* She squeezed a couch pillow into her churning stomach. *If only I'd have asked the hard questions when I had the chance.* The series of events that followed Janet's phone call replayed in fast forward motion. *No, that wouldn't have been a good time either. And had I brought Bobbie up before that, he might not have kissed me at all.*

No. I'd rather have his kiss than his explanation. Samira climbed up off the couch. *You over analyze everything!* Instead of reading, she decided to balance her checkbook. *At least that won't take any emotional energy.*

It was long into the night before Samira made her way back to bed. And by that time all of her thoughts were exhausted.

38

Joseph Phillip

The afternoon sunshine was beating in the windshield of the rented sedan. J.P. opened the car door and sat with one foot on the pavement and the other still inside the car. He scrutinized the row of brick houses along the narrow tree-lined street. *Looks like the same address.* He compared the house numbers to the return address on the worn envelope. He'd carried the letter from the Captain with him ever since Aunt Maggie insisted he take it. *Never had a desire to open it.* But it was with him all the time just the same.

Maybe I should have eaten something. The knots in J.P.'s stomach threatened to cramp. *No, on second thought, confrontation is usually better on an empty stomach.* Too many unpleasant memories plagued the drive down the coast. *It must be about twenty-four years since I've been face to face with the Captain. That's a hell of a long time, Ralston.*

J.P. finally climbed out of the car. *This would be a good time for one of Sparky's vodka shots.* He left the letter in his seat with his sport coat. *No reason to make this more formal than necessary.* He locked the car with the key control. *And no reason to drag it out either. Short and sweet and I'm on a plane to St. Louis.*

J.P. ascended the steps and raised the brass knocker. He turned and faced the front yard. There was a golden eagle glistening in the afternoon sun at the top of a high flagpole. *Not even a breeze today.*

There was no answer. *This might make the visit even easier. I could leave my business card and be gone.*

Just the same, I drove all this way . . . J.P. struck the knocker twice more. He moved to the edge of the porch and watched a pair of sparrows hop across the manicured lawn.

Very slowly, the heavy wooden door opened. A small, elderly man of Asian origin stood on the other side. *Who is he?* J.P. rechecked the house numbers. *They're the same.*

"Yes, Sir?" The elderly gentleman bowed slightly.

J.P. eyed him carefully. *Might as well get it over with.* "I'm here to see Captain Joe Ralston."

The little man looked J.P. up and down with pursed lips. "Do you have an appointment? Sir."

"No, I don't believe I do." *Do I need an appointment to see my own father?* "Does the Captain only work by appointment?" *That would be one way to get out of here without confrontation.*

"No, sir." The little man bowed his head momentarily. "Who shall I tell him is calling?"

Enough with the "sirs". "Tell him his son is here to see him."

"Yes, Sir."

J.P. stepped off of the porch as the man disappeared behind the closed door. *I don't know if this was a good idea or not.* His stomach was still churning

"The Captain will be up to meet you. Sir." The Asian man closed the door again.

J.P. judged the distance to the rented car. *There's still time to make an exit.* Deep down he knew he wouldn't leave, but the sting of being stood up an entire day at the St. Louis train station was suddenly fresh in his memory. *It wouldn't take much to get back in that car and drive away.*

The door opened again but J.P. couldn't bring himself to turn around. Footsteps crossed the porch but J.P. wouldn't face his father. *I have nothing to say to him.*

Short and sweet. J.P. heard the Captain walk down the steps. *I've made my appearance.*

The Captain crossed in front of his son. *He's a lot broader than I thought he would be at his age.* He walked straight and tall with his hands behind his back. *He's got to be pushing 80 by now.*

The Captain's head was high as he lifted his eyes to meet his son's.

I came here to see him. J.P. remained silent. *Surely he can think of something to say.*

The Captain's clean-shaven face was leathered and worn but his eyes were still the same blue.

He really doesn't look much different than I remember. A long silence occupied the space between the Ralston men.

Finally the Captain opened his mouth. "Joseph. Joseph Phillip."

J.P. glanced over the top of his father's shoulder into the empty street. No one had called him Joseph since . . . *since I don't know when.* It didn't sound right. *That name doesn't fit any more now than it did when I was growing up.* It was a name J.P. never grew into.

He knew his father's eyes were on him but he couldn't think of anything decent to say. *What do you say to the man who chose not to show up after promising you the world for your eighteenth birthday?*

"Joseph." The aging Captain spoke the name again. "It's good of you to come."

Is it? You don't look exceedingly pleased to see me. With his hands still inside his pants pockets, J.P. realized he was slightly taller than the Captain. *He used to be the tallest man I knew.*

The Captain didn't offer a handshake or any other form of greeting. His hands were tucked tightly behind his back. "You look good, Joseph. You're taller, more fit than your brother."

Does that have a bearing on my inheritance? J.P. caught his thought and tried to dismiss the negative connotations. J.P. stood still as the Captain walked all the way around him as if passing an inspection of sorts.

"What brings you to my quarters?"

What the hell is that supposed to mean? J.P. turned around to find his father facing away lighting a cigarette. *Does he think I'm here for my benefit?*

J.P. cleared his throat. "A letter, I guess."

The Captain nodded as he exhaled smoke through his nostrils. "The one to Maggie?"

J.P. nodded back.

"Did you read it?"

"No."

"I assumed as much." The Captain took another draw.

This is going nowhere! J.P. was beginning to plan his exit. *He can keep his goddamned assumptions to himself . . .* He looked up to find his father watching him very closely.

"Come on in. I'll introduce you to Tanganbang." With that the Captain started back up the steps to the porch. He motioned for J.P. to follow with a cigarette between his fingers. *I am not here to meet his friends.* "Look," J.P. glanced toward the rental car. "You don't have to entertain me or show me around." *I don't even know why I am here.* He ran his hand through his hair. "I had business in the Baltimore area and hooked up with Bobby. He thought . . ." *Shit, do I tell him this was all Bobby's idea? No.* " . . . He offered to drive down with me but . . ."

"You don't have to explain anything to me, Joseph." The Captain's eyes were surprisingly gentle. "It's good of you to come." He finished off the cigarette and stepped on the butt. With ease, the Captain leaned over and picked it off the floor of the porch.

I came this far. I might as well go inside. An awkward silence followed them. *Nothing feels right about being here.* He stepped inside his father's house. It was sparsely furnished but the walls were covered with photographs, recognition plaques and honorary medals. *Wow. That's a lot of memorabilia.*

"What can I get you to drink?" The Captain had stepped behind a make-shift bar.

Anything to calm my nerves. "J.D. and Coke."

Nothing more was said. The Captain put the drink in his son's hand and lifted his own drink to his weathered lips.

The whiskey burned all the way down. *I wonder what he's drinking.*

The Captain sank into an oversized leather recliner in the corner of the room.

His furniture looks a lot like mine.

Leather bound books lined the walls of the adjacent room. *I wonder how many he's actually read?* J.P. sat down on the edge of an ottoman. Much to his surprise the coffee table between him and his father was covered with photos. *There's James and Josh and all of Bobby's kids.* A glass top protected the prints.

"Maggie sends them to me periodically."

J.P. looked closer. *Some of these are more recent than what I have.*

"You have a set of good-looking boys, Joseph." The Captain's eyes were a darker blue than they had been outside in the sunshine. "Do you go by Joseph?"

I have a feeling he already knows the answer to that question. J.P. took another sip of the drink before answering. "No, I don't." The moment of truth was about to be known. "Professionally I use my initials. Aunt Maggie still uses my middle name." *Along with a few close friends.* Samira's face came into his mind's eye with that thought. *And I like the way she says my name.*

"Phillip." The Captain seemed to be mulling that over in his mind. "Your mother would have preferred Phillip over Joseph anyway." He blinked slowly.

And how would you know that or anything else about my mother? J.P. narrowed his eyes at his father. *All you cared about was climbing the ranks.*

"Leona." The Captain looked deep into his drink. "I still think about her everyday." He held his glass up toward the wall behind J.P. "She's there in my thoughts all the time."

Mom is all over that wall! J.P. stood up for a closer look.

"I have something I want to show you," the Captain rose from his chair and disappeared into another room.

J.P. took the liberty to look even closer. Some of the shots of his mother were familiar. *But most of these I've never seen.* His eyes studied her face and her hair and her hands. *I remember everything about her.* J.P.'s memory was lingering somewhere between the past and the present.

The little Asian man appeared silently and set a tray of cookies on the photo-strewn coffee table.

"Thank you, Tanganbang." J.P. heard his father's voice. "This is my son, Joseph Phillip. He goes by Phillip."

J.P. turned and faced the elderly man who folded his hands and bowed his head in silent greeting.

"Taganbang is from the Philippines. We've been together since sixty-eight."

J.P. nodded. *That's a long time for my father to maintain a relationship of any kind.* He took another sip of the whiskey before turning his eyes back to the photos on the wall.

"She was a beautiful woman," the Captain spoke again. "Here," his able hands took the cover off an old shoebox. "I told Maggie I had some things of your mother's for you and they're all here."

That's not why I'm here. "You don't need to give me anything of hers . . ."

"Hear me out," the Captain continued. "I gave a few things to Robert at Christmastime. These are yours. I didn't trust the U.S. Mail."

You don't trust the U.S. Mail? Now that's funny. But J.P. really didn't want anything of his mother's. *I don't want any of his baggage.*

The Captain lifted a stack of banded envelopes. "These are the letters Leona wrote to me over the years. I sorted them so you and Robert could get a feel for her thoughts while you were back in Missouri with her . . ."

And where were you in the world while we were back there? The whiskey was starting to mess with his mind on an empty stomach. J.P. helped himself to a plain cookie from the tray.

" . . . and these I saved thinking you might have a use for someday." The Captain hesitated before opening an old envelope. "I gave the other set to Robert." He poured the contents out in his hand and examined them as if for the last time. "These are her wedding rings, Joseph." He held them out for his son to take. "She'd want you to have them."

J.P. set his glass down on the table but he couldn't bring himself to accept the rings. *They're not mine and they don't represent anything that has ever been part of my world.*

"You should give them to Bobby . . ."

"Robert has the anniversary set. These belong to you."

I don't want them. "I didn't come here to take her stuff . . ."

The Captain raised his eyes and met his son face to face. "And I didn't invite you here to argue about it."

"You didn't invite me here period."

"Maybe you should have read the goddamned letter."

J.P. set his jaw. "It wasn't addressed to me." He watched the Captain turn away.

Behind his father he took note of more military honors. *Action in World War II, Korea, and Vietnam.* Another series of honors mentioned Captain Joseph Phillip Ralston's advisory roles in Desert Storm. Photos lined the walls with pictures of the Captain shaking hands with various presidents and other public figures. *All this yet he couldn't find any time to check in at home.* J.P. didn't want a part of anything that was written in those letters. *They're not addressed to me either.*

The whiskey on an empty stomach was taking full effect and J.P.'s temper was playing into it with ease.

"I don't know who Leona was to you, Captain. She was my mother and at some point in time I didn't get her back." J.P. scanned the photos of her again.

The Captain kept his back to his son but his voice was strong when he spoke.

"Neither did I. She didn't want to raise a family on military bases so we made the decision not to have children. But during one of the most memorable nights of my life she conceived. And at that point in time I gave her up for you and later for Robert because that was the way she needed it to be."

That's bullshit. J.P. balanced his weight with his hand against one of the book cases. *Nothing is making sense.*

The Captain turned and walked back to the leather chair leaving the wedding rings and letters in the cardboard box for J.P.'s taking.

"So that's it?" J.P. addressed his father from the dining room. "I drive all the way down here and walk away with Leona's thoughts and her rings."

"That's it." The Captain didn't show any emotion.

No apology for leaving us out there? No explanation for the flight that Never made it home? No excuse for not getting off the train in St. Louis?

J.P. fingered the banded letters. *Hell, I came all this way and gave up my flight home. I'd might as well take the box and be done with it.* He haphazardly replaced the lid on the box and started for the front door. *At least he won't be able to accuse me of never coming.*

But there was one obstacle yet to cross. *I have to walk in front of him to get to the front door.* J.P. tucked the box under his arm but couldn't force his feet to walk across the room.

"It was still good of you to come, son."

J.P. couldn't help but look at his father. *Why do I recognize the look in his eyes now?*

"If you don't have to rush right off, I'd like to take you to dinner." The Captain was studying his son's face. "It might be good to mix a meal with that whiskey."

The last thing I need to do now is get stuck socializing with the Captain at some Navy hangout.

"Nothing fancy. A good crab dinner and you'll be on your way." The Captain rose from his chair. "What do you say? My treat."

On the other hand, food won't hurt anything either. Especially before a long drive.

The Captain summoned Tangabang to bring his car around. J.P. was surprised to see a late model Lincoln pulled up out front. *Maybe an old Cadillac, but never a new Lincoln.*

The Captain drove into the country and stopped at what appeared to be a little shack. J.P. eyed the sign out front warily. *Big Daddy's Crab House. Great. Looks like a hole in the wall.*

"It might not look like much but Mobley fixes up the best crabs on the Eastern Coast." The Captain was obviously aware of J.P.'s demeanor. "Trust me."

Trusting you is not something I've ever done in the past. The attorney in J.P. was still very leery of the entire situation. *I don't like the way the Captain is trying to warm up to me and I don't like the fact that I'm still in Virginia when my flight is leaving from Baltimore.* Nevertheless, he allowed his father to order a plate of crab legs with the complete works.

It felt strange to be sitting across a table from a man he knew only from pictures and stories and distant memories. *I don't ever remember having a meal with the Captain.* J.P. watched. The Captain passed his fork from his left hand to his right. *That's odd. I wonder which hand he writes with?*

"You've done very well for yourself, Phillip . . ."

J.P. appreciated the Captain's purposeful use of his preferred name.

" . . . What made you choose law school over something else?"

"Money." J.P. answered honestly. "At the time of decision I went for the wage."

The Captain smiled for the first time. It was the same easy smile J.P. recognized in Josh. "Good motivator." He took a generous bite of crabmeat. "What made you stay in law?"

That's an interesting question. "I like to win and I'm good at it."

This time the Captain all but laughed. And then he did something that caught J.P. completely off guard. The Captain ran his hand through his thick gray hair. "I like your spunk, Phillip. That's what makes you a successful attorney."

Since he's asking questions, maybe I'll ask a few of my own. "What made you stay in the Navy?"

The Captain looked out from under his eyebrows. "I liked winning too and I was good at it . . ."

That's not a fair answer.

"But I lost a few too." With that, the Captain concentrated on his dinner for a moment. "Eventually winning doesn't mean as much in light of the losses."

About that time J.P.'s phone rang. *Of course it would ring now.* He excused himself from the conversation as politely as possible.

"This is J.P."

"Where the hell are you?" Denise sounded frantic on the other end. "I have called every airline from here to the East Coast!"

"Virginia. I'm in Virginia." *Didn't I call her?* "I'm flying in standby late tonight."

"Business endeavor or otherwise?"

Otherwise. J.P. answered in his mind. *No, it's more than otherwise. It's a little of everything.*

"So Sparky is in L.A. and you're in Virginia and I am totally in the dark here . . . You were supposed to be in a meeting with Jefferey Hughes and Sean Bridges an hour ago . . ."

Sean Bridges? When did she arrange that meeting? J.P. excused himself from his father's table. Once outside, he briefly granted permission for Denise to do whatever it was she needed to appease Jefferey Hughes and then explained that he was going to have to call her back. *I hate to do that to her, but I can't leave him sitting in there either.*

J.P. returned to the table, surprised by his sudden concern for his father.

"Business as usual?"

"Business anyway," J.P. admitted. "My assistant was expecting me back a couple of hours ago."

"Do you need to be back yet today?" The Captain checked his heavy chain link wristwatch. "It's an hour earlier there."

I'm well aware of the time change. "I fly out standby tonight. Business will resume then." *If Denise is still talking to me.* J.P. considered the ramifications of missing a meeting with Jeffery Hughes. *And if the city of Joplin hasn't cut all ties with the Hughes brothers for tampering with the city's new economic development plan . . .*

"But you know as well as I do that business runs smoother when you're there to direct the traffic." The Captain shared the easy Ralston smile again. "I know that look on your face. You're scheming."

He doesn't know anything about me. "What look?"

"I know because I've seen it in the mirror." The Captain mimicked his son's serious face for a brief moment.

I've seen that look in the mirror too. This time J.P. had to share the smile. *And I've seen it in Josh and James from time to time.* It was something Aunt Maggie always referred to as being in the Ralston genes.

A little while later J.P. watched his father sign for dinner. *Left-handed. I always wondered why I did some things right-handed and other things with my left.* Now he knew. *Another Ralston gene.*

Back at the Captain's house, J.P. picked up the cardboard box with less hesitation than he had before.

The Captain was in the kitchen making a phone call. J.P. took the liberty to once again admire the numerous photos of his mother. *She looks so happy.* The pictures above the Captain's desk included faded prints of him and Robert from days gone by.

"Jos—, I mean, Phillip," the Captain corrected mid-sentence. "I can get you out in an hour."

I need to be headed out now if I'm going to make my flight. "I'm going to need to . . ."

"No, on a flight." The Captain clarified. "There's a Fed Ex flight scheduled for take off at sixteen hundred. I can get you clearance into St. Louis."

What's he doing? I don't need to be a charity case.

The Captain squared his shoulders. "This is something I can do, Phillip," his eyes had turned a steel blue.

There were a lot of things he couldn't do. *Like go back in time and fix the broken and missing parts.* J.P. ran his hand through his hair. *Now I'll think of the Captain every time I do that!* Bobby's words suddenly replayed in J.P.'s mind " . . . *maybe it's what the Captain needs to say to you . . .* "

"All right. If it will make you feel better." J.P. resigned. *That saves me the drive back to the city.*

The Captain's face remained solemn. "It would. I'd like to do this for you."

J.P. granted permission for his father to follow through. Arrangements were made to have the rental car returned locally. The next thing J.P. knew, they were on their way to the airport. *I'm amazed how quickly the Captain is granted access to restricted areas simply by flashing his smile and his VIP badge.*

The Captain parked his car under the nose of a Federal Express jetliner. As soon as he stopped, uniformed men opened the car doors and escorted the Captain to the plane with proper salutes along the way.

Amazing.

A seasoned officer presented the Captain with official paperwork granting permission to board.

Now this almost beats the Hughes' perks at the Hyatt in Springfield. J.P. was slightly humored at the military's insistence on proper ritual.

The Captain led the way up the stairs to the open door on the jetliner. Three uniformed crewmen were saluting his father with highest regard. The Captain returned the salute and then put the men at ease. He handed over the paperwork and introduced his son using his full name.

"Joseph Phillip Ralston, the second." The Captain stood standing straight and tall.

I'll be damned. For the first time in J.P.'s life he felt slightly honored to be his father's son.

"You will have to pass security. Sir." J.P. realized the crewman was speaking to him. He had no idea what security entailed but he agreed. Immediately the crewmen took his garment bag and briefcase including his computer. *Interestingly enough, they don't seem to be concerned about the contents of the box the Captain is holding.*

J.P. lifted his arms as a metal detector scanned his entire body. He obediently removed his shoes when asked. And he showed them two forms of identification without resistance. When the crew was satisfied, they stamped the paperwork and informed the Captain of clearance.

Only then did the Captain proceed on into the cabin. Much to J.P.'s surprise, the airliner seats occupied only a few short rows. A partition stopped the view to the very back of the aircraft. Only three other men, all in uniform, occupied the cabin.

The Captain underwent the same security measures as his son and then took a seat in the first row and indicated that his son should sit next to him.

What's he doing? "Are you flying all the way to St. Louis too?"

"On the contrary, I am flying all the way to St. Louis and back." The Captain watched his son carefully. "The last flight carrying a family member never made destination . . ."

My mother's flight home . . .

" . . . This time I'm going to make sure the boys at home get their father back."

The Captain's presence thwarted J.P.'s wayward thoughts. No longer did he question the relevancy of his visit here. The old man was doing what he could. *And he's willing to go down with the craft if for whatever reason it doesn't make destination.*

J.P. sat down in the spacious seat next to his father. But there was more than two boys waiting back home. *And she's a damn good reason to make destination.*

There was no service crew aboard the jetliner. No one told him to buckle his seat belt. No one told him to straighten the back of his seat. But when the jet engines revved J.P. did those things anyway. He noticed the Captain doing the same.

They were high in the sky before either of them spoke again.

"Two other officers lost their wives in that same flight," the Captain remembered out loud. "Eventually the others remarried but Leona was all I ever needed. She's been enough for me over the years." His eyes had softened considerably. J.P. could feel the jetliner settle into cruising altitude.

J.P. listened as his father shared his most treasured memories. Stories of his mother's visits to stations all over the world filled J.P.'s mind with new insight on the long distance relationship that sustained both his father and mother for the better part of twenty years.

" . . . She was the only thing that kept me going in the heat of combat . . ."

J.P. dared not look at his father while he talked for fear of ruining the stream of memories that triggered some of his own treasured thoughts. Once, when J.P. looked at his father's hands he realized the Captain was holding Leona's rings.

"I'd raised up a lot of those boys by the time we got to Nam, Phillip . . ."

J.P. was surprised to hear his name mentioned in that sentence. *I figured by now he'd forgotten he was even speaking to me.*

" . . . sailing into the sea without most of my crew that night was one of the hardest things I ever had to do, next to putting your mother on a flight home every time my furlough was up."

In the archives of recollection J.P. remembered his father being home two, maybe three times during his childhood.

" . . . but the hardest thing I ever did was walk away from you boys on that Missouri farm." The Captain stopped talking and J.P. almost wondered if he had to compose himself before continuing. "Leona stood there proud and strong, holding your hands in hers"

That was the day I left teeth marks in his shoulder. The scar on his hand reminded him of another boy who needed a father.

The Captain ran his hand through his hair. "I went out there to bring Leona and you boys back to Virginia but Leona would have nothing of it. She knew what you needed." The Captain took a long pause. "You were better off without me there, Phillip . . ."

It's almost like he's read my thoughts.

" . . . I was brash and impatient and out of my territory. You needed your mother and her family more than you needed me."

That's exactly what I've told myself concerning Janet's insistence on taking custody of the boys. J.P. pressed his head back into the comfortable seat. *They needed their mother more than they needed me . . .*

" . . . Then after she was gone I was glad you and Robert were already comfortable with Maggie and Roy. They were your family more so than I ever could be . . ."

That's enough. J.P. closed his eyes and tried to lose himself in the roar of the jets. *I don't want to hear anymore.* But now the Captain was turning in his seat to face him.

"The last time I saw you," the Captain nodded his head indicating a clear memory. "You were leaning on the rail at the train station . . ."

So he was there.

"You were so handsome and strong and confident . . ."

Like hell I was. All I wanted was for you to step off that train and take me somewhere far away from that Missouri farm.

"I watched you for a long time before deciding you were better off without my interference . . ."

J.P. started to shake his head but the Captain continued.

" . . . you had a future where you were. You didn't need me coming in there passing judgment and making suggestions. And that's exactly what I'd have done . . ." The Captain leaned back in his seat once again. "No. You were better off there without me."

You're wrong, Captain. I needed you more that day than either one of us realized. Subconsciously, J.P. could feel the jetliner decrease in speed. *We don't have much time left.*

"Here," the Captain lifted J.P.'s hand off the armrest. Without any discussion he pressed Leona's rings into his son's hand.

J.P. closed his hand around them, honored to have them in his possession.

Several minutes later the Ralston men stood shoulder to shoulder at the top of the stairs. The sultry night air of summer in St. Louis was heavy.

"It was good flying with you, son."

J.P. shared his easy smile. "First class will never be the same."

The Captain mirrored his son's smile.

J.P. adjusted his garment bag on his shoulder as they started to descend the steps. Once on solid ground a band of Federal Express employees surrounded the Captain in honorary regard. The Captain acknowledged them as he continued to walk his son to a waiting car.

"Where do you need to go?"

"St. Louis International will have a hopper down to Joplin." J.P. started to put his bags in the backseat when a uniformed woman silently offered to take them for him. *Now this is service.*

The Captain looked apologetic. "I'm afraid we don't fly directly into Joplin but this driver will get you over to the connection."

J.P. was astounded at the service. *Especially on such short notice.* He looked up planning to offer a final thanks to his father, but the look on the Captain's face indicated there might be more. J.P. waited.

The Captain looked at the ground. "Winning is good, Phillip. But some things in life aren't worth losing. Some things you can't play to win." His father's eyes were clear and serious when he looked up. "Son, no matter how good your are at winning, there may come a time when winning isn't enough."

I don't believe he's ever called me 'son'.

"I hope you find something that will give you enough sustenance that the need to win will lose its power."

Give me enough sustenance that the need to win will lose its power . . .

"It was good of you to come, Phillip." The Captain placed the cardboard box in J.P.'s hands. Without an invitation, he wrapped his arm around his son's shoulder and gave him a good solid pat of approval.

I don't think he's ever done that to me before either. J.P. returned the gesture. But it feels right. He watched his father turn and cross the tarmac, obviously aware of where he needed to go to fly home. The Captain turned around when he reached a waiting vehicle. Standing straight and tall, he saluted his son.

He didn't have to do that. J.P. acknowledged his father's salute with a broad smile and a nod of the head. *But I'm glad he did.*

39

Around the Table

Samira clicked the remote control in her hand and displayed the final slide in the power point presentation. *The goal is to expand the online services at the library.* She had spent several weeks in preparation for today's meeting with the board of trustees. *Be careful not to let them divert the attention to other areas also in need of funding.*

Following a brief question and answer session, the board thanked Samira and began proceedings to adjourn. *I can't wait to get out of here.* She fastened the button on her suit jacket to calm the butterflies in her stomach.

"Ms Cartwright," a board member offered his hand. "Congratulations on the recent successes at Maple Street. Things are going very well. You keep it up and they're going to want you directing business downtown."

Samira accepted the compliment graciously. *It's nice to be recognized, but I prefer the branch down the street from my house.*

"Well done, Samira, as usual." The board chair, adjusted her wire-rimmed glasses. "I appreciate your time this afternoon."

"This was important," Samira pointed out. "It's time to see this proposal through."

"And that you did." The businesswoman knit her brow in thought. "We'll make our presentation to the board of supervisors in a week. I'll be sure to call you as soon as we hear anything back."

"Thank you Geraldine." Samira returned a firm handshake.

It's over, it's over, it's over! And I am so relieved! Not only was Samira finished speaking in front of a crowd, her days of research and number crunching could now turn to more exciting events. *Like preparing for the sculptor who's coming in for seminars next week.* Samira was totally lost in her own thoughts as she left the conference room.

"Hey Pretty Lady."

There's only one person who would have spoken that line. She turned but didn't see anyone. *I'm probably just hearing things.*

The next time she heard them, she stopped walking. *That has to be Phil.* She adjusted her purse on her shoulder and turned all the way around.

J.P. Ralston was standing just a few feet away. *He's clean-shaven, in a three-piece suit and carrying a briefcase.* Samira almost didn't recognize him. *He must be working.*

J.P. was holding a pair of glasses. "What brings you all the way to city hall on this fine afternoon?"

Last I knew he was still on the east coast somewhere. Suddenly she wondered how long he'd been back and why he hadn't called. *I should be furious.* In spite of her disappointment, Samira couldn't help but smile. *I'm still glad to see him.* "Business."

Phil lifted his chin slightly in understanding.

"And what brings you to city hall this afternoon?"

"Business." Phil returned the smile.

At least he didn't answer with another question. They were still standing several feet apart.

Phil's eyes came alive with energy. "But given an opportunity we could change that."

"Really?" *What makes you think I'd be willing to take that opportunity?* "And what would you change it to, Mr. Ralston?"

"Strictly pleasure."

Samira's cheeks suddenly burned with embarrassment. *I wonder if anyone heard that . . .*

Phil gently took a hold of her arm and led her across the foyer to a recessed doorway.

"You were incredible in there."

Samira was taken aback. "In where?"

"In that meeting."

I was so nervous! "You were watching me?" *He had no right to eavesdrop without my knowing!*

"Through the window in the door . . ."

Samira glanced toward the conference room. Sure enough there was a full-length pane of glass in the door. *It's a good thing I didn't know that at the podium!*

She tried to dismiss the subject. *It was nerve wracking enough without knowing Phil was watching!* "When did you get back?"

"Very late Tuesday night."

Samira watched Phil recalculate his answer.

"No, it was more like early Wednesday morning come to think about it." *And it's Thursday already.* "Did you have a good trip?"

"Let's just say it wasn't at all what I'd planned but . . ."

He's not telling me everything.

"But it was fruitful in several facets."

Phil's eyes were distant as he completed his sentence.

In personal or professional facets?

"I didn't get you called."

"I noticed." Samira tried not to sound hurt. "But that's okay." *I guess.* She thought again. *But if he's not going to call, then he shouldn't tell me he might.*

Phil ran his hand through his hair. "I've been booked solid . . ."

"You don't have to explain . . ."

"Does it help if I thought about calling every night?"

"A little." Samira smiled shyly. *How difficult is it to pick up the phone?* Out of the corner of her eye she caught him checking his watch.

"I need to be going," she offered. "I have a few things to finish up at the library before picking up the girls from the pool."

"Yeah, me too." Phil's eyes were searching hers as if he had more to say. "I meet with the city attorney here in about two minutes and Miles is rarely late."

A sudden thought occurred. *Unless he's too busy.* "Are you *booked* for dinner?"

"Tonight?"

Yes, tonight. "Six-thirty. You can eat and run if you need to." *Anything just to spend some time with him.*

Phil checked his watch again. Samira could tell he was beginning to shift into a business mode. *He's probably too busy.*

"I can give it a shot," Phil lifted his shoulders slightly. "It may depend on the results of this meeting."

"Fair enough," Samira let him off the hook. "I'll set the table at six-thirty. But leftovers warm in the microwave anytime." *It doesn't really matter when he comes, as long as he comes.*

"Fair enough," the attorney echoed her words. "I'll see what I can do."

"Are the boys with you?" *I can set plates for them too.*

Phil checked his watch again. "Not until tomorrow."

He really needs to go.

When the door across the way opened, Phil politely excused himself. "I'll shoot for 6:30."

What I wouldn't give for a pane of glass in the door of that office so I could watch him in action!

Back at the library Samira sorted through a stack of mail as she updated Mrs. Haddock and Daphne on the afternoon meeting.

"Now maybe we can get back to our regular agenda," Mrs. Haddock commented. She started to leave the office, but stopped in the doorway. "Oh, by the way, Ms Cartwright," she nodded her head toward the circulation desk. "The ladies from the historical society were here. They left a stack of resources they've decided not to use in their display. They wanted to know if there was a way to catalog and file them here with the other city historical records."

"I can take a look." Samira hadn't realized how much energy the presentation had actually used. *I'm exhausted!* The historical documents were sitting on the corner of the counter. Samira pulled a high stool next to the pile and sat down.

She read them with half interest and laid them aside as she sorted. *Hmmm. What's this?* Something near the bottom of the pile caught Samira's eye. *It looks very old.* It was a leather-bound book with yellowed pages. Very carefully Samira opened the cover. In antiquated script penmanship she read: *Diary of Mr. David C. Montgomery, Mayor of Joplin. 1933-39.*

Ever so carefully Samira turned the pages. *It appears to be a log of the mayor's daily appointments and schedules.* Some paragraphs were complete sentences. Others were fragmented thoughts and lists of things to be done. *I wonder if this was left in this pile on accident?* Samira marveled at the aged documentation.

"It's 4:00, Ms Cartright." Mrs. Haddock pointed at the clock. "I can take these to your office for tomorrow if you like."

It is time to be going. Samira ignored the clock. *But there are several references in here to a Mr. Lloyd Hughes.* She continued to turn the pages. *Without a doubt, Lloyd Hughes is the name I searched for extensively for Phil on his initial visit to the library. I should remember.* She ran her finger down the spine. *I typed it into the search engine enough times. I wonder if he's still working on that case?*

Samira gathered her purse to leave for the day. She was almost to the front door when she decided to go back for the diary. *If Phil is still working on the case, that book might be of significance. He can thumb through it and I'll bring it back tomorrow.*

I don't know what I was thinking! Samira scolded herself as she washed the seeds out of a green pepper. *How could I forget about Ellen picking up the girls tonight?* She placed the pepper on a cutting board and ran a sharp knife through it. Once sliced, she began chopping it into smaller pieces. *Phil does that to me . . . he scrambles my thoughts.*

"What's for supper?" Krissy reached for the cookie container.

"Company." *Oh, for heaven's sake!* "Stir fry."

"Who's the company?" Krissy

"I'd prefer you hold off on snacking until after supper. We're going to eat pretty quick here."

"With who?"

Samira glanced out the kitchen window and momentarily wondered if Mrs. Barnes would be watching the driveway all evening.

"Hello!" Krissy leaned into her mother's face. "I'm waiting!"

"With Phil."

"Cool. He can meet Aunt Ellen."

I hope NOT! Samira caught her thought. *That's the last thing I need.* Suddenly Samira regretted the dinner invitation altogether. *I am not ready for Tom's parents to know I have a man in my life!* "He's going to eat and run." *I hope.* "I doubt he'll still be here by the time Ellen gets in."

Krissy squeezed her shoulders together. "She said around eight thirty or nine. Oh, I can't wait to see her!" She wrinkled her nose when Samira took the skin off an onion. "Whew! That's strong!" She stepped back away from the counter. "Too bad we can't find that fashion magazine! We wanted to show Aunt Ellen those custom fingernail designs. I bet she could do something like that for us."

That magazine! Samira blinked her eyes at the onion. *Too bad I left it in such a precarious place!*

"Do you know where else it might be, Mama?"

Samira wiped an eye with the back of her hand. "I don't have it." *Anymore.*

Krissy sighed heavily. "Well we had it at Aunt Maggie's but I don't think we brought it home."

There it is again! This time from Krissy. *Aunt Maggie.*

"What about James?" Krissy was headed for her bedroom. "Is he coming?"

"No," Samira answered as she chopped the onion. "I assume James and Josh are still at Aunt Maggie's." *Oh for Pete's sake! She is NOT any relation to us. None!*

"I'm packed and ready to go." Kara flopped onto the sofa. "If my friends call, just tell them I'm with Aunt Ellen."

Samira noticed the excited grin on her daughter's face.

"I can't wait to see her!"

Ellen. She had somehow retained a magical affect on the girls. *That's probably because she still lives in a world of make-believe herself.* Samira checked the rice. *Ellen may never grow up.*

"Kara could you set the table please?"

Tom would be glad his sister still brings so much joy to the girls.

"Oh, for four." Samira corrected the number of plates in Kara's hands. "We'll need one more."

"Oh, really?" Kara reached for another plate. "And who might the other plate be for?"

Samira turned away to hide her smile. "Phil."

"Is that why you keep looking out the window?"

"I'm not looking out the window!"

Kara laughed. "Yes you are! Every time you do something you look out the window to see if he's here yet."

Samira looked out the window. "Well, he's not." But Mrs. Barnes was working in her front yard. *That's convenient.*

By the time Phil's truck was pulling in the driveway, dinner was almost on the table. Samira wanted it to be ready so he could just come, eat and go if he needed. *Besides, I really don't want him here when Ellen arrives.*

"Oh wow!" Krissy flew across the living room to the front door. "He brought his dog!" Without any hesitation she opened the door and welcomed Phil with a happy greeting.

He had changed but he was still wearing slacks and a long sleeved shirt with the cuffs rolled twice. *He looks more at ease now.* Samira enjoyed the way he interacted with Krissy. *But I miss the whiskers, just the same.* She watched Krissy take Chase down the front sidewalk and into the garage. Phil let himself into the front room.

"Hey, Pretty Lady."

Samira smiled. *I love the way he says that.* "Hey."

Phil closed the door. When she turned around with the hot food, he was standing in her kitchen. She paused for a moment, holding the hot dish between two hot pads. Phil took it from her and set it on the table.

"Okay, I think we're all set. I'll get the girls."

"No, wait," Phil intercepted her. Without asking permission he kissed her once on the lips.

He can't find time to call, but he can steal a moment to kiss me. Samira felt her frustration dissipate into desire. *But I can't stay here like this.* She wrapped her arms around his neck and allowed him to kiss her again. *We're on a deadline.*

"More business than pleasure?"

He knows I'm on edge. "Possibly." *He has no idea what I'm up against with Ellen coming tonight.* "What can I get you to drink?"

Phil leaned against the kitchen counter. "Water is fine."

Samira filled a glass with ice cubes. Just as she reached for the faucet she caught her hand on the edge of the sink. "Dang it!"

"Did you break a nail, Mama?" Kara asked the question as she entered the room. She looked at Phil. "Mama only swears when she breaks a nail."

I could live without her input.

"Let me see." Phil tried to take her hand.

"No, it's okay." *It's nothing, really.*

Phil didn't back down. Instead he raised her hand and examined the notched fingernail. "It doesn't look too bad," he commented almost with a tease. "Can I kiss it and make it better?"

I don't appreciate the sarcasm. If that's what it is. She pulled her hand away from his. "No, that won't make it better."

Phil kissed it anyway then offered to finish filling the glasses for dinner. Samira was slightly embarrassed by the petty issue. *It's just a fingernail.* She called Krissy to dinner.

Phil headed Chase back outside when Krissy came in. "He's been with Mike for a couple of days so he's more rambunctious than usual. I probably should have left him at the ranch with the boys."

"Oh, no!" Krissy interjected. "Don't make him stay out. Can't he stay in here while we eat?" She stepped around the dog and folded her hands in prayer before her mother. "Please, please, please? I can put a rug on the floor like Aunt Maggie did and he'll stay right on it. I bet you . . ."

There's that Aunt Maggie again! Samira glanced at Phil to see if he'd noticed. *If he heard it, he isn't letting on.*

"He'll be alright outside."

Samira put her hands on her hips. "He can stay if he'll stay on the rug . . ."

"Oh, thank you, thank you, thank you!" Krissy squealed. She hugged her mother around the neck then quickly turned to the dog and gave the 'Stay' command Phil had taught her at the ranch.

I can't believe I just gave into a plead for a dog! With that settled, Samira called Kara to the table and they gathered around for the evening meal. *It feels odd to have four sitting at my table for dinner.* Samira passed the chicken. *It used to be like this with Tom.*

Conversation flowed easily between Phil and the girls. He quizzed them about their experience at the ranch. Then he asked them about their week of babysitting. *If this pattern continues, he'll ask them about this coming weekend and I don't want him to know that Ellen is on her way!*

Samira was somewhat relieved when the telephone rang. It was easier to avoid the subject of in-laws than it was to try to explain.

"Mama, it's for you," Kara announced casually. She handed the phone to her mother. "It's Uncle Wes and he says he needs you . . ." Kara leaned over and whispered. "But you can't leave right now!"

Samira excused herself from the table. *Well he can't have me right now.* She put the phone to her ear feeling awkward talking to her brother with Phil within earshot.

"Hey, Sis," Wes' sounded concerned. "I'm stuck at the office but Pam is home with the kids. Are you busy?"

Busier than usual. Samira glanced at Phil. "We're eating dinner."

"Well, we don't need you right now."

Oh, Wes, please don't need me at all tonight . . .

"But I'm going to be here for awhile and Pam needs to pick up some allergy prescriptions for Mark before morning. It won't take too long . . ."

Samira sighed wondering why Pam couldn't have remembered that earlier in the day . . . *like maybe this morning while the girls were still there to watch the kids.* "I don't know Wes," she turned her back to table. "The girls are leaving later this evening and I need to be here with them until then . . ."

"The pharmacy is open until ten," Wes encouraged. "Even for just a few minutes would help tremendously."

But he's my brother. I can't turn him down. "Alright, I'll call you after Ellen leaves."

Before Samira had a chance to sit down again, Kara attacked. "He wants you to go over there to watch the kids tonight, doesn't he?"

Let's not have this discussion in front of Phil. Samira tried to head it off. "Maybe later for a short time."

"You should just tell him no, Mama . . ."

Krissy jumped right in. "Besides you can't leave us until we leave you anyway!" She smiled through her braces. "He'll just have to figure this one out on his own."

Even if it's not fair, they aren't going to talk about Wes that way. "Girls," Samira was standing next to her chair. "He doesn't call that often and he doesn't need me for that long. I don't know that you should be making decisions for me . . ."

"But you can't leave before Aunt Ellen gets here!"

"And you can't leave with company here . . ."

"And you shouldn't have to go back over there anyway . . ."

The onslaught of accusations starting coming simultaneously. Kara stood to make her point clearer than Krissy.

This is a fiasco! Samira held her hands out to stop the girls from saying anymore but they weren't backing down.

Ouch! Samira covered her ears. The shrill whistle came out of nowhere. The girls immediately stopped talking and Chase bound his way from the laundry room to his master's side.

"Sit!" Phil commanded.

And all three Cartwright women took their seats.

Phil chuckled. "I was talking to the dog but I guess it works both ways." He pushed away from the table and folded his arms. "If I'm hearing correctly . . ."

He has no right to analyze my family discussion. Samira couldn't believe what was happening. *And I can't believe I sat down at a command meant for a dog!*

Phil continued without permission. " . . . Your mother has a decision to make concerning her evening agenda. If you two aren't going to be here I'm not sure you have a say in how she chooses to spend her time . . ."

Krissy and Kara looked at each other guiltily. Kara lowered her head.

" . . . If you need to go Samira, I could stay for a short time . . ."

I don't know if I like him intruding on my decisions. "No, you're not going to stay while I go to my brother's." She caught the tone in her voice and backed off. "What I mean is, he doesn't need me right away and maybe by later he won't need me at all . . ." Samira searched for words of explanation. "And I need to be here with the girls anyway . . ." *Ellen is coming. Remember?*

Phil pulled back up to the table and picked up his fork. When he made eye contact with Krissy, she burst out laughing.

"How funny!" Krissy doubled over. "We sat down with the dog!"

It's not funny! Samira didn't appreciate Krissy's humor and she was frustrated with the way the whole evening was going. *This isn't anything like I pictured when I invited Phil to dinner.* Samira sighed. *I'm tired and Kara obviously has her feelings hurt.* Her eyes fell on the dog sitting on her dining room floor. *Who invited him in here?* She picked up her fork again. *And as if that isn't enough, I also still need to find a fingernail file.* She avoided Phil's questioning eyes. *What else could possibly go wrong?*

The phone that rang next came from Phil's hip. *If he carries a phone with him all the time, there really isn't an excuse for not calling me.*

"This one I need to take." Phil pushed away from the table. "If you'll excuse me." Phil snapped his fingers. Chase followed his master obediently out the back door.

Samira was relieved for the moment of privacy. She wanted desperately just to be herself. *But it never seems to work that way. There are always too many things working against me.* She tried to take a bite of supper. *Like Ellen's arrival later tonight.*

That thought had no more played in Samira's mind than Krissy was out of her chair bolting for the front door. "It's Aunt Ellen!"

No! No, not yet! Samira threw her hands over her head. *Nothing is working out right!*

Ellen made her usual boisterous entry, with compliments and hugs and questions for the girls. Both Krissy and Kara were instantly entertained and amused by Ellen's attention.

Samira rose from her chair and greeted Ellen properly—with a hug and a warm welcome. She couldn't help but return the natural hospitality in spite of the nervous cramp in her stomach.

"Have you eaten?" *Please say you're not hungry.*

"I had a late lunch so I'm good." Her eyes scanned Samira's front rooms. "Absolutely gorgeous what you've done with the place, Samira! Absolutely!" Ellen clapped her hands together. Her freckled face beamed with joy at seeing the girls. "Come here you two!" Another group hug followed. "I can't believe how much you've grown!" Ellen put her hands on top of Krissy and Kara's heads. "We're going to have to do something about your school wardrobe before I bring you home. I bet you've outgrown everything from last year!" Ellen's smile froze as she looked back toward Samira.

Samira followed Ellen's eyes to the kitchen. *Oh my God! Phil.*

"I don't believe we've met," Ellen offered her hand as she crossed the room headed toward Phil. Her long floral skirt brushed the hardwood floor as she walked.

Phil was standing next to the breakfast bar silently observing the situation. *How long has he been standing there?*

"J.P. Ralston." Phil introduced himself with reserve.

Samira hid her face in her hands. *This is the last thing I needed. She's two hours early for pete's sake!*

"I'm Ellen. And I'm here to kidnap these two teenagers for a couple of nights." Ellen turned back toward the table. "Don't let me interrupt your dinner!" Ellen pumped her eyebrows in Samira's direction.

You've already interrupted our dinner!

"Go ahead and finish and then we'll go." Ellen clapped her hands toward the table. "Come on, eat up! We have an agenda to plan!"

The girls obediently sat back down at the table. Samira quietly apologized to Phil for Ellen's intrusion.

Phil was watching the woman as he spoke. "That's alright." The acceptance sounded forced. "That phone call was a client. There's a new development in a case so I need to meet him downtown in a few minutes."

Samira was glad to have him leaving yet disappointed that he couldn't stay. *I don't know what I want anymore.* She watched Phil tell the girls goodbye and bid them a good time with Ellen. He politely acknowledged Ellen as he excused himself.

"How was the meeting?"

"It could have gone smoother." *How much can I tell her and still be honest?* "I have some backtracking to do in the morning to make sure the evidence stayed in tact."

"I'm sorry." Samira's reply was sincere. "That makes it hard when you've already been out of town, doesn't it?"

"It doesn't make it any easier anyway."

Samira pushed her hair out of her face with both hands. "Can I get you anything?"

She could get me about anything she wanted and I'd be satisfied. J.P. made Chase stay on the rug with a silent hand command. "You don't have to wait on me."

"Maybe I don't mind," Samira tilted her head and waited for an answer.

I am hungry. "Any chance there's any dinner left?"

"Chances of that are pretty good." Samira turned toward the refrigerator. "I noticed you didn't get to finish."

I usually try to finish what I start—especially where she is concerned. He watched Samira fill a plate with leftover dinner. *She's very much at home in her own space.*

"I didn't mean to rush off like that." *I should try to explain.* "I thought I had a longer block of time when I got here. But my investigator moved up the timeframe."

"That's alright," Samira removed a fork from a kitchen drawer and handed it to J.P. "I didn't know Ellen was going to arrive so early either . . ."

J.P. noticed dark circles under her eyes. *I don't think I've ever seen her so tired before.*

" . . . I'm sorry about her intrusion."

J.P. washed his hands in the kitchen sink. "Who exactly is Ellen, anyway?" *It's obvious the girls knew her well.*

Samira handed the warmed plate to J.P. He leaned against the counter and took a bite of the marinated chicken. *It's just as good this time as it was earlier.*

"Ellen is Tom's younger sister." Samira dropped several ice cubes into an empty glass. "She lives in Tampa so we don't see her often but when she comes home she always makes time for the girls." She turned around. "You can sit down and eat if you like."

Standing through a meal isn't as unusual as she might think. "I don't know what you put in this, but it's excellent." He took another bite and pulled out a barstool. *I could get used to meals like this.*

"I don't know what got into the girls tonight . . ." Samira put her hands over her face " . . . they were wound tight."

J.P. chuckled. *I love the way they all sat down when I whistled.*

"It's really not funny . . ." Samira's voice was low. She slid onto the barstool next to him. "I feel bad."

I wonder if she's been crying?

"Hey, you've had some challenging moments with me, right?" *Like that less than desirable confrontation in Aunt Maggie's yard.* "Let's just chalk it up for water under the bridge."

Samira moved her head in a nod but she didn't speak.

"So, how did the rest of your evening go?"

Samira put her elbows on the counter and crossed her wrists. "I went over to my brother's for a little while. My brother never has to work late." She paused. "Or at least he never used to have to work late . . ."

J.P. watched Samira think for a moment.

" . . . To be honest, I think my sister in law just needed to get out of the house and away from the kids for a little bit by herself." Samira sighed. "She was pretty stressed out. I got two of their three kids bathed and to bed before she got back."

"That's impressive." *No wonder she looks tired.*

"I haven't been home too long."

Another question had been on J.P.'s mind all day. "Tell me more about your presentation this afternoon."

Samira raised her eyebrows. "It's over!" There was a hint of relief in her voice. "I really don't like speaking in front of crowds."

"If you don't mind my saying, you seemed to handle it with a great deal of professionalism."

Now Samira frowned. "How long were you watching me?"

"Only from your first slide all the way to the end."

Samira didn't say anything. She seemed to be lost in her thoughts.

She doesn't give herself enough credit. "You were very polished, Samira."

"I spent about six weeks getting ready. We are in desperate need of more computer stations in our online center. In order to make that happen, I have to ask for money and that's always a hard thing for me to do." She was studying her fingernails. "Today's presentation was a request for funding."

"How much do you need?"

"About sixteen thousand dollars for the complete expansion."

I can think of several business owners who might be inclined to support such a cause. "So what happens next? Do they allocate the funds?"

"Oh, no." Samira's dark eyes met his. "This was just the board of trustees. They have to make a recommendation to the board of supervisors and then we wait to see what they decide. The funds aren't budgeted for this year so my guess is they'll approve the proposal for the next fiscal year."

J.P. finished the last bite of vegetables. "What other avenues of income do you have?"

"Private donations and gifts." Samira tucked her hair behind her ear. "But we don't have enough designated funds in those accounts for such a large project. And at this point, growing in stages doesn't reduce the number of customers we have waiting in line for a computer everyday."

Maybe I'll probe around and see what kind of interest I can generate. J.P. Started to get up, but Samira had his plate and was already on the way to the sink before he could stand. *She really doesn't need to wait on me.*

He watched her put his plate in the dishwasher. *She still looks really tired.* "How long are the girls staying with Ellen?" *That probably didn't sound right.*

"I don't know." Samira wiped the counter with a dishcloth. "Ellen is a free spirit. She's thinking she'll keep them at least two nights." Samira stopped and made eye contact. "Are you finished for the night?"

Either finished or just getting started. He reached out and gently pushed her hair behind a shoulder. "I'm finished working if that's what you're asking."

Samira took a step closer. J.P. wasn't going to turn her away. When he opened his arms she stepped into them willinging.

"I'm glad you came back." She rested her head against his shoulder.

"Thanks for supper." J.P. kissed her hair. "Both times."

He felt Samira's head move against him in acceptance but she didn't let go. *I can stay like this as long as she wants.* When she finally pulled away slightly he noticed her cheeks were damp.

What's up with the tears? "Hey, Pretty Lady . . ." J.P. lifted her chin with his fingertips and kissed her gently. "What's on your mind?"

Samira closed her eyes for a brief moment. "I'm just really tired."

I doubt it's that simple.

"The presentation downtown today took a lot out of me." Samira nodded as if she were trying to convince herself. "Then my brother needed me and I was already really tired but he doesn't ask very often so I felt I needed to be there for him."

J.P. wiped another tear with his thumb.

"And the girls," Samira sighed and looked away. "They were totally out of line at supper . . ."

Let her off the hook here. "They didn't bother me. Kids will be kids."

"I know." Samira lowered her head. "But then Ellen showed up early and I really hadn't planned . . ." she held her hair back with one hand. "Well . . . I hadn't exactly told Tom's family that I was seeing someone . . ."

J.P. couldn't resist. "You are?"

There was sudden hurt in Samira's eyes. "Sometimes I don't know . . ."

Bad timing, Ralston. J.P. wrapped his arm around her neck and pulled her in against him again. *Am I seeing someone?*

Samira wiped her cheek again. "And . . ."

Shit. I don't know if I can handle any more 'ands' tonight . . .

Samira's voice was very, very quiet. " . . . I can't give you what you're here for tonight."

Here we go. When he tried to see her eyes she turned away. *What does she assume I'm here for?* He tried to read her thoughts. *Nothing.*

J.P. pushed his weight off the counter. "Help me out here, Samira . . ." *Don't put her on edge.* "What do you think I came here for?" He ran his hand through her silky hair. "I came for my dog and it appears getting him back won't be a problem." He stroked her head again. "And I came for dinner. Twice. And that was excellent both times . . ." He could feel Samira's shoulders stiffen. "And I came here to see you."

Samira walked completely around the breakfast bar and stopped next to the dining room table. In the dimly lit room her face was shadowed. J.P. had to strain to see her eyes.

"Then maybe I can't give what I want to give you . . ." She crossed her arms over her middle. "And that was a really selfish thing to say."

Me or her? Who's being selfish? J.P. ran his hand through his hair. *This is why I don't get in too deep. Unspoken expectations.*

"I can't sleep with you tonight, Phil." Samira confessed from across the room.

What's she talking about?

"It would seem . . ." Samira's voiced trailed off for a moment. " . . . It would seem with the girls gone and James not back yet . . ."

No. Let's not make any assumptions here. "Listen, Pretty Lady . . ." *For whatever it's worth.* " . . . It's been a long day for both of us. What do you say we just call it a night." *Then I can go home with my dog and she can get some sleep.*

Samira looked away. "I'm sorry . . . ,"

Why is she always sorry? "No need to be . . ." J.P. crossed the room to where she was standing. "Come on, I'll tuck you in."

Samira shook her head. "You don't have to do that."

"Maybe I want to . . ."

"I know. But . . ." Samira looked up into his eyes. " . . . But, then you have to go." She sighed. "And that's a really selfish thing to say too."

"No it's not." *Why does she think that's selfish?*

"I don't want you to go, but I'm not in a position to . . ." Again Samira's voice trailed off.

It suddenly hit him. *Oh. She can't have sex tonight! That's it? She's worried about that?* "Who said I had to go?"

Tears were forming in Samira's eyes again.

I must say this will be a first for me. "My dog is here. I've had supper. And my work is done for the day . . ." *Or at least can be done.* "With the exception of a toothbrush I have everything I need until morning."

Samira took him by the hand and led him into her bedroom. J.P. looked around. *She moved his picture.* Samira disappeared into the hallway and returned with an unopened toothbrush.

She's good. He tapped the sealed box on her shoulder. "You're amazing." *In every way possible.* Samira closed the bathroom door between them.

I guess this is my invitation to stay. J.P. sat down on the edge of the bed and united his shoes. *His picture is over by the door.* He looked at his watch. *It's only ten.* He read the title of Samira's book on the bedside stand.

Samira returned and sat down on the edge of the bed. He watched her divide her long hair into three strands.

"I'm supposedly leading the literary club discussion on that book next week." Samira explained without being asked. Her fingers wove her hair in and out with expertise. "But I have a long way to go to be ready."

"I doubt it will take you too long." *Every time I've seen her she's been in a different book."*

"Reading for me and reading for group discussion are two different things."

"How do you do that?"

"Read for discussion? I have to outline and analyze the main plots and . . ."

"No, do this." He lifted her hair with his hand.

"My mother taught me when I was little. She still braids her hair every night." She smiled gently.

That's the first genuine smile I've seen out of her all night.

"I braid my hair when I know I don't want to wash it the next morning." Samira got up and walked across the room. As she turned off the lamp she leaned over and straightened J.P's shoes.

She'd get mighty tired of putting my bedroom in order every night. J.P. used Samira's bathroom and left the toothbrush on the counter to use again in the morning. *If I'm still here in the morning.* He still wasn't completely convinced he was staying the night. *Maybe I'll just stay until she goes to sleep. It's still pretty early for me.*

Samira was under the covers when J.P. returned. He unbuttoned his shirt as he crossed the room.

"Phil?"

I like the way she says my name. He looked at her over his shoulder as he sat down on the bed. Her hand ran across his shoulder blades. *And I like the way she touches me.*

"What exactly did you do while you were out East?"

I wonder where that came from? J.P. stretched out next to Samira and propped his head up with one hand.

"Well, let's see . . ." *What's she want from me here?* "I interviewed about fifteen possible witnesses. I met the judge and staff handling the case. I interviewed suspects in jail. Twice." *Is she looking for something else?* "Why?"

Samira's head was resting heavily in her pillow. "No reason, really." She yawned. "But earlier when I asked you about your trip you seemed, well . . . maybe a little distracted or something."

J.P. remembered. *I was thinking about the Captain.*

"See?" Samira lifted her head slightly. "You just did it again."

She reads me pretty quick. He ran his tongue over his bottom lip in thought. *If there's anyone I could talk to about the Captain, it's Samira.*

"I went to see my father before I came home." *I still can't believe I did that.*

"How is he?"

J.P. had to chuckle at his answer. "He's old." He pictured the Captain saluting him at the airport. "Older than I expected." *Much older.* "But he's good. He's strong and active and . . ."

By the time J.P. stopped talking about his experience with his father, the clock read eleven o'clock. Samira was still listening but she was starting to drift into sleep.

"How are you?"

J.P. thought for a moment. "I don't know yet." *Funny she would ask that.* "I don't know." He answered the second time more for himself.

Samira ran the back of her hand over J.P.'s cheek. Very slowly she cupped his head in her hands and kissed him gently on the lips.

"It's good that you went." She kissed him again. "But tonight I'm glad you don't have to go." Samira rolled over and reached for the light. "When should I wake you in the morning?"

J.P. pulled the backside of Samira's body closer to him. *I think that means I'm staying all night.* The covers separated them but he wasn't sure he was ready to stay in bed yet. *I need to sort this Mid America crap out before I can sleep.*

"I'll need to go home and shower . . ."

"And drop off your dog . . ."

"Oh yeah." J.P. remembered. *Chase.* He laid his head on the pillow next to Samira's. "Better have me up by seven."

"Okay." Samira whispered. Her breathing was getting heavier.

J.P. lay in the bed awake long after Samira had drifted off to sleep. His mind sorted through the evening meeting with Mr. Stephenson. Unable to sleep, J.P. slid off the edge of the bed and followed the light to the kitchen. *I wonder if she always leaves the counter lights on at night?* He poured a glass of orange juice. An empty wine bottle was sitting next to the sink. J.P. turned it toward the light. *That's interesting. Surely she didn't keep it on purpose.*

Another thought haunted him. *Am I really seeing her?* He rinsed his glass and set it next to the sink. *I guess maybe I am.* He'd claimed a bachelor status even before his divorce was final. *So if I'm seeing her, then am I still single?* As he crossed the kitchen the dated journal caught his eye again. *Maybe I'll take it in for Denise to review, just in case.*

He sat down on Samira's sofa and clicked the remote control. He muted the sound and flipped channels until he found Sports Center. *Single maybe.* J.P.'s mind was still churning while final scores scrolled across the bottom of the screen. *But I wouldn't exactly consider myself eligible anymore.* He continued to process. *At least not to anyone but her.* His eyes wandered from the tv to the hallway that led back to her bedroom.

"*Sometimes I don't know.*" J.P. replayed Samira's words in his mind. *Sometimes I don't know either. But what I do know is that woman has a hold on me I can't shake. Maybe I don't want to shake it. But if I'm not shaking her off, does that mean I'm falling for something I don't think I should have?*

He turned off the television. *The Cubs lost. Again.* There were files in need of review out in the truck but J.P. had no desire to go retrieve them in the dark of the night. *I'm too tired to think anymore anyway.*

J.P. went back to the bedroom where Samira was sleeping soundly. She hadn't moved since he'd climbed out of bed. *I could probably go on home and she wouldn't know the difference until morning.* He admired the serenity of her face in the dimly lit room. *But there's no way I am going to leave this Pretty Lady alone in her bed.*

J.P. draped his shirt and pants over the chair in the bedroom and slid under the sheets next to Samira. As he pressed his body into hers, Samira moved closer and linked her fingers into his as he draped his arm around her middle.

I'm beginning to think she may be all I need. J.P. thought about what his father had told him at the St. Louis airport. *But it depends on what it's going to take to win.*

41

Principle Matters

Samira ran her index finger over the sculptor's picture. "His name is Fabiano Uberti."

"He looks like a dream." Daphne fanned her hand in front of her face. "I have to make sure my husband doesn't come over while he's working here."

Samira studied the black and white press photo. "He looks like an artist." Samira turned the photo over and read the press release again. *Or maybe I'm just not looking anymore.* That thought caught Samira completely off guard. *I hope I only said that inside my mind!* Daphne's eyes were still glued to the photograph. *Back to business.*

"Here's a copy of the room layout. We'll need to have the conference center in order by noon." Samira placed the diagram on her desk. "Is Jim in?"

"Pretty soon," Mrs. Haddock interjected. "He's on break right now."

"Let me know when he gets back." *Jim is the best. It won't take him long to set up the room.* "Mr. Uberti will be here with his agent to survey the facility in a few minutes. Is there anything else you can think of before his arrival?"

"Have we ever hosted an international artist?" Daphne asked the question while she was still drooling over the photo.

Mrs. Haddock shook her head. "We've hosted lots of national artists, but never an international sculptor."

"This should be very educational." *I, for one, am ready to learn about a new art form.*

Fabiano Uberti arrived precisely at the top of the hour. Samira shook his hand. *Now I see why Daphne was so taken by his photograph.* Dark curls framed his olive features giving a greenish tint to his almost blue eyes.

The agent moved quickly and spoke without making eye contact. "We would like to tour the facility. The entire facility if you don't mind . . ."

I'd guess him to be about, what, mid-forties, maybe. Samira studied the artist's features. *But his modern suit gives him a very contemporary look.*

"We want to see everything!" Fabiano waved his arms out into the room.

Everything? Samira graciously offered a cup of coffee before beginning the tour. *I'll show him everything he needs to see.* She started with the online center and then worked her way around the entire main floor. The final stop was in the conference center. Jim had returned from lunch and was already starting to move tables and chairs in order to transform the room into a sculptor's studio.

Fabiano's eyes walked the entire parameter of the room. "De light is . . . , what shall I say? It is very soft." His Italian accent was apparent in his speech.

Samira suggested Jim open the blinds but the artist stopped her.

"No, no, soft is very good." He crossed his arms over his chest. Samira listened for several minutes as he conversed in Italian with his agent.

This is fascinating, even if I can't understand a word they're saying.

"Excuse me, Miss Samira." Helen Haddock was standing in the doorway. "I'm sorry to bother but I need you to take a phone call."

That's odd. Helen is quite capable of handling most telephone calls. Samira frowned in question.

"It's someone inquiring about an old journal but I don't know what journal she's referring to. She is under the impression you might know."

Samira thought for a moment. *The mayor's diary from 1933. But a woman?* She left Mrs. Haddock with the guests.

"This is Ms Cartwright. How may I help you?"

"Yes, sorry to interrupt your work," the woman's voice in Samira's ear was extremely professional. "My name is Denise Burke . . ."

How do I know this name?

"I'm employed by J.P. Ralston, attorney at law. J.P. handed me a journal from a former Joplin city mayor dating back to 1933. Do you know the book?"

Yes, I know the book. And I know J.P. Ralston. But I don't know Denise Burke. Yet.

" . . . This document contains information pertinent to a case we are currently trying to close, but J.P. is under the impression you need it back right away."

"That's correct." *I can't believe the book I gave J.P. might actually be useful!*

"In order for this document to be used in court we need physical accessibility. Is there a way we can check it out from the library under an extended agreement?"

Not until it's cataloged. "That diary is actually the property of the local historical society," Samira started to explain. "We haven't even cataloged it into the system for public viewing yet." *And even if it was already in the system it would be held as reference material only.*

"I see." There was a slight pause. "So there is no way we could keep it here for a few days?"

It was left in my care, which puts my reputation and working relations with the historical society on the line. "I'm sorry, Ms Burke." Samira knew the rules. "Until we have it cataloged and in the system it really needs to be here in the Maple Street facility."

"Is it possible the book might be somehow *misplaced* until about this time next week?"

Misplaced? I don't misplace items left in my care.

" . . . We only need it long enough to prove a point. Then we can return it in time to be *found.* And in the meantime we can guarantee its safety and protection."

"I'm sorry . . ." Samira was watching the sculptor across the room. It appeared he was preparing to leave the building. "I will need the book back right away." *Then I can get the proper permission and cataloging complete for their use.* "I can call you as soon as it becomes accessible to the public."

The tone in Denise's voice made it obvious she was not pleased with Samira's decision.

But I really need to get back to my guests. Samira hung up the phone. *At least she agreed to be in touch.* As she crossed the library, another thought crossed her mind. *I should have asked her how soon I could expect it back!*

A short hour later Mrs. Haddock stuck her head in the conference room door again. This time Samira was leaning over a table reviewing the room layout with Jim.

"Oh, Miss Samira, there is trouble. You need to come quickly!" She waved her hand quickly for Samira to follow.

What in the world? A uniformed police officer was standing at the circulation desk. "Go ahead with our plans, Jim." *Is it a friend of Tom's?* "I'll be right back."

"Good afternoon. Ms Cartwright, I presume?"

Samira acknowledged her identity and offered her hand in greeting.

"If I might have a minute of your time . . ."

Of course. Samira motioned him into her office and closed the door. *I don't recognize him.* Through the glass wall she could see the frightened look on Helen's face.

"How may I help you?" Samira sat down in the chair behind her desk but the policeman remained standing. He handed her a piece of paper.

"I have a subpoena from attorney J.P. Ralston for an historical book entitled, Diary of Mr. David C. Montgomery, Mayor of Joplin. 1933 . . ."

What? Samira was stunned. *What right does he have to stand here and order over historical records that aren't even eligible to the public yet? But that's not the half of it!* Samira was instantly angry. *I can't believe Phil would make such a demand without at least talking to me first!*

"Do you have this book in your possession Ms Cartwright?"

But that's not the half of it! "No, I don't." *Why would Phil make such a demand on me? He hasn't even talked to me about it yet!* "I believe Mr. J.P. Ralston has possession of that book."

"His office believes there is a copy here in your building."

Then his office is playing games because I just talked to Denise Burke. Samira pushed away from her desk. *I don't appreciate the way he's chosen to handle this.* She opened her office door and addressed her assistants.

"Ladies, the officer is here for a historical journal from a former city mayor. It belongs with the historical . . ."

"Oh . . ." Daphne interrupted. "Is it really old?"

Samira tipped her head slightly. *How would Daphne know about the journal? I hadn't shown it to anyone yet.*

"I'm sorry," Daphne began to explain. "I didn't know what to do with it." She reached under the counter and handed the journal over to Samira. "It was in the drive through book return but you were busy with Jim so I couldn't ask right then . . ."

So this is Ms Burke's idea of being in touch? Samira took a deep breath. *I asked Helen and Daphne knowing that book was at Phil's office.* She turned around and faced the officer. *Now I have no choice but to turn it over.*

"This book," Samira started to explain. "Is between ownerships. It was recently donated to the library for historical purposes only and I am not comfortable allowing you to take it off the premises without permission from the historical society."

"This book is needed by a court of law, Ms Cartwright."

"I understand," Samira clutched the diary with her hands. "But at the same time it needs to be officially documented and cataloged before it leaves here."

"How long will that take?" The officer crossed his arms.

Samira sighed. She could feel the agony of defeat already starting to settle into her stomach. "Well today and tomorrow we're getting ready for the resident artist to move his studio into the conference center . . ."

"If you prefer, you can wait in jail while your staff prepares for the artist in residence."

Samira opened her eyes wide. *Is he threatening me?* She stared at the officer. *I was married to a police officer long enough to know my rights!*

"Excuse me . . ." Samira read his name badge for the first time, " . . . Officer Centralis. I do believe I have rights above and beyond what you have just indicated and I would be willing to discuss them with your superior officer."

"You have twenty four hours to turn the evidence over to the courts. After that your presence will suffice in its place." Officer Centralis turned for the door. "Thank you for your time this afternoon, Ms Cartwright."

Samira was furious. Absolutely livid.

Mrs. Haddock came into the office, her eyes wide with worry. "What do we do now, Ms Samira? No one has ever come in here wanting a book that bad!"

"I'll tell you what we do now," Samira returned to her desk and pulled the bookmark out of her Clancy novel. "We call the attorney who ordered that subpeona." She flipped the bookmark over on her desk. Phil's phone numbers were written on the backside in pencil. Without a moment of hesitation she picked up the phone and dialed the number next to the lower case "c". *Let's see if he's answering his cell phone this afternoon.*

"J.P. Ralston."

I know this voice. Pure business. "J.P. Ralston, Samira Cartwright."

"Samira?"

"Yes, Samira." She could hear voices in the background.

His tone changed slightly. "Hey, Pretty Lady, what can I do for you?"

"What can you do for me?" *I'll tell you what you can do for me!* "You can tell your friends at the precinct that my books are not eligible for court orders! And furthermore, you can tell them that I am not substituting in its place!"

"Whoa . . . What are you talking about?"

I am NOT playing anymore legal games. "The officer that just left here expects me to hand over the historical diary by this time tomorrow. I told you I don't have formal custody of this book yet. There's no way I'm releasing it to the court! You could have handled this much differently!"

"What diary?"

"Come on, Phil!" Samira pounded her hand against the top of her desk. "You know what book I'm talking about. Your office ordered the subpeona!"

"You received a subpeona from my office?"

"From your office. I have it right here on my desk. Would you like me to read it to you? Your signature is on the line!"

"Look, I'm in the dark here."

He can sound as confused as he wants. I'm not buying into it.

"I haven't been in the office since first thing this morning and I'm about to step into jury selection right now . . ."

"J.P. Ralston, attorney at law. It's right on the line, Phil. But the book isn't leaving this premise! I loaned it to you in confidence and told you I needed it back right away. We haven't even cataloged it yet for heaven's sake!" *I have never been so furious!*

"Samira," Phil's voice was shifting again. "The bailiff is calling me, I need to go. But let me do some checking and I'll get back to you. Alright? Don't panic. Maybe there's just a misunderstanding or something."

Misunderstanding? Samira's thoughts were coming a million miles a minute. *And he has to go?*

"I'll call you back, alright?"

Is that anything like your assistant being in touch? "The sooner the better Mr. Ralston." *And who ever this Denise Burke is she'd best be ready to face the music as well.*

The rest of the afternoon passed in a blur. The sculptor's agent returned to oversee the preparations in the conference center and a woman from the historical society dropped by to discuss the items she had delivered a few days earlier. On top of all that Samira's mother called and invited her to dinner to celebrate Pam's birthday.

Great. Maybe I don't feel like celebrating a birthday right now. Just the same, Samira knew she would make an appearance for dinner.

Samira hung up the telephone from talking to her mother and looked through the glass wall to see J.P. Ralston enter the building through the front doors. *Nice he can make a personal appearance.* She watched him cross the room. *All business. Definitely J.P. Ralston. None of Phil in that walk.*

Samira folded her arms across her middle and allowed Mrs. Haddock the formalities of showing him to her office.

"Mr. Ralston."

"Samira." Phil pulled a chair up to the front of Samira's desk. "We need to get this issue over the journal cleared up."

"You first." *Let's hear this explanation.*

"First," Phil held up one finger. "I was not involved in the decision that sent a subpoena to your office today." Phil was looking her right in the eye. "Had I known how valuable the journal was going to be to the Hughes' case I would have discussed it with you in advance of legal action."

Well said. I hoped that would be the case.

"Second," Phil held up two fingers. "I can close this case with the book you put in my hands . . ."

" . . . Which you subsequently placed in someone else's hands . . ."

"Right." Phil didn't deny that fact. "Here's the deal. We summoned a jury today to hear this case beginning Monday morning at nine. I can avoid the court appearance and settle out with the city this weekend *if* I can show them the evidence in those dated documents."

Samira wasn't satisfied. *He has no idea what I've been through this afternoon! Not only did I have to face an officer of the law, but I also had to defend my own rights.* "Do you know what happened here this afternoon?"

"I'm presuming a local authority delivered the subpoena requesting the book." Phil sat back in his chair.

"Before that." *Let's tell him the whole story.*

"No, I don't know what happened before that."

Samira picked up the book from the top of the lateral filing cabinet behind her desk. She placed it on the desk directly in front of her. "I was tricked."

"How so?"

"I received a call from a Denise Burke . . ."

"That's my paralegal and personal assistant . . ."

"I assumed as much." *I've heard you on the phone with her.* "Denise Burke asked if your office could keep the book for awhile longer."

"That's because I told her it had to be back to you today."

"Very well." *Just hear me out.* "I told her we needed to catalog the book before it could be made available to the public."

"Which means we don't have access to it in the physical form for a few days, correct?"

"Correct."

"Denise actually insinuated that I might 'misplace' the book for a week, until your office could return it to me."

Phil didn't respond one way or the other.

"I'm sorry, but my reputation is on the line and I am not known for 'misplacing' anything—especially something of that magnitude! I told her that was not a possibility."

The attorney opened his hands in silent affirmation of her decision. "So what's the problem?"

What's the problem? "That was shortly after one o'clock. At three-ten a uniformed officer arrived here demanding that journal. I told him it was already in your custody." She held the book up for Phil to see. "And guess what? One of my librarians finds *this* book in the return cart!"

Phil narrowed his eyes. "So Denise returned the book like you requested?"

"No!" Samira could feel her blood pressure rising. *Don't you dare side with Ms Burke!* "She returned the book to trap me. I can't very well turn it over if it's not in my possession right?"

"Right."

"So now that it's here, I have to physically hand it over!"

"Right again."

"You don't get it do you?"

"Get what?" Phil had slid to the edge of his chair. "We need the book to close the deal. If you have it and we need it, we either ask to borrow it for a period of time, or we have to obtain legal permission to gain custody." His eyes were a steel blue as he explained.

I have only seen those eyes once. In Aunt Maggie's driveway when he was headed for James in the tent.

"It's a matter of having the right piece of evidence at the right time, Samira!"

"Is it?" Samira held his glare. "Does it make any difference that this book doesn't even belong to the library yet or that my reputation is on the line if something happens to it while it's 'missing?'"

"Okay . . ."

Samira crossed her arms. *All it will take to clear this up is an apology for the way I was taken advantage of by both Denise Burke and the police officer.*

" . . . Here's the deal. I've spent a solid eight months searching for the very evidence that is handwritten in that journal. If you're not going to allow it to be used for the purpose of aiding this case, then yes, I take legal action to obtain the evidence needed to get the job done. It's that simple."

This is anything but simple. Samira couldn't believe her ears. *There's no way this is the same man that woke up in my bed this morning.* She was angrier now than she was when the officer threatened her. *What happened to his tenderness and his compassion?* As confusing as this encounter was, protecting that diary suddenly seemed to take precedence over everything else.

"It's not that simple, Mr. Ralston." Samira crossed her arms again. "I was told that if I don't hand over the book for your case, that I would be taken into custody."

"According to the law, the person blocking the evidence from being obtained has an obligation to respond one way or another."

Let's get this straight! "So you would allow me to go to jail in order to get your hands on this journal?" Samira held the book up between them.

"It doesn't have to be that way, Samira. You're missing the point . . ."

"Missing the point?"

"Hear me out . . ." Phil stood up and walked around to the end of her desk. He knelt so he was just under her eye level. "Denise could have handled this differently, but she didn't. I left the book for her to review this morning. She ran across the exact dates and transactions that have been under scrutiny since the beginning of February concerning Lloyd Hughes' estate."

His eyes are so intense I can't even look away.

"If the case goes to court, it's highly probable the jury will side with the city. If I can keep it out of court and prove the case using that document tomorrow morning, or even first thing Monday morning, then the city gets fair settlement and we can finally close the estate."

I don't want an explanation. Samira frowned. *I want an apology.*

"You didn't answer my question. The officer stated I would go to jail if I didn't hand over the journal. Would you allow that to happen?"

"Would you withhold the evidence?"

"Don't answer a question with a question!"

"Then don't ask me to make a judgment call against my own case!"

The attorney stood up and ran his hand through his hair. "What's the worst thing that could happen if you allowed me to barrow that book?"

"The worst thing?" *Besides the fact that you've tested my integrity?* "The book belongs in this facility. It was placed under my care and I will protect it until it's cataloged properly or until I have permission to do otherwise."

"So who do I need to call?" Phil's frustration was beginning to show. "Give me a name and a number and I'll make the call."

"It's not that easy."

"To ask permission to borrow a book from the library?"

"No, to remove a historical reference item from the library."

"Excuse me," Phil put his hands on his hips and walked around in front of Samira's desk again. "If the Maple Street Library doesn't even own the book yet, how can you withhold the name of the person who can actually grant permission for the book to leave here?"

Samira leaned back in her chair. *If I give him the name, he'll make the call and get permission to use the book, there's no doubt in my mind about that.* She studied his face. *The part I don't understand is if he would actually allow me to be arrested if I refused to turn it over to the authorities!*

"So where do I stand in all of this, Phil?"

The attorney ran his tongue over his bottom lip. "You're the only thing preventing me from closing this case."

He could have thanked me for finding the evidence in the first place! Samira waited but he didn't say anymore. *He could admit that ordering a subpoena was an over-reaction to something a simple personal request might have solved.* Samira considered his last option. *Or he could have apologized and asked how we might remedy the situation.* He was watching her very closely. *But he didn't choose to do any of those things.*

"So that's it?" Samira stood. "I'm just a roadblock for the final goal?"

Phil shook his head. "Look, Samira . . . you don't see . . ." his tone had softened, but his eyes were still intense.

"No, I see very clearly." *Business always before pleasure.*

She leaned over her desk for a yellow sticky note. In an instant she wrote down the name of the lady from the historical society. *If he has the resources to order a subpoena, then he also has the resources to find the phone number.* "This should take care of your dilemma."

There was a long hesitation before Phil reached out and removed the note from the end of Samira's finger. His eyes were suddenly very dark and he held them low.

"I'll make the call."

"I'll wait to hear back then."

Inside Samira's chest her heart was screaming to let him off the hook. *All he had to do was say he was sorry.* Her head was holding firm. *I've given him every part of me, yet he can't even admit that he might be wrong. Now it's a matter of principle.* Samira put the book back behind her desk again. *He'll either realize he shouldn't have put me in the middle of his case, or he'll win the ruling.*

Phil opened her office door. Very slowly he turned around.

I don't want him to know how much this hurts me. Samira looked away. *Just go.* She started to shuffle a stack of papers. When she looked up again, Phil was leaving the building.

42

Making Amends

"Let me get this straight." J.P. put his fingers to his temple and closed his eyes as he attempted to understand Sparky's report. "If the money never left Joplin, then exactly how did the suspects turn up in Baltimore?" J.P. opened his eyes.

Sparky was standing across the room with his hands tucked deep into his pants pockets.

"Ah, listen carefully, J.P." He raised his dark eyebrows. "De suspects in Balteemore are still de ones who moved de monies." His face showed no expression. "But, I am led to beleev dat de money vas used right here in Joplin somehow."

"So that means the suspects are working for someone here locally?"

"Zat is my assumption." Sparky walked back to the small conference table and removed several sheets of paper from his briefcase. "I've traced every communication to and from de Mid-America computer mainframe." He pointed a finger to an email address on the top of the first sheet. "Dis address is fictional. It does not exeest. But dis one," Sparky indicated another address on the sheet. "Dis one answers in Caleefornia."

"How do you figure all this out?" Denise asked the question as she looked up from taking notes.

"Ah!" Sparky broke into a bright smile from under his moustache. "Dat is only for Sparky to know."

Denise returned the smile about the same time a bell rang announcing someone entering the front door.

Derek Danielson removed his glasses and rubbed his eyes with his thumb and forefinger. "So really this investigation is just beginning."

After the interviews in Baltimore I was sure I could indict the suspects without reasonable doubt. J.P. sighed. *If Derek is right, we've just barely scratched the surface of this case.*

Sparky seemed to understand their concern. "Nothing is ever as simple as it seems, J.P." The investigator rubbed his shiny head. "But, ve vill get the job done."

What do I tell Mr. Stephenson in the meantime?

"Hey, Boss?" Denise inquired from the other room. "I think you should come out here."

J.P. stepped into Denises' office. She handed him the Mayor's diary from 1933.

Damn it. "I thought I told you to cancel that subpeona." *This book is causing more trouble than it's worth.* J.P. was instantly angry.

"I did," Denise confirmed. "I called and cancelled late Friday afternoon." Denise sorted through a small stack of papers on her desk. "Here's the fax confirmation."

J.P. took the paper out of her hand. "Then where the hell did this come from?"

"A lady just dropped it off."

A Lady? J.P. immediately started for the door. "What lady?"

"A little gray-headed lady came in here and laid it on my desk."

"Just now?"

"Yeah, just now." Denise put her hands on her hips. "What's up with you anyway, Boss? First you tell me to skim the info to see if anything is pertinent. When I realize we can close the case using this evidence and go after the book you all but fire me for doing my job. And now you don't believe me when I say a lady just dropped the book off again?"

J.P. stopped in the open door. *The old woman from the library.* He ran his hand through his hair. *Having this book in my possession changes the dynamics of the nine o'clock court appearance considerably.*

"Call the judge and ask for a continuance," J.P. ordered. His mind shifted into high gear. "Tell him I'm sure we can settle without a jury."

Denise sat down in her chair and picked up the telephone.

"Derek . . ." *Let's get one thing off my plate.* "I need you to work with Sparky for the rest of the day. Maybe even the rest of the week. Give him whatever he needs to keep this investigation moving forward. Maybe we can have some answers by Friday."

Sparky stroked his moustache. "Maybe by de end of de day."

Wishful thinking.

Derek gathered his file folders and started for the door. "What do I tell Mike and Vince at the eleven o'clock meeting?"

J.P. sat down at his own desk. "I'll try to reach Mike right now." He reached for his telephone. "Chances are good you won't have an eleven o'clock with Benson and Barringer." He dismissed his intern without any further instructions. The clock read a few minutes past eight. *I've never known a private investigator who called meetings so early in the morning.*

"Mike Benson." J.P. opened a file folder on his desk.

"I'm sorry, he's not in yet. May I take a message?"

J.P. remembered the hour. "No message," he replied quickly. With the same intensity he redialed the phone. This time Mike picked up.

"Rise and shine, Counselor . . ."

"I'm up, already," Mike answered with forced enthusiasm. "And I'm finally done with your truck. I can bring it by on my way to the office."

I'm sick of driving that little sports car. "Took you long enough."

"She had a lot to move."

"I hope she's worth it." *And I hope she treats him better than the last one.* "Sparky just finished debriefing his investigation out west. He thinks the Mid-America scandal is still active here in Joplin. And, more importantly, he thinks the monies are being laundered right here under our noses . . ."

"Do tell . . ."

" . . . I've given Sparky full use of Derek for the rest of the week to see what they can uncover. That puts everything out east on hold and makes for some interesting conversations with Stephenson later today. Any chance you can sit in on that meeting."

"I'm free after ten. I'll drop your truck off in a few minutes."

"Keep it for now. I'll meet you at the gym at noon and bring you up to date on Sparky's report before meeting Stephenson at two."

"Noon is good."

J.P. buttoned the cuffs on his shirt. In full stride, he grabbed his suit coat off the back of a chair. "I'll be at the courthouse."

"I put the copies for the city attorney in your briefcase in the file marked *diary.*"

Thank you.

"Do we need to recognize the fact this book came back?"

I don't know. J.P. tapped the edge of the worn diary against Denise's desk. *She didn't answer her phone Friday night.* The weekend replayed in his mind. *I spent all day Saturday on the golf course with Hughes and the city planning commissioner trying to negotiate the misunderstanding that took place while I was out of town.* J.P. closed his briefcase. *And spent most of Sunday at Mid-America with Sparky.* He sighed. *And today is Monday.* The weekend was over. *And I haven't talked to her since the less than pleasant encounter in her office.*

"Shit."

"Gut feeling says something in the form of an apology might be in order. What do you want me to do, Boss? Send flowers or write a letter?"

Deep down inside J.P. knew what Samira wanted more than anything was to hear from him. *Tucking my tail isn't exactly my style.* He checked his watch. *And I'd better get moving or I'll be late to the courthouse.*

What the hell. "Both. And make the flowers roses."

"Roses?" Denise sounded very surprised. "I'm thinking I might deliver them in person just to see who's on the other end . . ."

J.P. caught the end of that statement as he stepped out onto the concrete balcony outside his office door. He turned around and retraced his tracks. "Just have them delivered." *The last thing I need is Denise snooping around Samira's territory.*

"Your keys, Counselor." Mike tossed them into J.P.'s gym locker.

J.P. dropped them in his gym bag.

"Christ, I had to park at the back of the parking lot!" Mike opened his locker and began to unbutton his collarless dress shirt. "That beast is so big I couldn't fit into the spaces up here."

J.P. put his toe on the edge of the bench to tie his shoe. "It was big enough to haul someone's shit though, wasn't it?"

Mike pulled a Nike tank top on over his head. "That it was." He held out his hand. "By the way, I believe you have my keys."

J.P. returned to his locker and removed the Corvette keys from his pants pockets. "Where'd she move to?"

"From the condos out by the airport to an apartment closer to the school where she teaches."

"Too much noise or what?"

Mike shook his head. "Nope. Not that simple." He sat down on the bench and tied his shoes. "She didn't like the new manager at the condos. Seems the complex was sold a month or so ago and she didn't appreciate the new corporate rules concerning where she could and could not park her Golf."

J.P. eyed his colleague warily. "How do you park a golf?"

Mike wiggled his eyebrows and danced his toes on the concrete floor of the locker room. "Much like you park my Corvettte—very carefully and close in so you don't have to walk a mile to your destination."

What kind of a woman drives a Golf anyway? "I'll see you out there."

J.P. was deep in his own thoughts when Mike entered the racket ball court.

"I hate to break the news but my new racket ball partner is going to bump you in thirty minutes." Mike slammed the little blue ball into the far wall with his racket.

"You've replaced me with a woman?" J.P. raised the racket in his left hand and returned the serve without any trouble.

"Yep." Mike took his turn again. "Not unlike the way you stood me up in exchange for a *lady's* company at the driving range."

J.P. ducked as the ball bounced back toward his head.

Mike missed the return. "How is your *lady* anyway?" He served a second ball into the wall.

"Pissed." J.P. returned the serve with more power than necessary. "Denise served a subpoena on a book from her library on behalf of the Hughes estate before I could intervene." He dodged left so Mike could make the play. When the ball came back he hit it again, but it skimmed the sidewall and stopped the play action.

Mike wiped the sweat from his face with his arm. "You sent a subpoena to Samira without warning?"

Oh yeah. I forgot Mike knows Samira. He picked the little blue ball up off the floor and hammered it into the wall with his racket. "Yep."

"Shit."

"Shit." J.P. echoed.

Several volleys were exchanged without comment. The first game was played and scored. Without a break in play J.P. served the second game. When there was finally a short break in volley, J.P. used the bottom of his holey shirt to wipe his face.

"But you've kissed and made up, right?"

J.P. served again. "Not exactly."

Instead of returning the serve Mike caught the ball with his free hand. "Excuse me?"

"Not yet." J.P. motioned for Mike to give him the ball. "That's game point."

"That's bullshit." Mike closed his hand over the ball. "You let a case rest between you and Samira?"

Basically.

Mike bounced the ball against the wooden floor and caught it again. "You're head is harder than this floor, good buddy." Mike was sounding serious. "You want my advice?"

This time when the ball bounced J.P. hit it out from under Mike's hand with his racket. "No."

"Screw you then." Mike let the ball rebound off the ceiling.

Since when does Mike Benson back away from sounding his own advice? J.P. missed the return. The ball bounced wildly against the glass behind him. *I do feel a little guilty about it, if that helps anything.*

Mike adjusted the sweatband around his head. "You have less than five minutes to brief me for Stephenson based on Sparky's investigation."

Fine. If he doesn't want the rest of the story with Samira, then he doesn't get it. The ball hit J.P. in the chest before he had a chance to return it.

"That's game. Again." Mike put his hands on his knees to catch his breath. "You lose."

Again. J.P. looked up to see a cheerful, red-head smiling down upon them from above.

"Three minutes. What's the scoop on Stephenson?"

Suddenly Mid-America has very little bearing on my life. J.P. stated the three main points of Sparky's discoveries in brief sentences.

"So it's basically in Stephenson's best interest to sit it out and wait to see where the monies turn up?" Mike straightened his back. Sweat was running off his face and dripping onto the floor.

"Basically."

"I can lean him in that direction." Mike waved at the redhead above them to come on down. "Anything else?"

J.P. started for the door. "Two o'clock."

"I'll be there."

"Shower first." J.P. stepped into the cooler air of the corridor. The red-headed woman was making her way down the steel staircase.

"And Counselor," Mike called from behind the glass.

What?

"Call the lady."

J.P. sat with his truck backed into the parking space two spots down from Samira's car. *I might not be able to read her thoughts, but she is predictable to some degree.* J.P. opened the Mid-America file across the console and began to document his mental notes from the meeting with Mr. Stephenson and the board president. *I know she gets off work at four.*

As anticipated, Samira appeared on the front steps of the library a little past four o'clock. *Who's the guy?* There was a man with her and he was talking to Samira using big hand motions. Samira was laughing. *She certainly seems to be enjoying the conversation.*

I can wait. J.P. finished notating his meeting and closed the file folder but Samira had only advanced two steps toward the sidewalk. *And he's still talking to her.*

Who the hell is he? The longer he watched, the more irritated it made him. *I could just leave and she'd never know I was here.* The man on the steps made a slight advance toward Samira. *Or I could get out of the truck and introduce myself.*

Just as he reached to turn the key in the ignition, the man turned and went back inside the library. J.P. watched as Samira descended the remaining stairs. Now it was decision time. *Do I get out of the truck or let her leave?*

Just talk to her. J.P. opened the door of the truck and stepped out onto the concrete of the parking lot. Samira looked up into his face with a bright smile.

I have missed that smile.

The smile quickly dissipated.

But this may be the last time I see it.

Samira glanced over her shoulder toward the front door of the library. "Phil." She tucked a loose hair back into her bun at the back of her head. "I didn't expect to see you here." She held her hand over her eyes to block the sun. "Have you been here long?"

J.P. decided to lie. *It will ease the tension to some degree.* "Not long."

"I got the note and the roses," Samira's dark eyes were looking directly into his. "I'm assuming they came from the office."

He'd hoped Denise sent them from him. *Obviously not the case.* "Thanks for the book."

"Maybe you can close the case now."

She's still distant and cautious. J.P. nodded. "Maybe." *Not that I blame her.* "I guess that would be the goal."

Samira nodded.

"So how was your day?" *Maybe she'll tell me who the man is.*

"Great!" Samira removed her hand from her forehead. "Today was a really good day."

Not a hint of insight. "Good start to the week then?"

"Lots better than last week!" Samira turned away from the direct sunlight but she kept her eyes on him. "Is there something I can do for you, Phil?"

I have a million things I want to tell her and don't even know where to start. He started to run his hand through his hair but Samira reached out and stopped the motion with her hand.

"You don't have to answer." Her face was suddenly very concerned.

"No, I do have to answer." *Say it, Ralston.* "I am here to offer ..." *an apology.* " ... Well, let's just say I was out of line." He looked beyond Samira into the row of bushes in front of her parked car. "And to answer your question, no, I wouldn't have let you go to jail in place of gaining custody of the book."

There. J.P. took a deep breath. *I answered that question.*

Samira's hand fell from his arm. "That takes a load off my mind."

Gotta love the sarcasm. "I don't know if we can go back and start this one over."

Samira's eyes were low. "I don't know either, Phil. This one is complicated."

The pit in J.P.'s stomach tightened. "I'd like to take you to dinner." *Or go anywhere to be alone with her for awhile.*

Samira shook her head. "I can't, Phil. Not tonight." She adjusted the strap on her purse. "I promised Mrs. Barnes I'd take her to the grocery store after work, which is now . . ." Phil watched as she fidgeted with her fingernail. "And tonight I'm coming back out here to work with our guest artist."

Guest artist? J.P. glanced over his shoulder. *Is that who she was talking to?* "It doesn't have to be tonight . . ." *I'd make anytime free to be with her.* J.P. watched her look away. *But the damage may already be done.*

Samira crossed her arms over her middle.

She looks nervous. "I just want a chance to . . ." J.P. stuffed his hands in his pockets. " . . . to make amends, Samira. I was wrong."

"I know." Samira agreed quickly. "And maybe I was wrong too." Her eyes were scanning the parking lot. "Maybe I was wrong for assuming too much."

How is it I can read these thoughts? "No . . ." *I don't like the way this is headed.*

"I'm sorry, Phil. But I do have to pick up Mrs. Barnes or she'll be calling out here looking for me." Samira checked her watch. "And I don't want to be late getting back out here either."

If anyone knows a time crunch, it's me. But gut feeling says she's just putting me off. J.P. weighed his options knowing his time was waning. *You can either lay it on the line with her right here, Ralston, or get in your truck and drive away.*

Always before J.P. Ralston had walked away. *But I've never lost anything I ever missed.* He inhaled deeply. *And I'm already missing her.*

J.P. opened his mouth. "I never meant to hurt you, Samira." *Why can't I just say it?* J.P. lowered his head. "I'm sorry too." *There. I said it.*

"I know, Phil." Samira's voice was just above a whisper. "But this one is going to take a little getting over." She paused briefly. "And I don't know . . ."

Here it comes.

" . . . if I can give you what you need."

J.P. closed his eyes. *There she goes blaming herself again . . .* "You already give me what I need, Samira . . ."

"Then I don't know if you have it in you to accept."

The reality of that statement hit like a ton of bricks. *Mike told me she was out of my league.* J.P. stood stock still as Samira kissed her fingertips and then pressed her fingers into his cheek. The emotions he felt were too strong for words and too powerful for a reaction of any kind. *She reads me like a book.* He held Samira's hand to his cheek until she gently pulled it away.

"I need to be going . . ." Samira turned toward her car. "Mrs. Barnes is waiting."

J.P. stood numb as Samira drove away. *Fact is, I'm out of her league.*

43

Baring her Soul

A caption on the business section caught Samira's eye as she cleared miscellaneous papers from her mother's table: ***Hughes Family Estate Closes with Fair Settlement.*** *So the diary I found for the defense paid off after all.* Samira leaned over the paper to read the details:

> The estate of the late multi-millionaire, Lloyd Hughes, of Springfield, Missouri, reached settlement with the city of Joplin. After many months of discrepancy, legal representation by the law office of J.P. Ralston was able to prove the estate did not owe back commercial tax as originally charged. The city of Joplin agreed to settlement of $125K in residential tax owed since 1944 . . . .

"Well, well," Samira's father entered the kitchen unannounced. "How's my girl?"

Samira greeted him with a hug. "Hi Daddy." Two little blonde girls caught up with happy squeals. "Where did you find these two?"

"I didn't find them . . ." Raymond rubbed their heads. "They found me!" With that he sent them towards the sun porch. "I bet Granny's in the garden."

"She is." Samira confirmed. "We needed a tomato for supper."

"Then you're staying?" Raymond filled a coffee cup.

Samira nodded. *Seems like I've been here a lot lately.* "Are we keeping Bonnie and Lizzie?"

"I'll take them home after dinner." Raymond was eyeing his daughter with care.

He knows I'm not exactly myself. To avoid being quizzed she went back to clearing the table.

"Your mother will want to eat in the dining room since the little girls are staying too." It wasn't long before Kara was in the kitchen helping Papa Ray set the table.

I just want a moment to finish that article. As soon as everyone was busy, Samira skimmed the details and focused on the summarizing paragraph.

> . . . The settlement was accepted by the now reigning brothers of the highly successful Hughes Corporation, with headquarters in Springfield. "This one has been a long time in coming to a close," said legal representation, Mike Benson. "Everyone involved feels the settlement is fair and in the best interest of the city as well as the Hughes family. It's a win-win." Miles Kelton, Joplin city attorney, expressed similar sentiments, "We are pleased with the outcome."

Mike Benson?

"What's caught your attention there, Sugar?" Raymond was leaning over his daughter's shoulder.

"Oh, Daddy." Samira jumped at the interruption. "I was just skimming the news."

Raymond looked doubtful. "I don't know that I've ever seen you take much interest in the business news." He shuffled some papers. "Now the Arts and Entertainment section sounds more like you. Have you seen it yet?"

So why didn't Phil close the Hughes Estate?

Raymond opened another paper over the top of the business news. "Here." He pointed a finger at the boxed announcement in the corner. "Now this is newsworthy." Samira followed along as her father read aloud:

> *"The sculpture gallery of Fabiano Uberti, Artist in Residence, is now open to the public at the Maple Street Library until the end of August. Uberti's work is known the world over for it's keen sense of reflective expression and life-like features. This is a must-see display. For a private showing or seminar with Uberti, please contact the library during business hours."*

Raymond stopped reading and looked up at his daughter.

"And it's not a bad photo of him either. Most newspaper photos don't come out so clear."

"This one happens to be a press copy so it's made especially for newspapers and such." Samira explained. *The original is still on my desk.*

"How's he working out? Are you getting a lot of traffic?"

Samira smiled. "Yes, Daddy. Lots of tours and on-lookers." She tucked her hair behind an ear. "And here's a little piece of information," she taunted her father on purpose. "Guess who he asked to be his model for his in-house piece?"

Raymond crossed his arms and puckered his lips in thought. "I only know one woman beautiful enough for that honor . . ."

"No," Krissy interrupted. "He picked Mama!" She threw her arms into the air. "Can you believe it? My mother is a model!"

Thanks, Krissy.

Raymond laughed heartily. "That is quite an honor, Princess."

I love the way Daddy still calls me Princess. He's never given that up. Even though Tom used to think it was childish.

"And I trust you are living up to his expectations."

Samira crossed the kitchen as she spoke. "He doesn't demand very much, that's for sure." She checked the meatloaf in the oven for her mother. "I simply show up wearing the same style of clothing from the day before, take my position, and read while he works."

"Isn't it marvelous, Raymond?" Ashleigh appeared from the sunroom with two big, ripe tomatoes. "Our daughter is a model for a world famous sculpture." The mother removed a large bowl of tossed salad from the refrigerator and handed it to her husband. "We need to go over tomorrow and see his work."

"Indeed." Raymond was still watching Samira with great interest.

Samira closed her eyes against the penetration of her father's thoughts. *Please don't ask any hard questions today, Daddy. I'm too tired.*

Kara and Krissy offered to take their little cousins to the park after dinner. The house was suddenly very quiet. Samira slipped to the back of the house where oversized windows in her father's study overlooked the back yard. *Daddy's read every word on every page of every book in this room.* She ran her hands over the covers of the books on the shelves.

I have needed the tranquility of this room for a while now. Without an invitation, Samira curled up in her father's reading chair and rested her chin on her knees. Through the window she could see her mother gathering an armful of cut flowers.

"I thought I might find you here." Papa Ray's shoes tapped softly on the hardwood floor.

Samira smiled gently. *I was half-hoping he'd come looking for me.* "It's quiet back here, Daddy."

Raymond took a seat on the loveseat adjacent to his daughter. He crossed his legs and followed her gaze into the back yard. "Is there a storm going on inside your pretty little head, Samira?"

Rarely did Raymond address his daughter using her first name. *Now I know he's reading my thoughts.* "I hadn't realized how consuming it would be to have this sculptor in, Daddy. He is a quiet man, but at the same time he is very demanding of my time and attention."

Raymond nodded his head once. His eyes were on Samira. But her eyes were still in the back yard.

"Being a still life model is hard work then?"

Samira rested her head on the chair. "He only works on the in-house piece after hours so I've had some late nights." *Later than I'm used to anyway.*

"Surely not alone!"

"Oh, no, Daddy." Samira waved her hand to calm her father. "Either Jim, our maintenance man, or one of my assistants has been in the building every time I've gone back for a sitting." Samira replayed the past few days in her mind. "But they're tiring of the overtime too."

"How much longer before he doesn't need a live model?"

"He's almost done with me." *But there's somebody else I'd rather be with.*

Raymond folded his hands behind his head. *He's satisfied with my answers.* When he spoke again so soon, Samira was caught completely off guard.

"And what about the man who stole your heart, Princess? Are you able to work him into your modeling schedule?"

How does Daddy read me like that? Samira pulled her knees tighter to her chest. *The whole summer has passed and I have never mentioned Phil to my parents.* She avoided her father's eyes completely. "Daddy," she tried to brush him off. "What makes you think someone stole my heart?"

"I'm your father, Sugar. The glow on your face tells me there is a man in your life that means something special. But the pain in your eyes tell me it must not be as easy as you'd hoped."

Transparency! Samira hated it when her family could read her so easily. She flipped her hair off the side of her shoulder. "It's not." *This is the part you weren't going to tell him, remember?* "He's a really busy man." *Just don't say anything to incriminate Phil before Daddy meets him.* "It's hard for him to take a break sometimes." *Why am I defending him?*

"Not exactly a family man then?"

Daddy is going to get to the bottom of my emotions. I can feel it coming.

"I wouldn't say that." Samira thought for a moment. "He's a father so that takes up his time and energy too. And he owns his own business so that takes most of the rest of him."

Raymond puckered his lips in thought. "I guess we know the repercussions of running your own business, don't we Ashleigh?"

Samira wasn't aware that her mother had joined them. *I wouldn't be surprised if they arranged this time alone with me.*

Ashleigh sat down and patted Raymond's leg. "We love having you, dear . . . ,"

But obviously they've noticed I'm hiding out over here. "Sometimes it's easier to be here than to wait for the phone to ring." *There. I said it. They shouldn't need any more information on Phil or any other part of my life.* Samira could feel her chest tightening with emotion. *But I really don't think he's going to call.*

"Waiting is difficult," Ashleigh admitted. "Very difficult." She patted Raymond's leg again. "Is he good for you, dear?"

Samira inhaled very deeply. She pulled her hair back in her hand and held it there. "He's passionate, intense, and playful, all at the same time." She let go of her hair. "He's really good with the girls and he takes me places and treats me like a queen." Samira felt a smile form on her lips. "And he has this really great smile . . ." *And I love the way he calls me Pretty Lady . . .*

"Yes," Ashleigh smiled genuinely at her daughter. "We've heard some things from Krissy."

Of course they have. She uncurled her legs and set her feet on the floor. "I like everything about him." A tear threatened to spill onto her cheek. *The only part I don't like is the way he couldn't separate me from his professional ambition.*

Raymond leaned forward and put his hand on his daughter's knee. "Then why the tears, Sugar?"

He hasn't even called me since that day in the library parking lot. Samira couldn't hold them in anymore.

In the distance she could hear Krissy and Kara returning with the little girls. Ashleigh silently excused herself.

"Oh, Daddy," Samira put her face in her hands. "I want everything he has to offer. Everything!" She reached for a tissue and held it to her nose. "But he scares me."

"In what way, darling?"

Samira found a smile through her tears. "Not like you might think." She wiped her nose again. "He scares me because I don't know if I can handle all of him." She thought some more. "And because if I give him my whole heart, I'm afraid he won't know what to do with it." *Am I afraid of being hurt?* "He doesn't know love yet, Daddy. Not like I do anyway." Another thought occurred to her. "Sometimes he's so focused on his work that I can't get to where he is even though I'm right there in the same room." *Like that day in my office.* "Yet if he'd just quit trying so hard to make it work . . ." Samira bit her bottom lip. *Love might have a fighting chance.* " . . . I don't know what to think anymore." Samira blew her nose. *But I do know I really miss him.* "What am I going to do, Daddy?" *I need to know what to do because I miss all of him.*

Raymond didn't wait any longer. He slid forward onto his knees. With one full swoop he gathered his daughter completely into his arms.

Just hold me, Daddy. Tell me there's a way to make this work again. She allowed her father to caress her hair and hold her until she gained a sense of composure.

Raymond let her sit back in the chair again. He moved a small footstool closer and sat down at Samira's feet.

"Well, Princess," he began. "It sounds to me like you need to share all this with him." Raymond was looking directly into his daughter's eyes. "You have the gift to know a person's soul, Samira. You understand people in ways that most miss. He might not know what to do with you either . . ."

Samira could see her father's face through her tears. *Only Daddy could remind me of my own intensity without hurting me.*

" . . . You're going to have to tell him how you feel and then give him the power to make the decision." Raymond's brow was wrinkled in concern. "And his decision might not be the one you're hoping for, Sugar."

Is that what I'm afraid of? Samira pushed her hair back again. *I'm afraid if I call him, he might not know how to handle me either.*

"I know." She choked out the realization against her own will.

"I'm sorry you have to go through this." Raymond's eyes were soft. "Love never comes easily."

"Nope," Samira wiped her face in her hands. "It never does."

"I wish I could do it for you, Samira."

"I know, Daddy." She forced a tearful smile. "Thank you."

"Do we know this man?"

Samira had kept her parents in the dark on purpose knowing it would be easier to let him go without their judgement. *They still don't need to know who he is.* "I don't think so." *It will be better if they don't know him.*

"Is he from around here?"

Samira nodded. "But his family is from northern Missouri."

Raymond seemed satisfied with that little bit of information.

"I'll be okay," Samira wrapped her arms tight around her middle to get a grip on her emotions. *I hope.*

Raymond nodded with assurance. "I know you will. You're a strong woman like your mother." He rose from his low seat and offered his hands to help Samira out of the chair. "You'll come out of this better for it either way." The father embraced his daughter as she accepted his assistance.

Samira inhaled her father's aftershave. *I wish I were a little girl again so Daddy could carry me into my room and tuck me in for the night without a worry in the world.*

"Why do things have to be so complicated, Daddy?"

"I don't know, Princess." Raymond stroked her hair as he answered. "But sometimes the things you fight hardest for are the things that bring you the most joy in life." He kissed her hair.

Suddenly reminded of Phil's kisses, Samira closed her eyes. *I fought hard the last time and I lost.* Memories of Tom's last days flitted through her mind. *What if I don't have the fight in me this time?*

"Everything will be alright."

I don't know if Daddy actually spoke those words out loud or just thought them hard enough I heard him. Samira nodded against her father's shoulder.

Monday morning came all too soon. Spent from the emotional outlet the day before, Samira still felt tired. *I just can't seem to get caught up on my sleep!* But her emotions were intact and the busyness of the library schedule was a welcomed retreat. Samira raised her elbows as an entourage of day care children skipped around in excited jockeying for a front row seat.

"There's plenty of space, children," Daphne assured. The assistant gathered a wayward group of students with her arms and began to guide them to the viewing area.

Fabiano Uberti was waiting patiently to speak to the children. He positioned himself on a tall stool and folded his hands in his lap. Surprisingly, his quiet presence drew the attention of the children and they began to settle down.

"Isn't it amazing how he does that?" Daphne asked of the artist.

"Does what?"

"Quiets them down without even speaking," Daphne was totally amazed by just about everything Fabiano had done during his two-week stay. *She's so smitten by him. Only a few more days and he'll pack his presentation and sculptures and be on his way.*

But Samira admired the way he worked with children too. *Most of all I admire the way he can capture someone's emotion and weave it into his work.* Her eyes moved to the incomplete sculpture sitting on a worktable behind Fabiano. What started out as a block of hard, formless clay was now a shapely character reflecting Samira's body. But more than that, the shape of the eyes and the position of the head allowed Samira to see a glimpse of her own soul.

"Miss Samira," Mrs. Haddock whispered from the conference room doorway. When Samira looked up, Mrs. Haddock moved her hand for Samira to follow. "There's a gentleman here who would like to see you in person."

The last visitor Helen interrupted an important meeting for turned out to be a police officer.

"He looked important," Mrs. Haddock explained. "So I seated him in your office."

Samira's eyes went immediately to the backside of a balding businessman. She didn't recognize him at first. But as she stepped into her office, the gentleman stood and greeted her with a warm smile. Samira offered her hand and instead of shaking, he raised it to his lips.

"Mr. Hughes," Samira was quite surprised to see him. "Would you care for a cup of coffee?"

"No, no, Ms Cartwright." He took a seat.

"I am here to return something that is of very important stature." Christopher Hughes opened his suit jacket and removed a worn journal. "I understand you are the mastermind who uncovered the winning piece of evidence to close my father's estate."

"A mastermind might be a stretch," Samira corrected honestly. "But I did happen to run across it about the same time the evidence became pertinent." *I wondered if I'd ever see that book again but I never expected it to be hand delivered by Christopher Hughes.* She accepted the book without hesitation.

Mr. Hughes smiled. "My brother and I certainly appreciate your role in this project. As you might already know, my father's estate has been tied up in legal battles ever since his passing." The gentleman's face grew more serious. "That journal allowed a fair settlement over what could have been an economic disaster for the company." Christopher Hughes rose from his chair. "We are in the notion to repay you for your help, Ms Cartwright . . ."

Oh, no. Samira put her hands out to stop the man from speaking. "That certainly won't be necessary . . ."

"On the contrary." Mr. Hughes was reaching for his interior pocket again. "You saved my brother and I several thousand dollars by discovering that journal." The man removed a sealed envelope. "It is our understanding that the library accepts donations on behalf of individuals. Is that correct?"

"We do." *Now payment on behalf of the library is another story.* "We accept designated gifts in memory of individuals if the family has a specific wish. Or we also accept undesignated gifts and allow the library board to use the gifts where they are most needed at the time."

Samira walked around her desk and opened a drawer. A glossy flier stated all the ways individuals and businesses might make a donation to the library. Mr. Hughes looked over the pamphlet with interest.

"This gift would be designated." He thought for a moment. "And we would like to give it in memory of our father, the late Lloyd Hughes."

"He was a very generous man from what I understand."

"He was indeed." Christopher punctuated the compliment. "Do you have a suggestion on the designation, Ms Cartwright?"

Samira's heart skipped a beat. *In all my years as the head librarian of the Maple Street Branch, no one has ever asked how I might designate a gift.* Immediately her thoughts went to the needs of the online center. Without hesitation Samira indicated that possibility.

"I would be interested to know more about this online center," Mr. Hughes replied with enthusiasm. "Is it on site?"

Samira offered Mr. Hughes a personal tour of the center. While she walked him through the area she restated most of the points she had presented to the board of trustees. *It's a good thing I worked so hard on that power point presentation!* It felt good to be able to say the words with such confidence.

As they made their way back into her office Mr. Hughes once again fingered the sealed envelope. He complimented Samira's informative tour as he began to open the flap. "Is it possible that our father's memoriam might be placed in the center?"

"I'm sure we could arrange for that, Mr. Hughes." Samira's heart was pounding hard in her chest. *Anything you wish.*

"That would be very nice." Christopher Hughes handed Samira a check made out to the city of Joplin on behalf of the Maple Street Library Branch for sixteen thousand dollars. "Do you think this might get the board of directors moving on the project a little quicker?"

"Oh, Mr. Hughes," Samira swallowed hard so her excitement would gush all at once. "This is a very generous donation for the cause."

"My father would be pleased to know he was still moving the city of Joplin into the future." Mr. Hughes stooped to pick up his briefcase.

Samira remembered the formalities. "I have some papers for you to fill out in order to make this official."

Christopher Hughes produced a business card without so much a turn of his hand. "Just fax the forms to my secretary. She will take care of everything." The gentleman smiled genuinely. "Once again, my brother and I appreciate your intervention immensely. If there is ever any other way we might be of use to you, please don't hesitate to let us know."

I have never had this kind of experience in my entire life! The next thing Samira knew Christopher Hughes was gone and she was left holding a check that would more than complete the online project.

Fabiano Uberti tipped his head in Samira's direction as she glanced in at the class through the glass windows. *Can he see my excitement from in there?* Samira felt like doing cartwheels all the way back to the circulation desk. She returned the artist's smile but ignored his silent invitation to join him. Instead she headed for the back room to find Mrs. Haddock.

Mr. Uberti will just have to wait!

44

Tough Love

Denise rattled off the phone messages. "I know it's getting late for a Friday, but Jessica Hutchison from Bridges Property is expecting to hear from you yet today. I checked the city council notes and it looks like they're set to close on the airport property next week. Her call may be in reference to that."

J.P. nodded as he skimmed the other messages. "What's from the Maple Street Library?"

"A woman called and asked for you. When I offered to take a message she said she'd try back later." Denise shrugged her shoulders. "Nothing more than that."

"She leave a name?"

"No name."

"Get her on the phone for me," J.P. dropped the clipboard on Denise's desk. *I haven't talked to Samira in over two weeks.*

"She didn't leave a name, Boss. Who should I ask for?"

"Ask for Ms Cartwright."

"Very well."

J.P. unpacked the contents of his briefcase onto the conference table behind his desk. *What am I supposed to say to her after so much time has passed?*

Denise called from the outer office. "Ms Cartwright on line two, Boss."

J.P. reached for the phone. *Just act casual.* He took a long, deep breath before he pushed the button to connect the line.

"This is J.P." *That was anything but casual.*

"This is Samira."

394

"Samira." *It's good to hear her voice.* "How are you?"

There was a slight hesitation on Samira's part. "I'm fine."

Is she fine?

"How are you?"

Swamped. Tense. Stressed. Insane without you. "Fine."

"Does your assistant make all of your calls for you now?"

It didn't even occur to me to dial the phone myself. "Only when I'm on the fly," he lied again hoping to redeem himself.

"Are you short for time?"

Damn it. Nothing is coming out right! "No." J.P. could feel tension in his chest. *Just relax and talk to her.* "Not anymore."

"That's good." Samira sounded relieved. "I know this might be short notice, but I received a gift today and I was thinking that if you had some time tomorrow . . ."

Name the time, Pretty Lady.

" . . . that I'd like to share it with you."

"What exactly do you have in mind?" *Dinner? Candlelight?*

"Lunch."

Lunch?

"I was hoping maybe you could meet me for lunch."

"Okay." *Whatever she wants.* "I can make that happen . . ." *with minimal rearranging.*

"Good."

Maybe she's ready to kiss and make up.

"Do you know where McClelland Park is?"

"At Shoal Creek?" *There's no place out there to eat.*

"Yes." Samira's voice was suddenly filled with renewed energy. "I'll be at the west parking lot at noon."

"Noon tomorrow." *I wish I knew what's on her mind.*

"And I'll bring the lunch."

"Like in a picnic?"

"Is that alright?"

"That's good." *It's not exactly a candlelight dinner, but it'll work.*

"Then you'll be there?"

I wouldn't miss it. "I'll be there."

Samira said goodbye but then caught J.P. with a parting thought. "Oh, Phil?"

Man, I like the way she says my name.

"Next time maybe you could make the call yourself."

J.P. closed his eyes. "Yeah. I can do that." *She could have called my cell. I'd have answered.*

He hung up feeling the same distance he'd felt the day she left him in the library parking lot. *She's a little out of your league.* Mike's words echoed again in ears. *Out of my league because she challenges my every motive.*

"Noon tomorrow?" Denise questioned as she entered the office with a note stuck to the end of her finger. "Do I need to add that to your calendar?"

"No." J.P. read the note. *Jessica Hutchison.* "I won't need a reminder."

"Be careful there, sport," Denise warned with a hint of sarcasm. "I think you're already booked at noon tomorrow."

This time my personal agenda comes first. "Then make adjustments."

"She sounds smart."

"She is."

"I don't think she liked me making the contact."

"She didn't."

"Do you need me to remind you of that in the future?"

"No." J.P. looked hard into Denise's eyes. "That will be all."

"What about Derek's study group?"

"When?"

"Noon tomorrow."

Shit. J.P. put his head in his hands. *He's only a week from the bar exam.* "Fix it."

"As in reschedule?"

"Yes, Denise. Reschedule the study." J.P. could feel the force in his voice.

"Maybe I should remind you that this study group includes more students than just Derek." Denise started to walk toward her own office. "And you sited the study group as one of the reasons you sent James home for the weekend."

I sent James home so I could have some peace of mind! J.P. Ralston had been inundated with the Mid-America case and Hughes business since the afternoon he last saw Samira. *My patience is growing thin.* "Just fix it, Denise."

Denise turned around in the doorway. "The last time you told me to *fix* something, I got my butt chewed for sending Mike to close your case." She clicked her thick fingernails on the doorframe. "Therefore, I'd prefer if you'd be a little more explicit this time."

She's right. But I couldn't close a case after spending a night with a bottle of Jack Daniels. "Tell Derek I can't make it at noon. In fact, I don't know exactly when I'll get there but tell him I'll stop by as soon as I am finished with my noon appointment."

"That I can do. Thank you for the clarification."

"Remind me again why I put up with you."

"Because I'm one of the few people in your life that can save your ass and your case all in the same day."

Point well taken. J.P. cued his computer screen to check the remaining items on his agenda. "Can you get . . ."

" . . . Jessica Hutchison on the phone?" Denise finished the question. "Done."

And because she's the only person in my life who reads my mind and puts up with me anyway.

"Line one, Boss."

J.P. picked up the phone prepared to listen to a new sales pitch aimed at the Hughes Corporation. He was right on the money with that assumption. *But the business Jessica Hutchison offered isn't nearly as high on my priority list as the business scheduled for tomorrow noon.*

The newspaper reiterated mostly old news from the day before. J.P. laid it aside as he finished off a glass of orange juice. This was the first morning he'd had completely alone in his own house since James had moved in early in the summer. The unusual stillness was as much a surprise as it was a welcomed retreat. *No boom box playing in the background and no one sitting in front of my computer.*

Instead of meeting Mike at the driving range, J.P. stretched out good and then headed down the bike path in a full stride. Chase ran dutifully along side his master. J.P. had been doing his workouts at the gym, which left Chase home without regular exercise.

"That's really not very fair, is it boy?" J.P. talked to the dog as they crossed the bridge at the end of the path. The steady rhythm of the run matched the evenness of his breathing. *I'm getting too old to give myself over to the bottle like that.* He stopped long enough to attach the leash. *Takes me too long to recover anymore.*

Chase spotted a squirrel in the distance. "Whoa boy! Let it go." J.P. gripped the leash tighter. *I'd feel a little better going into lunch knowing exactly what Samira has on her mind.* He shortened his stride to begin the cool down. *I don't know if she's ready to move on, pick up where we left off, or just call the whole thing off.* He slowed to a stop in front of his house. *Good run, Chase.* He unclipped the leash and let the dog into his backyard. *I could live with picking up where we left off or moving forward.* J.P. stretched his hamstrings. *But I don't think I want to call the whole thing off.*

It didn't take but a moment to spot her. J.P. parked his truck where he could see her even though she might not be able to see him. *She looks very much at peace sitting there with her book like that.* Samira was sitting cross-legged on a low park bench. *How does she get her hair to stay up like that?* J.P. stood next to his truck watching her for a long time. *I still can't read one single thought.*

Samira's eyes met his long before he reached the bench. They were full of energy. *I've missed those dark eyes.*

"Hey Pretty Lady."

Her smile came naturally. "Mr. Ralston. It's good of you to come."

Funny. Those are the same words my father said to me in Virginia.

"Are you hungry?" Samira closed her book.

For you? Yes. Famished. He wanted to touch her but didn't feel the same sentiments from Samira.

"I brought lunch but it's over there." She pointed to the edge of a hill.

I'd follow you about anywhere right now, Samira Cartwright. J.P. spotted a checkered blanket stretched out over the grass in the shade of an old maple tree. A picnic basket offered a silent invitation.

"This is the best view of the river . . ."

J.P. watched her eyes scan the area.

" . . . It's especially beautiful down here in the fall when the trees are in full color."

I have the only view I need right here.

Samira sat down and patted the space next to her.

There's an invitation I won't refuse.

A sudden array of cold cuts appeared. Then a bowl of red grapes. Then a bag of cookies. J.P. watched in amazement as Samira turned the area between them into a summertime buffet. Her quiet smile made him chuckle out loud.

Samira looked up. "What's so funny?"

J.P. shook his head. *You're funny. You just prepare this little meal like no time has passed between us at all.*

"I don't know that I've ever known you to not speak." Samira popped a grape in her mouth and offered one to J.P.

I hope this is a peace offering. "I don't know what to say to such a pretty lady." His eyes moved from her face to her hands where she was busy preparing a piece of bread for a sandwich. *Say something, Ralston.* "It's really good to see you, Samira." *And it is.*

"It's been awhile."

"Seventeen days."

Samira stopped spreading the mayonnaise but she didn't look up. *I wonder if she's kept track too.* He watched as she prepared her next thought.

"What would you like in your sandwich? Turkey or ham?"

"Both."

"Lettuce? Cheese?"

"I want everything." *Including the Lady preparing it for me.*

Samira proceeded to lay the cold cuts over the bread. "Maybe that's part of the problem." She made brief eye contact.

Either she's picking up where we left off, or she's about to call it off.

Samira handed him the sandwich without saying anymore.

Definitely not moving forward yet. J.P. held the bread in his hands. *I'd be perfectly satisfied to skip lunch and just have her.*

He waited to take a bite until Samira made her own sandwich.

If we're picking up where we left off, I might as well ask the question. "I noticed in the paper you were sponsoring a guest artist." *I also noticed the photo in the paper matched the face talking to her in the parking lot.* "How's that working out?" *I may not want to know the answer.*

Samira smiled easily. "It's working out really well . . ."

Just my luck. J.P. took a bite in spite of the pit that was slowly forming in his stomach.

" . . . Fabiano is very easy to work with. He handles the children well and has a way with the older generation as well." Samira's eyes scanned the horizon briefly. "Not all of our guest artists are so adaptable."

Fabiano. J.P. said the name in his mind with resentment. *I don't like the way her eyes change when she says his name.*

"I read the paper too. I see the Hughes estate settled with the city."

She's bright. J.P. swallowed. *Chances are good she also knows I wasn't present for the closing.* "It's good to have that case off my desk."

"The article mentioned Mike Benson." Samira wiped her mouth on a paper napkin. "Don't they interview you after cases?"

Yep. She knows. J.P. ran his tongue over his bottom lip. "I don't usually interview very well." *Which is true. But I know she wants an explanation.* A guilty conscience forced him to expand further. "I wasn't actually there when it settled."

Samira's eyes were gentle when she looked at him. "I'm sorry. I know it was a long time in coming."

Why does she apologize like that? Does she know I was deep into a bottle of Jack Daniels over my last meeting with her? "It was my own fault. I wasn't in any shape to be there that morning."

Samira didn't inquire any further and J.P. didn't offer further explanation.

"One of your clients stopped by to see me yesterday." Samira's face was suddenly bright.

I'm listening. "One of *my* clients?" *Maybe one I called pertaining to the funding for the library.*

"I think so. Mr. Christopher Hughes."

Professional training kept J.P. from showing the shock. *That wasn't one of the calls I made.* "Mr. Hughes?"

"I was quite surprised to see him myself . . ."

How is it she reads me like a book and I can't even read one single word of her?

" . . . He returned the mayor's diary."

"No kidding?" *How the hell did he get his hands on that? And who told him it belonged to the Maple Street Library?*

"No kidding." Samira offered a homemade cookie, which J.P. readily accepted. "And he made a donation to the library for helping settle his case."

"Mr. Hughes is a generous man." J.P. tried to sound casual. *Someone shared confidential information without my knowledge.*

"Generous enough to pick up the tab for the new online system at the library," Samira concluded. "I'm thinking I might owe you a commission on the gift."

That's a hefty gift. J.P. gathered a handful of grapes. "Not me."

"Your office, then?" Samira took a grape out of his hand.

"Not that I'm aware of." *I seriously doubt Denise was involved in that.* "But I'm not surprised that Mr. Hughes searched you out. That sounds like something he would do."

Samira was eyeing J.P. carefully.

She really thinks I sent Mr. Hughes over with the money. "Honest." J.P. put his hands up. "I did not have any knowledge of Mr. Hughes' intention." He shrugged his shoulders and offered another grape.

"You didn't even mention it to him?"

No, but I should have! "Not a word."

"Well, we're going to set up a memorial in his father's honor." Samira tried to hide her smile. "With his donation and a few that have come in since my presentation, we should be able to get started on the project much sooner than I'd anticipated."

"What's your completion goal?" *It's fun to see her so excited.*

She squinted her eyes into the branches of the tree above them. "Well, let's see, my original goal was to have it done by the time school started, but that's only a couple of weeks out now." She rearranged her legs and leaned back on one arm. "So now I guess I'm hoping for the first of the year."

J.P. wished he could accelerate the project for her. *I could write her a check, but I have a feeling that's not what she's wanting from me.*

"How are the boys?" Samira offered a handful of cookies.

Might as well fess up on that. "James wants to play football with Josh again this year."

"So that means he's going back to his mom's?"

He's gone. Practice has already started. "He's going to give it a shot." *It's not what I advised, but it's what he decided to do.*

Samira's eyes showed compassion. "And how are you doing with that?"

J.P. sighed. "I don't know yet." *I don't like it.* "I was getting used to having him around." *Turned out ok to be needed at home.* "We'll see if it lasts."

"I'm sure it's a tough adjustment." Samira tucked her feet up under her long skirt.

"Tougher than I anticipated." J.P. finished the last of the cookies. "And your girls? What are they doing to use up the rest of their summer?"

Samira shook her head. "That's a really good question." She looked off into the distance. "I've had a lot of overtime with Fabiano on site. I don't feel like I've been a very good mom these past few weeks."

She could never be a bad mom. "Give yourself a little credit." J.P. wished he could touch her, but wasn't sure if the invitation was open. "I'm sure the girls understand."

"Maybe . . ." Samira ran her finger over J.P.'s forearm sending excitement all the way to his toes.

Be careful, Pretty Lady. Touch me like that and I might not be able to control my instincts. J.P. opened his hand to hers. *I know what she wears to bed at night and how quickly a glass of wine affects her defenses, but I still don't know what she's thinking.*

Samira's eyes were thoughtful, almost serene when she looked up at him.

"There's a boardwalk that follows the creek . . ."

In the back of his mind J.P. knew he needed to touch base with Derek's study group. *But there is no way I'm turning down this invitation.* He helped Samira load the picnic into her car and then followed her down the hill toward the river.

The only sounds were the gentle tumble of the shallow creek and the birds in the trees. *Obviously she's been here before.* J.P. watched Samira carefully. *There's something on her mind.*

J.P. followed suit when Samira sat down along the edge. She crossed her legs and reached her hand into the water. A mature weeping willow shaded the walkway from the hot afternoon sun.

"I miss talking with you . . ."

"I do too." *I just hope I'm ready to listen.* He was afraid to look at her for fear he'd read something in her eyes he didn't want to see.

"I never know if I should call or not." Samira's voice was quiet. "I know you're busy . . ."

I'm never too busy for her.

"...and I know how much your work means to you."

Does my work mean that much to me? J.P. thought about it for a moment. "Maybe that's part of the problem. Maybe that's all I know."

Samira bumped him with her shoulder.

Is that an invitation to touch her back?

"That's not true."

"What? That my work isn't all I do?"

"No, that it's all you know." Samira looked out over the water. "You know a lot more than that!"

Here goes nothing. "I don't know much about hanging on to a pretty lady," He was afraid to say it out loud, yet just as scared not to say it at all. "I don't know much about that."

"Maybe not..." Samira looked over her shoulder at him. "But you know how to handle a pretty lady and I've missed that too."

I've missed that part too. J.P. couldn't resist. He lifted his hand and ran his fingertips down her arm. *More than she knows.* "So what do you think we should do about that?"

Very slowly Samira leaned into J.P.'s side. With guarded reserve he allowed her body to rest against him. *There is nothing I want more than to hang on to this.*

"I don't know..."

That's the part I'm afraid of.

"I think we need to work on the hanging on part." Samira looked up into his eyes.

I can't resist that look. The kiss that followed left J.P. speechless. *But why do I feel like it could be the last?*

Samira suddenly climbed to her feet. "I didn't mean for that to happen..."

"You don't have to fight it." J.P. stood as well. *Please don't fight it, Samira.*

She crossed her arms and closed her eyes. "Yes, I do," she answered quietly. "I do."

The last time she said those words to me I didn't know how to take them. A chill ran up his spine. *But this time they're even more confusing.*

Samira's now open eyes pleaded with him. "I do because..." She searched for words. "...because I need to know where you stand." She squeezed her shoulders together. "I need to know where I stand." She looked away. "I'm not very good at open-ended relationships and before..." Samira stopped talking and turned away.

"Before what?" *This is why she's out of my league. Her expectations are out of my reach.*

"... before I can give any more of me." Samira turned back around and faced J.P. "I need to know what your intentions are."

I don't have any intentions. J.P. put his hands in his pockets and studied the motion of the water as it passed under the boardwalk. *What the hell is she asking for? A proposal or something?* "Samira, if I knew for sure what it would take to hang on I'd give it to you on a silver platter." *Anything to hang onto what we had.*

"Hanging on doesn't mean you always give something away."

Here comes the saga. J.P. hung his head in dreaded anticipation. "Maybe not, but there isn't anything I wouldn't give to hang on to you."

"... I need you to hang on for yourself, Phil. Not for me. I need you to want me for your sake, not mine."

What's she mean, need her for me? When J.P. looked up, Samira was facing the river. *Is she asking me to give up everything I've worked for?* He didn't like the insinuations he was feeling. *She's stating her thoughts. I'm going to state mine.*

"Look, Samira, I've worked really hard to call my life my own." J.P. stared at her back. "And until you came along I've been extremely secure in the world I've created for myself." *No matter how I say this, it's going to come out wrong.* "And to be perfectly honest, I've never let anyone have this much control over me ..."

Samira turned her face into the breeze but she didn't turn all the way around.

"A long time ago I swore I'd never compromise my efforts again. So I don't know what to tell you, Samira. All I know is how to give you the parts of me that are the most easily detached from what I do." *And that's obviously not enough for her.* "Maybe you need to be free of me so you can live your own life." *But I hope to God I'm wrong.*

"I do live my own life. Everyday." Samira moved a step closer to him. "That's the easy part. But a huge part of me is incomplete and you ..."

First she tells me she wants me to need her, and then she says she can't live without me? "I'm not getting a real clear picture of what you're expecting of me here ..." *But if she wants total commitment, I can't do that.* "... I play by my own rules and always have. That's my problem. But if you're asking me to change the rules, I don't know if I can do that ..." *If I knew how, I would. But I tried that once and failed.* J.P. crouched down on the balls of his feet and reached for a foxtail that was growing up between the slats in the board. *Open-ended relationships are safer. Period.*

"Maybe your rules are what keeps you at a distance. Have you ever thought of that? Maybe you're so afraid of hurting you're also afraid to love! What you and I have shared doesn't come along everyday ..."

No it doesn't, but demanding more of me isn't the way to keep it coming. "I've told you, it's the only way I know . . ." *I am not afraid of hurting and seriously doubt I know how to love anymore.* "The things that come with a relationship don't come as easily for me as you might think . . ."

"Maybe you make them too hard . . ."

"I don't make them at all, that's part of the problem." *Just put it out there. She can take it or leave it.* "As much as I'd love to be able to promise you the moon, I can't even promise making dinner on any given night, Samira."

"Dinner can be re-heated."

"Not all dinners can . . ." *I've been down that road before. That's why I don't make promises anymore.*

J.P. felt Samira turn away from him. *No, we're not going to end like this.*

"What exactly do you want me to say?" *Tell me and I'll say it.*

Samira's eyes were damp when she faced him again.

That's just great. Now she's crying

Her voice was surprisingly calm when she spoke. "I don't want you to say anything."

This is why you live by SNSA rules, Ralston. "Then what do you need from me?" *Mike told you she was out of your league.*

She wiped a tear with her fingertips.

Maybe what she needs is to quit trying to figure me out so she can get on with her life.

"I think I just needed to know if you loved me . . ."

If I love her? "You may think that's all you need, but it won't be enough . . ."

"You're wrong, Phil." Samira was quickly gaining her composure. "It's not enough because you won't let it be. You think you have to control everything and keep your life divided into these convenient areas of interest. But you don't have to work that hard for me . . ."

"No, I do work hard. That's what I know." J.P. ran his hand through his hair. "I work hard to win and I'm good at winning . . ."

"I am not a trophy to be won, Phil." Samira's tears had stopped. "You don't have to win me . . ."

Then I am out of my league.

Samira sighed. "I don't really know where I stand at the moment, but I think I have a better idea of where you stand . . ."

"Then maybe you could enlighten me because I'm still in the dark here . . ."

"I know, Phil."

Phil could feel her starting to shift into another mode. "But you're the only one who can find you."

J.P. turned his face toward the motion of the water wondering what he should do or say next. When he turned back to Samira, she was halfway up the hill headed toward the parking area.

The running creek seemed louder than it had earlier in the afternoon. *Tell me who am I, Samira, because I don't think I know anymore.*

The pain that started in J.P.'s heart radiated through his entire body. *I don't know what this feeling is.* He put his hand on his chest. Very slowly, the colors of the world faded into hues of gray and white. *It can't be as simple as just loving her.*

Nothing was making sense. J.P.'s eyes went to the crest of the hill. *There's got to be more to it than that.* Suddenly nothing else seemed to matter. *Dad said there are some things you can't play to win.* He buried his face in his hands. *What if she's one of them?*

45

The Love Within

Samira looked up into the eyes of the artist.

"May I touch you?"

Fabiano had called her back to the library for one final modeling session. *He says it's time to put the finishing touches on the face.*

Samira nodded silent permission.

Fabiano Uberti gently touched her jawbones with his hands and positioned her face much like he had done in earlier sessions. Samira held her head exactly as he placed it.

"Mmmmm . . . ." Fabiano studied Samira's face thoughtfully. "I fear zhat I waited too long, Miss Samira." He tilted his head to the side as he raised a small scalpel to the terracotta figurine. "Zhe light I knew in your eyes is not zhere anymore." Very carefully the artist made a slight mark. "Zometing is different, hmmm?" Fabiano looked from his work back to Samira's face, then back to the figurine again.

I feel badly that I can't give him what he's worked toward all this time. The better part of a month had passed since she first sat in this position for him. During that time the lump of clay had taken on a life form. Samira studied the shape of the hands and the angle of the shoulders as Fabiano worked in silence.

He's very good. The figurine was in a sitting position with one knee up and one knee down. *He has captured my form.* Locks of hair were shaped into a loose weave at the nape of the neck and one hand held an open book against the lower knee. The other hand was resting out to the side.

"You don't need to respond if you don't want to." Fabiano continued to work. "Your silence speaks its own thoughts."

Forgetting her pose, Samira moved to the edge of the table and folded her hands in her lap. The transparency of her emotions seemed more evident in Fabiano's presence than with anyone else. *Even than with Wes or Daddy.*

Fabiano described the exuberance he saw in her eyes when he first mentioned the possibility that Samira might be his model. *That was the day he followed me outside and talked to me on the steps.* But there was more to that day than Fabiano's invitation to model. *Little did I know Phil was waiting for me too.* She thought some more. *And little did I know this was the piece Fabiano would choose as his main piece at the auction.*

Caught up in the initial excitement, Samira couldn't refuse. *But now I wish I could take it all back.*

Fabiano looked into her eyes with great intensity. "I once thought maybe marble for the finished work. Ahhh, but now . . ." he puckered his chin in thought. "Now maybe bronze to capture the sadness of your soul."

Maybe I don't want my soul captured.

"Yes, bronze. Bronze sets the stage for you now." Fabiano tipped his head indicating for Samira to turn hers slightly toward the light.

Remembering her purpose, Samira obliged. *I'll be glad to go home tonight.* "How long does it take to finalize a sculpture once you are finished carving?"

"Hmmm, she speaks but does not answer." Fabiano smiled quietly at the clay figure. "I must fire it next. When zhat is complete it will take a couple of days for the bronzing." The artist smiled with his eyes. "But don't you worry, Miss Samira, it will be ready in time for the auction."

"I'm not worried." *I trust him.*

"Maybe not about zhat," Fabiano replied casually. "But worried you are. Or saddened by zometing very near to your heart." He stopped and admired his work for a moment.

Hopefully he has this keen sense of emotions with all of his models.

"Yoor spirit is wounded tonight. Yes?"

Samira bowed her head. *Very much so.*

"Tis not good for a woman to keep it all inside." Fabiano stopped working and walked to the table where Samira was sitting. He held out his hand.

Unsure of what he was going to do, Samira hesitated to give him hers.

"Let me show you zometing." He invited her to follow his thoughts.

Reluctantly Samira put her hand in his and walked with him to the lobby where the finished pieces were on display.

"Look into zhere eyes." Fabiano released Samira's hand. "Tell me what you see." Samira looked into the faces of each piece. *An old lady in a swing. A child pulling a wagon. A girl holding a kitten. A mother and a daughter. A boy with a fishing pole. It is in their eyes.* Fabiano had captured the spirit of each model in his work. *I can see it.* She looked over the top of the display directly into Fabiano's anticipation.

"Do you know?"

Samira looked away.

"If you know what it is, you must say it to make it real." Fabiano walked around the display. His presence was very strong. "You will feel better to say it out loud, Miss Samira."

Samira looked once more into the eyes of the lady in the swing. "It's love."

"Hmmm, yes." Fabiano slowly put his hands out as if he might embrace her. Samira didn't know if she should move away or not. "And I fear it is love zhat has left your eyes." In his eccentric kind of way the artist reached out to Samira's face and positioned it like he had done many times in previous weeks. "Once it was zhere but tonight it is gone." He gently held one hand against her cheek. "Do you zhink it will come back?"

Samira tried to look away but his eyes held hers with a powerful gaze. She moved her head against his hand. "Not this time." She could see Phil's face clearly in her mind. *He's so confused yet so convinced that he has to do something more to win me.*

Fabiano's hand moved to Samira's arm. "I am very zorry." He spoke with compassion.

Somewhat surprised by the artist's empathy, Samira allowed him to squeeze her hand. "Thank you, Fabiano." Her eyes moved back to the woman on the swing. Aunt Maggie's porch swing came to mind. *Even that day I could sense the conflict of his spirit.*

Jim appeared in the back of the library. Samira dropped Fabiano's hand as she watched him weave his way through the sitting area toward the lobby.

"So all of these pieces go downtown on Monday, right?"

"Everyting." Fabiano waved his hand over the area. "Zhe ones in zhe studio will go too. I will tell you zhe ones we will sell and zhe ones we will keep."

"Very well." Jim seemed satisfied. "It's getting late, Miss Samira. Are you finished for the evening?"

Samira looked to Fabiano for an answer.

"Yes. We are finished for tonight." Fabiano was looking directly at Samira when he answered.

"Let me know when you're ready to leave and I'll lock the doors behind you. I'm going to run the buffer over the entryway after you go."

Samira thanked Jim as he turned to walk away. She could feel Fabiano's eyes still watching her as Jim disappeared behind the rows of books in the back of the library.

"I am finished working for zhe night," Fabiano informed quietly. "May I take you to dinner, Miss Samira?"

Caught completely off guard, Samira instantly put her hand to her chest. *This wouldn't be a good night to keep my company.* Another thought seemed to urge an acceptance.

"As a way to tank you for modeling," Fabiano clarified.

Samira tried desperately to gather her thoughts so they coincided with her logic. *Go to dinner with this passionate artist who just put the finishing touches on a sculpture of me?* "I don't know," she began to sort her thoughts out loud. Samira checked her watch. It was nearing eight o'clock. "I would need to check in with my girls."

Fabiano looked back toward the conference room where his work was still visible. "And I would need time to clean tings up here. Maybe half an hour?"

Samira calculated how long it would take her to get home and visit with the girls and then freshen up. She was still wearing the clothes she'd worn to meet Phil "I could meet you in an hour or so." *I have no idea what's motivating me to accept.*

Fabiano's eyes lit up with new excitement. "Do you know the bistro zhat is in zhe old hotel?"

"Andres?" A mental picture of the old inn formed in her mind. "It's French, you know."

"Hmmm, yes. I know." Fabiano kissed his fingertips into the air. "Zhe French have a way with entrées." He leaned in toward Samira. "In an hour zhen?"

Tipping her head in agreement, Samira confirmed the time, still wary of her underlying intention. Her mind played out the possibilities as she gathered her purse from her office. *I feel like I have something to prove. If Phil doesn't need me, then I should be open to new offers.* She located Jim in the back and informed him of her departure.

She crossed the parking lot with random thoughts boggling her mind. *But at the same time, I just walked away this afternoon. Isn't it a little too soon to be going out with someone else?* The sun was just dropping over the horizon as Samira pulled into her driveway. *And Fabiano is leaving town in a week! He's not someone I could ever form a long-term relationship with anyway.*

Samira raised a hand to the invisible Mrs. Barnes. Without looking she knew the old woman was somewhere within viewing distance on the other side of the street. *Maybe the fact that Fabiano is leaving town makes him even more appealing.* That thought caught Samira totally unaware. *If he's leaving, then whatever happens with him tonight leaves with him in a week.*

Samira put her hand to her forehead before opening the door into the kitchen. *I just need the voices to stop before I talk to Krissy and Kara.*

It's just a good thing the girls are home tonight. Dim lights flickered in the basement stairway indicating they were probably watching a movie. *I need them for accountability.* She knew her defenses were being challenged by Fabiano's presence. *And he is quite handsome in an artistic kind of way.* She pushed Phil's face out of her mind. *Mix Fabiano's looks with his talent and his passion and I might have a hard time resisting another invitation . . .*

Samira stopped in her tracks. *This time you have gone too far!* She buried her face in her hands and took a long, deep breath. *No. Absolutely not an option.* She sat down at the breakfast bar. *The decisions I may face later tonight could create an impact far greater than what I'm ready to face.*

You, Samira Cartwright, could have about any man you wanted if the choice were yours to make. Her eyes went to her daughter's school pictures on the bookshelf across the room. *But that's not who you want to become.*

Samira kicked her shoes off and listened as they made a hollow thud against the hard floor. *Dinner at Andre's would be romantic simply due to the atmosphere. But dinner is the only option. Nothing more.* Her thoughts tripped back to Fabiano's comment about the finishing glaze on the figurine. *Bronze is a better choice than marble.*

Sunday morning arrived much sooner than Samira hoped. She rolled over and checked the time on the alarm clock. It was after seven. She closed her eyes and put the back of her hand over her forehead. She was in her own bed, wearing her own nightshirt, and she was alone. *Completely alone. Just as it will be for the rest of my life.*

Samira wished she could stay in bed for the rest of the day. There was no motivation to get up. No underlying hope in a future with a whole family again. *Nothing left to make me think I could ever be whole again either.* She pulled the covers up over her shoulder as she turned over on her side and dozed off to sleep again.

"Yoo-hoo! Good morning, Mama!" Krissy pounced on the end of her mother's bed then crawled up to the empty pillow. "Time to wake up sleepy head! Granny is expecting us at her church this morning, remember?"

Samira moaned at the recollection. *I'd rather just stay here.*

"So did you stay out all night?" Krissy had her head perched up with a bent elbow.

"I came in about midnight." *Much later than I'd planned.*

"Did you have a good time?"

"It was okay," Samira yawned. She rolled over to face the freckled face of her youngest daughter. *It was actually very strange.*

"Was it like a real date?"

Samira questioned Krissy with her eyes.

"Like, I mean, did he take you to dinner and pay for your meal and then walk you to your car and kiss you goodnight?"

The mother thought for a moment before answering. "Yes, he paid for my dinner and walked me to my car and he . . ." *Yes, he kissed me, but it didn't feel right. It was all wrong!* " . . . kissed my hand." Samira felt terrible lying to her daughter. *But it just didn't feel right.*

The initial shock in Krissy's eyes blinked in guarded unbelief. "So he didn't really kiss you then, right?"

Samira frowned. "I would call that a gentleman's kiss." *He wanted it to be real. But it wasn't.*

"Not like the real thing though." Krissy popped up off the bed. "That's a relief!" She turned toward the bedroom door. "It's almost eight. You're going to be the one hurrying for a change!"

Is she really relieved? Samira buried her head in her pillow. *She has her hopes set on Phil.*

Samira sat next to her father during church. Throughout the service her mind played games with her heart. While the minister delivered the morning message, Samira pondered the events of the previous evening.

He would have kissed me again had I given him permission. But even now she could feel his narrow lips on hers. *It just wasn't right.* There was no doubt in her mind that she left him disappointed in the parking lot. *Dinner was fabulous—bon appetite without the mass of an American meal. The wine was a treat. His stories were enchanting. His attentiveness was flattering.*

Samira stood with the rest of the congregation at the announcement of the last hymn. *But there was something missing.* She opened the hymnal in her hands and began to sing the familiar words. *I wasn't drawn into his presence like I am—or was,* Samira instantly corrected that thought, *with . . .* It was hard to even think his name. A few stanzas later her father reached over and turned the page to the correct song. . . . *with Phil.*

The sanctuary was almost empty when Samira's mother remembered her flower vase downstairs.

"I'll go down and get it and just meet you outside."

Samira watched her mother exit through the glass doors into the narthex. As she walked along the aisle she ran her hand over the oak on the end of each pew. The wood was smooth with regular wear. As Samira neared the back she noticed a light in the chapel off to the side of the main worship area.

No one was in the room so Samira reached for the light switch that was higher on the wall the usual. *Daddy used to have to pick me up so I could reach this switch.* As the light clicked off, sunlight poured through a stained glass window casting a kaleidoscope pattern onto the neutral carpet. *That's beautiful.* Samira moved toward the center of the room. Her eyes followed the ray of light back to the window. Cut glass revealed figures of men and women joined in a circle, their faces gazing upwards toward a radiant ray of sunlight. Beyond the yellow streaks of glass was the figure of a descending dove. The glass seemed to shimmer in the sunlight as Samira studied the dove.

What I wouldn't do for that peace dove to touch me right now. I spent the better part of the past six years telling myself I could make it on my own, believing that I wasn't meant to be with a man. The light changed slightly illuminating the golden rays of light again. *But I was wrong. I was wrong to believe that! I was wrong to want to be alone.*

The light changed again and the people holding hands in the glass seemed to dance in a syncopated pattern. *I isolated myself from the world around me-from the world I used to know. I thought if I just stayed home I wouldn't be able to meet anybody,* Samira justified her actions. *But there's a huge difference between meeting just anyone and meeting the one you know loves you better than all the rest.* Samira felt her spirit tremble somewhere deep within her being. *How can I expect to be content now that I've known that kind of love again?*

A slight movement in the room caused Samira to catch her thoughts. The window instantly lost the animation. Staring at the now two-dimensional glass, Samira felt a presence move closer to her.

"It's a beautiful piece." The voice spoke from behind.

Pastor Bill. Samira turned around slowly. His once dark hair was all white, yet he still held the merriment in his eyes that had once reminded Samira of Santa Claus.

"I've seen it come to life more than once but it always seems to fade back into the single pane eventually."

Samira looked back to the window. The light had changed drastically and the window no longer appeared to have any resilience at all. *I see what he means.*

"Did you see the dove?" The pastor walked slowly into the room. "You can only see it when the light is just perfect . . ." he squinted his thoughtful eyes toward the top corner. "But it's not there now."

Samira looked too, expecting to see it descending right where it had been a few moments before. *Where did it go?*

"I've come to understand the movement of the dove to be a message of peace because I've only been able to see it when my soul was deeply troubled." The pastor turned and faced Samira directly. "And I sense maybe this is a good day for the dove to appear for you, Samira."

Samira questioned his observation with her eyes.

"I was watching you this morning." The wise, aging man looked deep into her eyes. "I've known you since you were born and I know from the pain in your eyes than you are working through something very important." The pastor raised his hand, placed it on Samira's shoulder. "Let's give it to the Lord in prayer together."

Samira obediently bowed her head as her lifelong pastor prayed openly and without contempt for her to find the peace her soul so longed to know. Moved by the depth of the pastor's perception, Samira remained still for several moments following his amen.

"I've known that peace before," she finally admitted. "But it seems like it's been a long, long time."

The pastor folded his hands against his suit coat buttons. "It's not as far away as you might think," he assured gently. "Look inside yourself, Samira, it is there, waiting for you to recognize it." The pastor paused. "The love within you is still there."

Samira shook her head. "It wasn't enough."

"Maybe you've overlooked its purpose."

"I chose to put it there and I can choose to take it out." Samira retaliated.

"But you can't choose love. Love chooses you."

"It must have made a wrong choice then because it isn't going to happen." Samira could feel a tinge of bitterness in her words.

The pastor looked back toward the window causing Samira's eyes to follow his. The sunlight outside had moved again and the rays of golden yellow were bright with intensity.

"Love doesn't know a wrong choice, Samira."

It did this time.

"Once the love is in your heart, you don't have a right to take it out." The pastor crossed his wrists behind his back. "Love always has a purpose and that's not something you can change."

So what am I supposed to do with it if I can't make it go away? The chapel was completely silent. *Even the people in Fabino's statues have love in their eyes. My love is gone. Vanished. All used up.*

"And if you can't change it or push it away, then you have to accept it." With that the pastor tipped his head in Samira's direction. His eyes twinkled in a silent revelation and then he made an exit through a single door on the far side of the chapel.

As Samira's eyes passed over the window again, the transparent dove flickered into motion and then faded back into the leaded glass as quickly as it had appeared.

If I can't change it or push it away, then I have to accept it? Samira thought for another moment. *He means I have to accept the love I have with Phil even if I don't understand its purpose?* She turned away from the window and started for the door.

Or maybe I'm supposed to keep loving Phil even if he doesn't have the capacity to contain it all. Samira could hear her mother calling her name.

"Coming, Mama!" Samira glanced back at the window. The white dove flickered into focus and then faded again immediately.

46

The Point of Decision

J.P. tucked his tie between two shirt buttons as he leaned over the chair. Sparky was monitoring online transactions at Mid-America.

"Dis is the vire I am vaiting for." The detective pointed his finger to a series of numbers moving along the top of the computer screen. "I predict dis transaction vill move from the holding company in Balteemor to Mid-America within a few minutes."

J.P. had no idea how Sparky had traced the transaction. *Nor do I have an inkling how it might relate back to the online tampering that took place at the beginning of the summer.* All J.P. knew was that it was high time to be drawing some concrete conclusions.

Sparky lunged suddenly. His eyes were fixed directly on the computer screen but his hand was scribbling out a line of numbers as they crossed the screen. *He's really a pretty amazing little man.*

Sparky keyed a command that opened up another window. "Vatch dis." He leaned back in the steno chair and crossed his arms.

What am I watching? J.P. stared at the screen. *What are these numbers?* Clearance was granted from another computer in the building, and then suddenly a sizable dollar amount appeared followed by an account number. *Whatever they are, the box says the transaction completed.*

Sparky jotted down the information and keyed in another code. "Ah-ha. Just as I tought." Sparky put the end of his stubby pencil to his lips. "Look at dis, J.P."

I'm looking.

"Look closer," Sparky encouraged. "See dis? Ve just vatched dis deposit come in over the wires from Balteemor." The detective tapped the pencil against the glass of the oversized screen. "But see? Today is not June fifth."

J.P. looked again. *Sure enough. It says June 5ᵗʰ.* "Are you sure it's the same transaction?"

"Positive." Sparky reached for the phone and dialed an extension. J.P. listened as he talked with a computer technician working on mainframe. "He vill be right over."

When the technician arrived with the report, the student intern was close on his heels.

What the hell is she doing here? J.P. shook his head. *That's the same student Stephenson allowed on board without security clearance earlier this summer.*

Sparky eyed the young woman and extended his hand. "I don't believe ve've met."

Sparky knows exactly who she is.

"Celia Monroe." She returned the handshake.

"And what brings you to my computer room?"

He means surveillance unit.

"What do you mean?"

Let's see how Sparky handles this.

"You tapped into my line . . ."

Ms Monroe shifted her weight from one foot to the other. "I don't know what you're talking about."

"Ah, I beleev you do, Ms Monroe." Sparky turned the page on the report and waited.

J.P. noticed that the color was beginning to drain from the woman's face.

"I . . . I wasn't even working on a computer."

Sparky raised his thick eyebrows and addressed the technician. "Vas Ms Monroe vorking vith you den?"

The technician seemed surprised to suddenly be involved in the conversation. "Uh, No, sir. Miss Monroe works in accounting. She followed me here after I picked up this report from the printer."

"Did you suspend the system like I requested?"

The technician affirmed the action.

"Den ve vill see in a moment who vas logged onto the system during de last few minutes." Sparky continued to skim the report in his hands. The only sound in the room besides the hum of active computers was the ticking of the wall clock above the door.

This is good. J.P. leaned against a computer workstation and waited. *I'd say Sparky has a tiger by the tail.* A long minute passed before another employee stuck her head in the door.

"I have the report you ordered, Sir . . ."

"Tank you very much." Sparky walked across the room and took the stack of papers from her hands. "Dis report vill tell me vhat I need to know." He began to skim and then looked up at the spectators in the room. "Oh, I am zo zorry. Do you vait on me? You may go now."

The computer technician excused himself quickly. But Miss Monroe hesitated. Her eyes were wandering back and forth from Sparky to the stack of papers he'd left laying on the computer desk.

"If you vant to read dem, go ahead . . . ," Sparky spoke without looking up. "You von't find vhat you are looking for."

Miss Monroe suddenly turned toward the door.

"Vhat time are you leaving today, Ms Monroe?" Sparky asked the question cautiously.

"I have been leaving at three o'clock, why?"

"No reason."

J.P. closed the door behind her.

"Dis is Sparky."

J.P. turned to see the little investigator talking into the telephone again.

"Yes der is zometing. Keep an eye on Ms Celia Monroe. Tell me de moment she leaves de building."

J.P. checked the clock above the door. *One thirty.* Curiosity was about to get the best of him. *I'd love to know what Sparky suspects.*

"Ah, yes, J.P. Patience. In due time I vill tell you."

J.P. smiled. *Funny he reads my thoughts.*

"In de meantime, you can tell Mr. Stephenson zhat de missing monies are back where zhey belong." The investigator put his hand up in a firm stop. "But! De must remain untouched and unmanipulated until I give de signal. Understood?"

J.P. was shocked. "All of the monies are recovered?"

"Every penny."

"Are you sure?"

"Yes. I am sure." Sparky's eyes were reading the report in his hands. "And I am sure Ms Monroe is de one hired to validate de transaction." He turned a page and smiled at the security camera in the corner above their heads. "Ve vill see."

"Hired by who?"

"Ah. Patience." Sparky worked his bushy black eyebrows. "Ve must be patient."

The telephone on the desk rang once and Sparky answered.

But I am not a very patient man, Sparky.

"Just as I tought." The investigator hung up the telephone and gathered both reports into one pile. "I must go. Ms Monroe is leaving de building and

I need to know where she is going." The investigator smiled with his lips closed and raised his bushy eyebrows. "I vill leave you to Mr. Stephenson."

Sparky made a quiet exit through a security entrance, but J.P. took the stairs two flights up and knocked against the open door to the president's office.

Mr. Stephenson looked up and motioned for the attorney to enter. "Any luck, J.P.? Sparky seemed confident something important was going to happen today."

J.P. took a seat in the leather chair across from Mr. Stephenson. "And Sparky is rarely wrong."

Mr. Stephenson leaned forward and crossed his arms on his desk.

What is it about his eyes that seem so familiar? "The missing monies have been returned to their original accounts, Mr. Stephenson. They came in from a holding company in Baltimore about a half an hour ago. Sparky has a wiretap on the accounts and has asked that they not be manipulated in any way until he gives the okay. He has already notified mainframe security so they're aware of the situation."

"Are you telling me the money came back?"

"That's what it looks like."

"That's incredible."

"Indeed." *Laundered, no doubt, but back just the same.*

"So what's next? Does he know where the money has been or how it came back?"

J.P. patted his hands against the arms of the big chair. "I don't know exactly what Sparky knows, but professional instinct tells me he knows enough that your case against the hackers in Baltimore may be bigger than we originally imagined."

Mr. Stephenson stood up and walked over to the window that overlooked downtown. "Amazing. It blows my mind that the money can disappear and reappear in these accounts without anyone here being aware of the transactions. And it is even more puzzling that a remote computer somewhere in the world can enter into my systems and manipulate data without anyone in this building granting access."

It will be interesting to see where Ms Monroe is going. "We just have to stay out of the way and let Sparky finish the investigation."

"How long are you thinking, J.P." Mr. Stephenson poured himself a cup of coffee and started back toward his own desk. "May I get you anything?"

"No thank you." J.P. watched his client take a seat again. "I don't have a timeframe from Sparky yet. Obviously we don't have much control of the situation at this time. Patience is the best we have to offer." *I can't believe I'm the one advising patience!*

Mr. Stephenson nodded. "Well, it's easier to be patient knowing the funds are back where they belong. Should I notify the investors?"

"Not yet." J.P. advised. "Right now we need to let everything settle so Sparky can validate the trace, which should eventually help lead us to the mastermind behind the crime."

Mr. Stephenson put his hand to his face. "It's very slow going, isn't it?"

"That it is, Mr. Stephenson. That it is." *No one is more tired of waiting than me.*

"I appreciate you sitting in on yesterday's board meeting, J.P." Mr. Stephenson held his coffee cup out in an informal toast. "I know you had other things you could have been doing." He took a sip. "So tell me . . . what are your thoughts? The property is prime development land but Mid-America is never going to use it. We have plenty of room for growth right here where we are and, to be honest, I like being in the heart of downtown. Even if we were to put up a branch we wouldn't need nearly that much land . . ." Mr. Stephenson was interrupted by a buzz on his phone. He held out a finger to excuse himself for a moment and pressed a button.

"Your wife on line 3, sir."

"If you'll excuse me, I need to take this call," Mr. Stephenson rose from his chair and crossed the room to another telephone.

J.P. watched Mr. Stephenson greet his wife and check his watch simultaneously. The attorney's eyes landed on a large framed photo of Mr. Stephenson and his wife. *She's pretty enough but she looks young compared to him.* J.P. had noticed the photo before but never paid much attention. But today he studied it more closely. *She looks vaguely familiar but I haven't the slightest idea where I'd have seen her.*

" . . . I might actually be out of here in a decent time today . . . I'll come home first and we can go over together . . ."

I wonder what it's like to have to stop working to take a call from a wife. For a brief moment his mind pictured Samira's gentle smile. *But it's not likely you'll ever have the chance to find that out.* J.P. caught his mental slip. *Nope. Not going back there.* He walked over to the full-length window and peered down upon the activity of the business district. His eyes followed the sidewalk to the law offices of Benson and Barringer. He thought about Mike's partnership with Vincent Barringer.

In the beginning J.P. had advised against Mike's decision to join a law firm fearing it might limit Mike's opportunities. *But twelve years later Mike's doing very well for himself. And he's able to enjoy some free time too.* J.P. sighed and dropped his hands into his front pockets. *That's another chance that has no doubt passed me by . . .*

" . . . I apologize for the interruption, J.P." Mr. Stephenson had joined him at the window. "At any rate, how would you advise the board to handle the land in question?"

J.P. faced the executive. At one time J.P. would have been eager to share his opinion but today he didn't feel the usual surge of energy that came with that opportunity. "I say if you're not going to use it for expansion of Mid America directly, then you have two options. You either develop it for industry or commercial lease, or you sell it." *Plain and simple.*

Mr. Stephenson nodded his head slowly. "I agree. But of the two options, what is your advice?"

Hughes will be more than interested, especially since they lost the final bid on the airport property. The attorney's mind continued to scheme. *I also know how slow Mid-America's board of directors move with big decisions.* It would take them months, if not years, to develop the land into anything profitable for their own benefit or the benefit of the city.

J.P. nodded his head. "I'd sell."

Mr. Stephenson chewed on his bottom lip and squinted his eyes in thought. "Would you list it through an agency?"

J.P. shook his head. "Not with that particular tract. If you're interested enough to sell, I might be able to drum up some interest." *Two phone calls. One to Denise. The second to Jefferey Hughes.*

There was more thoughtful silence between the two professionals. Finally Mr. Stephenson spoke again. "How long do you think it would take to find a buyer?"

The attorney smiled to himself. *A lot less time than it's taking to track down a computer hacker!* "I'd say within a month." *By morning.*

"Really?" Mr. Stephenson sounded surprised. He returned to his desk for his coffee cup. "I'm impressed."

Wait until he knows who is interested. Then he can be impressed.

"Tell you what," the president stood next to his chair. "Why don't you go to work on finding a buyer and I'll go to work on the board and together let's see if we can't at least progress one item of business toward some kind of closure."

J.P. could hear the hopefulness in Mr. Stephenson's voice. *He's bored with the lack of progress on the hacker's case too. We all are.*

"Sounds like a good plan."

Mr. Stephenson stuck out his hand. "Then it's a go. I'll call a board meeting first thing Monday morning."

"And I'll see what interest I can stir up before I go home tonight." J.P. returned the firm handshake.

"Can I offer you a word of advice, J.P.?"

Do I look like I need advice?

"No need to spend all night working on this. You've put in plenty of hours for Mid-America these past weeks. Take some time for yourself, J.P."

Is there something else I should be doing?

"Seriously." Mr. Stephenson's face was solemn. "Go home. Take a load off for a night."

Maybe my attitude is beginning to show. Lately he'd been fed up with the lack of forward motion in the hacker's case. And now Sparky was off on a new wild goose chase that only made limited sense. *Not to mention the fact that my personal life took a hit this week too.*

"Maybe I will." *More likely I'll go back to the office and work late into the evening. With James only around every other weekend now, there's little motivation to go home early.*

J.P. found Denise on the telephone when he walked into his office. She pushed a button on the base and smiled brightly at her boss.

"Lucky me," she quipped. "Or maybe I should say, lucky you."

J.P. stopped in front of her desk. *Probably neither.*

"You missed the initial onslaught of information from Sparky, but you're here in time to make a decision on this call."

"When did you talk to Sparky?"

"Just now. He's on his way back to Mid-America with new information on this Celia chic. And for your information, he's taking a cop back to the computer lab with him."

Now I'm interested.

" . . . but more on that in a second." Denise tipped her head. "Jessica Hutchison is on line two. She has a dinner invitation for you at Bridges' Condominiums later this evening."

"What's her motive?"

"She says she has information from her broker that might interest you."

J.P. started to walk away. "Six months ago I might have been interested."

"Then that's a no?"

"Yeah." *It might be worth checking out.* He went back to Denise's desk. "I don't know. What time?"

"Like that would matter?"

It might. "Find out."

Denise picked up the phone and inquired as to the nature and time of the engagement. Once again she asked the party to hold. "Eight o'clock. "She says you can expect to meet other real estate gurus as well."

"Are those her words or yours?"

"Mine," Denise smiled. "Are you in or not?"

"Get an address."

"I'll take that as an affirmative."

J.P. removed his suit jacket and hung it over the back of a conference chair in his own office.

"I don't think your little librarian would appreciate your having dinner with this Ms Hutchison woman." Denise was carrying a yellow sticky note as she entered J.P.'s office.

And maybe that's none of your business.

" . . . she sounds a bit too flirtatious to be serious about a business setup."

"Maybe that's just her nature."

"And maybe it's her nature to undermine any future you might have in a halfway decent relationship."

"What the hell is that supposed to mean?" J.P. felt new tension in his shoulders. He unbuttoned a shirtsleeve and started to roll his cuff.

Denise stuck the note on the edge of his desk. "That means you might want to practice saying 'no' all the way over there and avoid any alcohol she might offer."

J.P. was irritated at Denise's sudden concern over his personal discernment. He read the address on the note. *That's new condominiums on the edge of town.*

"Seriously, Boss," Denise continued. "I don't know if you should take a chance with her."

"Since when have you been so judmental of my personal decisions?"

"Since you had someone you might want to keep."

Had would be the magic word here. "Like you know a helluvalot about keeping someone anyway."

Immediately Denise's face fell and she set her jaw. "For your information, Phillip Ralston, I have kept a relationship for the better part of thirteen years. Just because I don't have a ring on my finger doesn't mean I don't know how to hang on to what I have!"

She's right. J.P. felt a sting deep inside. *She's been with Jerry far longer than I've ever been with any given woman.*

Denise turned abruptly to leave the room.

"I'm sorry." J.P. found himself apologizing, which felt terribly out of character. "I shouldn't have said that."

Denise stopped in her tracks. "You're right, you shouldn't have." She turned around briefly. "I think, if you're finished with me for the day, I'll go on home."

Maybe I should take the night off and just go home too. J.P. sat down in his chair and put his head in his hands.

"I'll see you Monday." Denise closed the door to his office.

J.P. shifted the files on his desk from one side to the other. *Hughes, Mid-America, Sparky . . . Shit. I don't even know what information Sparky called in about . . . Derek's casework for review . . .*

There was a lot to be done. He could work all night and still not be finished. *But I'm certainly finished with one thing. Samira.* J.P. leaned back in his chair. *And maybe with Denise if I don't watch it.* The attorney loosened his tie. Chances of her getting Jefferey Hughes on the line for him now were very slim. *I really should have talked to him before business closed today.*

A bell rang announcing someone's arrival through the front door. *Or Denise's departure.* Either way J.P. had to check. He opened the door to an empty office. The computer was shut down and the coffee maker was off for the weekend. Denise's desk was cleared in a very permanent kind of way. *Even Derek's desk is less scattered than usual.* J.P. sat down in a winged chair in the waiting area and put his feet on the chair across from him.

James isn't even at the house waiting for me to get home. Football practice had started in Harrisonburg. James had decided to try living with his mother and Bruce so he could play ball with Josh. *I won't see either one of the boys before Labor Day weekend now.*

Several minutes passed. And then a full hour went by. There was nothing motivating J.P. to go home. *And there's not much motivating me to go back to work either.* When he finally did go back to his desk the pile of folders turned his stomach.

You need to eat, Ralston. But eating at the club alone again wasn't appealing and fixing something at home had even less pull. J.P. opened a desk drawer and began to file the folders in the proper places for the night. The yellow sticky note on the edge of his desk caught his eye.

That's a possibility. J.P. filed his last folder under the *Hughes Corporation. I really don't feel like socializing, but Denise said it included dinner.* J.P. read the location again. It seemed innocent enough. *And it could be a good way to feel out some agents on a price for the Mid-America property.*

The attorney rethought his decision. *But then again, if Denise is right, you could end up in a compromising position.* He unrolled his cuffs and fastened the buttons. *On the other hand, what are you compromising at this point in time? Everything you hoped for walked away at Shoal Creek.*

He selected a sports coat from the armoire next to the bathroom door. *I'll drive over and check out the party and then go home.*

J.P. turned the key in the lock as he left the building. *If I can score dinner and a base figure for Mid-America's property in the same sitting, then I'm one up on the never-ending to-do list on my desk.*

Suddenly J.P. wished he were headed to Samira's for dinner around her table with Krissy and Kara. *But dinner wouldn't be enough.* J.P. felt his world fading into black and white again. *If I'm not supposed to win her, then what do I have to work for?* He unlocked the door to his truck. *Give it up, Counselor. You're not going to figure her out.*

The decision was made. *Let's see what's on Jessica Hutchison's agenda.*

47

The Cry of the Heart

The atrium of city hall was a buzz of activity as the final preparations were being made for the fundraiser auction. *Promote literacy.* Samira straightened the sign. *A few more hours and this event is a done deal.*

The library board sponsored this auction at the end of every summer. Throughout the year, local artists and artists in residence donated their work. Samira surveyed the artwork. *Good quality and excellent selection.*

"Everything looks great, Sis." Wes nodded his approval. "Is that statue on the pedestal supposed to be you?"

Samira glanced at the Fabiano's work, now covered with a bronze finish. "You have to ask?"

"No, it looks like you." Wes chewed on his bottom lip a moment. "Did you pose for him like that?"

"What do you mean like *that?*" *Just say it Wes.*

"Well," Wes raised his eyebrows. "Without anything on."

Samira avoided eye contact. "No!" *I suppose everyone is going to think that.* "I posed in that position with my clothes on. Fabiano imagined the rest."

Wes shook his shoulders uncomfortably. "What did the folks think?"

"They didn't comment one way or another." *It's just art, and he never saw me naked.* At first it had seemed like a great idea. *But I agreed under the influence of some very powerful wine.*

"The auctioneer just arrived," Daphne informed her supervisor.

"I'll be right over."

"I'll let you get back to work," Wes offered.

"Are you staying?"

425

Wes's eyes traveled toward the front doors of the building. "Yeah, I'm staying. Pam will be here in a few minutes with the kids. We'll keep Kara and Krissy with us until it's over."

At least I won't have to worry about where my girls are the whole time.

This is a much larger crowd than I remember from a year ago. The atrium was beginning to fill with people holding bidding numbers. Some had taken seats in the rows of chairs while others stood. An air of anticipation permeated the room.

Jim appeared at Samira's side. "Everything is ready, Miss Samira. Can I get you anything? A cup of coffee maybe?"

Samira's anxiety level was higher than usual. *It must be my adrenalin.* "How about a cappuccino, Jim?"

"A cappuccino it is." He turned toward the coffee vendor along the back wall.

Samira checked her watch and gave a nod to the board president. *I'm glad she's the mistress of ceremonies.* It was time for the auction to begin. *That's one job I would not want.* Introductions were made and credit was given to the appropriate parties. When Samira's name was mentioned the head librarian felt her face turn completely red. *I wouldn't mind if they'd just leave my name out of the program.* She covered her cheek with her hand.

"For you, Miss Samira." Jim returned with a styro-foam cup steaming with rich cappuccino. "Great crowd tonight."

The Café Ole. The logo on the cup caught Samira off guard.

"Is everything alright?" Jim looked concerned.

"Oh, yes, fine, thank you." She turned the cup in her hand. *Where in the world did he get this?* "It takes a huge team effort . . ."

"With a diligent leader." Jim tipped his cap to the librarian. "I'll be in the back if you need me."

I couldn't do this event without him. Samira listened to a detailed description of the first item. *Here we go.* The auctioneer cried out the first call. *I didn't realize the Café Ole won the bid to set up shop here tonight.* Samira took a sip of the hot beverage.

Across the way Samira could see her parents standing with Wes and Pam. *Krissy and Kara probably aren't too far away.* As usual, Pam had the little girls dressed to the hilt. *If there is one thing Pam loves, it's social outings.* That thought led Samira to another one. *Pam would have loved the high society party in Springfield.* She forced her mind back to the auction.

Time passed as the auctioneer cried on. Charcoal drawings, paintings, pottery, weaving . . . every kind of medium was for sale. A spotlight illuminated a table lamp accentuated with a leaded glass shade. Samira listened and watched as inconspicuous bidders pushed the dollar amount past a thousand dollars.

"Excuse me, ma'am?"

Samira turned and faced Mike Benson.

" . . . I understand this is your gig."

"Hello, Mr. Benson." *My gig? Mike has such a way with words.*

"Hello, Samira." Mike stood tall. "What exactly are we raising money for today?" The tall attorney whispered over the auctioneer as his eyes studied the crowd.

"Sold!"

Samira's eyes landed across the way on her brother. He was tucking something inside his jacket. *Surely he didn't pay that much for the lamp!* She remembered the question. "We're raising financial support for the literacy program to aide underprivileged children."

"Impressive," Mike nodded slowly. His eyes moved from the crowd back to Samira. "You bring in a wide array of Joplin society."

I'm not the one who brings them in. Samira looked away. "It's the quality of the artwork that brings the crowd."

"But every show needs a professional at the top."

And Mike Benson is a professional flatterer. Samira tucked a loose strand of hair behind her ear. *I'm really not in the mood for chit chat.* "What brings you to the art auction, Mr. Benson?"

Mike grinned. "Nothing. I've been in court and just stopped here to pick up some paperwork. Seems I happened upon this grand gala by accident."

"You should look around, maybe there's something here for your office." Samira half listened as the next item for sale was described in great detail through the speaker overhead.

"I thought about that." Mike squinted his eyes. "There's only one piece here that interests me."

Samira felt the lead. *But I am not going to give him the satisfaction of taking the bait.*

Mike crossed his arms over his designer suit. "Right there in the middle. Can you see it?" He nodded his head carefully. "That bronzed statue caught my eye."

I'm sure it's just a coincidence. Samira caught her breath. *There's no way he could know it's a replica of me.*

"There's rumor that the artist in residence just finished that piece." Mike's eyes were alive with energy.

"Last week." *Saturday evening.*

"He's good. I like his other pieces too but that one is different."

It's bronzed, unlike the others. Samira shifted her weight uncomfortably. She really didn't want to talk about it. *Not with Mike Benson.*

"It's almost as if . . . I don't know . . ." Mike's voice trailed off in thought. "Like Uberti captured a broken heart."

Surprised first that Mike used Fabiano's last name and secondly that he read right into her, Samira put her hand to her face. She tried to remember if she'd talked to Kelly Davis about modeling for Fabiano. *I didn't, but that doesn't mean Krissy didn't. I wonder how long Mike was in the atrium before making his presence known to me?*

"At any rate, it's a really nice work of art," Mike summarized. His quiet tone shifted gears. "So how are you, Samira?"

Totally taken aback by his candor, Samira closed her eyes.

"I was sorry to hear . . . well . . . that things went the way they did . . ."

So how long has it been since Mike talked to Phil anyway? It's only been a few weeks.

" . . . You look good."

I always do. I have to. Samira straightened her back. *It's my job to put up a front and look good, at least on the outside. Everyone expects me to be strong and happy . . .* "Thank you," Samira whispered as the auctioneer announced the sale of an oil canvas.

"Our mutual friend would be jealous of this little meeting."

Probably not anymore. "That's funny . . ." Samira decided to play the game. "I've never known Kelly to be the jealous type."

Mike pointed his finger at Samira. His face was more serious than she'd expected. "Me neither," he agreed with a long gaze into her eyes. "I was thinking of the other mutual friend."

"How is he?" *I can't even say his name.*

Mike hesitated. *He doesn't know what to say either.*

"Overworked and taking life way too seriously." Mike wiggled his eyebrows playfully. Then his face got serious again. "He's taking the boys to meet Bobby at the ranch over Labor Day weekend. A little R & R won't hurt him."

Samira had to look away. *Why would Mike bring Bobbie into this conversation?*

"He'd probably rather be in different company given the opportunity . . ."

Does he always need company? Samira crossed her arms against her now knotted stomach. "Then it's good he can get away from work for a few days." *Maybe he should stay away.*

Mike puckered his bushy moustache. His eyes were fixed on Samira.

I am not going to give him the satisfaction of eye contact.

"I guess if I'm going to be a serious bidder I need to register."

Samira could feel some tension building. "The registrar is at that booth by the coffee vendor." *But I doubt he'll follow through with a purchase.*

"Thanks," Mike nodded but he didn't move in that direction. "It's good to see you, Samira."

She didn't respond because she couldn't swallow the lump that had formed in her throat.

"Take care of yourself." Mike turned to go but took one last glance in Samira's direction as he made his departure.

The next item went up for bid. A set of colorful, oversized ceramic pots drew hushed exclamations from the crowd. *How am I supposed to take care of myself when every thought trips back to the man who is now taking Bobbie to the ranch?* Samira looked back over her shoulder, but Mike was gone. Across the way she could see his tall frame weaving in and out of the bidders. *Good he's leaving.*

A sudden sadness consumed Samira. *It took me all week to muster up a positive front.* But deep down her heart was still empty. Samira worked her way to the opposite side of the atrium. All of the chairs were taken and a large swarm of onlookers lined the back of the bidding area. *How is it I always end up feeling so alone in a crowd?* She stood in the middle of the most populated area.

A large spray of dried flowers sold for a hundred dollar bill. A black and white photo of a park bench at City Park brought fifty. An origami mobile auctioned for seventy-five.

"Things are selling so high!" Susan Olinger pushed her way through to Samira's side between items. "I can't believe someone would actually pay seventy-five dollars for a little mobile like that!" The woman's blonde hair bobbed against her shoulders. "But it's all for a good cause I guess." Susan applauded with the crowd when another small item sold.

Susan is always so critical, but I know she's here to support me.

"Samira," Susan whispered. She wiggled her finger for Samira to bend down to listen. Samira bent her neck slightly. "When I came in I saw Sam's golf partner here. The one who took you home that one time."

Samira straightened back up. *I know.* She didn't need Susan's meddling today. *Especially with Mike Benson.*

"He was over there." Susan pointed across the room. Samira grabbed Susan's arm to keep her from placing an illegal bid. A man standing next to them showed signs of annoyance. *It is always hard to keep Susan under control.*

"Here," Susan reached up and patted the bun at the back of Samira's hair. "You should freshen up a bit in case he sees you." The next thing Samira knew Susan was handing her a tube of lipstick and a mirror. *Susan! Stop it!*

"Just wait here," Susan instructed. "I'll see if I can find him."

He's long gone by now. But she can knock herself out looking for him.

The auctioneer was nearing the end of the sale. Only Fabiano's sculptures remained. Samira listened intently as the first item was described. She'd given her father firm instructions. Of the two pieces for sale, this was the one she wanted. *It reminds me of Aunt Maggie . . . who isn't even my aunt.* It was the one of the old woman in the swing. *I told Daddy no more than two hundred dollars. This can be my contribution to the reading program for the year.*

The auctioneer started the bids at seventy-five dollars, instantly shattering Samira's hope of securing this sculpture. Immediately it soared to three hundred and topped out at three-hundred and fifty dollars. Samira couldn't see her father from where she was standing and she was glad of that. *If he even gets a glimpse of my face he'll know I'm disappointed.*

Samira tried to console herself. *Some things just aren't meant to be. Maybe I'm not supposed to keep anything of Fabiano's around.* She challenged her personal motive for wanting one of the sculptures in the first place. *The less I think of his seductive initiation, the sooner I can move on.*

But standing there in the middle of that throng of people, Samira suddenly felt totally and completely alone. The applause at the close of that item reverberated loudly in her mind.

A firm hand gripped Samira's shoulder. *Thank God for Weston!* It was a hand that read her thoughts from afar and come to stand by her as the final sculptures were auctioned off.

The mistress of ceremonies described a finished Uberti figurine of a little boy with his fishing pole. Once again hushed approval rose above the crowd. Bidding began again.

Without permission Samira leaned into her brother's side. He tightened his hug. The terra cotta fisherman sold for four hundred dollars. People around Samira gasped.

"How'd you book Uberti?"

"I called his booking agent," Samira answered honestly. "His work was in an advertisement for an international art show in Springfield. I just dialed the number."

The final item up for bid was the bronzed statue of the woman. Again the crowd responded enthusiastically. Unable to stand the tension, Samira put her hands to her mouth. She felt Wes reach for his inside suit pocket for his bidding number.

"No, don't."

"Dad told me to."

"I don't want you to."

"But you're not Dad."

"I don't want him to either."

"He can't. He's outside entertaining Lizzie and Bonnie . . ."

Samira could feel panic in her chest. She didn't want to draw attention to herself or anyone in her family. *I want someone to buy my sculpture and take it far away where I won't be reminded of Fabiano's all too honest look into my emotions.*

The description stopped and suddenly the auctioneer was crying out in fifty dollar increments. Wes listened and watched but didn't enter a bid until the two-hundred fifty dollar cry.

"Wes, please!" Samira grabbed his bidding arm. *Dear God, please don't let him buy that statue!*

There must have been something urgent in her plea because Wes took his eyes off the auctioneer and looked down into his sister's eyes. Samira moved her head slowly from side to side. Wes let the next several bids go by without taking his eyes off his sister. Finally he put his number back inside his coat.

Thank you. Samira breathed a sigh of relief. Wes put his arm around her again. *I just want to be invisible.*

The auctioneer's cries continued to climb until they were well over the thousand dollar mark. Buyers were starting to hesitate and others were dropping out all together.

This is amazing!

"Dad's max was a thousand," Wes whispered in Samira's ear.

At least it wasn't me that prevented Daddy from getting his prized piece. At the same time she was in shock that the bid was still being raised.

The auctioneer slowed the rhythm of his cry as two lone bidders rose to the occasion. Samira could feel Wes's fingertips grip her shoulder. *He's nervous too.*

Everyone had stepped back away from the sculpture now. Only two men remained active.

"Who are they?" Samira asked her brother.

"The one on the left owns a gallery in Springfield. He's purchased several items today. I don't recognize the other."

The crowd gasped when the auctioneer reached two thousand dollars. Neither bidder seemed ready to back away. The gallery owner nodded his head to raise a hundred dollars, but before the other man could respond a single voice rang out from the crowd.

"I bid three thousand dollars."

Samira turned her head toward the voice.

Every person in the room seemed to catch their breath simultaneously. Even Weston stared in disbelief.

The auctioneer paused his cry until he had confirmation of a legitimate bid.

"The bid stands at three thousand dollars." the auctioneer offered the two remaining bidders a chance to raise again.

"Who is it?" Samira whispered to her brother.

Wes shook his head. "I can't tell."

"Going once . . . going twice . . ." Samira closed her eyes. *We have never sold a single piece for that much. Ever!*

"Sold! Three thousand dollars buys Uberti's latest work."

The auctioneer's gavel echoed into the microphone. Thunderous applause filled the atrium.

Unbelievable!

The crowd began to disperse but Samira remained frozen in her tracks. She suddenly needed to know who purchased her sculpture.

Wes frowned. "Are you alright, Sis?"

She nodded, unable to explain.

"That's a lot of money for one piece of art," someone exclaimed as they walked past. The library board president stopped and congratulated Samira by shaking both hands at once. Other well-wishers congratulated her too. But she couldn't concentrate. *I still need to know who purchased the bronze statue!*

"I'm going to close out," Wes told his sister between congratulatory wishes.

Samira was surprised he had made a purchase. "What did you buy?"

"The leaded lamp," Weston smiled, " . . . for my office."

"You paid over a thousand . . . ."

Wes smiled. "Pam said it was for a good cause."

It is, but oh my goodness!

Samira tried to see who was claiming her piece of art, but so far it was still sitting on the display in the middle of the make-shift gallery. The entire crowd was in motion. Some people were leaving, others were mingling casually, while yet others were in line to finalize their purchases. But no one seemed to be claiming the bronze statue.

It was late into the evening before the crowd thinned completely. As always, Samira stayed until the very last patron was gone before giving the okay for her crew to clean up the display area. The auctioneer and his staff were finalizing the details of the sale as well. The bronze statue still held its place on the pedestal in the middle of the atrium. *It's the only item left unclaimed.* Samira eyed it carefully.

"I must congratulate you, Miss Samira." The auctioneer's voice sounded tired after a long afternoon of crying. "This was a huge success!" He held his hands out in exclamation. "Your reading program should flourish this year!"

Samira thanked the man graciously for his donation of time and energy to the project as well.

"It's the least I can do. You taught my granddaughter to read, remember?"

Samira remembered the shy little girl very well. *She's probably almost ten years old by now!*

"We'll do it again next year." The auctioneer's wife promised as she signed a check for the total amount. "Here you are. Our pleasure."

The check was for several thousand over the previous year's earnings on this event. Samira double checked the amount and made comment about the difference.

"Sheldon Metzger was here from Springfield," one of the staff members began to explain. "He didn't hold anything back. If he wanted a piece, he went home with it."

"There were a couple of other dealers here too."

Samira couldn't resist. *I have to know.* "Who purchased the last Uberti?"

The two staff members exchanged a quick look but neither spoke. The auctioneer nodded his head and smiled slightly. "The final bidder has asked to remain anonymous, Miss Samira."

That's not fair! Suddenly Samira felt like she'd sold her soul to a total stranger. Her heart pounded hard in her chest. "Is that legal?" Samira tried not to sound as alarmed as she felt.

"I'm afraid it is," the auctioneer's wife answered with a sigh. He made that request when he registered so it's very legal."

"We're all finished, Miss Samira." Jim interrupted the moment. "What should we do with the remaining item?"

"The buyer has made arrangements to pick it up at a later time." The auctioneer explained cautiously, as if he sensed Samira's concern. "We'll crate it and keep it under lock and key until that time."

"Very well." Jim seemed pleased. "Then we're going to take the display props back to the museum and be done for the night."

Somehow Samira managed to respond to Jim. She also managed to drive herself to her brother's house where her parents and Krissy and Kara were waiting to congratulate the success of the auction. She even forced her way through follow-up conversations with her family concerning details about the auction. But all the while she fought against the unknown answers in her head.

Who bought my sculpture? And why in heaven's name did Mike Benson torment me so openly about Phil taking Bobbie to the ranch?

Back at her own house, Samira felt the fatigue of the day closing in around her. *It certainly didn't take Phil long to replace me.* Her mind's eye could see the model's body on the cover of the magazine wearing nothing but a skimpy thong. *Or maybe he never really intended to give her up for me in the first place.*

Samira finished the day in her own kitchen. The girls had retired to their rooms even though Samira was sure they were both still awake. She leaned over and peered through the window above her sink. *It looks like Mrs. Barnes has turned in for the night.*

She wiped the counter off. *You already wiped it down.* Samira always cleaned, and cleaned some more when her mind couldn't rest.

Just stop it!

I should have known better than to pose for Fabiano. But how was I supposed to know he could capture my soul in that work? She rinsed the dishrag. Again. *And how was I supposed to know a complete stranger was going to take me home?*

Samira left the light on above the counter and moved into the dining room. She rearranged the flowers in the middle of the table and then straightened the placemats.

And who is Mike Benson to come along and tell me that Phil decided to take Bobbie whatever her name is to the ranch for a long weekend?

She fluffed the pillows on the sofa with a heavy hand. Without hesitation she turned to the coffee table and picked up a magazine the girls had left out of place. *If I've told them once, I've told them a thousand times to put these back when they're finished!* Disgusted with the little bit of clutter, Samira flopped the periodical toward a basket in the corner of the room. The back page caught on the edge and fell to the floor. Samira bent over to put it more securely in its place. An advertisement for the famous lingerie company flashed an announcement for the fall television fashion show back in Samira's face.

Great. So now she's not only plastered in magazines with hardly any clothes on, but she's also strutting her stuff all over a runway for the whole world to see!

Fabiano's sculpture came into mind again. *Oh, who am I to judge?* Samira sat down in the corner of her sofa and pulled her legs to her chin. She wrapped her arms around her ankles. *Whoever took me home in the form of a bronze statue thinks I posed that way for Fabiano Uberti too.* Samira put her forehead on her knees and closed her eyes.

Very slowly a blanket of shame came over Samira. It started out so innocent. *But the more time I spent in position for him, the more his imagination worked through my good intentions.*

And it's not like I didn't know it. Samira covered her entire face with her hands. *I knew exactly what he was doing with me in his mind and I actually found it kind of flattering at the time.* Samira's heart grew heavier with each thought. *And the only reason he wined and dined me at dinner was to gain permission to undress me in the final moments of his stay in Joplin.*

The rhythm of the auctioneer's cry was once again alive in Samira's mind. *No. The reason he wined and dined me was to undress me in real life.* Darkness completely overcame Samira even though there was still a light in the kitchen. *I led him on by going to dinner and then stood him up in the parking lot unsatisfied.* Tears were beginning to dampen Samira's hands. *But he won in the end, didn't he? No matter who took that work of art home, Fabiano got the last word.*

Time passed but Samira didn't move. Images of her statue danced with the model in the magazine, playing tricks on her mind. Even after the tears stopped, the fragmented thoughts still taunted.

Feeling as if she was no longer alone, Samira lifted her face. *Kara.*

"Mama?" Kara approached her mother slowly, as if she could sense the delicate condition of her emotions.

Samira inhaled deeply. She felt numb as she shifted her weight against the sofa cushions. Kara sat down next to her.

"I saw Miss Davis' boyfriend at the auction tonight. He was talking to you."

"His name is Mike Benson . . ."

"Miss Davis says he knows Phil."

"He does." Samira swallowed hard. Neither of her girls had mentioned Phil's name since she'd told them she would no longer be seeing him. *Kara must still be thinking about him too.*

A long silence occupied the space between mother and daughter. Kara finally lifted her feet off the floor and curled into her mother's side. Samira put her arms around Kara's body and pulled her in tight. *Just hold me, darling, okay?* Tears ran down her cheeks as she pressed her face into Kara's silken hair.

"I miss you, Mama."

I miss me too, Samira cried in her heart. *I miss all of me.* She hugged her daughter tightly, hoping Kara's presence could stop the shadows of Phil's image from playing in her mind. *We danced here in this very room.* Samira remembered the candlelight and the music. *Did I lead him on like I did Fabiano?*

Kara didn't move. "Is there anything I can do, Mama?"

The mother shook her head and allowed the tears to fall openly. "No, baby. I think I have to get through this one on my own."

"Krissy and I prayed for you tonight." Kara put both arms around her mother's shoulders.

Samira nodded in approval. *That's the only way I'll ever get through this. He's the only one who can heal this broken heart.* Silent tears soaked Kara's hair.

"Everything's going to be alright," Kara assured with more confidence than her years. "I know it is."

Samira forced her head to move in a nod. "I hope so." *I really hope so.*

48

Old Habits

J.P. parked his truck between a new BMW and a shiny black Mercedes. It was eight o'clock exactly. *Just the way like it—right on time.*

Jessica Hutchison met him at the door wearing a short black skirt and a sleeveless white top that plunged deeply at the chest. *She's more casual than I've seen her in other settings.*

"Mr. J.P. Ralston," Jessica extended her arm into the room. "I'm sure you'll find this evening to your pleasure."

I'm here to observe, learn and leave. J.P. allowed Jessica to take his sports coat. He inventoried the guests as he rolled the cuffs on his shirt. *Mr. and Mrs. Armstrong from Armstrong construction. Clark Roberts, an architect from Springfield. Alan Goldstein from city council.*

"There's a self-serve bar just around the corner," Jessica announced. "Make yourself comfortable until the caterers are ready for dinner."

J.P. poured a glass of wine and helped himself to some crackers and cheese.

"J.P. Good to see you. It's been a long time." Clark Roberts was extending hand.

"That it has." J.P. returned the handshake. "What brings you to Bridges Condominiums tonight?"

"Ms Hutchison is presenting Bridges' proposal for the new condo development on the south side of town."

J.P. frowned. "On the south side? What development ground is available down there?"

"It's a tract overlooking Shoal Creek . . ."

Shoal Creek? J.P.'s mind instantly tripped back to the boardwalk with Samira. His still empty stomach turned uncomfortably.

" . . . At any rate, I'm looking forward to tonight's proposal." Clark Roberts lifted a brandy glass to his lips.

J.P. was caught off guard. "What proposal?"

Clark leaned in closer as if he might have a secret to share. "You must be working for the Hughes Corporation tonight?"

No, sir. I'm working for myself. J.P. forced the thoughts of Samira from his mind and refilled his wine glass. "No, I'm not working for Hughes or anyone else tonight. What kind of proposal are you talking about?"

Clark wrinkled his brow. "Ms Hutchison is laying out the proposal for Shoal Creek tonight. I assumed Hughes sent you here to take notes."

J.P. shook his head. "I'm here because Ms Hutchison invited me to dinner." *That didn't sound right.* Just as quickly as the words were heard, J.P. regretted having said them. "I mean, she thought there would be some kind of benefit for me here tonight."

"Any benefits she has to offer might be worth showing up for." Clark wiggled his eyebrows from behind his glass.

A few months back, that kind of a comment wouldn't have bothered J.P. In fact, it might have even fueled more incentive to pursue extracurricular activities. But tonight the comment toted an unfamiliar sourness. J.P. looked across the room at Jessica. She was very much in control of her party and she was quite easy to look at as well. *Maybe I should change the subject.*

"Clark, what's your relationship with Sean Bridges?"

Clark puckered his lips. "I've never met Sean Bridges. The only contact I have with the company is through Ms Hutchison."

That's interesting. J.P. was beginning to seriously wonder if Sean Bridges actually existed. His eyes took inventory of the guests again. *Tom Jones is in real estate here in town. Mary and Kurt Walters are commercial contractors, two of the best in the business. Richard . . . oh, what is his last name?* J.P. stared at the casually clad businessman across the room. *He's in marketing and sales.*

Jessica tapped a spoon on a water glass. J.P. kept an eye on the guests as they took their seats. *The only player missing in this lineup is an investor.* Jessica patted the chair next to her. *How convenient.*

Introductions were made while the caterers served. *Everyone seems to be aware of Jessica's purpose here tonight except me.* The hostess dropped her napkin. As she leaned over to pick it up, she ran her hand across J.P.'s thigh. A few moments later she took the liberty of brushing her hand over his when she reached for a fork. *If I didn't know better, I'd say she's trying to lead me on.*

The room was getting warm. *Too much wine before dinner, maybe.* The main course conversation flowed without J.P.'s input. He listened and took mental notes. *But nothing seems important.* When the caterers brought dessert, J.P. politely excused himself from the table.

I don't know what I'm doing here. The dinner conversation replayed in his mind. *I don't care what they decide to do with Shoal Creek and care even less about Jessica.* He stepped outside onto an oversized deck. J.P. leaned his hip into the railing. He could see Jessica preparing a presentation board in the sitting area. *If my sports coat wasn't inside, I'd have half a mind to make an early exit.*

Clark Roberts stuck his head outside. "Time for the presentation, J.P. Can I refill your drink?"

I'm driving. "How about half."

J.P. followed the architect back inside. He stood behind the sofa so he could see everyone in the room at once.

"Let's begin with the property itself," Jessica started into her presentation. With the press of a button on the wall, the lights in the room dimmed and an oversized television screen turned from blue to green and then a full-scale audio-visual production began to run.

The video opened with shots of the boardwalk along the creek under the canopy of trees. *I know that area all too well.* The voice on the television chattered on, but J.P.'s mind didn't hear anything. All he could make out was the replay of Samira's parting moment. *She just needed to know if I loved her.* The trees were swaying in the breeze on the screen. *I should have gone after her.* J.P. could still see her disappear over the top of the hill. *I shouldn't have let her go that easily.*

There was a pause in the presentation. Jessica turned the ceiling lights up a notch. "What do you suppose this tract of land would be worth if it were located in the heart of downtown?"

J.P. tuned in. *Here's a piece of information I can use for Mr. Stephenson.*

"How much land are we talking about?" J.P. asked from the back of the room.

Jessica looked doubtingly at him. "If you were paying attention at all . . ."

I wasn't.

" . . . you would know we're talking about 15 acres."

"How much of the land would actually be developed into residential housing?" Kurt Walters, the contractor asked.

"Exactly half." Jessica motioned toward a miniature model of the proposed development sitting on the large coffee table. "The other half would be divided between commercial services and common grounds."

"Seven and a half acres of residential development ground in downtown would run close to a million dollars." Tom Jones, the local real estate agent spoke up. "And the same in commercial could run double."

So five acres of commercial development could bring somewhere around three hundred and fifty.

"But wouldn't commercial development in Shoal Creek pull business away from established local merchants?" The marketing director questioned the motives forthright.

Hayes. That's his last name. J.P. finally remembered. *Richard Hayes.*

Councilman Goldstein put his nose in the air. "It's not our intent . . ."

What's with the 'our' part of the claim?

" . . . to take business away but rather to establish services that might not otherwise be convenient to folks living that far out of the way."

Tom Jones stood up and walked around to the backside of the sofa where J.P. was standing. "Shoal Creek isn't that far out of the way. I don't see why anyone would expect commercial services down there."

Jessica turned the model on the table so the commercial development side was closest to the guests. "We feel strongly that commercial services and conveniences enhance the motivation for sales. When people know they can stop at the dry cleaners or get a quick cup of coffee three blocks from home on their way to or from work, they are more inclined to make a move."

"It also creates a bigger market to bring people in from outside areas," the councilman added.

J.P. drank the last of his wine. *Since when does he know so much about this development? You'd think he'd be more interested in developing something inside the city limits. Let's see what he knows.*

"Where are the city limits in relation to this development?" J.P. walked closer to the model as he spoke.

Jessica Hutchison eyed him warily.

"If the property is within city limits . . ."

"It's not." Clark Roberts spoke up. "When I made the drawings I had to check with city hall for code requirements. Shoal Creek butts up to the city but it's unincorporated."

Jessica wasn't about to let that conversation go any further. "And as a result, the million dollars we could be investing in this caliber of property will run only about half that. That leaves more for commercial development."

If Bridges develops residential and commercial property outside the city limits, then the city gains nothing in taxes or otherwise. J.P. didn't like what he was hearing. *They're trying to market this proposal as if it is in city limits.* He reviewed the recent case facts between Lloyd Hughes' estate and similar taxing issues with the city.

"Don't get the wrong idea, J.P.," Councilman Goldstein attempted to explain. "The city has been trying to incorporate this area for years . . ."

Trying to develop or trying to incorporate it? There are two different motives here.

Hushed discussion began to permeate the room. *Nothing like opening Pandora's box.* Questions flew back and forth about the city's involvement over the proposed development. Jessica and Alan Goldstein replied with well-rehearsed answers. *I'd venture to say that I asked the one question Bridges hoped wouldn't be voiced in this particular company.*

J.P. listened to the discussion as it heated up. The longer he listened the more he wondered exactly what role the councilman was playing. *If the property in question is not within the city limits, then Goldstein shouldn't have any business at this party.*

Mr. and Mrs. Armstrong finally had enough. They excused themselves and explained they would need more information before making a final decision concerning their involvement. Richard Hayes followed quickly behind them.

One by one the guests began to explain their reason for needing to leave. J.P. was ready as well. He reached for his jacket but Jessica Hutchison held his arm.

"If you don't have to rush off . . ."

J.P. ran his free hand through his hair. *Denise warned me about this.*

" . . . I was hoping to give you a guided tour of the premium condominiums." Her hand moved from his arm to his waist. "It won't take too much of your time."

But I'm not in the market for a premium condominium. There was just enough wine left in him that his defenses were low, yet logic screamed at him to decline the invitation.

Jessica turned away as quickly as she'd appeared. Alan Goldstein was at the door. He and Jessica exchanged a few hushed words. J.P. removed his coat from the hanger and pulled it across his shoulders. As he stepped closer to the door, the councilman's glance turned to a definite sneer.

That confirms the hunch I had to not vote for him. Without another word, he passed through the front door onto porch.

"Wait," Jessica Hutchison was close on his heels. "Are you sure you can't stay, J.P.?"

J.P. turned and faced the woman. *She's unbuttoned her shirt further.* Her sultry smile was tempting. *Walk away, Counselor.*

"No." J.P. took a deep breath.

"No you're not sure or 'no' you can't stay."

Both. J.P. looked the woman up and down like he'd done with a thousand women in the past. *She's definitely something I could get interested in.* But she packed a lot of ammunition at the same time. *I don't know her motive. Play by the rules.* J.P. tried to hold firm. *Always know the motive. That was one reason playing with Bobbie Sommers had been so satisfying. I knew the objective up front. Sex. That was it.* J.P. stared at the exposed cleavage. *She's tempting. But she has a hidden motive.*

"No, I can't stay."

Jessica pouted her bottom lip. J.P. looked beyond her at the councilman who was still standing in the door. *The look on his face tells me he's already had her.*

"I'm really sorry," the woman touched the back of her finger to J.P.'s chest. "The master suite is a sight to behold."

I'm sure it is. "Thanks for dinner."

"I'm sorry you didn't want dessert." Jessica was still touching him.

The sound of high heels clicked behind him on the sidewalk. Jessica's eyes suddenly turned from flirtation to concern. J.P. turned to see who was coming. The woman on the sidewalk was digging in her purse. She looked up into J.P.'s face.

It looks like the chic from Mid-America.

"Excuse me." The woman continued along the way. Councilman Goldstein wrapped his arm around her shoulders the moment she stepped onto the porch. The door, which had been standing open up to this point, closed with a solid thud.

Now that's interesting. J.P. wished the woman would turn around so he could see her face through the window. *Maybe I should stick around.*

Jessica seemed to be reading his thought. "Maybe another time then." Without offering anything more, she crossed the porch and went inside. A few seconds later the outside lights clicked off.

So much for dessert. J.P. stood on the dark sidewalk only a moment longer. He knew the supposed identity of that woman. *She says she's Celia Monroe.* And he knew Jessica Hutchison still had to prove that Sean Bridges existed. *But I'm beginning to doubt his existence more all the time.*

Now the attorney wished he'd have settled for only a single glass of wine. *It's hard to keep all these details straight.* He started to walk to his truck, which was the only vehicle in the main parking lot now. *Obviously Goldstein and Jessica are working this Shoal Creek deal together somehow.* He climbed into the driver's seat. *And now I know Celia Monroe is connected to them as well.* J.P. turned the key in the ignition. *What I don't know is what my role was at this party.*

The attorney reviewed the silent communications he'd observed between Jessica and Alan Goldstein. *Hutchison wanted me there for reasons beyond sex, because there's no doubt in my mind she was going to get that from Goldstein no matter if I stuck around or not.*

J.P. drove out of the condominium complex back into the city. *I wonder if Goldstein's high society wife knows where he is and who he's with tonight.* The attorney was only a few blocks from his office. *So what was her purpose inviting me into that circle?*

It was late, but not too late. J.P. weighed his options. *I could go on home or I could go back to the office.* But he wasn't tired and he didn't feel like working anymore. J.P. checked the clock on the dashboard. *And Mike's probably not alone.*

Old habits were tempting. J.P. parked his truck in the lot behind Jimmy's Bar. He left his suit coat behind and entered the familiar pub from the rear entrance just like he'd done a thousand times before.

"J.P., ol' buddy!" Jimmy called from behind the bar. "I haven't seen you in months!" The experienced bartender slapped a napkin down in front of a barstool. "You drinkin' the usual?"

"Make it a double," J.P. slid onto a stool. The air was thick with smoke and the crowd around the pool table was rowdy.

Jimmy filled a bar glass with expertise. "What's been keepin' you away, partner?"

I can always count on Jimmy for decent counsel. "A pretty lady."

Jimmy spun his head around toward the back door. "I don't see her taggin' along. Where'ya leave her?"

J.P. sipped his drink but didn't answer. *I wish it were that simple.*

"Or did she leave you?" Jimmy crossed his arms and leaned his big black body back on his heels. His bald head glistened with sweat.

"Something like that."

"So what, we're talkin' three months? Maybe four since you've graced my establishment?"

"Somewhere in there." J.P. took another drink.

Jimmy shrugged his shoulders and snapped a bar towel in J.P.'s direction. "Not bad, J.P. Considering your record, I'd say that's one of the longest stints you've done in awhile." Jimmy threw his head back in laughter. "Drink up, counselor. There's more where that one came from."

J.P. knew Jimmy was talking about the drink. *But chances of finding another woman like Samira is slim to none.* What used to be friendly counsel felt more like a hit below the belt. Before J.P. finished his drink, Jimmy had another ready.

"Look over there." Jimmy took the empty glass and nodded his head toward the pool table. "See that brunette? A free drink says you can take her home."

J.P. shook his head.

Jimmy nodded excitedly. "Then two free drinks says she can take you home." He slapped his hands against the solid wood of the bar. "And three says that by morning she'll make you forget all about that pretty little lady on your mind."

The whiskey was beginning to take affect. J.P. turned on the stool and looked at the brunette playing pool.

"The only way to forget that pretty lady is to get back on the pony and ride," Jimmy counseled with a glint in his eye.

"She alone?"

"She is now. The guy she came with left with someone else over an hour ago."

Jimmy knows a good setup when he sees it. The attorney glanced around the crowded room. No one looked familiar, which was just the way he liked it. *But then again, nothing looks familiar anymore.*

Several shots later J.P. moved to a stool closer to the pool table. It didn't take long for the friendly brunette to make her move. Within the hour Jimmy gave a thumbs up. J.P. followed the woman out the front door to her car.

She talked to him all the way to the hotel. *I have no idea what she's talking about.* He gave her cash to pay for the room and waited until she came back with the key.

J.P. didn't remember actually going inside the room. What he did remember was her coming out of the bathroom wearing only a garter belt and stockings. *I don't even know her name.* The woman straddled his body on the bed and started to unbutton his shirt. Her face was deep into his stomach before he felt a sudden impulse to make her stop.

Confused by the alcohol as much as his own emotions, J.P. excused himself to the bathroom. He closed the door and leaned against it with all his body weight. *What the hell is wrong with you, Ralston?*

The voices inside his head were as vague as the reflection in the mirror. Jessica Hutchison's face flashed through his mind. Then Bobbie Sommers. And then Samira's. J.P. closed his eyes tight to make the images go away. *Any other time it wouldn't matter who was climbing on board.* He buried his face in his hands. *But tonight it matters and I don't know why!*

A sharp knock against the door startled J.P.

"Are you okay in there?"

Shit Ralston, you don't even know where you are! "Yeah, in a minute." *Does she have a name?* J.P. ran cold water into his hands and rinsed his face. *Of course she has a name. Everybody has a name.* He pressed his face into a dry towel. When he looked up he was eye to eye with his own soul.

Fatigue and confusion looked back at J.P. Ralston. He stared at the blank look. His father's steel blue eyes reflected a loneliness that he'd never allowed himself to claim. But tonight there was proof of that loneliness in the mirror. *Samira!* Very slowly he realized exactly what he'd let walk away. *Dear God, I didn't want her to walk away!* Very slowly he realized how much it really hurt to let her go.

"Mister! I have a surprise for you out here!"

I still don't know who she is, but I know she's annoying.

J.P. opened the door to the waiting woman. She was still topless, laying on her side on the bed. When he stepped into the room she sprang to where he was standing and wrapped her arms around his neck.

"I didn't think you were ever going to come out of there." Her lips touched J.P.'s neck.

Disgusted, J.P. pulled away. She moved with him. *Just give me some space, woman!* Finally he unlocked her hands from behind his neck and backed away. He picked up her shirt.

"Here . . ." J.P. struggled to find words as much as he struggled to keep his footing. The entire room was swimming around his head by now.

"Oh, you don't have to do that," the woman assured. "I'm good for whatever you want. And I won't tell a soul."

J.P. shook his head as he put his hand to his throbbing temple. "I'm not in any kind of shape for this." As much as he tried to control his speech, he could still hear the words running together.

The woman took her shirt but she didn't put it on. Instead she pushed her chest into his. "But I am, so you don't have to be."

"Look, this was a mistake." *My whole damned life is a mistake.* "You're going to have to leave."

Much to J.P.'s relief, the woman backed away slightly. But the relief was only temporary, for the next thing he knew her hand slapped into the side of his face.

What'd she do that for? J.P. closed his eyes against the sting on his skin. *I gave her permission to leave.*

In an instant the woman was behind the closed bathroom door. J.P. didn't care where she was as long as she wasn't against him. *I just need her to go away.* He sat down on the desk chair and put his head between his knees. He could hear the fast rhythm of the woman's voice behind the door. *I don't give a shit what she's saying, I just want her to go away.*

She emerged fully dressed with a cell phone stuck to her ear. She didn't speak to J.P. and he didn't offer any words to her either. She simply marched through the room and made a swift exit, all the while talking into her telephone.

"Good." J.P. tried to stand up. "Whoever she is, she's gone."

He started for the door, but his stomach had other plans. The next thing he knew he was hanging over the toilet.

J.P. awoke on a bed that wasn't his own and in a room he didn't recognize. He tried to get up but his head hurt to bad to move. He held his wrist over his eyes to check the time. Through blurred vision he finally decided it was around four o'clock. *Four in the morning? Or four in the afternoon?* J.P. forced himself onto his stomach and closed his eyes again.

49

Charades

Krissy dropped her backpack onto the dining room table with a loud thud. "Homework! I can't believe it! It's only the first week of school and I'm loaded!" She wrinkled her freckled nose. "English, math, AND reading!"

Math. Samira wasn't looking forward to Krissy's math homework. *Last year was hard enough, even with Kara's help.*

"I need you to sign on the line so I can play volleyball." Kara smoothed a piece of paper flat against the table.

"Do you need a physical in order to play sports again this year?" Samira signed her name in blue ink.

"The clinic is holding them next week."

"When does practice start?"

"Monday." Kara unpacked the rest of her bag. "And speaking of Saturday, are we doing anything?"

"Were we speaking of Saturday?"

"I guess not." Kara clarified. "But I was *thinking* about Saturday."

Samira watched her daughter break into a bright smile. *She's growing up all too fast.*

" . . . maybe I could go to the movies Saturday night?"

"And let's see if I can guess who else will be there . . ." Krissy interjected. "Could it be, Aaron Taylor?"

Kara's instant blush gave away the answer.

So much for Ryan Parkison. Samira sighed. *No matter how hard I try, I won't be able to keep the boys from calling.*

Krissy sprang from her chair when the phone rang. "I'll get it!"

"So, can I?" Kara's face was expectant.

How can I deny that smile? "I suppose."

Kara pantomimed a silent YES!

"It's for you, Kara! Guess whoooooo . . ."

Without hesitation, Kara swiped the phone from her sister and disappeared into her bedroom.

"Boys!" Krissy opened the refrigerator. "Who needs them?"

That won't last much longer. Samira carried a pile of clean laundry to her bedroom. *Boys. Who needs them?* She passed by Tom's picture on the cedar chest. *Me. I guess.* No matter how hard she'd tried to forget the feelings she had for Phil, they just weren't going away. *They're not even beginning to fade.*

Samira fingered Tom's rings as she passed by the ribbons hanging on the wall. *Still. I think I'm more inclined to being married than to being a single mom. I just talked myself out of it for a while.* She took off her skirt and hung it on a hanger. *But that doesn't mean I'm going to go searching for another right away either.* She took off her pantyhose and put them in the hamper. *It's not like I was even looking before. He just happened into the library and I fell for his invitation for a cup of coffee.* Samira unbuttoned her shirt and added it to the dirty laundry too. She felt a smile curl her lips. *A cup of coffee he didn't even drink.*

A knock at the bedroom door interrupted Samira's thoughts. "Mama? Miss Davis is here."

Kelly Davis? "I'll be right out." *That's interesting.* Samira dressed quickly. *I wonder what's on her mind.*

"Sorry I didn't call first," Kelly apologized right away. She was leaning over the newspaper on the dining room table.

Samira waved her hand. "You don't have to call before coming to my house! What can I get you? Lemonade? Tea?"

"Lemonade would be great."

"How was your first week of school?" Samira asked the question as she prepared two tall glasses of cold lemonade.

"Full!" Kelly smiled. "But we're off to a good start. I love my summers, but I love teaching too. I missed the kids."

Samira motioned toward the sunroom. Kelly took a seat in the rattan loveseat and pulled one leg up underneath. "How are you, Samira?"

"I'm good." Samira used her rehearsed response. "I'm glad for the school routine too." She took a drink. "But I can't say I miss the kids! It's nice having the library back after the summer programs." *Especially after Fabiano!*

Kelly's green eyes danced. She set the glass down on the end table and rewrapped her bulging curls back into a bun. "You do well to run as many programs as you do, Samira. And the paper reported that the art sale was a huge success a few weeks ago. You should feel good about that."

I do. Kind of. Samira simply nodded at the compliment. *I still don't know who bought my statue.*

"I was out of town that week," Kelly informed without being asked. "But Mike was there. He found it to be exceptionally well organized."

Mike Benson. "We talked briefly."

Kelly was watching her carefully. "So how are you really?"

Samira forced a smile, but she couldn't meet Kelly's eyes. "I am good, but . . ." *How do I express my thoughts without sounding pathetic?* " . . . but it hasn't exactly been easy."

Kelly's voice softened. "I'm really sorry, Samira. I know you might have liked things to work out differently."

Samira shrugged. "Maybe. But then again, you know, maybe it's all for the best this way." She glanced over her shoulder toward the living room. "Relationships take a lot of energy. As it is I can focus more on the girls now." *Even though they don't seem to be needing me as much as they used to.* "Kara signed up for volleyball so that means weaving in another schedule."

"I thought Kara might want to play junior varsity this year. I know she had a lot of fun last year."

I wonder why Kelly is really here? "I'm still getting used to the idea that she's really in high school!" Samira shook her head. *It seems like only yesterday that they were babies!*

Kelly smiled quietly but didn't offer any further comment.

"What about you?" Samira dismissed the melancholy moment. "Obviously you're still seeing Mike Benson."

Suddenly Kelly leaned forward and put her elbows on her knee. "I am. He's so much more fun than Brian Wilson!"

Samira had to agree. *The science teacher never seemed like Kelly's type.*

"He's funny and he's spontaneous and yet he's really caring too." Kelly's eyes widened as she grinned. "And so far he's remained very loosely attached, which gives me a lot of freedom. He comes and goes as he pleases and I do the same. But we have a really good time when we're together." Kelly leaned back again. "I like it this way."

Samira had to appreciate Kelly's honesty. *More straightforward than I could ever be.* "Any future plans tucked away in there?"

With that question, Kelly burst into melodic laughter. "I'm playing racket ball with him in the morning and golfing with him on Sunday. If I don't beat Mike too badly at his own games, I expect I might get dinner out of at least one of those outings." Kelly laughed again. "That's about as far as the future goes right now."

But don't you wish for more? Samira didn't understand Kelly's lack of long-term thinking. *She's just a year younger than me! I'd think she'd want to know what's in store beyond Sunday afternoon.* "Mike seems like a really great companion."

"Mike is a really good friend." Her voice became more serious. "He's loyal to a fault." She poked her finger at an ice cube in the lemonade. "Once he's attached, Mike has a hard time letting go." Kelly's eyes passed over Samira's. "And, to be perfectly honest, he sent me here today to check on you."

"Me?" *Why would he do that?* Samira was stunned. "Why me?"

"Because he's worried about you." Kelly unfolded her legs. "And to be honest, so am I." She licked her lips. "I just haven't seen you out and about lately. Not even at church . . ."

"I don't really even know Mike . . ."

"I know." Kelly was watching Samira closely. "But Mike has this knack for feeling people out and I think he's right that you're really . . . well, how do I say this? I just know that you must be hurting still, that's all."

"I've been over to my parents' church a couple of times recently . . ."

"It's okay, Samira. You don't have to explain."

Several moments of silence separated them. *What am I supposed to say now?* Samira sipped her drink.

Kelly knitted her brow. "You know, I've met J.P. a couple of times now. In fact, I've even taken a few days of dog duty when both he and Mike had to leave town on business . . ."

"You took care of Chase?"

"Afraid so. Long story." Kelly put her hands over her knees. "For being a lawyer, he doesn't communicate his thoughts completely. At least not his personal thoughts. I think he is probably highly effective in the court room, but he puts up a huge front when it comes to his personal territory."

Samira listened carefully. *If there's a point here, I don't want to miss it.*

Kelly shrugged her shoulders. "For what it's worth, and I don't want to sound petty or anything like that, but I just think . . ."

"Mama?" Krissy stepped through the French doors into the sunroom. "Mrs. Barnes wants to know if you can take her to the store tonight."

Can't it wait? Agitated at the interruption, Samira turned to face her daughter. "Is she here?"

"No, she just hollered across the street." Krissy grinned. "I told her yes."

"Then why are you asking me?"

"Because I thought you should know."

Of course I'll take Mrs. Barnes to the store. I'm so good at taking care of everyone else's needs . . . Samira half listened as Krissy babbled on with Miss Davis about a few school issues before disappearing back around the corner.

Kelly smiled. "Believe it or not, Samira, I miss Krissy when I don't see her all the time."

"That's very kind of you . . ."

"Well, it's a true statement. She makes me think and she makes me laugh all at the same time." Kelly finished the lemonade. "But, as I was saying about J.P . . ."

Phil. J.P. Samira thought about his names. Mr. Ralston. Why did he introduce himself to me as Phil, yet Kelly knows him through his best friend as J.P.?

" . . . what he said to you and what he meant might have been two different things." Kelly looked confused for a minute. "I mean, I don't know how things actually ended with you two, but the little I've been around him the more I'm inclined to believe that J.P. thought he was making the best decision when in reality he wasn't."

Samira put her hand to her head. *I don't know exactly where Kelly is headed with this conversation, but I'm not in any position to renew hope in whatever I had with Phil.*

"For whatever it's worth, Samira, I know through Mike, and Mike has a really good sense for things like this—especially with J.P., I know he didn't mean to hurt you."

I know that. I've known that all along. He was setting me free so his life issues wouldn't interfere with me. He was letting me go to separate me from his past. He watched me walk away so he didn't have to wonder if I'd stop loving him at some point in the future . . .

"And I'm sure that I have probably not communicated very clearly myself, but I'm still really sorry things didn't work out." Kelly's eyes were sincerely apologetic.

Samira appreciated Kelly's efforts, even if the words didn't help take the hurt away. *But it hasn't helped the emptiness in my heart.*

"I wish there was something more I could do."

"Me too." Samira sighed. "But that's okay. This is something I have to get through on my own."

Kelly started to say something and then hesitated. "Well . . . I'm already out here on a limb," she admitted. "And you can tell me to shut up at anytime, but your last statement might be completely wrong . . ."

Samira opened her eyes wide. Then she frowned.

" . . . I disagree. I don't think you have to work through these kinds of things on your own. I think if you'd just let someone else share in your pain you'd find out that you might heal a lot quicker." Kelly squished her face together, obviously afraid she'd said too much.

Samira wanted to walk away, but she couldn't. *Kelly is a guest in my home. I have to treat her with respect.* But at the same time, Samira strongly disagreed.

She'd always held back sharing her personal struggles with anyone. *I'm a strong woman.* She'd come through a lot already. *And I will get through this too.*

Somehow Samira finished the conversation with Kelly. And a little while later she managed to take Mrs. Barnes to the grocery store and back. After supper she retired to her garden while the girls entertained themselves with friends on the telephone. The summer vines needed trimmed back and it was time to clear away the dying branches of the rose bushes.

Samira worked diligently. Dusk was fast approaching and she'd really hoped to be finished in this area of the yard before the weekend. *But then again, I don't know what the hurry is. It's not like you have anything going on over the holiday weekend.* Samira worked the pruning sheers with ease. One after another, dead branches tumbled into the dirt. *Nor is it likely you'll encounter a knight in shining armor to rescue you from this Garden of Eden.* She trimmed another bush. *You really need to stop reading those medieval novels!*

A falling branch caught on a trellis. Without thinking Samira grabbed hold to pull it loose. A sharp pain shot through her hand. Quick examination showed an over-sized thorn from the rosebush protruding from her finger through the garden glove. Samira immediately removed the thorn but blood was already soaking through. *So much for finishing tonight.*

Samira held her finger under cold running water in the laundry room sink. It hurt, but it wasn't as bad as she'd suspected. *Only a little puncture.* She heard the walk in garage door close and assumed one of the girls had been out front. Samira turned her finger. *I think it's going to be all right.* She turned off the faucet and turned toward the kitchen just as her brother stepped through the entrance.

"Wes!" Samira gasped. "You startled me."

"I knocked, but no one answered. Is your doorbell working?"

Samira shrugged.

"Obviously your telephone is working. It's been busy all evening."

The throb in the finger was still prominent. Samira went on through the kitchen to get a band aide out of the hall closet.

"Let's see," Wes reached for Samira's hand. "What'd you do?"

Samira explained.

"You did this through a pair of gloves?"

"It was a big thorn."

"I guess." Wes examined the wound carefully. "Do you think Mom should take a look at it?"

"No." Samira didn't want her mother examining a cut from a thorn. She held still as Wes wrapped the bandaide around her finger. "See? It's better already." *It still hurts.* "So what brings you to my neighborhood, Wes?" *He has something on his mind or he wouldn't be here.*

"Are you busy in the morning?"

Babysitting. I knew it. Just because I don't have anything planned on my personal agenda doesn't mean I want to spend it babysitting. "I don't know yet, why?"

Wes turned a page in the newspaper, which was still open across the dining room table. "Here. Did you read this?" He pointed a finger. Samira walked back around the table to see what had his attention. "Shoal Creek. Are you tuned into this at all, Sis?"

Samira had heard mumblings from patrons at the library but didn't know the details. *I don't want anything to do with Shoal Creek. Nothing at all.*

Wes straightened his back and put his hands in his front pockets. "Alan Goldstein wants to bulldoze the entire area for development." He shook his head in disbelief. "I don't understand it."

Samira pretended to skim the article as Wes attempted to sort through his thoughts. "Mid-America is getting ready to sell our property on that end of town. And no doubt, whoever buys it will develop it for commercial investment. But Shoal Creek isn't protected by city code. I'm afraid they'll destroy the natural beauty of the land."

The picture in the paper showed the boardwalk along creek. *A little further down was where I sat with . . . well anyway . . .* "So they want to take out all these trees?" Samira ran her hand over the full-color photo. The trees in the picture were still green, but in a few short weeks they would be turning to rich shades of autumn. *They shouldn't take the trees out.*

"Every last one if I'm understanding correctly." Wes leaned over the paper again. "Here," He rested his finger on a paragraph at the end. "There's a public meeting on Tuesday for citizens who wish to protest Goldstein's plan."

Samira was still confused. "Why isn't city council fighting against Councilman Goldstein's ideas?"

"Because Shoal Creek isn't within the city's limits."

Oh wow. Without the protection of the city, this could be devastating for the whole area. "You mean it's not protected by parks and recreation regulation or anything?"

"Apparently not." Wes stuffed his hands back in his pockets. "Right now it's privately funded. But if Goldstein gets a hold of it, Shoal Creek as we've known it will be no more."

"Are you going to the public meeting?"

Wes nodded. "But tomorrow another member of city council is offering a guided tour of Shoal Creek for those interested in trying to protect the area from being destroyed."

"And you want to go to that?" *That's why he needs me to babysit.*

"Yes." Wes answered forthright. "But I want you to go with me."

Samira was taken aback. *I can't go back to Shoal Creek. It's too soon.*

"Come on, Sis. I need your expertise. I'm willing to fight this thing, but I need you there to see the natural beauty for me. I'm going to look at it through the eyes of an investor. You're going to see it as a gardener."

Samira crossed her arms over a now churning stomach. "I can't, Wes."

"What could you possibly have going on in the morning?"

"What business is that of yours?"

"I didn't mean it that way," Wes tried to apologize. "This is something I would like to see you sink your teeth into, that's all."

Suddenly his motive was becoming clear. "So you want me to adopt this project?"

"You'll want to if you go down there and take a look."

"I know what it's like down there."

"I know you do. That's why I want you to go on this tour with me and hear what they have to say about Goldstein taking it all away."

"I have plenty on my mind without taking on a city council member," Samira retorted. "Do you think I don't have enough to keep me busy or something?"

"I know what's on your mind, Sis, and you need to let it go."

So that's it, isn't it? Even my own brother is here to help me get over this man I should never have had in the first place.

"I can live without your advice." *Wes is my brother. Unlike Kelly Davis, I can walk out on him!* She turned for the door.

"Where do you think you're going?"

"I left my pruning sheers in the rose bed . . . "

"Get them later."

"I'm getting them before it gets dark."

"You have enough lights out there to make it look like daytime if you flip a switch."

Samira let the door slam a little harder than necessary as she marched into the garden. *This is my retreat!* Not even Wes's snide remark about her outdoor lighting effects could take away the hallowed presence in her garden.

The door slammed again. Samira looked back. Wes following her.

He has no right to come here and taunt me with an ecological issue in an effort to distract me from whatever it is I choose to hide myself behind . . .

Samira reached for her sheers, careful not to bump the newly fallen stems from the rose bushes. *If I only knew exactly what I was hiding behind . . .*

"Just stop it, Samira." Wes's voice was stern. "Stop the charade and the lies you're telling yourself and face the music once and for all."

Samira refused to face him.

"You work so hard at being strong and able and secure, Sis, but you're no stronger than the rest of us." Wes paused but he didn't move any closer. "You don't have to be perfect and secure. Hell, you don't even have to be happy." He paused again. "But there's a bunch of us out here in the real world waiting for you to come back around, and it's about high time you give up your pride and admit that things didn't go the way you'd planned."

"I didn't plan . . ."

"Then you hoped," Wes corrected immediately. "We all feel badly about the way things happened. But as long as you're shutting yourself off from the world, we can't help."

Samira hung her head. Dead limbs from the rosebushes were scattered at her feet and on the sides of the raised beds. She knew how quickly those branches would dry up and disintegrate now that they were cut from the mother bush. *Just like me. It wouldn't take much for me to disintegrate right now either.*

"It was just a matter of time, Wes," Samira started to speak her thoughts. "I needed more commitment than he could give."

"Maybe you can't manipulate everything out like you want to. Maybe some things you have to allow to evolve on their own."

"I took a chance and look what happened."

"You took a chance and look what you'd never have known had you not tried?"

"Like what?"

"Like the fact that you have the capacity to love someone again."

Samira closed her eyes. "But it was all wrong. I made some hasty decisions."

"Yeah, well, love will do that to a person. No reason to beat yourself up for that one."

Now Samira turned around and looked up into her brother's eyes. "But Wes, I let him move me in ways I'd forgotten I could be moved."

"And it was a very good thing."

"No! It wasn't. Because I almost let it happen again with someone else for all the wrong reasons."

"The artist?"

I knew Weston figured that one out. She hung her head in shame.

"So what? I figure he's halfway around the world with another project working his art into someone else's soul by now." Wes reached out and put his hand on his sister's head. "It's your soul I'm concerned about."

You and everyone else it seems. "Dang it, Wes. I don't want to talk about this." She gripped the sheers tightly in her hands. "I'm tired of thinking about it. I'm tired of replaying the good memories in my head only to have them end in disappointment. I'm tired of being nice and being happy." Samira sighed heavily. "I'm even tired of pruning the vines."

"Then it must be time to take off the mask and just be yourself." Wes let go of her head. "So, how are you now, Sis?"

"Mad."

"Good, now we're getting somewhere . . . "

The dark cloud that had been shadowing Samira's ability to move suddenly lifted. She opened her mouth and breathed in the thick, humid air of the evening.

" . . . So will you go with me in the morning?"

It feels so good to be free! Samira didn't know exactly what happened, but she suddenly knew there were better days ahead.

"I guess." She nodded her head. "I don't have anything better going on."

Wes smiled a genuine smile. "You should get mad more often, Samira." He wrapped his elbow around his sister's neck. "It does you good to vent."

Is that what it is? Samira walked back to the house tucked inside her brother's arm. *Somehow I think it's more than that. Does my love for Phil have to stop because he can't accept it?*

Samira waved goodbye to her brother as he backed his car out of the driveway.

I think I can love him still. Even if he doesn't know how to accept it.

She turned to go back inside. Somehow there was freedom in that realization.

50

Letters of a Name

J.P. opened the door to the outside. Bright sunshine flooded the darkened motel room burning his eyes. He put his hand to his forehead and took in the surroundings of the building. *Second floor balcony.* The sign over the parking lot read: Welcome to the Capri.

He scanned the parking lot as best as he could against the sunlight. *That's what I figured.* No truck. *Not that I could drive it anyway.* He closed the door and sat down in the chair at the desk. Surprisingly he was still dressed. *But I have no idea how I arrived in this hellhole.*

J.P. reached for his cell phone. *Nothing.* He closed and opened the lid again. *Dead battery.* He ran his hand through his hair and leaned back into the chair. *Just my luck.* The clock on the desk read 1:22. *Obviously P.M.*

The numbers on the desk phone blurred as J.P. struggled to recall Mike's phone number. *Shit, Ralston. Just remember one of them.* Ever so slowly he pushed the buttons one at a time, hoping against hope that a familiar voice would answer.

"Mike Benson at your service."

Relieved, J.P. pressed the phone hard into his ear. "Mike . . ."

"Hey, good buddy, where are you man?"

J.P. put his pounding head in his other hand. "At the Capri."

"Are you alone?"

"Yeah. As far as I know."

"Do you need a ride?"

"Yeah." It hurt his head just to speak out loud.

"Anything I can bring you?"

J.P. closed his eyes. "A clean shirt and a quart of milk."

"Alright. Here's the deal. I'm on the green at the 4ᵗʰ hole. It's going to take me a while to get down there. Are you going to be alright for awhile longer?"

"Yeah." *I'm going to lay back down.*

"What room?"

I have no idea what room I'm in.

"J.P.?"

"I don't know."

"Check the door."

J.P. pushed himself off the chair opened the door. *211.* He went back to the phone and gave Mike the room number.

"Sit tight. I'll be there as soon as I can get there."

I'll be here. J.P. looked around the room. *I guess.* It was cheap and dingy. The curtains hung haphazardly and the furniture was dated and worn. *Nothing like waking up at the gates of hell without a rope to grab onto.*

J.P. stretched out on the musty bed and closed his eyes.

A loud thud brought him back into consciousness. He tried to sit up on the bed but his muscles didn't respond.

"Holy moly, J.P.," Mike emerged from the bathroom.

Has he been here awhile or is he just getting here? J.P. put the back of his hand over his forehead.

"Let's get you out of this flophouse."

"How'd you get in here?"

Mike offered a helping hand. "I paid for the extra day and they gave me a key to come find you." Mike tossed a large metal key on the desk.

The metallic ring sent a throbbing pulse through his temples.

"Sorry." Mike apologized. "Here, change out of that . . ."

I know. I'm a mess.

". . . Just put this on and let's go."

Obediently J.P. unbuttoned his soiled dress shirt and exchanged it for a clean t-shirt. Mike took the dirty shirt and nodded his head toward the door. Without speaking J.P. forced himself off the low bed. It took a few seconds to get his bearings, but eventually he followed Mike onto the balcony and down the concrete stairs.

"How'd you get my truck?"

"Jimmy called." Mike closed the door and walked around to the driver's side. "He thought you might not want it towed first thing this morning."

"Jimmy who?"

Mike started the engine and adjusted the air conditioner vents. "Jimmy the bartender." He opened a quart of milk and handed it to J.P. "The bartender who bragged up the brunette he sent you away with."

J.P. took a drink of milk without any discussion. *I remember a little about being at Jimmy's bar. But I don't have any recollection of a brunette.* The motion of the moving vehicle was causing J.P.'s stomach to work against him. He grabbed onto the armrest with all the strength he had left.

"You gonna make it or do I need to stop?"

J.P. couldn't answer. He just shook his head and closed his eyes again.

They drove in silence for awhile.

"I called your aunt so she knew not to expect you this morning."

J.P. squeezed his eyes tight. *Oh shit! I was supposed to be at the ranch sometime this weekend with Bobby's family.*

"Whad'ya tell her?" Mike turned the truck into the sun causing J.P. to turn his face.

"I lied through my teeth . . . ."

What do you tell her in a case like this?

" . . . I told her you were in the middle of a case and couldn't break free quite yet." Mike looked back to the road. "You owe me double for that one." Mike continued to explain. "She said Bobby and his family got in yesterday and are looking forward to seeing you."

Not today. Not like this.

Once inside his house, J.P. sat in a kitchen chair and watched as Mike let Chase back inside and checked for telephone messages.

"Sparky's on a hot trail, J.P." Mike paused. "You do remember Sparky don't you?"

J.P. managed a nod. *Kind of.*

"He tried reaching you last night on your cell without any luck. So I'm going down to your office with him this afternoon. We're going to set a trap for . . ."

J.P. knew Mike was trying to brief him on a case, but he was talking way too fast for comprehension.

"Shit, J.P." Mike headed for the door. "Sleep it off. I'll be back later. And don't forget to call your aunt."

The slam of the screen door caused J.P. to grab his head again.

The sun was still shining when J.P. awoke. This time he was in his own bed. Chase was asleep on the rug by the bedroom door. J.P. rolled over and sat up. *Ten o'clock.* J.P. read the clock again. *Ten o'clock what?*

It doesn't matter what day it is anymore. J.P. took his time getting into a hot shower. His beard had grown considerably but he had no motivation to shave. Instead he rested his hands on the top of the shower stall and let the water pound against his aching muscles.

Dressed only in a pair of sweat pants, J.P. found his way to the kitchen and let Chase out into the back yard. *I'm hungry but I don't dare eat too much.* He filled a glass with water, drank it down and then filled another. *I wonder where Mike is?* J.P. leaned into his kitchen window. *The truck's here so he must have had a way to get home.*

J.P. took a piece of dry toast to the living room and sat down on the couch. Thursday's morning paper was still open on the coffee table. He flipped it over and found the remote control. With a click he turned on the pre-game show on ESPN. *It must be Sunday.* J.P. rubbed his rugged face in his hands. Mindlessly he watched the commentators on television give their opinions of the NFL lineups for the day. Some days he might care. *But not today.* He clicked off the tv and went into his office.

Message lights flashed on his computer and on the answering machine. He moved a small stack of papers to the side and uncovered a reminder to call the boys before heading up to the ranch. *Shit, Ralston. You can't hold yourself together even long enough to make an appearance at the ranch.*

Disgusted with himself he went back to the bedroom and put on his running shoes. Unsure of his strength, J.P. decided to take Chase out on the street instead of down to the walking path. *I don't need to go far. I just need to get outside and breathe in the fresh air.*

Thirty minutes later J.P. returned to the house sweaty and tired, but somewhat refreshed. He drank another glass of water and returned to his desk. *I need to call Aunt Maggie.* J.P. picked up the phone, but couldn't force himself to dial. *She's the one person I can't lie to.* He put the phone back into the cradle. *I have no idea how I'm going to fix this one.*

The shoe box from his father caught his eye. After a moment's hesitation, he carried it into the living room and sat back down on the sofa. Trying not to be too curious, J.P. flipped off the lid and picked up a bunch of banded letters. Some had red, white, and blue stripes around the edge indicating airmail delivery from days gone by. Others were plain envelopes with colorful stamps in the corners. But all were yellowed with age.

J.P. allowed his fingers to unwrap a stack. He sorted through taking note of the postmarks and addresses. They'd been delivered all over the world at different times. One envelope in particular caught his eye. It was dated October 22, 1965. *Mom's birthday.* J.P. removed the contents of the envelope and opened a hand-written letter.

Dear Joe, It's my birthday! Can you believe I'm 25 years old today? I received your package a week ago but Maggie won't let me open it until tonight. That will be the highlight of my day!

The skies are blue in Missouri today. I took the boys over to Maggie's early this morning and we busied ourselves making birthday cake for tonight's party. What I wouldn't give to save you a piece! Angelfood from scratch. Your favorite! The Langford's and Annabelle Campbell are joining us at Maggie's for dinner. After that we'll play cards and celebrate with cake and ice cream. Joey is so excited about the shindig. He knows there will be kids to play with and candles on the cake.

Little Bobby is cutting teeth this week. Poor little guy is miserable most of the time. I stayed up with him rubbing his gums until he fell asleep on my lap last night. Maggie helped me with him this morning. A few more days and those two-year molars should be through the gums. That will make all the difference. Roy took Joey fishing this afternoon so I could rest. But I wanted to get a quick note off to you before I lay down.

Joe, I've been thinking about our time together in Washington a few weeks back. We were so fortunate to be able to steal a few precious hours. I can still feel your arms around me and sometimes when I'm up with the baby in the night I can sense your steady breathing next to me once again. I miss you more than I can express, but I love you even more than that. The thought of you facing the heat of the battle is almost more than I can bare some days. But then I say my prayers and I know you are safe in God's care once again. I don't doubt God's protection over your life—not for one minute. And I don't want you to doubt it either. Know that wherever you are and whatever you're facing, that God is between you and the enemy.

I must go for now. Bobby will be awake before my head ever hits a pillow. But you are in my heart and in my prayers. I will write after the party tonight. And then again in the next day or so. I love you Joe Ralston. Don't you ever forget that. ~Leona

After that the letters came one right after another. Constant news from home bridged the distance between the Ralston boys and their father. And every letter was punctuated with words of loving, tender care. J.P. felt his eyes well up with tears when he read about his mother's pride when he won his first boy scout medal. *I remember that day.* And he felt his stomach knot when he read about Bobby's close call with a neighborhood dog. *Yeah, I remember that day too.*

His emotions became one with his mother's words until he could no longer separate himself from their history. Aunt Maggie's constant presence in his upbringing became more apparent and for the first time in his life he realized how attentive his mother was to their every need.

. . . Joey started kindergarten today, Joe. You should have seen him all dressed up in his shorts and button shirt. I walked him all the way to school with a brilliant smile for the little guy. But I cried all the way home, Joe. Why is it we cry when something so wonderful is happening? I didn't understand any of it. I was the first mother at the school when the day was done.

J.P. remembered his mother crying that day. He remembered her lingering hug before she turned away to walk back home. . . . *I took Joey to the doctor today. It seems the spots on his back are poison ivy. Must have been from an outing with Roy . . . And a nasty case of it too,* J.P. recalled. *Missed a whole week of school getting over that. Joey came home from school today with a black eye! I couldn't imagine what had happened. But the other boy's mother didn't hesitate to call and fill in my curiosity. I never liked that little boy anyway. He's such a bully . . .*

Timmy Houston. And I took him down too. J.P. still felt the satisfaction of that moment.

Joey asked me about the war today, Joe. He worries about you—wonders where you are and if you're safe. I tell him only the Navy and God know where you are in the ocean. And I tell him God is watching out for your safety. He prays for you every night before bed . . .

J.P. put the letter down on the table. He didn't remember ever saying a prayer for his father. *But I remember praying.* He remembered praying for his mother to come back. He remembered begging God to fix the plane crash so his mother could come home again. And he remembered taking off into the woods at a full stride toward the lake screaming at God for taking her away. But he didn't remember any prayers after that. *There wasn't anything to pray for after that.*

Scenes of his childhood, of his mother's funeral, of his father standing alone at a distance at the graveside; scenes of Aunt Maggie's ranch and of playing games with Roy in the living room; scenes playing catch with Bobby in the backyard at the house where they lived in town; and scenes of the time he decked his brother for asking his sweetheart to the spring dance . . .

J.P. dropped his head between his knees and locked his fingers behind his head. He tried to shut out the flood of memories that were now coming at him faster than his mind could possibly comprehend.

J.P. laughed at the last memory. *Damn it. I had my heart set on Suellen Jackson but she chose my scrawny little brother over me.* He shook his head at the recollection playing in his mind. *And if I'm not mistaken, Bobby got about what he deserved out of that night.*

Chase nudged his master gently, bringing J.P. back to the present. The dog pressed his furry face into his master's uneven beard.

J.P. accepted the affection and returned the favor with a firm grip around Chase's broad shoulders. "Well, ol' boy. What do you think?" J.P. looked his dog in the eye. "I think it's about time this sorry, old master of yours got his shit together."

Chase cocked his head to the side with canine interest.

"I've spent my whole life fighting wars I can't win." J.P. sighed. "I haven't been able to win against any odds, ol' boy, but I gave it a fair shake."

With that command, Chase put his front leg in the air. J.P. smiled. He reached out and shook Chase's paw with satisfaction.

J.P. went to the sink and filled a water glass. *I couldn't win my father's attention. And I couldn't win my mother back. And I couldn't even win custody of my boys.* He swallowed the water in one long drink. "But I could win in court." J.P. made the announcement to his dog who was now standing at attentive anticipation. "And for a helluva long time that's been enough."

Back in his bedroom, J.P. opened his top dresser drawer and removed the envelope that contained his mother's wedding rings. A single marquee diamond graced the engagement ring while the band held a row of twelve smaller cut diamonds. J.P. turned the rings in his hand. They were small compared to his own fingers.

His father's words replayed in his head. "*She's all I ever needed*".

And he's all she ever needed. J.P. made that realization for the first time in his adult life. He'd always assumed his mother suffered great hardship over his father's commitment to the Navy. *But her letters tell me something different.*

"*She knew what was best for you boys.*" The Captain's face was resolute when he'd made that statement. *Obviously he trusted her to let her stay home like that time and time again.* J.P. put the rings back in the envelope. *I don't think I've ever trusted anyone that much. Not even Mike.*

A sudden urge to be near his mother gripped J.P.'s soul. He pulled an old t-shirt from his drawer and grabbed a change of clothes and his shaving kit. His duffel bag was packed in less than five minutes.

As he turned for the door he snapped his fingers for Chase to follow.

"Come on, Chase. We have a reservation at the ranch."

J.P. drove in silence, unaware of the passing time. The miles passed under his tires as childhood memories continued to play in his mind. Close to three hours later J.P., turned his truck off the main highway onto a low maintenance gravel road. Dust rolled in his rearview mirror but J.P. didn't mind. *I haven't been here for a million years.* He knew exactly where he was going. *When was the last time I was here anyway?* He brought the truck to a stop in the shade of a massive oak tree overlooking a deep valley. *I came here after the Captain stood me up at the depot.*

Chase bounded out of the truck excited to have new territory to explore. But J.P. sat still in the driver's seat. His eyes passed over the rows of headstones. *I came here that day so she could fix the broken parts.*

J.P. took his time. He walked the row all the way to the far fence and then turned and faced his mother's epitaph. A beloved wife and mother. Leona Elena Ralston 1940-1972. The space next to his mother's was incomplete. Joseph Phillip Ralston 1930 ~ An American Bald Eagle graced the corner of the tombstone.

He stood there staring at his father's name and for the first time in his life, Joseph Phillip Ralston felt no bitterness. *I'm not even angry.* There wasn't even bottled resentment shouting false accusations at the father he never knew.

The grown boy knelt down and put his hand on the cool marble that marked his mother's place of burial. J.P. could feel tears well up in his eyes. "I'm sorry, Mom. I didn't know. I didn't know how much you loved him." J.P. thought again. "Hell, I didn't think you loved him at all. And I didn't know how much he depended on you back home either." J.P. took a deep breath as his tears spilled over and mixed into his whiskers. "I just didn't know."

Chase passed by with his nose to the ground. "I've spent my whole life fighting for the love I never knew you had. I figured if you didn't get it then I didn't deserve it either." J.P. sat down on the grass and pulled his knees to his chest.

Time passed.

All I've ever known, or at least all I remember knowing is that I didn't have what it took to bring my father home. Ever. And the few times he was home, he wasn't the father I wanted him to be.

J.P. stared at the sandblasted eagle on the stone. *Eventually I took matters into my own hands. Figured if he didn't need me, then I didn't need him either.* He wiped his nose on the back of his hand. *But the things I thought I needed never brought me any lasting satisfaction either.* He recalled his college days of carousing and partying. *But Mike, now he had a sense for the finer things in life.* J.P. smiled and leaned back on his hands. *Still does. He'd let me flail, then he'd reel me back in. Somewhere in there I figured out I could win at something, so I latched on and curtailed the party life long enough to get into law school.*

J.P. noticed a hawk circle high in the sky. *Then that ordeal with Janet. That was just a stupid mistake. I never intended to get her pregnant. And I never intended to love her either. But I think I did for awhile.* He remembered some happy moments. *It's hard not to love the woman who gives birth to your own flesh and blood.*

He leaned all the way back on his elbows so he could watch the hawk.

"But you know what?" J.P. spoke into the space between him and his mother's tombstone. "Even though I gave her all I had, it still wasn't enough."

The hawk made one last circle then flew off into the distance. *I wasn't the man she hoped I'd be. I had to finish law school and pass the bar. And then I went to work for Lloyd Hughes so I could pay off my school loans.* Chase padded by in the overgrown grass. *Hughes became my escape from the onslaught of discontent and demands Janet unloaded on me every night.* J.P. nodded his head. *Hughes was probably the best thing that happened to me back then.*

You're wrong.

J.P. sat up in the grass. He looked around to see if anyone was there for he knew the words he'd heard in his head were not his own.

What do you mean, I'm wrong? He directed the question to the unseen voice.

Joshua Thomas and James Allen Ralston.

J.P. picked a long blade of grass and twisted it in his fingers. Slowly he began to understand. *Yeah, they're the best things that ever happened to me. But I couldn't be the father they needed either.*

You're wrong again.

"I am not wrong again!" Now J.P. was standing, screaming into the valley. "I tried, but I couldn't make their mother love me back!"

J.P. could see James's face in his rearview mirror the day he left him standing in the driveway. *God, don't make me go back there!* He closed his eyes, but the image wouldn't leave. *Don't you know I tried to make that work?*

Guilt and remorse conjured up scenes of angry tantrums and irresponsible decisions.

But you didn't have to earn their love, did you?

Again J.P. looked around for the voice, but this time he knew it came from within his being. *No, I didn't.* He rubbed his damp eyes with his hands. *But I was afraid if I accepted it I wouldn't be able to live up to their expectations either.*

Suddenly aware of his immediate surroundings again, J.P. snapped his fingers. Chase stopped digging at the base of a fencepost and trotted up to his master's feet. "You don't require very much of me, do you boy?" J.P. knelt beside his dog. "A little exercise, a scoop of chow, and a bucket of water. That's all you need."

"But people," J.P. dug his hand into Chase's thick fur as his thoughts shifted again. "People are different than that." *To make people happy you have to do things that don't necessarily fit your character.* He continued to massage the dog's shoulder. *Janet needed me to be someone I wasn't and when I didn't fit that mold she found someone that did. So I figured he was probably the one the boys needed too.*

The big black dog rolled over on his back. "Yeah, I'll rub your belly if you'll rub mine." *It's a great concept, but it's no rule to live by. I simply prefer to take care of my own endeavors. It's safer that way.*

And you can control it.

Now J.P. was beginning recognize the voice in his head as something more powerful than his own thoughts. *Is that what it is? Control?* He puckered his lips in thought. *No, it's not control. It's the front I use to be who people need me to be. It's not Joseph Phillip Ralston II that answers to Christopher Hughes, nor it is Joseph Phillip that wins in court.* The attorney's eyes fell on the engraved letters again. *Joseph Phillip Ralston. I wanted to be just like him—independent, strong, brave, brash . . .*

Chase flopped over onto his feet and wagged his tail. *But I didn't like who he turned out to be in real life or in my mind, so I gave up the name and became J.P. Ralston, Attorney at Law.* J.P. picked up a short stick and tossed it into the air. Without a moment's hesitation Chase took off after it.

I must admit, ol' J.P. does damned well for himself. He considered his court record. *But anymore the satisfaction of winning isn't as motivating as it used to be.* J.P watched his dog retrieve the stick. *Joseph Phillip II must have more to learn about life.* Suddenly Samira's sweet smile appeared in his mind. *And she may be the one thing I can't fight to win.* He knelt down and took the stick out of Chase's mouth.

By now J.P. wasn't surprised to hear the voice inside his head speak again. *Maybe she's the reason there's no fight left in you.*

Chase jumped against J.P.'s knees and knocked him off balance. When J.P. rolled into the grass, the dog took advantage.

"Quit it!" J.P. pressed against the eighty-pound dog with his arm. He couldn't help but laugh. "Chase! Stop!" J.P. tried without success to deter Chase's wet tongue from licking his face. The master finally gave in. Chase barked excitedly and pounced at his master, thrilled at the spontaneous wrestling match.

"You win, boy," Phil rolled into a fetal position to protect himself from the dog's happy attack. "I'm all yours! You win! I don't want to play this game anymore!"

Bottled tears of guilt and regret welled up in J.P.'s eyes and ran out onto his face. In spite of Chase's affection, J.P. couldn't hold them back any longer. *I don't want to play this game!* He took advantage of a lull in Chase's attack and pushed himself up into a sitting position. Chase nudged him again, but this time J.P. was ready. He tossed the stick into the air, relieved to have his canine friend occupied with something other than him.

God, I've spent over half my life fighting battles I couldn't even see. But I don't want to do that anymore. Chase returned with the stick, but this time he stretched out in the grass, seemingly content to be still for a moment. J.P. wiped his face with the hem of his shirt. *So exactly what did the Captain mean when he wished for something of sustenance to take away my will to win.*

Chase was panting hard. J.P. continued to review his parting conversation with his father.

No, he didn't wish for something to take away my will to win. The color of the sky suddenly seemed more blue. *He said he hoped I'd find something of sustenance so the need to win would lose its power.*

Suddenly life didn't seem to be an empty chasm. For the first time, Joseph Phillip Ralston felt an invisible weight lift from his chest. *So the will to win isn't the driving force! Or at least it shouldn't be.*

Time passed again. But how much time passed, J.P. didn't know. But he was aware when the sun began to drop lower in the sky. And he was also aware that Chase was now sleeping in the grass next to him.

"So what I am supposed to do now?" J.P. questioned his dog in the stillness of the moment. "What do I do if I'm not playing that game anymore?"

And then, in an echo of his mother's thoughts, he heard her voice inside his head again. *Know that wherever you are and whatever you're facing, that God is between you and the enemy.*

But the enemy has been in my own mind. The realization came slowly. *The enemy has been talking me out of the life meant for Joseph Phillip Ralston, II.* With that thought came the assurance that maybe, just maybe there was a bigger purpose to his life than winning women and court battles. *And maybe, just maybe, I haven't been fighting these battles alone all this time.*

J.P. stood up and let his eyes take in the beauty of the valley before him. *If the Captain trusted her, then I have to trust her too. I think I can do that. I can trust her.*

But as he walked away he knew that he was trusting more than the words of his beloved mother. He was trusting in her belief that God was between him and his self-imposed enemy. *All this time I thought God was the enemy.*

The master snapped his fingers and Chase appeared obediently at his side. "Come on, Chase. Let's go see if Aunt Maggie has supper on." He opened the driver's door and waited for Chase to bound across the console to the waiting passenger seat. "And we'd better hurry up 'cause we've got a lot of explaining to do when we get there." *Especially to Bobby. There's no way he'll let me off the hook.*

J.P. felt good making a showing at the ranch. *It would be far too easy to just head back home and chalk the whole damn weekend up to another lost bygone.* But this time J.P. knew there was more to it than that. *I owe it to the boys.* He thought again. *No, I owe it to myself.* He put the truck into reverse. *I need to show my ragged face and give them whatever is left of me.*

But as he started to back away, another thought caused him to take one last look at the valley below. J.P. put his foot on the brake and held it there. He squinted his eyes into the distant sky that was now fading into shades of lavender and orange. *My God, what have I done? What if I just let the last prayer of a chance walk out of my life? What if she's the sustenance I need to take away the power of winning?* In his mind's eye, J.P. could still see Samira walking up the hill away from him.

He heard Chase sigh a heavy breath indicating a deep canine sleep. Very slowly J.P. understood the implications of his decision not to go after Samira at Shoal Creek.

Heaven save me from myself.

51

Making Contact

"What's the matter, Mama? You look confused." Kara passed by the dining room table.

Samira pushed her hair to the back of her head. "I am." She turned the page of the document she was trying to understand. "I think I need an interpreter to understand all this legal jargon!" She was exasperated. *I've been through this policy about Tom's trust three times and I still don't understand.* "I have to sign these papers before the end of the month but I don't want to sign them if I'm not sure what I'm signing."

"Maybe you could call someone to help you."

Krissy looked up from her math homework. "Let's see, who might we know that's a lawyer?" She grinned. "Miss Davis knows someone. We could ask her to ask him . . ."

Definitely not Mike Benson. "No. I'll figure it out. I just need to focus more . . ."

"You could make an appointment with Papa Ray's lawyer if it's still confusing," Kara made another suggested.

I've always called my parent's attorney for things like this. "Thanks for your concern, ladies, but I'll figure it out." She looked first at Kara and then at Krissy. *They don't believe me.* "Really, I will." With that Samira closed the document and stashed it back in the legal sized envelope. *Later, when I'm alone.*

Kara poured a glass of milk then pulled out a chair adjacent to her mother. "I have to turn this in tomorrow and I don't know who to write on the line." Kara handed a single sheet of paper to her mother. "It's for Career Development class."

Annual Career Exploration Banquet.

Kara looked defeated. "I don't know who to invite. Everybody is taking someone with really exciting careers and I don't have a clue who I should take."

"What's the assignment?"

"We're supposed to invite an adult with a career we or someone in the class would like to learn about. There's this big banquet and all the adults are introduced and then we divide up into smaller groups and learn about people's careers that might interest us. Then the next day we write a report on our favorite ones."

That doesn't sound so bad. "So what careers interest you?"

Kara rolled her eyes. "That's not it, Mama. Don't you see? I don't have anyone I can invite."

"Like, you mean, you don't have anyone you *want* to invite," Krissy interjected.

"No one with an exciting career!" Kara crossed her arms. "Danielle is taking her father who's a medical technician. Kacey is taking her uncle who designs bridges. Jennifer's dad is in publishing and he's going . . ."

"Is anyone taking a librarian?" Krissy was still working on her math.

"No. But everyone is taking their dad."

"I thought Kacey's uncle was going . . ."

"He is, but he's a guy, isn't he?"

"Don't mom's have careers too? Or aunts?"

"Not my friend's moms!" Kara's impatience with her sister was showing.

Samira listened trying to understand more fully. *What is really bothering Kara?* "Uncle Wes and Papa Ray are in banking. I'm sure they would represent the career world from a male's perspective if you wanted . . ."

"I don't want to take them. Banking is boring."

"What about Miss Davis' boyfriend? He's a . . ." Krissy tried again.

"I don't even know him!"

Krissy shrugged her shoulders at her mother.

"What career would you like to represent that night, Kara?"

"I don't know." Kara stood up and walked back to the kitchen. "Something exciting and challenging and helpful."

"Like a nurse? Granny was an emergency room nurse! That's pretty exci . . ."

"No!" Kara's voice was sharp. "That's a woman and all my friends are taking men!"

Okay, she's not interested in a woman's career tonight. "Name a career that interests you then."

Kara dropped her eyes and lowered her voice. "Like someone in law enforcement."

She's thinking of her father.

"Cool!" Krissy seemed to like that idea. "Just like Daddy!"

Just like Tom. Samira clarified in her mind. *But she can't take him.* She watched her daughter's face fall. *I don't know if I can fill this void for her.*

"What about that guy from Granny's church that worked with Daddy? Do you remember him?" Krissy was determined to find a date for her sister now.

Samira knew exactly the man in Krissy's memory. *But David is NOT an option.* She couldn't stand the idea of even contacting him again. *Besides his wife just had a baby.*

Kara sat down in one of the barstools at the breakfast bar. "No, not him." Her eyes were still low.

Krissy shrugged her shoulders again and pushed her math notebook toward her mother. "Here. Done. Will you check these for me while I shower, please?"

I hope I can do the math enough to check them! So far this year she'd kept up with Krissy's assignments but they were into new algebra and it was getting more and more difficult with each assignment.

Krissy left her pencil on the table and headed for the hallway. "I'll let you know if I think of anyone else, Kara. Okay?"

I know what Kara's thinking, but I don't know how to help. "I'm sorry you can't take your father, Kara."

The young woman looked away. "Yeah. Me too." She took a deep breath. "It just seems like all my close friends have a dad to take. Kacey is taking her uncle, but she's not someone I hang around with much. Tia and Brittney at least have step dads to take. I don't even have that."

"There's still a couple of weeks before the actual banquet," Samira pointed out. "What if I call the teacher and tell her we're working on this and will have an answer by the end of the week?"

"For one thing," Kara began to correct her mother. "The teacher is a guy. Mr. Wilber. And for another, I don't want anyone to know I don't have anyone to take."

You just don't have the one you want to take. "So how can I help?"

Kara slid off the stool and started to walk away. "I don't know if you can, to be honest."

And I don't know if I can either. Without another word she disappeared behind the door to her bedroom.

"Too bad Phil didn't stick around. He'd have been a great date," Krissy surprised her mother from behind. She was wrapped in a towel. "Forgot my sweats! They're in the washroom!" She tiptoed across the hard floor to the laundry room and returned carrying a folded sweat suit in her arms. As she passed by the desk, she answered the ringing telephone.

Samira took her empty coffee cup and walked away from the table. *They've both talked about the lack of a father's presence in our lives lately.* Prior to her relationship with Phil, neither Kara nor Krissy had ever mentioned wanting a father-figure in their lives. *Obviously they've gotten a glimpse of what things could be like with a dad around now too.*

Samira rinsed her cup in the kitchen sink. *But it isn't likely to happen.* Still, she felt awful about Kara's predicament. *Maybe one of Kara's teachers would go with her. Or maybe we could ask Pastor Bill . . .*

"Mama, the phone is for you . . ." Krissy stretched the spiral cord as far as she could.

Samira had been so lost in her thoughts she already forgotten that the phone had rung.

" . . . and it's a man!" Krissy punctuated with a loud whisper.

Samira frowned. "Hello?"

"Ms Cartwright? My name is Marty Brown. I'm on staff out at the university."

Marty Brown. Samira was sure he was calling to raise funding for the school. *Maybe he could go to the banquet.*

"I apologize for calling you at home, but under the circumstances we thought it might be more professional this way . . ."

Yep, he's asking for money.

"We have been made aware of your work at the Maple Street Library and the more we hear, the more interested we are about talking to you concerning an opening we are anticipating at the end of this year . . ."

He's not going to ask me for money?

"Before the university foundation launches a broader search for a program director, we wondered if you might be willing to meet with us?"

A moment of silence passed before Samira realized she was supposed to reply.

"Exactly what are you asking of me?" *I don't understand.*

Marty Brown cleared his throat. "We would like to interview you for the opening."

Samira laughed. "Me? But I have a job!" *This is really quite humorous.*

"That's why we thought it better to call you at home."

He's serious. She put her hand to her mouth. "Oh, my. This is quite interesting." Samira needed to think. *Did he say program director?* "Do you know I'm a librarian?"

"Yes, Ma'am. But we are impressed by what you've accomplished with the Maple Street branch." The voice paused. "We would appreciate your taking the time to visit with us in the near future."

They're impressed with my success at the auction, that's all. Samira tilted her head in thought. "How near are we talking into the future?"

"As soon as next week if you have the time."

No, Samira. You need to think about this before answering. You always think about these kinds of things before answering, remember? "Is there a way I can think about this and call you back with an answer?"

Mr. Brown sounded more serious when he spoke again. "It would be better if we could go ahead and set up a time to meet. There will be plenty of time for questions then."

Samira couldn't believe her ears. No one ever told her she couldn't think about something important before she answered. *They want to interview me for a job I'm not even seeking.*

"Ms Cartwright?"

"I guess that will be alright."

"This is very good," Marty Brown confirmed. "Shall we say Tuesday evening at seven o'clock? That would be one week from tonight."

Samira checked the calendar on the kitchen wall. "My daughter has a volleyball scrimmage until 7:30."

"Would eight o'clock be better?"

He's not going to back down, is he? "Eight o'clock is better. Where exactly should I meet you?"

"We'll be in the meeting room at the university library. Just tell them at the desk who you are and someone will show you the way . . ."

Samira listened as Marty Brown gave her a few more details about the possible position and then he reiterated the meeting time and place before ending the call.

"Who was that?" Kara asked as she returned to the kitchen.

Samira didn't know how to answer. *I certainly don't want anyone to know about this yet!* She flipped her hair over a shoulder. "It was someone from the university. They want to talk to me about the programs at the Maple Street Library." *Which isn't exactly untrue.*

"Sounds serious," Kara replied half-heartedly. She picked her library book up off the table and returned to her bedroom.

It is serious, I think. Samira leaned over the math book to check Krissy's problems, but her mind was still on the telephone conversation. The last time she'd been offered a job when she wasn't looking she took it. *And I still have that job!*

A week later, Samira sat fidgeting in a folding chair next to her brother. *This is a huge meeting. A much larger crowd than I anticipated!*

Councilman Goldstein was at the microphone stating his case concerning the development of Shoal Creek from the podium at the city council meeting.

"... Development of that property could mean huge revenue for the surrounding area. The longer we delay this decision the longer before we will see any profit ..."

"Thank you, Councilman." The mayor interrupted Alan Goldstein politely.

Wes put his hand on Samira's knee. She stopped bouncing her heel against the floor.

"...The fact is, we as a council do not have a right to make a decision on this property ..." another councilmember began an explanation but Samira's mind was wandering.

The university offer is so different from what I do now, yet it sounds intriguing. I wouldn't be in the library, but I could use the library resources to build a strong program for the foundation. She glanced at her brother wishing for his full attention in order to process the opportunity with him. *But I'm not even looking for a job. Remember? I have a good job. And I'm right in the middle of our new online project.*

"The city attorney has advised us to proceed with caution, Mr. Goldstein ..." The mayor spoke deliberately. Samira could feel the tension rise in the room. "There will be no more discussion over property outside the city limits. However, development plans for the same tract of land will be heard by the county commissioner at next week's public hearing."

Loud whispers permeated the overcrowded room. Samira leaned forward in her seat as the mayor dismissed the forum.

"Now that was a heated debate!" Wes announced. "I don't see how Goldstein can push this through the county commission without public support."

I don't know either, but I really came here to talk to Wes about more personal matters.

"Weston!"

Samira turned her head to see a suit-clad businessman reach out to shake her brother's hand. Wes returned the greeting and engaged in politics while the crowd began to close in around Samira. *Now I'm going to have to wait even longer for his attention.*

She made her way to the room divider then turned and scanned the room. *If I stand here I can see the whole room and still keep an eye on my brother.* All of a sudden Samira's eyes stopped on Mike Benson. He was standing on the far side of the room obviously deep in discussion with a small group of people. *He's the last person I'd expect to find in this crowd!*

Although Samira tried to keep her eyes away from Mike Benson, she couldn't help it. *Just a glance.* Her eyes passed over that side of the room again. But Mike had moved slightly to one side and Samira looked directly into the face of J.P. Ralston. He was wearing a business suit and tie and his dark blue eyes were focused directly on her.

Oh my goodness! Samira caught her breath but she couldn't look away. If Phil had been engaged in conversation, he wasn't saying anything now. He was just standing there. His jaw was set deep in thought.

"Ms Cartwright." A man about her same height offered his hand. Samira looked into his face and recognized him.

"Mr. Brown." *I hope he's not expecting a response! I just interviewed with him last night!* Samira forced a smile and returned the handshake.

"You can call me Marty. This issue over Shoal Creek has created quite a stir among the community," Mr. Brown continued.

I wonder what business Phil has here?

"Are you in favor of Goldstein's proposal?"

Samira knew better than to speak her thoughts about a public proposal in a public arena. *Especially with someone who has the potential to become my employer.* "I am still drawing my conclusions."

"I see." Marty Brown studied her face carefully. "I trust you are still considering our position . . ."

"I am." *Now maybe he'll let me be. I'm not ready to discuss anything about the interview until I talk with my brother.* Marty Brown was standing square in front of her view to the far side of the room. *And I will also talk to my parents, although I know Daddy will want me to spread my wings and take the job.*

Mr. Brown nodded politely. "Very well. I look forward to hearing from you then."

Good. He's gone.

Immediately Samira turned her attention to the far wall, but there was no one there whatsoever. Wes was still talking in the same spot Samira had left him, but there was no sign of Mike Benson or Phil Ralston anywhere. *I know they were both there a minute ago.* Suddenly the room became very warm.

It looks like Wes is going to be awhile. Samira stepped into the corridor where it was cooler. Several clusters of concerned citizens were still discussing the impact of the Shoal Creek debate.

"Buona tardes, Senorita."

It wasn't the voice she'd hoped for but she stopped walking and turned around anyway.

"Do you speak to all the ladies in Spanish, Mr. Benson?" Samira found him looking quite smart and professional in his double-breasted, pinstriped suit. *No tie though. He seems to like these collarless shirts instead.*

"Only the really pretty ones." Mike puckered his bushy blonde mustache in a playful manner that made Samira forget he was wearing a suit. "I'm surprised to see you at such a heated political extravaganza."

"You just never know where I might appear."

"Obviously." Mike grinned. "We're representing some clients tonight, in case you're wondering."

"I wasn't," Samira lied. "But thank you just the same."

Mike opened his mouth to say something but his eyes suddenly shifted to a spot just beyond her. His tone changed dramatically. "If you'll excuse me . . ."

Samira turned to see where Mike's eyes had gone. Standing just a few short feet from her was J.P. Ralston. He had his phone to his ear but his eyes were watching her. He seemed taller than she'd remembered. *Or is it the suit? Much more conservative than his friend.* Whatever it was, there was something different about him. *Now what do I do?*

Phil finished the call. Samira wondered about the whereabouts of her brother but she was too close to Phil to turn away now.

"It's good to see you." Phil spoke into the space that separated them.

Samira smiled easily. She couldn't help it. "And you."

"Are you coming, Boss? I'm picking up Sparky . . ." A woman wearing a black pantsuit and high heels was fast approaching the attorney from behind. Samira watched the woman slow to a stop. Her eyes went from the attorney to Samira and back again. "J.P.," she tapped a long fingernail on the face of his watch. "Three minutes."

"I'll be there."

J.P. acknowledge the woman's insistence with a silent gesture. Without another word she turned and started off in the direction from which she'd come.

"Busy night." Samira decided it would be best to let him off the hook. *Maybe that's why Mike told me they were working, so I wouldn't be disappointed.*

Phil closed the space between them by taking a few short steps in her direction. "I didn't expect to see you here."

"Funny, that's what Mike said as well." *But I am disappointed he has to go, just the same.* Samira watched Phil run his hand through his hair.

"I'd like to say great minds think alike but that would be an understatement in Mike's case."

Samira inhaled deeply. *I've never been very good at small talk.* She wanted to ask him how the boys were and if he was okay. *I want to know everything about him. But this isn't the time or the place.*

"I'm on my way out of town on business . . ."

Phil was sounding more like an attorney than Samira wanted him to. "Don't let me keep you." *This is the attorney I need to help me with the legal papers on my desk.*

"We're on our way to the airport now." Phil nodded, but it was obvious he was either still deep in thought or completely distracted by business matters. "It really is good to see you."

"It's too bad you have to go."

J.P. looked beyond Samira into the distance of the corridor. "Maybe sometime we . . ." His voice trailed off in an unfinished thought.

Samira could see the woman in high heels coming toward them again. "Maybe we could . . ." *She's definitely intent on keeping him on schedule.* "I'm not hard to find." *As long as I'm still working at the Maple Street library.* The click of the high heels on the polished floor was getting closer.

Phil held his hand out in acknowledgement of the time. His eyes were a dark shade of blue when he looked back at Samira.

"Then maybe I'll come find you . . ."

"Maybe so." *I hope he means that.*

The main part of city hall had cleared considerably. Samira watched the woman at the end of the hall wave her arm for Phil to hurry. He picked up his pace into a gentle jog and then disappeared through the glass doors into the dark of the night.

I wonder where he's going?

"Hey, Sis, sorry I took so long," Wes apologized as he came up behind Samira. His eyes followed hers to the double doors. "Are you ready to go? The girls are probably starting to wonder where you are."

Wes conversed freely about the debate all the way back to the house. Instead of asking for his opinion on the job at the university, Samira decided to enhance her brother's stand against Councilman Goldstein. *Now I don't know if I want his opinion. Or even Daddy's for that matter.*

If there was even a remote possibility that Phil Ralston might actually come and find her, Samira didn't want to jeopardize his effort by taking another job. *Maybe I'm just looking for an excuse to turn it down. But even if I accepted the new job I wouldn't even start until the first of the year. That should give Mr. Ralston plenty of time to come looking.*

52

The Facts of the Matter

J.P. ducked his head as he slid into Mike's Corvette. "Are we set to go?"

"As far as I know," Mike took off diagonally across the parking lot.

"What about Chase?"

"Kelly's checking on him."

"Are you sure?"

"Of course I'm sure?"

J.P. snapped his seatbelt into place. "I should have boarded him."

"Kelly doesn't mind. She'll let him out on her way to school in the morning and put him back in when she gets done at the gym at night." Mike patted his hands against the steering wheel while he waited at a red light. J.P. could see the taillights of Denise's car driving away on the other side of the intersection.

"Do we have the case documents?"

"Denise has them. Sparky wants to prep us as soon as we get in the air."

"What are your thoughts on Goldstein?" *The entire proposal seems preposterous if you ask me.*

Mike glanced in his rearview mirror. "I don't know yet. It's fishy but I can't put a finger on it."

"Everybody knows the county planning commission will shut him down cold, so I don't know why the mayor is letting it get all blown out of proportion now."

"Our fine mayor is going to let the voices speak. He always does."

Always. J.P. thought this might have been one time the mayor should have shut down public opinion before it got out of hand.

476

Mike interrupted J.P.'s thoughts. "So, how'd it go?"

J.P. looked sideways at his friend. *He's not talking about Goldstein anymore.* "How'd what go?"

"In there. With Samira."

"What's it to you?" *I don't like the way Mike can converse so easily with a woman whose name I can barely speak.*

J.P. could feel the sudden acceleration as Mike shifted into a higher gear. "Is it a crime to ask a personal question?"

No, it's not a crime, it's just that I didn't know what to say to her. "Ask away. You didn't have any trouble striking up a conversation with her."

"Hell, it didn't appear that you were going to open your mouth. I figured one of us should be polite and acknowledge her presence."

"Josh called about the football game this weekend. I was going to finish talking to him then go talk to her." *If she was still there.*

"Could have fooled me." Mike sounded disgusted. "So what did you say to her?"

J.P. watched the white line of the highway streak by the side of the car. "Not much you can say in three minutes or less."

Mike pulled the Corvette into the parking lot at the airport. Denise and Sparky were already walking across the parking lot toward the entrance. "You either say nothing or you say it all."

Great. J.P. opened the door. *Then chances are good I said absolutely nothing.* He heard the alarm set on the Corvette as he walked away. "I told her I'd look her up." *And I will.*

Mike caught up to J.P. on the sidewalk. "When?"

As soon as I get back. "Why? Are you going to ask her out if I don't?"

"Maybe not me, but if you don't, guaranteed, someone else will."

What's this maybe shit? J.P. knew that fact very well. *I know she's one of the hottest commodities on the market.* But there was business at hand and he needed to clear his mind of everything that didn't pertain to the case. *That's the way I work.*

Denise handed both Mike and J.P. a newly assembled folder as they boarded the chartered jet. "Vince will meet us at the airport. He wants these court documents memorized by then." Derek was already fastening his seat belt.

"Don't wait too long," Mike whispered as J.P. began to settle into a seat next to him.

I just need to get through this case. Then I'll be able to give her my full attention. He chose a seat. *Or maybe I should call her in the morning at work.* He clamped the thick metal tongue of the seatbelt in place. *At least then she'd know I was serious. I have every intention of looking her up, but maybe I didn't communicate that very well.*

J.P. opened the file folder as the jet engines prepared for takeoff. He skimmed the updated reports from Vince Barringer. *But it was damn nice to see her tonight.* He could still see her in his mind's eye. *Damn nice in every way possible.*

Sparky wasted no time. Once the jet was at cruising altitude, the little investigator stood up in the aisle and indicated for everyone to follow along in the folders.

"As you know, ve are at the heart of dis investeegation," Sparky informed with his hesitant, broken English. "Ve must be exactly prepared in de morning." He knitted his bushy, black eyebrows. "De Balteemore suspects have taken the plea bargain. De evidence is weighted against dem." Sparky made eye contact with all four team members in the plane. "Dey know who is de culprit behind the Mid-America heist and it is time for dem to tell us."

"By now Vince should know who the mastermind is." Mike leaned his head into the airplane seat. "Do you know who it is, Sparky?"

The little man raised his eyebrows. "I tink zo."

"Are you going to share that information with us?" *I hate playing Sparky's waiting game.*

"De suspects are vorking for the same person Celia Monroe is vorking for . . ."

"Celia, the student banker at Mid-America?" Derek asked.

"Dat is de one," Sparky assured.

"Celia, othervise known as Melinda Lynn Jones," Sparky paused and allowed the newly revealed alias to hang in the air. "And I beleev J.P. knows who she is vorking vith because he bumped into her at a party."

J.P. frowned. *I went to a party with Celia Monroe?* He looked over at Mike.

"The dinner party," Denise realized out loud. She leaned across the aisle toward her boss. "You went to that dinner party with Jessica Hutchison. That must be where you saw her."

Sparky nodded his head once.

"I didn't go *with* Jessica Hutchinson . . ."

"When did all this transpire?" Mike cast an accusing look in J.P.'s direction.

Give it up, Counselor. I didn't do anything with anybody.

Denise filled in the blanks. "That Friday night. Late dinner."

Mike focused in harder. "That Friday night before the Saturday I picked you up?"

That would be the one.

"Jimmy said it was an unknown party . . ."

"It was." *As far as I know.* J.P. still remembered very little of that night.

"She approached you as you vere leeving." Sparky tried to give a hint.

"As I was leaving where?"

"De party."

"What?" *Was he following me?* "How do you know that?"

"Ah . . ."

J.P. shifted in his seat and ran his hand through his hair. *Don't 'ah' me now, Sparky!*

"My suspect vas under surveillance, but you appeared dere too."

Denise laughed out loud.

"Bag it, Denise," J.P. instructed.

"Told you he was good," Mike interjected. "As good at investigation as Vince is in interrogation." Mike put his arm over the divider that separated his seat from J.P.'s "Imagine that. Our investigator finds his own employer at the scene of a surveillance."

J.P. flipped Mike a choice finger. *What's up with Mike's sudden disgust with my personal life?* J.P. forced his mind to remember the dinner party. *That dinner party is what initiated this city-wide discussion concerning Shoal Creek.* His mind's eyes followed Celia Monroe up the stairs onto the wooden porch of the condominium office suite. *Now I remember, Celia passed through the door right past Alan Goldstein and Jessica Hutchison.*

"And who does Miss Hutchison vork for?" Sparky continued to lead J.P.'s memory.

"Sean Bridges."

"Beengo."

The plane bounced slightly in an air pocket.

Mike leaned forward in his seat. "Bingo what, Sparky? Jessica Hutchison works for Bridges. We know that. Does Celia Monroe, or whatever her other name is, work for him too?"

"Tomorrow ve vill know for sure. Tonight ve only speculate."

"We don't even know who the hell Sean Bridges is!" *I've been trying to land a face-to-face meeting with that man since the onset of issues between Hughes and the city.*

Sparky raised one eyebrow. "But, ve know dat Bridges needed monies to make land purchases for his developments. And ve know dat Jessica Hutchison is pushing for more development, but I tink dat is just a red herring . . ."

"You think Bridges is funding the Shoal Creek proposal?"

"No, I tink de Shoal Creek proposal is designed to turn your attention avay from de matter at hand . . ." Sparky was looking directly at J.P. "De more interest you show to the Shoal Creek development, de less dey tink you vill pay attention to de on-going investeegation for Mid-America."

J.P. closed his eyes. *So the mastermind is right under my nose, watching my every move, hoping to lead me astray?*

"Dis one is very compleecated, J.P.," Sparky knitted his brow again. "I tell you everyting, but only when it is time."

"Do I know Sean Bridges, Sparky?" *I need to know who he is!*

Now even Denise was leaning into the aisle to hear the answer.

"I beleev you do."

Denise cocked her head to the side in thought. "We've never met him face to face. The only person we know who has seen him in the flesh is Jefferery Hughes."

"When in God's name did Hughes meet him?" J.P. demanded.

"While you were out gallivanting somewhere off the shores of the eastern coast with another unknown party!"

Enough accusations! "I was gallivanting with my Father."

"Holy shit, J.P." Mike looked shocked. "Why didn't you tell me?"

"Because it wasn't relevant." J.P. unbuckled his seat belt and stood up.

"I figured you'd connected with Bobbie Jo Sommers." Denise informed. "She called looking for you that day."

Am I ever going to lose that woman? He rubbed his temple between his thumb and forefinger. *She's the biggest red herring I've ever encountered!*

"Sparky," J.P. addressed the investigator directly. "How do I know Sean Bridges?"

"You ate dinner with him at his own dinner party." Sparky leaned on the seat and crossed his hairy arms over his chest.

J.P. forced his mind back to the guest list. *Armstrongs were there, that architect, Clark Roberts, Tom Jones in real estate . . .* So far these guests didn't seem to have any direct relation to Sean Bridges. *Had I realized the impact that meeting had on this case, I'd have ended that night much differently.*

"Who is it?" J.P. continued to run the guests through his mind. *That marketing and sales guy who works with Hutchison . . . Hayes, Richard Hayes.* "Bridges wasn't there that night, Sparky. I wasn't introduced to him whatsoever."

"Dat's because you already know him."

There was only one other person there that night besides Hutchison—"Alan Goldstein."

"Two beengos!" Sparky's eyes flashed like lightning. "And I tink he vants you fighting against Shoal Creek for the city's interests instead of vorking dis case."

Now Mike was standing too. "Are you sure, Sparky?"

Sparky had to look way up to see the faces of both attorneys. "Only speculation tonight, remember? Tomorrow ve learn for sure."

Denise spoke up again. "Then what's the scoop in California? What cover up did you find clear out there?"

"Dat is vhere the holding company kept de funds. A real estate company is de umbrella to cover the holding company's assets. Ingenious, but very simple."

"That makes perfect sense," Derek finally remarked from his seat. "Bridges only needed funding long enough to purchase the land out by the airport. When the land sold to the city, the money was returned in hopes that no one missed it."

That's pretty good coming from an intern.

"But it took longer to close on the property by the airport than Bridges thought it would. Mid-America discovered the missing funds in the meantime . . ." Mike continued.

"Greed."

Everyone's eyes turned to Sparky for an explanation.

"De airport property vas a done deal until Bridges found a higher bidder . . ."

The Hughes Corporation.

" . . . den he tried to make more dan vas coming to him. De delay created just enough time for Mid-America to run quarterly reports. Vhen dey deescovered de money vas gone, dey reported it." Sparky shook his head sadly. "Greed."

"And you really think Sean Bridges is the same in one with City Councilman, Alan Goldstein?" *He's been on city council a long time to be under an alias.*

Mike sat down in another seat. "I don't doubt it, J.P. Look at what Goldstein was doing tonight at the forum? He knows he's proposing something totally against public opinion. He's creating a stir big enough that the media and city government are going to be totally focused on Shoal Creek when the Mid-America case comes to a peak."

So I was invited to the party as part of a plan to distract me from the Mid-America investigation?

"Tomorrow ve vill know everyting," Sparky reminded. "But tonight ve must try to rest."

Rest? With information like this pounding around in my head? J.P. sat down in a row of seats by himself and tried to settle into his own thoughts. He couldn't even close his eyes without Samira's face appearing in his mind.

And God, she looked good. Not good like I need to have her, but better than that. Like I . . . J.P. closed his eyes to find the right word . . . *like what?*

He opened his eyes and looked around the cabin. His closest comrades were all in the air with him. Derek was absorbed in the contents of the file folder containing the court documents. Everyone else in the small cabin was at least pretending to be asleep. Even Mike seemed extremely relaxed.

But Mike can go to sleep at the drop of a dime. These are the people who know me the best, put up with me, save my ass over and over again, work my agenda, and yet the only face in my mind when I close my eyes is Samira's.

Alan Goldstein's involvement in the Mid-America case caught J.P.'s thoughts again. *This could turn out to be the biggest case in my entire career. I should be strategizing and preparing . . . normally I would be.*

He closed his eyes again. Samira was still there. He wondered how she was getting along, and if Kara had decided to play volleyball at school. He wondered why Samira attended the Shoal Creek forum. *Mostly I wonder if she missed me as much as I've missed her.*

Face it, Ralston. J.P. put his face in his hands. *You can't even have sex with anybody else now that you've had her. You tried and it didn't work. She's the only one you want.* J.P. turned in his seat. *But it's more than that. It's lots more than that.* J.P. stretched one leg out into the aisle. *Until I met her I thought a woman was something to be won, but this woman is something to behold.* He rested his head into the high-backed seat.

There used to be this feeling of victory every time I mastered a new woman, especially if there was a little competition for her attention. I won Samira, but there wasn't any victory march. J.P. laid the folder aside. *It's like she's a part of me all the time now. I thought if I let her walk away that I'd be able to just pick up my life where I left off. But it's not working out that way.*

I'm really tired. He squeezed his eyes shut tight and tried to lose himself in the roar of the engines. *Ralston, tomorrow you're going to wake up, that is if you ever get to sleep, and lead this legal team into an opportunity that could turn into a whale of a case. You should be ecstatic.*

But he wasn't. The case was right there to be had. And J.P. Ralston knew exactly what he needed to do to blow it wide open. *With the suspects taking the plea bargain and testifying against the mastermind of this heist, I've got the world by the tail.* J.P. thought about the possibilities. *It's still going to take some doing, but with Vince and Mike onboard, we should be able to nail them without a shadow of doubt.*

J.P.'s thoughts shifted again. *But she's right there too.* He pictured Samira's contemplative face. *It's like I don't live alone anymore—like she's one of my missing pieces. I know this case. I know its potential on my future.* The prospects were extremely enticing. *But what about the potential with Samira? What bearing does she have on my future?*

J.P. rubbed his weary face in his hands. *I knew something was different about her that first night. But what I didn't know then was how she was still going to be affecting me now! She was so fragile that night. Always is. It wasn't like I was having sex with someone new. I know that feeling. It was more like the night moved with us somehow . . . like I'd known her my whole life.*

J.P. wished he weren't trapped in an airplane. *I thought if I ever found the perfect match there'd be a flash of light or something to alert all the senses to move in that direction.* J.P. remembered her fresh scent. *And it's not like I have to out draw someone who's shooting for her too.* His eyes studied Mike's sleeping face. *Unless Mike knows something I don't.*

Derek turned off the reading light above his seat creating a new degree of darkness in the cabin. *But it wasn't like that at all.* The drone of the small jet consumed J.P. for a while. In his mind he was with Samira at the waterfront again—*Or was she with me?* Her dark eyes and subtle smile brought a deep sense of contentment he'd never known with a woman. *I think it's more than being together—not just standing there together, but immersed in one another's . . . what? What is it?*

"You were immersed in one another's soul."

The thought came out of nowhere. J.P. lunged forward in his seat. *Who said that?* He looked around but no one was sitting near him. *We were immersed in one another's soul?*

The walls of the plane seemed to be closing in around him. J.P. stepped into the aisle. There was no escaping the thoughts of Samira. *Or is it her thoughts within my mind?* She felt just as close to him now as she had been when he kissed her at the edge of the lake. *Or did she kiss me?*

There was nowhere for J.P. to go. He walked to the back of the short jet and took a seat with his back against the bathroom wall. His mother's letters to the Captain were fresh in his mind again. *She was all he ever needed because she prayed him through. That's what she kept saying in her letters.* At first that thought felt foreign. But the more J.P. pondered the notion, the more it made sense. *If there is a God above, then He's the only one that could have kept them connected over the miles and through the years.* He considered the hardships his parents must have faced during those times. *Only something that big could have connected them like that.*

J.P. closed his eyes again and tried without success to relax with the hum of the engines. *"Maybe Samira is praying you through."*

Once again J.P. was on his feet. Again no one was there, but the words were so clear in his mind he was sure someone in the plane had spoken them. J.P. checked every passenger. They were all asleep. He sat back down in the same seat.

Maybe she is. Maybe that's why she feels close enough to be right here with me right now. Somehow that thought was very comforting. J.P. inhaled deeply and closed his eyes. *I would like that—if she were right here with me . . .*

J.P. awoke as the small plane bounced onto the runway in Baltimore. Vince would pick them up and take them immediately into preliminary meetings. The deposition was scheduled for nine o'clock and there was still much preparation to do.

The new case facts swirled in J.P.'s mind as he descended the steps of the small aircraft. He breathed in the smell of jet fuel and hot rubber that permeated the air as he pulled his suit jacket over his shoulders.

"This is the big day, Counselor," Mike slapped his colleague on the shoulder, obviously refreshed and ready for the day ahead. "If all goes well we should leave here ready for pretrial hearing and thus launch the beginning of the end to a very powerful case."

How does he wake up all chipper and everything? J.P. was still groggy from the abbreviated night. He could see Vince waiting with a passenger van along the fence of the private runway.

I know this case inside and out. The new evidence felt solid and J.P. felt confident they could advance at a very rapid pace. But in spite of the familiar pump of adrenalin in his veins, he couldn't feel the underlying drive that always came with new energy in a big case.

The fact of the matter is, Counselor . . . Vince opened the door to the waiting van. . . . *that the facts of the case don't matter as much as the matter of fact back home.* Samira's smiling face appeared in his mind as J.P. slid across the bench seat so Sparky could sit next to him. *And she's a very comforting matter of fact.*

53

Wearing Hats

The book club ladies were mingling in her living room. Samira took silent attendance. *Everyone's here tonight.* She surveyed the women she'd shared books with for over a decade. *We represent four generations of female perspectives.* Pam was one of the youngest in the group.

Mrs. Haddock clapped her hands together. "Gather around, ladies. Let's get started."

Samira had her furniture arranged around the fireplace. Everyone started to find a place to sit.

"I started another pot of coffee." Pam sat down in the chair next to Samira. "It will be ready shortly."

What would I do without Pam? "Thanks. I didn't realize the pot was empty already."

Mrs. Haddock began the discussion with a short review from the New York Times.

Helen always does such a great job when she leads. Samira listened as the women began to talk about the novel. *Their faces are familiar and their thoughts are intriguing, but aside from Pam and Helen, I really don't know these women very well.*

" . . . Personally, I thought the author stretched the truth a little too far to be considered historical fiction. She had a tendency to imagine facts that I know to be false . . ."

"I disagree. I thought the historical facts were very accurate. It made the story line more believable for me . . ."

"Samira, what are your thoughts? Did you enjoy the story?"

I've never held my opinions from this group. "Personally?" The ladies turned their attention to Samira. "No. I have to say I didn't enjoy it very much. I found

485

myself skipping here and there over parts that didn't hold my attention." *But that might have been my unsettled spirit more than the book itself.*

"That's exactly how I felt," someone chimed in. "It just didn't grab me like most best sellers."

"What made it reach the best seller's list anyway?"

"The author's reputation had to have been a factor there . . ."

"I agree. Her last book was much better . . ."

The phone rang. *The girls will get it.* It only rang once. *I knew they'd pick up.* Samira tried to turn her attention back to conversation. *How is it every time the phone rings now I wonder if it's going to be Phil looking me up.* She listened to Pam make a point. *I thought I was over waiting for the phone to ring.*

Usually Samira was more involved in the discussion, but not tonight. Her mind jumped from work to Krissy's schoolwork to the job offer from the university. Nothing held her attention very long, with the exception of her chance meeting with Phil.

He was so serious that night. She took another sip of her coffee. *But he was still very intense.* She replayed their brief conversation in her mind again. *I should be terrified of a man who packs so much power in his character.* Samira smiled. *But I'm not.* She frowned. *At least I don't think I am.*

The corporate conversation was beginning to divide into smaller groups.

I'm not afraid of Phil, but J.P. Ralston might be another story. I don't know him as well. She placed her now empty cup on the edge of the coffee table and sighed. *I hate to get my hopes up though.*

"Do you think she ever really understood the motive behind his denial?"

Samira looked around. *Are they talking to me?* "Whose denial?"

"Jonathan's." Pam grinned. "Francine's lover . . ."

"Oh!" Samira remembered the topic at hand. "Oh him. No. Francine was too worried about her own motives. She didn't have the capacity to figure Jonathan out . . . ."

One of the ladies sitting across from Samira shook her head. "We were wondering if the author had a clue, not Francine. But I agree with you, Samira. Francine was totally self absorbed from the very beginning."

Oh.

"Don't you think that's one of the reasons the book didn't hold our attention?"

Maybe it's time to warm their coffee. When Samira headed for the kitchen, Pam followed.

"I can't believe I answered like that."

"Me neither!" Pam bumped her sister in law with her hip.

"I don't know where my mind is tonight." *Well, yes I do.* "Not only did the book not holding my attention, the conversation isn't either!"

Pam chuckled. "Let's play hostess. Maybe they'll burn themselves out of chit-chat and go home early."

Samira jumped when the phone rang again. Krissy came flying up the stairs into the kitchen with the portable phone. Samira lifted the coffee pot above her head to avoid a collision. Krissy all but ran through the dining room then slid in her sock feet into the hallway.

"Must be an important call."

Must be.

Krissy tip-toed back into the dining room, this time without the telephone. Her cheeks were a bright red.

Very curious behavior. But when have I ever known Krissy to act normal in front of an audience?

"It didn't turn out too bad," Pam spoke with a matter of fact as she helped Samira clean up. "I was expecting the discussion to end on a negative note, but Mrs. Haddock did a good job bringing it back around."

Samira lined up the cups up in the dishwasher. "That's Helen's gift. She knows how to bring people together."

"She brought almost everyone together at the end . . ." Pam rinsed the dishrag under a running faucet. "Every body except for our hostess."

Me? "Why do you say that?" Samira poured the remaining coffee into her own cup.

"I don't know," Pam grinned. "Maybe the way your thoughts seemed to be a million miles away tonight—like you were thinking of someone . . ."

"Is it that obvious?"

"Not to anyone else in the room. But I'd venture to say I know you better than most of these women."

Transparency. "That you do." *Helen probably noticed too.*

"Sometimes it's nice to be with a group of women who don't know you very well, yet appreciate you for who you are." Pam ran the dishrag over the countertop. "But you are always who you are . . . you don't wear masks Samira. And tonight I know you were no where near this room for the better part of the evening."

She read me like a book! "Maybe not."

"Definitely not!"

"What's his name?"

"I don't know, Pam . . ."

"You don't know his name?"

"No, I know his name, but I don't know if I want to talk about him."

"Do we know him?"

"No."

"Have you known him long?"

"Awhile now."

"Has he asked you out yet?"

"Not in awhile."

Pam paused. "So you've been out with him already?"

And a lot more than that with him.

"Obviously you'd like to go out with him again. Has he asked you again?"

I don't want to lead her astray. "No." Samira sighed. "It's the same one I was seeing in the summer. I bumped into him last night for the first time in awhile."

Suddenly Pam looked concerned. "He didn't restore any hope did he?" She recovered the accusing remark quickly. "I don't know all the facts, but Wes told me that things didn't end up like they . . . well, like they should have."

Samira leaned against the counter. "I don't know what I hoped for before!"

"Yes you do!" Pam answered immediately. "You hoped for the opportunity to complete your family again!"

Is that it? Samira hadn't thought of it quite that simply. *Am I simply hoping for a man to complete my family again?* "Maybe I hoped for someone to take care of me again."

"Oh, Samira. There's nothing wrong with that!" Pam put her hand on Samira's shoulder. "In fact, I'd say it's rather healthy to wish for someone you can care for and receive care from just the same. Don't you think?"

"Maybe." *But what I hoped for and what happened were two different things.* "It just caught me off guard to bump into him like I did."

"But that's all it was, right?"

"Right." *Pam's still worried about me.* "We just talked for a couple of minutes then he had to go."

"It's probably better that way."

Krissy poked her head around the corner "Is the coast clear?"

"Except for me, everyone is gone." Pam cocked her head. "What's up?"

"Ohhhhh, nothing . . . ." Krissy disappeared again.

"Something is definitely up." Pam joined Samira at the breakfast bar. "Your mom is having Wes's birthday dinner Friday night. Did she call you?"

"Yes. She left a message late last week."

"And you'll be there, right?"

It's not like my calendar is bulging with other commitments. "Of course we'll be there."

"It's possible you might have plans."

Krissy hurried through the kitchen going the other way.

Pam watched with curiosity. "They're up to something!"

"They'll be back." *One of them won't be able to keep a secret for very long.* In fact, Krissy returned almost immediately with Kara close on her heels.

"Mama, we need you to come over here." Krissy gently tugged on her mother's arm. "There is someone that wants to talk to you."

"Did the phone ring?" *I didn't hear the phone ring.*

"Not just now," Kara answered from the computer. "But earlier it did." *What are they up to?*

"Give me just a minute . . ." Kara typed on the keyboard a minute and then clicked on the mouse a few times. "Okay. I think I have it ready."

"Have you ever done an instant message?" Krissy asked.

By this time Pam had joined them at the computer desk.

"No."

"It's really easy," Kara began to explain. "You just type like you're on the phone or something. Then you hit enter and the message sends right to the other person so they can type right back." Kara stood up and indicated for her mother to sit down in the steno chair.

"Who called earlier?" Pam asked casually.

Krissy couldn't hold it in anymore. "James."

"James who?" Samira asked quickly.

"James. You know, Phil's James." Kara clarified.

James Ralston?

"He called to see if you were on instant mail. I told him I could set you up after the women were gone." Kara leaned over the computer keyboard and clicked the mouse. "So here. Now you're set up."

Pam was humored. "And who might James be?"

"Mom's old boyfriend's son." Krissy shrugged her shoulders.

"Well, he's not that old," Kara corrected. "But he's the son of the man Mama dated for awhile." Kara wrinkled her face at her mother. "Is it okay to explain him like that?"

I guess. The computer played a faint tone and a screen popped up.

Hey, pretty lady . . .

"Oh, my gosh, he's online!" Krissy squealed.

"James?" Pam asked.

"No. Phil! James called to find out mom's email name so his dad could talk to her. And he actually did it!" Krissy was excited. "But Mom doesn't have a screen name so she's talking on Kara's."

Samira's heart was pounding hard in her chest.

"Are you going to say something back?" Kara sounded concerned.

"I don't know what to do."

"Type, for pete's sake! Say anything!" Krissy was getting frantic. "If you don't answer he'll think you're not on!"

Not on what?

"Just say anything," Kara encouraged with more patience than Krissy. *"Hey back."*

Samira's fingers were shaking when she typed. Krissy reached in and pushed the enter key.

"Are you busy?

"Not at the moment." Samira remembered to press enter this time.

"Can you talk?"

"Can I type or can I talk?" Samira looked at her over-interested audience.

"Let's help your mother tidy up the living room, girls!" Pam sprang into sudden action. "Let's put the furniture back where it goes and get this day wrapped up so I can go home . . ."

Thank goodness for Pam's insight. "For a few minutes." Samira typed back.

"I've been doing a lot of thinking about that question you asked me."

Exactly what question is he referring to? "Refresh my memory."

"The one about needing to know if I loved you."

Oh my.

Another line of dialog popped up before she could respond. *"I'd like to revisit that question when I get back if you have the time."*

Obviously he's not home yet. "Where are you now?"

"I'm on the east coast working a case. I fly back tomorrow."

Samira reviewed the next day in her mind. *"I'll be home tomorrow after work."*

"I'm actually not free until Friday and then it's complicated. Are you free Friday night?"

With the exception of Wes' party. "I could be."

"If you are, I'd like to take you to the boys' football game."

Football? I was hoping for something more intimate. "I don't know anything about football." *Why isn't he saying anything? Oh. Press send.*

"Football is secondary. I was thinking the drive up to the game might be a good time to talk."

"Okay." *Talking is a good idea.*

"I'll call you when I'm out of my last meeting."

"Okay. Is there anything I need to know about football games before I go?"

"Dress warm, it's supposed to be cold."

It's not exactly what I expected for an answer, but okay.

"What's he saying?" Krissy asked as she and Pam pushed the easy chair back into its normal position.

Samira answered without thinking. "He invited me to a football game."

"Cool. Very cool." Krissy sounded excited. "Are you going to go?"

Oh, wait. I don't want Krissy involved in this conversation. "Hold on, Krissy, let me finish this."

"But you don't even like football!" Kara chimed in.

Just let me concentrate. Samira waved her hand for her girls to be still. *"I'll dress warm."*

"I'll call you as soon as I'm free . . . late in the afternoon probably."

Another computer screen popped up with an instant message to Kara from somebody named "Sweet Anthony".

"Kara, come take care of this. Someone else is trying to talk to you."

Kara appeared at her mother's side instantly. When she saw the name she quickly closed the window. She shrugged her shoulders. "I don't know why he always pops in on me like this."

It's a boy, obviously. "Can you talk to more than one person at a time?"

"Oh yeah!" Kara was nodding her head. "But go ahead and finish up."

Suddenly Samira felt vulnerable. *Instant mail does not feel very private.* She had to reread Phil's last comment again before replying.

"I'll be home."

Nothing happened. *Oh, that darned enter.*

"Sounds good. Sleep tight, Pretty Lady."

I doubt I'll be able to sleep at all now! "You do the same."

"It's hard to sleep with you in my mind all night long."

Funny, he has the same affect on me. "I'll talk to you Friday then."

"Friday."

"When's the game?" Krissy passed by the computer.

"Friday."

"Friday?" Kara interrupted. "That's when we're going to Granny's for supper. Remember?"

Samira turned all the way around in her chair. *I know.*

"If I were your mother and had a chance to spend the evening doing something new and entertaining, I think I would have to choose the evening out." Pam winked at Samira.

"But it's Uncle Wes's birthday!" Krissy added with a hint of drama. "Don't you think she should go eat cake and sing the song for her brother?"

Pam looked knowingly at her sister in law. "I think your mother needs to follow her heart."

Samira appreciated Pam's permission to miss the family gathering. *I just hope my folks and Wes feel the same way!* She turned the chair around to face the computer again. In light gray type along the bottom of the message screen it read: J.P. appears to be offline and might not respond to a message.

Samira brushed her fingers over the keyboard wishing he weren't hundreds of miles away. *But at least he found me.* She smiled at the computer screen. *And he called me Pretty Lady again.*

Pam finished tidying up and headed toward the coat closet. "Thanks for the entertainment, Samira. I'm going to head on home."

Samira closed the instant message window and left the computer.

"It was fun." Pam pulled her coat over her shoulders. "And if I were you, I'd go to the game Friday night."

"Thank you for understanding," Samira spoke candidly. "He just wants to talk and I'm ready for that too."

Pam patted her sister in law's arm. "Why don't you let me come get the girls after school and keep them for the night. Then you won't have to worry about what time you get home."

"You want my girls on Wes's birthday?"

"Think about it Samira, having the girls around might actually give Wes and me some badly needed time alone!" Pam winked. "This is the same guy that arrived on your doorstep in a partial tuxedo, right?"

Samira smiled. "That's the one."

Pam opened the door. "I'd be willing to go just about anywhere with him."

Samira waved to her sister in law as she backed out of the driveway. *I'm willing to go, but he's right, we need to talk first.*

Krissy was hot on her mother's trail as soon as Pam was out of sight. "Does this mean you're dating Phil again, Mama?"

"No." *I don't want to get their hopes up again. Or mine for that matter.* "We're going to watch Josh and James play football and talk. We're definitely not dating." She tried to sound and appear calm and in control. *Even though my heart is pounding in my chest.*

"Well," Krissy flopped over the back of the sofa and landed out of sight on the cushions. "If you hurry up and go steady with him again, Kara could take Phil to that banquet party. I think a lawyer would make a very interesting career guest!"

I forgot all about Kara's dilemma over that. "Have you thought any more about who you want to invite, Kara?"

"Yes." Kara looked directly at her mother. "I've decided I want to take you."

Krissy popped up over the back of the couch.

"But I thought all your friends were taking their dads . . ."

"They are. But you're like a mom and a dad to me. And I've decided I'm okay with that."

Oh, Kara, I've waited a long time to hear those words. Samira walked across the room and pushed Kara's silky hair back from her face. "And I would be honored to be your guest at the banquet."

Kara smiled and leaned into her mother's hands.

"Even if I am a boring librarian." *Unless I have a new job by then.*

"You are a lot of things, Mama," Kara stated. "But you are NOT boring!" She sat up straight in the barstool. "You'll probably give the best career talk of the whole night."

Krissy shook her head as she left the room. "You guys are too mushy for me!"

"Did Krissy tell you who the other phone call was from?" Kara was whispering.

Samira whispered back. "No. Who?"

"Ben Applegate." Kara raised her eyebrows. "A boy actually called Krissy to talk!"

That is amazing. Too bad Pam's not here to tease Krissy about that now.

Krissy returned. "What?"

"Oh, nothing." Kara smiled at her mother. "I'm really glad you want to go with me to the career banquet."

"And I'm glad you decided to invite me."

"We'll be a great team."

Samira was left to her own thoughts as she prepared for bed. *There's the decision about the university job offer.* She'd hoped to discuss it with Wes and her parents at dinner Friday night. *But now that's not going to be a possibility.* She changed into a long nightgown and returned to the kitchen to turn down the lights for the night. *I don't know why I want to talk to them about the university, really. They'll want me to take it, and I don't think that's what I really want to do.*

Samira passed by the computer and realized she was nervous about being with Phil again. *Maybe more excited than nervous.* Samira clicked the mouse to close the open windows in preparation to shut down the computer. *No, definitely nervous. It's like having a first date all over again.*

I'm glad I got to talk with Phil. Samira turned off the living room light. *But the best part of my day is having Kara invite me to her career banquet.*

I like being the Pretty Lady almost as much as like being both a mother and a father to my girls. She glanced at her face in the mirror as she passed through her bedroom. *It's kind of fun to wear different hats and still feel like me.*

54

Breaking the Dam

Tension was high in the conference room at Benson and Barringer's Law firm. J.P. sat at the foot of the table directly opposite a federal agent.

Who would have known Mid-American's scandal was going to end up working with the FBI?

"Gentleman," the agent cleared his throat. "And lady." He paused again. "I must say I am impressed with the amount of research you have completed regarding the business of Sean Bridges, but I am here to tell you this is a highly complex case. I've been on his trail for over three years now and I still don't have enough hard evidence to prove his guilt."

"But you do agree that Sean Bridges is definitely Alan Goldstein." *He only shares enough information to keep us out of his way.*

The agent's eyes were steel blue when he answered. "Yes, this time. He has many identities. And many accomplices."

I need to understand further. "But so far none who were willing to testify against him, correct?"

"Pardon my doubt, Mr. Ralston, but it is going to take more than two witnesses to put Sean Bridges, currently a.k.a. Alan Goldstein, behind bars for any length of time. He has a monopoly on underground banking scams, including laundering in this particular case."

"How many witnesses will it take?" Mike spoke up.

"More than two." The agent began to close his briefcase.

Mike didn't back down. "Define *more*. Are you talking six? Twelve? Twenty-four?"

"Mr. Benson, I know what you're thinking because I've studied his puppets personally. He pays them extremely well and hides them even better when he's done with them. The best we can do right now is keep a close eye on your local suspects." The agent snapped the latches. "And it is extremely important that your knowledge of this case be kept entirely confidential. One slip and we both lose him."

"Excuse my ignorance, Agent Roderick," Vince leaned forward in his chair. "But based on the evidence we can provide, it would seem the court could at least detain him while you finished the job."

"I have boxes full of evidence that could have detained the man." Agent Roderick rose from his chair. "Our goal is to put him away. Not detain him."

"Then our goal is the same," Vince pointed out. "What more would you need from us in order to begin federal prosecution?"

Agent Roderick didn't back away. "I would need no less than ten affidavits stating direct involvement in this given case. In addition to that I need hard evidence—be it computer files, banking files, signatures, anything that directly link Goldstein or Bridges back to the current case."

Vince was nodding in understanding. "The current case being the scam within the Mid-America accounts."

"As you know, the events of the Shoal Creek proposal are also linked in somehow. We are watching him with extreme caution." Agent Roderick's eye passed over the attorneys.

Vince was thoughtful. "Would you agree that Goldstein's biggest obstacle concerning Shoal Creek is raising funding?"

"It's not as simple as you're thinking, Mr. Barringer. Like I said, I have boxes of evidence, but attaining it in a timely fashion is the missing link to date. By the time we've been able to gather enough information to press charges, he manages to wrap up the lose ends and move on to another job under a new name."

He's already moved on to a new job. Shoal Creek. But this time he's moved on within the same community.

"But you said earlier he always appears to start a new job to distract the officials before the original scam is completed, right?" Mike was thinking out loud.

"That has been his pattern to date."

"And we believe he is hoping to distract us from the original scam right now, which would lead us to believe with even more confidence that his work with Mid-America is almost complete."

"I don't disagree, Mr. Benson." Agent Roderick was still standing. "But in order to hold his interest with the Shoal Creek proposal, he's going to need considerable revenue. My prediction, based on past history, is that once the final transactions are complete at Mid-America, any possibilities with Shoal Creek will dissipate immediately."

What about this? "From what you described to us concerning previous scams, Bridges never followed through with the red herring. In other words, the distraction served its purpose and then he walked away, correct?"

"That is correct." Agent Roderick seemed uninterested.

But agent Roderick doesn't know Bridges' character as well as Sparky does. "What if the funding became available for Shoal Creek? Do you think he would attempt to keep the Shoal Creek proposal alive?"

"What would be his motive?" The agent frowned. "He's already profited on job A. Why jeopardize his identity further by trying to force another lump sum within the same infrastructure?"

Nope. Roderick does not know Bridges. "For the sake of speculation, let's say he did secure funding to develop Shoal Creek. With that said, do you think it's possible to catch him in the act of laundering?" *Let's see where he goes with this.*

"In the act?" The agent looked doubtful.

"For example, what if we made it possible to catch him in the act of a direct transaction?"

Now the agent frowned. "You humor me, Counselor. His work is invisible. It happens in cyberspace . . . ."

Some of it happens in cyberspace. The rest happens through his trusty accomplices.

" . . . Again, why would he jeopardize his identity by putting his undercover operation at risk again so soon?"

Greed. Sparky said it. "For the sake of speculation . . ."

"I would encourage you to call me if you run across something that sure."

At least he left the door open.

The meeting broke up quickly with that last remark.

The FBI's been monitoring Mid-America for three years. J.P. watched Agent Roderick shake hands with Vince. *I'd place my vote of confidence in Sparky's investigation over the FBI any day.*

Denise followed J.P. out of the conference room and down the hall. "I'll have these notes ready in the morning . . ."

"I'll be in late since I'm going up to the boys' game tonight." J.P. turned around to make eye contact. " . . . So don't stay up all night getting them ready."

"Thanks, but I'd rather type them while they're fresh in my mind." Denise stopped in Mike's office long enough to pick up her coat. "How soon are you leaving? Should I pick up a sandwich for the road."

It is getting late. J.P. checked his watch. "Within the hour." *And I need to make a phone call along that line as well.* "I'll get something on my way out of town but thanks for the offer." "What time tomorrow, J.P.?" Vince was removing his necktie, apparently headed out for the day. His assistant was close on his heels.

"Let's make it one o'clock."

"One o'clock, Betty." Vince nodded his head. "Alright. I'm going to pick my girls up here in a few minutes, but I think you might be on to something, J.P. Let's hash it out tomorrow and get it on paper."

Mike was sitting on the corner of his desk. "I think you're on to something . . ." Mike mimicked his partner. "Do you really think Sparky can set the trap?"

"If anyone can, Sparky is the man."

"Wouldn't that piss off the FBI if a former KGB agent provided proof for their case?" Mike laughed. "I think it's worth a shot." He spun off the desk and landed in his leather executive's chair. "So you're still headed north?"

J.P. nodded in the affirmative. "I'd rather stay here and work on the case . . ." *but the company is too good to turn down.*

"But the case will be here tomorrow."

"Yeah."

"Mike," a petite assistant knocked on the open door. "Kelly is on the line. Can you still meet her at 5:00?"

Mike gave two thumbs up.

"Dinner?"

"Racket ball."

J.P. shook his head. "Then dinner?"

"Only if she's buying."

There's no way I'd let a woman pay my way.

"Excuse me again," the assistant interrupted. "If you have a minute she wants to talk to you. Line four."

Mike exploded into the phone. "Of course I have a minute!"

J.P. turned away to give Mike a moment of privacy. *Not that Mike knows that much about privacy . . .* His eyes passed over a statue on the bookshelves. *I've never noticed that before.* He walked closer. *A nude woman, reading a book.* J.P. took the liberty to move it a quarter of a turn. *And look at that.* He studied the bronzed piece further. *Her hair is in a knot like . . .*

"So what do you think?" Mike appeared at J.P.'s side.

J.P. didn't take his eyes off the statue. "Is it new?"

"Brand new. And it's an original too."

Mike has always had an eye for art, but I've never known him to be interested in sculpture.

"Do you recognize anything . . . ?"

"Where'd you get it?"

"At an art auction."

"Where?"

"At city hall . . ."

"Who did it?"

"Who did it or who is it?"

It looks like Samira. J.P. stared at his friend. "Why do you have it?'

"Because I knew you wouldn't want anyone else to have it."

"What the hell is that supposed to mean?"

"Think about it, good buddy. Your woman sitting on anyone else's shelf just didn't seem right."

Then it is Samira. J.P. looked at her again. "How'd you get it?"

"I outbid the artist himself."

I don't understand. "What artist?"

"The one who formed this body." Mike gently ran his hand over the statue. "He wanted it bad, man."

The statue or her? "What'd it run you?" *Wait. I know the answer to that question.*

Mike laughed his hearty laugh and walked away. "You don't want to know."

"Yes, I do." J.P. left the statue and followed Mike across the office.

"No, trust me on this one."

"Come on, Mike . . . I'll write you a check . . ."

Mike put his hands out and stopped J.P.

"Here's the deal." He crossed his arms. "You figure out what you need to do to win Samira back, and I'll let you have it for free."

J.P. didn't like being blackmailed. *And I don't like being denied something I want either.* "You can't do that!"

"Ah! But I can!" Mike wasn't backing down. "That's the deal. Take it or leave it. Just be thankful she's on my shelf instead of entertaining Fabiano Uberti."

"Fabiano Uberti is a . . ."

"Spare me the explicts, Counselor. And use your energy to win her back."

J.P. ran his hand through his hair. *Mike's going to win this one.*

"And I tell you what, I won't even hold this favor for payback."

He's serious. "You really think I did her wrong, don't you?" *I don't know if I want to hear his answer.*

"I think you forced your trump card assuming she'd tag along for the ride."

"But you're the one who said she was out of my league."

"She is. Or at least she was." Mike puckered his moustache in thought. "But maybe you've shown some major progress in your character here lately."

Without hesitation Mike pushed a button on his cell phone and handed it to J.P. "She's probably home."

Mikey doesn't know I've already made contact. J.P. had the upper hand now. *I'll accept that challenge.* J.P. turned his back to his friend as the phone began to ring in his ear. "Samira, It's Phil." J.P. watched Mike listen with interest. "I told you I'd call . . ." *Mike is doubtful, I can tell.* "I should be there to pick you up in about . . ." he checked his watch, " . . . about 45 minutes."

After she hung up, J.P. handed the phone back to Mike.

"You're taking her to a football game?"

"You're playing racket ball."

Mike shrugged his shoulders under his long blonde curls. "Okay. I give. Get the wrinkles ironed out and she can grace your shelf."

"Does she know you have it?"

"Highly unlikely."

"Who did your bidding?"

"Some thug I met in the parking lot."

"You're full of shit."

"Yeah, I am." Mike smiled. "Clint Barr was with me. He works here. I had him do the dirty work."

J.P. only needed one more answer. "What was your cap?"

"I told Clint to come home with the prize."

"How much, Mikey?" *I really want to know what he paid.*

"More than Uberti was willing to pay."

"How much?"

"More than you keep in your checking account."

"How much?!"

"Three grand."

"Holy shit, Counselor!"

"She's worth it, isn't she?"

"Three grand?"

"But it's an original Uberti!"

That's its only drawback! J.P. admired the work again. "Now I do owe you."

"No, you owe *her*." Mike folded his arms as he sat down in his chair. "And if you don't get your ass out of my office you're going to make us both late."

In spite of the chill in the air, J.P.'s hands were sweating when he rang Samira's doorbell. *It feels like my first date, or something.* His heart skipped a beat when the doorknob turned.

"Come on in," Samira covered the mouthpiece on the telephone as she answered the door. "I'll just be a minute."

J.P. stepped inside. *I didn't know if I'd ever be back here.* Samira motioned for him to follow her.

"Okay, Daddy, I'll call you in the morning when I get up . . ." She crossed the kitchen and removed the lid on a crock pot. She held a bowl in J.P.'s direction.

She doesn't have to feed me. J.P. started to deny the offer. *But I am hungry and it smells really good . . .*

"Chicken and dumplings." She handed him a ladle. "Go ahead."

J.P. helped himself. Before he sat down at the breakfast bar, Samira had a glass of water at his place.

"No, I don't have a number where I can be reached." Samira was still talking into the phone. "But I won't be gone all night."

J.P. opened his cell phone. *She can give him this one.* He pushed a button to display his own number.

"Oh, wait," Samira corrected. "Here's a number you can call if you need anything . . ."

J.P. took a bite as Samira read his number off.

" . . . I know, I am too. Yes, I talked with Wes . . . I will . . . You have fun tonight too . . ."

Whoever she's talking to isn't very pleased she's leaving town tonight.

"Sorry," Samira apologized as she hung up the phone. "I'm missing a family birthday dinner tonight for the first time ever!" She put both of her hands in her hair. "My father is having a hard time with it."

Great. Now I'm in the middle of a family discrepancy. "Excellent meal, by the way."

"Thanks." Samira still looked distracted. "It's easy and I figured you'd need something quick."

Does she always plan ahead like this? Instead of sitting down, J.P. leaned on the counter. "What about you?"

"I ate already." Samira turned off the crockpot. "Before Daddy called."

J.P. processed his next thought as he ate. *Mike says I owe her a fair shake.* "You know, Samira, if you need to go to the family dinner . . ."

"Oh, no. It's okay . . ."

" . . . We can do this another time," J.P. finished his sentence.

"Can we?" She looked doubtful. "I'm okay with it. But Daddy doesn't know what to do with an extra plate at the table."

J.P. rinsed the empty bowl and set it in the kitchen sink. "I don't like the idea of ruffling your father's feathers." *Any grown woman who still calls him Daddy obviously has a tight relationship with the man . . .*

"Thank you." Samira sighed. "But I've made up my mind. My girls are taken care of and my brother doesn't mind. It's his birthday. Maybe we should just go before I talk myself out of it again."

"Are you sure?" J.P. stepped aside as Samira rinsed the bowl again and placed his dirty dishes in the dishwasher.

"Yes." Samira dried her hands on a dishtowel. "Let me get my coat." She locked the deadbolt on the front door then picked up a long woolen coat from the back of the sofa. *She still looks stressed out.*

Once inside the pickup there was no place to hide from the thoughts that were bouncing around in his head. *I've wanted to talk to her for so long now, I don't know where to begin.* They spent the first several miles in small talk about Krissy and Kara's activities and James and Josh's busy lives. Then several miles passed in silence as he worked up the nerve to open the conversation.

When J.P. finally opened his mouth to speak, Samira started to say something at the exact same time.

"Go ahead."

"No, that's okay. You go."

"Ladies first."

Samira looked away. "I was just thinking . . ." she paused in thought. "I guess I just didn't know if we'd ever be alone long enough to talk again . . ."

I had that same feeling. "That's my fault." J.P. decided to let her off the hook. "I have a nasty habit of not knowing how to sustain healthy relationships."

"Do you think what we had was a relationship?"

J.P. thought for a moment. *We had sex. We had dinner. I couldn't focus at work because of her. Still can't focus . . .* He glanced in her direction. "I'd have to answer in the affirmative. Do you think otherwise?"

"Sometimes I don't know," Samira leaned her head into the headrest. "It was definitely more than a one night stand but I can't exactly decide if it was a full blown relationship or not. Everything moved so fast for awhile and then it suddenly stopped."

"I didn't mean for it to stop like that . . ."

"I think that was my fault. I got in a hurry to . . ."

"No, you didn't . . ."

"Hear me out . . ." She put her hand on the console. "I pressed you for answers you didn't have yet. I should have been more patient."

"And I should have given you more of my time." *I have a hard time separating work from home.* J.P. thought for a moment. *That's the main reason I couldn't stay married. At least according to Janet.*

They rode with in their own thoughts for a mile or so.

"Tell me about the game tonight . . ."

Is she asking that to pass time, or because she doesn't want to talk about us? "It's away. Against one of their biggest rivals. According to Josh, it should be a good game." *Might as well give her the rest of it.* "Last I knew Aunt Maggie and Uncle Roy were planning to drive over so we may see them there." He noticed a slight smile on Samira's face with that comment. "I didn't talk to them this week, but that was the plan last weekend."

Oh yeah. "And it's possible Bobby might be there too. If the work schedule played out the way . . ."

Sudden tension caused J.P. to stop talking in mid-sentence. *What caused that?*

Samira turned her shoulder away from him.

He drove a ways further before asking the dreaded question. "Is it something I said?"

"Maybe . . ."

Great.

"There's something I've needed to talk to you about and should have talked to you about a long time ago but it just never seemed like the right time, but now . . ."

I love hidden agendas. "I'm all ears."

"Well, I seem to have a knack of running into your friend Mike . . ."

"I've noticed."

"Either that or he has the knack of running into me . . ." Samira fidgeted in her seat. "But one of the last times I talked to him he told me Bobbie was going to be at the ranch over Labor Day weekend."

J.P. frowned. *Why would she be concerned over that? And why would Mike share my personal agenda without my permission?*

Samira wasn't saying anything.

"And you're upset because . . . ?" *She's looking at me as thought I should already know the answer to that question.* "For whatever it's worth, that weekend left a lot to be desired." *It's probably better to fess up than muddy the waters at this point.*

"This is a really hard thing to say out loud," Samira spoke with a great deal of caution. "But I need to get it out of my system, and to be honest, you're the only one I can to say it to."

Shit, Ralston, here it comes. J.P. gripped the steering wheel

"I didn't appreciate knowing that someone else had already taken my place . . ."

Taken your place how?

"I mean, maybe I jumped to a few conclusions, but the time I spent with you at your aunt's ranch meant something to me . . ."

And to me.

"and, well . . . it just seemed, well, like a slap in the face that you'd turn around a few short weeks later and take somebody else to that same place."

Samira stopped talking, but J.P. kept listening.

So she didn't want me to take my brother and his family to the ranch? He hoped she'd explain more because he was missing a big part of something she wasn't explaining. *To my knowledge, no one has ever felt slighted by my brother's presence. Well, with the exception of Janet.* He glanced at Samira and found her watching him very carefully. *Does she know about the brunette from Jimmy's bar?*

"Am I speaking out of turn here?"

I don't know. "No, I don't think so." *I can cross-examine a witness on the stand with great success. But I have no idea what to say to her.* "I don't know exactly what you want me to say."

Samira's eyes dropped, telling him even saying that was a mistake.

Come on, Ralston. Get a clue, would you? He forced his mind back to that weekend to see if he'd missed any incriminating details. *Maybe I just need to come clean.*

"I'm not sure how much Mike shared with you, but I didn't even make it up to the ranch until late Sunday and I had to have the boys back to their mother by nightfall on Monday . . ." *And I'm not sure James has forgiven me yet for my absence that weekend.*

" . . . I spent a day and a half with them and Bobby and then drove back home." He looked over at her to see if her body language had relaxed any. Her arms were crossed. *Obviously that didn't help.*

You're damn lucky she can't walk out on you now. Samira was looking out her window but he knew she was still listening. *Just lay it out there. I have nothing to lose now.* J.P. reran the entire weekend in his mind. *Either that or I have everything to lose.*

"Alright . . ." *Lose the defensiveness.* "Here's what I remember from that weekend. Do you want the shorten version or the whole nine yards?"

Samira shrugged.

The whole thing. "I left the office late in the afternoon and attended a business dinner that ended up pertinent to my highest priority case . . ." *Even if I did have ulterior motives at the onset of that party.* He decided that was all she needed to know about that appointment.

" . . . On my way home, against my better judgment, I stopped in at an old hangout, one I hadn't been to in several months now . . ." *Not since I met you.* "I hooked up with an old friend, a bartender, actually, who fell into step with my old habits and set me up with a woman at the pool table."

Samira still hadn't looked at him. *I really don't want to tell her about this part.*

"And to be perfectly honest . . ." *This may be the end of what could have been.* " . . . I don't remember much else until I woke up in a place I shouldn't have been without transportation and had to call our now mutual friend, Mike, for a ride home."

There, it's out there for whatever she wants to make of it. "But if it matters to you at all, I couldn't do what I set out to do there." *How honest do I dare be?* J.P. drew a deep breath. "I didn't . . ." the words wouldn't come.

Samira turned in her seat.

Sure, now she's going to look at me. "I didn't have sex with her." He couldn't force himself to look at Samira. *I might as well finish it off now.* "And to my recollection, I don't think I even kissed her." *My guess is I made a pretty shitty date that night.*

"What about Bobbie?"

Who is she referring to? Now he looked at Samira. "Bobby who?"

Samira wrung her gloves in her hands. "I should have asked you about it earlier. I'd planned to talk to you at the ranch, but like I said, it didn't happen and . . ."

Bobbie Jo Sommers. "But you took her magazine to the ranch, didn't you . . ."

"Yes. And I felt really stupid. Like I was prying into your private life somehow. But when Mike said you were taking her to the ranch I . . ."

Whoa! "Wait, wait, wait . . . ." *I need to get off this highway.*

"I took the magazine so I could ask some questions . . ."

"Just, wait, Samira . . . ." J.P. took the next exit ramp and pulled off to the side of the road. *Let's get this cleared up once and for all.* "Bobby—the one at the ranch, was my brother, Robert. I didn't take the model in the magazine to Aunt Maggie's."

The look on Samira's face was mixed. *So is she relieved, or doesn't she believe me?* "But I saw you with her in Springfield . . ."

J.P. ran his tongue over his bottom lip. *I knew Bobbie Jo was trouble there, but I didn't know Samira saw me with her.* This was far more serious than he'd imagined it could be. *You have no choice but to come clean now, Ralston.* J.P. put his hands behind his head and leaned as far back into the truck seat as possible. "Bobbie Jo Sommers is a model . . ."

"I know. I've done my research. In fact, I get those magazines in the mail every month or so . . ."

She is definitely out of my league. "Alright." *I'll give her credit for doing her homework.* "I met her at a club after some kind of a fashion show her agency put on at the mall last spring . . ."

"Probably the spring bridal show . . ."

Does she want me to tell this story or not? "Maybe, I don't know. I didn't go to the show, I met her afterwards . . ."

"That's the show the chamber sponsored in the spring."

"Okay. Then that's the one she was in town for." J.P. took a breath. "Do you want me to finish this or not?"

Samira was completely facing him now. "I'm waiting."

No, you're forcing the issue. "At any rate, Bobbie—that would be Bobbie Jo, and I hit it off and spent some time together while she was in town. Then later in the spring I spent a week with her in Mexico." *I never thought I'd share that information with her.*

Samira slid up to the edge of the seat.

So now what? Is she going to get out or what?

Samira did not speak.

"And that's it." *Besides the fact Bobbie was incredible in the sack and a handful in the gentleman's club.* "That's how I know her."

Samira blinked but she still didn't speak.

I wish she'd say something. "And if it matters, and I'm thinking it might . . ." *Maybe I don't want her to say anything.* "I haven't spent any time with her since then." The scene at his office suddenly came to mind. "Wait, before I get myself in any deeper, let me clarify that. She did come by the office when she was in town mid-summer but I let her know I was seeing someone and sent her away." *Or at least I didn't let her have her way.*

"So the meeting in Springfield was what then?"

"Chance! What do you want from me? I didn't plan it if that's what you're thinking." J.P. was finished being accused of something he hadn't done. "I didn't know she had a show going on there, and she didn't know I had meetings with the Hughes Corporation."

"Had you known would you have still invited me to go along?"

If that isn't a loaded question, I've never heard one. J.P. leaned on the driver's door and thought for a minute. *She doesn't back down does she?* "Here's the bottom line, Samira, take it or leave it." *I doubt this is what Mike had in mind when he suggested I win her back.* "I invited you to Springfield because I wanted to spend time with you. I wanted to get to know you better and thought that would be a good way to do it." The memories of his time with her in the hotel came back easily. "And I have no regrets."

"And Bobbie?"

And Bobbie . . . that could prompt about a million different responses. J.P. ran his hand through his hair. *Tell her the truth.* "With Bobbie I have a few regrets." He nodded in new understanding. "When I took her to Mexico I thought the way to a woman's heart was with really good sex. And, I'll be perfectly honest with you here . . ." *I'm to the point now I really don't care what she's thinking.* " . . . Bobbie Jo and I had good . . ." *. . . great . . .* " . . . sex together."

His eyes scanned the roof of his vehicle hoping to find words to finish his thoughts. "But she was before I met you." *I have never told a woman what I'm about to tell her.* There was a lot of risk in his next series of thoughts. *She*

can either *hear me out or shut me down.* "Samira . . ." *How do I explain this?*
" . . . before I knew you I lived alone and led a life that was all mine. I did
whatever I pleased whenever I wanted to do it. But you've given me something
no woman has ever offered before . . ." *Be careful, Ralston. This could sound
extremely shallow.* "I don't know if I can even explain . . ."

Samira sighed.

"When I'm with you something moves deep within me." *Deeper than
I've ever felt anything move in my entire life.* "Hell, even when I'm not with
you, I'm moved by your presence. And lately you haven't even been part of
my life, but yet you're there in my thoughts and my decisions, and habits . . ."
J.P. looked down at her hands that were resting uneasily in her lap.

"No one has ever permeated my every waking and sleeping thought like
you do, Samira. I'm still single and I still live alone, but it's like you're here
with me all the time." J.P. felt his hand move to his chest. "No one has had
this kind of power over me before."

Samira's head was bowed when J.P. finally dared to look at her again.
He couldn't tell if she was deep in thought or crying. *I've said everything I
know to say.*

He glanced at his watch and then back to Samira. *We'll be lucky to make
the start of the game now.* "If you want me to, I can take you back home." *I
don't know what else to offer.*

Samira slouched into the seat. Her hair was over the most part of her
face. "If you take me home I won't get to see Maggie and I won't get to meet
your brother, Bobby."

I don't care what we do anymore. His emotions were spent. J.P. had bared
his soul in ways he'd never planned on doing. *At least she's not screaming
obscenities at me.* "Whatever you want to do. It's your call."

"I'm sorry," Samira pushed her hair back as she apologized.

"No, we're not going there," J.P. shook his head. "This whole thing is
far more complicated than I ever imagined it could be. But we're not going
to be sorry over it." *I hate apologies that have no blame.* "It's just one huge
misunderstanding on many different levels."

"Then if we're not going to be sorry we can't rehash it in the future."

"What the hell is that supposed to mean?"

Samira looked spent too. "It means we call a truce." She turned her
face toward him. "That means it's water under the bridge. We leave this
whole misunderstanding right here along the side of this road and move
forward."

I don't like the idea of permanent closure. "And move forward into what?"

"That question brings us back to the whole point of this road trip."

J.P. hated games. "I have no idea what you're talking about . . ."

"Think about it, Mr. Ralston . . ."

J.P. almost smiled at Samira's formality. *She's going to make her point now.*

" . . . in that email thing we did the other night with the help of our children, you told me you wanted to revisit the question from Shoal Creek." She tipped her head. "Here we are."

But I've just aired all of my bullshit. How do I answer a question like that now?

Samira was still waiting.

"So what are you suggesting, Pretty Lady?" *Even though she's tired, she's still the most beautiful woman I've ever known.*

"I think we have a game to catch, that's what I'm suggesting."

"Are you sure?"

Samira nodded.

J.P. put the truck back in gear. A wave of relief washed over him. It was as if he'd been set free from a bondage he didn't know he carried.

"So, tell me more about Bobby."

There's no way in hell I'm going back there again. "Which one?"

"Your brother."

"Maybe we should call him Robert."

"So, tell me more about Robert."

That I can do. "He's in telecommunications, lives out east with his wife, Megan, who's an investment broker. They've got three kids . . ."

55

New Beginnings

Phil pointed to a glow in the sky. "My guess is that would be the stadium."

"You've never been here before?"

"Not here." He turned the truck in the direction of the lights. "On the average I miss more games than I see each season."

I can't imagine missing any of the girls' activities. "Is it alright to leave my purse in the car?"

Phil opened the console.

Samira laid her purse inside. *This way I don't have to keep track of it on the bleachers.* She slid out of the truck. *I wish I wasn't so tired.*

"Ready?"

"Sure." *My family is probably just sitting down to dinner about now.*

"Watch your step." Phil took her elbow as they stepped up onto a wooden bridge that led them across a ditch.

It feels good to have him touch me. Even if we are separated by coats.

"That'll be six dollars, sir." The man at the entrance held out his hand.

Phil handed over a fifty dollar bill.

The gatekeeper frowned. "I can't break this sir. They've already taken my money pouch."

Phil is a little on edge. "I have a ten in my purse."

"How close can you come?"

"Well, let's see," the ticket taker counted some ones. "If I give you my twenty and all my ones I'm still three dollars short."

Phil held out his fifty. "Keep the change."

"Well, then I won't have any change for the next person." The man seemed frustrated. "There's a convenience store a block down the road. They'll have plenty of change for you there."

"But I'm here now and I'd like to get in to watch my boys play ball before anymore time ticks off the clock."

I could fix this. "Just let me get my purse."

He shook his head. "Here, give me a twenty and as many ones as you can part with then donate the rest to the cause."

The gentleman sighed. "I don't feel right about it." He took the fifty with a great deal of hesitation. "Here's my twenty. If I give you ten ones then I've shorted you fourteen dollars and that just isn't right, mister."

"Am I complaining?"

He's used to getting what he wants.

"Well, I'm sorry about that and I'm sorry they took my extra programs too. They'll have some of those at the concession stand."

"That's just great."

Samira turned her collar up to block the cold north wind. *A ten-dollar bill would have eliminated the issue.* She watched as Phil accepted the short change.

"You'd think they could break a freakin' fifty-dollar bill."

Phil stopped and read the scoreboard. Samira looked too. *First quarter. No points on the board yet.* They walked to the edge of the visitor's bleachers.

"Uncle Roy will be seated at the fifty yard line about half way up the bleachers." Phil's eyes were searching the crowd.

He's so tense. Samira watched him for a moment. *Maybe I should have had dinner with my parents.*

Phil guided Samira with his hand on her waist.

"Over here!"

Samira looked up to see Aunt Maggie waving her hands. *There's a familiar face.* The people on the end of the row began to shift so Samira could pass through. Phil held her arm as she stepped over the knees of the people between her and Aunt Maggie.

"My, my!" Aunt Maggie exclaimed. "I didn't expect to see you here tonight!" Aunt Maggie lifted up the corner of an old quilt. "Move down, Roy, so Samira can be warm with us."

I didn't mean to make such a stir.

Phil crouched in the aisle so people in the stands could see around him. *I feel bad I'm in here and he's over there.* She felt Aunt Maggie's hand pat her leg.

"How are you, darlin'? We missed you over Labor Day."

Oh, wow. I didn't expect to begin with that discussion. Samira chose to keep things simple. "I'm doing fine thank you." *But it's nice to be missed just the same.* Samira looked out over the football field. "What numbers are we watching for?"

Uncle Roy leaned over Maggie. "James is on the offensive line. See him? He's wearing a number twenty-four jersey." Roy pointed with his gloved finger. "But Joshy, we can't see him so good. He's on the far side lined up as a receiver. We'll see him in a minute. Look for number eighty."

"Oh, honey, you can't really see too much from way up here." Maggie adjusted the quilt. "We just come here to support the team and pretend like we know what's going on."

At least I'm not the only one who doesn't know the game.

There was another break in play and the entire team left the field. *Where are they going?* People around Samira began to move around too. Phil took the opportunity to squeeze in directly behind Samira. He put his hands on her shoulders as he settled in. Samira straightened her back. *I think I'm going to like him sitting behind me like this.*

"Hey, bro. Nice you could make it."

There's a familiar tone in that voice.

"Are you going to introduce me? Or should I call her Sue?"

Must be Bobby.

Samira leaned back as Phil spoke into her ear. "Meet *Robert*."

Funny. She smiled in Robert's direction.

"Bobby, Samira Cartwright." Phil finished the introduction.

Maggie chimed right in. "She's such a nice girl, Robert." She turned and patted her nephew's knee. "It's good to see you, too, Phillip!" Maggie's face beamed with a genuine smile.

Aunt Maggie sure loves these boys. Samira ran her gloved hands over the patchwork quilt covering her lap. *I should be home helping in the kitchen.*

Maggie caught her studying the pattern on the quilt. "My sister made this a million years ago."

Samira gave the worn blanket more deliberate attention. *It reminds me of the quilt on the bed at the ranch.* "Do you quilt, Maggie?"

"No, I left the sewin' to my sisters." Maggie wriggled a little under the cover. "I took to the kitchen."

And a fine cook she is! "How many sisters do you have?"

Maggie waited to answer until the crowd around them finished a cheer. "There were four of us. We were alphabetized. Leona, me, Naomi, and Opal. In that order." Maggie nodded her head. "Naomi is the quilter. Leona used to sew too."

Leona. Samira remembered the photo in Maggie's living room. *Phil's mom.*

"This here is a log cabin pattern," Maggie explained further. "But it's so worn and patched you can't really tell anymore."

Samira admired the miniature stitches. *It's cozy at any rate.*

They watched the game in silence for several minutes. When the buzzer rang, the crowd began to disperse around them. Samira felt Phil stand.

What's he doing?

"It's halftime." Phil explained without being asked. "We're going to go try to catch the boys when they come back from the locker room. Do you want anything from concessions?"

Samira couldn't think of anything.

"Then we'll bring you a cup of coffee." Robert smiled the easy Ralston smile.

Very strong resemblance. Samira had to smile back.

Robert tapped his uncle on the shoulder. "Come on, old man, let's go find those boys."

It's funny how they call Uncle Roy "old man".

"I'm going to walk down to that bathroom." Maggie wiggled out from under the blanket too. "Do you mind sitting here with our things?"

Samira suddenly felt very vulnerable. In the distance she could see Phil and Robert walking towards the school. *I'm glad volleyball is an indoor sport.* She pulled the quilt in tighter around her legs. *I wonder how the birthday party is going?*

A man wearing a long coat and a wool hat was making his way up the bleachers toward her. *I wonder who that is.* He walked on the empty seats and stopped right where Samira was sitting. Without asking for permission, he sat down right next to Samira in Maggie's spot.

"I'm sorry, sir." Samira tucked the quilt in around her legs. "Someone is sitting there."

"No one is sitting here right now."

I don't like his attitude. "But she is coming back." *I wish he would go away!* Samira looked around hoping someone was on their way back.

"Not to worry . . ." the man had a sly grin on his face. "I came up here to talk to you for a minute."

Well, I don't have anything to say to you . . .

Without warning, the man slid his hand under the blanket and put it on Samira's knee.

Samira instantly slid into the empty space next to her. *What does he think he's doing?*

"You're pretty jumpy for being a companion of J.P. Ralston's . . ."

What business does he have knowing I'm with J.P. Ralston? "I have no idea what you're talking about." Samira spoke through clenched teeth. *If Aunt Maggie's purse wasn't on the other side of that quilt, I'd walk away.*

"Of course you don't know . . ." The man leaned in closer. "I've been watching you. You seem mighty refined to be in J.P.'s company . . ."

He's disgusting!

The man picked at his teeth with a toothpick. " . . . I happen to know a little about the man who is escorting you tonight and feel obligated to offer a word of warning . . ."

Samira turned away. *I don't need advice or anything else from this man!* The man slid closer to her again. *I'm going to have to get out of here.* She started to stand, but a woman carrying a bag of popcorn and a steaming Styrofoam cup returned and took a seat one row behind Samira. *I don't know her either, but at least I feel less vulnerable now.*

Samira slid even further onto the metal seat. Much to her horror, the man moved when she did. When he leaned in to speak again, Samira could smell alcohol on his breath.

"You are out of line . . ."

"I'm not out of line any more than J.P. is . . ." the man gazed into Samira's eyes. "His idea of a relationship is to love 'em and leave 'em. Think about that the next time he gets you in the sack."

This time when the man put his hand on her knee, Samira bolted from her seat. Strong arms caught her in the aisle, but coffee spilled over the bleachers as a result of the collision.

"Whoa there, girl."

Samira's heart was pounding hard in her chest and she knew if she said anything at all that tears would spill out of her already damp eyes. Samira was unaware of anything other than the sheer terror of the man still sitting on Maggie's blanket.

"It's okay." The calming tone of his voice caught Samira's attention. She looked up into Robert's concerned face.

Oh, thank you, God! Samira put her gloved hands to her face. "I don't know who he is . . ." Samira tried to explain, " . . . but he's . . ."

"Shhh," Robert put his arm around Samira's shoulders and pushed her head into his chest. "That's Bruce Hamilton." Robert whispered into her ear. "And I don't doubt you for a minute."

Who's Bruce Hamilton?

"What the hell?" Phil stopped a few steps below where Samira and Robert were blocking the stairs.

Robert let Samira go. "We've had a breif encounter with . . ." He nodded his head. Samira watched Phil's eyes go from Robert to the man sitting on Maggie's blankets.

I have never seen his eyes like that. The look frightened Samira. But the face of the woman hurrying up behind Phil was just as frightening.

"Get your ass off these blankets and out of these stands," Phil demanded.

The man crossed his arms and raised his eyebrows.

"Hold this." Robert handed Samira the half empty coffee cup. She watched Robert turn and face his brother. Phil tried to step around Robert.

Oh, no. He's going to get physical.

"Phillip, this isn't your ballgame." Robert was speaking very calmly. "You're here to support James and Josh, not make a scene in their stands." He took a sideways step blocking Phil's view.

The woman standing behind Phil put her hands on the back of Phil's coat. "Don't do anything stupid." Samira could hear trembling in the woman's voice. "I didn't know he was coming over here or I would have warned . . ."

Who is she?

Phil stepped out of the woman's hold. His eyes were still glaring.

Samira looked around. The football team was beginning to gather on the sidelines again and the stands were beginning to fill up. She could see Maggie making her way back across the grassy lawn between the bathroom and the bleachers. *This could get ugly.*

"Don't do it, Phillip," Robert warned quietly. "He's not worth the price you'd pay."

Uncle Roy was now standing at the bottom of the steps and he appeared to be well aware of the conflict. He put his hand out to keep Maggie from starting up the stairs.

Phil's eyes were a cold blue and his jaw was set. Samira had seen that look only one other time. *And that time he was on his way to reprimand James for something his mother accused him of . . .* Suddenly Samira realized who the woman was behind Phil. *So that must be Janet's husband.* She looked back at the man who was still inviting a fight simply by his stubborn presence. *They know exactly how to push Phil's buttons!*

He's creepy. No wonder James has trouble living with him.

"I only touched her a couple of times," the man purposefully explained to the audience gathering in the stands. "I don't know what he's all worked up about."

He touched me to provoke, Phil!

Phil took a quick step toward the man.

Oh, no. We're not going to do this. "Excuse me," Samira held the coffee cup out to the woman sitting in the bleachers. "Will you hold this?" Without waiting another second she stepped between Phil and Bruce Hamilton. *Now what am I going to do?*

"Don't get in the middle of this."

"I'm already in the middle." Samira took a deep breath. "But you and I need to talk and if you get tangled up here, we're going to lose our chance."

Phil's eyes moved to Samira. *Hold his eye contact.*

"He's the biggest bastard this side of the Mississippi." Phil's voice was loud enough most of the people gathered around heard.

"I know." *And I believe you.* She stepped into Phil's personal space. "But this isn't the time or the place to make that fact known." She flattened her hand against his coat. Her voice was almost whispering when she spoke again. "Just walk with me off these bleachers and let Bobby deal with him."

Phil set his jaw again, but he kept his eyes on hers.

"Come on." Samira added a little pressure to his side and much to her relief, Phil moved with her. Together they stepped over the fallen quilt.

Samira dared to turn around, but only long enough to know Robert was indeed going to handle whatever was left of the conflict. She had to skip several steps to catch up with Phil who was now headed out into the open lawn.

I have no idea what Phil's mindset is now, but I'm glad he didn't follow through with whatever he was thinking back there!

Phil stopped walking when he reached the chain-linked fence that separated the parking area from the stadium.

"He's an asshole."

"I know . . ."

"I hate him."

"I understand."

"I should have cleaned his clock when I had the chance."

I can't agree with that one. "You did the right thing."

"I let him steal my family away. Is that the right thing?"

Oh, I didn't know that's what he was talking about. "No. But you can't win battles by beating people up."

"He's no fighter."

Especially when he's drunk. "Not in that condition."

"What condition?"

Do I tell him or not?

Phil stopped right in front of Samira and addressed her directly. "What condition are you talking about?"

I'm not going to lie to him now. "He's been drinking." *And he's creepy.* Samira watched Phil's eyes go back to the stands. "He's not in his right mind." *Even though I'm not sure he'd be any better in a sober state.* Samira shuddered at that thought.

She watched Phil's face. *His mind is suddenly a million miles away.* She turned her back to the wind and pulled her hood up over her head.

Samira watched two full minutes tick off the scoreboard in addition to the time the clock was stopped completely. A few times she heard the fans in the stands cheer. But Phil's eyes stayed in the distance with his thoughts.

Samira wrapped her arms tighter around her middle in an effort to keep warm. The wind was stiff. *I could be sitting in front of my father's fireplace but instead I'm here with this man I hardly know, waiting for him to say something. Anything.* In the stadium light his face looked more chiseled than usual.

Ever so slowly, Phil's thoughts came back to the present. "I'm sorry . . ."

That's the most sincere thing he's ever said to me. Samira waited but he didn't say anymore. "No harm done." *With the exception of frostbite in my toes.*

"No, I mean . . . ," Phil's thoughts were still more distant than Samira realized. " . . . I'm sorry for not being in my right mind." He ran a bare hand through his hair.

His eyes were cloudy when he looked at Samira again. *Has he been drinking too?*

Phil put his hand back in his pocket. His eyes were turned toward the playing field now. "I haven't been a father to those boys for over half of their lives . . ."

Samira stepped closer to Phil so she could be sure to hear.

" . . . I've had opportunities and backed off because I thought I was doing the right thing by letting Janet and that bastard raise them as a family. But I was wrong."

Samira saw number twenty-four run off the field to the sidelines.

"You know, I met my father a few weeks back."

I remember.

"I mean, I knew him, but I didn't understand who he was while my mother was alive . . ." Phil's eyes were focused somewhere deep in the distance. " . . . I always thought he was Navy brat out there saving the world while his wife and kids were struggling along back on the Missouri homeland . . ."

Phil paused and Samira waited. " . . . But I was wrong about that too. The Captain and my mother had an understanding between them that allowed them to raise us up according to what my mother thought was best. It turns out he's the one who gave us up in order to maker her happy."

I had no idea . . .

" . . . The result is I never really knew my dad. But I thought I did and I held a grudge against him for too long. Somehow in the distance of their relationship there was a strong bond of . . . I don't know how to explain it, but something held them together even when they were apart."

Maybe like a bond of love?

"But now . . . now I understand that what was between my parents was the reality of something I've never personally known . . .

The hue of Phil's eyes softened drastically when he looked at Samira.

" . . . until maybe now."

I think he's addressing the question from Shoal Creek.

"You've changed the way I think, Samira."

Is that a good thing?

"I wasn't in my right mind, so to speak, the Friday and Saturday of Labor Day weekend." Phil looked away and ran his hand through his hair again. "I wasn't any better off than the bastard in the stands."

So that's what happened the night he was supposed to be with his family.

Samira watched Phil chew on his bottom lip a minute. "I put a case at risk, exposed my professional reputation again, and jeopardized the trust between me and James that I spent the entire summer establishing . . ."

The lump in Samira's throat was finally too big to swallow. *At least now I know he was drinking the night I thought he was out with that magazine model.* She could feel the weight of Phil's realization before he was even finished. *But he's still a better man than Janet's creepy husband.*

"I've spent my whole life getting even." Phil looked away. "But I don't think that matters anymore."

When he looked back to Samira, she felt it was time to say something. "Then what does matter, Phil?" *I hope that's the right question.*

Phil rubbed his face in both hands, then slowly reached out and pulled Samira into his chest. "You matter a whole helluvalot . . ."

Samira allowed his embrace to warm her from the inside out.

" . . . And if you really want to know the truth, you also scare the shit out of me."

"Maybe you have much the same effect on me." Samira lifted her face so she could see his. *Although it's doubtful I would ever phrase it quite that way.* She'd never known anyone with such power of character, both destructive and constructive. *But I've never known a man with such depth to his soul either.* Samira pressed her face into his chest again. She wished she could feel his heart beat, but his coat was too thick. *How will I ever explain him to Daddy?*

"I owe you a cup of coffee."

Samira made a worried face. "Just don't leave me alone again, okay?"

Phil draped his arm over Samira's shoulder and started toward the concession stand. "Highly unlikely I'll ever leave you alone again."

That's sounds promising.

Robert intercepted their route. He removed his stocking hat and knelt on one knee before them on the gravel walkway. "My hat is off to you, Lady Samira. In my entire life I've never seen anyone handle my brother with such grace."

"Get up, Bobby." Phil kicked his shoe at his brother's bent knee.

Bobby stood up. "She's a keeper, big brother."

"Yeah, I know."

Phil answered with such confidence that Samira's heart skipped a beat. "The coffee is on me."

Robert handed the first cup to Samira and the next one to Phil. Samira was stunned to see Phil accept. *I've never known him to drink a cup of coffee. Ever.*

"It's always a pleasure to bump into your ex-wife and her entourage, Phillip." Bobby snapped a lid on his cup and then turned to do the same for Phil and Samira.

"Is it now?" Phil allowed his brother to cover the coffee. *So that must have been Phil's pre-game tension.* Samira noted that there was no tension in Phil's voice at all when Janet was mentioned this time. *Maybe we've made some progress here after all.*

"She has always held me in such high esteem." Bobby rolled his eyes at Samira. He lifted his cup in a toast. "Here's to new beginnings."

"To new beginnings." Phil raised his cup. When his eyes passed over Samira's they stopped.

She allowed Phil's quiet gaze to penetrate. *He's still serious, but the earlier torment is gone.* She lifted her cup. *Maybe if he's coming to terms with his past, he'll be able to move into his future.*

"Yes. To new beginnings."

56

Freedom

J.P. clicked the computer mouse and waited for the document to print while Samira changed into his clothes. *At least she agreed to come home with me.* J.P. took the papers out of the printer tray and sorted them back into numerical order. *Even if she stipulated her own terms.*

"I found some hot chocolate mix," Samira called from the kitchen. "Do you have cups?"

"Yeah . . . somewhere . . ." *Where are they?* "Try the cupboard above the stove." He carried his papers out to the living room. *I really need to go over Denise's notes at least once before morning.*

"Found them . . ." A few minutes later Samira appeared in the archway between the kitchen and living room. She was wearing a pair of his sweatpants and a long-sleeved t-shirt James had left behind.

And she looks damn good.

Samira set one of the mugs down amidst the scattered newspapers on the coffee table.

"Sorry about the mess. Maria didn't come in today."

Samira lifted her cup to her lips. "Who's Maria?"

Let's get this one out in the open from the get-go. "My housekeeper."

"She doesn't pose for magazine covers or anything like that, does she?"

J.P. had to smile. "No, I doubt Maria has even been considered for a cover shot." He pictured the elderly Hispanic woman in his mind. "But she does stop in a couple times a week to tidy up, and do my laundry." J.P. looked around his front room. *It's been worse.* "She's probably glad James isn't here."

"Do you miss him?" Samira curled into the corner of the sofa and pulled her knees to her chest.

"Sometimes." J.P. spoke honestly. "But right now my casework is heavy enough that he's better off playing football and sticking to familiar routine." *Or am I just talking myself out of fatherhood again?*

Samira nodded and sipped the hot chocolate.

She looks tired. J.P. looked back to the notes. *I should get this done so we can call it a night.* He felt Samira's feet slide in between him and the couch. *It feels good to have her touching me.*

J.P. finished reviewing. Much to his surprise, Samira hadn't spoken a word while he was reading. *She's either totally lost in her own thoughts or extremely polite.* He dug a pencil out from under the corner of a newspaper. *Most likely the latter.* He jotted a quick note: How much does Goldstein need to purchase Shoal Creek? He tapped the stack of papers on the coffee table.

"Finished?"

"For now." *Tomorrow will be a long day at the office.*

J.P. stood up and offered a hand to Samira. She pulled herself off the couch. J.P. went back into his office. *If I were alone, I'd go over the FBI report one more time.* He glanced in Samira's direction. *But I am definitely not alone.*

As he turned out the overhead light in the office, Samira became silhouetted in the doorway. *I don't know if I want to play by her terms.* He'd never had a woman stay the night in his own home.

"What are you thinking?"

"I'm thinking . . ." *How honest should I be here?* " . . . that you move me in ways I may not be able to control."

"And I'm thinking if you don't put me to bed I'm going to fall asleep standing up."

Putting you to bed won't be a problem. But not undressing you? That could be a problem.

J.P. crossed the kitchen and checked the lock on the back door. *She did my dishes.*

"Do you leave a light on at night?"

"No. Why?"

Samira shrugged. "I always leave a dim light in the kitchen. It just makes it feel more homey . . ."

"Would you be more comfortable if I left one on?"

"No, I'm okay." Samira yawned. "Do you have that toothbrush you promised me?"

"I put it on the counter." He pointed to the bathroom off his bedroom.

J.P. took a deep breath and held it in as Samira disappeared behind the closed bathroom door. He exhaled as slowly as he'd breathed in. *How do you put a woman like that in your own bed and not finish what you're dying to start?* He reached behind his head and grabbed his sweatshirt. With one swift motion he pulled it off and tossed it into the dirty clothes hamper. *After all the crap at the game, it's amazing she even agreed to come home with me.*

J.P. opened his top dresser drawer looking for an old t-shirt. The worn envelope his father had given him was folded along the edge. He poured the contents out in his hand. *Mom's wedding rings.* J.P. turned the diamond so he could see it in the dim light of the room. *"Some things in life aren't worth losing . . ."* His father's words played in his mind. *". . . there may come a time when winning isn't enough."*

J.P. closed his hands around the rings and looked at the closed bathroom door. *She's definitely not worth losing but if winning isn't enough, then what is?*

The door opened and Samira stepped out into the light. Her hair was hanging over her shoulders. *Just like in Springfield.*

"Your turn." Samira stepped into the bedroom. "Which side do you usually sleep on?"

J.P. shook the rings in his hand. "Both."

Samira raised her eyebrows. "Well, tonight you need to pick a side."

"I pick your side." *She can think on that for a minute.* J.P. closed the bathroom door before she had a chance to retaliate.

He laid his mother's rings on the shelf. *Geez, Ralston. You like tired.* He ran his hand over his chin and decided not to shave until morning. He took care of business and brushed his teeth. When he left the room, he took the rings with him again.

Samira was already curled up under the covers. Her hair fanned the entire pillowcase.

Someday these rings are going to mean something. J.P. set the rings on the nightstand as he sat down on the edge of the bed. Samira's hand touched the base of his neck, then moved slowly down the length of his spine sending signals to every nerve ending in his body.

"You're making your terms very difficult to play by . . ." *But I'm not playing to win her. Am I?*

"Don't put a shirt on . . ."

I don't put anything on to go to bed. "I don't know if I can leave anything on under the circumstances." *Maybe she'll grant me permission . . .*

Her hand moved to his waist. "But you promised."

J.P. turned so he could see her. "That I did." He pulled the covers down and slid between the sheets next to her. *She took off the sweatpants.* "You should know, this is the hardest promise I've ever had to keep."

Samira's fingertips touched his cheek. "I like it when you don't shave."

"I like it when you talk to me in bed." J.P. dared to pull her closer to him. He had yet to kiss her tonight, but he was afraid a single kiss would only make it harder to keep his promise.

"Turn off the light . . ."

J.P. clicked the switch at the bottom of the lamp like he did every night. But tonight he had a woman to hold. *A very special woman.*

His eyes adjusted to the darkness of the room. *I want to watch her fall asleep.*

"Did your aunt make the quilt?"

"What quilt?"

"The one we're sleeping under." Samira moved closer. Her hands were now flat against his bare chest.

Oh. "Yeah, I guess she did." *I'd never stopped to think about who made this quilt.*

"Aunt Maggie said her sisters are the quilters."

"Naomi and my mother. They were the sewers." *Why do I know that piece of information right now?*

"I know. It's very cozy under your family quilts."

It's not the quilt making it cozy.

"Do you remember the first time you slept with me?"

How could I forget? "Every detail . . ."

"I was so scared."

J.P. ran his fingers through her hair. "You didn't seem scared to me."

"I was. I was terrified I'd forgotten how to make love to a man."

He still couldn't explain the way she moved him. *But I'd never made love to a woman before either.*

" . . . And then the next morning I was afraid I'd never see you again." Samira completed her confession.

"Is that why you wouldn't let me kiss you?"

Samira's head was instantly off the pillow. "Ohhh . . ." She sat up and put her face in her hands. "I didn't want you to remember that part!"

J.P. laughed at her reaction. "I remember all the parts."

"Even the part when I cried?"

Yeah, that part too. He nodded knowing she could see him well enough to see his answer.

"I didn't mean to hurt you . . ." Samira pushed her hair back over her shoulder. "I was afraid of being hurt."

I wondered what that was all about? "If it makes you feel any better, I felt guilty for staying that night."

"Why?" Samira was laying down again with her head propped up on an elbow.

"Because I felt like I'd taken advantage of you."

"But I wanted you to stay."

"I know." He could see her dark eyes searching his in the dark. "And I wanted to stay too." *You might as well lay it out there.* "But I was afraid I wasn't ready for a woman like you."

Samira rolled onto her back and put her arms over her face. "I hate it when people say that about me."

Now J.P. was up on his elbow. "When they say what?"

"*A woman like you.*" Samira threw her arms into the air. "What is that supposed to mean anyway? It's like I can't be who I am because I'm like *that!*"

"Come here." He took a hold of her hand and pulled her back toward him. "I'll tell you about the woman like you." He slid one of his legs between hers so she was right up against him. Placing his hand in the small of her back he held her tight. "There is only one woman like you. You're compassionate and beautiful. You're spirited and sophisticated and independent and strong . . ."

Samira began to shake her head and tried to pull away.

"I'm not finished yet." *And she needs to hear me out.* "But at the same time you're stubborn and vulnerable and sexy. And if you want to know the whole of it, I didn't know if I could handle all you had to offer that night."

"I am not stubborn."

J.P. smiled into the dark. "Oh, yes you are, Pretty Lady."

"Strong-willed, maybe, but not stubborn."

"I beg to differ." *This is kind of fun.* He moved his hand up the inside of the t-shirt and felt her tenderness against his hand. *She's not wearing anything underneath this shirt.*

"You promised . . ."

"Yes, I did." *But the promise only stipulated sex. She didn't mention anything about making love and that's exactly what I want to do with her.* J.P. pressed his pelvis into hers as their lips touched. Consumed by her presence in the darkness he kissed her again. And then again.

But you promised! J.P. heard his conscience through the heat of the passion. *Oh shit.* As much as he hated to, he knew this was a promise he had to keep.

Samira was lost in her own passion. J.P. felt her bare legs rise up over his body. Straddling his hips she started to remove the t-shirt. *I owe her my integrity if nothing else.* J.P. moved his hands up her thighs and hung on to the hem of the shirt. Her eyes searched his.

"I have a promise to keep."

Samira pulled on the shirt again but J.P. held it tight. He sat up into her and wrapped his arms all the way around her. "These are your terms, Pretty Lady." *Definitely not terms I'd agree with for anyone else!*

"Maybe I changed my mind . . ."

And she says she's not stubborn! "Maybe you did," J.P. allowed her to kiss his neck. "But I'm a man of my word." *And I'm not going against my better judgment like I did the first time I was with her.*

Samira stopped kissing him and threw her head back. J.P. held her body weight as she fell away. *I could work my way down this pose . . .*

She was smiling playfully when she leaned forward again. J.P. caught his breath as she ran her hands through his hair.

"Then just kiss me good night."

I don't have to because you're kissing me! J.P. opened his eyes expecting to find himself standing in the shallow waters of the lake at Aunt Maggie's ranch. He'd always attributed the power of that kiss to Samira's passion. *But it's more than that . . . It's more of a power between us.* Samira gently eased off his lap. *I've felt chemistry before. But this is even more evocative than that.*

J.P. watched as she turned her back to him and slid her legs back under the covers that had almost fallen off the end of the bed. J.P. caught the quilt and pulled it over Samira's shoulder. Then he stretched out and wrapped his arm around her middle.

What I wouldn't do for this sensation to last a lifetime. Her body warmed him from the inside out. *Some things aren't worth losing . . .*

"Phil?"

"Yeah?" He linked his fingers with hers under her breasts.

"Next time can I stay under your terms?"

J.P. chuckled. *Anything you wish, Pretty Lady.*

Morning came with clarity of mind and a rejuvenated spirit. J.P. awoke early. *I'm going to let her sleep.* He dressed as quietly as possible and took Chase out the back door. J.P. was completely consumed with thoughts of Samira as he worked up to a full stride. *How is it that I feel more committed to this woman than I've ever felt before yet at the same time I feel completely free?* The gravel crunched under his running shoes. *I don't feel like I have anything to prove.*

By the time he reached the turn around point at the bridge, he was ready to get back to her. He removed his sweatshirt and tied it around his waist. *It took me all of ten years to actually bring a woman home to stay with me. I don't want her to wake up alone!* J.P. threw a large stick into the timber for Chase to retrieve as he took off again.

Samira was just beginning to stir when J.P. returned to the bedroom. He watched as she rolled over and opened her eyes. *She's just as beautiful in the daylight as she is in the moonlight.*

"Mornin', Pretty Lady."

"What time is it?"

"Almost eight."

Samira sat up with an abrupt jerk.

"Too early or too late?" He removed his sweaty t-shirt.

Samira was climbing out of bed. "I told my father I'd call him when I got up."

"Go ahead." J.P. pointed to the phone by the bed. He sat down on the edge of the chair and removed his running shoes and socks. *Does she call him every morning?*

"No, you don't understand." Samira pushed her hair back out of her face with both hands.

I have no idea why this is so important. At the same time he was humored by the way she was standing there.

"I'm usually up long before this. Daddy would have expected my call before now."

Then call him. "Tell him you slept in." *Which is exactly what she did.*

"But what if he's already been to the house to check on me?"

He would do that? J.P. stood up and used the damp t-shirt to wipe his face again. "How will you know if you don't try to get a hold of him?"

"What do I tell him?" Samira put her hands on her hips, obviously in a state of panic.

I don't know if it's healthy for me if she's this concerned about her father after one of the best nights of my life.

Samira was still looking panicked.

J.P. reached over and handed the handset to Samira. "Dial the number and get the facts before you set yourself up for something that might not even have happened."

Samira looked at him and then at the phone. "I guess you're right." She started to push the numbers on the keypad then stopped. She looked up at J.P. like maybe she didn't want him listening.

J.P. threw his arms out to his sides. "Alright, I'm going to take a quick shower while you sort this out, okay?" *I'd rather not hear what she tells him anyway.*

Samira's face softened. "I'm sorry."

"Don't be." *What is it with her father anyway?* He started to run water in the sink. While the temperature of the tap warmed, he lathered his face. *I don't know if I want to know the answer to that question.* J.P. adjusted the faucet to a slow stream and ran the razor over his cheek with his left hand like he did every morning. *A simple "good morning" would have sufficed.*

There was a faint tap on the door.

"Come in . . ."

Samira's dark eyes peeked through the crack.

I could tell her there's another bathroom. J.P. passed the razor from his left hand to his right and started down the other cheek. Samira was still watching him in the reflection.

"You can come in . . ." he stopped shaving long enough to focus on her eyes in the reflection. She stepped all the way through the door, still wearing Josh's shirt. It hung just below her panty line. *Too bad it's not a little shorter.*

"Have you been out already?"

He rinsed the blade under the running water. "Chase and I took our morning run."

"I didn't mean to sleep so long."

J.P. lifted his chin in the reflection and ran the razor over the edge of his jaw line. "Didn't do any harm, did it?" *I hope everything's in order with her father.*

"I guess not." Samira put the seat down on the toilet and sat down. "Daddy wasn't looking for me yet, thank goodness. He's a worrier."

Obviously. J.P. rinsed his blade again. He could feel Samira's eyes on him.

"I told him I'd be over for brunch in an hour or so."

Works for me. I need to be at the office by then anyway. He turned off the water and set the razor down in its place by the medicine cabinet.

"But it's still awhile before an hour is up . . ."

So what's she suggesting? He decided not to give her the satisfaction of eye contact. Instead he buried his face in a dry towel and wiped the remaining shave cream off his face. Before he looked up again, Samira's arms were around his middle from behind. *I'm going to need a cold shower instead of a hot one.*

"I'm glad you're a man of your word." Samira tucked her fingers under the waistband of his shorts.

I'm not so sure I'm as grateful. "What about your terms of agreement?" He put the towel over the edge of the sink and turned around. *I am not going to terminate an agreement without reading the face of the one who drafted the conditions.*

Samira's hands moved over his bare shoulders and locked behind his head. "The terms of the original agreement ended at daylight," she said slowly. "And as far as I'm aware, no new terms have been set for the new day."

J.P. ran his hands over her hips. *No panties. Now there's a silent invitation if I've ever known one.*

"I'd hate to keep you from your family again . . . " *The last thing I need to do is piss off her father before brunch.*

"Krissy wasn't even awake yet, and Mama and Kara had gone to the store for eggs."

J.P. ran his hand up her backside and cupped it behind her ear right before he kissed her.

Samira broke the kiss gently. She took his hand as she turned around. Almost on tip-toe, she led him back to his bed.

When she reached to remove the t-shirt, he didn't stop her like he had before.

"What time do you have to be at the office?"

J.P. could feel her hand pressing against the small of his back.

"It doesn't matter . . ." *Nothing is going to rush this moment.* He'd waited for it for too long. He felt the curves of her body with his hands as he kissed her again. *Nothing has ever felt this right.* He rolled slowly onto his back, pulling her with him as he moved.

"I don't want to make you late . . ."

She's still talking to me in my bed. J.P. pulled her leg over his hips and moved her back into the same position he'd experienced in the darkness of the night. "You won't."

Samira leaned over him and balanced her weight on her forearms. He enjoyed the sensation of her hair when it brushed against his bare chest. He didn't dare close his eyes for fear he'd miss the passion in her dark eyes.

"I think we've been this far before . . ."

The passion J.P. was hoping to see in her eyes was overshadowed by a fresh playfulness that brought an easy smile to his lips. She kissed his smile.

We have, but this time it's daylight and I can see all of you. He allowed her next kiss to linger. *And I like everything I see.* J.P. sat up into her just as he'd done the night before, but this time, he didn't have to hold back. The delayed response of this moment was sweeter than it would have been had they rushed into it the night before. J.P. realized that fully as the warmth of her body consumed his entire being.

She is very much worth the wait. J.P. pulled her slightly forward and moved gently within her. *Without a doubt she's all I'll ever need.*

57

Seeking Victory

The afternoon had been long, and it wasn't over yet. Samira leaned into the mirror in the ladies room to reapply her lipstick. She hoped it would make her look fresher than she felt. *Another hour,* she told herself. *Then I can go home and get off my feet!*

It was Thursday. She'd spent all morning on the telephone confirming the library events for the next quarter in preparation for the noon board meeting. *That meeting lasted way longer than I anticipated.* Now she was at the high school gym waiting for Kara to play her fourth volleyball match.

A loud buzzer from the gym announced the start of another game. Samira inhaled deeply and gave her reflection a weary nod. *Smile.*

"Samira! Come here!"

Oh no, not Susan. Samira stopped in her tracks. *Be polite but firm.* Much to her surprise, Susan was pulling a man toward her. *How does he always seem to show up?*

"Look who I found wandering the halls!" Susan was proud of her catch.

"I wasn't exactly wandering," Mike Benson raised his bushy eyebrows at Samira. "I'm late and have a feeling I might be too late."

"Oh, don't be silly. It's never too late . . ." Susan was still pulling on his arm.

Poor Mike. He doesn't need Susan's meddling. "Mike Benson," Samira stuck out her hand. "It's good to see you again." His hair was wet. *He obviously walked a ways in the rain.*

Susan let Mike's arm go and clapped her hands together. "Oh, and you remember each other too! How perfect!" She reached with both hands and

527

straightened Samira's suit jacket from the bottom. "Well, I'll let you two chat. Take your time. I'll keep stats on Kara for you." Susan began to walk away slowly. Twice she turned around and made encouraging gestures in Samira's direction.

Mike rolled his neck from side to side. "She's a case, isn't she? I think she gave me whiplash."

He's obviously here to see Kelly. "May I help you find your date?" *I just talked to her a few minutes ago. Funny, she didn't mention Mike.*

Mike adjusted the loose watch around his wrist. "Well, let's see. I told her I'd be here forty minutes ago."

Samira stepped aside so a group of high school girls could pass by. "She's probably watching the game."

Mike seemed very distracted. He pushed a button on his cell phone and put it to his ear. "I didn't know there was a game today." He sounded rushed. "Hang on."

Samira looked through the open gym door. Kara was still sitting on the bench next to her coach. *I don't want to miss her game!* Her eyes went on up into the bleachers and stopped on her mother. *And I told Mama I'd be right back.* Samira tuned into Mike's end of the telephone conversation.

" . . . No, trust me and just come in here a sec, alright?" Mike's voice was forceful. He punched another button on his phone and dropped it into his suit pocket. "Our mutual friend is sitting in my car in the parking lot . . ."

"Phil is here? At the school?" *Really?*

"It's a long story, but he's without transportation and I'm without my date so we're both a little stressed. Is she in there?" Mike nodded toward the gym.

"Probably."

Mike's face was already searching the bleachers. "What are you doing here anyway?"

"It's my daughter's game." Samira looked back into the gym. Kara was still next to her coach. *Fortunately.*

"Miss Samira, you may have just saved my hide and my date." Mike Benson looked from the crowd back to her. "If that red-headed English teacher is still talking to me when I finally work my way to the top of those stands, I owe you a favor."

"You don't owe me anything." Samira knew Kelly was patiently waiting. *She's not the type to be bent out of shape over a late appointment!*

There wasn't a minute's hesitation in Mike's step. He stopped inside the door, paid his entrance fee and then took off in full stride for the bleachers. *I wonder if he's been here before.* Samira watched Mike climb effortlessly to the very top of the stands where he bent one knee on the bleacher in front of Kelly. *There goes the explanation and dramatic apology.*

Her eyes went back to the game just in time to see Kara trade places with another player. *That's my girl.* She stepped inside the door so she could see better.

They put her in to serve! The ball left Kara's hand and bounced near the baseline of the opposing court. *12-13.* The line judge rolled the ball under the net and Kara served again. *13-13. Nice going!* Samira clapped with the crowd. *14-13. You go, Kara!* The next serve went into play and the home team lost the serve.

"She's good."

Samira's eyes went to Mike in the stands. *I don't know if I'm ready to face that voice in public.* She turned and faced Phil who was standing several feet directly behind her. *Especially in a public that includes my mother.*

"She gets her athletic ability from her father."

"She gets her poise from her mother."

The ball was back in play. "Not hardly." *I really want to watch this. 14-15. Come on, girls.* Samira could feel Phil's presence move closer. "Tom had nerves of steel." She remembered well. "That's what made him so valuable on the police squad." *14-16. Win the serve back, ladies!* She was relieved to see Kara's coach call a time out. "They play the best of five. This is game four."

"Poise and nerves are two different things." Phil picked up the conversation. "And the poise she gets from you. It's very becoming."

Samira blushed. She stepped out of the doorway, hoping her mother wasn't paying any attention. *Or Susan for that matter.*

Mike Benson appeared suddenly.

"I hate to prolong this situation . . ." Mike tried to apologize. " . . . But it seems my date would like to stay and watch the end of this match." Mike's face was extremely serious. "And being the gentleman I am, I'm inclined to give her the benefit of my presence through the remainder of this game."

The look on Phil's face was total frustration, yet the way Mike addressed him was so comical.

These two are funny together.

Phil looked from Mike to Samira, and then back again. "Counselor, it would seem that you've forgotten one major detail of a promise you made earlier today."

Mike crossed his fingers behind his back so Samira could see. "And what promise might that have been?"

"The promise that you would run me back to the office immediately following the afternoon meeting."

I think Phil is far more serious than Mike realizes.

Mike continued to hold his hand behind his back. "The stipulation to that promise was that the meeting needed to end on time." The damp curls on

Mike's head bobbed as he talked. "Seeing as how you were in charge of that ever-so important business maneuver, it would seem you should have ended it in a more timely fashion to accommodate the original agreement."

Samira was trying to concentrate on the game, but with Mike's final comment, she burst out laughing.

"Then give me the keys to your car and I'll come back and get you."

He really wants to go.

"By the time you get back to the office, the game will be over and I'll be ready for my car again. What's another twenty minutes anyway?"

"Maybe you could catch a ride to my office from your date . . . ."

"Here, tell you what, Counselor . . ."

Samira listened to Mike's voice amidst the crowd noise. "Let's just call this a return favor. You owe me a couple of doosies anyway and this one will only cost you a few minutes of your time . . . ."

"Mike, come on," Phil was beginning to plead. "I have a shit load of paperwork to complete by morning and you know it."

Samira continued to listen.

"You'd take a dinner break and work out, right?"

"Later!"

"Just consider this an early break."

"I don't see a place to eat anywhere near this volleyball game!"

"Ah, you're just not looking hard enough."

Samira turned around just in time to see Mike place a green bill in Phil's hand.

"There's a concession stand down that hall. I passed it when I was looking for Miss Davis." Mike sounded very matter of fact. "And I'm almost certain the popcorn was fresh."

Mike turned and spoke to Samira. "He'll be fine. He just needs to unwind a minute. Way too intense today." Samira's eyes followed him all the way to the top of the bleachers where Kelly was contentedly watching the game.

And I need to be paying closer attention too! In spite of that desire, she turned just long enough to make eye contact with Phil again. His face was less than comfortable.

"This is the third time I've been stranded today." He ran his hand through his damp hair. "And to be honest, it's starting to play against my patience."

I understand. Noise from the crowd took her eyes back to the scoreboard. *If Kara weren't playing, I'd take him myself. 20-18. And Paula is serving.*

"Do you want to take my car?"

For the first time since he'd walked into the building, Phil's face looked hopeful. But then he seemed to have a second thought. "Then how would you get home? It's raining."

"My mom is here. She could take us home." *I don't know how I'll explain that to her, but I'm sure she'll give us a ride.*

"My truck should be back at the office by now . . ."

Phil started to explain but Samira's attention shifted back to the game. Paula lost the serve and the opponents were tied again. *I really need to get off my feet.* "Do you want to sit down for a minute?"

Phil looked blankly into the gym, then ran his tongue over his bottom lip. "Sure." He threw his hands out in surrender and started to follow Samira.

"Excuse me, sir. That will be three dollars." The ticket taker held out her hand.

Phil handed over the bill Mike had given him and waited for change. "That was easier than changing a fifty." Phil sat down beside Samira.

I wonder if anyone in this crowd will recognize J.P. Ralston. She lifted her feet out of her dress shoes and placed her nylon toes on the bleacher in front of them. *That feels better.*

And Kara is serving again! Samira sat on her hands and watched as Kara served the first point. *22-20. They have to win by two.* "If we win this game, they'll play one more to fifteen." *23-20.*

"Hey there, stranger!" Krissy was suddenly seating herself directly in front of them. "Where did you come from?" Krissy's friend plopped down directly in front of Samira. "Tif, meet Phil. Phil, Tif—short for Tiffany but she hates her real name."

Krissy hasn't seen Phil since the ranch, yet she picks up like they just left off.

Phil yanked Krissy's ponytail playfully. Samira looked in time to see his easy smile. "Pleased to meet you, Tif. I understand about the name thing." Phil played the game politely. He winked at Samira.

Kara missed the serve and the opponents took over again. Samira buried her face in her hands more in reaction to Krissy's arrival than to Kara's missed serve.

"Don't worry, Mama, they'll get it back!" Krissy nodded toward the home team. "See? Christine Jackson is up next. She'll ace the next serve."

First they have to win the serve back!

"I'm starving!" Krissy held out her hand. "Can I have some money, please, please?"

"Krissy, it's less than an hour now and we'll be home . . ."

"But my stomach can't wait an hour . . ."

Can't she just leave me be until after the game? Samira thought again. *That's a very selfish thing to think!* She reached for her purse. *And they're tied again! I can't stand it!*

"Here," Phil took Krissy's hand and handed over Mike's change. "Go. Be happy."

"Oh, my gosh!" Krissy squealed. "You're awesome! Thanks!" Without a moment's hesitation, Krissy threw her arms around Phil's neck and hugged him.

In front of God and everybody! "How much did you give her?"

"Two bucks."

"That's it?" Samira was shocked. *She thinks he's awesome for two bucks.*

"That's it, why?"

"Because she's never reacted that way when I've given her money!" Samira watched as Christine Jackson aced a serve over the net. 24-23. The crowd went wild causing Samira to wish she wasn't sitting in a busy gym. *I can't even hear myself think! And thinking would be very helpful right now!*

"That's game."

"There's one more." Samira stated over the cheers. "For the match."

"I figured as much."

She remembered her offer. "Are you sure you don't want to take my car?"

Phil looked over his shoulder. Samira looked too. *Mike and Kelly don't look like they're ready to leave yet.* The people in the stands around them sat back down in their seats.

"You know, if you really don't mind, I'd be inclined to do just that."

"I don't mind," Samira reached for her purse. *Anything to relieve his tension.*

"I can call you later or stop by so you can take me back to my truck."

Whatever works for him. "That's fine." Samira handed him her keys. "I'm in the second row on the south side."

Phil nodded. "You're sure you're okay with this?"

"Positive!" *I'll think of something to tell Mama.*

"Then I'll give you a ring in what, about an hour?"

"Whenever. I'm just going home after this."

Phil thanked her and started to stand up.

"Wait!" Krissy was suddenly present agin. "Don't go yet."

Samira followed Krissy's backward glance and spotted her mother walking directly toward them. *Oh, Krissy, how could you?* The clock on the gymnasium wall was ticking off a ten-minute break between the games. *That's way too much time!*

Phil waited politely as Krissy helped her grandmother up onto the bottom bleacher. "This is where Mama went, Granny." Krissy was beaming from ear to ear. "Phil, this is my grandmother, Ashleigh . . ."

Samira closed her eyes. *Why am I so embarrassed for Mama to meet Phil?*

" . . . And Granny, this is Phil, the one I've been talking to you about."

The one she's been talking to Mama about? Samira opened her eyes to see Phil kindly greet her mother. *He is very gentle and professional and calm. And sexy . . .* The last thought caught Samira totally off guard.

Phil excused himself from the introduction very casually and then turned to face Samira again. He held out her car keys. "I'll be in touch later."

Okay. Samira nodded. She was so tongue-tied now she didn't know if she would ever recover. *And there's still five minutes of break.*

"I'm going to go to the restroom, Samira," her mother patted her knee. "I'll be right back."

Krissy disappeared as quickly as she'd appeared leaving Samira to her own thoughts. The whole turn of events was too much too fast!

"Would you just look at him, Samira?" Susan was making her way down the bleachers in Samira's direction.

She's just what I don't need!

"I can't believe it! But I think we've lost your window of opportunity!" Susan was thoroughly disgusted. "Just look at the way he's talking with Miss Davis! You'd think he's known her for some time the way they are carrying on!"

Samira turned around and made eye contact with Kelly and Mike. They waved and she waved back. *Maybe that will keep Susan out of my love life for a while!*

"I'm telling you Samira, the way you scare them off . . . well, it's safe to say that you're going to end up an old maid." Susan's eyes went to the top of the bleachers again. "He was quite the catch and you screwed it up!" Susan continued on down the bleachers without fully stopping.

Thank you, God, for taking her away!

"This is an exciting afternoon." Ashleigh took her seat. The teams had switched sides and now the serving corner of the home team was right in front of Samira and her mother. "Kara didn't think they would have a chance and just look at the way they're playing!"

But what she's saying and what she's thinking are two different things. Samira knew her mother meant well. *The excitement she's referring to is more than the game.*

I might as well tell her the truth. "I didn't know Phil was going to be here . . ."

"I assumed as much," Ashleigh's eyes were on the game. She clapped with the crowd as the home team scored a point. "I'm sure you might have wanted me to meet Phil in a different setting, but it's alright honey." She clapped again when they scored. "He seems like a very nice man."

I can always count on Mama to hold her thoughts until she processes them further. Samira tried to concentrate on the game but it was difficult to think about volleyball when the man she loved had just appeared at her daughter's game.

"He rode over here with his best friend, but his friend decided to stay for the rest of the match. Phil needed to get back to work so I loaned him my car."

"That was very nice of you, dear." Ashleigh smiled politely. "So you and the girls will need a ride home?"

Samira nodded.

"I can stir up some beef and noodles quick after the game and you won't have to fix a meal."

Samira's first reaction was to decline, but the thought of not having to put a meal on the table was very inviting. On a second thought she accepted the invitation.

Ashleigh clapped again. "Wonderful! Your father will be home by then. We've been missing you."

Kara was next to serve.

I know, ever since I missed Weston's birthday party. Samira put her elbows on her knees and rested her chin in her hands. *Had I known how long they'd hold that over my head, I might have made a different decision.* Samira watched her daughter drop a serve near the baseline scoring for her team again. *But then again, I'd have missed that whole night and the next morning with Phil.* Samira forced her mind back to her mother's voice.

"Where does this Phil work, honey?"

"He's an attorney. Self employed." Now Samira was glad for the noise of the crowd.

Ashleigh nodded slightly. Her salt and pepper hair was tucked back into her regular bun. "He looks very professional. And a very nice smile too."

But you should see him in the morning when he hasn't shaved and he's all sleepy and unaware. Samira smiled. "Yes, he does have a great smile, doesn't he?"

"And he makes you smile." The mother looked directly into her daughter's eyes. "I haven't seen you smile like that in a long while, Samira."

Samira looked back to the game. "Like what?"

"I'm your mother, Samira." Ashleigh also looked back to the game. "I know your expressions and the one you wore in the doorway over there was a genuine smitten look."

So she was watching me. Samira sighed, once again very aware of her transparency. *It's just as well Krissy brought her over now!*

"Just be careful, dear."

Samira closed her eyes. *I know Mama's going to finish that thought.*

" . . . It seems he could spare a few minutes to finish a freshman volleyball game."

Samira rocked back on the pads of her hands against the bleachers. She had no desire to hear the rest of the observation.

" . . . . I don't want you to be hurt by his commitment to his job."

But Tom was committed too. Remember? That's what you used to like about him—the way he was always ready to respond to a call or emergency. Kara finished serving with the team up by five points. *They don't even know Phil yet so I don't dare defend him.*

"Now I just hope they can hang on!" Ashleigh's excitement for Kara's team was sincere.

I hope I can hang on.

They finished the match. *15-10. Excellent game for freshmen girls.* The season was already drawing to a close. *They've come so far this year!* Samira stood up in applause with the rest of the crowd. Just the thought of putting her feet back in her heels made her feet hurt again.

"Do you want to stop at home and change?"

Oh, thank you! "That's a good idea. My feet are killing me."

"You look tired, dear." Ashleigh stepped down a bleacher. "I'll go get my coat and meet you in the hall."

I am tired. I've been tired since last weekend when I stayed up too late Friday night. Reluctantly she slipped her foot back inside the leather pump.

"Am I correct in assuming that our mutual friend made an independent departure?"

Mike Benson was standing on the gym floor in front of Samira. Kelly was a few feet away chatting with a group of parents. "Yes, he did."

"Sorry about that." Mike folded his hands in front of his jacket. "I thought maybe he'd relax and stick around a few more minutes if I stayed."

"That's okay." Samira started to walk toward the steps but Mike offered his hand. She accepted and stepped down off the bleacher seats. She looked around the room. "This is a lot for Phil and me to juggle . . ."

Mike was listening with his eyes.

" . . . It's like, I don't know." Samira buttoned her suit jacket. "When we're alone together we're great. Everything is good." She thought a minute more. "But then when other people are around we're on guard somehow and it's not very comfortable for either one of us."

Mike was nodding his head and smiling gently. "I know. You'd think with J.P. being an attorney and all he'd be great in a crowd, but he's always on edge . . ."

Kelly was still visiting as Samira and Mike started toward the door into the hallway. " . . . And so are you."

"Do you think?" *Boy he reads me like a book.* In the distance she could see Krissy talking with her grandmother.

"Pretty sure about that." Mike wiggled his eyebrows and without looking away he lifted his arm for Kelly to step under.

How did he know she was coming? The sunny smile of the English teacher made Samira smile.

"He couldn't take the crowd, could he?"

"That's okay . . ."

"So do you need a ride home?"

"What the hell?" Mike was stunned. "He took your car?"

"I offered." Samira corrected. "He needed to go and I needed him to be gone." Her eyes went back to her mother. *As much as I love my mother, how do I explain this intense, passionate man?*

"I saw you hand over the keys," Kelly admitted. "I'm going with Mike. You can have my car."

"Oh no!" Samira was surprised at the offer. "My mom will take us home. We're just waiting on Kara."

"Are you sure?"

"Positive." *For the most part.* Samira thanked her friend for the offer. *That's far more than Susan would have ever offered.*

"Okay, then we're out of here. We have a racket ball court with our name on it," Mike announced. "Catch you later?"

"More than likely." Samira was surprised how often she bumped into Mike.

Kara emerged from the locker room, changed and ready to relive the game. All the way home, Samira participated in the excitement of the big win with guarded detachment.

My greatest victory will be winning Phil over to my parents. He's going to challenge every thing they've ever imagined for me and the girls.

58

You Belong to Me

The garage door was already open when J.P. arrived at Samira's house. He pulled the Camry inside and turned off the engine. The headlights of his pickup pulled in behind him. Mike's Corvette was parked in the street at the end of the driveway.

"I can't believe you let a girl drive your car." J.P. snagged his truck keys out of the air.

"It was either let her drive my car or your truck . . ."

"Good decision." J.P. grinned. "You and Kelly seem to be getting on . . ."

Mike shook his head. "I don't know what you're talking about. We're strictly business, nothing more." He pointed toward the house. "But that one in there, she's one to be getting on with . . ."

"I'll take care of my own business, thank you." J.P. was slightly humored. "Thanks for bringing the truck."

"It's the least we could do after the mess at the school." Mike narrowed his eyes in thought. "Contrary to what you might be thinking, I really had no idea Samira would be there . . ."

Mike doesn't aplogize often. "I know. No harm done."

"I know, but . . . well, it just didn't go like I thought it might . . ."

"It's a done deal, good buddy." J.P. nodded toward Mike's car. "Kelly's waiting."

"Alrighty then . . ."

He's either stalling, or his woman has put him up to saying something . . .

"Kelly and I were talking . . ."

Here it comes.

537

"... and we'd like to go out with you and Samira Saturday night after Stephenson's cocktail party. You know, maybe have dinner somewhere ..."

We don't take our women out together, Mikey. Remember our rules? J.P.'s first instinct was to decline the offer. "I don't take women with me on local business, Mikey."

"I usually don't either, but this is only a cocktail party with Stephenson." He shrugged his shoulders inside the bulky sweatshirt. "I'm planning to take Kelly."

"You're taking Kelly over me?"

"Maybe, but it's not like we have an official role there. We'll make an appearance strictly for a professional presence. So, I thought I'd invite her along. If you invited Samira then we could make a quick appearance at the gathering and then go find a decent dinner somewhere."

Kelly definitely put him up to this. J.P. still didn't like the idea, but Mike was speaking so earnestly J.P. couldn't bring himself to say no. "Let me talk to her about it."

"That's fine, take your time." Mike was getting anxious. "But we're set for tomorrow, right?"

"Yeah, everything is a go. Sparky will be in position early in the morning at Mid-America. The Hughes Corporation is sending their CFO with the deposit at ten. And everything after that should be a cakewalk."

"Do you really think Bridges is going to take the bait?"

"We have nothing to lose by trying."

"Gotta like it," Mike clapped his hands together. "Hey, that property closing between Hughes and Mid-America was sweet!" Mike patted J.P. hard on the shoulder. "That's a business fusion Joplin's been needing for too long."

Considering Bridges almost severed the relations between the city's business world and Hughes last summer, this is a very amazing turn of events. "Things are starting to come together." *I finally feel like I'm making progress after a long summer of setbacks.*

"I can't believe you kept it quiet long enough to pull it off."

Easier said than done. Mike was starting to fidget. J.P. was amused.

"So, I guess I'll see you tomorrow then?"

"Don't let me keep you, Counselor."

"Okay." Mike started for his car. "I'm going to go then."

The look on Mike's face made J.P. laugh out loud. *He's either extremely anxious to be alone with Kelly, or he's scared to death to be alone with her.*

Mike turned around as he reached the end of the driveway. "Don't forget to ask about Saturday."

I can't believe he's letting his girl chauffeur him in his own car. He's crazy! If it's my truck, I'm going to drive it.

All three Cartwright women were gathered at the dining room table. Samira had changed from her business suit into a warm up outfit of some kind. *She looks far more comfortable, but the suit was a nice touch.*

"Hey ladies . . ." Phil pushed the garage door button as he stepped into the kitchen.

"Hey." Samira looked up and forced a tired smile. "Come on in." She stood up. "Can I get you something?"

Always a hostess. "No, I'm fine, thanks." *The fireplace is a nice touch tonight.*

"Did you eat supper?"

Dinner. Remember to ask her about dinner. "Yeah, I did. On the way back to the office." Phil looked back to the girls. Kara had moved closer to her sister. Krissy had her face buried in her hands.

"We're struggling with last minute homework." Samira explained the situation wearily. "I didn't think to ask them about homework before I accepted my mother's invitation to dinner. So now we're cramming it in last minute."

It looks serious. "What are we working on?"

Samira closed her eyes. "Math. And it's math beyond me!" She opened her eyes again. "Kara is trying to check them so we can do the next problem. She only has three left."

At least it's not science. He leaned over the girls. "Having any luck?"

"Not really," Kara replied. "I get two different answers every time."

"Let's see," J.P. sat down in another chair and motioned for Kara to slide the book over. Krissy looked up. *Poor kid's been crying.*

"Only the even numbers." Kara ran her hand over the problems.

J.P. took his reading glasses out of his interior jacket pocket.

"I didn't know you wore glasses." Krissy seemed to perk up.

"Only when the numbers on the page are too small to see with normal eyes." J.P. wiggled his eyebrows at Krissy. He read the problem in the text and compared it to Krissy's work as he rolled the cuffs on his shirt. *She's set the problems up backwards.* He could feel Krissy watching him.

"You look very distinguished wearing glasses."

"Why thank you." *They make me feel old.* He picked up the pencil on the table and wrote out the numbers on a piece of scratch paper.

"You play a wicked game of volleyball, Kara."

Kara's face lit up immediately. "Thanks! Were you there?"

"I saw part of a game."

Kara launched into a recap of the final game as J.P. worked the problem in his head.

"Keep practicing and you'll be the clinch server on varsity." *There, that's the way the problem should look.* "Okay, Krissy, look at this . . . ." J.P. turned the book so she could see what he'd done. "You need to rearrange your problem to look like this. You had the formula backwards. You can get the answer that way, but it will take a lot longer."

He watched Krissy study the numbers.

"I'm going to go shower and get ready for bed, okay, Mama?" Kara pushed her chair back under the table.

There she goes, calling Samira Mama again. It's very southern.

"Can you work it from here?"

"I think so." Krissy took his pencil and went to work.

J.P. turned around to find Samira at the breakfast bar with her head bent over a pile of papers, seemingly deep in thought. Krissy finished the problem and turned the paper back around.

J.P. checked the answer against his own. "That's right." He pointed to the next one. "Now set this one up the same way."

"We're only doing the evens."

"I know, do the odd ones for practice."

Krissy's swollen eyes challenged him. "But I can't check the answers in the back on the odd ones."

"I have the answers, Krissy."

"Where?"

J.P. chuckled. "In my head. Now just do it." He pointed to the next problem. "It's only going to take a minute and you'll be better for it." J.P. leaned back in his chair and crossed his arms behind his head. "I'll wait."

"You're crazy." Krissy went back to work.

No, Mike is crazy. I'm just a hard ass.

"Maybe you can help Mama with her papers while I'm working on this."

He looked over his shoulder at Samira. *Does she have homework too?* J.P. left his glasses on the table and stepped around to see what she was working on. "Math?"

Samira sat up straight and pushed the papers away. "It's nothing really."

"It's due tomorrow, isn't it? You said you needed a lawyer to figure it out!" Krissy made the statement without looking up.

Samira closed her eyes again. "Yes, it's due tomorrow, Krissy. Thanks for your concern."

She's really wishing Krissy would mind her own business. J.P. put his hands on Samira's shoulders and pressed his thumbs into the base of her neck.

Tense. Very tense. Samira pulled her hair over a shoulder and allowed him to continue the massage. *If we didn't have company I could do the whole body.* He couldn't help but notice the return address on the legal sized envelope. *I thought he retired.*

"Done with that one." Krissy pushed the book to the end of the table.

J.P. returned to the dining room table for his glasses. He checked her work. "Good. Do the next three."

"The next three in a row or just the next three even?" Krissy turned her crystal blues eyes up to his.

It's getting late. "Even."

"Good." Krissy bent over her book with renewed understanding. "Then I'll be done." J.P. watched her write a set of numbers. "It's easier this way."

"This is the correct way, that's why it's easier."

"Well, it works anyway."

Samira picked up her papers and carried them to the table. "I do need a lawyer to figure these out." She pulled out a chair and sat down. There are a lot of big words in here that I don't understand." Her dark eyes met his with a sense of surrender.

J.P. sat back down in the same chair. "Well, let's see, I happen to know a good attorney who might be able to help you, but I think he's out on a date right now . . ." *Remember to ask her about dinner on Saturday!* He pulled his telephone off his belt. "But I might be able to reach him if you really need assistance . . ." J.P. rested his elbows on his knees and flipped open the phone.

Samira took the phone out of his hand.

"That isn't exactly the one I had in mind . . ."

"You're a lawyer, aren't you?" Krissy asked as she pushed her paper toward J.P.

"You know, Krissy, I am." He started to check the math in his head.

"Then maybe you could just do it for her."

I love the way Krissy just puts it out there. J.P. couldn't hide his smile. *She's a handful, but I like the spunk.* "You set it up right, but did the math wrong." J.P. turned the paper around again. "Check your sums."

"Oh great." Krissy took the paper back. She found her error and fixed it. "Is that better?"

J.P. read upside down. "That's the right answer. Is that better?"

"You mess with my mind."

J.P. laughed out loud. *Any mind as busy as hers needs a challenge.* "Two more and you're done."

"Good, because I'm tired."

So is your mother. J.P. looked back at Samira who was quietly watching the exchange between him and her daughter. "I really don't mind."

"Krissy?"

"No, looking at your papers." He opened his hand. *I don't really want her working with Cramer anyway. He's clueless about ninety percent of the time.* "What are we looking at?"

Samira put her elbows on the table and rested her chin on her hands. "I get these once every three years concerning the girls' investments from Tom's estate . . ."

"Tom was my dad." Krissy clarified.

" . . . I have to agree to the changes, sign, and return in the envelope provided by tomorrow to avoid penalties."

"You don't have to agree." *She doesn't have to agree to anything if she doesn't want to.*

"I do if I don't know what the other options are," Samira explained. "That's where I'm stuck."

Krissy spun her paper around again. "Done. And I double checked the math this time . . ."

She's quick.

"I'm going to go get ready for bed while Phil checks them."

"I know it's the end of the day, Phil." Samira touched his arm. "You don't have to read this if you don't want to."

It's the least I can do for a Pretty Lady. "I don't mind." *Besides, I owe her a favor.* He set the legal papers aside to check Krissy's math. "It's what I do, you know." He circled a wrong answer.

"I do know, but you're off the clock."

"A good attorney is never off the clock."

"Really?" Samira sounded doubtful. "Does that mean I'll get a bill in the mail later?"

Only if I mention the favor to Denise. "Yeah. It'll read, 'services rendered'." J.P. refused to look at Samira's face.

"Mr. Ralston."

"Yes ma'am?" J.P. could feel the tension lift. But Samira didn't respond right away. Samira was biting her bottom lip and her face was thoughtful. *I don't know if I should interrupt her thoughts or not.*

Krissy reappeared wearing flannel pajamas. "How many did I miss?"

"One."

"Good." She picked up the pencil. "Easy one, too." She made the correction. "That's the kind of mistake that costs me points in tests."

"Work the problem then double check your math." *I feel more like a father than I do an attorney.* J.P. thought about that for a minute. *Now there's a frightening thought, Mr. Ralston.*

Samira was still watching him.

"What?" *Talk to me, Pretty Lady.*

Krissy put her math book away.

"I'll keep that a minute," Phil snagged the pencil before Krissy put it away.

"I just realized something."

Phil leaned back in his chair and stretched his legs out far enough to touch her sock feet with his. "Can you share that realization?" *Now I feel like an attorney again.*

"Not just yet," Samira pulled her feet away and stood up. "I'm going to see if Kara is in bed yet." She disappeared in the hallway leading to the bedrooms.

"I'll wait."

"You already said that once." Krissy was gathering up the stray homework items off the table.

"I'm a man of my word, then, right?"

Samira was suddenly in the archway of the hall again. She tipped her head to the side just enough to let Phil know he'd been heard. *I'll keep my word anytime, but especially whenever that lady is involved.*

"Good night, Phil," Krissy was following in her mother's footsteps. "Thanks for the popcorn at the game and for the help with my math. Next time I'll call you before I stress out."

And I'll answer. "Anytime, Krissy. Sleep tight."

"You too," Krissy said with a yawn.

J.P. picked up Samira's papers and the pencil and took them to the sofa. He turned on a lamp so he could see better. *These don't look too intimidating.* He skimmed the first part. *She just needs to make an educated decision and sign. You'd think Cramer could take time to at least walk a client through the options instead of just mailing them out for a signature.*

A phone rang but J.P. didn't respond. *It's not my house.*

It rang again.

"Is this your phone?"

Kara was walking toward him. The phone in her hand rang again.

Oh yeah, it is my phone.

"Yeah, this is J.P."

"Dad . . ."

I can't tell their voices apart anymore.

" . . . It's James."

Thanks for the clue. He set the papers aside. "James, what's up?" *He sounds defeated.*

"Not much."

"Are you home?"

"Not yet. I'm at a friend's house waiting for Mom to pick me up."

J.P. checked his watch as he removed his reading glasses. It was nearing ten o'clock. *You'd think she could pick them up in a timely matter.*

"What's up for your weekend?"

I gotta remember to ask Samira about Saturday. "I'm working, that's about it. Might have plans Saturday evening. Might not." *But I hope I do.*

"All night plans?"

Only by God's grace. "Doubtful." J.P.'s eyes followed Samira across the room. She stopped at the kitchen sink.

"Josh and I were thinking about coming down after the game."

"Come on down." He watched Samira fill a coffee cup and dim the kitchen lights. *She always leaves a light on at night.* "Do you need me to come get you?"

"Don't know yet." James's voice was more distant than usual. "I'll find out and call you."

"Is everything alright?" *Something doesn't sound right.*

"Yeah, for the most part." There was a long pause on the other end. "I just need to get out of here for awhile."

"Where's your game?"

"Home."

"I'll come get you if need be." *I don't like the tone of his voice.* He fingered the papers as Samira curled up in the corner of the sofa. "Just say the word." *God, she is beautiful.*

"Thanks, Dad. My calling card is getting low too."

I hear that. "Alright. I'll pick up a new one for you." *I just need to put them on my cell plan.* He was listening to James, but his eyes were on Samira as she sipped a cup of coffee. *How can she drink coffee this late in the day?*

"Well, it looks like Mom's headlights. I'd better go."

He's only told me half of what's on his mind. "James, call me back tomorrow, alright?"

"Alright."

"Hang in."

"Yeah, I will. Later."

"Later." A few seconds later the phone went dead in the father's hand. Samira's toes pressed into the side of his thigh. "James?"

"James." J.P. closed his phone and set it on the coffee table. "He's ready for a break."

"I can understand that."

I guess she can. Bruce Hamilton is a bastard. "I need to get the boys transportation so they can come and go as they please."

"Do you think James can stick it out a whole year?" Samira's eyes were genuinely concerned.

Doubtful. "I don't know." *But what would I do with him all the time down here?*

Samira wrapped both of her hands around the mug. "You'll figure it out when the time comes."

How does she know what I'm thinking?

"You really don't have to look over those papers. I know it's late."

"It's late for you," J.P. corrected. *I'm usually checking Sports Center on ESPN about now.* He glanced at her silent television screen. *I don't think I've ever seen her watch tv.* "I'm usually home in front of the television reviewing a pile much deeper than this." He put his glasses back on and flipped the front page over the clip at the top. "Besides, I'm halfway through it already."

"That's amazing," Samira set her cup on a ceramic coaster. "I've lost sleep just trying to get through the first page!"

J.P. rubbed her feet with his hand. "This I can do." *It would be easy to do more than her feet.* "Just don't ask me to fix your sink or change the oil in your car."

Samira laughed unexpectedly.

"What?"

"You're so funny!"

"No, I'm serious." J.P. corrected. "I don't do plumbing or cars."

"But you do this!" Her hand slapped the papers hard.

"Yes, I do."

"That's funny."

No, it's not. He felt Samira's fingertips against his scalp. *And neither is that. If she wants me to get through this, she's going to have to stop doing that.*

J.P. skipped a page. *Let's just cut to the chase.* "Here, this is the part you need to understand." He leaned forward so Samira could follow along. "Do you want the girls to have access to the funds at age eighteen or twenty-one. And . . ." J.P. moved his finger across a line so she could see where he was reading. " . . . do you want to specify what they can and cannot use the money for?"

"That's it?" Samira sounded unsure.

"Basically. There's more investment options, but you'd need to talk to a professional investor before making any changes there." *Too bad my sister-in-law lives so far away.* "You're other option is to check this box and request an extension on the deadline so you can make a more educated decision."

Samira looked directly into Phil's eyes with that remark. "I have a decision to make." There was a sudden heaviness in her remark.

"Not tonight . . ."

"No, I do, really." Samira picked up her coffee cup and sat back into the corner of the sofa again. "And earlier I realized you're the one I've been needing to talk to about it."

Oh, this is the revelation from the table. He set the papers down again. "Alright." *Personal or business?* He set his glasses on top of the papers and rubbed the bridge of his nose with his thumb and forefinger. *I hope this isn't too complicated. I still have to ask her about Saturday night.*

Samira stared into her coffee cup like Phil had seen her do many times before.

I can wait. Again.

"When I got home tonight there was a message on my machine from Mr. Marty Brown."

Who the hell is that? Phil had to work hard not to be defensive at the mention of a man's name. *And what does he have to do with me?*

"Do you know him?"

"No, I can't say that I do."

"Well, he needs an answer by tomorrow afternoon," Samira unfolded her legs and left the sofa. J.P. followed her with his eyes to the dining room table where she started to straighten the few loose papers leftover from Krissy's homework.

"And I don't know what to tell him . . ." Samira sorted the papers and tossed the scratch into the trashcan by her desk.

What is she talking about? It was all J.P. could do not to force her to get it out. *This is one time I could use Krissy's input to move this thing along.* Unable to stand the suspense, J.P. left the sofa too. Samira started to wipe down the breakfast bar with a rag. J.P. put his arms around her and stopped the motion.

"The counter is clean." *Very clean.* "And I can't really be of much assistance to you if I don't know what you're talking about."

"I know." Samira leaned heavily in his arms.

Obviously I'm going to have to ask questions to get the answers.

"What do you know?"

"I know that the counter is clean." Samira lobbed the damp rag toward the sink. "I already wiped it off."

J.P. couldn't help but smile in disbelief. *I was hoping for a subject matter on the previous conversation.* Her hesitation was beginning to make him wonder if Mr. Marty Brown had personal interests in Samira. *I'm not going to take a chance.*

"What kind of decision, Samira?" J.P. loosened his hold around her middle.

Samira's dark eyes were sad. "He offered me a job at the university."

What university? "And this is a bad thing?" *Usually a job offer is more exciting than she's letting on.*

"No." Samira frowned. "Well, yes." She rolled her eyes. "I don't know if it is or not."

"Come on." J.P. couldn't take her indecision anymore. He took her by the hand he led her back to the living room and sat her down in the easy chair. J.P. sat down on the coffee table directly in front of her. "Talk to me. Start at the beginning."

He watched Samira take a deep breath. "Usually I talk these things through with my brother but I already know his advice, so I didn't want to tell him about the offer."

Okay, it's not the beginning, but at least she's talking.

"And I always talk about things like this with my parents, but I know their answer too . . ."

"So you didn't bring it up with them either?"

"No." Samira looked straight into his eyes. "Because now I know you're the reason I can't talk to them."

How do you end up in the middle of these things, Ralston?

"It's a really nice offer, Phil. It's more money, a nice office, a generous expense account, and exciting potential . . ."

I'm still waiting.

" . . . but, I like what I do now. In fact, I really like what I do now. I know what's expected of me and I'm successful. There's no hidden incentives and nothing to take me out of my comfort zone, and I like it that way."

She doesn't want to change jobs. "So, what's the issue?"

"Until tonight I didn't know. But now I understand."

Understand what?

Samira folded her hands tightly and leaned forward in the chair. "I understand that you accept me just like this . . ." She flung her hands out to her side. " . . . just like I am!" Her eyes lit up a little. "I don't have anything to prove to you because you don't demand that of me."

Is this a good thing?

"Don't you see?" She started to stand up.

No, let's not wipe down an already clean counter again. He gently put his hands on her hips to put her back into the chair.

"Mr. Marty Brown learned about me from several different sources within the infrastructure of my supervisory board. He decided I was the one he wanted to direct the programs—that would be fundraising efforts, for his alumni foundation. So all of a sudden he has this idea of who I am and what I can do for him."

Makes sense. She's got a clear picture of Brown's motives.

"But I'm not the person he thinks I am. I'm a librarian who loves her work!" Samira put her hands in her hair. "I really like what I do, in spite of my misgivings with this last guest artist . . ."

Uberti. I knew he was trouble from the get-go.

"But, if I talk to my brother about it, he's going to tell me I'm boring and too safe, yet he's not much better than me. He's Mr. Conservative from the word 'go'! Still he'd think I was a fool for not taking the extra money and the challenge and at least giving it a whirl." Samira crossed her arms over her middle. "And my parents, well, they would encourage me to follow my heart. But really what they want me to do is follow my heart if it leads to the same conclusions they come to!" She was talking very fast. "And my decision might not be the same as theirs." Samira rolled her eyes.

I've seen Kara do that hundreds of times.

" . . . Don't get me wrong, they'd support my decision, but I know for a fact that after I'm out of ear shot they talk about their disappointment in me because I didn't do what they preferred." Samira sighed and hung her head. "What kind of support is that?"

Agreed. She's onto something here.

"But not you, Phil." Now she looked up into his face. "Not you. You say, 'what's the problem?' And there isn't one really. Because you trust me to just be me."

This is an absolutely amazing one-sided conversation. J.P. reached out and took Samira's hands. They were perfectly manicured as always. "Samira, this is the you I know. I wouldn't want any part of you to change."

"Wow." Samira sighed. "I don't think anyone has ever said that to me and meant it." Her fingers gripped his tighter.

"You gotta be who you are, Pretty Lady. And it's obvious you're family has some notion of who you might be, but the fact is, they must think an awful lot of you because even if you don't do exactly as they would, they still let you hang around, right?"

Samira nodded.

How far can I take this without going too far? "There's going to come a time when you have to break away from your family's expectations and live according to your own rules and your own ideas. In fact, over time my guess would be that they'd learn to love the real Samira just as much if not more." *I know I do.*

Samira's hands were still holding on for dear life. "Do you think?"

"I do." J.P. said those words again. "Yeah, I do." *In more ways than you know, I do.*

Samira's eyes were damp, but he knew her well enough by now that he knew she wasn't going to let them spill over into tears. "Then I do, too."

Now this is intense. Yet the hopefulness that had filled Samira's eyes brought an easy smile to his face. *How could they not allow this Samira to be who she is?*

"Come here," Phil put his hand behind Samira's hair and pulled her now smiling face toward his. Without asking permission he kissed her gently on the lips.

"I don't want you to leave," Samira whispered between kisses.

No more than I want to go.

Samira pulled away from his kiss. "I mean ever." The look in her eyes was completely sincere.

A very slow realization surfaced somewhere deep within. "I know." He ran his tongue over his bottom lip. "Me either." *I have no desire to spend the rest of my days across town in a house by myself knowing she's over here.* "We might have to figure this whole thing out."

Samira's face was suddenly full of light. Phil laughed at her bright smile and reveled in the way her eyes scanned the room as if a whole new concept was developing in her mind.

"I want to show you something." Phil stood up and slipped his hand into his front pocket. Mixed in with loose change and keys, he felt his mother's wedding rings with his fingers.

"I've been thinking about this for awhile now, but, uh . . ." Phil couldn't believe he was about to say the words he'd rehearsed a million times in his mind since leaving the ranch. "These were my mother's wedding rings." He placed the two separate rings in Samira's hand and watched as she turned them gently in her fingers. "She was everything my father ever needed even though they lived thousands of miles apart for the whole of their marriage. It's taken me most of my life to figure that out." Phil inhaled very deeply. "I came extremely close to letting the only thing I ever needed walk out of my life, and I'm not willing to make that mistake twice."

Samira's eyes were full of wonder when she looked up into his.

You'd better say it now, Ralston, before you lose your nerve! J.P. took a deep breath. "Someday, I want to give those rings away." *Nothing has ever seemed so right.* "And I'd like for Krissy to have one and Kara to have the other."

Samira was still watching him, but now her eyes were moist. *I don't think she's going to be able to hold the emotion in this time.*

"And I'd like to put a different set of rings on their mother's hand." *Finish it off, baggage and all.* "That is if she'll have me." *Not exactly how I rehearsed, but it's out there now.*

There were no words or sounds whatsoever. Samira simply rose from her chair and wrapped her arms tightly around his neck and held him.

Phil reciprocated, completely consumed by her presence. "It's taken me a helluva long time, Samira," Phil spoke quietly as he held her. "But I know you belong to me." Her arms held on tighter around his neck. "It doesn't matter where I am or what I'm doing, you'll always belong to me."

She's definitely all I'll ever need. Phil heard her sniffle. *Yep, the tears spilled over.*

59

Playing for Keeps

The cashier behind the counter radiated a familiar smile. "Well, hallo!" The southern accent brought a smile to Samira's face. "Ya'll haven't been in for a bit!"

"No, I haven't."

"But I bet you'd like a Cappuccino."

"Yes, thank you." *I feel connected to this woman even though I don't know her name.*

"Are you meeting that handsome Joe in a few minutes?"

Does she know his name, or is she just using Joe as a catch phrase? "As a matter of fact, I am." *We haven't been here for a long time. I'm surprised she remembers.*

"I was afraid maybe it didn't work out between ya'all, but I musta been wrong." She placed a lid over the steaming beverage and snapped it into place. "Shall I just put this on his tab? I 'member how he likes to take care of you and all."

He does like to pick up the tab, doesn't he? "That would be fine." *But I didn't know he kept one at the Café Ole!*

"I see ya'all's table is vacant too." The woman pointed to the front corner.

Boy, she does remember us! Samira thanked her again. She opened her book against the wrought iron tabletop.

"Am I late?"

Samira looked up into Phil's deep blue eyes. "No, I'm early."

"I knew that," Phil sat down in the chair across from her. "It's been awhile since we've graced this place."

"But the cashier remembered me."

"Of course she did. You're not easy to forget." Phil smiled easily. "Besides. Shondra and I have a special agreement."

Samira raised her eyebrows on purpose. "Shondra?"

Phil placed his right hand over his chest. "It's on the nametag."

"Of course." *I should have known.* "What kind of an agreement might you have with your friend, Shondra?"

"She keeps the tab, I pay the bill."

"You're just lucky I'm a light eater . . ."

"No, I'm just lucky." Phil leaned across the table. Samira was sure he was going to kiss her, but his lips only touched her forehead. "What can I get you?"

"I was thinking of the French Onion soup."

"Anything else?" Phil was already headed for the counter where people were beginning to wait in line.

Samira shook her head as he walked away. *I like the way he takes care of me, even when he's not here. He makes me feel important.* She tried to go back to her book but had trouble concentrating. *More later.*

Phil returned with two bowls of soup and a glass of water. He set the tray between them and went back to the counter for napkins. *I bet he tips Shondra well for taking care of me.* Samira smiled at that thought. *No wonder she remembers me.*

Samira dipped a metal spoon into the rich soup. *I've missed this place.* But mostly, she'd missed the company. "Did you sleep well last night?"

"Not really." Phil stirred chicken and noodles around in a bowl. "It's hard to be content knowing you're across town alone in another bed."

"Well, it's better than thinking I'm not alone in another bed." *I couldn't resist.*

Phil's feet wrapped around hers under the table unexpectedly.

"That is not an option, Pretty Lady." The hue of his eyes darkened a shade with that thought.

"No, it's not, but I had to say it." *It doesn't take much to make him jealous.* She savored her first bite of broth. *But I really don't mind him staking his claim on me either.*

"How was your morning?"

"Well, I called Mr. Marty Brown and officially declined the offer."

"And how does that make you feel, Ms Cartwright?"

I don't feel guilty. I don't feel responsible. "Very free, thank you for asking."

"Then you made the right decision." Phil raised his water glass to her in an unofficial toast.

"Are the boys coming down tonight?"

"It sounds like it." Phil was nodding his head. "Jan is going to meet me half way."

He didn't sound defensive when he mentioned her name this time.

"I've got somebody checking into a car for them. Hopefully I can give them a little travel independence and relieve myself of making those late night trips north."

"Are they staying the whole weekend?" *Before I extend the invitation, I need to know what his weekend looks like.* She broke a saltine cracker in half and dipped it into the broth.

"I'll meet Jan again Sunday night, unless the boys have a car by then."

He's not wasting any time with this decision!

"Well . . . ," *I have no idea how he's going to react.* "My mother has invited you and the boys for Sunday dinner." *This certainly takes us into new territory.*

Phil stopped chewing and looked doubtingly in her direction. "Why would she do that?"

Samira scanned the parameter of the small café. "Let's see, maybe she's curious to know more about the man with whom her only daughter has been spending time . . ." Samira blew gently on the soup in her spoon. "Or, maybe she just wants to be hospitable to a man she's only briefly met at a volleyball game."

Phil finished chewing the cracker that was already in his mouth.

"More than likely it's the latter," Samira clarified. "She called me this morning and made the invitation."

"You're going to be there, right?"

Samira laughed. *I would never send him in there alone!* "Yes. And Krissy and Kara too." *He's taking this more seriously than I expected.*

"Alright." Phil wiped his fingers on a paper napkin. "I'll go if you'll go."

"I'll RSVP in the affirmative then." She tipped her head to one side. "My mother is a wonderful hostess."

"Based upon what I know of her daughter, I don't doubt that for a minute." Phil complimented easily. "Is this a formal occasion?"

That's an interesting question. "I don't know." Samira frowned in thought. "I guess we'll all be coming from church, but Mama won't expect you to be dressed up." She thought some more. "No, just come as you are."

Phil shook his head and grinned mischievously. "Probably not. You don't know my normal Sunday morning attire."

" . . . I can promise you one thing, Mr. Ralston," Samira set her empty bowl off to the side. "You won't go away hungry."

Phil ran his tongue over his bottom lip. "You always leave me just a little hungry because I always go away wishing for more . . ."

"I was speaking of the meal . . ."

"I was speaking of you . . ." Phil stacked his empty bowl underneath hers and began to gather the used napkins.

He must have a tight schedule. He told me last night he might not have a lot of free time. She helped him gather what little trash was left on the table.

"Do you have a few more minutes?"

So maybe a tight schedule isn't the urgency. Samira checked her watch. "A few."

"I have something I want to show you."

Now I'm curious. "Okay."

"Not here." He stood up and picked up the tray full of dishes. "Let's go for a walk."

What in the world? Samira picked up her coat as she stood up. A moment later Phil was holding it while she slipped her arms into the sleeves. *He's always a gentleman. Always.*

It must not be far. His truck was nowhere in sight and he wasn't wearing a coat other than his sports jacket. *The same one he had on last night.*

Without hesitation Phil linked his fingers between hers and led her across the street. An alleyway led to the back of an office building. Samira noticed Phil's truck at the far end of a small parking area.

Where in the world is he taking me? Samira walked with him up a flight of concrete stairs. At the top she read the cursive lettering across a glass door. *J.P. Ralston, Attorney at Law.*

So this is his office! There was something urgent in his step that accelerated her adrenalin as well. He opened the door and motioned for Samira to enter.

That's the woman I saw at the Shoal Creek Meeting.

The woman looked up and began speaking at the same time. "Oh, hey, Boss, can you take a call from Sparky? He's been calling your cell but . . ." Suddenly the woman's greenish brown eyes stopped on Samira. "Oh, sorry . . ."

Phil was very much in a business mode. "Yeah, I need to talk to him . . ." He left Samira's side and reached for the phone.

"Sparky, J.P., what's going on?"

Sparky? Now there's an interesting name. Samira crossed her wrists and smiled at the lady.

"Excuse me, I didn't know J.P. had company." The woman rose from her seat and offered to take Samira's coat. "Can I bring you something? A cup of coffee maybe?"

"No, I'm fine, but thank you." Samira allowed the woman to hang her coat on a brass hook along the wall. *This is a very elegant room. A little too formal for me, but highly professional.* She scanned the sitting area. *A few plants would make it even more inviting.*

"I'm Denise Burke. I don't believe we've met."

She's the one who issued the subpoena on Lloyd Hughes' diary! Now I can put a name with a face.

"Samira Cartwright." Samira exchanged a firm handshake with the woman.

She's older than I imagined, but obviously highly efficient. Phil was still talking on the phone.

"Would you like to sit down?"

He shook his head quietly in Denise's direction.

A gentle bell rang as the door to the outside opened. A tall, slender man walked in with a hand full of file folders. He nodded silently to Samira as he entered.

" . . . Derek is here now . . . Alright . . . We'll get on it and I'll see you in a few minutes."

Obviously this will be a short visit. Samira watched Denise sort through folders from the man.

"Derek," Denise addressed him without looking up. "This is Samira Cartwright."

The young man turned and greeted Samira properly. "Very pleased to meet you." He shook her hand. "Derek Danielson. Have you been helped?"

"Undoubtingly." Denise sounded sarcastic.

Oh my. Samira noticed Phil send a silent look of warning toward Denise.

Denise smiled at Derek. "She's here with the boss."

That's funny that she calls him 'the boss'. Maybe she doesn't know which of his names to use either.

Phil handed the phone back to Denise. "He's going to walk you through the formula."

"This one." Derek had a file open over his hand.

I'm impressed with the way they're all on the same line of communication.

"Why me?" Denise raised her eyebrows in Phil's direction.

"Because I'm busy." Phil motioned for Samira to follow, but his eyes were still on his secretary. "Give me ten and hold the calls."

Samira's shoes left an imprint in the plush carpeting as she crossed the room toward an open door.

"Ten and counting." Denise covered the mouthpiece on the phone and addressed Phil one more time. "Derek's on his way back over there. Do you need him to take anything?"

Phil allowed Samira to step into the interior office before he answered Denise's question. "No, I'll be right behind him."

"I'll believe that when I see you leave."

Phil closed the door behind them. *If he's bothered by her remarks, he's not letting on.*

"She's a damn good paralegal . . ." Phil answered without being asked. "But she speaks every thought that crosses her mind." He smiled easily.

I wouldn't put up with it, but obviously he's used to it. Samira dared to let her eyes travel around the book lined office. *Very elegant and very beautiful at the same time.*

"So this is where you spend your time . . ."

"And plenty of it." Phil concurred. "But that phone call considerably diminished my lunch hour."

Samira heard new urgency in Phil's voice. "Don't let me keep you."

"You're not keeping me." Phil took Samira by the hand and led her to the window behind his desk. "But I want you to see something."

She followed his gaze down the alley to the Café Ole. Samira laughed out loud. *The café is in full view from anywhere in his office.* "So this is why you knew the name of a coffee shop so quickly that first time you came looking for me!"

"Exactly." Phil seemed pleased that he'd given away his secret. "So these last few months when I've been sitting here at my desk, I've been wishing you could meet me over there again."

Samira watched him run his hand over the glossy edge of a conference table that matched the rest of his furniture. Her eyes went from the tips of his fingers to a single object on the table.

"Oh dear God!" Samira put her hand to her mouth. *That's my statue!* She couldn't speak. Nor could she take her eyes off of it.

"It's an original, so I've been told."

Samira forced her eyes to his. *Doesn't he know Fabiano carved that of me?*

"It's quite a find, isn't it?" Phil was studying Samira's face.

He has to know! Samira swallowed hard but there was an air pocket stuck in her throat. She swallowed again.

"It's a beautiful piece of art." He admired the bronzed statue openly, running his fingertips over the woman's head and following the form of her body all the way down her back.

Samira backed up and sat down in a chair. *I have to explain.* "She didn't pose that way." *I mean, I didn't pose that way!*

"It looks very natural to see her reading." Phil's eyes were on the sculpture.

"No, I mean, like . . ." *I mean, it's totally obvious the statue is nude!* " . . . like *that!*"

"But that's the way I like her."

He does know it's me.

Phil turned the figurine one half turn. "But here's the biggest mystery of the whole work." He pointed to the bundle of hair at the nape of the statue's neck. "How does she get it to stay like that all day long?"

At least now I know where I am. Samira threw her head back and let all of her tension out with one long sigh.

Phil was suddenly over her, helping her into a standing position. Samira was completely consumed by the passion in his kisses and the tenderness of his touch. When he released his hold and gave her room to catch her breath, Samira had to remind herself of her surroundings.

How does he do that to me? She touched the bun at the back of her head to see if it was still in place. She remembered his agenda and the urgency with which he'd expressed a diminished noon hour. *But I have to know . . .*

Phil turned the figurine back around on the table and admired it with genuine interest.

"How? . . ." *How do I ask this?.* " . . . Who? . . ." She put her hand to her forehead to try to organize her thought. " . . . Where did it come from?"

Phil's eyes were intense. "She was here when I came in this morning."

"No . . ." *I don't mean your secretary.* "I'm talking about the sculpture."

"So am I." Phil cupped Samira's face in his hands gently and kissed her again. "I said, She was here when I came in this morning."

I don't like not understanding. There had been too much mystery with this piece of art already. "But where was it before it came here?"

Phil smiled softly. "It was in good hands."

Oh my gosh! "Mike had it then, didn't he?" *It's so obvious now. He had it all along.*

Phil didn't answer, but he didn't deny Mike's ownership either. "I had to earn the right to own it."

It was Samira's turn to smile now. *Mike must have raised the stakes.* "And what exactly were the measurements upon which you were judged?"

Phil grinned and wiggled his eyebrows. "Someday, Pretty Lady, we'll go there. But right now I have a business associate dying for my input on a very big case, and I have an assistant out there who doesn't know the word 'knock'. And if I stay in here alone with you one more minute, you're going to be more like that statue than you ever intended to be . . ."

Samira took a step away from Phil's presence. *And I'm afraid I might not fight against the notion very hard either!* When Phil started to kiss her again, Samira put her fingers gently over his lips.

He laughed right out loud.

It is so good to see him laugh like that! Samira walked around to the front of his desk, forcing even more space into the passionate moment.

A buzzer sounded somewhere in the room, causing Samira to catch her breath.

"That's my ten minute warning."

More like twenty.

He was still chuckling. "Um . . . I failed to carry through on a promise last night and I don't want to jeopardize a friendship so I need to follow it through now."

I have no idea what he's talking about. She lifted her purse off the corner of the desk and wrapped her hands through the straps.

"I have a business engagement here in town tomorrow late in the afternoon . . ."

Samira watched Phil open a hidden armoire on the wall. He selected a necktie. Without looking in a mirror, he slid it under his collar and began to tie it.

I know that pattern. I used to have to do that for Tom.

"But after I'm done over there, Mike and Kelly have invited us out to dinner."

Oh, I can't stand it. Without asking permission, she intercepted the motion of Phil's hands and finished the knot in a perfect Windsor. *That's very nice.* But the satisfaction vanished as she ran her schedule through her mind. *I told Wes I'd babysit Saturday evening.*

Phil opened a door and stepped into a bathroom. "Thanks. It looks good." He came back out. "So, what do you think about dinner?"

Samira felt a familiar pang in her stomach. *I really do need to distance myself further from my family.* "What time?"

Phil shrugged his shoulders and adjusted the knot to fit better. "I don't know. Not before eight."

That's late, but maybe not late enough. "I'm going to have to check." She hated turning him down. *Besides, it would be good to be out with Mike and Kelly.* "I've promised my brother a few hours of child care tomorrow afternoon and evening." Samira bit her lip. *But maybe I can talk Kara and Krissy into taking over later on.* "Let me see what I can work out."

"It doesn't matter to me either way." Phil seemed satisfied. "Don't knock yourself out over it. If it works, we'll go. If not, we'll meet up with them another time." He reached for the brass handle on the solid door between the offices. "I'll call you tonight and let you know what's up with the boys, alright?"

I like being behind this closed door with him. Samira closed her eyes and allowed him to kiss her one more time before he opened the door to the outside world. *But I like being in any room with him, even if it's a noisy volleyball game.* She smiled into his eyes.

"Pretty Lady, you need to leave my office before we're busted." Phil opened the door slowly and Samira stepped through.

"Ten minutes?" Denise was sitting at her desk typing away on a computer keyboard. "I'll open some windows to let the steam out of your office."

Samira watched Phil show a middle finger in his assistant's direction. Much to her own surprise, Samira had to stifle a laugh.

Phil opened the door to the outside. "Talk to you tonight."

Samira nodded, completely comfortable parting ways independent of his escort. *My guess is there will be an exchange of some choice words once I'm out of ear shot.* All the way back to her car Samira felt a lilt in her step.

He's the only one who should have that statue. Because he's the only one with viewing rights. Samira knew she was smiling on the inside as well as on her face. *And other rights.* She closed her eyes with that thought. *My parents would be horrified.* She pressed the button on her key chain to unlock her Camry. *As if they haven't figured it out already.*

Samira slid behind the wheel of her car. *I have to remember to thank Mike for looking out for me.* She started the engine and backed out of the parking space. *Unless he was simply looking out for Phil.* Samira laughed out loud as she pulled into traffic. *What on earth is my father going to think of this man? He's nothing like they would choose for me! He's too passionate. Too spontaneous.*

She stopped at the red light next to the Mid-America parking lot. *Oh, and then there's Wes who's going to drill him about investments and personal issues.* Samira waited for the light to change. *God help us!* Slowly she followed the car in front of her across the intersection. *But they're just going to have to get over their hang-ups, because I'm playing for keeps.*

60

The Moment of Truth

J.P. sat down hard on the bench at the end of the gym and wiped the sweat off his face with the tail of his t-shirt. *I'm getting too old for this!* He leaned forward and placed his elbows on his knees to catch his breath.

"You in, Dad?" James yelled from the center of the basketball court.

J.P. shook his head and motioned for them to start without him. *Two games back to back and I'm done.* He wiped his face again. *I used to be able to go all morning!* J.P. watched as Josh and James worked the offense.

"Good morning, J.P.!"

That voice is way to cheery for me. He looked up as Kelly Davis sat down next to him.

"You're up and at 'em early for a Saturday."

Tell me about it. "The boys wanted to play ball."

Kelly's eyes went to the action under the hoop. "Which one is yours?"

"Two of them are mine." *It feels good to claim them both.* J.P. pointed. "Josh is a senior, he's taking the shot." *Damn. He should have had that.* "And James, his brother recovered his rebound." *Nice shot, James.*

"How old is James?"

"He's a sophomore." *Turning sixteen pretty soon. He needs his license.*

Kelly flashed her sunny smile. "Good looking boys. I bet it's fun having them around."

More than I realized. "Yeah, it's good to have their energy around the house."

"Hey, what did you and Samira decide about dinner tonight?"

J.P. shook his head. "She had plans with her family. We'll catch you another time." *It's just as well with the boys being here.*

"Samira is very faithful to her family . . ."

Is she telling me that on purpose?

" . . . But faithful to a fault, sometimes."

She said that for my benefit, obviously. J.P. refused to go there. *Tomorrow could be interesting though.* Sunday dinner didn't quite seem like his style. *I fit in better at a cocktail party like Stephenson is having tonight.*

"We'll try again."

As long as she's sitting here, I might as well ask a few questions of my own. "What brings you to the club so early this morning?"

Kelly laughed heartily. "This isn't early! It's after nine!"

It's after nine? I need to shower so I can check Sparky's progress over at Mid-America . . .

"I'm meeting a girlfriend for aerobics here in a few minutes."

I wonder if she ever takes a break? "How many times a week do you work out anyway?"

Kelly was watching the game on the court. "I do cardio everyday. What about you?"

I thought I was asking the questions. "I'm in the weight room with Mike three times a week."

"What about cardio? That's what your heart needs, you know."

Yes, I know. J.P. stood up to give indication he was about finished chatting. "I run a few times a week with Chase."

Kelly stood up too. "That's funny. You run with Chase." She grabbed a handful of her bushy curls and pulled them into a wrap behind her head. "That's like having two verbs and no subject."

Who else compared my dog to a verb? J.P. put his hands on his hips. *It was Samira and one of the girls at the ranch. What's up with women and verbs?*

Kelly started to walk away. "Sorry we won't see you tonight, but have a good time at the cocktail party."

The security guard at Mid-America's back entrance recognized J.P. before he presented his identification. Ever since Sparky moved the makeshift surveillance unit into a secured area, badges had become standard procedure. J.P. slid his badge into the magnetic pocket on the door.

Sparky was sitting in front of two large computer monitors.

"What do you know this morning, Sparky?"

"Tings seem to be right on schedule." Sparky pointed to an in-house security screen. "Our suspect, Celia Monroe requested to vork overtime today. Ve vill see vhat she is up to."

J.P. could see the suspect at work in every angle of her cubicle. *It's amazing how detailed we can get,* he thought to himself. "Any other activity?"

"Monies from de new account are secure. Quarterly reports ran at the close of business yesterday. And now ve vait."

Waiting is always the hardest part.

Sparky swiveled in his chair. "Mr. Stevenson came by dis morning. He said I should come to his house tonight for a drink." The little man stood up and refreshed a cup of coffee. "Dat all depends on vhat is going on inside de mainframe."

"I understand." *Besides, I hired you to work this case. Not make social appearances.* J.P. didn't like the idea of his private investigator mingling with Joplin business society.

Sparky continued as if J.P. hadn't spoken. "Our suspect vill be dere. I tink she is going dere for an alibi." His eyes went back to Celia Monroe on the screen. "And if dat is de case, den I vill need to be here."

Up until now J.P. had assumed Stephenson's cocktail party was simply to celebrate the sale of property and new business agreements between Mid-America and The Hughes Corporation. "Stephenson didn't plan this party as a distraction, did he?"

Sparky eyes became animated. "On da contrary, it turns out de party is timed perfectly to be a distraction. But Mr. Stephenson doesn't know dat yet."

At least that gives me a little more incentive to show up and mingle.

"Vhile ve have time, shall ve go over da chain of command once again?"

"I'm at your beckoned call, Sparky."

The investigator pulled up a chair and opened a well-worn folder. "It vill vork like dis . . ."

J.P. sat down and watched as Sparky moved his hand over the typewritten page, complete with English misspellings.

" . . . de monies vill be authorized from dis building. Computer number seventy-two . . ."

The only in-house computer, other than Sparky's, enabled to authorize this particular account.

"Our friends in Balteemore are standing by . . ."

The one time suspects, now working undercover in order to save their own asses in court.

"When notified, dey vill transfer de funds to de holding company in Caleefornia."

The one disguised as a real estate company.

"At vhich time ve vill trace de transaction back to dis system and prepare to secure de account from further tampering zo dey cannot even attempt to move de monies back."

In the event they get skittish. "Is this the first time Bridges has attempted to move funds from the same institution more than once?"

Sparky shook his head. His eyes were still fixed on the schematic in the folder. "No. He's tried it before, *but . . .*" Sparky accented that little word by raising his right pointer finger. " . . . at least according to de FBI reports, by de time the transaction was complete, Bridges suspected a tail and cancelled." Sparky turned a few loose pages of notebook paper in the folder. "Dat happened at least two times."

"Third time's a charm." *In more ways than one.*

"Ah, ve are dangling a sizeable revenue. Bridges is no fool. De money vill talk and he vill move cautiously at first. When he is sure of clearance, click-click, ve seal de account."

If you say so, Sparky. J.P. still didn't understand how Sparky had been able to track all the details of the online hoist in the first place.

Late in the afternoon J.P. found himself leaning over his bathroom sink with a razor. He'd tried to call Samira, but no one had answered. Now it was time to be thinking about the cocktail party.

"So, Dad . . ." James was laying sideways across his father's bed. "Did you ask mom if you could buy us a 4-Runner this weekend? Or are we going to, like, totally surprise her when we pull in the driveway with it."

J.P. rinsed his razor. "I told her you were driving yourselves home in your own vehicle." *I don't ask my ex-wife anything.*

"That is so sweet!" Josh hollered from the hallway! "I can't believe we finally have a little freedom!"

"Don't abuse it." J.P. glanced at James in the mirror. "Do you hear me?"

Josh appeared in the bathroom doorway. "Loud and clear, Dad." He grinned. "Thanks."

It's the least I can do for them.

"So, You really don't care if we, like, go to the movies tonight?"

J.P. rinsed the shave cream out of the blades. "Depends on what movie you're planning to see."

"It's rated R, but I'm seventeen," Josh reminded. "Action flick. Schwarzenegger."

"Which theater?"

"The new one at the mall."

"Ten-thirty curfew. I'll be home by then." The father gave them a heads up on the deadline.

"Cool!" James jumped off the bed. "And we don't have to call for a ride home, right?"

"Not if you take the 4-Runner." J.P. could see the excitement on the boys' faces in the reflection of the mirror. *It feels good to trust them.* "Temporary plates are prone to scrutiny . . ."

"I have yet to have a traffic violation," Josh offered.

But the excitement of a new vehicle can change all that. J.P. wiped his face in a towel. "Just don't test it. That truck can go away as fast as it appeared." He stepped out of the bathroom. James and Josh gave silent understanding. "Ten thirty."

"When do you have to leave?"

J.P. glanced at the digital clock next to his bed. "Mike's picking me up in a few minutes."

"Any dinner plans?" James rubbed his stomach.

Oh yeah. They probably need to eat. J.P. opened the wallet. "Order a pizza."

"Or, we could drive through somewhere . . ." Josh hinted.

Either way they take my cash. J.P. grinned at his boys. "Suit yourself." The series of whoops and hollers that followed was well worth the permission granted.

J.P. finished dressing. He hadn't worn his tux since the weekend in Springfield with Samira. It seemed strange to be putting it on for such a brief engagement. *I'll be there an hour at the most. Just long enough to take guest attendance and make good on the public appearance for Stephenson.*

James appeared in the bedroom doorway again. "I'd think with a getup like that you'd have a date or something."

One would think. "She's busy with her family tonight."

"No other options, huh?"

"Nope." *There's no other woman I'd go with anyway.* "And to be honest, I'm not really looking for another option."

James balanced his weight on the top of the doorway with his hands. "So, you and Samira must be a couple now, huh?"

The father straightened his bow tie in the reflection. *I hadn't exactly thought of it that way.* "I guess maybe so."

"Sweet!" James gave his father two thumbs up. "She's good for you."

"Do you think?"

"Oh, yeah. She keeps you, like, way mellow." James grinned. "Makes me think, well . . . You're just not as irritable with her around."

Not as irritable, huh? J.P. laughed. "That is a good thing, then." He lifted his tuxedo jacket off the dry cleaner's hanger. "We're having Sunday dinner at Samira's parents' house tomorrow."

James made a face with that news. "Why would we do that?"

"Because it keeps peace in the family." *Her family. I could live without family relations.* J.P. thought again. *Hell, I do live without family relations.*

"Wait til I tell Josh." James started to leave but turned around. "You look hot, Dad. You deserve a date. Maybe you should call her again."

I tried that. J.P. had dialed Samira's number only to get the answering machine right after they got home with the new truck. "The tux is to impress a client or two."

"You're call . . ."

"Whoa!" Mike entered through the kitchen door. "Nice wheels!"

"Nice duds!" James circled Mike.

"When do I get my ride?"

Josh fished the keys out of his pocket. "Name the time!"

Mike pounded the counter in a rhythmic pattern. "How about when I bring your Dad back?"

"What time will that be?"

Mike shrugged his shoulders. "Movie night for you guys, eh?"

"Schwarzenegger." Josh grinned. "Since you and Dad didn't find dates you have to go out together, huh?"

"I'm taking your ol' man so he doesn't feel stupid being there alone." Mike lowered his voice and turned his shoulder to J.P. "My hot date is after this business affair!"

Josh raised his eyebrows.

The phone on J.P.'s hip rang. He checked the caller ID before answering. "Sparky, this is J.P. What's up?"

"Ve have activity on the new account. Vhen are you going to de party?"

"We're on our way now." J.P. made eye contact with Mike.

"I need you to keep a close eye out for our honored guests. Vatch for Goldstein, Jessica Hutchison and our Celia Monroe. Dhey are de most important."

I can do that.

"Ve need to know vhat time dey come and vhat time dey go." Sparky finished giving the instructions and then disconnected the call without any further discussion.

"Alright, guys," J.P. clapped his hand together. "Ten-thirty. Be here. No later. And one stop before the movie to eat."

J.P. put his hands in the air and met James's open palms with high fives as he started to leave the house. *It's fun to set them free.*

He followed Mike out the kitchen door and climbed into the low seat of the Corvette. *I wouldn't want to slide into this thing every day of my life.*

"I brought you a present," Mike reached behind his seat and fished out a plain paper bag. He handed it to J.P. as he buckled his seat belt. "Couldn't resist."

"What is it?"

"Had your name written all over it!"

J.P. didn't like the way Mike was avoiding eye contact. *It's a movie.* He turned it over and read the title. "Meet the Parents."

"I thought you might want to watch it after I bring you home!"

Up until this moment the thought of meeting Samira's parents hadn't bothered J.P. too much. He read the title of the movie again. "You're full of shit."

Mike laughed heartily.

"There's been some activity on the new Mid-America account. Sparky needs us to inventory the crowd and note arrival and departure times."

"Very cool," Mike widened his eyes as they pulled into Mr. Stephenson's neighborhood. "The usual suspects?"

J.P. felt the slowing of the engine as Mike geared down. "Goldstein, Hutchison, and Monroe."

There was a line of guests entering Mr. Stephenson's house when Mike turned the corner. "We can do that." Mike had slowed way down. "It's not hard to find this place, but finding a place to park might be another story."

J.P. admired the gated community that surrounded the newest golf course in the area. *Big houses. Fancy cars.* The three-story brick house was impressive. *Stephenson isn't as conservative as he lets on.* The clock on the dashboard indicated five-twenty. *Fashionably late along with the rest of the guests.*

Mr. and Mrs. Stephenson greeted Mike and J.P. at the front door with great enthusiasm. "I've heard a lot about your legal counsel in these past days," Mrs. Stephenson announced with a handshake. As her eyes met J.P.'s, she started to speak and then stopped. Mr. Stephenson made a formal introduction, seemingly unaware of her hesitation.

J.P. looked at the cheerful blonde. *I know her face from the picture in his office.* He studied her face again. *But I've seen her somewhere else.*

He followed Mike further into the house, but glanced back for one more look at Mrs. Stephenson. *Face it, Ralston. You could have met her in one of a million places.* Their eyes connected again. *I know she's seen me, I can read that much from her face.*

Mike bumped J.P. in the arm with his elbow. "The Hughes brothers seem right at home."

J.P. looked into the formal living room just off the entryway. *I'll make my presence known.* Christopher and Jefferey Hughes were mingling among the gathering crowd. *Casual conversation like this saves phone calls later.*

"Any news today?" Christopher asked under his breath.

J.P. knew the businessman was talking about Sparky's surveillance at Mid-America. *But Sparky says no public conversations on the topic.*

"Nothing yet today." *I'll check in with our little investigator a little later.*

"Oh, J.P.!" Mrs. Hughes appeared from around a corner with her arms spread open wide. "It's so good to see you!" She initiated a ceremonial hug, which J.P. returned formally. Her eyes scanned the room behind him. "Where is that beautiful woman I met in Springfield? She is with you, isn't she?"

J.P. ignored Mike's accusing look. "No, she's not here tonight."

"But she is *with* you, tell me she is." Mrs. Hughes looked over her wire-rimmed glasses.

She's as eccentric as ever. J.P. watched as his best friend made a silent escape from the conversation. *Good, he can scout out the crowd while I entertain the Hughes.*

"Elizabeth . . ." Christopher Hughes joined his wife.

J.P. smiled. "That's alright." He looked back at the high society woman. "Yes, she's just not here tonight."

"Oh, wonderful, wonderful!" Elizabeth Hughes threw her arms out to her sides again. "I knew you could keep her if you would just step it up a bit." J.P. watched the her hurry over to a corner table and reached for a small black purse. "Here," she said returning with something in her hand. "I've had this for her ever since I last saw you. Would you be so kind as to deliver this for me?"

It was a new audio release of the Springfield Symphony in concert. *Leave it to Mrs. Hughes to drop a subtle reminder of the concert we missed.* His eyes scanned the room hoping to catch a glimpse of Mike somewhere in the crowd.

Mrs. Hughes chattered on. "She didn't get to go hear the symphony live that night and they were playing Copland." J.P. was humored by her. "And they played very well, I must say."

If she's trying to make me feel guilty, it's not going to work. J.P. thanked her for the gift and promised to give it to Samira at his earliest convenience.

Christopher Hughes interrupted his wife's conversation, almost as if he had news of his own to flaunt. "I paid Ms Cartwright a visit of my own on behalf of my father's estate," he publicized the information without reserve.

I'll handle this one with care. "I understand you were able to assist with a new addition to the library."

Christopher nodded. "A fine woman, J.P. Do encourage her to call if the library has needs in the future."

I didn't realize Samira had made such an impression on the Hughes. J.P. noticed Denise and Derek at the front door and excused himself from the Hughes' company. *I could stand for a few more minutes with Christopher, but under the circumstances, I think it's best to leave Mrs. Hughes to mingle with someone else.* J.P.'s eyes happened upon Mrs. Stephenson again. *She's very familiar . . .*

Mike reappeared before J.P. could get to Denise. "Mixed crowd here tonight," he reported. "High society, low society, and great servers." Mike held a mixed drink out for J.P. to take. "This is for you."

"What is it?"

Mike sipped his own drink. "Your usual. JD and Coke."

Seems a bit harsh for this early in the evening. J.P. accepted the drink anyway. Across the room he noticed Celia Monroe mingling through the crowd with another bank employee. *Very interesting.* He noted the time as Sparky had requested. *Five forty-five.*

"Two city council members and the mayor are present in the other room." Mike held his glass out toward the room behind the kitchen. "Gorgeous two-story fireplace in the family room." He sipped his drink again. "You need to check this place out."

"Not exactly as conservative as I'd expected."

"Quite extravagant, I'd say," Mike complimented the décor. "They say he is heir to his father's throne."

J.P. turned around so he could see the people mingling behind him. Mr. Stephenson's father was engaged in conversation with a group of people just inside the French doors of what appeared to be an office. "He already has the throne. His father retired from Midland Mortgage four years ago, at which time Midland Mortgage and American Savings merged." *There's a couple of my clients over there.* "Young Mr. Stephenson has been in the driver's seat since then. His father has input through the board of directors."

"Impressive," Mike stared at J.P.'s historical account. "You've done your homework, J.P. Ralston."

J.P. smiled and nodded his head toward a woman in the far corner. "Now there's a familiar face, Mikey." Derek was on the make with a woman dressed in a tight-fitting black mini skirt and revealing blouse.

J.P. watched Mike's eyes widen with the recognition. *Now I know why he didn't bring Kelly here.*

"Rachel Radochovich." Mike whistled quietly through his teeth. "She's still a looker, isn't she?" Mike grinned broadly under his mustache. "I do know how to pick 'em don't I?"

It suddenly occurred to J.P. that he didn't recognize anything extremely sexy about Kelly Davis. *At least not like the one standing over there.*

"Looks like Derek is wanting a piece of Rachel tonight." Mike finished his drink.

J.P. watched Derek on the make. "Think we should tip him off?"

Mike shook his curly head. "I say let him take the plunge. He'll be a better man for it."

J.P. laughed. *I seriously doubt she made Mike a better man for any of the shit she handed him.*

Denise wasn't far away and for the first time J.P. realized Jerry was with her. "I need to talk to Denise a minute." He excused himself from Mike's company and joined Denise mid-conversation with an editor from the Tribune.

J.P. offered his hand to Denise's long time companion. "Jerry, it's good to see you. How's the beat?" *Denise and Jerry have been together longer than I've worked with Denise.*

Jerry's crew cut and button down shirt gave him an ultra conservative appearance. "It's good, J.P. And your office never seems to be too far out of the loop of current affairs."

J.P. smiled. Jerry was always good to keep the media focused on the positive side of the law. *But, I'd think, after all this time, he would want something a little more permanent with his woman.*

"You've done well to keep up with the riff-raff surrounding Shoal Creek." J.P. spoke in recognition of Jerry's recent press concerning the venture. *And there may be more to that story soon.*

"Shoal Creek has some interesting twists. Do you think Goldstein can pull it off?"

Ask me again in a week. "It's hard to tell. Just keep your ears open and your eyes peeled."

Jerry raised a cocktail to his lips. "I always appreciate an insightful tip."

"Anytime I can be of service." He raised his glass to meet Jerry's toast. But when the whiskey went down it burned more than usual. J.P. swallowed hard, trying not to choke on the drink. *Who in the hell mixed this drink anyway?*

J.P. glanced at the entryway and immediately recognized the guest entering the front door. In spite of Sparky's warning, he really didn't think he'd have the guts to show his face in this crowd. J.P. checked his watch. *Six o'clock straight up. Very interesting.* But even more interesting was the guest's companion. *Jessica Hutchison.* J.P. watched Mr. and Mrs. Stephenson greet them just as they had all the others.

Now I need to stick around until they leave. J.P. was very intrigued by their appearance. *If he is indeed Sean Bridges, then Jefferey Hughes is going to know him by that name.* J.P. turned around and searched the room for the younger Hughes brother.

The attorney wound his way through to the far door of the formal living room and entered an oversized kitchen that overlooked the family room. The outside wall was all glass overlooking the golf course and lake. Mr. Stephenson senior was entertaining yet another band of businessmen. *A very wise businessman to work the crowd like he does.*

J.P. continued on into the family room. *There's Jefferey.*

J.P. waited and watched. He made his way up to Mr. Hughes and turned around so he could see Alan Goldstein in the kitchen.

"You've done a fine job with the business details between the corporation and Mid-America, J.P." Jefferey complimented J.P. before he had a chance to speak. "I want you to know we appreciate all you do for us." The executive sipped the drink in his hand. "You know, if you ever change your mind and decide you want to give up a private practice, you have a place with us."

Nice offer, but it won't happen. J.P. thanked Mr. Hughes for the kind words. *I'd lose too much independence working for one client.* J.P. thought again. *And I'd be bored out of my mind.*

"Mr. Hughes," J.P. changed the subject. "Help me out. There's a man in the kitchen I recognize, but I can't place his name. I'm thinking you did some business with him while I was out of town last summer."

J.P. watched Mr. Hughes narrow his eyes to scan the faces of the guests in the kitchen.

Black suit, black tie, just like everyone else in the room.

"Oh, yes, I see," Jefferey was focused on the middle of the crowded room. "I can't see all that well, but it appears to be that real estate broker who wanted to sell us the airport tract."

That would be the one.

"He goes by Bridges, I think . . ."

Jefferey went on to describe the details of the meeting J.P. had missed. But the only detail he needed was the one he already had. *Hands down Jefferey Hughes would testify in a court of law if I need his witness.*

Mike appeared out of nowhere looking more animated than usual.

Derek must have gotten a bite out of Rachel.

"You are not going to believe this," Mike started talking before he even reached J.P. "You've got to see this." He started to lead J.P. back through the throng of formally clad people.

"You're not going to believe this either . . ." *Wait til I tell him we have our witness . . .*

"No, me first this time." Mike had a hold of J.P.'s elbow. "Is that still your first drink?"

"Yeah." J.P. made a face. "What'd you put in it?"

"I didn't. The bartender mixed it." Mike was leading J.P. back through the living room. They passed the French doors that led into an oversized study.

"Well, it's plenty strong."

"I didn't notice anything wrong with mine." Mike stopped at the bottom of a grand staircase. "Since when was Jack Daniels ever too strong for you?"

I don't know. J.P. looked into his drink. *But it tastes like hell.*

"Take a look up there."

J.P. followed Mike's eyes up the stairs. "Where?"

"On the wall."

"What were you doing up there?" J.P. noted a gallery of photos hanging on the wall.

"Mingling." Mike nudged his shoulder. "Go up to the landing and take a good hard look at the picture on the left."

J.P. felt stupid going up the stairs. *No one else is up here.*

"Just go." Mike nudged him again. "That whiskey will taste better once you see what I saw."

What the hell? Reluctantly J.P. made his way up to the first landing. He stopped and glanced at the photograph on the left. *Looks like Stephenson's wedding picture.* He turned around and shrugged his shoulders at Mike.

"Look closer!" Mike was coming up the stairs now.

Before he turned back to the picture, Mike had his finger on a bridesmaid.

J.P. looked once. Then he looked again. Then he reached for his glasses.

"Don't bother . . ." Mike stopped J.P.'s hand. "It's her."

J.P. looked again, stunned. *What is Samira doing in Stephenson's wedding picture?* He suddenly wondered if she might be in the crowd. *No, she had family obligations tonight.*

"What the hell?"

Mike shrugged his shoulders under his blonde curls. "I don't know, but if you like, being the friend that I am, I could make some inquiries."

I definitely need to know. He gave Mike permission to ask some questions.

Suddenly it didn't seem important that Jessica Hutchison was there with Alan Goldstein, or who ever that man claimed to be. And it didn't matter if Rachel Radocovich screwed Derek. Celia Monroe's presence no longer had an impact on J.P.'s agenda either. He no longer cared if Elizabeth Hughes approved of his date. *The ONLY thing that matter right now is the relationship between Samira and the Stephenson family.*

"Got it!" Mike came up from behind and handed J.P. another drink.

"I don't need it." J.P. declined.

"Trust me, you need it." Mike handed it over anyway. "This is one time you should have done your homework."

I already have a bad JD.

"Take the goddamn drink, and I'll give you the information you need." Mike lowered his head and looked out from under his bushy eyebrows.

J.P. took the drink. "What's the scoop?"

"You're not going to believe it when I tell you."

"Try me."

"Take a drink first. It will help."

Just give me the friggin' information!

Mike waited stubbornly.

Oh, fine. J.P. sipped the drink. It was just as bitter and hard as the last one. He made a face and wiped his mouth on the back of his hand.

Mike was nodding his head eagerly. "He's her brother."

"Who?"

"Stephenson."

What?

"Do I have to spell this out?" Mike took J.P. back to the photo. "Samira Cartwright, your woman in waiting, is the honorable Weston Stephenson's sister. Get the picture?"

J.P. stared at the photograph. *Oh, my god! That's the familiar look I see in his eyes when he questions my judgment.* He looked closer. *And he's the brother who'd tell her to take a job for the money.* The realizations were starting to come faster than J.P. could control. *And it was probably his birthday party Samira missed last weekend.*

"Counselor?" Mike interrupted the onslaught of connections that were blinding J.P.'s vision. "Are you alright?"

J.P. couldn't answer. He lifted the whiskey to his lips and drank it down. All the way down. And it burned all the way to his toes but J.P. Ralston was too stunned to notice.

Mr. and Mrs. Stephenson were still greeting incoming guests near the front entryway a few feet from where Mike and J.P. were standing. *And I know I've seen her face somewhere other than on Stephenson's desk—and oh holy shit, their kids! I know his kids! They were at Samira's once when I went to pick her up!*

Mike pounded J.P. hard on the back. "Breathe, buddy, breathe."

"J.P.," a voice greeted from behind. "I'm glad you could make it." J.P. turned to face the voice but when he went to shake hands, he realized he had a glass in each one. Completely embarrassed, J.P. tried to stack the empty glass under the full one. Much to his relief, Mike held out a hand. J.P. handed the full one to his friend and then offered his hand in greeting.

"Great party." *Stupid thing to say. But what do I say to the father I dared to piss off before brunch last Saturday morning.* J.P. swallowed hard as the handshake released.

"It's wonderful to have the Hughes brothers with us as well. They are going to be fine contributors to city commerce."

"Indeed." J.P. had noticed the similarities between the Stephenson men before, but to put Samira in the mix was overwhelming. *Do I need his permission to date his daughter?* Reality set in. *And I've done far more with her than simply take her to dinner! Shit.* J.P. swallowed hard.

"Harold Reinholdt is here from the Reebock Company. He is one of our most highly esteemed investors. It might do your business well to introduce yourself if you get a chance." Raymond Stephenson discreetly pointed out the executive across the room.

Funny. I wonder if Mr. Stephenson would be so eager to endorse my services if he knew what I've been doing with Samira.

Raymond Stephenson excused himself, leaving J.P. to his confusion. Mike put the full glass back in J.P.'s hand. Without thinking, J.P. raised it to his lips and drank it down.

"Damn!" J.P. choked. "This is wicked."

Mike frowned and shrugged his shoulders. "It's your usual, man. What's up with you and the Jack Daniels?"

Everything is up with me. Suddenly the room felt very crowded. *This puts a whole new twist on meeting the parents.*

61

Family

Krissy grinned and rolled her eyes. "I know why you want to sign on to your email account."

Samira waved her hands for Krissy to move out of the chair. "I won't be here long." *I just want to see if he wrote in today.* I like being in touch this way. *I wonder if he found a car for the boys?* In the background, Samira could hear little Mark crying. *He's getting sleepy.* Samira accessed her email from her parents' computer.

No new messages. Samira sighed. *I know I talked to him yesterday, but it seems like longer.*

"I don't know what to do with Mark!" Kara looked exasperated. "Granny has the girls in the tub and I can't make him happy."

Samira signed off. "I'll take him." She gave her seat up to Kara. *She'd rather be chatting with her friends right now anyway.*

Mark was laying in the middle of the family room floor sucking his thumb when Samira got to him. His little eyes were puffy from crying.

"Come here, little guy," Samira put him over her shoulder. *Almost two years old already.* Samira stooped to pick up his blanket. *My how times flies. Seems like yesterday I was visiting Pam in the hospital.*

Samira could hear joyful screeches coming from behind the bathroom door. *I bet Mama's as wet as the girls by now.* Samira crossed her parent's bedroom and sat down in the platform rocker. Very gently she turned Mark in her arms so he was leaning up against her. "You, little fella . . ." Samira whispered to her nephew, " . . . need to close your eyes."

Samira began to hum. *Just like I used to do for the girls.* The words to the song played in Samira's mind even though she didn't sing them out loud. Little Mark snuggled in. He was asleep almost before Samira finished the first stanza. *Sometimes I miss these quiet moments at the end of the day.* Mark had a new little boy haircut. *I miss his curls too. Tom always hoped we'd have a little boy someday, but I'm not sure he would have approved of a Mama's boy . . .* She cuddled Mark closer. *But that's exactly what my little boy would have been.*

Samira stayed in the rocking chair until the house was quiet from bath time. She was just starting to get up when her mother came to find them.

"He's getting to be a handful, isn't he?" Ashleigh held out her hands.

"I can get him, Mama." Samira shifted Mark's weight against her shoulder and carried him across the room to the crib. *Sweet dreams, little guy.*

A Bach Invention was playing on the radio when Samira joined her mother in the kitchen again. Ashleigh handed her daughter a cup of coffee. "I do appreciate your assistance tonight, dear. I can take care of the kids, but it's so much easier when your father is home to assist."

"What time do you expect Daddy home?" Samira looked at the clock. It was well past eight o'clock. *I could be getting ready for a dinner date right now.*

"Oh, anytime. He didn't think he would be too late." Ashleigh leaned across the kitchen counter and wiped it clean with a damp rag.

It's already clean, Mama. Samira almost laughed out. *Funny, that's what Phil said to me the other night.*

"I think everything is in order for tomorrow. The salads are in the refrigerator, the meat is seasoned and ready to put in the oven, and the green bean casserole is mixed and ready to bake All I have to do in the morning is make the bread and peel the potatoes." Ashleigh smiled at her daughter.

"I wish you'd let me bring something," Samira offered again. "I really don't mind."

"You are bringing the guests."

"And lots of them!" Krissy appeared in the kitchen. Without asking permission, she helped herself to an apple out of the fruit basket on the counter. "Three, to be exact."

"Tell me again. How old are the boys?" Ashleigh started to count out plates.

"Josh is a senior. What is he, Mama? Seventeen?" Krissy was talking between bites.

"I think he's eighteen." Samira watched Krissy pick a piece of apple from between her braces. "Be careful, Krissy. I'd like those brackets in place when we see the orthodontist this week."

"I know." She took another bite. "James is going to be sixteen like next month or something." The girl took another bite and smiled at her mother. "I hope you have lots of food because they'll eat a lot!" Krissy chewed for a moment. "And they are big boys! James is taller than his dad!"

Ashleigh laughed. "There will be plenty."

Mama will have more than enough food for all of us.

Kara stuck her head around the corner. "The girls want to watch 'Pete's Dragon'. Is there enough time before bed?"

"That's a long one." *But that's the one Krissy always picked too.* "Bonnie and Lizzie might fall asleep before it's over."

"Fine with me." Kara disappeared as quickly as she'd appeared.

"I never know what she's thinking anymore."

Ashleigh's eyes were warm when they met her daughter's. "And you may never know again." She cocked her head to the side as she counted out silverware.

"Am I really that hard to read?" *I always feel like I'm so transparent.* Samira picked up the stack of plates and carried them to the dining room table.

"You're not hard to read, dear, I just never know exactly what you're thinking." Ashleigh joined her daughter in the dining room.

"You should have gone over to Wes and Pam's party tonight, Mama." Samira started to space the plates evenly around the oversized oak table. "The girls and I could have handled the kids."

"Not with so much to do!" Ashleigh looked around her spotless house. "No, I am more comfortable getting things ready for tomorrow. Your father will represent us both just fine."

She smiled genuinely. "You know how I feel about social gatherings anyway." She followed her daughter, placing the silverware in appropriate positions along side the plates.

Mama loves social gathering as long as she's the one in charge! She finished arranging the plates, but there were two left over. Samira started back to the kitchen.

Ashleigh stopped her work and studied the table. "Oh, wait, dear. We need to shift the side plates to add two more."

Samira silently named off the guests as she counted the plates already on the table. "There are eleven plus Mark's high chair."

"I know, but I decided to seat the little girls out here with us."

Wait. She watched as Ashleigh made room for the extra two plates. She counted again in her head. *Eleven. Right?*

Ashleigh pointed. "One here, and one there."

"Phil only has two boys."

"Yes, I know." Ashleigh smiled sheepishly. "But I invited Pam and Wes to join us. With the party going on at their house tonight, Pam won't have time to put a meal together." Ashleigh turned away. "Besides, two more at the table just helps complete the picture."

Complete what picture? Samira was irritated. "You should have told me." *Now I have no way to inform Phil of the changes. Meeting my parents is one thing. Meeting my entire family is another!*

"I didn't think about it until just tonight." Ashleigh went back to setting the silverware. "I couldn't leave them out!"

Why not? Samira sighed heavily.

"I don't understand, Samira." Ashleigh finished with the silverware. She opened a drawer on the china hutch and extracted a stack of cloth napkins. She began folding them into shapes on the corner of the table. "It only made sense."

Samira left the dining room. *Mama always says, if you can't say anything nice, then don't say anything at all. It's not fair for Phil to walk in unaware of the extra guests!*

"Do you need to call and let him know your brother and sister-in-law will be joining us?"

"It won't do any good now," Samira answered. "I won't talk to him before morning."

"You can call from here if you like."

Nice gesture, Mama, but it won't work. "He's out for the evening." *On a date I should have accepted!* "I won't talk to him before he gets here."

"Isn't he meeting us at church?"

Church? Oh, heaven's NO! Samira put her hands in her hair. She couldn't believe her mother expected her to invite Phil and the boys to church! *I wasn't even planning on going to church in the morning!*

"He does go to church, doesn't he?" The mother skillfully hid her face behind her coffee cup.

Church? No, not Phil. Samira let her hair go. *Now I suppose Mama is going to pass judgment before she even really gets to know him.* "I don't know."

"I thought that would be one of your priorities when you started dating someone."

It's not exactly like I planned to meet this man, Mama! Samira started to wipe down the counter. *Stop. The counter is already clean.*

"So he had plans tonight?"

He has a name, you know. "Yes." Samira had to guard the bite in her tone. "Phil had a business engagement tonight."

"On a Saturday night?"

Samira stared at her mother. "Wes has a business engagement tonight and Daddy went over there!"

"But it's not a regular business affair. I'd say it's more of a social event. Wes hosted the party to celebrate one of his newest clients at the bank . . ."

"That's business!" Samira couldn't help but raise her voice a notch. "Phil is a very successful businessman. I'm sure he is meeting with some important clients tonight too."

Ashleigh met her daughter's glare with soft eyes. "I'm sure that's right, dear." She lowered her head slightly. "I didn't mean to upset you."

Now I'm glad she doesn't know exactly what I'm thinking. Samira looked away. *But I know what she's thinking and I don't appreciate her passing judgment so soon. He's not going to be who they want him to be anyway.*

"Krissy tells us he's a lawyer . . ."

Phil. Learn his name, please. "Phil has a private practice here in town."

"I wonder if your father knows him?"

"Highly unlikely."

"Well, I'm sure he's a very good lawyer." Ashleigh's voice was soft.

How does she do that? She knows I'm upset, yet she softens her tone and takes the conversation back to a neutral zone every time. "He's very active in city government and also works for a large corporation out of Springfield on a regular basis."

Ashleigh offered to fill Samira's cup again, but Samira politely refused.

"We're all looking forward to spending time with Phil and his family."

We are, are we? Samira rinsed her cup in the sink. *At least she used his name.*

"Weston was quite concerned about you when it didn't work out between you and Phil a few weeks back . . ."

How nice of Wes to break confidentiality.

"I think it will help ease his mind if he can sit and visit with this man in your life."

Now we have the real reason Mama invited Wes and Pam to dinner. It had very little to do with their personal agenda. In fact, it has everything to do with mine. Samira decided to go out on a limb.

"I just hope you haven't set your expectations too high, Mama." She watched her mother's face carefully. "I like Phil a lot." *More than I'd like to admit, actually.* "He makes me laugh." *He makes me cry.* "He supports my decisions." *He lets me think for myself.* "He's always a gentleman." *Especially when we're alone together.* "And he seems to enjoy spending time with Krissy and Kara." *Just as much as I enjoy being with James and Josh.* "I don't want you to be disappointed in him because he doesn't go to church or because he chooses to work on a Saturday evening."

Ashleigh leaned her hip on a kitchen stool. Her face was serene and thoughtful.

"Phil's a very good man, Mama, even if he doesn't add up to yours and Daddy's standard of measurement." *I like everything about him.* Samira felt her face redden as she continued to explain. *Even if he has a tendency to lose his temper.* "I don't want you to be worried about me." *He's good for me because he needs me in ways I didn't realize I could be needed.* "I just want you to be happy for me." *He makes me whole again.*

The mother placed her coffee cup on the tile counter. "We are happy that you're dating again, Samira. We just don't want to see you get hurt."

I figure that's just a chance I have to take. "I know, Mama." *But I'm not dating again. I'm keeping Phil.* Samira's deep brown eyes reflected her mother's sentiments. "I know." *But it hurts just as much to not have anyone at all.*

The church service lasted much longer than Samira wished to wait. *I only came this morning to deter any repercussions later.* Even the familiar hymns stuck in her throat.

I can't believe I'm this worked up about Phil meeting my parents. She passed the offering plate. *Phil is so independent, yet he's so passionate about his work.* She studied her father's profile in the stillness of the sanctuary. *And in that way he's not so much different from Daddy.* She stood with the congregation to sing the traditional doxology.

Samira's mind was still wandering during the morning message. Wes and Pam were seated across the aisle and one row up. Samira watched her brother draw Pam closer to him in the pew. *Wes would tell me to follow my heart. But he'd also tell me to be cautious and not to give away too much before I knew for sure.* Samira's mind tripped back to the ranch. For a moment she could see Phil walking up Aunt Maggie's sidewalk after his morning run. She felt her mouth curl into a silent smile. *No, his passion isn't just in his work. It's in the way he walks. It's in his voice and in his smile.* Samira remembered his arms around her as they rode Toby back to the house together. *It's in his anger as much as it's in his kisses.* She squeezed her arms around her middle. *I hope they can see all that about him.*

Samira admired her mother's loose bun at the back of her neck. *They wouldn't be so critical except for the fact that they worry about me way too much.* Samira bowed her head at the pastor's invitation.

Maybe it's because we love you so much. That thought came out of nowhere. Samira lifted her head to see who was thinking the inaudible thought. Very gently, Samira felt her father's hand slip under hers. She returned the loving gesture by linking her fingers into his.

Oh, Daddy, you always seem to know me the best. Samira continued to hold her father's hand as they stood to sing the last hymn. *I just want you to give Phil a chance.* Raymond let go of her hand and instead wrapped his arm around her shoulder.

Samira allowed him to pull her close as he sang. "Amazing Grace, how sweet the sound, that saved a wretch like me . . ."

Maybe that's what we need at dinner today. Samira joined in. *Amazing Grace . . .*

Ashleigh didn't waste any time exiting the sanctuary. She had a family dinner to put on the table and no one was going to detain her efforts. Samira skipped a step to keep up with her mother's stride.

"I'm thankful the table is set already," Ashleigh commented as she unlocked the Cadillac. "We can fill the glasses and pop the bread in the oven and everything else should be ready."

Samira motioned across the churchyard for Krissy and Kara to hurry. *They're going to have to walk in the rain if they don't hustle!* Krissy waved back and pointed to Wes and Pam. Samira understood. *That way they can help with the kids.* She climbed into the backseat while her father took the seat next to Ashleigh.

"Mama's on a mission, Daddy."

"Don't I know it!" Raymond laughed as he fastened his seatbelt. "If it weren't so drizzly we could walk our sidewalk path home."

Samira smiled. *I loved those walks with Daddy as a child.* Her eyes followed the path they'd walked back to the house together hundreds of times over the years.

Ashleigh was in high gear the moment they entered the house. Samira watched her mother stop in the entrance hall and rearrange a bouquet of fresh cut flowers. *It won't matter, Mama. I doubt Phil and the boys would have noticed if one stem was too long.*

"Twenty minutes is all we need on the rolls . . ."

Samira looked at the grandfather clock next to the bouquet. *Plenty of time.* Still, she couldn't keep her eyes from going back to the dining room windows. She'd parked her Camry in the driveway before church, just like she'd promised. *As if Phil can't read street addresses.*

Wes and Pam's van pulled in the driveway while Samira was putting ice in the glasses. *Here we go.* Samira tried to steady her nerves, but her hands were shaking. *For pete's sake, it's only your brother.* Samira thought again. *No, it's more than that.*

Suddenly the aroma of freshly baked bread mixed with the smell of burning wood. Samira smiled. *Daddy built a fire in the fireplace*

"Thank you, Daddy."

"You're welcome, Princess." Raymond kept poking at the fire. "It's just cool enough outside I thought a little fire might help warm our spirits."

I wonder if he knows I'm a wreck over all this? Samira returned to her task. *Probably.*

The hall was suddenly filled with happy commotion. "Leave your shoes at the door." Pam ushered the little girls in out of the rain. "We don't want to get Granny's carpet muddy." Samira watched Pam help Lizzie remove her coat.

Wes ducked in out of the rain carrying little Mark under a blanket. The moment the door closed, Mark pulled the cover off his head.

"Boo!" He cooed at his father.

Samira smiled as she took Mark. "Let's get you out of those wet clothes."

Wes removed his trench coat and hung it on the hall tree. "I imagine his diaper is about as wet as my raincoat." He held his hands out to take Mark back, but the toddler leaned back into the security of his aunt's shoulder. "Since when did I play second fiddle to my little sister?" Wes poked the little boy in the tummy with his finger playfully. "So, are you excited for us to meet this man in your life, Sis?"

Samira tugged on the sleeve of Mark's jacket and pulled it off one arm. "I don't know if I can call it excitement." *More like nervous anxiety.*

"It can't be that bad, can it?" Wes leaned back on his heels. "You've been seeing him long enough now I'd think you'd be ready to let us in on your secret."

"Maybe." *He's not really a secret.* Samira pulled Mark's coat completely off and hung it next to his father's on the hall tree.

"Why the worried face?"

There he goes, reading my emotions again. "I just want you to like him, that's all."

"Sis, I trust your judgment." Wes squeezed her arm. "Relax."

Easier said than done. "I'll go change him." *I really don't mind.*

Samira changed her nephew's diaper with ease. *Just like riding a bike, little Mark. You never forget how to change a diaper either!* He was content and playful as she carried him back down the hall into the main part of the house.

Wes was standing with the front door open when Samira came around the corner. She overheard her brother's voice.

"Hey what can I do for you? We're just getting ready for a family dinner."

That sounds funny. Samira stepped into the entrance hall. Her eyes came into contact with the visitor behind the door.

Phil!

"I'm actually not here to see you . . ."

He's letting in the cold air! "Come on in." Samira made the invitation much to her brother's dismay.

Wes moved over and allowed Phil to step inside. "Then you're here to see my father?"

Why would he be here to see Daddy? "Wes . . ." Samira tried to set Mark on the floor but he was holding on to her necklace. She straightened again and loosened his hold on the sterling chain.

"I'll get Dad."

I really don't understand. "I'm sorry I didn't get you told earlier. Did you get my email?"

Phil shook his head.

"Phone message?"

He shook his head again.

Samira sighed. Mark was examining her earring. "I tried to warn you ahead of time. I'm sorry."

Phil looked concerned. "It's an amazing turn of events. To be perfectly honest, I'm not sure how we missed it."

How we missed the fact that my mother invited Wes and Pam to dinner? Samira pulled her head away from Mark's busy little hands. *He's more nervous than I thought he would be.*

"My mother didn't tell me until last night so I didn't have much time to inform you."

Phil shrugged. "It's probably just as well I didn't know any sooner."

Probably. One night of sleeplessness is plenty for me! Suddenly Samira missed James and Josh. "Are the boys coming?"

Phil turned around and ducked enough to see through the leaded glass windowpane. "Yeah, they should be here shortly. I came from the office so they're meeting me here."

I could be hospitable! "Can I take your coat?"

"Looks like your hands are full." He slipped out of his leather jacket.

Samira took the coat with her free hand and hung it on the hall tree. "This is Raymond Mark. But we just call him Mark." *One introduction out of the way.* Mark was trying to get Samira's necklace in his mouth. "Come on in."

Samira's eyes locked with Phil's for an extended moment. She could feel his presence moving somewhere deep within her soul. *Oh, I know that look and it makes me nervous.* "If I could get both of Mark's hands free at the same time, I'd put him down." *Please don't kiss me here.*

Finally Mark lost interest in his aunt's jewelry. Samira took advantage of the moment and quickly put him on his feet. "Where's Papa Ray?" Mark balanced for a moment before wobbling off toward the living room.

"Why there you are!" Pam appeared from the dining room with a happy smile. "I wondered what happened to my little guy!" She knelt long enough to get a hug from Mark as he passed by. When Pam stood up she was surprised to find a visitor in the hall.

"So that's where I've seen you before!" Pam exclaimed. "I knew I'd seen you somewhere but I couldn't figure it out." Samira watched her sister in law shake Phil's hand without reserve.

"Same." Phil nodded his head. "It didn't dawn on me either."

"I was at the house . . ."

"When I picked up Samira once . . ."

"Exactly." Pam was nodding her head as well. "Samira you should have told me."

Told you what? Samira looked over her shoulder to see her father and brother crossing the living room. Her father was removing the gloves he always wore when he worked with firewood.

"J.P. Ralston."

How does Daddy know that name?

Raymond stuck out his hand in greeting. "This is a surprise." Raymond was smiling but Samira knew he was all business. "What can we help you with?"

Help him with? Samira was confused. "Daddy, this is Phil."

"I know J.P., Princess." Raymond excused his daughter's introduction gently.

Not J.P., Phil. I know him as Phil. Well, most of the time. Her father was waiting for a response. *Maybe they do know each other from the business end.*

"I'm here to see Samira . . ." Phil tucked his hands in the front pockets of his khaki pants.

Raymond seemed worried. "Is something the matter?"

"Not that I know of . . ." Phil looked to Samira who in turn looked to her father.

"He's here for dinner." *He knows Pam. Does he know my father?*

"Dinner?" Wes looked confused.

The doorbell chimed, causing a stir of commotion behind them. Krissy appeared out of nowhere and made a beeline for the door. "Hey guys!" She turned around with a bright smile. "Oh, hey! When did you get here?" She stopped long enough to address Phil. "Here." Krissy was holding out her arms. "I'll take your coats."

"Papa Ray, this is Josh, and this is James." Krissy turned toward Phil. "And I guess you guys have already met, right?"

"Yeah," Wes looked at Phil. "We've met."

Not officially! I don't know what's going on here!

"Great!" Krissy turned toward the boys. "This is my uncle Wes, and my grandfather, Raymond Stephenson." Without waiting for another second, she grabbed James by the sleeve. "Come on. Let's go meet my grandmother and aunt."

Maybe I should just let Krissy make all the introductions.

Bonnie and Lizzie came flying down the hallway hot on Krissy's heels.

"Be careful!" Samira tried to slow them down, but it was too late. They knocked little Mark onto his knees. He was instantly in tears but the girls ran a full circle eight pattern between Phil and Samira preventing her from helping Mark.

"Girls, please," Wes tried to gain control of the situation, but by then the girls were clear across the living room. He turned back toward Phil and Samira and apologized.

"Doesn't bother me."

He looks uneasy.

And Samira was still completely in the dark.

"So, let me get this straight," Wes pointed his finger at Phil. "You're here to eat dinner with my sister?"

"I believe that was the invitation."

Raymond crossed his arms. His eyes were focused on his daughter. "You should have told us you invited J.P. Ralston to dinner, Princess."

Sometimes I wish he wouldn't call me Princess! Besides I didn't make any of the invitations. Mama made them all!

"This is quite a shock . . ."

Phil's trying to smooth things over, but it's not his fault. "I tried to get a hold of Phil last night so he would know everything, but we missed each other, so here we are!" Samira threw her arms out to her side.

"Here we are, indeed." Raymond took a hold of Phil's elbow. "Come on in. Fine young men you have with you . . . ."

They didn't get two steps into the living room before Bonnie and Lizzie were the center of attention again. "I'm Bonnie and I'm almost seven," she introduced herself easily. "And this is my sister, Lizzie." She put her arm around her little sister's shoulder. "She's four." Bonnie looked around. "And I don't know where my baby brother went, but his name is Mark."

Samira's heart almost melted when Phil crouched down and greeted the little girls. "Very pleased to meet you, Bonnie and Lizzie. My name is Phil."

Bonnie giggled as Phil shook her hand but Lizzie ducked her head out from under her sister's arm and sped away into the living room.

"No running in the house!" Krissy gave instruction from somewhere out of sight.

Samira put her face in her hands. *This is NOT at all what I was expecting.*

Pam was starting to fill the water glasses from a crystal pitcher. "Samira, he's much more handsome in khakis and a denim shirt than he was in half a tux."

I know. But I liked the tux too. She could see Phil in the living room. He was examining a toy with little Mark. *It's strange to see him interacting with a toddler.*

Samira caught Phil's glance and returned a nervous smile. *I can't believe we're actually going to sit down to dinner with my family.*

Ashleigh stepped into the dining room and removed her apron. "I think everything is ready." Her eyes passed over the table. "Shall we gather the family?"

Family. Samira's eyes went directly to the man sitting in her parents' living room. *That's a comforting thought.*

62

Dessert

J.P. turned the plastic truck in his hands. *Mark.* The little boy who had given it to him had tottered off to get another object. *They said his name was Mark.* The fire in the fireplace was warm. *Nice ambiance, anyway.* But even the fire didn't ease his nerves. *I still can't believe I missed this vital family connection.*

"So, J.P.," Weston Stephenson was sitting in the easy chair. "I had no idea you were the one my sister was, um . . ."

Sleeping with?

"Seeing." Wes smiled a little. "How long have you known her?"

I don't know what she wants them to know and what she wants to keep to herself. J.P. set the toy truck down on the floor. "Since last summer." *Vague answers are better than no answers at all."*

"No kidding?"

No kidding.

J.P. watched Mr. Stephenson's wife cross the room behind him.

"I just assumed . . ." Mr. Stephenson stopped talking to help Mark with a toy.

Extremely awkward here. J.P.'s eyes skimmed the spines of the books lining the wall between the living and dining rooms. *Copperfield, Melville, Dickens, Kipling, Twain. Extremely well-read people.* Mark toddled over and pushed a stuffed rabbit into J.P.'s hand. *I don't know what to do with a person this size.*

" . . . Anyway, I just assumed the lawyer my sister was seeing was one I didn't know."

At least you knew my occupation; that's more than I can say about what I knew about you. *J.P. had to remind himself not to be defensive.* After all, she did say she tried to give me a little warning.

"So what is your intent, anyway?" Wes shrugged his shoulders. "I mean, do you have plans . . . ?"

I have plans to eat dinner with her family. J.P. didn't like the insinuating tone. *At least for this afternoon . . .*

Mark's little hands were starting to examine the phone hanging on J.P.'s belt. *He sure in an inquisitive little thing.*

Wes's dark brown eyes reflected the same depth of thought as his sister's. "Well, at least I know she's been in good hands."

J.P. didn't dare look up. *What he means is at least he knows whose hands she's been in.*

"J.P . . ." Raymond entered the living room unannounced. "I want you to know, I had a wonderful visit with Christopher Hughes last night. Fine gentleman."

J.P. leaned back in his chair and made eye contact. *It's his house. He can set the tone.*

"Tell me, how do you know the Hughes brothers?" Raymond sat down on the sofa.

Is this is a professional interview or a personal one? J.P. weighed his options. *Either way my answers could be used against me.*

"I went to work for Lloyd Hughes . . ."

"The brothers' father?" Wes clarified.

"That's right. Lloyd hired me right out of law school. I worked directly with the Hughes Corporation until I went into private practice." *That was a long time ago.*

"Well, I'm impressed with their knowledge in commerce and their interest in local business development." Raymond narrowed his eyes in thought. "They're a fine asset to Mid-America."

The Hughes are fine assets to anyone they deem worthy. J.P. recalled their business history. *Don't do anything to piss them off.* "Keep Hughes happy, and they'll perform well for Mid-America."

Weston raised an eyebrow behind his newspaper.

He heard me.

"Didn't you take my sister to a Hughes event in Springfield awhile back?"

Interesting that he knows that. "Last summer." Samira's image in the hotel bathtub suddenly came into vision. "That was a major event."

"I remember she had to find formal wear and get her hair done and everything."

*I remember the black dress as it came off . . .*J.P. tried not to grin. "Christopher Hughes announced his daughter's engagement that night."

"Were you there on business or pleasure?"

Now there's a loaded question. Business until midnight, then strictly pleasure. "I was under the Hughes' employ to oversee the prenuptials." J.P looked from one Stephenson to the other and matched their corporate tone.

Wes frowned momentarily.

"Where'd you go to law school, J.P.?" Raymond fired another question.

The only answers he's going to get today are the ones on my resume. "Columbia."

"University of Missouri?"

"Yes, sir." *He already knows the answers to some of these questions.*

Raymond's look was sincere. "Why a private practice over joining a firm or continuing with a corporation?"

He knows my work ethic. This is a personal question. "I prefer to be in control of my casework and my clientele." *Take it or leave it. I don't play well with others.*

"It takes guts to set out on your own," Weston pointed out.

"More discipline than guts." *Anything else you want to drill me on while I'm at your disposal?* Mark had wandered into the middle of the living room and was busily sorting a stack of professional magazines into disarray.

By now the aroma of fresh bread was permeating the entire house. *Reminds me of Aunt Maggie's.* J.P. watched Raymond straighten the stack of periodicals. *He tidies up, just like his daughter.*

Raymond lowered his head. "J.P., what are your feelings concerning Councilman Goldstein's plans for Shoal Creek?"

I had no idea what to expect here today, but Shoal Creek never crossed my mind. J.P. leaned forward and put his elbows on his knees. *Sean Bridges?* "I think he's climbing an uphill battle." *He doesn't have enough revenue to make it happen. Yet.* Little Mark bounced a stuffed rabbit happily over J.P.'s hands.

"But what do you think about the actual development plans? Do you think people would eventually buy into property down there?" Weston almost sounded hopeful the plans might really work.

J.P. shook his head. *Doesn't matter what his master plan projects.* "I don't think he'll get that far." *Especially if he falls into the electronic trap that's set in the basement of your bank for later today.*

"Alan Goldstein is a new name to these parts. He came to town about six years ago and the next thing we know he's holding a seat in city government." Raymond was obviously puzzled. "I wonder where he came from?"

California. "Out of state." *With illegal cyberspace ties all over the nation.* "Somewhere out west, I've heard."

Two little girls went blazing through the front room full speed ahead. Raymond reached out and snagged one of them around the waist with his arm. J.P. was sure the child was going to be reprimanded, but instead Raymond pulled her into his lap and tickled her until she couldn't breathe.

This isn't exactly like I'd pictured Samira's father. I expected a man of high integrity, but I didn't expect it to be Raymond Stephenson.

Weston still had his nose buried behind the Sunday paper.

J.P. could see Samira arranging food on the dining room table. She blushed when he caught her eye. *I like being able to draw that response from her without saying a word.*

"All right, fellas, gather the troops. I think we're ready to eat." Ashleigh emerged from the kitchen. *She is a very elegant woman.* J.P. admired the way she motioned everyone to the dining room with a graceful turn of her hand. *Samira certainly has her mother's grace.* Ashleigh smiled. *And her dark eyes.* When those dark eyes fell on J.P., he couldn't hold them. *It's like she's reading something beyond my thoughts.*

J.P. started to stand up, but little Mark was leaning on his leg. *So what do I do with him?* Mark raised his arms to be picked up. *Well, alright.*

"Come on, little fella . . ." J.P. held his finger out and Mark took a hold. "Let's go eat."

I don't know when the last time was that I had contact with a person this small.

"Are you Auntie's boyfriend?" One of the little girls was pulling on J.P.'s pants.

J.P. stopped walking and studied the little girls' face. *How do I answer that?* "I guess maybe I am."

The girl rolled her little blue eyes and put her hands over her mouth. Then she spun around and disappeared.

"Lizzie, let's go wash up!" Krissy grabbed hold of the back of the girl's shirt and guided her toward the hallway. "Mark goes in the high chair."

She wants me to put him in there? Wes was still behind the newspaper and his mother was nowhere to be seen. J.P. looked from Mark to the high chair. *It doesn't look all that complicated.*

Mark walked right up to his chair and then turned and put his chubby little arms up for J.P. to pick him up. *I don't have a clue what I'm doing.*

J.P. looked around hoping to find Samira. No one was there so he crouched down to Mark's eye level. "Here we go, little fella." Mark didn't weigh any thing like J.P. expected. He lifted him off the ground without any effort at all. *James was probably the last little guy I picked up like this.* Yet he couldn't recall a single moment holding either one of his boys for any length of time at all. *I worked too hard blocking those memories.* J.P. pulled his head away when the little boy tried to grab his ear. *It wasn't exactly the most gratifying time of my life.*

"Oh, here, let me help you." Mrs. Stephenson's wife appeared out of nowhere. J.P. watched her skillfully remove the tray on the high chair. "I'll buckle him in for you."

"Well, well, well," Krissy announced her arrival. "Look who found you!" She was speaking to the toddler.

More like, who found me! J.P. observed Mark in the chair. *Kinda like riding in a car but you don't go anywhere.*

"Where do you want to sit, Pam?" Ashleigh was helping the older of the two girls into a chair.

Pam. Her name is Pam. J.P. dared to look closer at her face. *She's got to be a good ten years younger than Stephenson.*

"Why don't you put the girls between you and me." Pam was arranging the water glasses so the crystal was not in front of the little girls.

Krissy purposefully bumped into J.P. as she passed. *Thank God for Krissy.* He caught her ponytail enough to give it a slight tug. Krissy stuck out her tongue before scooting around the edge of the table.

"Krista, is that any way to treat our guests?" Ashleigh disciplined gently.

What is up with this Krista business? J.P. winked at Krissy.

"He started it, Granny."

J.P. felt his own cheeks warm as Mrs. Stephenson's dark eyes questioned him. *Are they always this formal?* J.P. ran his hand through his hair. *A retired nurse. And a very intense retired nurse at that.*

"J.P., why don't you sit here next to Samira." Ashleigh put her hand on the back of a polished chair at the corner.

I bet she kept an orderly emergency room too. J.P. watched Samira help the other little girl into a chair and push her up to the table. *I like the way her skirt sways with her motions.* J.P. ran his hand through his hair again. *I shouldn't be thinking about her skirt with her father in the room.*

"Weston!" Ashleigh called into the living room. "You can finish the business section later. Come and find your seat."

Weston. J.P. watched the man rise from his chair and sheepishly make his way into the dining room. *He looks more like a Mr. Stephenson than a Weston.*

"A word to the wise . . ." Weston spoke to J.P. as he started for a chair.

Obviously he knows where he is going to sit.

" . . . my mother doesn't allow any business talk at the table." Weston raised his eyebrows. "Mealtime is sacred."

Considering the company, that's a very good thing to know. J.P. stood behind his assigned seat and waited for the others to sit down first. *Mrs. Stephenson has this all planned out.* When Samira appeared at his side, he automatically pulled out her chair.

"Well, J.P., it is an honor to dine with you." Raymond took the seat at the end of the table.

"Indeed." J.P. slid his chair up to the table. *What do I say, non-business related, to the father of the woman . . .*

"I don't want to sit here!" One of the little girls was whining.

J.P. found himself sitting between Samira and her father. *Holy Toledo! I'm dining with him, but I'm sleeping with her.*

"Bonnie, just sit still," her father instructed.

"No. I want to sit by him!" She climbed off the chair and pointed at Josh across the table. Her her father put her back on the chair.

Well, I'm dining with both of them.

Raymond Stephenson was patiently waiting for his granddaughters to get situated.

I wonder if he'd be that calm if he knew where his daughter was last Saturday morning?

"It's okay, Weston." Pam seemed to have a calming affect on her husband. "Do you mind?" She looked across the table at Josh.

Josh shrugged his shoulders. "I'm cool."

Bonnie was instantly on the move. She eagerly climbed onto the chair between James and Josh.

"Now we can pray," she announced happily.

Oh, great. We're going to pray? J.P. swallowed hard. *Of course we're going to pray.*

Kara was the last one to sit down. "I guess that puts me over here."

She looks less than pleased to be sitting by Krissy. J.P.'s. eyes circled the faces. *I don't think I've ever sat at a family table that would hold this many people at once.*

Samira's mother was seated closet to the kitchen door. She spread her hands and everyone followed suit, linking fingers. J.P. bowed his head according to the family tradition, but his senses were instantly triggered when Samira touched his hand.

I'd love to be holding more than just her hand . . . Those thoughts dissipated instantly when Raymond Stephenson took his other hand. *I don't like being in the middle.* J.P. had a hard time concentrating on the prayer.

"I understand we have some football players dining with us," Raymond passed the roast beef to his son. "What positions do you play?"

Josh took a warm roll out of the basket and passed it to Samira. "Wide receiver."

James accepted the green bean casserole from Ashleigh and helped himself to a generous serving. "Offensive line."

"Cheerleader!" Krissy added cheerfully.

"You cheer for volleyball," Kara corrected.

"I know." Krissy passed the potatoes.

"What's your record so far this year?" Raymond seemed genuinely interested.

Both boys looked up to see who was being addressed. And then they answered in unison. "Five and two."

J.P. took a helping of everything that was passed.

"What's the forecast for the rest of the season?" Weston jumped into the conversation.

Josh shrugged his shoulders. "We have one more competitive opponent. The other three should be easy wins."

"Last game of the season will be the toughest one," James added. "Excellent dinner, by the way."

Ashleigh thanked the young man with a warm smile.

J.P. was more than a little surprised to hear the compliment come out of James so naturally. *Could be a reflection of too much take out pizza!*

Just as Weston had foreshadowed, there was no business discussion at the table whatsoever. But conversation flowed easily among the family members. Every grandchild was given equal opportunity to share.

These people listen to each other. Even the little girls were well-mannered while the others talked around them. *And they're all polite too.* He tried to remember back. *James and Josh never knew this kind of family continuity. Still don't.*

"I think Mark is about ready for his nap." Ashleigh started to remove the high chair tray. "Shall I take him?"

Nothing better than a Sunday afternoon nap after a great meal. J.P. glanced at the sleepy eyes. *He's trying to stay awake.* The rolls passed again, so J.P. helped himself to another. *Almost as good as Aunt Maggie's.*

"I'll take him." Pam pushed away from the table calmly. "That way I can change him before I lay him down."

Pam. I need to remember her name. He watched the women work together to free Mark from the straps that held him in.

Ashleigh sat back down in her chair. "I bumped into Ginny O'Brien at the grocery store yesterday . . . ."

Who? J.P. didn't hear very clearly. He looked up when no one responded right away.

" . . . We were waiting in line at the meat counter together."

Surely she didn't say who I thought she said . . .

Weston frowned across the table. "Do we know Ginny O'Brien?"

A wave a relief passed over J.P. *I thought she said, Jimmy the bartender!* J.P. wiped a drop of sweat from his forehead with his napkin.

"Well, she knows us." Ashleigh filled in the blank. J.P. watched her eyes stop on Samira. "We used to play cribbage together. Ginny sits on the board of directors at the university."

J.P. could feel Samira's sudden tension without even touching her. *She never told them about the job offer.* The look on Ashleigh's face told him the cat was just about to be let out of the bag. *Here it comes.* He reached under the table and patted Samira's thigh in silent support.

"I remember Ginny," Raymond lifted his fork as he spoke. "Short woman. Kind of plump?"

"Well, yes," Ashleigh agreed. "She tells me the university contacted Samira about a possible position."

"No kidding," Weston was instantly interested. "A position as in a job?"

Samira nodded.

"That's great, Sis!" Weston was obviously excited. "What kind of a position?"

"Mama has a job already!" Kara interjected. "And it's a really good one."

Fine point, Kara.

"That doesn't mean she isn't open to new opportunities," Weston pointed out. "What's it about?"

Mr. Stephenson likes thinking for his sister. J.P. noticed Samira fidgeting with her silverware. "It's a not for profit position within their alumni association. Sales and marketing for the most part."

Fundraising and events.

"Full time? Part time? Out with it, Sis! This sounds like something you might need to explore."

Samira's eyes scanned the table. "James, would you please pass the butter?" She sliced the end off the stick of margarine.

She doesn't have anything to put butter on . . .

"I don't know, Wes . . ." Samira was still holding the knife with the butter, obviously flustered.

She'd be a mess on a witness stand. J.P. pulled his roll in half. Without saying anything he placed it in Samira's free hand. *With a little coaching she could learn to think on her feet.*

"Thank you." Samira stared at the bread. Then she stared at J.P.

He smiled his easy smile. *Good luck with the interrogation.*

"Um . . ." Samira buttered the bread. "I thought about it for a long while, but I'm not in the market for a new job . . ."

J.P. watched her take of bite of his bread. When she finished chewing she finished the thought. "I turned them down."

"Already?"

Obviously her brother isn't too thrilled about that.

" . . . How can you make that decision without weighing the advantages?"

By this time Krissy and James had a conversation going on of their own, which was good because it took some of the tension out of the adult discussion. J.P. finished his last bite of potatoes. *It'd be nice if someone came to her rescue.*

The little girls were finished eating. First one asked to be excused, and then the other. It didn't take but a moment for Krissy and Kara to follow suit.

Amazing how they all carry their plates to the kitchen. I can't even get the boys to throw away an empty pizza box! He looked around the table. His boys were still finishing their dinner. But no one else was eating anymore. All eyes were on Samira. *No wonder she has trouble making decisions for herself.*

Samira finished her bite of bread so J.P. silently offered her his other half.

"I did weigh the advantages." She was obviously in mid-thought, but she stopped talking to take the bread.

" . . . But the disadvantages added up faster than the advantages." Samira took a bite. For the first time she looked across the table at her brother with confidence.

He crossed his arms. Not a good sign.

"I'd think you'd at least want to bring it up for discussion first."

"I did."

J.P. decided to finish eating. *This may be the last meal I ever eat in this house if they find out she discussed it with me.*

"When?"

He doesn't back down, does he?

Raymond Stephenson put his hand gently against his son's shoulder but his eyes fell on his daughter.

Pick a side, Mr. Stephenson. Which one are you going to support?

"Do you know how difficult it is to get on the staff at the university?" Weston was looking at his father, but was obviously talking to his sister. "There is a waiting list of people a mile long who would like to be employed out there?"

I know what I'd like to say. J.P. glanced in Wes's direction. *But gut feeling says to hold my tongue.*

" . . . I can name three people right off the top of my head who would give their right arm to teach at the university."

But this wasn't a teaching job. This was sales and marketing.

Weston shot an irritated look across the table at his sister. Samira lowered her head.

Enough. J.P. made his decision. *Time for the closing argument.* "That's good." J.P. wiped his mouth on a cloth napkin. "If there are that many people waiting to get on board, they won't have any trouble finding the right person to fill the vacancy."

Samira's eyes widened, but she didn't speak. Instead she lifted her water glass and took a drink. J.P. watched Weston's eyes go from his father to his mother, but no one chose to speak.

Case closed.

"I'm sorry, Samira." Ashleigh folded her hands politely. "I was wrong to bring Ginny up at the table."

Samira's voice was steady when she spoke. "I just hadn't had a chance to bring it up yet." Without hesitation she touched Josh on the arm. "Does that new vehicle out in front of the house happen to belong to you?"

Nice recovery!

Suddenly the boys were animated and alive again.

And good confidence too. He put his arm over the back of Samira's chair, making sure to touch her shoulder as he did so. *She's definitely coachable.*

Samira's father was instantly involved in the new conversation and Ashleigh was beginning to gather dirty dishes at her end of the table.

J.P. felt his phone vibrate on his belt. The grandfather clock read almost one-thirty. *This could be Sparky.* He thought again. *Or it could be Janet.* The phone vibrated a second time. This time J.P. quietly excused himself from the table. He stepped into the living room and answered. *Check the ID. Good.*

"What's going on, Sparky?"

"Dere is activity as ve speek. I beleev de monies vill be moved to de holding company vithin de hour."

I'd like to see this go down with my own eyes. "We need to notify Agent Roderick."

"Denise has done dat already."

Chances are good this phone call will put an end to the family affair. J.P. glanced around the room. *But if this surveillance plays out it will put and end to Sean Bridges.*

"If you vant to vatch, you vill need to arrive quickly."

"Alright." J.P. spoke with hesitation. "I'll see what I can do."

The call ended without a formal goodbye. All eyes, including Pam's, were on him when he re-entered the dining room. *Obviously not a family who approves of business calls in the middle of Sunday dinner.* Nonetheless, J.P. could feel his adrenalin starting to pump.

I should take Stephenson with me. J. P. sat back down on his chair knowing he couldn't stay there very long. *He's going to need to understand this chain of events in order to inform his board of directors.* Samira's hand brushed his leg under the table. *How does she do that? One little touch sets off every nerve ending in my body!*

"Is everything alright?" Weston was gathering his plate and silverware.
I haven't been one to mince words up to this point. No reason to do so now.

"Hey, Dad." Josh was standing in the entryway door. "James and I are taking Kara and Krissy for a ride in the 4-Runner. Be back in twenty."

J.P. looked at Samira.

"They have my blessing." Samira rose from the table.

J.P. Ralston fixed his eyes on the bank president. "Mr. Stephenson . . ."

"Wait." He shook his head. "Under the circumstances, I think *Wes* would be in order."

Wes. It didn't sound right. *He's my client.* J.P. felt Samira's presence as she walked behind his chair. *This could get complicated.*

"Okay, Wes," J.P. stumbled over his tongue a little. "That was Sparky."

Wes was suddenly very alert.

" . . . He is picking up some activity on the new account."

Samira had returned from the kitchen for more dishes. *I hate to run out on her, but the impact of this is huge.*

Wes was very serious. "Do we need to go down there?"

"Boys," Raymond Stephenson jumped in. "This is Sunday. Surely there is someone else who can go."

"Go where?" Ashleigh asked the question innocently enough.

"Downtown," Wes answered quickly.

"To the bank?" Pam sounded irritated. "Today?"

Shit.

"Oh, Weston," his mother was talking again. "This is Sunday, son."

"I know what day it is." Wes sounded defensive.

And all the while the clock is ticking.

"It shouldn't take too long, should it?" Wes started to carry his plate into the kitchen.

"No way of knowing." *Let's not mislead them.*

Samira returned for the third time. "No way of knowing what?"

J.P. picked up his own plate and silverware and followed Wes.

"How long this might take."

"Might what take?" Samira looked confused.

J.P. put his plate in the stack with the others. "We need to run down to the bank."

"Now?" She looked surprised.

"Yeah." *Come on Samira, give me the go ahead. I need this.*

"The bank isn't even open." Samira poured leftover green beans into a smaller container.

Good point. "That's precisely why we need to get down there." *Only one computer is running in the entire building other than Sparky's. It's critical we monitor everything that happens in the next few minutes.*

Samira frowned at her brother. "Can't it wait until tomorrow?"

J.P. threw his head back. *I can't believe how many people are involved in this conversation!*

Wes was shaking his head. J.P. could see his focus shifting as well. "No, this isn't something we can control."

"Who's we?"

"The legal team." Wes wasn't backing down. "I need to see what J.P. is building on here so I can explain it to my board on Monday."

Samira was still frowning, but now she was looking at Phil. "J.P.?"

That would be me. "Maybe it won't take long." *It could take a split second. Or it could take the rest of the day. Shit. I can't lie to her.* "This is business, Samira. And I need to be there. It would be a great advantage to have Mr. Stephenson . . ." J.P. corrected himself, " . . . Wes down there with me."

"You need to be at the bank?" She was obviously confused.

"As soon as possible."

"Do you bank there?"

What is she talking about? "No."

Samira looked worried.

This is taking way too long.

Raymond carried the breadbasket and an empty casserole dish into the kitchen. "If J.P. Ralston says he needs to be down there, then I think we should let him go."

Let me go? J.P. shook his head. *Excuse me?* He looked back at Samira who now had her face hidden behind her hands.

"I won't be all day." J.P moved her hands with his. *I hope.* The emotion behind her eyes was almost ready to spill over. He bent his knees so he was standing at her eye level. *I can't leave her like this.* He lifted her chin with his forefinger. "What's the matter, Pretty Lady?"

"I don't understand."

"Don't understand why I have to go to work?" *Make it quick, Ralston.*

"And why does my brother have to go with you?"

She's not making any sense. J.P. wanted to close his eyes to think. But he was afraid to look away. *How do I make this any clearer without breaking confidentiality?*

"I'm going down to check on the case at Mid-America. Once the meeting is over, I can come back."

Weston walked past and tapped J.P. on the shoulder. "I'm ready when you are."

J.P. nodded but he didn't take his eyes off of Samira's.

"What case?"

"The Mid-America case." *This shouldn't be so hard!*

"You're on a case?"

I'm always on a case. That's what I do! "Yes." *Make it clear.* "I'm representing Mid-America on a case and the lead investigator needs me down there to monitor some activity."

Samira's emotion spilled out of her eyes and onto her cheek.

Don't cry, Samira. He wiped her tear with his thumb.

"You're my brother's attorney?"

No, he's my client. Or at least his company is my client! "Yes."

"That's how you know my brother?" Now the tears were coming in a stream.

J.P. was the one who didn't understand now. "Yes."

"Why didn't you tell me?"

How could she not know this? "Because I didn't know until last night."

"How did you know last night?"

"Because I went to a party at his house and saw a picture of you on his wall!" *Good God! I'd rather be having this conversation in private. The whole damn family is gathered around!*

"Princess . . ."

Raymond was butting into J.P.'s conversation. *I can handle my own business! And what's with the Princess?*

"J.P. Ralston is our attorney down at the bank. Didn't you know that?"

"You went to his party while I was babysitting his kids?" Samira was questioning Phil with a sadness he'd never heard in her voice.

You were babysitting his kids? J.P. moved his hand from her face to her shoulders.

Samira pulled completely away from his touch. "How could you not know that Wes was my brother?"

Maybe because you are so damned secretive about your private life. J.P. took a deep breath. *I didn't mean that. There was just no reason for this discussion to come up.* "I don't know." *How was I supposed to know you were a Stephenson?* J.P. took a step back and ran his hand through his hair. "You said you tried to let me know . . ." *Why are all these people standing here?*

"I tried to let you know my brother and his wife were coming for dinner." Samira wiped her face with her fingertips.

Okay. J.P. still didn't get it. *Oh, god I need to be going.* The phone vibrated again. "I didn't check any messages."

"Is that my fault?" Samira was still crying.

"Sis," Wes reached out and touched her shoulder, but she pulled away abruptly. "I've been working with J.P. on a particular incident down at the bank for months now . . ."

"Am I the only one here who doesn't know what's going on?" Samira was openly frustrated.

"No, dear. I'm afraid I don't know either." Ashleigh mother was quietly confused as well.

"I think I know . . ."

Everyone's eyes turned to Pam.

" . . . I think J.P. Ralston has been working for Wes . . ."

For the bank . . .

" . . . and I think Phil has been dating Samira . . ."

I don't know if we can officially call it dating . . .

" . . . but I don't think J.P. knew Wes was Samira's brother . . ."

Not until last night . . .

" . . . and it's obvious Samira didn't know Phil was working at Mid-America." Pam shrugged her shoulders. "At least until now."

At least.

Samira still had tears in her eyes, but when she looked at J.P., he could see a hint of something that wasn't there before.

"So you just found out too?"

There was so much he wanted to explain, but J.P. didn't know where to start. *I just figured she knew when she said she left a message . . .* He nodded his head once.

"Well, this is a small world, isn't it?" Asheligh seemed relieved to know the details, even if she didn't fully understand.

"But if you don't mind," Wes was getting impatience. "I need to take my attorney and scadaddle or we may both lose our jobs!"

"Go!" Ashleigh waved the men out of her kitchen. "Go do what you have to do so you can come back for dessert!"

There's more to this meal? Suddenly J.P. remembered his manners. "Thank you for . . ."

"Go!" For a quick moment, Ashleigh's eyes were the exact reflection of her daughters. "You can thank me later. Sounds like you have work to do."

Wes appeared with J.P.'s coat. "If we're coming back here together, you might as well ride over with me."

J.P. slid his arms into his jacket. *I hate riding with someone else!*

"Phil?"

He stopped and turned all the way around. Samira was right behind him. Her eyes looked exhausted from fatigue of the misunderstanding.

"Are you coming back for dessert?"

She looks so frail and so beautiful all at the same time. J.P. couldn't help but smile. *I don't care whose house I'm standing in.*

"Come here." He reached for her hand but when she reached out, he pulled her all the way to him. "I'll come back if you'll be my dessert." J.P. whispered in her ear.

The tears in her eyes suddenly glistened with new understanding. And much to his surprise, Samira kissed him. Gently at first. But then with more passion. Not once. And not twice. But three times. Right there in her parent's dining room.

The impact of Sparky's activity on the Bridges' account suddenly had very little relevance. He laughed out loud and returned Samira's embrace. For the first time in his life, Joseph Phillip Ralston understood that some things were more important than all the rest.

"J.P. are you coming?"

I know I'm coming right back here for dessert when this is all said and done. He stole another quick kiss, then reluctantly let Samira go. J.P. followed Wes out into the dismal weather. But J.P. Ralston didn't notice the rain or the clouds. The only thing he noticed was the freedom he felt somewhere deep inside. *A freedom like I've never known before.*

63

The Defense

Samira ran her hands over the front of her skirt. Through the dining room window she watched Wes cover his head and run all the way to the driveway. *If Phil minds the rain, he's not letting on.* Samira watched him walk calmly to Wes' car.

I didn't plan to kiss him. Samira smiled. *But I couldn't stop either.* She heard his whisper again. *"I'll come back if you'll be my dessert."*

Samira began to gather the remaining odds and ends. Salt and pepper shakers. Loose silverware. *Anything to keep my thoughts private and my hands busy.* She took a step toward the kitchen and bumped into her father. *Oh. How long has he been there?* His hands were tucked deep inside his pants pockets and his eyes were studying her very carefully.

Instantly, Samira's cheeks reddened and her heart began to pound against her sternum. She had to look away. *I haven't done anything wrong!* She set the miscellaneous tableware down on the buffet. *Was he standing there when I kissed Phil?*

Her father's voice was calm and gentle when he spoke. "You should have told us you were seeing J.P. Ralston, Princess."

Samira chose not to face her father. "I didn't know it mattered so much." *Besides, I don't know him as J.P. Ralston.*

Raymond Stephenson puckered his lips in thought. "He's a very powerful man, Samira."

Powerful? Samira frowned. "How so?"

"Come with me."

Samira watched her father cross the dining room and start down the hall. *No, Daddy. Not today.* She knew he was going to his study. *But he's my father so I'll go with him.*

Raymond opened a drawer in the bureau and sat down in his chair. Very intentionally he selected a large envelope and pulled the contents out.

What's he doing? Samira watched her father flip the corners of the pages until he found the exact paper. He put that set aside and the rest went back in the envelope.

He patted the seat next to him. "Here, Sugar." He placed his reading glasses on the end of his nose and tipped his head to read through the lenses.

Reluctantly Samira sat down. She had no idea what her father was thinking, nor did she have a clue what the papers might reveal about Phil. *But the way he's acting, they could be incriminating.* She curled into the corner of the loveseat.

Raymond folded a few pages back over the stapled corner and turned the packet so Samira could see. "This is a list of cases J.P. Ralston has successfully closed on behalf of his clients in the past five years, many of them before litigation was required." Raymond indicated multiple pages. "Then, we get to the cases that closed unsuccessfully during the same amount of time." Raymond revealed a single sheet of paper. He handed the whole packet to his daughter.

I still don't understand. Her eyes skimmed the list of businesses and individuals J.P. Ralston had represented. *Wow.* She turned to the second page. She was surprised how many names she recognized. *These are big businesses. Or at least people with a lot of money.*

"He's a very powerful man, Samira."

"He's powerful because he wins cases?" *And why does Daddy have a list like this anyway? With a record like this, I'd think he'd be making an extremely sound living!*

Raymond shook his head slightly as he gazed over his glasses into his daughter's eyes. "He's powerful because he knows how to get his way."

Suddenly Samira didn't want to see anymore of the list. *I feel like I'm spying on him.* She flipped back to the top page. *But if he's as successful as this printout shows, his lifestyle sure doesn't reflect his earnings.* She smoothed the papers flat. The top sheet was a copy of J.P. Ralston's resume. *Or at least his house is humble enough.* She reviewed the furnishings of his house in her mind. *He doesn't even have a dishwasher!*

Samira frowned. "Daddy, why do you have these?" *But I guess Maria washes his dishes.*

"Because we hired him to represent Mid-America." Raymond lifted the large envelope off the bureau. "These are the attorneys we didn't hire."

Samira couldn't help it. She had to read further. *Business, corporate, probate, wills, trusts, real estate, lawsuit matters . . . I didn't realize he did all of that. No wonder he could help me with the paperwork for Tom's trust.*

"He seems to be very capable." Samira continued to read. *Education . . . Bar Admissions . . . Professional Activities . . . Community Involvement . . .*

"J.P. is very capable." The father linked his hands over his crossed knee. "That is, capable of handling the legal matters for the bank."

Now Samira looked up at her father. *I don't appreciate his tone.* "What exactly are you suggesting, Daddy?"

"I'm not suggesting anything. But it occurs to me that you might not be aware of his reputation . . ."

His legal reputation looks pretty good. Samira ran her hand over Phil's resume. *Is Daddy talking about his personal reputation?*

"Companies hire him to represent their issues because they want to win. Right or wrong, they expect J.P. Ralston to bring them out of the thick on top." The business tone in Raymond's voice was very apparent. "That's why the board hired him for Mid-America. We knew he could get the job done." Now the father's eyes softened a degree. "My fear is he may very well use those same powers to win my daughter."

Am I a prize to be won? Samira looked away from her father's eyes. They were too deep. Too personal.

"So is Mid-America right for hiring him if he wins for the wrong reasons?"

"That's not the point, Samira." Raymond lowered his head a degree. "Mid-America needs their rights protected and J.P. Ralston has the credentials to make that happen."

"But you just insinuated that J.P. Ralston will do whatever it takes for the victory, right?"

Raymond nodded. "According to his resume and references, yes."

Samira skimmed the front page of the resume again. *I am simply amazed at all he has accomplished in sixteen years.* She sighed. "Remember when I told you I didn't know if I could handle all of him?"

"Yes. And had I realized J.P. Ralston was the man you were referring to, I would have advised you differently."

But you didn't know so you have to hear me out now.

"You told me I needed to tell him how I felt inside," Samira reminded. "So I did." She didn't want to look at her father. "And you know what happened? I expressed my feelings to Phil. But I was answered by J.P. Ralston." *Maybe you should just level with him.* "Daddy, I don't know J.P. Ralston as well." She handed the resume packet back to her father. "In fact, it doesn't even sound right to me when you call him J.P. I know him as Phil Ralston . . . ." *And it took me forever to even find his last name!* "I met him as Phil and that's who I've come to know. His business life is a segment I'm not as familiar with . . ."

"That's just it, Princess." Raymond leaned forward to make his point. "What about his other life? There isn't a businessman in Joplin who doesn't know J.P. Ralston. And I can assure you, there are plenty that would prefer not to do business with him . . ."

"Then why did you hire him?"

"Because we knew he could handle the multi-faceted legalities at the bank."

Then the ones who don't like him must have been on the other side of his cases. "So the fact that I am seeing him is a bad thing?"

"No. Not necessarily." Raymond took a deep breath and removed his reading glasses. "Samira, I trust J.P. Ralston to get to the bottom of the business issues at the bank. Hands down I believe he is the man for the job." Raymond sighed again. "But I don't know if I want my daughter in those same hands. You said yourself that he scares you."

He does! "But he scares me because there is so much of him to understand. Not because of the way he treats me or anything like that." Samira closed her eyes as she searched for the right words. "He scares me because I don't know if I can be all he needs me to be for both Phil and J.P." *They can be two totally different people sometimes!* "Am I making any sense at all?"

"You're telling me the man you love and the man that works for Mid-America are two different personalities. I don't see that as a healthy situation . . ."

Did I say I loved him? "But it's not exactly like that!" Samira was frustrated at her own lack of understanding. "Phil Ralston is a very . . ." *Choose your adjectives carefully, Samira!* " . . . sensitive, quiet, caring man. But J.P. is strictly business. He thinks in business terms and acts with authority and is quick to judge . . ." *yet he can be angry in an instant.*

"He has no right to pass judgment!" Raymond snapped.

"I didn't say he passed judgment!" Samira corrected her father firmly. "I meant that he's quick to make decisions." *And he'll defend a case to its death—even if I'm caught in the middle!*

"But you don't know him that well . . ."

"I know him well enough to know that what we have together is an amazing connection . . ."

"Connecting what, Samira?"

"Connecting everything!" Samira heard her voice raise a notch. "We connect as parents. We connect as people, as a couple." *Stop. Don't go any further.*

"J.P. Ralston will connect with someone as long as he is in charge and getting his way."

"Maybe in business, Daddy, but I've not experienced that kind of manipulation from him." *Well, except for when he filed a supeana against me.* Samira remembered that all too well. *But I stood my ground. He didn't budge my decision.* She gave herself credit for standing strong.

"Yet. Not yet, maybe." Raymond was obviously worried. "It's just a matter of time."

Samira couldn't believe her ears. Her father had never spoken so candidly to her about anything. Everything about her screamed to defend the man. But something in her father's face caused Samira to hold her tongue. She pulled both knees up under her skirt.

"Don't you see, Princess?" Raymond leaned forward on his elbows. "I see the way you look at him and I know you think he's good for you. But he's a man . . ."

" . . . of his word." Samira finished her father's sentence. *He's been nothing less than a gentleman with me.*

Raymond became very quiet. Samira could feel his eyes on her as she watched the rain run down the outside of the windowpane.

"He let me go, Daddy." Samira leaned her head into the back of the loveseat. "I told him how I felt about him. And do you know what he told me?" Her eyes followed a single raindrop all the way from the top of the glass to the bottom. "He told me he wasn't fit for a woman like me." Samira hugged her knees tighter. "He told me he couldn't make it home for dinner all the time and that I deserved better than that. He told me he was too intense and he had a hard time separating his work from his personal life . . ." *At least that's what he meant.* "And he allowed me to make my choice."

Samira looked at her father. "And I walked away."

Raymond dropped his eyes to the floor. "I'm sorry we have to talk about this."

"I'm not." Samira swung her feet to the floor. "I'm not, Daddy." She touched her father's knee. "I lived without him for almost three months." *I need him to understand.* "But I wasn't really living anymore. Don't you see, Daddy? He honored my decision. He didn't even try to talk me out of it. But I made the wrong decision."

"Kind of like the university decision, then?"

"No. Nothing like that." *How can he compare a life decision with a job offer?* "No, what Phil and I have together is bigger than a career option." Samira searched for words again. "He makes me laugh. Do you know how long it's been since I had someone to really laugh with, Daddy?"

Raymond was listening.

"He takes time to help Krissy with her math. And he asks Kara about her ballgames. And he wants to know how my day went." *But there's so much more . . .* "And I trust him. I trust him for the whole of who he is, both in the business world and in his personal life." A commotion in the hall let Samira know Josh had returned with the girls. "Just like you trust him to handle Mid-America's legal affairs."

An intense silence permeated the room.

Tell him what you need. He's not going to know if you don't spell it out. Samira took a deep breath. "Daddy, I need you to get to know Phil. J.P. aside, there's a man that you don't yet know."

Raymond was chewing on his bottom lip. Samira knew he was trying to decide how to respond without hurting her feelings. When he finally spoke his words were soft.

"I guess the things you know him by wouldn't be listed on a resume."

Samira smiled at her father's wit. "No. But his clients might be able to list some of those qualities." *Like the Hughes brothers, for instance.*

"I don't know about that yet," Raymond replied. He patted his daughter's knee. "But I trust you, Samira."

Footsteps were coming down the hall toward the study.

"Thank you, Daddy."

Raymond's eyes were sincere.

"Here you are!" Krissy exploded into the book-lined room. "Josh is wondering who owns the chess set in the sunroom."

Samira smiled again. *Daddy won't be able to turn down a game of chess on a Sunday afternoon.*

"I reckon that would be me." Raymond rose from his chair.

"I told him no one played until they played against you!" Krissy poked her grandfather in the arm.

"How did you get to be so smart?"

"It just comes naturally," Krissy quipped.

Samira watched her father and Krissy disappear into the hall arm in arm. *Sometimes I think he loves me too much.* She stood up and crossed her arms over her middle. *But really, I wouldn't want it any other way.* Phil's resume was laying face up on the bureau. Samira returned it to its place inside the envelope with the others. *You can't judge a man by what it says on a piece of paper.*

The rain had intensified considerably. The sky was very dark now and thunder claps were coming closer together. Samira found her mother and Pam visiting in the living room. She could hear the dishwasher running in the kitchen and the dining room table was wiped to a high gloss.

"Sorry I didn't help you clean up." Samira curled into the corner of the sofa.

"You had more important matters at hand," Ashleigh observed.

Maybe. I didn't really have a choice. Daddy kind of dictated that whole situation.

"Samira. I owe you an apology." Ashleigh's dark eyes came to rest on her daughter. "I did not bring my friend Ginny into dinner conversation to put you on the spot."

Samira started to shake her head. *It wasn't her fault. I should have told them earlier . . .*

"You know how we like to catch up on the news around the table." Ashleigh's face was quite serious. "We'd heard from all the grandchildren so I thought you might need a way to bring your news to the forefront. I didn't realize you'd already made a decision."

Well, at least now I understand she wasn't intentionally trying to incriminate me. Samira reached back and removed the clip from her hair. *Why is it I can always speak my mind to Daddy, but when it comes to Mama I can't ever seem to find the right words?* Samira's hair fell against her shoulders in a bunch.

"I knew from the start I was not designed for the job at the university." She shook her hair loose with her fingertips. "But I went and heard what they had to say and then made my decision."

"I'm sure you made the right choice, Samira." Pam's face was sincere. "You're always so cautious."

Always? Samira thought of her quick decision to allow Fabiano to carve her in the nude. *Not always!* "Can you see me organizing fundraising events and giving motivational speeches on a regular basis?" *I would be miserable!*

"Yes." Pam spoke up very quickly.

Samira rolled her eyes. *No way!* "You're very kind, Pam, but I don't think so! I'm lucky to survive the art auction once a year!"

"Speaking of the auction, did you ever find out who purchased that statue of you?" Pam's eyes were alive with new energy.

Samira was speechless. *What do I tell her?* She rearranged her hair again. *Do I want them to know Phil has me on his table?* She felt her cheeks warm with color. *No. I don't want them to know.*

"It's the oddest thing. Someone would pay that much for it and then remain anonymous." Pam shrugged her shoulders.

Ashleigh was watching her daughter carefully. "It was a beautiful work of art."

If only I'd have told Fabiano to leave my clothes on! Samira stopped herself from smiling. *But now that I know who has the piece, I really don't mind.*

"Hey, Mama." Kara came up behind her mother and touched her shoulder. "Can you help James? He's stuck on his homework."

"Sure." *Anything to get out of this discussion.* Samira slid forward and stood up. *But at least now I know what Phil bought with some of his hard-earned cash!* She couldn't help but smile now. *Unless Mike actually made the purchase.* Suddenly Samira wondered about that entire turn of events. *Someday I'm going to ask for the whole story.*

James was slouched into the corner of the bench.

"What are we working on?"

His eyes were doubtful. "English." He leaned forward and put his elbows on the table. "Diagramming sentences." He tapped his pencil on his textbook. "And it sucks."

Samira smiled and sat down. *It's been a million years since I've diagrammed a sentence.* "Let's take a look." *When the train goes through, the windows rattle noisily and the whole house shakes.* Samira began to analyze the problem. *Compound/Complex sentence with all the components.* "How many subjects are there?"

"Three."

"So set the first two up on separate lines, one above the other."

James drew two lines and listed the two subjects.

"Divide the line for the action of each subject."

Samira watched James study the sentence. *He's a thinker.* Then he listed each action word after the dividing line. *Good concentration.*

"The connecting word goes between the two lines."

"But what about the other words in the first half?"

"We'll come back to them. First let's set apart the major functions of the sentence."

James listed the conjunction and underlined it correctly.

"Connect the two parts with dotted lines."

"Like this?" James dotted the lines.

"Good." Samira put her fingernail on the paper. "Now list out the subject of the last part of the sentence over here."

James was nodding his head as if he was suddenly beginning to understand. "This is good," he stated with a little more confidence. He worked the sentence all the way to the end. "Now I go back for the adverbs and stuff, right?"

"Right." Samira patted him on the shoulder. *Wow! His shoulders are much more developed than I expected!* "I think you've got it!" Her memory tripped back to the summer. *No wonder his father had a few injuries from the fight.* Samira thought again. *But Phil isn't exactly a lightweight either.*

"Coffee Samira?" Ashleigh was pouring a fresh cup.

"Please." It gave Samira great satisfaction knowing she had repaid a favor to his father. *Hopefully we've both learned from these experiences.*

Josh came into the kitchen rubbing his face in his hands. "Excellent chess player out there, man. Boggles my mind!"

"But you played a fine game, son." Raymond was obviously pleased with his competition. "Who taught you how to play?"

"Dad at first but after I started beating him, my uncle Roy tweaked my strategy."

"Someday I would like to play against your uncle Roy."

You might just meet your match in Uncle Roy, Daddy. It suddenly felt perfectly comfortable to know Roy and Maggie as an aunt and uncle.

"Uncle Roy is intense at the chess board," James interjected. "His games last for hours!"

The grandfather beamed. "Every perfect chess game is meant to last hours!"

Ashleigh put a cup of hot coffee in front of her daughter. Samira breathed in the rich aroma with anticipation. *Nothing like a fresh cup of coffee to warm the spirits . . .*

A sudden flash of lightning caused the electricity to flicker. Screams could be heard from another room.

Raymond turned and headed for the basement stairs. "Don't want those girls to be frightened if the lights go out."

"Did Dad say what time he was coming back?" Josh was sitting on the stool in front of Ashleigh's eating bar.

Samira shook her head. "I don't think he knew."

"He said he was coming back for dessert," Ashleigh answered.

That's not all he said about dessert. Samira didn't like Josh's worried look. "Do you need to talk to him?"

"He probably forgot we had to leave today," James added. He was still working on his English assignment.

Surely he wouldn't forget that, would he? Samira thought about Phil's one-track mind when it came to business. *Well he might.* "Should you call him?"

"Maybe." Josh was thinking. "I don't want to leave too late. Mom's already not very happy that we're driving home alone."

Samira looked out the window. *I can certainly understand her concern!* "I hope the rain lets up."

"Me too."

Ashleigh handed a portable phone to the teenager. "Why don't you call him? Tell those boys the peach cobbler is just about ready to come out of the oven."

"So that's what I smell!" Kara entered the kitchen from the dining room. Bonnie was close on her heels.

"The lights went out!" The little girl was animated. "Even the tv went off!"

Samira watched Josh dial his father's number then listened to the one-sided conversation.

"Dad. It's Josh . . . Yeah, they went out for a second and came back on . . . only once . . . When are you coming back? . . . No, but James and I need to be headed home pretty quick . . ."

Samira watched Josh turn toward the window.

" . . . No, it's still coming down hard . . . okay, I'll call her when you get here . . . How much longer? . . . Mrs. Stephenson says the peach cobbler is just coming out of the oven . . ." Josh covered the mouthpiece with his hand. "He wants to know if you have ice cream."

"Of course!"

"Yes . . ." Josh went back to the telephone conversation. "Alright. Bye." Josh laid the phone on the counter. "He says they had to shut down because of the lightning so they should be here in a few minutes."

I wouldn't want to be in that building without electricity! Samira shuddered at the thought. Another flash of lightning announced the thunderous clap that followed. Bonnie screamed again, causing everyone in the room to jump.

"Come here, Pumpkin." Raymond picked up the seven-year old. "Let's go in the living room and play a game." As the grandfather passed the sunroom he suggested that Kara join them.

In other words, Daddy doesn't want anyone in the glass room with all this lightning!

"Finished." James pushed his English book toward Samira.

"Should I look them over?"

"Yeah." James looked pleased. "But I think they're okay. I didn't know to set each part up separately. Makes a huge difference."

I'm sure it does. Samira took the notebook and text and began to compare notes. It suddenly occurred to her that James held his pencil in his left hand. "Which hand do you write with, James?"

"Left." James looked uneasy. "That's why my letters slant the wrong way."

"There's nothing wrong with the way your letters slant," Samira encouraged. "Which hand do you eat with?"

"Both!" Krissy piped up as she entered the room eating a banana.

"Krista!" Ashleigh reprimanded.

"Well, he does when he's really hungry!"

James lunged at the girl but she darted just out of reach. "I hold silverware in my right hand."

Samira smiled. *Just like his father.* The answers in his notebook were correct. *That's really interesting.*

James followed Krissy into the other room.

"Samira, if things ever become more permanent between you and Phil, or do you call him J.P.?" Pam stopped in mid-thought. She had Mark perched on her hip.

"Phil." Samira closed the English book.

" . . . between you and Phil, you're going to have your hands full!"

Josh accepted a glass of orange juice from Ashleigh. "No, she's not. I can handle Krissy, no sweat!"

"That's exactly my point." Pam laughed.

Samira tapped the eraser of the pencil against the oak tabletop. From where she was sitting she could see James and Krissy in the living room and Josh at the counter. And Kara was in the dining room on the other side. For the first time, she could see the makings of a family on a broader scale.

Brothers would be very good for my girls. Samira studied Josh's face. *He looks so much like his father!* Her eyes traced his young cheekbones. *Sisters probably wouldn't hurt the boys' perspective either.* Samira was suddenly aware of Josh's status. *Although he'll be off to college by this time next year.* That thought caused her to stop and think about how fast her own children were approaching that age.

Samira slid off the bench behind the kitchen table and joined Kara in the dining room. She was leaning over a piece of paper on the table.

"What is it?" Samira studied the penciled image.

"It's the sky over Granny's garden before it rained hard. I sketched it after church when it was still just sprinkling."

Samira looked again. She could recognize approaching clouds in the distance behind an array of flowers. *She has a gift.* "Kara, it's very good."

"I'm going to take it to my art teacher tomorrow." She cocked her head to the side in thought. "You're really happy today, aren't you Mama?"

Samira thought for a minute. "Well, I guess I'm not in a bad mood."

"No, not like that." Kara lifted her drawing off the table. "I mean, like, you just seem really satisfied or something."

Funny that Kara would say that. Samira looked into her daughter's dark eyes. *Funnier still that she even noticed.*

"I think it's because Phil is here." Kara looked around the dining room. "Or, I mean, was here." Her eyes met her mother's again. "He makes you happy, doesn't he."

There was nothing Samira could do about the smile that was forming on her lips. It came so naturally and so easily. "I think he must." She tucked her hair behind her ears and tried to look away.

"I remember when you were so sad." Kara's was deep in thought. "I didn't know if we'd ever get you back when you stopped seeing him."

I didn't realize how much those days affected my girls. "I'm so sorry, Kara."

"I'm glad he's back." Kara smiled slightly.

"Really?"

"Really. He makes you happy . . ."

Samira pushed Kara's hair behind her shoulder. *I needed to hear that.*

" . . . and Phil seems pretty happy when he's around you too." Kara pulled her own hair away from her face. "Actually, when you're around he kind of forgets everyone else is here . . ."

Samira frowned.

" . . . don't be mad. It's just what happens." Kara shrugged her shoulders. "It's actually kind of funny . . ."

"Daddy, Daddy, Daddy, Daddy . . ." Lizzie came bouncing into the dining room, interrupting the intimate conversation. *I don't know if we'll get back to this talk again!* She wished for more time alone with Kara.

Samira looked up in time to see Wes run from the driveway to the shelter of the front porch. He stopped in front of the door and blocked Samira's view through the window. A few moments later, Samira heard the front door open, but not before another strike of lightning took the electricity for good.

Phil stood in the entry hall, soaked from the pouring rain. The only light came from the window behind him. Samira studied his form as he removed his jacket and hung it on the hall tree.

In spite of the excited commotion in the living room due to the lack of electricity, Asheligh was still in top form. "Let me get some towels!"

Phil lowered his head and ran both hands through his hair. Samira felt her heart stop the moment his eyes connected with hers. His easy smile warmed Samira from her head to her toes.

"Hey, Pretty Lady."

He makes me more than just happy. The man in the hall looked so familiar, yet something about him caused Samira to search his eyes for a deeper identity.

Ashleigh returned quickly and handed over two small towels. Wes took his and playfully dried Lizzie's dry hair before using it on himself. But Phil just stood there. Samira knew he had taken in all of her from the bottom up. She'd felt the movement of his eyes on her body and now they were once again looking deep into her eyes.

He still scares me. Samira inhaled very deeply. *But I need him to keep me satisfied.*

"Peach cobbler by the fire," Ashleigh announced with authority. "Who wants ice cream?"

Samira felt the entire family move toward the kitchen. Happy conversation and playful exchanges were loud in her ears. But Phil didn't move. He stayed in the entry hall just watching. Very slowly he ran the towel over the back of his neck and dried his face.

This is the Phil Ralston I know and love. He's quiet and peaceful, and yet he's so intense, all at the same time. Samira grinned playfully. *And I think he's thinking about dessert.*

"Samira?" Ashleigh poked her head around the corner. "Ice cream?"

"No thank you."

"Phil?"

"Absolutely."

Samira watched Phil's eyes go from her to her mother. Now he was moving toward her.

He didn't speak, he simply took her hand when she reached for him. The warmth of his skin penetrated Samira's senses. Goose pimples formed on her arms and the back of her neck. As she took a step toward the kitchen, Phil let go of her hand and draped his arm over her shoulder. *Just like he did at the driving range in Springfield.* She pressed her head into his shoulder as they moved together. Very briefly his lips touched her temple, but he still never said a word.

Samira couldn't hide the smile that was begging to be shared. *Daddy still kisses me like that.* Everything felt right. *Everything.* She stepped out from under Phil's arm as she entered the kitchen. It was then she realized her father's watchful eye upon them.

Raymond offered a single serving of peach cobbler to his daughter. *I should have known Daddy was watching us again.*

"Phil?"

Samira's heart skipped another beat. But this time it was for love of her father. *Oh, Daddy!* She grabbed his arm and pecked him on the cheek. "You're the best, Daddy."

Raymond winked at his daughter, but his eyes went right back to Phil. "Ala mode, right?"

"Yes, Sir." Phil accepted the china plate overflowing with cobbler and ice cream. Samira watched him exchange an appreciative glance with her mother. "This is just the way I like it."

Me too, Samira concluded. She looked from her mother, to her father, to Phil. *This is just the way I like it too.*

64

A Chance to Explain

Three Weeks Later . . .

The grand jury foreman dismissed the session for a two-hour lunch break. J.P. checked his watch. *That gives us just enough time to review with Sparky and prep Agent Roderick one final time.* He reviewed the morning testimonies. *Celia Monroe, our two ingenious hackers from Baltimore, and Jessica Hutchison.* He was pleased with the way things had gone so far. *Hutchison's the only one who needed to consult with her attorney, but if she's shacking up with Goldstein as I suspect, then she has the most to lose no matter how the court rules.*

Vince caught up with J.P. as they exited the courtroom. "Tell me, Counselor. What made you lean toward a grand jury summons in the first place?"

"Expediency more than anything." The attorneys crossed the street to the civic center plaza. "If Agent Roderick is right about Goldstein's disappearing acts, then we don't have much time to hold him."

"Here's the part that still boggles my mind . . ." Mike's eyes were narrowed in thought. "Goldstein moved to Joplin seven years ago and wasted no time marrying Angelica Juervas. If he was already on the run, or at least involved in these other laundering operations, why would he hitch himself to a prominent society figure like Angelica?"

It's obvious, isn't it? "To hideaway. No one's going to look for a professional thief in society's spotlight."

"I suppose not." Mike was still baffled. "But why take up relations with someone else if you've got the society queen by the tail?"

"Maybe he didn't like playing by the queen's rules." Vince ran a room key through the magnetic strip at the private elevator.

I don't like playing by anybody else's rules.

Denise and Sparky had completely transformed the Hughes' suite into command central.

"Lunch is on the counter." Denise didn't look up from her computer screen. "We've eaten so you go ahead."

Vince and Mike removed their suit jackets and hung them in the closet next to the door. J.P. hung his on the back of a high barstool and rolled his shirt sleeves.

"How did it go dis morning?" Sparky perched himself on a stool and crossed his hairy arms over his chest.

"Very well." Vince answered without hesitation. "The witnesses were very cooperative."

Sparky raised his stubby chin toward the ceiling. "Dey must be. Dey have everyting to lose."

"Jessica Hutchison didn't like answering questions concerning Goldstein." Mike accepted a clipboard from Denise.

Put yourself in her shoes. If she testifies against him she loses her cohabitation ticket. J.P. sank his teeth into a club sandwich. *If she testifies on our behalf she reduces her charges. Either way you look at it she loses.*

Denise handed a clipboard to Vince. "Betty needs you to check in at the office before you go back into session."

"Denise, what am I supposed to do with this call from Kelly? Should I call her back?"

This stint with Kelly Davis is lasting longer than I thought it might.

"She said you could call her cell phone between twelve twenty and one o'clock, or leave a voice message at home." Denise pointed. "I wrote that down on the bottom of the note."

"So you did, Ms Burke. Forgive me for missing that . . ."

"I charge double for repeating information," Denise handed another clipboard to J.P. "No news is good news from Derek. He's handled all the incoming calls." Denise tapped a fingernail on a specific message.

Call Bobby. I know. Aunt Maggie told me he'd be calling about Thanksgiving.

"That's the only one of urgent matter." Denise made eye contact. "Derek says it's getting more urgent each day."

Since when was Thanksgiving so urgent for my brother?

Denise lowered her voice. "Have you decided how to handle the Stephenson-Cartwright connection? It would be a shame for the media to exploit whatever it is you have going with the librarian."

I'll deal with that issue in private, thank you very much.

"I'm telling you, boss. I talked to Jerry this morning. He senses some kind of a storm brewing. You'd best take care of business before your business takes care of you."

"Does she really charge double?" Mike spoke to J.P. under his breath. "How do you afford to keep her?"

"I get it right the first time."

"Sometimes." Denise straightened up the dishes from lunch. "The information that's about to leak could cost you more than double."

I heard you the first time, Denise.

"Hey, J.P." Mike covered the mouthpiece on his cell phone. "What time you figure we'll be out of the courtroom tomorrow afternoon? Four? Five?"

"At the latest." *We'll go back in session with Roderick and Sparky this afternoon. Tomorrow kicks off with the investment officers from California and Stephenson. After lunch we'll hear from Jefferey Hughes.* J.P. nodded his head in satisfaction. "Yeah. Closing arguments should be done by close of day."

"Cool." Mike disappeared behind a bedroom door.

Unless Sparky's testimony takes longer. Then that puts closing arguments first thing the next morning.

Mike reappeared. "Kelly's thinking about driving over tomorrow after school."

"Why?"

"Counselor! It's a night on the town! Where's your sense of adventure?"

At home. I'd rather be on my way to see Samira.

"So here's what we're thinking. You and Samira still owe us a night out . . ."

We do?

"You turned us down the night of Stephenson's party . . ."

How does he keep track of everything?

"Kelly is going to invite Samira to join us for dinner."

Samira won't accept. She'd rather I come home.

"It's only dinner." Mike grinned. "Then the evening is all yours."

Plan all you want, Mikey. She won't do it.

Late the next afternoon

"That was a fine closing argument, Counselor!" Mike slapped J.P. hard on the back. "You sealed the indictment with Jefferey Hughes! His testimony brought down the house."

J.P. was smiling. *That was a damned good way to end the day wasn't it.* "By the time we're into our main course, Sean Bridges, alias Alan Goldstein, should be behind bars."

"And as usual, Sparky knew exactly where he'd be."

"He's an amazing investigator." J.P. nodded his head in approval. "He'll be invaluable as we prepare for trial."

"You owe me for that one too."

I will never get out of debt with Mike.

"Anything you weren't satisfied with?" They crossed the intersection into the French Quarter.

"I don't know." J.P. rewound the testimonies in his head. "I don't like Hutchison's hesitations." *It's a damn good thing I walked away from that dinner party when I did.*

"She'll burn her own bridges . . ."

"As in *Sean Bridges?*"

"Most likely." Mike pointed at a sign further up the street. "Kelly made reservations at The Chardonnay."

I can't believe Samira accepted this invitation. J.P. examined the elegant script on the sign. *Looks nice enough.* "I suppose I have to speak French and leave my tie on?"

"Just for that, I'll let you buy dinner." Mike held the door open for J.P. to enter first. "VISA is an international language, isn't it?"

"I'll buy your dinner after we win the case."

"Fair enough." Mike approached the short man with a waxed moustache.

"Bienvenue au Chardonnay. Avez-vous une réservation ?"

I was just kidding! I didn't think they'd really speak French!

"Welcome to the Chardonnay . . ." the host started to translate.

Mike replied. "Oui. Quatre à diner sur le balcon supérieur. Benson et Ralston."

"Ampèreheure, oui. Vous voici. Y a-t-il d'autres qui vous joignent ?"

I get the "oui". But everything else is Greek to me.

"Oui. Nous avons deux dames nous joindre. Vous pouvez les montrer à notre table quand elles arrivent." Mike answered again.

Okay, this time I picked up the dames. I know what they are.

"Très bien. Redressez de cette façon, svp."

J.P. followed Mike up a set of decorative wrought iron stairs.

"Frederick sera avec vous sous très peu."

"Merci." Mike thanked the host. "He says our server will be with us shortly."

I could use a cold draft. J.P. slid up to the table.

"So what do you think?"

"Very classy." *Not exactly my style.* "How'd you know about this place?"

"Kelly knew about it." Mike wiggled his eyebrows. "She's got a knack for fine dining."

No doubt. "And I suppose the two of you can converse in French as well as Italian and Spanish,"

"Oui." Mike grinned. "l'italiano di Kelly's potrebbe usare una poco più pratica. Ma il suo francese è molto fluent."

I have no idea what he just said.

"In other words," Mike continued. "She needs to work on her Italian. But her French is fluent enough."

"So you two must be getting on fairly well these days."

"Pourquoi vous inquiétez-vous ?" Mike raised his bushy, blonde eyebrows in a question.

I'll take a stab. "Because she's still hanging around and you don't seem to be wishing she'd go away."

Mike's eyes lit up. J.P. turned to see what had caught his attention. *Very timely.*

"Let's just say I have no desire to see anyone else in the near future."

Fair enough. J.P. rose from his chair as Kelly and Samira approached. *And let's just say I have no desire to see anyone else at all.* He took Samira's hand as she stepped up to the table. 'Hey Pretty Lady." *She's more beautiful every time I see her.*

Samira smiled quietly and allowed him to kiss her on the forehead.

"Samira?" Mike pulled out her chair.

Kelly was already seated.

It's like time stands still when she walks into a room.

A tuxedo-clad waiter appeared at the table. "Bonsoir, dames et messieurs. Mon nom est Frederick. Je serai votre serveur ce soir. Est-ce que je peux vous commencer au loin par quelque chose de la liste de vin ?"

Samira raised her eyebrows at her date.

"We'll let Mike handle the formalities."

"Wine, J.P.?" Mike handed him the list. "You choose, I'll order."

J.P. skimmed the list. *Merlot, Petit Bistro.*

Mike nodded and placed the order.

"Ainsi que ce soit." Kelly conversed with the waiter easily. "Veuillez commander la immersion d'artichaut et d'épinards de Parmesuan."

That's just great. Now we have two French—speaking parties at our table.

"He'll be back with the wine." Mike translated again. Then he turned back to Kelly. "Le Chardonnay est très amusement. Excellent choix pour diner, Mlle Davis."

"Much obligé, M. Benson."

Some things we won't understand. *J.P. admired the way Samira's black dress wrapped it's way around her body and disappeared under the tablecloth.* The only language I need to know is hers.

"Very enchanting." Samira made eye contact.

"The company or the setting?"

"Both. Maybe . . ."

The waiter returned with four wine glasses and a bottle of wine. He poured a sample into a single glass. J.P. went through the ceremonial gestures before taking a sip. "Very good." *Smooth and rich.*

"Les apéritifs seront dehors momentanément." The waiter carefully filled the remaining glasses.

"May I offer a toast?" Mike lifted his glass. "To friendships and the future."

Friendships and the future, huh? J.P. lifted his glass. *I figured he'd toast the indictment.* "To friendships and the future," Kelly repeated.

This is really good wine.

Samira was studying the menu.

I could just order her for the rest of the night. Samira blushed when their eyes connected. *I like being able to do that without saying a word.*

"Queest-ce que je peux apporter à votre pour le diner ?"

J.P. listened to Mike order their entres in French. *I'll order for us in English.*

"Your French is very impressive." Samira smiled across the table.

It's annoying if you ask me.

"You should hear his Italian and Spanish!" Kelly was patting Mike on the arm.

"I've experienced a little of his Spanish . . ."

What the hell? J.P. shot a wary look at his friend.

Mike put his hands up in defense. "Only in public, man. I've never said a foreign word to her in private!"

Now Kelly was frowning at Mike.

"I swear!" Mike frowned at J.P. "See what you started?"

"I didn't say a word."

"How did your day turn out?" Kelly changed the subject.

I'd rather not discuss this case with Samira here. It is her brother's case we're on. I have enough issues between Samira and my client as it is. If Denise is right about the media picking up on that . . . I don't need the Tribune publishing my private affairs . . .

" . . . Wouldn't you think, Counselor?"

"Think about what?" *I have no idea what they're talking about.*

"Well," Kelly explained. "I talked to Samira and we planned ahead just in case."

"In case of what?"

Mike was leaning toward his date in a playful manner.

"In case you were off duty." Kelly smiled brightly. "We don't have to go back until tomorrow unless you guys need to go back tonight."

"Vous dites-vous pouvez-vous rester la nuit avec moi dans la suite luxueuse d'hôtel, ma dame ?"

Obviously Kelly is the only one who can understand that.

"If you don't want to stay over tonight, I can go back . . ." Samira's eyes were searching J.P.'s.

"Go back where?"

"Home." Samira shrugged her shoulders. "Either way is fine with me. I don't want to put you out . . ."

Either way? Is she planning to stay in Springfield tonight?

"Oui." Kelly spoke into the middle of the table. "Then it's settled! We'll all stay over and go home in the morning!"

"But I don't want to impose . . ." Samira was still speaking only to J.P.

Where did I get lost in this conversation? "You're not imposing . . ." *They are.* "Do you want to stay tonight?" *If she wants to, I'm not going to turn her away.*

"Only if you do."

Only with her. Not them. "What about Krissy and Kara?"

"Pam and Wes have them."

I don't know if I like my client knowing who I'm with and where I am.

The waiter appeared at their table again, this time carrying a tray full of entrees. "Bon appetite!" He presented each meal with a formal flare.

"Est-ce que je peux vous apporter toute autre chose ?"

Mike seemed to take an inventory of the table.

"Rempliriez-vous svp son verre de l'eau ?"

"Devons-nous diner?" Mike picked up a steak knife and a fork. 'Shall we dine?"

"Oui." Samira answered in French, catching everyone off guard.

That was good. J.P. took a bite of his steak. *Does she speak French, or is she just playing along?*

"Rumor has it the library is putting in a new online system this fall." Mike purposefully engaged Samira in conversation.

Samira rested her knife on the edge of her plate. "We are. It's very exciting, but I'll be glad to be finished with the construction! It's a mess to work around."

"But it's going to be really nice when it's done," Kelly chimed in. "You guys need to stop and see it sometime."

J.P. watched Samira take a drink of water. *She hasn't touched her wine.*

"You know, Mike, I've had something on my mind for quite some time now," Samira began cautiously.

This could be interesting.

Mike wiggled his eyebrows and tipped his head in a playful manner. "Maybe we can help ease your pretty little mind."

"I'm thinking that might be a possibility."

Where's she headed?

"For the longest time I didn't know who won the final bid at the art auction."

"Exactly what art auction are you referring to, ma'am?"

Spare us the drama, Counselor!

"I'm referring to the art auction at city hall to raise money for the reading program."

"Oh, yes. *That* art auction." Mike was nodding knowingly now. "How might I be of assistance?"

"Until that day, I didn't know anonymous bidding was allowed at a public auction."

"Really? I wasn't aware of that either."

Fess up, Mikey. She's got the tiger by the tail.

"That surprises me since you turned out to be the final, *anonymous* bidder."

"That surprises me too since I left moments after talking to you."

Samira raised her eyebrows. "Then you must have friends in high places."

Now Mike was shaking his head. "I wouldn't exactly call it a high place, but I do have friends who are willing to assist me with worthy causes." Mike wiped his mouth and moustache with a cloth napkin. "Did the current owner happen to tell you what the stipulation was for entitlement to that piece?"

Leave it be, Mikey.

"No, I'm not aware of any stipulations!" Now Samira was looking at J.P.

"Let's see, maybe you'd like to tell the rules of the bargain . . ." Mike hid behind his wine glass.

"There was a bargain?" Samira tipped her head.

Oh, Mikey. You'll pay for this later! J.P. avoided Samira's eyes. *How do I explain this?*

"Go on, Counselor!" Mike raised his glass in encouragement.

Just put it out there. What do I have to lose? "Mike wouldn't allow me access to the statue until I figured out how to win you back."

"Am I a prize to be won?"

The sharpness in Samira's tone caught J.P. off guard. *Maybe I have more to lose here than I thought.* His father's words were suddenly making sense. *"Some things in life aren't worth losing . . ."* He sighed heavily. *Anything I say at this point can or will be used against me.*

Samira's eyes were doubtful.

This must be what the Captain meant when he said sometimes winning isn't enough.

"Let me clarify . . ." Mike stepped in. "I had my doubts that our mutual friend had given you a fair shake." Mike waited for Samira to make eye contact before he continued. "So I made him get his shit together before he could have access to the art."

I don't know if that helped or hindered. J.P. passed his fork from his left hand to his right. *She's not responding.*

"And I must say, I think J.P. has done rather well untucking his tail, don't you think, Samira?" Kelly was totally focused on Samira.

Even Kelly knows we're in over our heads this time. J.P. continued to watch Samira but she wasn't looking in his direction.

"Est-ce que tout est bien ?"

How long has he been standing there? The waiter looked on hopefully.

"Any complaints?" Mike translated.

Yeah, the topic of this conversation.

"Excellent, merci." Mike dismissed the waiter politely.

Dinner continued, but the lightness of the evening was lost. J.P. was glad to finally get his check. *It's time to end this charade.*

"We're going to walk the French Quarter," Kelly announced.

"You're more than welcome to join us," Mike assured. "Or you're free to meet up with us to get Samira's luggage later."

I fulfilled my end of the deal by having dinner with them. "Why don't you call the suite when you get back to the hotel?"

"Fair enough. Merci." Mike thanked the waiter as he delivered a steaming cup of coffee to Samira. "In the meantime we'll find some entertainment of our own."

Why don't you do that? J.P. reviewed his ticket. *Ten to one, Mike put the wine on his tab.* He put a charge card in the pocket of the leather pouch.

That would be correct. He smiled to himself. *Now I'll probably owe him for that too.*

Mike put his hand on Samira's shoulder as he stood. "Samira, thanks for the privilege of dining with you. We'll have to do it again soon."

If I ever recover from the comment about winning her back. "Kelly." J.P. stood up and offered his hand. "You have my condolences on the rest of your evening."

"On the contrary, we'll get on just fine." Kelly smiled brightly. "We'll call you in awhile, Samira."

I'm sure they won't have any trouble getting it on. J.P. grinned to himself as he sat back down.

Samira's disposition was still contemplative. "Mike is a good friend, isn't he?"

J.P. watched Mike and Kelly make an exit on the main level. "Yes, he is." *The best.*

"Kelly really enjoys his company."

J.P. rested his eyes on his date. "They must be good for each other." He watched Samira sip the coffee.

"I'm sorry about the wine," Samira turned the still full glass with her fingertips. "And I shouldn't have brought the statue up like that."

"It's no problem." *There's no reason for her to apologize about anything.*

"Well, there is, really." Her dark eyes were sad.

J.P. watched her stare into her coffee cup.

"The last time I dined in a French restaurant I gave a man permission to do something I regretted later."

I have never taken her to a French restaurant. He thought again. *Unless she's talking about the Café Ole, but they don't serve wine.* Now he was curious. *Who took her to a French restaurant?*

Samira was deep in thought.

J.P. waited.

"I didn't want the wine making any decisions for me tonight . . ."

"Okay . . ." *I don't like the direction this might be headed.*

Samira spoke with a faraway look in her eye. "Fabiano Uberti took me to the Bistro 712 the last night he was in Joplin."

J.P. swallowed hard. *I knew he was trouble the day I saw him on the library steps!*

"I allowed the wine to . . . well, I just had a little more than I should have . . ."

Probably no more than the Jack Daniels I had that night. But I was alone!

"That's the night I gave him permission to . . ."

To what?

"To undress the clay model." Samira took another drink of the coffee. "He talked me into it before I realized what the repercussions could be. I didn't think about my statue being on display for the whole world to see!" She rolled her eyes but refused to look at J.P. "He didn't really see me that way, you know."

No, I didn't know. But I wondered.

"I posed with my clothes. The whole time. But at the last minute he used his imagination . . ."

At least I can say I have more than my imagination.

"I didn't realize how heavy that was weighing on my mind." Samira forced a smile. "But tonight's experience was much more fun with Mike and Kelly and all the French . . ."

"Hey, Pretty Lady." J.P. put his hand over hers. "You didn't have to tell me that."

"I know." Samira looked away. "But I needed to." She set her coffee cup aside. "I'm ready whenever you are."

I'm ready, you just say the word. "Did you have anything in particular in mind?"

Samira raised an eyebrow. "Dessert maybe."

I'd almost given up on dessert! He took a deep breath as he studied Samira's chocolate brown eyes. "I've been thinking about this dessert since dinner at your parents' house."

"Me too." Now Samira's smile was sincere. "They took my coat at the door."

"Then by all means, we should pick it up as we leave," J.P. suggested. He stood and helped Samira with her chair.

The walk back to the civic center was comfortably quiet. Without any resistance Samira allowed him to gather her in tighter than necessary. *This must be what the Captain meant about my mother being enough . . .* J.P. closed his eyes as he kissed her hair. . . . *Because right now she's enough just like this.*

"I really don't mind if you need to go back home tonight."

And give up an entire night with this beautiful woman? "You're the only reason I wanted to get home." *But I didn't figure we'd have a chance to be alone even then.*

"Really?"

"Really."

"Kelly told me it was my call."

J.P. considered Samira's situation as they crossed the courtyard. "Are you comfortable staying?"

She stepped into the revolving door with him. "I think so. It was strange because this time Wes and Pam know who I'm with . . ."

I know exactly how she feels.

"It took Wes a little bit to get used to the idea that I was spending a night with his attorney."

This is obviously a difficult situation for all of us. "Would you be more comfortable if we went back home?"

Samira gently shook her head. "No. I want to stay."

It's good to hear her say that out loud. "So you're okay knowing that your family knows you're here with me." *She's studying the artwork again.*

"They knew I was coming over to meet you for dinner."

So she's going to let them wonder about her full intent. I don't know if I like being in the middle. *J.P. pressed the call button for the main elevator.* Especially with her father being who he is . . .

Samira's hand suddenly slipped out of J.P.'s. *What the . . . ?*

"Good evening, J.P."

J.P. spun around and faced the voice. *Stacked heels, short skirt, tight sweater . . . Holy Shit. Where did she come from?*

"I've been trying to reach you all week." Bobbie's eyes were sultry.

She's been drinking. Her presence caused a knot to form in J.P.'s stomach. *Obviously this is the "Bobby" call that was getting more urgent by the day.*

The elevator doors opened and J.P. stepped aside. *Denise tried to warn me but Derek spelled it wrong in the email!* He glanced at Samira, who had now taken several steps away from him. *This isn't at all what she's thinking.*

"J.P., I thought we had something special."

If she were sober I could at least reason with her. J.P. jerked his head away as Bobbie tried to touch his ear like she did before in this very same lobby. "S-N-S-A was your call, Bobbie Jo. And it ended a long time ago." *Like in April, when I left you at a photo shoot in Mexico.*

"But baby . . ." Bobbie Jo cooed. "I thought you'd always have something in reserve for me . . ."

"Good evening, J.P." Vince Barringer stepped off the elevator.

"Vince." *I know what he's thinking too. And it's not the case!* J.P. glanced in Samira's direction but she wasn't there.

Bobbie took a step toward J.P. "She left."

Who left?

"You look a little out of her league, baby." Bobbie ran her hand along J.P.'s arm. "Maybe she's expecting more out of you than you know how to give."

That's it! J.P. turned all the way around. *Maybe what she's expecting is exactly what I need to give!* Samira was no where to be seen. *Come on, Pretty Lady! Give me a chance to explain!* Panic began to set in. *Dear God, don't let this be the end!*

65

Staking a Claim

Where in the world is he going? Samira started to follow, but Phil was moving too fast. She watched Bobbie Jo Sommers and her friends get on the elevator. *Good. Maybe they'll leave him alone now.*

Phil turned both ways in the lobby. Samira smiled. *I've seen him speechless before. But I've never seen him completely frazzled.* She crossed her wrists and waited patiently. *He'll notice me eventually.*

Intuition proved successful. When Phil turned all the way around she was in full view. Very slowly Phil started into the courtyard where Samira was standing. *I could meet him part way, but I think I'll let him come all the way over here instead.* She grinned playfully. *That way Bobbie will be able to see us.*

"I didn't know where you were." Phil sounded more like J.P. Ralston when he spoke.

That's the same thing he said to me at the Hughes party. "I didn't go very far." *I was still within earshot.*

Phil stopped a short distance from Samira. "I still didn't know where you were."

Samira closed the space between them with a single step. "Well I'm here now."

"I owe you an explanation . . ."

"No you don't . . ."

"Yes, I do." Phil put his hand out. "That was unfair and unexpected . . ."

Three stories above, Samira could see the model and her friends leaning over the balcony making taunting motions with their bodies. *Perfect. They're just where I want them.*

"She's the last person . . ."

"Phil . . ." *Having those women up there is kind of like having Mrs. Barnes watching; only I don't have anything to hide here.* "I called a truce on this topic. Bobbie whatever her name is is not open for further discussion."

"I still need to explain . . ."

"Truce." Samira took a hold of his tie. "That means the case is closed. You explained before and unless something has changed, there's no reason to go back over it."

Samira could feel him trying to read her motives. *He'll never read me on this one.*

"Truce." She moved her hands along his sides on the inside of his jacket.

"I'm sorry, Samira."

I do believe that's the first time he's said those words to me.

"I'm really sorry."

His eyes were deep blue when Samira looked into them. She smiled knowing full well they still had an audience up above. "I know." She pressed her body in against his and moved her hands to guide him even closer. *Let's show them whose league he's in now.* Without waiting for permission, Samira kissed him on the lips. At first Phil didn't respond, but it didn't take him long to change his mind.

This is kind of fun. She felt Phil's arms pull her in even closer. *He has no idea I'm staking my claim.* Samira didn't pull away and Phil didn't offer to let her go either.

"Whoa, whoa, whoa! Break it up!"

Mike.

"For God's sake, this is why you have a room!"

Samira caught her breath and turned into the crook of Phil's arm. She smiled at the women in the balcony. *He's mine, Bobbie.*

Mike was shaking his head. "What's with you two anyway? Don't you have any sense of ethic responsibility here?"

Samira could still feel the excitement of Phil's body against her hip.

"Back from your walk already?"

Nice try, changing the subject.

Kelly appeared at Mike's side with a brilliant smile. "I figured you two would be in the room by now!"

"They need to be!" Mike shook his head again. "You wouldn't believe what I just caught them doing in the lobby!"

Kelly cast an accusing look in Samira's direction.

Guilty as charged.

"We're on our way . . ."

"Well, so are we." Mike lifted a strap off his shoulder. "We're headed out so here's Samira's bag."

"You mean you'd come to my room without calling first?" Phil was teasing and Samira knew it.

Mike didn't miss a beat. "After what I just witnessed I'm not sure you'd have made it to the room without my intervention!" He handed Samira's bag to Phil. "This little lady of yours packs lighter than any woman I've ever traveled with!"

Hey! That's what Phil told me at his aunt's ranch last summer!

"I know." Phil put the bag over his free shoulder. "What do you mean you're headed out?"

I thought the plan was for us to stay over.

"Headed out, like nos estamos yendo. You know, Nous partons de la ville. In other words, see ya later . . . ." Mike lifted his hand in the air in a fictitious wave. "We decided to sleep at home. There's a racket ball court reservation at the club first thing in the morning."

Samira opened her eyes wide. *Kelly knew I'd never arrange a night out of town like this on my own so she did it for me.* She dared to make eye contact with Kelly. *It's been a long time since a girlfriend took it upon herself to look out for me!*

"Now this is an interesting turn of events." Phil still had his arm around Samira's waist. "If I didn't know better, I'd think maybe you two planned this all along . . ."

"J.P., you never know any better so you might as well give it up while you're ahead." Mike's eyes were suddenly wide with wonder. He turned his head and followed a group of women with his eyes.

I think she got the picture. Samira knew Mike had spotted the scantly dressed models.

"Uh, Counselor . . . ," Mike looked panicked. "Might I have a word with you . . . in private?"

Oh, now this could be interesting.

Phil let go of Samira. "No need to."

"But, uh, I would strongly advise a moment in confidence . . ." Mike was now looking directly at Phil.

Obviously Mike knows Bobbie. But he doesn't know I know.

"Like now . . ." Mike insisted.

Phil was starting to laugh. "I'm good . . ."

"Not good enough . . ."

"For what?"

"For a surprise of this magnitude." Mike took Phil's arm. "It will only take a second." He started to pull Phil away from Samira.

Samira decided to play her card. *The only one I have.* "Is that how long it takes to define S-N-S-A?" *I have no idea what that stands for but I'd love for these two clowns to explain it to me.*

Both Mike and Phil froze and stared at Samira.

Samira raised an eyebrow.

"What's SNSA?" Kelly chimed in. "And who were those girls that walked by?"

Obviously it's something more revealing than I presumed.

"It's a dry cleaning term," Mike answered quickly. "Starch, non stain . . ."

" . . . Aerosol." Phil finished.

Now they're scrambling.

Kelly put her hands on her hips. "I've done a lot of business at the dry cleaners over the years and I don't ever recall having the option of no stain aerosols."

Kelly's on to them too. Samira crossed her arms and cast a look that indicated the dupe was up.

"Aerosol?" Mike squished his face.

Phil shrugged his shoulders. "It was the first thing that came to mind."

"I told you, you never know better!" Mike shook his head. "Next time let me finish my own sentence."

"So let's see, you would finish with . . . . ?" Kelly was tapping her foot.

Mike looked at Phil and Phil look back at Mike.

It's possible this is the one time we will ever witness both of these able attorneys speechless at the very same time!

"We used to be better at this."

"No, we just used to be faster. Much faster." Mike answered without looking at the women. "J.P., did I tell you what we saw as we walked through the French Quarter after dinner?"

"No, I think that conversation was interrupted . . ."

These two are quite the pair!

"I don't think they're buying it." Mike glanced in Samira's direction.

"I feel terribly out of practice."

"We are out of practice." Mike was starting to laugh. "And we're old!"

"Hey, hey . . ." Kelly interrupted the play. "You two might be old, but we happen to be quite young and sprite. If you're too old and out of practice to finish what you started, Samira and I may have to find some younger, more refined dates for the rest of this affair."

This is an affair?

"Okay, okay. You've got us over a barrel." Mike winked at Phil. "Let's just tell them what it means so we can be on with our evening."

Dessert is resting on this one last explanation, Counselor.

Phil motioned for Mike to speak first.

"It's a sex word," Mike lowered his voice. "I don't know if we should talk about it in public."

Kelly leaned toward Mike in playful retaliation. "After what you witnessed from these two love birds awhile ago, I don't think it's going to matter if you talk about sex in public."

Samira blushed all the way to her toes! *I only did that to stake my claim!*

"You're call, Miss Davis."

You're on, Mr. Benson."

These two make a really great couple!

Mike faced his date. "Sex. No strings . . ."

Sex, no strings what?

"Shit." Mike swore. "I can't remember the rest."

"Try harder," Kelly encouraged.

"Attached." Phil answered.

"Yeah! That's it. Sex, no strings attached."

No way!

"You've got to be kidding!" Kelly laughed loudly. "That's what that means?"

"You insisted." Mike reminded.

"You should have lied." Kelly suggested. "That's disgusting."

"We tried . . ."

"But we're terribly out of practice," Phil added.

"With the sex strings part or the lying?" Kelly asked.

Wow! Kelly's just going to put it all out there, isn't she?

"Both!" Mike and Phil answered in unison.

"Now that was damn good." Mike commented under his breath.

"Not bad, Mikey. Maybe we haven't lost our touch completely."

Mike and Phil exchanged a high five.

Samira laughed right out loud. *They're just too funny together.*

"Enough already!" Kelly pointed her finger. "All sex has strings attached. I'd think you'd both know that by now!"

"It does?" Mike had a look of total surprise plastered on his face.

"Mr. Benson, your ride home balances on the remainder of this conversation . . ."

"Ah, Kelly. I didn't mean it, really . . ." He turned to face J.P. "Look, I'd love to stay and see the next chapter of your heated affection, but it's been a helluva long day and my ride is leaving."

"Call me tomorrow, Samira," Kelly reached out and squeezed Samira's arm. "And enjoy the rest of your *uninterrupted* time together."

Now I know for sure Kelly set me up intentionally. "Thanks, Kelly."

"Anytime." Kelly grabbed Mike by the hand. "Good night, J.P."

"Kelly." Phil nodded in their direction. "Counselor."

Mike turned around and waved his free hand. "Goodnight John Boy . . ."

Phil was shaking his head when he turned back to face Samira. "A twenty dollar bill says Mike either finished the wine by himself, or they found another nightcap on their way back here."

"I'm not really a gambling woman," *But I sure seem to take a lot of risks with Phil.* " . . . But, if I had to gamble tonight, I'd say you're pretty close to the mark."

"Right on the mark." Phil reached for Samira's hand and took a step toward the private elevator.

"The Hughes' suite?"

"The Hughes' suite." The doors opened. "So where did you run off to, Pretty Lady?"

He's not going to let this one slide, is he? Samira looked down on the courtyard. "Over there," she pointed. "I went to see the paintings while you took care of business. I thought you'd be more comfortable if I stepped away." She could feel Phil's eyes on her even though she wasn't looking at him.

"You didn't have to do that."

"Yes, I did." Samira turned and faced him. "Is that really what the SNSA comment referred to?" She fell into step as Phil started to walk.

"Yep."

That's unbelievable.

"After you, Pretty Lady." Phil opened the door to the suite.

I remember every detail about the night we spent here. Phil's things were packed and organized on the foot of the bed. "Mike must not have told you Kelly and I had made arrangements to stay tonight."

"Let's just say Mike withheld pertinent information." Phil set Samira's bag on the bed next to his.

I'd put a twenty-dollar bill on the table that says he's going to hang the jacket over the chair and roll the cuffs on his sleeves. Much to her surprise, Phil hung the jacket on a hanger and loosened his tie. *That's why I'm not a gambling woman!*

"What are you thinking, Pretty Lady?" Phil was removing his tie.

Samira stepped into his personal space and began unbuttoning his dress shirt. "I'm thinking this is the first time I've spent an entire evening with J.P. Ralston."

"Really?"

She pulled his shirt tail out and unbuttoned the last button. "Really."

"What makes you think that?" Phil pulled the tie out from under his collar and draped it around Samira's neck.

"It doesn't match my outfit." *He's still very much in a professional mode.* "Are you tired?"

Phil shook his head and slipped out of his shirt. "Why?"

He answered a question with another question. "You're just really quiet." *I can't believe he hung up his shirt too.* Samira handed him the tie.

"I'm just waiting on you to answer my question, that's all."

Samira frowned. "What question?" She stepped out of her shoes and sat down on the edge of the bed.

"What makes you think you just spent an entire evening with J.P. Ralston?" Phil unzipped his shaving kit.

He really wants an answer, doesn't he? Samira thought for a minute. "Well, let's see, for starters, you refused a refill on the wine after only one glass. I've only seen you do that when you were officially on duty . . ."

"Tonight I was honoring your lead . . ."

Oh, I see, this is going to be a defense match. "That was very thoughtful of you." *Let's see where he goes with this one.* "J.P. Ralston is the only man I know who can be spotted and picked up by a supermodel at the entrance to an elevator in a fancy hotel."

Phil was squeezing toothpaste onto his toothbrush. "And I walked away so I could spend the rest of my evening with you."

"And I must say you did so with a great deal of integrity."

Phil put the toothbrush in his mouth and disappeared into the bathroom. The door closed for a few minutes.

Samira stretched out sideways across the king sized bed. *I always feel very small on a bed this size!*

Phil asked another question upon his return. "Anything else?"

Only one more thing, J.P. Samira propped her head up on an elbow. "I've never seen Phil hang up a coat and a tie." *I don't think he has an answer this time.* "Ever."

Phil was shirtless. He stretched out on his stomach between Samira and the luggage. "Maybe there's some other things J.P. Ralston needs to hang up."

Samira assumed he was still playing the game. "Like what?" She ran her fingertips down the length of his spine.

"Like anything that hinders what you and I could have together." Phil turned his face toward hers. "Like casework and cover models."

I don't know how serious he is, but he seems to be contemplative! Samira thought for a moment as she continued to move her hand over his bare shoulder.

"You don't have to give up anything for me." *Well* . . . "Except the supermodel."

"Maybe I have to give it up for me." Phil rolled onto his side and ran his hand over Samira's shoulder. He linked his fingers into hers. "I think I need to give some things up for me so I can be more of who I need to be for you."

This is exactly the point I was trying to make at Shoal Creek. "And what exactly does that mean, Mr. Ralston?"

Phil looked deep into her eyes. "That means I need to be less of J.P. Ralston and more of Joseph Phillip."

So there's even more of him to know than I realized. "I don't think I know Joseph Phillip very well, yet."

"Maybe we can get to know him together." Phil leaned in close.

Maybe we can. Samira closed her eyes as Phil kissed her. *If this is the introduction, then so far I like him very much.* She rolled onto her back and allowed Phil's body to press into hers.

"J.P. did a great job staking my claim in the courtyard." Samira ran her fingers over Phil's check bone. "Once he understood I was serious, he didn't seem to mind being kissed like that in public."

The grin that appeared on Phil's face made the spontaneous moment even more worthwhile.

"Let's talk about that. J.P. didn't mind much, but it was totally out of character for the Samira Cartwright I've known."

It was Samira's turn to smile. "I think the audience on the third balcony brought an ornery streak out in me."

"What audience?"

He's looking into my eyes but I know he's thinking about other body parts. "Bobbie and her friends were in full view over your left shoulder. I decided to give them a little something to talk about."

"Now that's funny." Phil laughed easily. "I didn't know you had it in you to be so forthright and impulsive."

Samira shared the laughter. "Does it bother you?"

Phil held her head in his hand and pulled away slightly.

Maybe that was the wrong question.

"No. But I do have one major concern," Joseph Phillip turned serious again. He put his knee over her leg as he talked.

I like the way he's communicating. "And that would be?"

Phil kissed her gently on the lips.

Samira wrapped her arms around Phil's neck.

"My dog." He spoke between kisses.

"Derek is taking care of him," she snuck an answer into the foreplay.

Suddenly Phil was laughing.

"What?" Samira moved with him as he started to sit up.

"I know Derek is taking care of him right now." Phil pulled her up beside him on the edge of the bed.

Then what? Samira didn't want the playful moment to end.

"But what about him in the long term?"

What is he talking about? "Derek?"

"No." Now Phil was shaking his head. He stood up and helped Samira to her feet.

"What?" *And why are we standing up?*

Phil put his hands under Samira's ears and turned her face toward his and kissed her again. "What about Chase when Joseph Phillip gets his act together?"

"I don't think Chase will mind knowing Joseph Phillip."

"Chase is probably the only one who knows Joseph Phillip completely." Phil skillfully unzipped Samira's dress.

She could feel Phil's hands against her bare back. *I like where this is leading, but I'm still not sure about the dog.*

"I can give up a lot of things, Pretty Lady," Phil kissed her again. "But I don't think I can give up my dog."

"Oh, Phil!" Samira pushed away slightly. "Is that what you're afraid of? Do you think you have to give up Chase to have me?"

Phil pulled her back in. "My dog and your back yard are not exactly a match made in heaven."

Well, he has a point there. Samira put her arms around Phil's neck. "But if our match is made in heaven, don't you think everything else will fall into place?"

"Can you learn to live with a dog and a husband?"

A husband? Samira's heart skipped a beat. *Is he proposing?* "If that's what it takes to gain a husband I'm sure I could make adjustments." Her dress was hanging loosely around her body.

"Then I'd like to make a proposal." Phil linked his hands behind Samira's waist.

For some reason I never pictured this moment like this! She held her breath.

"I'd like to propose that you, Samira Stephenson Cartwright, become my wife."

Oh, Dear God! This is the answer to my prayers! And all I had to do was agree to take in his dog!

"Pretty Lady, you are everything I need."

"Everything?"

Phil's face was radiating the same joy Samira was feeling. "Absolutely everything." With that statement he drew her in to his body. "You are the lady I desire."

"And you are the only one I desire, Joseph Phillip Ralston." Samira confessed between his kisses.

"Then you accept my proposal?"

Samira rested her head against Phi's bare shoulder. "Yes, I accept." She could feel his heartbeat against her collarbones.

A few moments later Samira stepped out of her dress and allowed Phil to remove the remaining articles of clothing. *He's always a gentleman.* She pushed the covers back on the bed. Samira watched her future husband finish undressing as she slid between the crisp sheets. When he joined her, his hands were warm and smooth against her hips.

She gave silent permission for him to continue. *I don't know that I've ever seen his eyes so intent.* The depth of his focus caused Samira to melt even further into his spell. Phil's lips were soft against her skin and his hands had a magical affect as he continued to discover her.

If this is Joseph Phillip, then he's the one I want to know more . . .

Very slowly Samira opened the whole of her being to his.

Phil spoke as he became one with her being. "I love you, Samira Stephenson."

Samira didn't dare close her eyes. "And I love you, Joseph Phillip." *More than I even knew was possible.*

The next afternoon found Samira in her brother's family room. She could see the kids playing in the backyard through the wall of glass.

"Well, this is certainly an unexpected turn of events," Raymond Stephenson spoke with trepidation.

It's not unexpected if you're me!

Weston was staring out the window.

I wish he'd say something. Anything.

"It's like we've been hung out to dry."

That's not what I wanted him to say. Samira was totally disgusted with her brother. *Maybe he should have just stayed quiet.* Samira glanced into the kitchen wishing Pam would come to her rescue. *Or Mama, or anyone!*

"Well, not exactly hung out to dry," Raymond seemed to be attempting to comfort his son. "J.P. just said he wasn't going into litigation. He'll still give legal counsel as we proceed into trial."

Wes cast an accusing look at Samira.

You'd think he could be happy for me. But he's stuck in his own world. Samira crossed her arms over her middle. *How was I supposed to know Joseph Phillip was going to give up litigation in order to free J.P. Ralston?* She felt her heart sink lower into her stomach.

Samira's mother appeared at the sliding glass door with Mark on her hip. "Weston, could you bring me a dry diaper please?"

"Where's Pam?"

Oh, for pete's sake! "I'll go get a diaper!" *He's so lost in his own concern he can't even take care of his son for a minute!* Pam was folding towels at the top of the stairs.

"Have you told the girls yet?"

At least someone is interested. "Not yet. Phil's boys are coming down tonight. We wanted to talk to all four of them together."

"Well, of course." Pam snapped a towel. "Are you excited?"

Obviously she can't tell by looking. "I was until I came over here." Samira stepped into the nursery and took a diaper out of the bag next to the changing table. "Had I known Wes and Daddy were going to blame me because their attorney pulled out of litigation, I'd have stayed home!"

Pam wrinkled her face empathetically. "I know. It doesn't seem fair, does it?" She folded her arms. "Maybe it won't be as disastrous as they're thinking."

"Maybe." *I'm sure Benson and Barringer will carry them through just fine.* Samira went back downstairs and handed the diaper over to her mother.

"Thank you, dear." Ashleigh's face showed signs of concern.

I highly doubt she's concerned about Mark. Samira could hear her father and Wes talking in the office. Samira turned her head so she could make out their words.

"Dad, we hired J.P. because we knew he'd get the job done."

"And he did, Wes. He exposed an underground laundering business right under our noses."

"But the job's not finished."

"He didn't say he wouldn't help. He just said he wasn't going to litigate."

"Why? Because it conflicts with his personal life?"

"No, because it conflicts with your personal life."

What is that supposed to mean, Daddy? Samira watched her mother fasten Mark's britches.

"Since when has my attorney had the right to determine my rights to privacy?"

Samira could hear the change in her father's tone. "Since he decided your sister was more important than a case, Weston."

Phil told them that? Samira put her hand to her heart.

"There you are, little fella. Run and play!" Ashleigh put Mark on his feet and watched as he toddled back outside. "We won't have too many more nice days to play outside."

"No, we won't." Samira hadn't taken notice of the beauty of the day. She jumped a little when her mother put her hand on her shoulder.

"You're just going to have to be patient with them, Samira." Ashleigh nodded toward the office door. "This news is quite unsettling for the business."

Go on, Mama. Tell me you're really happy for me, in spite of the Mid-America crisis. Samira watched her mother's thoughtful face.

"Thanksgiving is really quite soon. Are you sure you shouldn't wait a little longer?"

Samira put her hands in her hair! *Why am I even here?* "Does it matter that Phil's family will be here then?"

"This is an important event, Samira." Ashleigh walked across the kitchen and put the wet diaper in the trash. "Surely they wouldn't mind coming back again."

They just don't get this, do they? Samira spun around on her heels. *There is no reason for us to wait!* She picked up her purse by the front door. *The only thing waiting will do is keep us apart when we really are ready to be together.* Samira put her hand on the front door handle. *Why can't they see this?*

"Where are you going?" Ashleigh was following a few steps behind her daughter.

"I don't know." *And even if I did, I wouldn't tell anyone!*

"Don't go, Samira." Ashleigh's voice was pleading. "We still need to talk about some things."

"Talk to Daddy. And Wes." Samira turned around in the open door. "Obviously what I have to say isn't nearly as important as their issues today."

Samira took one last, long look at her mother before she closed the door.

66

Breaking News

I've never done this to him so I don't know how he's going to react. Mike was sitting at his desk with his hands folded in silent thought.

Time was passing, but Mike still wasn't speaking. He finally made eye contact with J.P.

"So you're walking away from a chance to litigate the biggest case of your life before a federal judge?"

"I have to, Mike." J.P. leaned forward in the chair. "I don't have any choice."

"Yes, you do." Mike stood up and walked across the room. "You could wait until after trial to tie the knot."

"It's not that simple . . ."

"She's not pregnant is she?"

"No, for God's sake, Mike!" *It only took once to learn that lesson!* "No!" *I can't believe he even said that!* "But there's no reason for us to wait. I don't want to go home alone at night anymore. And I don't want to wake up alone either."

"Surely you could figure it out."

"You're right, I could figure it out." J.P. crossed the room and faced his best friend. "But I'm tired of figuring it out . . ."

Mike's eyes softened a little.

"I can't have this case and Samira too. You know that as well as I do. The significance of this conflict of interest is too risky." J.P. thought some more. "Even if I wasn't going to marry her I'd need to pull free of one or the other until after trial."

"You don't make things easy, do you J.P.?"

"Not this time."

"Not ever! Face it good buddy, you're a hard ass all the way around."

At least he's loosening up. There for a while I thought he was going to blow.

"That puts Vince in position for opening arguments. When do you want to talk to him?"

"The sooner the better. Goldstein's arrest will make Sunday headlines. It won't take long for legalities to follow." *At least he's thinking strategy.* "And I'll leave Denise and Derek at your disposal."

"And Sparky."

"And Sparky." J.P. chuckled. "He was yours to begin with."

"I know. You still owe me for that one." Mike turned and faced his friend. "I'm happy for you man, but I didn't think about it pulling you off Mid-America."

"Neither did I." *I've spent my whole career striving for a case of this magnitude.* "But it has to be, Mikey."

"Yeah, I know." Mike stuck out his hand.

J.P. hesitated. When he put his right hand into Mike's he received a genuine handshake.

"Hats off to you, buddy. I don't think I could do it . . ."

Do what? Get married?

" . . . I'd have to finish the job first, then go back and pick up the relationship."

Things change, my friend. "I'd have said the same six months ago." J.P. shrugged. "There's not a doubt in my mind I could go in there and win this case, Mikey. But this time winning isn't enough."

"She's not worth losing is she?"

"No, she's not." *I wonder if he's thinking the same thing about Kelly.* "Some things you can't play to win."

"Amen, brother." Mike raised his head in a thoughtful gesture. "So, what? You going to stand before Judge Parker or do the whole walk down the aisle thing?"

"It's her call." *Makes no difference to me as long as the end result makes her my wife.*

"Unbelievable." Mike turned back toward his desk. "How'd Stephenson take it?"

Which one? "Not very well." *Neither one of them, really.*

"I assumed as much." Mike sat down in his chair and rolled back up to his desk. "How'd you go about it?"

"I went to see her parents first."

"That was noble of you."

"Samira's got this tight little family thing going. I figured I'd best be in the clear with her father before making her my wife." *The last thing I need to do is piss him off.*

"So you really asked *permission* to marry her?"

"Basically." *But not in so many words.* "I just told them . . ."

"Them?"

"Yeah, her mother was there too."

"No shit?"

"No shit." J.P. grinned. "I asked for their blessing on my proposal and told them I'd take good care of her."

Mike threw his head back and covered his face with his hands. "My buddy, J.P. Ralston, not only proposed to a woman who has him all melty and mushy, but he even asked her parents for her hand in marriage!" Mike laughed as he made eye contact with his friend. "This is really too much, J.P.!"

I know.

"Oh, hell." Mike picked up the phone. "I need to find Vince and tell him what's up." The attorney pushed a button. "Shall we say three o'clock?"

"That's good." J.P. checked his watch. "The boys are coming down tonight so I'll want to be out of here by about four thirty."

"Sure, play the family man now . . ." Mike held out his hand to stop J.P. from responding. "Hey Vince. We have some late-breaking news on the Mid-America case. Our trusted colleague has pulled out of litigation so he can marry the Stephenson heir."

How is it Mike can make something with life-changing implications sound so trivial with a simple flip of his tongue? J.P. ran his hand through his hair.

"No, I'm not joking! He's standing right here in my office looking more guilty than Goldstein feels . . . we're thinking the three of us need to sit down yet today to go over business before the media gets wind of the arrest . . . No. Goldstein's held without bail . . . it's a done deal if you ask me . . . We're aiming for three o'clock . . . Good. See ya then."

Mike hung up the phone. "It's a date. Be back here at three."

"Sounds like Vince took it with a grain of salt." *Getting Vince to work on a Saturday isn't always an easy task.*

"You know Vince, he's steady. He knows the media hype is coming too." Mike rose from his chair. "I guess congratulations are in order, Counselor."

"Thanks."

"Tell Denise I appreciate her willingness to stay on board."

I'll tell her, after I tell her my news.

"You haven't told her yet, have you?"

"I will." J.P. cringed.

Mike pressed his finger into J.P.'s chest.

"Honest! She's next on the list!" *Like as soon as I leave here.* "Unless you'd be willing to talk to her for me . . ."

Mike grinned and shook his head full of curls. "You don't pay me enough to deliver that kind of news to Denise. She's all yours, good buddy. And spare me the details."

Mike answered his phone when it rang.

Kelly. The look on his face is a dead giveaway.

"I'm outta here." J.P. whispered. "I'll be back at three."

Mike nodded in understanding and waved J.P. out the door.

I wonder how long it will be before ol' Mikey takes the plunge? Once inside his truck, J.P. pressed a button on his cell phone. *Hard to tell where I'll find Bobby.*

"Bobby, this is J.P."

"I'll be damned! You actually returned my call!"

Maybe that message was Bobby after all. "Did you call?"

Familiar laughter filled J.P.'s ears. "Yeah. Several times. I'm bringing the whole fam-damily out for Thanksgiving. Did Aunt Maggie tell you?"

"I caught wind of something along that line." J.P. turned onto Main Street. "How much flexibility do you have that weekend?"

"Flexibility is the name of the game, big brother. What do you have in mind?"

Plenty. "I was thinking maybe you could bring your brood down here to Joplin to sit in on my wedding."

"Holy shit, J.P.!"

No kidding. The more times I hear myself say that out loud, the more surprised I am all the way around.

"You mean like in three weeks?"

Is that all it is? "Three weeks." *Wow. That's going to go fast!*

"Same girl, right?"

"Same one."

"We'll be there!" Bobby was laughing again. "I knew she was a keeper when her finesse saved your ass in the bleachers."

That was a nice save, wasn't it? J.P. pulled into his personal parking place. "I knew before that."

"No doubt you did."

"I'll send the details through Aunt Maggie." J.P. locked his truck.

"Wait, J.P. There's one more thing."

There always is. J.P. started up the stairs.

"Did Maggie happen to mention that the Captain is coming with us?"

"With you where?" J.P. unlocked the front door of his office.

"To Thanksgiving."

I think he's serious. "To Aunt Maggie's?"

"Yeah, to Maggie's . . ."

No. She didn't happen to mention that major detail.

" . . . I thought you might want a heads up."

That sheds new light on the weekend . . .

"J.P.?"

"Yeah, I'm still here."

"That may play into your plans to a degree."

"To a major degree." *It didn't occur to me to invite the Captain.*

"Why don't you process that for awhile and get back to me so I know how to handle it, alright big brother?"

"Alright." J.P. turned on the lights and booted the computers.

"I'm headed into a tunnel, J.P. Call me back later."

"Will do, Bobby . . ." A click on the line alerted J.P. that the call had dropped.

The makeshift office from Springfield was in boxes around office. *At least they got things unloaded.* J.P. looked around the room. *I wonder how hard it's going to be to convince Denise I'm doing the right thing.* The message clipboard was waiting on J.P.'s desk.

"Bobby called. Return the call." J.P. ran his hand through his hair. *Maybe it was my brother.* He set the clipboard back down on his desk. *If that's the case, then it was strictly happenchance to bump into Miss Sommers in Springfield. How unlikely is that?*

"J.P.? Are you here?"

Denise. I should have known she'd come in to organize today.

"I thought I'd come up and unpack the Mid-America files so we could get a clean start on Monday." Denise met her boss in the doorway between the offices. "When did you get back? Derek said he fed your dog last night."

Now I know she's been in touch with Derek today. "We came back early this morning."

"We? Who's we?" Denise disappeared into her own office.

"I came back with Samira."

"Oh really?" Denise lifted a file box onto the counter in the workroom. "That's a pretty risky thing to do considering her connection to Mid-America."

There's a segue if I've ever had one. J.P. lifted the second box onto the counter for Denise. "About that connection." *I have no idea how she's going to take this.* "I've resigned from Mid-America's prosecution team."

"Yeah, right." Denise tucked her hair behind an ear. "Tell me something I can believe, Boss."

J.P. took a stack of file folders out of the box and sorted them into two piles on Derek's desk. "Believe it or not, Denise, it's true."

Denise put her hands on her hips. "This is federal prosecution, J.P. You don't just walk away."

"You do if there's a conflict of interest that could jeopardize the integrity of the case." *Or the integrity of the relationship.* He accepted another small stack of files from his assistant.

"In that case you stop seeing her until after trial, right?"

"Not in this case." He waited until Denise looked at him. "In this case I'm pulling out of litigation."

"You can't do that, Boss! You have too much riding on the outcome!"

"I already did because I have too much riding on it." *Personally and professionally.*

Denise sank into one of the winged backed chairs in the waiting area. "So that's it? We're done? Mid-America just stops after all this?"

J.P. walked over and sat down in the chair adjacent to Denise. "Not exactly. I'm done with litigation. But I'll stay on as legal counsel for Mid-America until the end of the trial. However, you are still on the case, as is Sparky, and Derek if he's needed." *She's listening, but she doesn't want to hear this.* "I personally won't have direct involvement in the trial."

"How can you do this?" Denise's eyes showed signs of betrayal. "All this time and effort and you're just going to walk away?"

Tell her the rest, Counselor. "I'm not exactly walking away, I asked Samira to marry me, Denise."

Stunned silence permeated the room. Denise didn't say anything. In fact, she didn't react in any way whatsoever.

This is worse than waiting on Mike. At least I had confidence that Mike would come around.

Very slowly Denise rose from the chair and walked over to her desk. "So just like that, you decide to cancel your ticket to federal litigation and get married." She flashed an accusing look in J.P.'s direction. "All for the little librarian?"

No. For far more than that! "Not exactly *just like that,*" J.P. defended. "I've given it a great deal of thought . . ."

"Your thoughts obviously didn't include me or the practice . . ."

"That's not true, Denise." *I didn't anticipate this.* "I weighed all the options, I just didn't happen to include anyone else's opinion, including Samira's. We can't afford to put the case at risk over a relationship, and I can't afford to put my relationship with Samira at risk over a case either." *Especially after the way she reacted to the subpoena over the Hughes' diary.* "But nothing else around here will change . . ." *With the exception of fewer weekends and holidays at the office.*

"We'll see about that over time." Denise's tone was sarcastic. "So now I report into Mike and Vince? Is that what I'm hearing?"

J.P. shook his head. "No, you don't report in to them any more than you report into me. You're on the case with them. You're a part of the team."

"Somehow I can't see either one of them buying into that." Denise sat down in her chair with an air of defeat.

J.P. knelt in front of Denise's desk so he was just below her eye level. "They can't win the case without you." *And that's the truth of the matter.* "Hell, I couldn't even win it without you, Denise. You're the best paralegal in the business. They need to secure the court's favor and you're the only one who has enough skill and information to make that happen."

Denise looked across the desk doubtfully. "But it's not the same. You won't be there reading my mind."

"I'll be there, I just won't be at the bench."

"So you're really going to go through with this aren't you?"

I already have. "I am." *As far as I'm concerned, the only thing left is the formalities.*

Denise sighed and rearranged a few loose papers.

"It will be okay, Denise." J.P. stood up and walked around the desk. "I'm not going anywhere and neither are you."

Denise looked up.

Is she crying?

"Can you guarantee that for me, Boss, because I'm feeling a little slighted here."

"You have my word."

Denise rolled her eyes.

"Have I ever let you down before?"

Denise blinked.

Yep, she's crying.

"No."

"Then I won't this time either."

Denise forced a quick smile. "So what now? Business as usual?" The phone rang. "It's for me."

I knew she would take it hard. I just didn't know she'd take it personally. J.P. sat down in his chair and turned around very slowly. *So what am I supposed to be doing if I don't have trial prep on the top of the pile?* The cell phone on his belt vibrated.

J.P. checked the I.D. *That would be the boys.* "What's up?"

"Hey Dad, we're headed out . . ."

Sounds like James.

"We should be there in a couple of hours."

Yep, it's James. "Tell your brother to drive carefully and call me if you need anything along the way."

"Like gas?"

"Get gas before you leave town!"

"We already did that. I was just messing with you."

It's good to hear him laugh.

"Oh, and Josh says we'll need food."

"Save up, Samira's cooking tonight." And I'm sure it will be worth the wait.

"Alright. We'll see you at the house."

"Be safe and keep the shiny side up, alright?"

"Bye, Dad."

J.P. clicked the phone off. *You know, Ralston, it feels good to be called Dad.* He fingered the phone in his hand. *It wouldn't hurt to call mine and let him know what's going on.*

J.P. opened his briefcase and pulled out the worn envelope. Once again J.P. scanned the aged handwriting on the lined paper. It's really more of a note of appeal than a letter. He turned the paper over in his hand. *He just wanted to plead his case with me one more time.* J.P.'s eyes stopped on the footer underneath the formal signature. Very slowly he pushed the numbers on the cell phone.

J.P. took one long breath before sending the signal. Two rings sounded in the attorney's ear. Then three. *Maybe he's out for the afternoon.*

"Captain Joe."

The crisp baritone voice resonated in J.P.'s ear. "Captain, this is J.P."

There was no immediate response.

"Your son."

"I know. Joseph Phillip."

More Joseph Phillip today maybe than yesterday or the day before that.

"I didn't expect your call."

Nor did I expect to be calling. J.P. ran his hand through his hair. "I talked to Bobby today. He says you're thinking about joining us for Thanksgiving." *Seems odd I'd say it that way. I've missed more Thanksgivings than I've made over the years.*

"Robert invited me and Maggie agreed." The Captain sounded reserved.

I should put his mind at ease. "That's good. You'll get to meet my boys." *They're eighteen and sixteen years old and don't even know the Captain exists.*

"I'm looking forward to that, Phillip."

I need to tell him what's been running through my mind. J.P. drew a deep breath. "I've been thinking a lot about what you told me on the tarmac in St. Louis . . ."

The Captain seemed to be listening so J.P. continued.

" . . . You told me there might come a time when winning wouldn't be enough."

"I remember."

"Well," J.P. paused to gather his thoughts. "I'm there."

"We all get there eventually." The Captain paused as if he was still thinking. "So what are you going to do about it?"

J.P. chuckled at his father's direct reply. "There's only one thing to do."

"What's that?"

He seems genuinely interested. "I'm going to marry the one thing in life that isn't worth losing." J.P. couldn't help but smile. He ran his hand over Samira's bronzed statue on his desk. *She looks almost as good in bronze as she does in nothing at all.*

"I'm happy for you, son. I hope she's all you'll ever need."

"She is." *That's the second time he's called me son.* J.P. could picture his father's face. *He's probably looking at one of my mother's pictures as he says that.* "I'd like to have you join us that day if you're up for a road trip from the ranch down to Joplin."

"Are you thinking around Thanksgiving?"

"I am."

"I'd like that very much."

So would I. "I'll get the details up to Aunt Maggie and we can go from there."

"Very good." The Captain's voice was stronger now. "You be in touch now, you hear?"

"I will." *But there's more.* "Hey Dad?"

"Yes?"

It feels as good to call him 'Dad' as it does to be called that. "Thanks." *For the advice.*

"You're welcome, Phillip. You take care now."

J.P. nodded contentedly. "You do the same and we'll see you in a few weeks."

Denise was standing in J.P.'s office when he disconnected the call. *She looks mellow enough. Maybe she'll surrender the fight.*

"Your dad, huh?"

"Yeah." *Believe it or not.* "He's coming out for Thanksgiving."

"For the *wedding?*" Denise started to organize the loose papers on J.P.'s desk.

"For Thanksgiving. But we're thinking we might use that holiday to everyone's advantage." *Especially our own.*

Denise nodded. "Well, let me know if you need anything. I'd be glad to help."

I don't think I've ever seen her so sad. "Are you okay?" J.P. walked around his desk and stopped her from sorting unimportant papers.

"Yeah, I'm fine. I just never thought . . ." Denise flipped her short hair behind her ear. " . . . well, you know. Who would have guessed you'd be getting married before me?"

So that's what all this is about. He sat down on the edge of his desk.

"It's just that . . . " Denise was obviously searching for words. " . . . that I could always justify my situation against your . . . what should I call it?" She tapped her acrylic fingernails on the desk. "Your elusiveness to commitment?"

Is that what that was? J.P. had to stifle a smile.

"But if you're getting married then that leaves me without a comparison and it makes my situation with Jerry seem very, well, . . . hollow."

"Jerry's a good man, Denise." *And you're a good woman.* "Maybe you need to decide what you need from one another."

"I don't know if we know anymore." Denise blinked away a tear. "We've been like this for so long that I don't know if there's a definition of need. It's all a matter of convenience and comfort levels now. Stepping out of them seems like a huge threat to whatever it is we've established."

J.P. thought about Denise's common law status and realized her quandary. *I need more than a common law commitment from Samira just as much as she needs more from me.*

"But I'm happy for you." Denise reached out and touched J.P.'s arm. "Samira seems like a really nice lady."

"She is." *And she's a helluva lot more than that too.* J.P. put his hand over Denise's. *It's not very often Denise is this candid with me.*

"I guess this means I can burn the little black book in my desk drawer, huh?" The glint in Denise's eye seemed more in character.

J.P. stood up and shook his head. "You're not off duty yet. Derek is coming along. He may need your scheduling services."

"Speaking of Derek . . .

She's starting to shift back to business.

" . . . He's losing the lease on his apartment. He's living in one of the Bridge's condos." She started back toward her own office and stopped in the doorway. "Bridges' Property Management isn't exactly the most stable place to be paying rent at the moment. But maybe, if you're moving out of your place, he could rent your house."

Am I moving? That thought caught J.P. off guard. *Yeah, I guess maybe I am.*

Denise frowned. "You are moving in with her aren't you?"

"I don't know," J.P. chucked to himself. "I guess I hadn't thought much about that."

"Well, think about what you want to do. Derek has until the first of December to make a decision." She clicked her nails on the doorframe. "Are you going to be here much longer?"

Now she's starting to sound like the Denise I know and depend on. "No. I need to be back over at Benson and Barringer at three."

"Do you need me to be there?"

I don't need her to be there, but maybe she needs to be there for herself. "Are you free? I don't want to mess up your whole Saturday."

"No, I'm good. If you need me I'll go with you and keep you men in order."

J.P. nodded his head. "Three o'clock straight up." He thought again. "And here's the deal, I need to be out of there no later than four thirty to meet the boys." *So we can be on time for dinner at Samira's.*

"I'll see to it that we're done by then . . ."

I can always count on Denise to bust me out of a meeting.

" . . . I assume our focus is a handoff from you to Vince?"

"Exactly." *Now she's talking.* "Vince will open. Mike will close."

"And Mike will cross-examine."

"Most likely." J.P. held out his hand. Denise slapped it with her palm. *Things are going to transition very easily.* He watched Denise open the main file for Mid-America. *Thanks, Denise.*

J.P. leaned forward on the downstairs sofa and put his elbows on his knees. He was holding his mother's wedding rings in his hand, but he had yet to reveal them to anyone in the room. *I think I need them for my own security somehow.* All four children were seated around them.

" . . . And so we'd like you to all stand up with us at the wedding."

"Oh! My! Gosh!" Krissy was the first one to react. "Like at the wedding where he'll become your husband?"

Samira glanced at J.P. "Yes, Krissy."

"So that means he'll like be our step dad kind of thing?" *That's funny, I hadn't exactly thought of myself as a step dad.* J.P. felt the rings roll from one side of his palm to the other. *I'm just figuring out how to be a regular dad!*

Krissy threw her hands into the air. "Always the bridesmaid, never the bride!" She grinned mischievously at her mother.

Maybe that's how Denise felt earlier today.

"Pretty cool you two are getting hitched," James stretched out on the carpeted floor. "But, it's not like we didn't see it coming."

Samira's eyes flew open wide.

"That's not what he means . . . ," Josh kicked his brother playfully.
What did he mean?
" . . . he means it was pretty obvious you two belonged together."
"Well, duh!" Krissy exclaimed. "It's written all over them."
J.P. knew if he looked at Samira she'd blush. *I'll let her off the hook this time.*
Krissy flew off the other couch. "So did he give you a ring?" She grabbed her mother's hand.
Leave it to Krissy to bring that up.
"No." Samira pulled her hand away.
"What?!" Krissy pounded J.P. on the leg. "Don't you know how it works? When you ask a woman to marry you, you're supposed to get down on one knee and put a ring on her finger."
"You watch too many Hallmark movies, Krissy." Kara spoke for the first time.
I wonder what she's really thinking?
" . . . In real life it might not happen exactly like it does in the movies."
"But you are going to give her one, right Phil?"
There's another detail that will need some attention on my part. "If that's what your mother wants." J.P. squeezed the rings in his hands.
"Well, of course she wants one!" Krissy threw her hands into the air again. "Every woman wants a diamond! They're a girls' best friend, you know!"
"Just like a dog is a man's best friend," James added.
We could have done without that.
Chase was suddenly at attention. *He must hear something.* Before J.P. could intervene Chase was barking and bounding up the stairs.
J.P. motioned for James to follow the dog.
"Sure, send me into unknown territory!"
That's what he gets for spouting off!
Krissy followed James and the dog up the stairs. Samira was suddenly flustered.
We're going to have to establish some canine rules for this household.
"Mama!" Krissy called from the top of the stairs. "Papa Ray and Granny are here!"
The sudden look of shock on Samira's face caused J.P. to worry. *Evidently they didn't come around as easily as she'd hoped.*
"What in the world?" Samira seemed to be addressing herself more than anyone else. "I hope they're not here to try to talk us out of this!" She rolled her eyes at J.P. and headed for the stairs.
Surely she wouldn't allow them to alter her decision. J.P. rose to follow Samira and motioned for Josh to come along. Kara was slow to getting out of the

beanbag chair. *I think I'll wait for her.* She had yet to make eye contact with him.

I have no idea how to communicate with this young woman. J.P. held out his hand for Kara to go up the steps first.

She stepped onto the first one and then turned around and faced J.P. Even standing on the step she was still below his eye level.

And I thought Samira was intense sometimes.

"I think it's okay that you're marrying my mother." Kara's voice didn't waver. "She needs you more than you probably know."

Intense. But extremely insightful. "You know what, Kara? I need your mother about that much too."

The young woman didn't blink or move. "She was really sad when she wasn't with you." Kara spoke without pretense. "But lately she's been really happy again and she is very calm now too."

Takes guts to speak her observations like this.

"But I don't want her to be hurt anymore."

That is a very bold thing to tell the man who is about to marry your mother. J.P. had to look away for a moment to compose his thoughts. "Kara . . . "

I'm not exactly sure what to say but I think I'd better be as honest with her as she's daring to be with me. "I love your mother more than I've ever loved a woman." He chose his words very carefully. "I'll do whatever it takes to be a good husband . . . "

" . . . and not hurt her anymore . . . "

Okay. "And not hurt her anymore."

"Promise?" Kara raised her eyebrows.

She's just like her mother. "I promise." His eyes traveled up the stairs to Samira. *I had no idea she was standing there.*

"Cross your heart and hope to die?"

"Cross my heart and hope to die." He crossed his heart with his finger.

"Okay then." Kara turned around and started up the steps. She stopped short when she came to her mother's feet at the top.

J.P. watched the Cartwright women communicate without saying a word. *I don't know if that's a woman's intuition or simply the way Samira has connected with her daughter's over the years.*

J.P. ascended the steps slowly. He also hesitated at the top.

"That's about all the approval you'll get out of her for the time being."

J.P. put his hand under Samira's hair and kissed her on the forehead. "Then that's about all I need for the time being." *That's plenty for starters!*

"I didn't expect my parents tonight."

"I knew that from the look on your face."

Samira sighed. "I don't know why they're here."

"Maybe we should find out." J.P. was almost humored at Samira's lack of control in her own house. *She likes to have more time to plan.*

"What if they don't want me to get married?"

He shrugged his shoulders. "Who are you going to listen to?"

"You?"

J.P. shook his head.

"Them?"

Nope. He shook his head again but this time he looked deep into Samira's eyes.

"Me." Samira exhaled very slowly. "I have to listen to my own heart."

"You know, Pretty Lady," J.P. lowered his voice. "There are things you'll cling to all your life. But maybe it's time to let some things go so you can become my wife."

Samira looked over J.P.'s shoulder and nodded her head in understanding. J.P. glanced into the other room. Krissy was making conversation with her grandparents in the living room. James and Josh were politely conversing as they were included. *Family is a good thing.*

"I'm going to make a pot of coffee." Samira crossed the kitchen and began to run water in the carafe. "Would you like anything?"

She needs the coffee to calm her nerves, but I don't think she has anything strong enough for me tonight. In spite of Samira's concerns, he crossed the dining room and offered his hand to Raymond Stephenson. *Might as well get this over with.*

67

The Secret Door

Samira sat between Phil and her father, anxiously awaiting the close of the service. *Had I known Mama's intent was to invite us all to church today, I'd have steered her in another direction.* She opened the hymnal to the page indicated in the bulletin. *Church is something Phil and I can work through later.* Samira's eyes passed over the stained glass in the window at the end of the pew. *But I am glad he's here with me this morning.* She breathed in deeply, noticing a hint of Phil's aftershave. *Especially if we're going to have Pastor Bill marry us.*

"Please stand for the closing hymn." The song leader raised his arm for the congregation to rise.

Normally Samira would share her hymnal with her father. But today she was slightly confused. *Oh good. Daddy is going to share with Mama.* Across the way she could see Krissy and Kara entertaining Josh and James. *I hope they're behaving.*

Tom knew all these songs, but my guess would be that they are unfamiliar to Phil. Samira opened her mouth to sing the opening stanza. *As far as that goes, this entire setting is probably unfamiliar territory.* Her father's tenor harmony blended with the congregational voices. Samira smiled to herself. *I will never tire of hearing Daddy sing these songs.*

Samira bowed her head for the final benediction. As she looked down, it was obvious Phil didn't know what to do with his hands. He started to tuck them in his pants pockets, but Samira slipped her hand inside his.

"Amen." Raymond straightened his back. "It's always good to have you join us for worship, Princess." He pecked his daughter on the cheek. "And a nice treat to have you sitting with us this morning as well, Phil."

Daddy is making a genuine effort here. Samira suddenly wondered how she should introduce Phil when people came to greet her. *He has so many names to choose from!*

"J.P."

Samira turned to see old Mr. Price offer his hand in greeting.

"Glad to have you with us this morning."

Samira watched Phil exchange a handshake. "It's good to see you, Mr. Price. It's been awhile."

How does Phil know my father's tailor?

"Anytime I don't need you is a sign things are going well, don't you think?" The old man laughed cordially. "Are you here with Miss Samira?"

"I am."

Samira felt her cheeks warm when Phil looked at her.

"Excellent company, that young woman." Mr. Price winked at Samira causing her blush to intensify. "We should meet for lunch and catch up sometime."

Phil nodded his head. He was in direct eye contact with the elderly gentleman. "Give me a call and we'll work it in."

"Very well." The man turned and raised his hand in a silent wave.

Before Samira got to the end of the pew, another man had stopped her fiancé to visit. *How in the world do they know him?* She stepped out in the aisle and turned to wait for Phil to join her. *Or maybe I should ask how he knows them?*

"Mama?" Kara was standing at her mother's side. "Can we catch a ride to Papa Ray's with Josh? He offered to drive us."

Samira looked over Kara's shoulder at Phil's boys. Krissy was busy introducing them to other teenagers. "I guess." *This is a new phenomenon! I'm not used to having other drivers in the family.* Phil was still talking to the couple in the pew behind him. *And it won't be long before James has his license too!* "As long as he takes you straight to the house. No scooping the loop."

Phil finally stepped into the aisle. The look on his face told Samira he was ready to be out of the crowd.

"How do they know you?"

Phil put his hand against Samira's waist and began to direct her through the mingling parishioners. "Clients."

Oh! I never considered that possibility. "Yours?"

"Mine."

"Pastor Bill said he'd meet us in the chapel when he's finished greeting the people." It was Samira's turn to guide Phil. She took his hand and led him around the end of the last pew.

"And Pastor Bill is . . . ?" Phil was looking around the room.

"He's the one shaking hands in the black suit at the door." *I keep forgetting Phil doesn't know this place.* "The man wearing the robe is Pastor John. He's new. But I've known Pastor Bill since I was a baby." *Or maybe I should say he's known me that long.*

Phil raised his chin giving indication he was following Samira's explanation.

"Come in here." Samira stepped into the chapel off the side of the sanctuary. "This is my favorite room." She closed the door behind them. "It's peaceful in here." *And if the light hits that window just right, maybe the dove will appear!* Phil looked less than comfortable. "Is something wrong?"

"No." Phil took the liberty to walk into the middle of the room. "But to be perfectly honest, I have a hard time finding anything peaceful inside a church building."

He's really not very comfortable here. Samira smiled gently and met Phil in the middle of the room. "I guess if you're not used to it, a church can be kind of intimidating."

"I just never feel like I belong here." Phil's eyes were on the stained glass windows.

I wonder if he even went to church as a child? "When I was little, I used to sneak in here to get away from all the grown ups who always wanted to visit with me after the service." Samira chuckled. "Some of them are out there chatting away right now!" *Like Mr. Price.* "They used to ask me all kinds of questions I never really wanted to answer so I'd come in here to escape the interrogation." *They still do that to me when I visit.* Samira was smiling at the memory.

"They have good intentions." Phil was looking around.

"They do, but if you're like me, you'd rather be in here where it's quiet and still." Samira glanced at the window hoping against all odds to see the dove flicker across the pane.

Phil nodded his head. "I must be a lot like you because it's much more comfortable in here than it is out here."

Samira pointed at a child-sized pew along the far wall. "When I was little I'd sit on that bench and stare at the window." She wanted desperately to tell Phil about the dove, but was afraid to reveal the image before he had a chance to experience it for himself. "Sometimes, if I was very still, I could hear God talking to me."

Phil looked less than convinced.

Samira raised her eyebrows. "You don't believe me?"

"Somehow I do believe you." He ran his hand through his hair. "I can't say I've ever heard the voice of God."

Samira was curious. "So what can you say then?" *I'd like to hear this side of Joseph Phillip.*

Phil's eyes met hers again. "Let's see, I can say I've heard a voice in my head, but I don't know I could attribute it to be The Voice." His eyes looked into the distance behind Samira.

"I remember one time I was in here by myself, and Daddy came to get me. I could still hear the grown ups talking out there and I wasn't ready to leave." Samira's heart warmed with the memory. "Instead of picking me up and carrying me out like he usually did, Daddy sat down with me and we stayed in here until I couldn't hear so many people talking." *I was probably about five or six years old then.* She could remember swinging her feet off the edge of the little pew. *Daddy prayed with me that day. I know he did even though he didn't say a word out loud.*

Phil dropped his hands into his pockets. "Sometime you'll have to read the letters my mother wrote to the Captain when Bobby and I were little." His eyes were distant, yet focused. "My dad sent a box of them home with me and I finally gave myself permission to read some." Phil puckered his lips in thoughtful silence for a moment. "I didn't realize how much faith my mother had in those days."

Samira was standing only a short distance from Phil, but she could feel the distance of his thoughts.

"She closed her letters by reminding the Captain that God was between him and the enemy." Phil's blue eyes came back to Samira's.

"And obviously He was." *Your father certainly had great success facing the enemy over and over again.*

Phil slowly nodded his head but Samira doubted he was nodding in agreement. "It's taken me awhile but I think I misinterpreted the enemy's identity."

This is going much deeper than I expected. "Who did you think the enemy was?" Phil's eyes had darkened considerably. *Maybe I shouldn't have asked that.*

"For a long time I thought it was God." Phil's eyes went back to the window.

I've wondered from time to time if that's what he thought. "Can I tell you something very personal?"

Phil blinked slowly and cast his eyes back on Samira.

Samira put her hands on his waist under his open jacket. "I believe you are the answer to my prayers."

"Can I tell you something very personal?" Phil's voice was very quiet.

She felt Phil take a deep breath and waited for him to exhale.

"I believe I've been my own worse enemy over the years. And it's a damn good thing you were praying because I don't think I'd have ever found you any other way."

"Oh, Phil." Samira caught her breath. *It took a lot of courage for him to tell me that.*

"True statement, Pretty Lady."

"Ah, Samira!" Pastor Bill entered through the double doors that led back to the sanctuary. "I knew I would find you here." He moved to the center of the room and reached out his right hand. "I'm Pastor Bill."

"Phil Ralston."

Interesting. Samira shared a look of surprise with her fiancé. *Not J.P. today?*

"Very pleased to meet you." Pastor Bill was motioning toward a small round table. "Shall we sit down for a moment?"

"I know this isn't the best time," Samira apologized to the pastor.

"Now, now," The elderly gentleman took a seat. "You're both here and I am here. This must be the perfect time."

Pastor Bill always knows how to put people at ease. Samira admired Phil's composure as he sat down in the chair next to her. *He seems more at peace now too.*

"I was not surprised to get your call, Samira." Pastor Bill's eyes danced with merriment. "It wasn't so long ago we were here in this room leaning toward a glimpse of the future."

Is that what we were doing? Samira couldn't help but smile at his choice of descriptive words. *He's such a poet.*

"I sense you've found the peace you came seeking that day." Pastor Bill was looking only at Samira.

Subsequently, Samira realized Phil was also looking at her. "I believe I have." She felt her cheeks warm with her confession.

"I believe you have as well." Pastor Bill nodded in satisfaction. "Shall we get down to business then?"

Samira could see Phil run his tongue over his bottom lip and she knew he was humored by the conversation so far. *I just hope he holds that thought until we're out of this building!*

"I understand the two of you are planning to be married?"

"And I . . ." Samira stopped to correct herself. "Or rather, we would like for you to perform the ceremony."

The minister's eyes twinkled again. "It would be my honor."

"We don't want anything as fancy as my mother is thinking," *I don't want to sound harsh, but I need to be honest.* "So I'm thinking the best way to satisfy everyone is simply to have the ceremony after church."

"And how do you feel about this, Phil? Do you have any concerns about such a service?"

Phil was shaking his head. "I have only one concern and I suppose this is as good as any place to voice it . . ."

What in the world is he going to say?

" . . . my only concern is that I leave that day with this Pretty Lady as my wife. Everything else is of secondary priority."

Whew! Samira let out all of her air. *I had no idea what he was thinking!*

"I know for a fact we can accommodate that." Pastor Bill smiled broadly. "And I know from our phone call that we don't have much time in which to prepare, but I would like to meet with the two of you at least once before the ceremony." The minister paused.

Of course we would want to meet with Pastor Bill! Samira was nodding her head in agreement and she sincerely hoped Phil could spare the time to meet with them too.

"As you know, it takes three to get married. And it takes three to stay married. It's important we remember to include the third and most important party in our preparation."

Phil tipped his head as if he was contemplating the pastor's comment. Pastor Bill answered the silent question. "You, Samira, and God."

Much to Samira's relief, Phil smiled.

"Do you agree?"

"I do." Phil put his arm around the back of Samira's chair.

"Very well." The minister turned toward Samira. "As you may recall, I told you once that Love doesn't make a wrong choice. I trust you are ready to embrace its purpose for the greater good."

I am so thankful Love doesn't make a wrong choice. She knew Phil was wondering what they were talking about. "I am." She answered easily. Without hesitation, she leaned into Phil's arm. *The warmth of his body permeated hers immediately.*

"Shall we say Thursday at seven then?"

Samira looked at Phil for approval. *His schedule is much more complicated than mine!*

"That works for me." Phil sat up straighter in his chair as if he was anticipating the end of the conversation.

"Me too." Samira also slid forward on her chair. *Now I'm glad Mama is cooking! I'm getting really hungry!*

Pastor Bill rose from his seat and offered his hand to Phil one more time. Before he walked away he squeezed Samira's shoulders with his aged hands. "Until then."

Samira watched her lifelong pastor walk the length of the chapel and disappear through the single door at the back. *In all my years of coming to this room, I still have no clue where that door leads.* For the first time in her life, Samira wondered what was concealed on the other side. *I'm going to investigate that here in the near future.*

When her thoughts came back to the present, Phil was standing in front of the stained glass window. Her eyes followed his to the very top.

Phil pointed to the top of the glass but he didn't say anything.

"Did you see the dove?"

Phil nodded his head with sudden excitement. "Yeah! Did you see it?"

"I just know it's there." Samira's heart was pounding in her chest. "Did the people dance?"

"I don't know about that," Phil tipped his head to study the window again. "But I know I saw a dove swoop across the glass lengthwise."

Samira was excited with Phil's revelation. "Now you know why I used to sneak in here when I was little!" *I don't know that I've ever seen him so taken by artwork before!* "It's the dove of peace. Pastor Bill says he's only known it to appear as a symbol of peace to troubled souls."

Phil laughed out loud! "Yeah, well, my soul certainly fits that category." He looked at the window again.

It's magical. "You can't make it happen, you just have to be patient and allow it come."

"That's interesting." Phil ran his hand through his hair. "I've spent most of my life forcing things to happen only to learn if I give it up the control, the best things in life will come."

That's what Pastor Bill meant when he said Love would come to me.

" . . . Trouble is, I'm not the most patient man in the world."

Samira put her arms around Phil's neck. "I would beg to differ with that statement. Joseph Phillip Ralston happens to be the most patient man I've ever known."

Phil grinned. "Some things are certainly worth the wait." He kissed her quickly. "Isn't somebody cooking lunch for us?"

"My mother." *But I'm not quite ready to go.*

"Then what are we waiting for?"

Peace maybe? Phil returned Samira's kiss but it was obvious he was ready to leave. She let go and watched him cross the room toward the single door.

"Where are you going? We came in over here." Samira pointed to the double doors that led back to the sanctuary.

"I know, but the parking lot is out here." Phil pointed to the single door at the back of the room.

How does he know that? Samira decided to prove him wrong. "Okay, then I'll follow you." *It probably leads into the pastor's study or something.*

Much to Samira's surprise, the door led into a dark entry hall. She watched Phil turn another doorknob. When he opened the second door, sunlight flooded the entire area!

"Hey, how did you know that?" *All my life I've assumed a magical passageway to heaven behind this door!*

Phil allowed Samira to step outside first. "It's not too hard to figure out. When we parked I noticed the main entryway and this one. I assumed from the inside that this one led back out doors."

This is too funny. She scanned the parking lot for Phil's truck. "But where did you park?"

A funny look came over Phil's face. "I guess I didn't. Josh did."

Samira grinned at the realization. "And I came over with my parents." *Maybe this is more like a passageway to heaven than I originally thought!*

"So we're stranded?"

"Better than stranded!" Samira took him by the hand as she started across the brown grass in the churchyard. "Now I get to take you anywhere I want to go." Samira laughed into the sunshine. *I am so thankful I was patient enough to let this Love come back to me!*

Phil followed without any reluctance whatsoever. Samira tucked herself into his arm. *Now I can show him some more of my favorite places.* Until today, this path had been reserved only for her father. *But today I get to share it with the man who loves me better than the rest. Maybe even better than Daddy.*

68

Peace

Mike patted the inside pocket on his suit coat. "Shit. I left the license in my car."

J.P. slapped him on the arm. "Don't swear in here!" He looked around the chapel. *I wonder if that dove is going to appear?* "Lightning is nearer striking here than anywhere else."

Mike laughed. "Okay, Counselor. But I still need to get outside to get your legal document."

J.P. pointed to the single door at the back of the room. "That leads to the parking lot and as far as I know you can come back in by the same route."

"Huh. A groom's room with a chicken exit." Mike nodded his head. "Gotta like it." He started for the door.

"Hey, Mike." J.P. waited for his friend to turn around. "You do have the ring, don't you?"

Mike's blonde curls bobbed on his head. "Not to worry." He held Samira's ring out for J.P. to see. "Right here in my hot little hand."

Just checking. Mike slipped quietly out the door. The congregation was still singing the last hymn. *Pastor Bill told me he'd come for me at the end of the service.* J.P. paced the length of the room. *I don't remember being this nervous the first time I got married.* He thought some more. *Fact is, I don't remember being this sober the first time around.* Samira's dark brown eyes came into focus in J.P.'s mind. *There's no way in hell, or heaven for that matter, that I'd do anything to jeopardize this day.*

The stained glass window caught J.P.'s attention again. The sunlight was illuminating the image as it had before, but there was no animation. *He said it takes three to get married and it takes three to stay married.* J.P. ran his hand through his hair. *I may have had three present when I got married before, but I certainly didn't have three following the ceremony.*

The entire first year of his marriage to Janet had always been a blur. *I don't know how it all works, but I'll do whatever it takes to be the husband . . . "And father . . . "* J.P. turned his head. A voice had sounded in his hear. *And father?* He smiled to himself. *I guess it's a package deal, huh?* The voice spoke again. *"That it is."*

J.P.'s eyes went to the top of the windowpane. *Maybe that's what Samira means by hearing the voice of God.* He chuckled slightly. *How do you know it from your own?* Without warning, the light behind the window shifted and the image of a dove flitted across the glass toward the people who seemed to be dancing at the bottom of the design.

The dove of peace. He waited another moment hoping for the dove to appear again. *Peace for a troubled soul.*

Mike reappeared as silently as he'd slipped away. "Got it." He waved the paper in the air. "I'd hate to get out of here without all the right signatures."

That's not an option.

"Nice job with her ring," Mike was examining the diamond in his hand. "It's unique but classy all at the same time.

"It's the one she liked." *Wait 'til he sees it on her hand. That's where it really takes on her personality.* J.P. took the ring out of Mike's fingers and studied it one last time. "Once she saw this one, her mind was made up."

Mike grinned. "Do you have any idea how tightly you're wrapped around her little finger?"

J.P. gave the ring back to his best friend. "Yes, I think I do." *And I'm thinking I like it that way.*

"I can't believe you're actually going to let her put a ring on your finger!" Mike slid onto the little round table and crossed his ankles. "You fought tooth and nail to *not* wear a ring the first time around."

"Wrong woman." J.P. remembered that fight. *But I'll wear this Pretty Lady's ring.*

"Amen to that!" Mike stroked his moustache. "I bet she picked out your ring too."

"Actually, she let me choose my own."

"Really?"

"Really." *Well, not exactly.* J.P. grinned. *I chose my own with her approval.* "I let her pick it out."

"I figured as much." Mike was suddenly contemplative. "You know, I think I owe you one, good buddy . . ."

"I'm sure you do, but in light of everything I owe you . . ."

Mike shook his head. "Seriously, J.P. Hear me out." He looked J.P. square in the eye. "In the beginning of all this I assumed Samira was way out of your league. You know, she had her life together, she was smart, she was steady . . ." Mike chewed on his moustache for a moment. "You weren't ready for a woman like that. You were in a league of your own, working the courtroom, catering to your clients, enjoying your weekends . . ."

"Things change, Mikey . . ."

"Yeah, I know." Mike crossed his arms. "You've changed."

Yes, I have. "So, you're saying . . ."

"I'm saying I'm proud of you, brother! You broke free of the past and stepped into the present with, well . . ." Mike was thinking. "Well, with a dignity I haven't seen in you since I met you."

"Thanks. I think." J.P. was studying Mike's face. *What's he telling me here?*

"No, really, J.P. Think about it. She was out of your league, but you played yourself out. I must say, you came into this kicking a screaming, but once you surrendered to yourself, you figured this whole thing out."

I hope he's right.

Pastor Bill opened the double doors and stepped inside. "Almost time, fellas." He crossed the room wearing a full-length white robe.

No one said anything about the robe thing. J.P. glanced at Mike. *I just hope he keeps his observations to himself.*

"The ushers are rearranging a few things and making sure the family is all seated appropriately." Pastor Bill patiently explained the slight delay. "When we get the signal that the women are ready, we'll enter the sanctuary and walk up the side aisle like we practiced yesterday."

Mike jumped up off the table. "This would be my cue to become a fly on the wall."

Mike is always Mike.

Pastor Bill turned back around and peered through the double doors.

Mike offered a his hand, but as J.P. started to return the shake, Mike pulled hard and embraced J.P. with his free hand. "You're doing the right thing, Phil. Trust yourself on this one."

There's not a doubt in my mind, Mikey.

Mike lowered his voice. "But you owe me big time for making me sit through church first!"

J.P. laughed as he returned the embrace. "Fair enough."

"I'm going to give this rock in my pocket to Josh." Mike winked as he walked away.

"You have a good friend in that man," Pastor Bill observed out loud.

"The best."

"Few men are so fortunate.'

No one knows me as well as Mike Benson. J.P. couldn't pull his eyes from the minister's face. *He reminds me of somebody but I can't quite place him.* When Pastor Bill smiled J.P. realized who it was. *I think he reminds me of Santa Claus!*

"It is time, Phil. Are you ready?" Pastor Bill was now holding J.P. by the elbow.

"Yes, I am." *In spite of the butterflies in my stomach.*

The sanctuary looked more crowded than it had been. *That's Mr. and Mrs. Barnes.* The ushers were still helping an elderly couple up the aisle on the far side of the room. *Samira was worried they would be so far away they couldn't hear.* He glanced at the back of the sanctuary. *She probably made special arrangements to have them moved closer to the front.*

Pastor Bill waited for the elderly couple to be seated, and then led Phil up the side of the church. They took their places at the front of the center aisle.

As the music began to play, J.P. scanned the faces in the crowd. Samira's parents were seated in the same row as Aunt Maggie and Uncle Roy. *It's been a long time since I've seen Uncle Roy this dressed up.* The Captain was seated next to Roy. His dress uniform was sharp and professional. *He looks good. And it's good to have him here.* Wes and Mark were seated in the next row back. Bobby winked as their eyes connected. *I'm just glad he and Mike aren't seated anywhere next to one another!*

I wonder where the fly on the wall is? J.P. dared to search the room looking for Mike's smiling face. *There's Kelly.* She was at the back of the church watching through the glass. *Chances are good Mike's not too far out of her jurisdiction.*

The music changed. Suddenly James and Krissy were standing next to Kelly. *Oh, she must be the one giving directions.* He folded his hands and watched as Krissy and James started up the aisle. James walked about halfway and then gave his father a big thumbs up sign. They shared the Ralston smile. *Leave it to James to cheer me on in my own wedding!*

Josh and Kara were close behind. *They look good all dressed up like this.* His sons had chosen black slacks with black collarless shirts. *Very professional. And these young women look like a million bucks in those fancy dresses.* J.P. considered the voice he'd heard in his head a few minutes earlier. *Any boy wanting to take them out will have to go through me first.*

"Are you nervous?" James whispered as he stepped into his place.

Not anymore. J.P. shook his head slightly. *But I was a few minutes ago.*

Krissy was beaming a brilliant smile across her freckled face. "Here comes the bride!" she whispered as she turned to take her place.

Breathe, Counselor. Breathe.

His eyes went to the back of the church and connected with Mike's. Mike threw his hands high above his head and grinned back. *Behave, Mikey!*

Two little blonde girls appeared at the back of the aisle. Pam was still doting over their hair. With a little prompting Lizzie and Bonnie started to drop flower petals as they walked the aisle. *They look a lot like their mom all dressed up like that.*

His eyes happened to fall on Denise and Jerry as the little girls passed their pew. *She looks a little sad. She knows what she needs but doesn't know how to get there.*

Lizzie and Bonnie stepped up next to the pastor and turned around to face the congregation. Their faces beamed with joyous anticipation.

This time when the music changed the entire congregation stood. *Okay. Now I'm nervous.* J.P. took a deep breath and held it in. His bride stood at the back of the church wearing a dress he'd never seen before. *Dear God, she is the most beautiful woman I've ever laid eyes on.* J.P. glued his eyes to Samira's as she walked toward him. *She's perfect.* The blush that appeared in Samira's cheeks told J.P. she knew exactly what he was thinking.

I don't know if I can wait for permission to kiss her or not. Even as J.P. exhaled, he didn't feel any relief in his lungs. *Tonight isn't going to come soon enough.* It seemed like it took forever for Samira to reach his side. All the while he held eye contact. *She's poised, confident . . .* Samira's dark eyes penetrated J.P.'s . . . *And she's all I'll ever need.*

Her palms are sweating. J.P. took a hold of her hands like they'd practiced.

"Dear Friends, we are gathered here in the presence of God to witness the marriage of Samira Susanne Cartwright and Joseph Phillip Ralston. Who gives this couple in holy matrimony?"

"We do." All four children responded as they'd been instructed.

The pastor smiled his Santa Claus smile and motioned for everyone to be seated. When they turned to face the minister, J.P. felt Josh briefly put his hand on his shoulder. *He knows I'm about ready to hyperventilate.* But Samira's dark eyes brought a calming affect to his whole being. *She does have a way with me like none other.*

Pastor Bill offered a prayer, but J.P. didn't close his eyes. *I don't want to take my eyes off of her for one minute.*

"Repeat after me," the minister spoke quietly as he made brief eye contact with Phil.

Just go slow because I want her to hear every single word . . .

"I, Joseph Phillip Ralston, take you Samira Suzanne Cartwright, to be my wife . . ."

"To have and to hold . . ."

J.P. finished his vows, still holding Samira's eyes with his own. She was gripping his hands with all of her might.

When it was Samira's turn to state her vows she hesitated.

Just concentrate, Pretty Lady . . . We're almost finished here.

"I, Samira Suzanne Cartwright, take you Joseph Phillip Ralston, to be my husband . . ."

For just a brief moment J.P. glanced over Samira's shoulder in his father's direction.

I do believe this is the first time in my life I've felt worthy of that name.

"To have and to hold . . ."

It suddenly felt exactly right that the Captain was seated in the same row as Aunt Maggie and Uncle Roy. J.P. swallowed a lump of emotion he hadn't expected.

" . . . This is my solemn vow." Samira's eyes were damp but they hadn't spilled over yet.

J.P. shared his easy smile with his bride. *Neither one of us likes being the center of attention like this!*

Pastor Bill seemed to be taking his time getting the rings from the children. He even stooped to show them to the curious Lizzie.

Just give us the rings and get on with the show! J.P. held out his hand as Pastor Bill placed the diamond in his hand. Obediently he repeated the words after the minister.

"I give you this ring . . . as a sign of my vow . . . and with all that I am . . . and all that I have . . . I honor you . . . in the name of the Father . . . and of the Son . . . and of the Holy Spirit."

It takes three to get married. The impact of that statement suddenly made sense. J.P slipped Samira's ring onto her finger. *I'm all yours, Pretty Lady.*

He held out his hand and listened as Samira did the same for him. *She's the only one for whom I'd wear a ring.*

Samira finished without further prompting from the pastor. " . . . in the name of the Father, and of the Son, and of the Holy Spirit."

Her smile calmed every nerve in J.P.'s being. He knew the pastor was still talking, but he had no idea what he could possibly be saying. Somewhere in the midst of the moment, J.P. knew he was kissing his bride. He didn't even care if he'd waited for permission or not. The next thing he knew the congregation was on their feet and applauding. Mike was standing at the back waving for J.P. and Samira to walk down the aisle.

"Did he announce us as man and wife?" Samira asked the question as they started to walk arm in arm.

"I don't have a clue." When he looked at Samira her cheeks were glowing.

At the end of the aisle J.P. turned his bride toward him and kissed her again. *In the name of the Father and the Son and the Holy Spirit.* He punctuated his vow. Samira's arms were wrapped around him on the inside of his jacket. *I like the way she does that.*

"A-hem!" Mike interrupted the intimate moment by pulling the couple apart. "You're blocking traffic, Mr. and Mrs. Ralston."

Mr. and Mrs. Ralston. That has a nice ring to it. J.P. reluctantly allowed Mike to hug his bride. *Go easy there, fella, that's my wife . . .* He turned to face his sons who were already in line to embrace Samira.

"Way to go, Dad!" Josh exchanged a high five with his father and then paused for a fatherly hug. "That was sweet!"

Krissy turned around like a ballerina. "How do you like the dresses? We picked them especially for you!"

"They're perfect." J.P. wrapped the young woman in his arms. *But only made perfect by the ladies wearing them.*

J.P. noted a few tears in the corner of Kara's eyes. He hugged her with both arms. Surprisingly, she hugged him back. *She is so much like her mother.*

"Welcome to the family," Weston Stephenson grasped J.P.'s hand. "I must say, this union is a win-win for the whole family."

A banker first. A brother second. "Indeed." J.P. accepted a warm embrace from Pam.

He looked beyond Pam's shoulder into the dark eyes of his new mother-in-law. *She does her hair the same way Samira does hers.*

"Ashleigh," he offered his hands, but the woman lifted her chin and kissed him on the cheek. She didn't speak, and J.P. didn't offer any words. But there was an understanding that passed between them. *How does she communicate like that?*

Raymond Stephenson stepped back and admired Samira. "It's not everyday a father gets to see his beautiful daughter pledged in holy matrimony."

Samira was beaming at her father.

Now I'm out of my league.

"I love you, Princess." Raymond hugged his daughter. "Don't you ever forget that."

J.P. knew Samira spoke, but he wasn't able to make out her words. *Surprisingly enough, she's not crying.* J.P. admired his bride's composure. *If anyone would make her cry, I'd think it would be her father.*

Raymond offered his hand to J.P. "Phil, I'm putting my daughter in good hands."

Now I am totally out of my league! J.P. nodded. *His expectations are higher than any I've ever had to earn.*

"In fact, I can't think of any hands I'd rather have her in." Raymond stepped closer and squeezed J.P.'s shoulder with his free hand.

"Thank you, sir." J.P. was completely serious. *He may always be Mr. Stephenson to me.*

The line kept moving and people continued to greet J.P. and Samira. *Surely we're about done with this formality.*

The next hand wasn't unfamiliar, however. J.P. paused for a moment and then opened his arms to hug Denise. *I wish she wouldn't cry.*

"It was a beautiful ceremony," Denise sobbed. "Just beautiful."

J.P. lifted her chin with his finger. "You deserve the same."

Denise nodded. "I know. We've been talking." She wiped her eyes with a damp tissue. "I'll see you at the Stephenson's in a few minutes."

Jerry's handshake was sincere. "Congratulations, man. You've given us plenty to think about."

J.P. smiled. "Take all the time you need, but don't wait too long."

Jerry's eyes were thoughtful. "Thanks for the advice, Counselor."

"Phillip?" Aunt Maggie stretched out her arms. "I am so happy for you . . ."

She's been crying, but her real tears will be shed in private.

"I knew God wasn't finished with you yet."

J.P. bent in half to hug his aunt. *And somehow I knew she never stopped praying for me.*

J.P. embraced Uncle Roy.

"Well done, Phillip. I knew she was a keeper."

"Not before I did though." Bobby was ready for a brotherly hug. "You done good, big brother. Life has much in store!"

J.P. greeted Bobby's family one after the other. Megan was also crying.

Why do people cry at weddings? J.P. looked at Samira. She was in a full body embrace and tears were streaming down her face. The Captain had his eyes closed as he hugged his new daughter-in law..

That's intense. J.P. had to look away to keep his own emotions from overflowing. Time stood still as he made eye contact with his father.

The Captain saluted his son in military fashion. J.P. stood tall.

"I'm proud to call you my son, Joseph Phillip."

J.P. nodded once but the lump in his throat kept him from speaking. *And I'm proud to wear your name, Dad.*

The Captain held out his hand, but J.P. ignored the handshake and opened his arms.

"To hell with the Navy."

I think he waited to be last in line on purpose. J.P. hugged the Captain long and hard.

"Your mother would be proud." When they separated, the Captain's cheeks were wet. "That grandson of mine has offered to drive me to the reception after family pictures." Captain Joe wiped his face with a white handkerchief.

Family. I didn't realize how much I needed it. "That grandson of yours is mighty proud to be your chauffeur."

"The pleasure is all mine."

J.P. turned and watched Josh meet his grandfather. Mike and Kelly were engaged in animated conversation just inside the door. *There's no reason to hold back, Mikey.*

And then Joseph Phillip turned around into Samira's waiting arms.

And this pleasure is all mine. Joseph Phillip kissed Samira uninhibited by their surroundings. *She's all I'll ever need.*